Andrew Taylor

Andrew Taylor is the award-winning author of a number of crime novels, including the Dougal series, the Lydmouth books and *The Barred Window*. He and his wife live with their children in the Forest of Dean.

Requiem for an Angel is the omnibus edition of the acclaimed Roth Trilogy – a unique literary achievement that, like an archaeological dig, strips away the layers of the past to expose the roots of present evils.

Andrew Taylor won the CWA Ellis Peters Historical Dagger 2001 for *The Office of the Dead*, the third novel in the trilogy.

For more information about Andrew Taylor, visit his web site at http://www.andrew-taylor.co.uk

D1150220

Praise for *Andrew Taylor* and the *Roth Trilogy*

'This author knows precisely how to wield suspense'

Independent on Sunday

'Taylor is a major thriller talent'

Time Out

'As Andrew Taylor triumphantly proves . . . there is still room for excellence'

Irish Times

'Taylor is marvellous and devilishly clever'

Frances Hegarty, *Mail on Sunday*

'Like Hitchcock, Taylor pitches extreme and gothic events within a hair's breadth of normality'

TLS

'There's no denying Mr Taylor's talent . . . exciting, readable and thoroughly amoral'

Daily Telegraph

'Skilful, elegant, powerfully atmospheric [trilogy] in which ancient evil shimmers like images trapped in a corridor of mirrors'

Philip Oakes, *Literary Review*

'Andrew Taylor is a master of the corrosive passions that fester beneath conventional façades . . . A fascinating unravelling of the horrors that the past can visit on the present'

Val McDermid, *Manchester Evening News*

'A highly praised trilogy of novels whose ecclesiastical background adds to the intense nature of the suspense. They inform not only the heart but the brain since Taylor is a writer blessed with great compassion as well as an unerring eye for historical detail. His flawed heroes and heroines and narrators are people you have met before in the street. Their dilemmas are murderously mundane, but the scale of their tragedies, devastating'

Frances Fyfield, *Sunday Express*

'I find it hard to understand why [these novels] are not better known, more hyped, filmed by European film directors. As well as being unputdownable, they are most unusual in their structure, style and content . . . Each book is an example of a different sort of suspense novel. *The Four Last Things* is a modern story and concerns a serial killer. The Wests' unimaginable doings in Gloucester are brought to mind in many subtle ways. *The Judgement of Strangers* is an Agatha Christie novel but with all the simplicity gone . . . as though a kaleidoscope of the separate elements has been given an extra twist so that the result is as dark, passionate and dramatic as an opera. *The Office of the Dead* is a Gothic novel . . . and it is the genteel, civilised manner of the telling that makes the story all the more appalling . . . I was bowled over by them'

Adèle Geras, *Books and Company*

'A trilogy which spans both history and geography . . . which will have the reader turning back to check the identities of Taylor's ambiguous characters and relish his fine writing'

Gerald Kaufman, *Scotsman*

'Finely crafted . . . Taylor has established a sound reputation for writing tense novels that perceptively penetrate the human psyche. His ingredients are doubt, guilt and moral ambiguity, intermingling with the more usual trappings of crime detection' Marcel Berlins, *The Times*

'Each [book in the trilogy] illuminates the others, and the depth and amplitude of this study of crime and retribution in a world in which literature, religion, obsession and long-concealed secrets interact with human needs and relationships, cannot be appreciated until the last few pages of [. . .] the final volume . . . A major literary undertaking' James Melville, *Ham & High*

'It deals in the quietest, most civilized way with abominable suffering . . . a highly sinister piece of work'

Natasha Cooper, *TLS*

'Complex, with lots of sinister implications . . . moves the traditional crime novel on to some deeper level of exploration'

Jane Jakeman, *Independent*

Andrew Taylor

REQUIEM FOR AN ANGEL

THE FOUR LAST THINGS
THE JUDGEMENT OF STRANGERS
THE OFFICE OF THE DEAD

Foreword by Frances Fyfield

HarperCollins*Publishers*

HarperCollins*Publishers*
77–85 Fulham Palace Road, London W6 8JB

The HarperCollins website address is
www.**fire**and**water**.com

This paperback edition 2002

1 3 5 7 9 10 8 6 4 2

First published in Great Britain
in three volumes

The Four Last Things published by HarperCollins*Publishers* 1997
Copyright © Andrew Taylor 1997

The Judgement of Strangers published by HarperCollins*Publishers* 1998
Copyright © Andrew Taylor 1998

The Office of the Dead published by HarperCollins*Publishers* 1999
Copyright © Andrew Taylor 1999

Andrew Taylor asserts the moral right to
be identified as the author of this work

ISBN 0 00 713436 3

Typeset in Meridien and Bodoni by
Palimpsest Book Production Limited, Polmont, Stirlingshire

Printed and bound in Great Britain by
Clays Ltd, St Ives plc

CONTENTS

FOREWORD

Writing a foreword to a series of books is a difficult job to do, especially if the task is complicated by admiration. How to start? Spluttering with praise? Turgid with analysis? Wordy with wisdom, or prefacing the whole damn thing with an essay of the place of the trilogy in history, from 30,000 BC, to date? Andrew Taylor certainly has a place in history, but nothing occurs to me in these opening sentences, apart from humble enthusiasm and the wish to impart a fraction of the pleasure these novels have given me.

He is a storyteller, a true practitioner of that ancient art which many mainstream novelists forget. Above all, these are stories, which means that the element of suspense is paramount. As a consequence, whatever is learned in the meantime is absorbed with the ease of fine alcohol and likely to give rise to great, possibly rowdy, excitement. There is plenty to learn, because on one level, this trilogy is a history of social habits and attitudes from 1958 to the present day, giving Taylor the opportunity to evoke three successive eras with uncanny, atmospheric accuracy. (Those old enough to remember uneven lino floors, grim, food-free pubs and the rationing of hot water, are in for particular delights.) On another level, the narratives reflect the changing state of the Church of England and the altered status of its sometimes hapless clerics. Never have the servants of God been so sorely tried, tempted and diminished. Like many of the protagonists, Taylor is erudite, an erudition so lightly worn in his case that it becomes positively infectious. The prose is tense without being weighty, often poetic and frequently funny, perhaps inevitable with books which, quite apart from the cunning embroidery of themes and curses, deal with the diversity of real lives. For here is a Taylor who cannot dress dummies, only real, convincing people.

The Four Last Things features the Appleyards, present-day inner-city dwellers, potentially happy, despite the vicissitudes of their opposing careers as a woman cleric and male police officer, until their beloved child is abducted. The reader knows by whom, and into what appalling danger: the victims do not, and God is silent on the subject. In *The Judgement of Strangers*, when a sternly handsome and passionate priest faces the torture of a sexless and sterile marriage against the cacophonous background of the licentious 1970s, God is equally reticent. Again, there is a child, omnipresent, but often silent. In *The Office of the Dead*, set in 1958, an element of godlessness prevails in the character of Wendy, the narrator, guest of the Reverend Byfield and his wife and an uncomfortable adornment to the Cathedral Close. She is the sinner, taking refuge from her adulterous husband and frivolous life, inseparable from her bottle of gin and as fine an example of the decent scarlet woman as literature can provide.

On that note, it could be said of Taylor's characters, *that by their decency, so shall you know them*. They are you and me, born innocent, but not for long, formed only as our Gods can judge us.

The books may be read separately and in any order, although I should include the warning (or do I mean advice?) that reading them in sequence reveals an extra layer of interconnections and subtleties, plus a few cataclysmic and truly breathtaking shocks. The war between good and evil does not operate on a level playing field in this trilogy and the devil has a facility for recruiting those with the very best intentions.

I envy the reader who has yet to begin, for these are novels of heavenly virtues and perfectly wicked goodness.

Frances Fyfield

THE FOUR
LAST THINGS

'. . . nor can I think I have the true Theory of death, when I contemplate a skull, or behold a Skeleton . . . I have therefore inlarged that common *Memento mori*, into a more Christian memorandum, *Memento quattuor Novissima*, those four inevitable points of us all, Death, Judgment, Heaven and Hell.'

Sir Thomas Browne, *Religio Medici* (1642), Part I, Section 45

For Caroline

PROLOGUE

'In brief, we all are monsters, that is, a composition of Man and Beast . . .'

Religio Medici, I, 55

All his life Eddie had believed in Father Christmas. In childhood his belief had been unthinking and literal; he clung to it for longer than his contemporaries and abandoned it only with regret. In its place came another conviction, another Father Christmas: less defined than the first and therefore less vulnerable.

This Father Christmas was a private deity, the source of small miracles and unexpected joys. This Father Christmas – who else? – was responsible for Lucy Appleyard.

Lucy was standing in the yard at the back of Carla Vaughan's house. Eddie was in the shadows of the alleyway, but Lucy was next to a lighted window and there could be no mistake. It was raining, and her dark hair was flecked with drops of water that gleamed like pearls. The sight of her took his breath away. It was as if she were waiting for him. An early present, he thought, gift-wrapped for Christmas. He moved closer and stopped at the gate.

'Hello.' He kept his voice soft and low. 'Hello, Lucy.'

She did not reply. Nor did she seem to register his use of her name. Her self-possession frightened Eddie. He had never been like that and never would be. For a long moment they stared at each other. She was wearing what Eddie recognized as her main outdoor coat – a green quilted affair with a hood; it was too large for her and made her look younger than she was. Her hands, almost hidden by the cuffs, were clasped in front of her. He thought she was holding something. On her feet she wore the red cowboy boots.

Behind her the back door was closed. There were lights in the house but no sign of movement. Eddie had never been as close to her as this. If he leant forward, and stretched out his hand, he would be able to touch her.

'Soon be Christmas,' he said. 'Three and a half weeks, is it?'

Lucy tossed her head: four years old and already a coquette.

'Have you written to Santa Claus? Told him what you'd like?'

She stared at him. Then she nodded.

'So what have you asked him for?'

'Lots of things.' She spoke well for her age, articulation clear, the voice well-modulated. She glanced back at the lighted windows of the house. The movement revealed what she was carrying: a purse, too large to be hers, surely? She turned back to him. 'Who are you?'

Eddie stroked his beard. 'I work for Father Christmas.' There was a long silence, and he wondered if he'd gone too far. 'How do you think he gets into all those houses?' He waved his hand along the terrace, at a vista of roofs and chimneys, outhouses and satellite dishes; the terrace backed on to another terrace, and Eddie was standing in the alley which ran between the two rows of backyards.

Lucy followed the direction of his wave with his eyes, raising herself on the toes of one foot, a miniature ballerina. She shrugged.

'Just think of them. Millions of houses, all over London, all over the world.' He watched her thinking about it, her eyes growing larger. 'Chimneys aren't much use – hardly anyone these days has proper fires, do they? But he has other ways in and out. I can't tell you about that. It's a secret.'

'A secret,' she echoed.

'In the weeks before Christmas, he sends me and a few others around to see where the problems might be, what's the best way in. Some houses are very difficult, and flats can be even worse.'

6

She nodded. An intelligent child, he thought: she had already begun to think out the implications of Santa Claus and his alleged activities. He remembered trying to cope with the problems himself. How did a stout gentleman carrying a large sack manage to get into all those homes on Christmas Eve? How did he get all the toys in the sack? Why didn't parents see him? The difficulties could only be resolved if one allowed him magical, or at least supernatural, powers. Lucy hadn't reached that point yet: she might be puzzled but at present she lacked the ability to follow her doubts to their logical conclusions. She still lived in an age of faith. Faced with something she did not understand, she would automatically assume that the failure was hers.

Eddie's skin tingled. His senses were on the alert, monitoring not only Lucy but the houses and gardens around them. It was early evening; at this time of year, on the cusp between autumn and winter, darkness came early. The day had been raw, gloomy and damp. He had seen no one since he turned into the alleyway.

Traffic passed in the distance; the faint but insistent rhythm of a disco bass pattern underpinned the howl of a distant siren, probably on the Harrow Road; but here everything was quiet. London was full of these unexpected pools of silence. The streetlights were coming on and the sky above the rooftops was tinged an unhealthy yellow.

'You look as if you're going out.' Eddie knew at once that this had been the wrong thing to say. Once again Lucy glanced back at the house, measuring the distance between herself and the back door. Hard on the heels of this realization came another: perhaps she wasn't afraid of Eddie but of outraged authority on the other side of that door.

He blurted out, 'It's a nice evening for a walk.' Idiotic or not, the remark seemed to have a relaxing effect on Lucy. She turned back to him, peering up at his face.

He rested his arms along the top of the gate. 'Are you going out?' he asked, politely interested, talking as one adult to another.

Again the toss of the head: this time inviting a clash of wills. 'I'm going to Woolworth's.'

'What are you going to buy?'

She lowered her voice. 'A conjur—' The word eluded her and she swiftly found a substitute: 'A magic set. So I can do tricks. See – I've got my purse.' She held it out: a substantial oblong, made for the handbag not the pocket; designed for an adult, not a child.

Eddie took a long, deep breath. Suddenly it was hard to breathe. There always came a point when one crossed the boundary between the permissible and the forbidden. He knew that Angel would be furious. Angel believed in careful preparation, in following a plan; that way, she said, no one got hurt. She hated anything which smacked of improvisation. His heart almost failed him at the thought of her reaction.

Yet how could he turn away from this chance? Lucy was offering herself to him, his Christmas present. Had anyone ever had such a lovely present? But what if someone saw them? He was afraid, and the fear was wrapped up with desire.

'Is it far?' Lucy asked. 'Woolworth's, I mean.'

'Not really. Are you going there now?'

'I might.' Again she glanced back at the house. 'The gate's locked. There's a bolt.'

The gate was a little over four feet high. Eddie put his left hand over and felt until he found the bolt. He had to work it to and fro to loosen it in its socket; it was too stiff for a child of Lucy's age, even if she could have reached it. At last it slid back, metal smacking on metal. He tensed, waiting for opening doors, for faces at the windows, for dogs to bark, for angry questions. He guessed from her stillness that Lucy too was waiting. Their shared tension made them comrades.

Eddie pushed the gate: it swung into the yard with a creak like a long sigh. Lucy stepped backwards. Her face was pale, intent and unreadable.

'Are you coming?' He made as if to turn away, knowing that the last thing he must seem was threatening. 'I'll give you a ride there in my van if you want. We'll be back in a few minutes.'

Lucy looked back at the house again.

'Don't worry about Carla. You'll be back before she notices you're gone.'

'You know Carla?'

'Of course I do.' Eddie was on safer ground here. 'I told you that I worked for Father Christmas. He knows everything. I saw you with her yesterday in the library. Do you remember? I winked at you.'

The quality of Lucy's silence changed. She was curious now, perhaps relieved.

'And I saw you at St George's the other Sunday, too. Your mummy's called Sally and your daddy's called Michael.'

'You know them too?'

'Father Christmas knows everyone.'

Still she lingered. 'Carla will be cross.'

'She won't be cross with either of us. Not if she wants any Christmas presents this year.'

'Carla wants to win the Lottery for Christmas. I know. I asked her.'

'We'll have to see.'

Eddie took a step down the alleyway. He stopped, turned back and held out his hand to Lucy. Without a backward glance, she slipped through the open gate and put her hand in his.

1

'Who can but pity the merciful intention of those hands that do destroy themselves? the Devil, were it in his power, would do the like . . .'

Religio Medici, I, 51

'God does not change,' said the Reverend Sally Appleyard. 'But we do.'

She stopped and stared down the church. It wasn't that she didn't know what to say next, nor that she was afraid: but time itself was suddenly paralysed. As time could not move, all time was present.

She had had these attacks since childhood, though less frequently since she had left adolescence behind; often they occurred near the start of an emotional upheaval. They were characterized by a dreamlike sense of inevitability – similar, Sally suspected, to the preliminaries to an epileptic fit. The faculty might conceivably be a spiritual gift, but it was a very uncomfortable one which appeared to serve no purpose.

Her nervousness had vanished. The silence was total, which was characteristic. No one coughed, the babies were asleep and the children were quiet. Even the traffic had faded away. August sunshine streamed in an arrested waterfall of light through the windows of the south-nave aisle and the south windows of the clerestory. She knew beyond any doubt that something terrible was going to happen.

The two people Sally loved best in the world were sitting in the second pew from the front, almost directly beneath her.

Lucy was sitting on Michael's lap, frowning up at her mother. On the seat beside her was a book and a small cloth doll named Jimmy. Michael's head was just above Lucy's. When you saw their heads so close together, it was impossible to doubt the relationship between them: the resemblance was easy to see and impossible to analyse. Michael had his arms locked around Lucy. He was staring past the pulpit and the nave altar, up the chancel to the old high altar. His face was sad, she thought: why had she not noticed that before?

Sally could not see Derek without turning her head. But she knew he would be staring at her with his light-blue eyes fringed with long sandy lashes. Derek disturbed her because she did not like him. Derek was the vicar, a thin and enviably articulate man with a very pink skin and hair so blond it was almost white.

Most of the other faces were strange to her. They must be wondering why I'm just standing here, Sally thought, though she knew from experience that these moments existed outside time. In a sense, they were all asleep: only she was awake.

The pressure was building up. She wasn't sure whether it was inside her or outside her; it didn't matter. She was sweating and the neatly printed notes for her sermon clung to her damp fingers.

As always in these moments, she felt guilty. She stared down at her husband and daughter and thought: if I were spiritually strong enough, I should be able to stop this or to make something constructive out of it. Despair flooded through her.

'Your will be done,' she said, or thought she said. 'Not mine.'

As if the words were a signal, time began to flow once more. A woman stood up towards the back of the church. Sally Appleyard braced herself. Now it was coming, whatever it was, she felt better. Anything was an improvement on waiting.

She stared down the nave. The woman was in her sixties or seventies, small, slight and wearing a grubby beige raincoat which was much too large for her. She clutched a plastic bag in her arms, hugging it against her chest as if it were a baby. On her head was a black beret pulled down over her ears. A ragged fringe of grey, greasy hair stuck out under the rim of the beret. It was a warm day but she looked pinched, grey and cold.

11

'She-devil. Blasphemer against Christ. Apostate.' As she spoke, the woman stared straight at Sally and spittle, visible even at a distance, sprayed from her mouth. The voice was low, monotonous and cultivated. 'Impious bitch. Whore of Babylon. Daughter of Satan. May God damn you and yours.'

Sally said nothing. She stared at the woman and tried to pray for her. Even those who did not believe in God were willing to blame the shortcomings of their lives on him. God was hard to find so his ministers made convenient substitutes.

The woman's lips were still moving. Sally tried to blot out the stream of increasingly obscene curses. In the congregation, more and more heads craned towards the back of the church. Some of them belonged to children. It wasn't right that children should hear this.

She was aware of Michael standing up, passing Lucy to Derek's wife in the pew in front, and stepping into the aisle. She was aware, too, of Stella walking westwards down the nave towards the woman in the raincoat. Stella was one of the churchwardens, a tall, stately black woman who appeared never to be in a hurry.

Everything Sally saw, even Lucy and Michael, seemed both physically remote and to belong to a lesser order of importance. It impinged on her no more than the flickering images on a television set with the sound turned down. Her mind was focused on the woman in the beret and raincoat, not on her appearance or what she was saying but on the deeper reality beneath. Sally tried with all her might to get through to her. She found herself visualizing a stone wall topped with strands of barbed wire.

Michael and Stella had reached the woman now. Like an obliging child confronted by her parents, she held out her arms, giving one hand to Michael and one to Stella; she closed her mouth at last but her eyes were still on Sally. For an instant Michael, Stella and the woman made a strangely familiar tableau: a scene from a Renaissance painting, perhaps, showing a martyr about to be dragged uncomplainingly to the stake, with her eyes staring past the invisible face of the artist, standing where her accuser would be, to the equally invisible heavenly radiance beyond.

The tableau destroyed itself. Stella scooped up the carrier bag with her free hand. She and Michael drew the woman along the pew and walked with her towards the west door. Their shoes clattered on the bright Victorian tiles and rang on the central-heating gratings. The woman did not struggle but she twisted herself round until she was walking sideways. This allowed her to turn her head as far as she could and continue to stare at Sally.

The heavy oak door opened. The sound of traffic poured into the church. Sally glimpsed sunlit buildings, black railings and a blue sky. The door closed with a dull, rolling boom. For an instant the boom didn't sound like a closing door at all: it was more like the whirr of great wings beating the air.

Sally took a deep breath. As she exhaled, a picture filled her mind: an angel, stern and heavily feathered, the detail hard and glittering, the wings flexing and rippling. She pushed the picture away.

'God does not change,' she said again, her voice grim. 'But we do.'

Afterwards Derek said, 'These days we need bouncers, not churchwardens.'

Sally turned to look at him combing his thinning hair in the vestry mirror. 'Seriously?'

'We wouldn't be the first.' His reflection gave her one of his pastoral smiles. 'I don't mean it, of course. But you'll have to get used to these interruptions. We get all sorts in Kensal Vale. It's not some snug little suburb.'

This was a dig at Sally's last parish, a predominantly middle-class enclave in the diocese of St Albans. Derek took a perverse pride in the statistics of Kensal Vale's suffering.

'She needs help,' Sally said.

'Perhaps. I suspect she's done this before. There have been similar reports elsewhere in the diocese. Someone with a bee in her bonnet about women in holy orders.' He slipped the comb into his pocket and turned to face her. 'Plenty of them around, I'm afraid. We just have to grin and bear it. Or rather them. We get worse interruptions than dotty old ladies, after all – drunks, drug addicts and nutters in all shapes and sizes.'

He smiled, pulling back his lips to reveal teeth so perfect they looked false. 'Maybe bouncers aren't such a bad idea after all.'

Sally bit back a reply to the effect that it was a shame they couldn't do something more constructive. It was early days yet. She had only just started her curacy at St George's, Kensal Vale. Salaried parish jobs for women deacons were scarce, and she would be a fool to antagonize Derek before her first Sunday was over. Perhaps, too, she was being unfair to him.

She checked her appearance in the mirror. After all this time the dog collar still felt unnatural against her neck. She had wanted what the collar symbolized for so long. Now she wasn't sure.

Derek was too shrewd a manager to let dislike fester unnecessarily. 'I liked your sermon. A splendid beginning to your work here. Do you think we should make more of the parallels between feminism and the anti-slavery movement?'

A few minutes later Sally followed him through the church to the Parish Room, which occupied what had once been the Lady Chapel. Its conversion last year had been largely due to Derek's gift for indefatigable fund-raising. About thirty people had lingered after the service to drink grey, watery coffee and meet their new curate.

Lucy saw her mother first. She ran across the floor and flung her arms around Sally's thighs.

'I wanted you,' Lucy muttered in an accusing whisper. She was holding her doll Jimmy clamped to her nose, a sign of either tiredness or stress. 'I wanted you. I didn't like that nasty old woman.'

Sally patted Lucy's back. 'I'm here, darling, I'm here.'

Stella towed Michael towards them. She was in her forties, a good woman, Sally suspected, but one who dealt in certainties and liked the sound of her own voice and the authority her position gave her in the affairs of the parish. Michael looked dazed.

'We were just talking about you,' Stella announced with pride, as though the circumstance conferred merit on all concerned. 'Great sermon.' She dug a long forefinger into Michael's ribcage. 'I hope you're cooking the Sunday lunch after all that.'

Sally took the coffee which Michael held out to her. 'What happened to the old woman?' she asked. 'Did you find out where she lives?'

Stella shook her head. 'She just kept telling us to go away and leave her in peace.'

'Ironic, when you think about it,' Michael said, apparently addressing his cup.

'And then a bus came along,' Stella continued, 'and she hopped on. Short of putting an armlock on her, there wasn't much we could do.'

'She's not a regular, then?'

'Never seen her before. Don't take it to heart. Nothing personal.'

Lucy tugged Sally's arm, and coffee slopped into the saucer. 'She should go to prison. She's a witch.'

'She's done nothing bad,' Sally said. 'She's just unhappy. You don't send people to prison for being unhappy, do you?'

'Unhappy? Why?'

'Unhappy?' Derek Cutter appeared beside Stella and ruffled Lucy's hair. 'A young lady like you shouldn't be unhappy. It's not allowed.'

Pink and horrified, Lucy squirmed behind her mother.

'Sally tells me this was once the Lady Chapel,' Michael said, diverting Derek's attention from Lucy. 'Times change.'

'We were lucky to be able to use the space so constructively. And in keeping with the spirit of the place, too.' Derek beckoned a middle-aged man, small and sharp-eyed, a balding cherub. 'Sally, I'd like you to meet Frank Howell. Frank, this is Sally Appleyard, our new curate, and her husband Michael.'

'Detective Sergeant, isn't it?' Howell's eyes were red-rimmed. Michael nodded.

'There's a piece about your lady wife in the local rag. They mentioned it there.'

Derek coughed. 'I suppose you could say all of us are professionally nosy in our different ways. Frank's a freelance journalist.'

Howell was shaking hands with Stella. 'For my sins, eh?'

'In fact, Frank was telling me he was wondering whether we at St George's might form the basis of a feature. The Church of

England at work in modern London.' Derek's nose twitched. 'Old wine in new bottles, one might say.'

'Amazing, when you think about it.' Howell grinned at them. 'Here we are, in an increasingly godless society, but Joe Public just can't get enough of the good old C of E.'

'I don't know if I'd agree with you there, Frank.' Derek flashed his teeth in a conciliatory smile. 'Sometimes I think we are not as godless as some of us like to think. Attendance figures are actually increasing – I can find you the statistic, if you want. You have to hand it to the Evangelicals, they have turned the tide. Of course, at St George's we try to have something for everyone – a broad, non-sectarian approach. We see ourselves as –'

'You're doing a fine job, all right.' Howell kept his eyes on Sally. 'But at the end of the day, what sells a feature is human interest. It's the people who count, eh? So maybe we could have a chat sometime.' He glanced round the little circle of faces. 'With all of you, that is.'

'Delighted,' Derek replied for them all. 'I –'

'Good. I'll give you a ring then, set something up.' Howell glanced at his watch. 'Good Lord – is that the time? Must love you and leave you.'

Derek watched him go. 'Frank was very helpful over the conversion of the Lady Chapel,' he murmured to Sally, patting her arm. 'He did a piece on the opening ceremony. We had the bishop, you know.' Suddenly he stood on tiptoe, and waved vigorously at his wife. 'There's Margaret – I know she wanted a word with you, Sally. I think she may have found you a baby-sitter. She's not one of ours, but a lovely woman, all the same. Utterly reliable, too. Her name's Carla Vaughan.'

On the way home to Hercules Road, Michael and Sally conducted an argument in whispers in the front of the car while Lucy, strapped into the back seat, sang along with 'Puff the Magic Dragon' on the stereo. It was not so much an argument as a quarrel with gloves on.

'Aren't we going rather fast?' Sally asked.

'I didn't realize we were going to be so late.'

'Nor did I. The service took longer than I expected, and –'

'I'm worried about lunch. I left it on quite high.'

16

Sally remembered all the meals which had been spoiled because Michael's job had made him late. She counted to five to keep her temper in check.

'This Carla woman, Sal – the child minder.'

'What about her?'

'I wish we knew a bit more.'

'She sounds fine to me. Anyway, I'll see her before we decide.'

'I wish –'

'You wish what?'

He accelerated through changing traffic lights. 'I wish she wasn't necessary.'

'We've been through all this, haven't we?'

'I suppose I thought your job might be more flexible.'

'Well, it's not. I'm sorry but there it is.'

He reacted to her tone as much as to her words. 'What about Lucy?'

'She's your daughter too.' Sally began to count to ten.

'I know. And I know we agreed right from the start we both wanted to work. But –'

Sally reached eight before her control snapped. 'You'd like me to be something sensible like a teacher, wouldn't you? Something safe, something that wouldn't embarrass you. Something that would fit in with having children. Or better still, you'd like me to be just a wife and mother.'

'A child needs her parents. That's all I'm saying.'

'This child has two parents. If you're so concerned –'

'And what's going to happen when she's older? Do you want her to be a latchkey kid?'

'I've got a job to do, and so have you. Other people manage.'

'Do they?'

Sally glanced in the mirror at the back of the sun visor. Lucy was still singing along with a robust indifference to the tune, but she had Jimmy pushed against her cheek; she sensed that her parents were arguing.

'Listen, Michael. Being ordained is a vocation. It's not something I can just ignore.'

He did not reply, which fuelled her worst fears. He used silence as a weapon of offence.

17

'Anyway, we talked about all this before we married. I know the reality is harder than we thought. But we agreed. Remember?'

His hands tightened on the steering wheel. 'That was different. That was before we had Lucy. You're always tired now.'

Too tired for sex, among other things: another reason for guilt. At first they had made a joke of it, but even the best jokes wore thin with repetition.

'That's not the point.'

'Of course it's the point, love,' he said. 'You're trying to do too much.'

There was another silence. 'Puff the Magic Dragon' gave way to 'The Wheels on the Bus'. Lucy kicked out the rhythm on the back of Sally's seat, attention-seeking behaviour. This should have been a time of celebration after Sally's first service at St George's. Now she wondered whether she was fit to be in orders at all.

'You'd rather I wasn't ordained,' Sally said to Michael, voicing a fear rather than a fact. 'In your heart of hearts, you think women clergy are unnatural.'

'I never said that.'

'You don't need to say it. You're just the same as Uncle David. Go on, admit it.'

He stared at the road ahead and pushed the car over the speed limit. Mentioning Uncle David had been a mistake. Mentioning Uncle David was always a mistake.

'Come on.' Sally would have liked to shake him. 'Talk to me.'

They finished the journey in silence. In an effort to use the time constructively, Sally tried to pray for the old woman who had cursed her. She felt as if her prayers were falling into a dark vacuum.

'Your will be done,' she said again and again in the silence of her mind; and the words were merely sounds emptied of meaning. It was as if she were talking into a telephone and not knowing whether the person on the other end was listening or even there at all. She tried to persuade herself that this was due to the stress of the moment. Soon the stress would pass, she told herself, and normal telephonic reception would be restored. It would be childish to suppose that the problem was caused by the old woman's curse.

'Shit,' said Michael, as they turned into Hercules Road. Someone had usurped their parking space.

'It's all right,' Sally said, hoping that Lucy had not heard. 'There's a space further up.'

Michael reversed the Rover into it, jolting the nearside rear wheel against the kerb. He waited on the pavement, jingling his keys, while Sally extracted Lucy and her belongings.

'What's for lunch?' Lucy demanded. 'I'm hungry.'

'Ask your father.'

'A sort of lamb casserole with haricot beans.' Michael tended to cook what he liked to eat.

'Yuk. Can I have Frosties instead?'

Their flat was in a small, purpose-built block dating from the 1930s. Michael had bought it before their marriage. It was spacious for one person, comfortable for two and just large enough to accommodate a small child as well. As Sally opened the front door, the smell of burning rushed out to greet them.

'Shit,' Michael said. 'And double shit.'

Before Lucy was born, Sally and Michael Appleyard had decided that they would not allow any children they might have to disrupt their lives. They had seen how the arrival of children had affected the lives of friends, usually, it seemed, for the worse. They themselves were determined to avoid the trap.

They had met through Michael's job, almost six years before Sally was offered the Kensal Vale curacy. Michael had arrested a garage owner who specialized in selling stolen cars. Sally, who had recently been ordained as a deacon, knew his wife through church and had responded to a desperate phone call from her. The apparent urgency was such that she came as she was, in gardening clothes, with very little make-up and without a dog collar.

'It's a mistake,' the woman wailed, tears streaking her carefully made-up face, 'some ghastly mistake. Or someone's fitted him up. Why can't the police understand?'

While the woman alternately wept and raged, Michael and another officer had searched the house. It was Sally who dealt with the children, talked to the solicitor and held the woman's hand while they asked her questions she couldn't or wouldn't answer. At the time she took little notice of Michael except to think that he carried out a difficult job with more sensitivity than she would have expected.

Three evenings later, Michael arrived out of the blue at Sally's flat. On this occasion she was wearing her dog collar. Ostensibly he wanted to see if she had an address for the wife, who had disappeared. On impulse she asked him in and offered him coffee. At this second meeting she looked at him as an individual and on the whole liked what she saw: a thin face with dark eyes and a fair complexion; the sort of brown hair that once had been blond; medium height, broad shoulders and slim hips. When she came into the sitting room with the coffee she found him in front of the bookcase. He did not comment directly on its contents or on the crucifix which hung on the wall above.

'When were you ordained?'

'Only a few weeks ago.'

'In the Church of England?'

She nodded, concentrating on pouring the coffee.

'So that means you're a deacon?'

'Yes. And that's as far as I'm likely to get unless the Synod votes in favour of women priests.'

'A deacon can do everything a priest can except celebrate Communion: is that right?'

'More or less. Are you –?'

'A practising Christian? I'm afraid it's more theory than practice. My godfather's a priest.'

'Where?'

'He lives in Cambridge now. He's retired. He used to teach at a theological college in the States.' Michael sipped his coffee. 'I doubt if Uncle David approves of the ordination of women.'

'Many older priests find it hard to accept. And younger ones, too, for that matter. It's not easy for them.'

They went on to talk of other things. As he was leaving, he paused in the doorway and asked her out to dinner. The invitation surprised her as much (he later admitted) as it surprised him. She refused, but he kept on asking until she accepted, just to get rid of him.

Michael took her to a Chinese restaurant in Swiss Cottage. For most of the time he encouraged her to talk about herself, either evading or returning short answers to the questions she lobbed in return. She told him that she had left her job as a careers adviser in order to go to theological college. Now she was ordained, she had little chance of finding a curacy in the immediate future, all the more so because her father was ill and she did not want to move too far away from him.

'Besides, a lot of dioceses have no time for women deacons.'

Michael pushed the dish of roast duck towards her. 'If you're a deacon – or a priest – well, that has to come first, I suppose? It has to be the most important thing in life, your first allegiance.'

'Of course.'

'So where do people fit in? I know you're not married, but do you have a boyfriend? And what about children? Or would God be more important?'

'Are you always like this?'

'Like what?'

'So pushy.'

'I'm not usually like this at all.'

She bent over her plate, knowing her thick hair would curtain her face. In those days she had worn it long, and gloried in it.

'You're not celibate, are you?' he asked.

'It's nothing to do with you.'

'Yes, it is.'

'As it happens, no. But it's still nothing to do with you.'

Three months later they were married.

It was ridiculous, Sally told herself, to read significance into the malicious ramblings of an unhappy woman. To see them as a portent would be pure superstition. Yet in the weeks that followed Sally's first service at St George's, the old woman was often in her mind. The memory of what she had said was like a spreading stain. No amount of rubbing would remove it.

May God damn you and yours.

When Sally had been offered the curacy at Kensal Vale, it had seemed almost too good to be true, an answer to prayer. Although she was not personally acquainted with Derek Cutter, the vicar of St George's, his reputation was impressive: he was

21

said to be a gifted and dedicated parish priest who had breathed new life into a demoralized congregation and done much good in the parish as a whole.

The timing had seemed right, too. Sally's father had died the previous winter, bringing both sorrow and an unexpected sense of liberation. Lucy was ready to start school. Sally could at last take a full-time job with a clear conscience. And Kensal Vale was geographically convenient: she could walk from Hercules Road to St George's Vicarage in forty minutes and drive it in much less, traffic permitting. The only drawback had been Michael's lack of enthusiasm.

'What about Lucy?' he had asked in an elaborately casual voice when she mentioned the offer to him. 'She won't be at school all the time.'

'We'll find a child minder. It could actually do her good. She needs more stimulation than she gets at home.'

'Maybe you're right.'

'Darling, we've discussed all this.' Not once, Sally thought, but many times. 'I was never going to be the sort of mother that stays at home all day to iron the sheets.'

'Of course not. And I'm sure Lucy'll be fine. But are *you* sure Kensal Vale's a good idea?'

'It's just the sort of parish I want.'

'Why?'

'It's a challenge, I suppose. More rewarding in the end. Besides, I want to show I can do it, that a woman can do it.' She glared at him. 'And I need the stimulation, too. I've been freewheeling for far too long.'

'But have you thought it through? I wouldn't have said that Kensal Vale's particularly safe these days.' He hesitated. 'Especially for a woman.'

'I'll cope,' Sally snapped. 'I'm not a fool.' She watched his mouth tightening and went on in a gentler voice, 'In any case, jobs like this don't grow on trees. If I turn this down, I may not be offered another for years. And I need to have experience before I can be priested.'

He shrugged, failing to concede the point, and turned the discussion to the practical details of the move. He was unwilling to endorse it but at least he had not opposed it.

As summer slipped into autumn, Sally began to wonder if Michael might have been right. She was sleeping badly and her dreams were going through a patch of being uncomfortably vivid. The work wasn't easy, and to make matters worse she seemed to have lost her resilience. In the first week, she was rejected by a dying parishioner because she was a woman, a smartly dressed middle-aged man spat on her in the street, and her handbag was stolen by a gang of small boys armed with knives. Similar episodes had happened before, but previously she had been able to digest them with relative ease and consign them to the past. Now they gave her spiritual indigestion. The images stayed with her: the white face on the pillow turning aside from the comfort she brought; the viscous spittle gleaming on her handkerchief; and, hardest of all to forget, the children, some no more than five years older than Lucy, circling her in their monstrous game with knives in their hands and excitement in their faces.

Nothing went right at home, either. Michael had retreated further into himself since the squabble on the way back from church and the subsequent discovery that Sunday lunch had turned into a burnt offering. There were no open quarrels but the silences between them grew longer. It was possible, Sally thought, that the problem had nothing to do with her – he might be having a difficult time at work.

'Everything's fine,' he replied when she asked him directly, and she could almost hear the sound of the drawbridge rising and the portcullis descending.

Sally persevered. 'Have you seen Oliver lately?'

'No. Not since his promotion.'

'That's great. When did it happen?'

'A few weeks back.'

Why hadn't Michael told her before? Oliver Rickford had been his best man. Like Michael, he had been a high-flier at Hendon police college. They had not worked together since they had been constables, but they still kept in touch.

'Why's he been made up to inspector and not you?'

'He says the right things in committee meetings.' Michael looked at her. 'Also he's a good cop.'

'We must have him and Sharon over for supper. To celebrate.'

Sally disliked Sharon. 'Tuesdays are usually a good evening for me.'

Michael grunted, his eyes drifting back to the newspaper in front of him.

'I suppose we should ask the Cutters sometime, too.'

'Oh God.' This time he looked up. 'Must we?'

Their eyes met and for an instant they were united by their shared dislike of the Cutters. The dislike was another of Sally's problems. As the weeks went by, she discovered that Derek Cutter preferred to keep her on the sidelines of parish work. He made her feel that wearing a deacon's stole was the clerical equivalent of wearing L-plates. She suspected that in his heart of hearts he was no more a supporter of women clergy than Michael's Uncle David. At least David Byfield made his opposition perfectly clear. Derek Cutter, on the other hand, kept his carefully concealed. She attributed her presence in his parish to expediency: the archdeacon was an enthusiastic advocate of the ordination of women, and Derek had everything to gain by keeping on the right side of his immediate superior. He liked to keep on the right side of almost everyone.

'Lovely to see you,' Derek said to people when he talked to them after a service or at a meeting or on their doorsteps. 'You're looking blooming.' And if he could, he would pat them, young or old, male or female. He liked physical contact.

'It's not enough to love each other,' he wrote in the parish magazine. 'We must *show* that we do. We must wear our hearts on our sleeves, as children do.'

Derek was fond of children, though he preferred to look resolutely on the sunny side of childhood. This meant in effect that his benevolent interest was confined to children under the age of seven. Children grew up quickly in Kensal Vale and the area had an extensive population of little criminals. The picture of him in the Parish Room showed him beaming fondly at a photogenic baby in his arms. In his sermon on Sally's second Sunday at St George's he quoted what was evidently a favourite text.

'Let the children come to me, Jesus told his disciples. Do not try to stop them. For the kingdom of God belongs to such as these. Mark ten, fourteen.'

There should be more to being a vicar, Sally thought, than a fondness for patting people, a sentimental attachment to young children and a range of secular skills that might have earned him a decent living in public relations or local government.

Sally knew that she was being unfair to Derek. As an administrator he was first class. The parish's finances were in good order. The church was well-respected in the area. There was a disciplined core congregation of over a hundred people. As a parish, St George's had a sense of community and purpose: Derek deserved much of the credit for this. And some of the credit must also be due to his wife. The Cutters, as Derek was fond of telling people, were a team.

Margaret Cutter was a plump woman who looked as if she had been strapped into her clothes. She had grey hair styled to resemble wire wool. Her kindness was the sort that finds its best expression in activity, preferably muscular. She invited Sally for coffee at the Vicarage on the Tuesday after Sally's first service at St George's. They sat in a small, overheated sitting room whose most noteworthy features were the bars on the window and the enormous photocopying machine behind the sofa. On top of the television set stood a toy rabbit with soft pink fur and a photograph of Derek and Margaret on their wedding day. Sally thought that she looked older than her husband.

'Just us two girls,' Margaret said, offering Sally a plate of digestive biscuits, which proved to be stale. 'I thought it would be nice to have a proper chat.' The chat rapidly turned into a monologue. 'It's the women who are the real problem. You just wouldn't believe the way they throw themselves at Derek.' The tone was confiding, but the dark eyes flickered over Sally as if measuring her for a shroud. 'Of course, he doesn't see it. But isn't that men all over? They're such fools where women are concerned. That's why they need us girls to look after them.' Here she inserted a pause which gave Sally ample time to realize that, astonishing as it might seem, Margaret was warning her that Derek was off limits as a potential object of desire. 'I knew when I married him that he was going to be a full-time job. I used to be a lecturer, you know, catering was my subject; they begged me to stay but I said, "No, girls, I only wish I could but I have to think of Derek now." Well, that's marriage, isn't it, for better or

25

for worse, you have to give it top priority or else you might as well not do it.' She stroked her own forearm affectionately. 'You must find it very hard, Sally, what with you both working and having the kiddie to think of as well. Still, I expect your Lucy's grown used to it, eh? Such a sweet kiddie. In some ways it's a blessing that Derek and I haven't had children. I honestly don't think we would have had time to give them the love and attention they need. But that reminds me, I promised to give you Carla Vaughan's phone number. I must admit she's not to everyone's taste, but Derek thinks very highly of her. He sees the best in everyone, Derek does. You do realize that Carla's a single parent? Two little kiddies, with different fathers and I don't think she was married to either. Still, as Derek says, who are we to cast the first stone? Did he mention she likes to be paid in cash?'

The following day, Wednesday, Sally took Lucy to meet Carla. She lived in a small terraced house which was almost exactly halfway between St George's and Hercules Road. Half West Indian and half Irish, she had an enormous mop of red curly hair which she wore in a style reminiscent of a seventeenth-century periwig. The house seethed with small children and the noise was formidable. Carla's feet were bare, and she was dressed in a green tanktop and tight trousers which revealed her sturdy legs and ample behind; she was not a woman who left much to the imagination.

Carla swept a bundle of magazines from one of the chairs. 'Do you want a Coke or something? And what about you, Lucy?'

Lucy shook her head violently. She kept close to her mother and stared round-eyed at the other children, who ignored her. Carla took two cans from the refrigerator and gave one to Sally.

'Saves washing up. You don't mind, do you?' She stared with open curiosity at the dog collar. 'What should I call you, by the way? Reverend or something?'

'Sally, please. What a lovely big room.'

'One of my fellas did it for me. He was a builder. I told him to knock down all the walls he could without letting the house fall down. And when he'd finished I gave him his marching orders. I'm through with men. If you ask me, you're better off without them.' She leaned forward and lowered her voice slightly. 'Sex. You can keep it. Mind you, men have their uses when you need a bit of DIY.'

Sally glanced round the room, ostensibly admiring the decor. She noticed that most of the horizontal surfaces held piles of washing, disposable nappies, toys, books, empty sweet packets and video tapes. The back door was open and there was a sunlit yard beyond with a small swing and what looked like a sandpit. Sally thought that the place was fundamentally clean under the clutter and that the children seemed happy; she hoped this was not wishful thinking.

While she and Carla discussed the arrangements, Lucy feigned an interest in the twenty-four-inch television set, which was glowing and mumbling in a recess where there had once been a fireplace; she pretended to be absorbed in an episode from *Thomas the Tank Engine*, a programme she detested.

'Why don't you leave her for an hour or two? Trial run, like.'

Sally nodded, ignoring the sudden surge of panic. Lucy lunged at her arm.

'You just go, honey.' Carla detached Lucy with one hand and gave Sally a gentle push with the other. 'Have you ever made gingerbread robots with chocolate eyes?' she asked Lucy.

The crying stopped for long enough for Lucy to say, 'No.'

'Nor have I. And we won't be able to unless you can help me find the chocolate.'

Sally slipped out of the house. She hated trusting Lucy to a stranger. But whatever she did, she would feel guilty. If you had to list the top ten attributes of modern motherhood, then guilt would be high up there in the top three.

Sally Appleyard could not say when she first suspected that she was being watched. The fear came first, crawling slowly into her life when she was not looking, masquerading as a sense of unease. Her dreams filled with vertiginous falls, slowly opening doors and the sound of footsteps in empty city streets.

Rightly or wrongly she associated the change in the emotional weather with the appearance in mid-September of Frank Howell's feature in the *Evening Standard*. In his idiosyncratic way the balding cherub had done St George's proud. Here, Sally was interested to learn, was the real Church of England. Two photographs accompanied the piece: one of Derek equipped with dog collar, denim jacket and Afro-Caribbean toddler; the other of Sally. In the text Howell described the incident at Sally's first service.

'Pity he had to choose St George's,' Michael said when he saw the article.

'Why?'

'Because now all the nutters will know you're there.'

She laughed at him but his words lingered in her memory. There was no shortage of rational explanations for what she felt. She was tired and worried. It was not unnatural, particularly for a woman, to equate a sense of unease with being watched. She knew that a solitary and reasonably attractive woman was vulnerable in parts of the parish. To a certain type of male predator her profession might even add to her allure. Perhaps Michael had inadvertently planted the idea in her mind. Besides, to some extent she really was under observation: she was still a novelty in Kensal Vale: the woman with the dog collar was someone to stare at, to point out, sometimes to laugh at, and occasionally to abuse.

She-devil. Blasphemer against Christ. Apostate. Impious bitch. Whore of Babylon. Daughter of Satan.

One evening near the end of the month she was later home than expected. Michael was watching from the window.

'Where the hell were you?' he demanded as he opened the door to her. 'Do you know what time it is?'

'I'm sorry,' she snapped, her mind still full of the room she had left, with the bed, the people, the smells and the chattering television and the view from a high window of Willesden Junction beneath an apocalyptic western sky. 'Someone was dying and there wasn't a phone.'

'You should have sent someone out, then. I've phoned the Cutters, the hospitals, the police.'

His face crumpled. She put her arms around him. They clung together by the open door. Michael's hands stroked her back and her thighs. His mouth came down on hers.

She craned her head away. 'Michael –'

28

'Hush.'

He kissed her again and this time she found herself responding. She tried to blot out the memory of the room with the high window. One of his hands slipped round to the front of her jeans. She shifted back to allow his fingers room to reach the button of the waistband.

'Mummy,' Lucy called. 'I'm thirsty.'

'Oh God.' Michael drew back, grimacing at Sally. 'You go and see her, love. I'll get the drink.'

The following evening, he came home with a personal alarm and a mobile phone.

'Are you sure I need all these?'

'*I* need you to have them.'

'But the cost. We –'

'Bugger the cost, Sal.'

She smiled at him. 'I'm no good with gadgets.'

'You will be with these.'

She touched his hand. 'Thank you.'

The alarm and the phone helped at least for a time. The fact that Carla could now contact her at any time was also reassuring. But the fear returned, a familiar devil. Feeling watched was a part of it. So too was a sense of the watcher's steady, intelligent malevolence. Behind the watching was a fixed purpose.

But there was nothing, or very little, to pin it to. The evidence was skimpy, almost invisible, and capable of innocent interpretations: a small, pale van which one afternoon followed her car round three successive left turns; someone in a long raincoat walking down Hercules Road late at night and glancing up at the windows of the flat; warm breath on the back of her neck in a crowd swirling down the aisle of a supermarket; Lucy's claim that a man had winked at her in the library when she went there with Carla and the other children. As to the rest, what did it amount to but the occasional shiver at the back of the neck, the sense that someone might be watching her?

To complicate matters, Sally did not trust her instincts. She couldn't be sure whether the fear was a response to something in the outside world or merely a symptom of an inner disturbance. This was nothing new: since her teens, she had trained herself to be wary of her intuitions partly because she did not understand them and partly because she knew they could be misleading. She lumped them together with the uncomfortably vivid dreams and the moments when time seemed to stand still. They were interesting and disturbing: but there was nothing to show that they were more than freak outbreaks of bioelectrical activity.

The scepticism was doubly necessary at present: she was under considerable strain, in a state which might well induce a certain paranoia. In the end it was a question of degree. Carrying a rape alarm was a sensible precaution against a genuine danger: acting as if she were a potential terrorist target was not.

In November, leaves blew along the pavements, dead fireworks lined the gutters, and mists smelling of exhaust fumes and decaying vegetables softened the outlines of buildings. In November, Uncle David came to lunch.

The 'Uncle' was a courtesy title. David Byfield was Michael's godfather. He had been a friend of his parents and his connection with Michael had survived their deaths and the cooling of his godson's religious faith. An Anglo-Catholic, he was often addressed as 'Father Byfield' by those of the same persuasion. The November lunch in London had become a regular event. In May the Appleyards went to Cambridge for a forbiddingly formal return fixture at the University Arms.

This Saturday was the worst yet. It began badly with an emergency call from Derek, who had gone down with toothache and wanted Sally to take a wedding for him. Sally abandoned the cooking and Lucy to Michael. Neither the service nor the obligatory appearance at the reception did much for her self-esteem. The bride and groom were disgruntled to see her rather than Derek, and the groom's mother asked if the happy couple would have to have a proper wedding afterwards with a real clergyman.

When Sally returned to Hercules Road she found the meal over, the sink full of dirty plates, the atmosphere stinking of David's cigarettes and Lucy in tears. Averting his eyes from her dog collar, David stood up to shake hands. Lucy chose this moment to announce that Daddy was an asshole, an interesting new word she had recently picked up at Carla's. Michael slapped her leg and Lucy's tears became howls of anguish.

'You sit down,' Michael told Sally. 'I'll deal with her.' He towed Lucy away to her room.

David Byfield slowly subsided into his chair. He was a tall, spare man with prominent cheekbones and a limp due to an arthritic hip. As a young man, Sally thought, he must have been very good-looking. Now he was at least seventy, and a lifetime of self-discipline had given his features a harsh, almost predatory cast; his skin looked raw and somehow thinner than other people's.

'I'm so sorry not to have been here for lunch,' Sally said, trying to ignore the distant wails. 'An unexpected wedding.'

David inclined his head, acknowledging that he had heard.

'The vicar had to go to casualty. Turned out to be an abscess.' Why did she have to sound so bright and cheery? 'Has Lucy been rather a handful?'

'She's a lively child. It's natural.'

'It's a difficult age,' Sally said wildly; all ages were difficult. 'She's inclined to play up when I'm not around.'

That earned another stately nod, and also a twitch of the lips which possibly expressed disapproval of working mothers.

'I hope Michael has fed you well?'

'Yes, thank you. Have you had time to eat, yourself?'

'Not yet. There's no hurry. Do smoke, by the way.'

He stared at her as if nothing had been further from his mind.

'How's St Thomas coming along?'

'The book?' The tone reproved her flippancy. 'Slowly.'

'Aquinas must be a very interesting subject.'

'Indeed.'

'I read somewhere that his fellow students called him the dumb ox of Sicily,' Sally said with a touch of desperation. 'Do you have a title yet?'

'*The Angelic Doctor*.'

Sally quietly lost her temper. One moment she had it under firm control, the next it was gone. 'Tell me, do you think that a man who was fascinated by the nature of angels has anything useful to say to us?'

'I think St Thomas will always have something useful to say to those of us who want to listen.'

31

Not trusting herself to speak, Sally poured herself a glass of claret from the open bottle on the table. She gestured to David with the bottle.

'No, thank you.'

For a moment they listened to the traffic in Hercules Road and Lucy's crying, now diminishing in volume.

The phone rang. Sally seized it with relief.

'Sally? It's Oliver. Is Michael there?'

'I'll fetch him.'

She opened the living room door. Michael was sitting on Lucy's bed, rocking her to and fro on his lap. She had her eyes closed and her fingers in her mouth; they both looked very peaceful. He looked at Sally over Lucy's face.

'Oliver.'

For an instant his face seemed to freeze, as though trapped by the click of a camera shutter. 'I'll take it in the bedroom.'

Lucy whimpered as Michael passed her to Sally. In the sitting room, Lucy curled up on one end of the sofa and stared longingly at the blank screen of the television. Sally picked up the handset of the phone. Oliver was speaking: '. . . complaining. You know what that . . .' She dropped the handset on the rest.

'It's a colleague of Michael's. I'm afraid it may be work.'

'I should be going.' David began to manoeuvre himself forward on the seat of the chair.

'There's no hurry, really. Stay for some tea. Anyway, perhaps Michael won't have to go out.' Desperate for a neutral subject of conversation, she went on, 'It's Oliver Rickford, actually. Do you remember him? He was Michael's best man.'

'I remember.'

There was another silence. The subject wasn't neutral after all: it reminded them both that David had refused to conduct their wedding. According to Michael, he had felt it would be inappropriate because for theological reasons he did not acknowledge the validity of Sally's orders. He had come to the service, however, and hovered, austere and unfestive, at the reception. He had presented them with a small silver clock which had belonged to his wife's parents. The clock did not work but Michael insisted on having it on the mantelpiece. Sally stared at it now, the hands eternally at ten to three and not a sign of bloody honey.

Michael came in. She knew from his face that he was going out, and knew too that something was wrong. Lucy began to cry and David said he really should leave before the light went.

The last Friday in November began with a squabble over the breakfast table about who should take Lucy to Carla's. As the school was closed for In-Service Training, Lucy was to stay with the child minder all day.

'Can't you take her this once, Michael? I promised I'd give Stella a lift to hospital this morning.'

'Why didn't you mention it before?'

'I did – last night.'

'I don't remember. Stella's not ill, is she?'

'They're trying to induce her daughter. It's her first. She's a couple of weeks overdue.'

'It's not going to make that much difference if Stella gets there half an hour later, is it?'

'It'll be longer than that because I'll hit the traffic.'

'I'm sorry. It's out of the question.'

'Why? Usually you can –'

Michael pushed his muesli bowl aside with such force that he spilled his tea. 'This isn't a usual day.' His voice was loud and harsh. 'I've got a meeting at nine-fifteen. I can't get out of it.'

Sally opened her mouth to reply but happened to catch Lucy's eye. Their daughter was watching them avidly.

'Very well. I'd better tell Stella.'

She left the room. After she made the phone call she made the beds because she couldn't trust herself to go back into the kitchen. She heard Michael leaving the flat. He didn't call good-bye. Usually he would have kissed her. She was miserably aware that too many of their conversations ended in arguments. Not that there seemed to be much time at present even to argue.

On the way to Carla's, Sally worried about Michael and tried to concentrate on driving. Meanwhile, Lucy talked incessantly. She had a two-pronged strategy. On the one hand she empha-sized how much she didn't want to go to Carla's today, and how she really wanted to stay at home with Mummy; on the other she made it clear that her future happiness depended on whether or not Sally bought her a conjuring set that Lucy had seen advertised on television. The performance lacked subtlety but it was relentless and in its primitive way highly skilled. What Lucy had not taken into account, however, was the timing.

'Do be quiet, Lucy,' Sally snarled over her shoulder. 'I'm not going to take you to Woolworth's. And no, we're not spending all that money on a conjuring set. Not today, and not for Christmas. It's just not worth it. Overpriced rubbish.'

Lucy tried tears of grief and, when these failed, tears of rage. For once it was a relief to leave her at Carla's.

The day moved swiftly from bad to worse. Driving Stella to hospital took much longer than Sally had anticipated because of roadworks. Stella was worried about her daughter and inclined to be grumpy with Sally because of the delay; but once at the hospital she was reluctant to let Sally go.

The hospital trip made Sally late for the monthly committee meeting dealing with the parish finances which began at eleven. She arrived to find that Derek had taken advantage of her absence and rushed through a proposal to buy new disco equipment for the Parish Room, a scheme which Sally thought unnecessarily expensive. Despite his victory, Derek was in a bad mood because during the night someone had spray-painted a question on the front door of the Vicarage: IS THERE LIFE BEFORE DEATH?

'Infuriating,' he said to Sally after the meeting. 'So childish.'

'At least it's not obscene.'

'If only they had come and talked to me instead.'

'There are theological implications,' she pointed out. 'You could use it in a sermon.'

'Very funny, I'm sure.'

He scowled at her. For a moment she almost liked him. Only for a moment. She walked back to her car in the Vicarage car park. It was then that she discovered that she had left her cheque book and a bundle of bills at home. The bills were badly overdue and in any case she wanted to draw cash for the weekend. Skipping lunch, she drove back to Hercules Road where to her surprise she found Michael. He was sitting at his desk in the living room going through one of the drawers. There was a can of lager on top of the desk.

'What are you doing?'

He glanced at her and she knew at once that their quarrel at breakfast time had not been forgotten or forgiven. 'I have to check something. All right?'

Sally nodded as curtly as he had spoken. In silence she collected her cheque book and the bills. On her way out, she forced herself to call goodbye. Once she reached the car she discovered that she had managed to leave her phone behind. She didn't want to go back for it because that would mean seeing Michael again.

She drove miserably back to Kensal Vale. It wasn't just that she knew that Michael was capable of nursing a grudge for days. She worried that this grudge was merely a symptom of something worse. Perhaps he wanted to leave her and was summoning up the strength to make the announcement. Not that there was much to keep him. Their existence had been reduced to routine drudgeries coordinated by a complicated timetable of draconian ferocity. At the thought of life without him her stomach turned over.

She was down to visit a nursing home for the first part of the afternoon, but when she reached the Vicarage (IS THERE LIFE BEFORE DEATH?) she found a message in Derek's neat, italic hand.

Tried to reach you on your mobile. Off to see Archdeacon. Margaret at Brownies p.m. Please ring police at KV – Sergeant Hatherly – re attempted suicide. Paint apparently indelible.

She picked up the telephone and dialled the number of the Kensal Vale police station. She was put through to Hatherly immediately.

'We had this old woman tried to kill herself last night. She's in hospital now. Still in a coma, I understand. I think she's one of your lot so I thought we'd better let you know.'

'What's her name?'

'Audrey Oliphant.'

'I don't know her.'

'She probably knows you, Reverend.' Hatherly used the title awkwardly: like many people inside and outside the Church he wasn't entirely sure how he should address a woman in holy orders. 'She's got a bedsit at twenty-nine Belmont Road. You know it? She's one of the DSS ones, according to the woman who runs the place. Very religious. Her room's full of bibles and crucifixes.'

'What makes you think she's one of ours?'

'She had one of your leaflets. Anyway, I've checked with the RCs. They don't know her from Adam.'

Sally pulled a pad towards her and jotted down the details.

'Took an overdose, it seems. Probably sleeping tablets. According to the landlady, she's a few bricks short of a load. Used to be in some sort of home, I understand. Now they've pushed her out into the community, poor old duck. Poor old community, too.'

'I'll ring the hospital and ask if I can see her. I could go via Belmont Road and see if there's anything she might need.'

'The landlady's a Mrs Gunter. I'll give her a ring if you like. Tell her to expect you. I think she'll be glad if someone else will take the responsibility.'

That makes two of you, thought Sally.

'I knew that one was trouble,' Mrs Gunter said over her shoulder. 'People like Audrey can't cope with real life.' She paused, panting, on the half-landing and stared at Sally with pale, bloodshot eyes. 'When all's said and done, a loony's a loony. You don't want them roaming round the streets. They need looking after.'

They moved slowly up the last flight of stairs. They were on the top floor of the house. Someone was playing rock music in a room below them. The house smelled of cooking and cigarettes. Mrs Gunter stopped outside one of the three doors on the top landing and fiddled with her keyring.

'I phoned that woman at Social Services this morning. I'm sorry, I said, I can't have her back here. It's not on, is it? They pay me to give her a room and her breakfast. I'm not a miracle-worker.' Mrs Gunter darted a hostile glance at Sally. 'I leave the miracles to you.'

She unlocked the door and pushed it open. The room was

small and narrow with a sloping ceiling. The first thing Sally noticed was the makeshift altar. The top of the chest of drawers was covered with a white cloth on which stood a wooden crucifix flanked by two brass candlesticks. The crucifix stood on a stepped base and was about eight inches high. The figure of Christ was made of bone or ivory.

'If you met her on the stairs she was always muttering to herself,' Mrs Gunter said. 'For all I know she was praying.'

The sash window was six inches open at the top and overlooked the back of the house. The air was fresh, damp and very cold. The single bed was unmade. Sally stared at the surprisingly small indentation where Audrey Oliphant had lain. There were no pictures on the walls. A portable television stood on the floor beside the wardrobe; it had been unplugged, and the screen was turned to the wall. In front of the window was a table and chair. Against the wall on the other side of the wardrobe was a spotlessly clean washbasin.

'She left a note.' Mrs Gunter twisted her lips into an expression of disgust. 'Said she was sorry to be such a trouble, and she hoped God would forgive her.'

'How did you find her?'

'She didn't come down to breakfast. I knew she hadn't gone out. Besides, it was time for her to change her sheets. And I wanted to talk to her about the state she leaves the bathroom.'

They found a leather-and-canvas bag with a broken lock in the wardrobe. As they packed it, Mrs Gunter kept up a steady flow of complaint. Meanwhile her hands deftly folded faded nightdresses and smoothed away the wrinkles from a tweed skirt.

'She's run out of toothpaste, the silly woman. I've got a bit left in a tube downstairs. She can have that. I was going to throw it away.'

'Do you know where she went to church?'

'I don't know if she did. Or nowhere regular. If you ask me, this was her church.'

Sally picked up the three books on the bedside table. There was no other reading material in the room. All of them were small and well-used. Sally glanced at them as she dropped them in the bag. First there was a holy bible, in the Authorized Version. Next came a book of common prayer, inscribed 'To Audrey, on the occasion of her First Communion, 20th March 1937, with love from Mother'.

The third book was Sir Thomas Browne's *Religio Medici*, a pocket edition with a faded blue cloth cover. Sally opened the book at the page where there was a marker. She found a faint pencil line in the margin against one sentence. 'The heart of man is the place the Devils dwell in: I feel sometimes a Hell within my self; Lucifer keeps his Court in my breast, Legion is revived in me.'

As Sally read the words her mood altered. The transition was abrupt and jerky, like the effect of a mismanaged gear change on a car's engine. Previously she had felt solitary and depressed. Now she was on the edge of despair. What was the use of this poor woman living her sad life? What was the use of Sally's attempt to help?

The despair was a familiar enemy, though today it was more powerful than usual. Its habit of descending on her was one of those inconvenient facts which she had to live with, like the bad dreams and the absurd moments when time seemed to stop; just another outbreak of freak weather in the mind. While she was driving to the hospital she tried to pray but she could not shift the mood. Her mind was in darkness. She felt the first nibbles of panic. This time the state might be permanent.

On one level Sally continued to function normally. She parked the car and went into the hospital. In the reception area she exchanged a few words with a physiotherapist who sometimes came to St George's. She took the lift up to the seventh floor. A staff nurse was slumped over a desk in the ward office with a pile of files before her. Sally tapped on the glass partition. The nurse looked at the dog collar and rubbed her eyes. Sally asked for Audrey Oliphant.

'You're too late. Died about forty minutes ago.'

'What happened?'

The nurse shrugged – not callous so much as weary. 'The odds are that her heart just gave way under the strain. Do you want to see her?'

They had given Audrey Oliphant a room to herself at the end

38

of the corridor. The sheet had been pulled up to the top of the bed. The staff nurse folded it back.

'Did you know her?'

Sally stared at the dead face: skin and bone, stripped of personality; no longer capable of expressing anger or unhappiness. 'I saw her once in church. I didn't know her name.'

On the bed lay the woman who had cursed her.

Sally found it difficult not to feel that she was in one respect responsible for Audrey Oliphant's death. It made it worse that the old woman now had a name. Perhaps if Sally had tried to trace her, Audrey Oliphant might still be alive. The pressure must have been enormous for a woman of that age and background to kill herself.

She phoned Mrs Gunter from the hospital concourse and gave her the news.

'Best thing for all concerned, really.'

Sally said nothing.

'No point in pretending otherwise, is there?' Mrs Gunter sniffed. 'And now I suppose I'll have to sort out her things. You'd think she'd be more considerate, wouldn't you, being a churchgoer.'

Sally said she would return Audrey Oliphant's bag.

'Hardly seems worth bothering. Audrey said she hadn't got no relations. Not that they'd want her stuff. Nothing worth having, is there? Simplest just to put it out with the rubbish. Except Social Services would go crazy. Crazy? We're all crazy.'

During the afternoon the despair retreated a little. It was biding its time. Sally visited the nursing home. She let herself into St George's and tried to pray for Audrey Oliphant. The church felt cold and alien. The thoughts and words would not come. She found herself reciting the Lord's Prayer in the outmoded version which she had not used since she was a child. The dead woman had probably prayed in this way: 'Our Father, which art in heaven.' The words lay in her mind, heavy and indigestible as badly cooked suet.

Halfway through, she glanced at her watch and realized that if she wasn't careful she would be late picking up Lucy. She gabbled the rest and left the church. The Vicarage was empty but she left a note for Derek, who was still enjoying himself with the archdeacon.

It was raining, sending slivers of gold through the halos of the streetlamps. As Sally drove, she wondered whether Lucy had forgotten the conjuring set. It was unlikely. For one so young she could be inconveniently tenacious.

Sally left the car double-parked outside Carla's house and ran through the rain to the front door. The door opened before she reached it.

Carla was on the threshold, her hands outstretched, her face crumpled, her eyes squeezed into slits and the tears slithering down her dark cheeks. The big living room behind her was in turmoil: it seethed with adults and children; and the television shimmered in the fireplace. A uniformed policewoman put her hand on Carla's arm. She said something but Sally didn't listen.

Michael was there too, talking angrily into the phone, slashing his free hand against his leg to emphasize what he was saying. He stared in Sally's direction but seemed not to register her presence: he was looking past her at something unimaginable.

2

'I am naturally bashful; nor hath conversation, age, or travel,
been able to effront or enharden me . . .'

Religio Medici, I, 40

Eddie called her Angel and so had the children. He knew the
name pleased her but not why. Lucy Appleyard refused to call
Angel anything at all. In that, as in so much else, Lucy was
different.

Lucy Philippa Appleyard was unlike the others even in the
way Angel chose her. It was only afterwards, of course, that
Eddie began to suspect that Angel had a particular reason
for wanting Lucy. Yet again he had been manipulated. The
questions were: how much, how far back did it go – and why?

At the time everything seemed to happen by chance. Eddie
often bought the *Evening Standard*, though he did not always
read it. (Angel rarely read newspapers, partly because she had
little interest in news for its own sake, and partly because they
made her hands dirty.) Frank Howell's feature on St George's,
Kensal Vale, appeared on a Friday. Angel chanced – if that
was the appropriate word – to see it the following Tuesday.
They had eaten their supper and Eddie was clearing up. Angel
wanted to clean her shoes, a job which like anything to do with
her appearance was too important to be delegated to Eddie.

· She spread the newspaper over the kitchen table and fetched
the shoes and the cleaning materials. There were two pairs of
court shoes, one navy and the other black, and a pair of tan
leather sandals. She smeared the first shoe with polish. Then

41

she stopped. Eddie, always aware of her movements, watched as she pushed the shoes off the newspaper and sat down at the table. He put the cutlery away, a manoeuvre which allowed him to glance at the paper. He glimpsed a photograph of a fair-haired man in dog collar and denim jacket, holding a black baby in the crook of his left arm.

'Wouldn't like to meet him on a dark night,' Eddie said. 'Looks like a ferret.' Imagine having *him* running up your trousers, he thought; but he did not say this aloud for fear of offending Angel.

She looked up. 'A curate and a policeman.'

'He's a policeman, too?'

'Not him. There's a woman deacon in the parish. And she's married to a policeman.'

Angel bent her shining head over the newspaper. Eddie pottered about the kitchen, wiping the cooker and the work surfaces. Angel's stillness made him uneasy.

To break the silence, he said, 'They're not really like vicars any more, are they? I mean – that jacket. It's pathetic.'

Angel stared at him. 'It says they have a little girl.'

His attention sharpened. 'The ferret?'

'Not him. The curate and the policeman. Look, there's a picture of the woman.'

Her name was Sally Appleyard, and she had short dark hair and a thin face with large eyes.

'These women priests. If you ask me, it's not natural.' Eddie hesitated. 'If Jesus had wanted women to be priests, he'd have chosen women apostles. Well, wouldn't he? It makes sense.'

'Do you think she's pretty?'

'No.' He frowned, wanting to find words which Angel might want to hear. 'She looks drab, doesn't she? Mousy.'

'You're right. She's let herself go, too. One of those people who just won't make the effort.'

'The little girl. How old is she? Does it say?'

'Four. Her name's Lucy.'

Angel went back to her shoes. Later that evening, Eddie heard her moving around the basement as he watched television in the sitting room above. It was over a year since he had been down there. The memories made him feel restless. He returned to the kitchen to make some tea. While he was there he reread the article about St George's, Kensal Vale. He was not surprised when Angel announced her decision the following morning over breakfast.

'Won't it be dangerous?' Eddie stabbed his spoon at the photograph of Sally Appleyard. 'If her husband's in the CID, they'll pull out all the stops.'

'It won't be more dangerous if we plan it carefully. You've never really understood that, have you? That's why you came a cropper before you met me. A plan's like a clock. If it's properly made it has to work. All you should need to do is wind it up and off it goes. Tick tock, tick tock.'

'Are we all right for money?'

She smiled, a teacher rewarding an apt pupil. 'I shall have to do a certain amount extra to build up the contingency fund. But it's important not to break the routine in any way. I think I might warn Mrs Hawley-Minton that I may have some time off around Christmas.'

During the next two months, from mid-September to mid-November, Angel worked on average four days a week. Sometimes these included evenings and nights. Mrs Hawley-Minton's agency was small and expensive. Word of mouth was all the advertising it needed. Most of the clients were either foreign business people or expatriates paying brief visits home. They were prepared to pay good money for reliable and fully qualified freelance nannies with excellent references and the knack of controlling spoiled children. The tips were good, in some cases extravagantly generous.

'It's a sort of blood money,' Angel explained to Eddie. 'It's not that the parents feel grateful. They feel guilty. That's because they're not doing their duty – they're leaving their children to be brought up by strangers. It's not right, is it? Money can't buy love.'

They were very busy. On the agency days, Angel took the tube down from Belsize Park and made her way to Westminster, Belgravia, Knightsbridge and Kensington. She looked very smart in her navy-blue outfit, her blonde hair tied back, the hem of her skirt swinging just below the knee. Mrs Hawley-Minton's girls did not have a uniform – after all, they were ladies, not servants – but they were encouraged to conform to a discreetly professional house style. Meanwhile, Eddie saw to the cooking, the cleaning and most of the shopping.

In their spare time they made their preparations. For one thing, Angel insisted on repainting the basement, a refinement which Eddie thought unnecessary.

'What's the point? We only did it eighteen months ago.'

'I want everything to be nice and fresh.'

They shared the outside research. Angel liked to say there was no such thing as useless knowledge. If you gathered all the information that could possibly be relevant, and tried to predict every contingency, then your plan could not fail. Working separately, they quartered the broad crescent of north London between Kentish Town in the east and Willesden Junction in the west. They went in the van, on foot and by public transport. Afterwards Angel would set little tests.

'Suppose you're travelling from Kensal Vale: it's rush hour, and there are roadworks on Kilburn High Road, and you want to cut down to Maida Vale: what's your best route?'

The riskier part of the research involved the surveillance of Lucy and her parents. Angel insisted that they be even more cautious than they had been on other occasions because of Michael Appleyard's job. It was easier once they had worked out the geography of the Appleyards' routine. Like the majority of Londoners, the Appleyards spent most of their lives at a handful of locations or travelling to and from them; their city was really an invisible village.

Angel spread out the map on the kitchen table. 'Four main possibilities. St George's, the flat in Hercules Road, the child minder's house, Kensal Vale library.'

'What about shops?' Eddie put in. 'She and her mother often go down West End Lane. And they've driven up to Brent Cross at least twice since we started.'

Angel shook her head. 'I don't like it. Too many video cameras around, especially at Brent Cross. Remember that boy Jamie. Jamie Bulger.'

That year a dank autumn slid imperceptibly into a winter characterized by cutting winds and relentless rain; pedestrians wrapped up warmly and hurried half-disguised along the pavements. On research trips Angel usually wore her long, hooded raincoat, often with the black wig and glasses.

'It makes you look like a monk,' Eddie said with a chuckle as she checked her appearance in the hall mirror one evening. 'Or rather, a nun.'

She slapped him. 'Don't ever say that again, Eddie.'

He rubbed his tingling cheek and apologized, desperate as always for her forgiveness. However hard he tried, he sometimes managed to upset her. He hated himself for his clumsiness. It made everything so uncomfortable when Angel was upset.

Eddie worried about Angel going out alone in the evening. These days no one was safe on the streets of London, and beautiful women were more vulnerable than anyone. One night in October she returned home towards midnight with a torn coat, her colour high and the glasses missing. She told Eddie that a drunk had pawed her in Quex Road.

'It was disgusting. It's made me feel physically sick.'

'But what happened?' Eddie drew her towards the sitting room. For once the roles were reversed. He felt fiercely protective towards her. 'How did you get away?'

'Oh, that wasn't a problem.' She drew her right hand out of her pocket. Silver flashed before his eyes.

'What is it?' He looked more closely and frowned. 'A *scalpel*?'

'I cut open his hand and then his face. Then I ran. If people behave like animals, they have to be treated like animals.'

On another occasion they went together to St George's and stared at the grubby red brick church with its sturdy spire and rain-washed slate roofs. Angel tried the door but it was locked. Eddie was surprised how angry this made her.

'It's terrible. They never used to lock churches when I was young. Not in the daytime.'

'Did you go to church?' Eddie asked, suddenly curious. 'We didn't.'

'Didn't you?' Angel raised her eyebrows. 'Shall we go?' By the middle of November, Angel had decided that it would be best to take Lucy while she was in the care of the child minder. According to the Voters' List, her name was Carla Vaughan.

Angel summed up the woman with three adjectives: fat and vulgar and black.

'You think it'll be easier if we take her from there?' Eddie asked.

'Of course. The Vaughan woman takes far too many children. There's no way she can keep track of them all the time.'

'She was giving them sweets when they were at the library. I bet *she* doesn't make them clean their teeth afterwards. And they were making a dreadful racket in there. She was almost encouraging it.'

'She's a disgrace,' Angel said. 'When she's at home with them, she probably sits them in front of the television and feeds them chocolate to keep them quiet. I'm sure she hasn't any professional qualifications.'

'Lucy'll be better off with us,' Eddie said.

'There's no question of that. She's just not a fit person to have charge of children.'

By the afternoon of Friday the twenty-ninth of November their preparations were almost complete. That was when Eddie acted on the spur of the moment; as so often, it seemed to him that he had no choice in the matter. The sense of his own helplessness outweighed even his fear of what Angel might say and do when she discovered what had happened.

Circumstances played into his hands – forced him to act. Rain, a cold dense blanket like animated fog, had been falling from a dark sky for most of the afternoon, persuading people to stay inside if they had any choice in the matter. At Angel's suggestion, Eddie set out to explore the geography of Carla Vaughan's neighbourhood.

The prospect of plodding through a dreary network of back streets between Kilburn and Kensal Vale would have been boring if it had not scared him so much. In his imagination, this part of London was populated almost exclusively by drug addicts, dark-skinned muggers, gangs of uncontrollable teenagers and drunken Irishmen with violent Republican sympathies.

Shivering at his own daring, he parked the van in the forecourt of a pub called the Rose of Connemara. With the help of a map he navigated his way through the streets around Carla's house. Much of the housing consisted of late-Victorian terraces, with windows on or near the pavement. Lights were on in many of the windows. He glimpsed snug interiors, a series of vignettes illustrating lives which had nothing to do with him: a woman ironing, children watching television, an old man asleep in an armchair, a black couple dancing together, pelvis to pelvis, oblivious of spectators. He met few other pedestrians and none of them tried to mug him.

The way he found Lucy – no, the way Lucy came to him – seemed in retrospect little short of miraculous; if he believed in God he could have taken it as evidence of a divine providence hovering benignly over his affairs. He had been exploring an alley which ran between the back gardens of two terraces. One of the houses on his right was Carla's, and he had carefully counted the gardens in order to establish which belonged to her. He saw no one, though at one point an Alsatian flung itself snarling against a gate as he passed.

He identified Carla's house without trouble. The windows were of the same type as those at the front – UPVC frames with the glass patterned to imitate diamond panes; wholly out of period with the house but typical of the area and the sort of person who lived in it.

The little miracle, his present from Father Christmas, was waiting for him, her dark hair gleaming with pearl-like drops of rainwater.

'It was Lucy's fault,' Eddie told Angel later. 'She's such a tease. She was asking for it.'

Angel was furious when they reached Rosington Road. She didn't say much, not with Lucy there, but she suggested in an icy voice that Eddie might like to go to his room and wait there until she called him. Angel took Lucy to the basement. By that time Lucy had started to cry, which increased Eddie's misery. It made him so sad when children were unhappy.

'I'm too soft for my own good,' he murmured to himself. 'That's my trouble.'

Eddie sat on his bed, hands clasped over his plump stomach, as though trying to restrain the sour ache inside from bursting out. On the wall opposite him was a picture, a brightly coloured reproduction in a yellowing plastic frame. It showed a small girl in a frothy pink dress; she had a pink bow in her dark hair, a mouth like a puckered cherry and huge eyes fringed with dark lashes. The picture had been a Christmas present to Eddie's mother in 1969.

The girl, now seen through water, blurred and buckled. *Oh God. Why don't you help me? Stop this.* There was no God, Eddie knew: and therefore no chance of help. He thought briefly of Lucy's parents, the policeman and the deacon. Let the woman's God console them. That was his job. In any case, Eddie was not responsible for the Appleyards' pain. It had been Angel's decision to take Lucy. So it was her fault, really, her fault and Lucy's. Eddie had been no more than the agent, the dupe, the victim.

Time passed. Eddie would have liked to go down to the kitchen and make himself a drink. Better not – there was no point in upsetting Angel any further. He heard cars passing up and down Rosington Road and snatches of conversation from the pavement. The house itself was silent. The basement was soundproofed and Angel had not switched on the intercom.

'Lucy,' he said softly. 'Lucy Philippa Appleyard.'

Eddie stared at the picture of the girl and stroked his soft little beard. He had been five that Christmas. Had the artist been lucky enough to have a real model, someone like Lucy? He remembered how his mother slowly unwrapped the picture and stared at it; how she picked a shred of tobacco from her lips and flicked it into the ashtray; how she stared across the hearthrug at his father, who had given her the picture. What he could not remember was whether she had spoken her verdict aloud, or whether he had merely imagined it.

'Very nice, Stanley. If you like that sort of thing.'

What had Eddie's father liked? If you asked different people you received different answers: for example, making dolls' houses, taking artistic photographs and helping others less fortunate than himself. All these answers were true.

Stanley Grace spent most of his life working at the head office of Paladin Assurance. The company no longer existed – it had been gobbled up by a larger rival in one of the hostile takeovers of the late 1980s. In the days of its independence, the Paladin had been a womb-like organization which catered for all aspects of its employees' lives. Eddie remembered Paladin holidays, Paladin Christmas cards, Paladin pencils, Paladin competitions and the Paladin Annual Ball. Stanley Grace bought 29 Rosington Road in 1961 with a mortgage arranged through the Paladin, and promptly insured the house, its contents, himself and his wife with Paladin insurance policies.

Eddie never discovered what his father actually did at Paladin. The relationship between his parents was equally mysterious. 'Relationship' was in fact a misleading word since it implied give and take, a movement from one to the other, a way of being together. Stanley and Thelma did not live together: they coexisted in the wary manner of animals from different species obliged by circumstances beyond their control to use the same watering hole.

Eddie remembered asking his mother when he was very young whether he was human.

'Of course you are.'

'And are you human, too?'

'Yes.'

'And Daddy?'

'Oh, for heaven's sake. Of course he is. I wish you'd stop pestering me.'

Stanley was a large, lumbering man built like a bear. He towered over his wife. Thelma was skinny and small, less than five feet high, and she moved like a startled bird. She had a long and cylindrical skull to which features seemed to have been added as an afterthought. Her clothes were usually drab and a size or so too large for her; her cardigans and skirts were dappled with smudges of cigarette ash. (Until the last year of her life she smoked as heavily as her husband.) When, later in life, Eddie came across references to people wearing sackcloth, he thought of his mother.

She was nearly forty when Eddie was born, and Stanley was forty-seven. They seemed more like grandparents than parents. The boundaries of their lives were precisely defined and jealously guarded. Thelma had her headquarters in the kitchen, and her writ ran in the sitting room, the dining room and all the rooms upstairs. The basement was Stanley's alone; he installed a five-lever lock on the door from the hall because, as he would say jocularly, if he left the basement door unlocked, the Little Woman would start dusting and tidying, and he wouldn't be able to find anything. Stanley also had a controlling interest in the tiny paved area which separated the front of the house from the pavement, and in the wilderness at the back.

Gardening was not among Stanley's hobbies and in his lifetime the back garden remained a rank and overgrown place, particularly at the far end, where an accidental plantation of elder, ash and buddleia had seeded itself many years before. Over the tops of the trees could be seen the upper storeys of a block of council flats, which Thelma said lowered the tone of the neighbourhood. At night the lighted windows of the flats reminded Eddie of the superstructure of a liner. He liked to imagine it forging its way across a dark ocean while the passengers ate, drank and danced.

As a child, Eddie had associated the tangle of trees with the sound of distant trains, changing in direction as the wind veered from Gospel Oak and Primrose Hill to Kentish Town and Camden Road. He heard their strange, half-animal noises more clearly than in the house or even in the street – the throbbing of metal on metal, the rush of air and sometimes a scream. When he was very young indeed, he half-convinced himself that the noises were made not by trains, but by dinosaurs who lay in wait for him among the trees or in the patch of wasteland on the other side of the fence.

Though Stanley had no time for gardening, he liked to stand outside on a summer evening while he smoked a cigarette. His head cocked, as if listening carefully to the rumble of the trains, he would gaze in the direction of the trees and sometimes his pale, sad face would look almost happy.

In those days, the late 1960s and early 1970s, Rosington Road was full of children. Most of the houses had been occupied by families, whereas nowadays many of them had been cut up into flats for single people and couples. There had been fewer cars, children played in the street as well as in the gardens, and everyone had known one another. Some of the houses had belonged to the same families since the street was built in the 1890s.

According to Thelma, the house had been Stanley's choice. She would have preferred somewhere more modern in a nice leafy suburb with no blacks or council housing. But her husband felt that his leisure was too important to be frittered away on unnecessary travel and wanted to live closer to the City and the head office of the Paladin. The house was semi-detached, built of smoke-stained London brick, two storeys above a basement. The ground sloped down at the back, so the rear elevation was higher than the front. The other older houses in the road were also semi-detached, though the gaps between each pair and its neighbours were tiny. During the war the area had suffered from bomb damage. One bomb had fallen on the far end of the road and afterwards the council had cleared the ruins to make way for garages and an access road for blocks of flats, newly built homes for heroes, between Rosington Road and the railway line.

Adult visitors rarely came to the house. 'I can't abide having people here,' said Thelma. 'They make too much mess.'

When his mother went out, she would hurry along Rosington Road with her head averted from the windows, and her eyes trained on the kerb. When Eddie was young she would drag him along in her wake, her fingers digging into his arm. 'We must get on,' she would say with an edge of panic to her voice when he complained of a stitch. 'There's so much to do.'

Stanley was very different. As he was leaving home he picked up another persona along with his umbrella, hat and briefcase. He became sociable, even gregarious, as he strolled along Rosington Road on his way to the station. Given a choice, he walked slowly, his chest thrust out, his feet at right angles to each other, which gave his gait more than a suspicion of a waddle. As he progressed down the street, his white, round face turned from side to side, searching for people – for anyone, neighbour or stranger, adult or child.

''Morning. Lovely day. Looks like it's going to last.' He would beam even if it was raining, when his opening gambit was usually, 'Well, at least this weather will be good for the garden.'

At the office Stanley had a reputation for philanthropy. For many years he was secretary to the Paladin Dependants

Committee, an organization which provided small luxuries for the widows and children of former employees of the company. It was he who organized the annual outing to Clacton-on-Sea, and the week's camping holiday, also once a year, which involved him taking a party of children for what he called 'a spot of fresh air under canvas'.

Eddie never went on these outings. 'You wouldn't enjoy it,' Thelma told him when he asked to go. 'Some of the children come from very unfortunate backgrounds. Last year there was a case of nits. Do you know what they are? Head lice. Quite disgusting.' As for his mother, Eddie found it impossible to imagine her in a tent. The very idea was essentially surreal, a yoking of incongruities like a goat in a sundress – or indeed like the marriage of Stanley and Thelma Grace.

His parents shared a bedroom but to all intents and purposes there might have been a glass wall between them. Then why had they stayed together at night? There was a perfectly good spare bedroom. Thelma and Stanley must have impinged on each other in a dozen different ways: her snoring, his trips to the lavatory; her habit of reading into the early hours, his rising at six o'clock and treading ponderously across the room in search of his clothes and the contents of his pockets.

Loneliness? Was that the reason? It seemed such an inadequate answer to such a complicated question.

As it happened, Stanley enjoyed his own company. He spent much of his time in the basement.

The stairs from the hall came down to a large room, originally the kitchen, at the back of the house. Two doors opened from it – one to the former coal cellar, and the other to a dank scullery with a quarry-tiled floor. Because of the lie of the land, the scullery and coal cellar were below ground level at the front of the house. A third door had once given access to the back garden, but Stanley screwed this to its frame in the interests of security.

The basement smelled of enamel paint, turpentine, sawdust, photographic chemicals, cigarettes and damp. Always good with his hands, Stanley built a workbench across the rear wall under the window overlooking the garden. He glued cork tiles to the wall to make a notice board on which he pinned an ever-changing selection of photographs and also a plan of the dolls' house he was working on. He kept free-standing furniture to a minimum – a stool for use at the workbench; a two-seater sofa where he relaxed; and a low Victorian armchair with a button back and ornately carved legs. (The latter appeared and reappeared in many of Stanley's photographs, usually with one or more occupants.)

Finally, there was the tall cupboard built into the alcove on the left of the chimney breast. It had deep, wide shelves and was probably as old as the house. Stanley secured it with an enormous padlock.

In the early days, the basement was forbidden territory to Eddie (and even later he entered it only by invitation). Usually the door was closed but once, as he passed through the hall, Eddie noticed that it was half-open. He crouched and peered down the stairs. Stanley was standing at the workbench examining a photograph with a magnifying glass.

His father turned and saw him. 'Hello, Eddie. I think Mummy's in the kitchen.' With the magnifying glass still in his hand he came towards the stairs, smiling widely in a way that made his cheeks bunch up like a cat's. 'Run along, now. There's a good boy.'

Eddie must have been five or six. He was not usually a bold boy – quite the reverse – but this glimpse of the unknown room had stimulated his curiosity. In his mind he cast about for a delaying tactic. 'That door, Daddy. What's the padlock for?'

The smile remained fixed in place. 'I keep dangerous things in the cupboard. Poisonous photographic chemicals. Very sharp tools.' Stanley bent down and brought his cat's smile very close to Eddie. 'Think how dreadful it would be if there were an accident.'

Eddie must have been about the same age when he overheard an episode which disturbed him, though at the time he did not understand it. Even as an adult he understood it only partly.

It happened during a warm night in the middle of a warm summer. In summer Eddie dreaded going upstairs because he knew it would take him longer than usual to go to sleep.

Pink and sweating, he lay in bed, holding a soft toy, vaguely humanoid but unisex, whom he called Mrs Wump. As so often happens in childhood, time stretched and stretched until it seemed to reach the borders of eternity. Eddie stroked himself, trying to imagine that he was stroking someone else – a cat, perhaps, or a dog; at that age he would have liked either. His palms glided over the curve of his thighs and slipped between his legs. He slid into a waking dream involving Mrs Wump and a soft, cuddly dog.

The noises from the street diminished. His parents came upstairs. As usual his door was ajar; as usual neither of them looked in. He was aware of them following their usual routine – undressing, using the bathroom, returning to their bedroom. Some time later – it might have been minutes or even hours – he woke abruptly.

'Ah – ah –'

His father groaned: a long, creaking gasp unlike any other noise Eddie had heard him make; an inhuman, composite sound not unlike those he associated with the distant trains. Silence fell. This was worse than the noise had been. Something was very wrong, and he wondered if it could somehow be his fault.

A bed creaked. Footsteps shuffled across the bedroom floor. The landing light came on. Then his mother spoke, her voice soft and vicious, carrying easily through the darkness.

'You bloody animal.'

One reason why Eddie liked Lucy Appleyard was because she reminded him of Alison. The resemblance struck him during the October half-term, when Carla took Lucy and the other children to the park. Eddie followed at a distance and was lucky enough to see Lucy on one of the swings.

Alison was only a few months younger than Eddie. But when he had known her she could not have been much older than Lucy was now. The girls' colouring and features were very different. The resemblance lay in how they moved, and how they smiled.

Eddie did not even know Alison's surname. When he was still at the infants' school at the end of Rosington Road, she and her family had taken the house next door on a six-month lease. She had lived with her parents and older brother, a rough boy named Simon.

The father made Alison a swing, which he hung from one of the trees at the bottom of their garden. One day, when Eddie was playing in the thicket at the bottom of the Graces' garden, he discovered that there was a hole in the fence. One of the boards had come adrift from the two horizontal rails which supported them. The hole gave Eddie a good view of the swing, while the trees sheltered him from the rear windows of the houses.

Alison had a mass of curly golden hair, neat little features and very blue eyes. In memory at least, she usually wore a short, pink dress with a flared skirt and puffed sleeves. When she swung to and fro, faster and faster, the air caught the skirt and lifted it. Sometimes the dress billowed so high that Eddie glimpsed smooth thighs and white knickers. She was smaller than Eddie, petite and alluringly feminine. If she had been a doll, he remembered thinking, he would have liked to play with her. In private, of course, because boys were not supposed to play with dolls.

Eddie enjoyed watching Alison. Gradually he came to suspect that Alison enjoyed being watched. Sometimes she shifted her position on the swing so that she was facing the hole in the fence. She would sing to herself, making an elaborate pretence of feeling unobserved; at the time even Eddie knew that the pretence was not only a fake but designed to be accepted as such. She made great play with her skirt, allowing it to ride up and then smoothing it fussily over her legs.

Memory elided the past. The sequence of events had been streamlined; inessential scenes had been edited out, and perhaps some essential ones as well. He remembered the smell of the fence – of rotting wood warmed by summer sunshine, of old creosote, of abandoned compost heaps and distant bonfires. Somehow he and Alison had become friends. He remembered the smooth, silky feel of her skin. It had amazed him that anything could be so soft. Such softness was miraculous.

Left to himself, Eddie would never have broken through the back fence. There were two places behind the Graces' garden, both of which were simultaneously interesting and frightening, though for different reasons: to the right was the corner of the plot on which the council flats had been built; and to the left was the area known to adults and children alike as Carver's, after the company which had owned it before World War II.

The council estate was too dangerous to be worth investigating. The scrubby grass around the blocks of flats was the territory of large dogs and rough children. Carver's contained different dangers. The site was an irregular quadrilateral bounded to the north by the railway and to the south by the gardens of Rosington Road. To the east were the council flats, separated from Carver's by a high brick wall topped with broken glass and barbed wire. To the west it backed on to the yards behind a terrace of shops at right angles to the railway. The place was a labyrinth of weeds, crumbling brick walls and rusting corrugated iron.

According to Eddie's father, Carver's had been an engineering works serving the railway, and during a wartime bombing raid it had received a direct hit. In the playground at Eddie's school, it was widely believed that Carver's was haunted by the ghost of a boy who had died there in terrible, though ill-defined, circumstances.

One morning Eddie arrived at the bottom of the Graces' garden to find Alison examining the fence. On the ground at her feet was a rusting hatchet which Eddie had previously seen in the toolshed next door; it had a tall blade with a rounded projection at the top. She looked up at him.

'Help me. The hole's nearly large enough.'

'But someone might see us.'

'They won't. Come *on*.'

He obeyed, pushing with his hands while she levered with the hatchet. He tried not to think of ghosts, parents, policemen and rough boys from the council flats. The plank, rotting from the ground up, cracked in two. Eddie gasped.

'Ssh.' Alison snapped off a long splinter. 'I'll go first.'

'Do you think we should?'

'Don't be such a baby. We're explorers.'

She wriggled head first into the hole. Eddie followed reluctantly. A few yards from the fence was a small brick shed with most of its roof intact. Alison went straight towards it and pushed open the door, which had parted company with one of its hinges.

'This can be our place. Our special place.'

She led the way inside. The shed was full of rubbish and smelled damp. On the right was a long window which had lost most of its glass. You could see the sky through a hole in the roof. A spider scuttled across the cracked concrete floor.

'It's perfect.'

'But what do you want it for?' Eddie asked.

She spun round, her skirt swirling and lifting, and smiled at him. 'For playing in, of course.'

Alison liked to play games. She taught Eddie how to do Chinese burns, a technique learned from her brother. They also had tickling matches, all the more exciting because they had to be conducted in near silence, in case anyone heard. The loser, usually Eddie, was the one who surrendered or who was the first to make a noise louder than a whisper.

There were other games. Alison, though younger than Eddie, knew many more than he did. It was she who usually took the lead. It was she who suggested the Peeing Game.

'You don't know it?' Her lips formed an O of surprise, behind which gleamed her milk-white teeth and tip of her tongue. 'I thought *everyone* knew the Peeing Game.'

'I've heard about it. It's just that I've never played it.'

'My brother and I've been playing it for years.'

Eddie nodded, hoping she would not expose his ignorance still further.

'We need something to pee into.' Alison took his assent for granted. 'Come on. There must be something in here.'

Eddie glanced round the shed. He was embarrassed even by the word 'pee'. In the Grace household the activity of urination was referred to, when it was mentioned at all, by the euphemism 'spending a penny'. His eye fell on an empty jam jar on a shelf at the back of the shed. The glass was covered on both sides with a film of grime. 'How about that?'

Alison shook her head, and the pink ribbons danced in her hair. 'It's far too small. I can do tons more than that. Anyway, it wouldn't do. The hole's too small.' Something of Eddie's lack of understanding must have shown in his face. 'It's all right for you. You can just poke your willy inside. But with girls it goes everywhere.'

Curiosity stirred in Eddie's mind, temporarily elbowing aside the awkwardness. He picked up a tin. 'What about this?'

Alison examined it, her face serious. The tin was about six inches in diameter and had once contained paint. 'It'll do.' She added with the air of one conferring a favour, 'You can go first.'

His muscles clenched themselves, as they did when he was about to step into cold water.

'Boys always go first,' Alison announced. 'My brother Simon does.'

There seemed no help for it. Eddie turned away from her and began to unbutton the flies of his khaki shorts. Without warning she appeared in front of him. She was carrying the paint tin.

'You have to take your trousers and pants down. Simon does.'

He hesitated. His lower lip trembled.

'It's only a game, stupid. Don't be such a baby. Here – I'll do it.'

She dropped the tin with a clatter on the concrete floor. Brisk as a nurse, she undid the snakeskin buckle of his elasticated belt, striped with the colours of his school, green and purple. Before he could protest, she yanked down both the shorts and his Aertex pants in one swift movement. She stared down at him. He was ashamed of his body, the slabs of pink babyish fat that clung to his belly and his thighs. A boy at the swimming baths had once said that Eddie wobbled like a jelly.

Still staring, Alison said, 'It's smaller than Simon's. And he's a roundhead.'

To his relief, Eddie understood the reference: Simon was circumcised. 'I'm a cavalier.'

'I think I like cavaliers better. They're prettier.' She scooped up the tin. 'Go on – pee.'

She held out the tin. Eddie gripped his penis between the forefinger and thumb of his right hand, shut his eyes and prayed. Nothing happened. In normal circumstances he would have had no trouble in going because his bladder was full.

'If you're going to take all day, I might as well go first.' Alison glared at him. 'Honestly. Simon never has any trouble.'

She placed the tin on the floor, pulled down her knickers and squatted. A steady stream of urine squirted into the can. She raised the hem of her dress and examined it, as though inspecting the quality of the stitching. So that was what girls looked like down there, Eddie thought, still holding his penis; he had often wondered. He craned his neck, hoping for a better view, but Alison smiled demurely and rearranged her dress.

'If you keep on rubbing your willy, it goes all funny. Did you know?' Alison raised herself from the tin and pulled up her knickers. 'At least, Simon's does. Look – I've done gallons.'

Eddie looked. The tin was about a quarter full of liquid the colour of pale gold. Until now he had assumed that he was shamefully unique in having a penis which sometimes altered shape, size and consistency when he touched it; he had hoped that he might grow out of it.

'It's nearly half-full. I bet you can't do as much.'

As Eddie glanced towards Alison, he thought he caught a movement at the window. When he looked there was no one there, just a branch waving in the breeze.

'What did I tell you? It's going stiff.'

Eddie was still holding his penis – indeed, his fingers had been absent-mindedly massaging it.

'Empty my pee outside the shed,' Alison commanded. 'Then you can try again.'

Eddie realized suddenly how absurd he must seem with his shorts and pants around his knees. He pulled them up quickly, buttoned his flies and fastened his belt.

'I don't know why you're bothering to do yourself up. You'll only have to undo it all again.'

He went outside the shed and emptied the can under a bush. The tin was warm. The liquid ran away into the parched earth. It didn't look or smell like urine. He wondered what it would taste like. He pushed the thought away – *disgusting* – and straightened up to return to the shed, his mind full of the ordeal before him. For an instant he thought he smelled freshly burned tobacco in the air.

*   *   *

Eddie and Alison played the Peeing Game on many occasions, and each time they explored a little further.

Fear of discovery heightened the pleasure. When they went into Carver's, there was often a woman on the balcony of one of the council flats. The balcony overlooked both Carver's and the garden of 29 Rosington Road. Sometimes the woman was occupied – hanging washing, watering plants; but on other occasions she simply stood there, very still, and watched the sky. Alison said the woman was mad. Eddie worried that she might see them and tell their parents that they were trespassing in Carver's. But she never did.

Eddie's memories of the period were patchy. (He did not like to think too hard about the possibility that he had willed this to be so.) He must have been six, almost seven, which meant that the year was 1971. It had been summertime, the long school holidays. He remembered the smell of a faded green short-sleeved shirt he often wore, and the touch of Alison's hand, plump and dimpled, on his bare forearm.

The end came in September, and with shocking suddenness. One day Alison and her family were living at number 27, the next day they were gone. On the afternoon before they left, she told Eddie that they were moving to Ealing.

'But where's Ealing?' he wailed.

'How do I know? Somewhere in London. You can write me letters.'

Eddie cried when they parted. Alison forgot to leave her address. She slipped away from him like a handful of sand trickling through the fingers.

3

'I feel sometimes a Hell within my self; Lucifer keeps his Court in my breast, Legion is revived in me.'

Religio Medici, I, 51

Sleep caught Sally in mid-sentence, as sudden as a drawn curtain or nightfall in the Tropics. One moment she was lying in bed, holding the hand of a policewoman she had never met before; the policewoman's lips were moving but Sally wasn't listening because she was too busy wondering why she was holding the hand of a total stranger. Then the sleeping tablets cut in, blending with whatever the hypodermic had contained, probably a tranquillizer.

Michael had not been there. She hadn't seen him for hours.

Her mind went down and down into a black fog. Smothered by chemicals, she slept for hours, so deeply asleep that she was hardly a person any more. In the early hours of Saturday morning, the fog began gradually to clear. She slept on but now there were dreams, at first wispy and insubstantial – a suspicion of raised voices, a hint of bright lights, a sense of overwhelming sadness.

Later still, the images coalesced into a whole that was neither a picture nor a story. Afterwards, when Sally woke bathed in sweat on a cold morning, she remembered a bell tolling, its sound dulled by the winter air. She saw dirty snow on cobbles, mixed with fragments of straw and what looked like urine and human excrement. A spire built of raw, yellow stone and surmounted by a distant cross rose towards the grey sky.

In the dream a man was speaking, or rather declaiming slowly in a harsh, deep voice which Sally instinctively disliked. She could not make out the words, or even the language they were spoken in, partly because she was too far away and partly because they were distorted by hissing and cracking and popping in the background. Still in the dream, Sally was reminded of the 78-r.p.m. records she played as a child on the wind-up gramophone in her grandparents' attic; the scratches had overwhelmed the ghostly frivolities of the Savoy Orpheans and Fats Waller.

When Sally woke up, her mouth was dry and her mind clouded. The dream receded as she neared consciousness, details slipping away, drifting downwards beyond retrieval.

'Come back,' she called silently. Her eyes, still closed, were wet with tears. Something terrible was happening in the dream, which at all costs had to be put right. But at least it was only a dream. For a split second relief touched her: only a dream, thank God, only a dream. Then she opened her eyes and saw a woman she had never seen before sitting by her bed. Simultaneously the truth hit her. *No, it's not true, NOT true, NOT TRUE.*

'You all right, love?' the woman asked, bending forward.

Sally levered herself up on one elbow. *Not true, please God, NOT TRUE.* 'Have they found Lucy?'

The woman shook her head. 'They'll be in touch as soon as there's any news.'

Sally stared at her. It didn't matter who the woman was. Who cared? She was younger than Sally, her face carefully made up, her brown eyes wary, the teeth projecting slightly, pushing out the lips and giving the impression that the mouth was the most important feature in this face. The *Daily Telegraph* was open on her lap, folded to one of the inside pages. She did not wear a wedding ring. Sally clung to these details as though they formed a rope strung across an abyss; and if she let go, she would fall.

'It's true, isn't it?' she heard a voice saying, *her* voice. 'All true?'

'Yes. I'm so sorry.'

Sally let her head fall back on the pillow. She closed her eyes. Her mind filled with a procession of images that made her want to scream and scream until everything was all right again: Lucy crying for her mother and no one answering; Lucy naked and bleeding in a narrow bedroom smelling of male sweat; Lucy lying dead on a railway embankment with her clothes strewn around her. How could anyone be so cruel, so cruel, so cruel?

'She might have just wandered off,' Sally said, trying to reassure herself. 'Got tired out – fallen asleep in a shed or something. She'll wake up soon and knock on someone's door.'

'It's possible.'

Possible, Sally thought, but highly improbable.

The woman stirred. 'They say no news is good news.'

Sally opened her eyes again. '*Has* there been no news? Truly?'

'If there had been news, any news at all, they'd have told you and your husband straightaway. I promise. I'm DC Yvonne Saunders, by the way. I took over from Judith.' The woman hesitated. 'You remember Judith? Last night?'

Sally's head twitched on the pillow. More memories flooded back. A plain-clothes policewoman, Judith, holding her arm while a doctor with ginger curls pushed a hypodermic into the skin. Herself saying – shouting – that she wasn't going to stay with friends or go to hospital: she was going to stay *here*, at home in Hercules Road because that was where Lucy would expect to find her; she and Michael had made Lucy memorize both the address and the phone number.

'They'll find her, Sally. We're pulling out all the stops.' Again a hesitation, a hint of calculation. 'Doctor left some medicine. Something to help you not to worry. Shall I give you some?'

'No.' The refusal was instinctive, but the reasons rushed after it: if they tranquillized her she would be no use to Lucy when – *if* – they found her; if they turned her into a zombie, she wouldn't be able to find out what was happening, they wouldn't tell her anything; she needed to be as clear-headed as possible, for Lucy's sake. Sally leant back against her pillows. 'Where's Michael? My husband?'

The eyes wavered. 'He's out. He'll be back soon, I should think. I expect you'd like to freshen up, wouldn't you? Shall I make some tea?'

Sally nodded, largely in order to get the woman out of her

bedroom. Michael – she needed to think about him but she couldn't concentrate.

Yvonne stood up, her face creasing into an unconvincing smile. 'I'll leave you to it, then.' She added slowly, as if talking to a person of low intelligence, 'I shall be in the kitchen, if you need me. All right, love?'

No, Sally wanted to say, it's not all right; it may never be all right again; and I'm not your love, either. Instead, she returned the smile and said thank you.

When she was alone, she pushed the duvet away from her and got out of bed. The sweat cooled rapidly on her skin and she began to shiver. They had given her clean pyjamas, she realized, clinging to the security of domestic details. She was ashamed to see that the pyjamas were an old pair: the material was faded, a button was missing from the jacket, and there were undesirable stains on the trousers. The shivering worsened and once more the impact of what had happened hit her. Her knees gave way. She sat down suddenly on the bed. *My baby. Where are you?* The tears streamed down her cheeks.

She dared not make a noise in case Yvonne came back. *This is all my fault. I should have kept her with me.* She fell sideways and curled up on the bed. Her body shook with silent sobs.

Water rustled through the pipes. Sally, familiar with the vocabulary of the plumbing, knew that Yvonne was filling the kettle. The thought galvanized her into changing her position. At any moment the policewoman might return. With her hand over her mouth, trying to prevent the terror from spurting out like vomit, Sally scrambled off the bed and pulled open the wardrobe. She avoided looking at the accusing faces in the photographs on the chest of drawers. She selected clothes at random and, with a bundle in her arms, sneaked into the bathroom and bolted the door.

Boats, ducks and teddies had colonized the side of the bath. One of Lucy's socks was lying under the basin. Automatically Sally picked it up, intending to drop it in the basket for dirty clothes. Instead she sat on the lavatory. She held the sock to her face, breathing its essence, hoping to smell Lucy, to recreate her by sheer force of will. Did Lucy at least have Jimmy, her little cloth doll? Or was she entirely without comfort?

Tears spilled down Sally's cheeks. When the fit of crying passed, she sat motionless, her fingers clenched round the sock, and sank into depths she had not known existed.

There was a tap on the door. 'How are you doing, love? Tea's ready.'

'I'm fine. I'll be out in a moment. I might have a shower.'

Sally brushed her teeth, trying to scour the taste of that long, drugged sleep from her mouth. She dropped the pyjamas on the floor, stepped into the bath and stood under the shower. Making no move to wash herself, she let the water stream down her body for several minutes. Last night, she remembered dimly, she had given way. She remembered shouting and crying in Carla's house and later at the flat. She remembered Michael's face, white and accusing, and police officers whom she did not know, their expressions concerned but somehow detached from what was happening to her and to Lucy. The ginger-haired doctor had been tiny, so small that he came to below her shoulder. She must not let them give her drugs again.

She turned off the shower and began to dry herself. There was another tap on the door.

'How about a nice slice of toast, love?'

Seeing if I'm still alive. 'Yes, please. There's a loaf in the fridge.'

The thought of food disgusted her but she would be no use to anyone if she starved herself. She dressed quickly in jeans, T-shirt and jersey. In her haste, she had provided herself with two odd socks, one with a hole in the heel. She ran a comb through her hair. As an afterthought she pushed Lucy's sock into the pocket of the jeans. The routine of showering and dressing had had a calming effect. But as she unbolted the door the fact of Lucy's disappearance hit her like a flail, making her gasp for air.

She could not face Yvonne. She staggered back to the bedroom. Directly opposite the doorway was the crucifix on the wall above the mantelpiece. She looked at the little brass figure on the cross and realized as if for the first time how terribly pain had contorted the miniature face and twisted the muscles of the legs, the arms and the stomach. How could you forgive God for inflicting such suffering? But God hadn't forgiven God. He had crucified him. And if he had done that to his own child, what would he do to Lucy?

The unmade bed distracted her. She pulled up the duvet and plumped the pillows. After making the bed, she reminded herself, she normally tidied the room. But it looked tidy already. Usually there would have been Michael's dirty clothes flung over the chair, a magazine or a book on the floor by his side of the bed, a glass of water and his personal stereo on the table: he was a man who left a trail of domestic chaos behind him.

A pile of books on the chest of drawers caught her eye. They were small, shabby and unfamiliar. She picked up the first of them, a prayer book, and as she did so she remembered where they had come from. She turned to the flyleaf. 'To Audrey, on the occasion of her First Communion, 20th March 1937, with love from Mother.'

Audrey Oliphant's suicide seemed no more real than a story read long ago and half-forgotten. Sally could hardly believe that she had seen the woman dead on a hospital bed less than twenty-four hours earlier. She remembered the cheerless bedsitter, a shrine to lost beliefs. Most of all she remembered the woman standing up in St George's as Sally began to preach her first sermon.

She-devil. Blasphemer against Christ. Apostate. Impious bitch. Whore of Babylon. Daughter of Satan. May God damn you and yours.

She dropped the Prayer Book as if it were contaminated. *May God damn you and yours.* She almost ran from the room, shutting the door behind her. Yvonne was no longer someone to be avoided but a potential refuge.

This feeling vanished as soon as Sally reached the living room. Yvonne had laid the table in the window; usually Sally and Michael ate breakfast in the kitchen, often on the move. She had managed to find the wrong plates, the wrong mugs and the wrong teapot. There were paper napkins, a choice of both jam and marmalade, and a tablecloth which the Appleyards had last used on Christmas Day. Sally thought of little girls playing house and tried to suppress her exasperation. She also wished that she had remembered to wash the cloth.

'Perhaps you prefer honey?' Yvonne was poised to dash into

the kitchen. 'And is there any butter? I can only find margarine. That's what I have, but perhaps –'

'That's fine,' Sally lied. 'Margarine's fine. Everything's fine.'

She drank a glass of fruit juice and then sipped a mug of sweetened tea. The first mouthful of toast almost made her gag. She allowed Yvonne to pour her a second mug of tea and used it to moisten her throat between mouthfuls. Yvonne made her feel a guest in her own home, confronted by an overanxious hostess.

Parish reflexes came to Sally's rescue: automatically she asked questions. Yvonne told her that she worked at Paddington, that her boyfriend, also a policeman, was a sergeant in traffic control, and that they had a small flat in Wembley, but were hoping to move to somewhere larger soon. The illusion of intimacy lasted until Yvonne used the phrase 'living in sin' to describe what she and her boyfriend did.

'Sorry.' A blush crept up underneath her make-up. 'Perhaps I shouldn't be talking like this. What with you being a vicar and all.'

'Before I decided to become ordained, I lived with two men.' Sally inserted a practised pause and then slipped in her usual punchline: 'Not at the same time, of course.'

Yvonne tittered, and the mask slipped, revealing the youth and vulnerability behind. Usually, Sally thought, she would not have talked so readily to a stranger. But Michael was a police officer, which made Sally an honorary insider, at least on a temporary basis. And Yvonne was nervous – perhaps she had not done this job before. The flail of memory slapped her again: *baby-sitting*, they might call it, or *child minding*. For the next few seconds Sally fought the urge to bring up her breakfast over Great Aunt Mary's linen tablecloth.

The telephone rang.

'I'll get it.' Yvonne was already on her feet. She picked up the phone. She listened, then said, 'I'm a police officer, sir . . . Yes, Mrs Appleyard is awake . . . I'll ask her.' She covered the mouthpiece of the handset. 'Someone called Derek Cutter. Says he's your boss. Do you want to talk to him? Or he says he'd be pleased to come over.'

Sally opened her mouth to say that she didn't want to see

Derek, or talk to him; and if she never did either again, she for one would not waste any tears. Instantly she restrained herself. This wasn't Derek's fault. She had a duty both to him and to the parish. And, more selfishly, it was important to create the illusion that she was in control; otherwise they might starve her of information.

'Ask him to come over if he can spare the time.' Sally decided to kill two birds with one stone: Derek could take Miss Oliphant's belongings.

Yvonne relayed the message and put down the phone. 'He won't be long. He's over at the community centre in Brondesbury Park.'

'What's that phone doing? It's not ours.'

'No. We're taping and tracing all calls.' Yvonne stiffened. 'It's standard procedure. Nothing to get worried –'

Sally pushed back her chair and stood up. She was shaking so much that she had to support herself on the table. 'You're sure Lucy's been kidnapped. Aren't you? *Aren't you?*'

Derek took both Sally's hands in his and said how very, very sorry he was. He had ridden over from Kensal Vale on the Yamaha. Sally thought he fancied himself in motorcycle leathers. As she introduced him to Yvonne, he loosened the white silk scarf around his neck, revealing the dog collar beneath.

With unnecessary tact, Yvonne retreated to the kitchen, leaving Sally unwillingly alone to savour the experience of Derek in full pastoral mode.

'We are all praying for you, my dear.'

'Thank you.' Sally didn't want prayers, she wanted Lucy.

Still holding her hands, Derek went on to say that there must be no question of her coming in to work until Lucy was safe and sound. She need not worry, they could manage perfectly well.

'Would you and Michael like to come to stay with us? Margaret and I would love to have you. The bed's made up in the spare room.'

Sally's mind filled with an unwanted picture of Derek in his pyjamas. Would the hair of his chest be as white-blond as the hair on his head? Had he any hair on his chest at all, or just pink skin stretched over his bony ribcage, with the two nipples as the only points of interest to break the monotony? She wanted to giggle and she felt sick. She heard herself thanking Derek for his (and Margaret's) kind offer, and promising to discuss it with Michael. Certainly, she said, they would bear it in mind.

'Lots of people send their love. Stella in particular.'

'Stella.' It was little more than twenty-four hours since Sally had driven her to the hospital. 'Has her daughter had her baby?'

There was a pause. 'Yes. Last night. It's a girl. Mother and baby are doing fine, I gather.'

Sally concentrated very hard on Stella's joy. 'Lovely. Tell Stella how pleased I am.' She made an intense effort to blot out the rising hysteria and the knowledge that Lucy needed her. 'Audrey Oliphant?'

'Eh?' Derek released her hands. 'Who?'

'The woman who tried to kill herself. You remember? You asked me to see her yesterday.'

'I remember.'

'She died before I reached the hospital.'

'Was she one of ours?'

'Yes. In a sense.' Sally sat down. 'She was the woman who made a disturbance when I preached my first sermon.'

'Oh, yes. Poor woman. Where did she worship?'

'I don't know if she went anywhere. Her landlady thought not. But I think we should see she gets a proper burial.'

'Better make sure it's a man who conducts the service.' Derek began to smile, then stopped, remembering why he was here.

'Anglo-Catholic for choice. Her room was like an oratory. I've got a bag of her clothes.' She looked wildly round the room, wondering where the bag was. 'And also some books.' Had she taken the books out last night? If so, why?

'It doesn't matter now. We'll sort it out.'

Derek's voice was so soothing that Sally realized she must be sounding overwrought. She made an effort to turn the conversation back to the parish and the arrangements which needed to be made.

Derek slipped from the pastoral mode to the managerial. Here he was in his element; his efficiency was a virtue. He had already arranged cover for her services. Margaret would see to the Mothers and Toddlers and the Single Mums for as long as needed. As he went through her responsibilities, Sally had a depressing vision of Derek rising unstoppably, committee by committee, preferment by preferment, up the promotional ladder of the Church. It wasn't the meek that inherited the earth but people like Derek. She told herself that the Church needed the Dereks of this world, and that she had no reason to feel superior in any respect.

'And if there's anything that you or Michael need,' he was saying when she pulled her mind back on course, 'just phone us. Any time, Sally – you know that. Day or night.'

He stood up, tied the silk scarf round his thin neck and slipped the strap of his helmet over his arm. In its way, it had been a polished performance, and part of Sally was able to admire its professionalism. It made her squirm. Yvonne had almost certainly been eavesdropping through the open door of the kitchen.

'Look after yourself, my dear.' He seized her hands again and pressed them between his. 'And once more, if there's anything I can do.' Another, firmer squeeze, even the suggestion of a stroke. 'You have only to ask. You know that.'

Good God, Sally thought, as her skin crawled: I think he fancies me. With a wave of his hand, Derek called goodbye to Yvonne and left the flat. Too late, Sally remembered Miss Oliphant's bag but could not bear to call him back.

Yvonne came into the living room. 'Quite a charmer.'

'He does his best.' Sally forgot about Derek. 'Who's in charge of the case?'

'Mr Maxham. Do you know him?'

Sally shook her head.

'He's very experienced. One of the old school.'

'Shouldn't he be asking me questions? Shouldn't someone ask me something?' She heard her voice growing louder, and was powerless to stop it. 'Damn it, I'm Lucy's *mother*.'

'Don't worry, love, they'll send someone round soon. Maybe Mr Maxham will come himself. They're doing everything that can be done. Why don't you sit down for a bit? I'll make us a nice hot drink, shall I?'

'I don't want a drink.'

Sally sat down and started to cry. Yvonne dispensed paper handkerchiefs and impersonal sympathy. In a while the tears stopped. Sally went to the bathroom to wash her face. The reflection in the mirror showed a stranger with moist, red-rimmed eyes, pinched cheeks and lank hair. She went back to the living room. Being with Yvonne, with anyone, was better than being alone. Solitude was full of dangers.

The minute hand crawled round the clock, each minute an hour, each hour a week. Everywhere Sally looked there were reminders of Lucy – photographs, paintings, toys, clothes and books.

The worst reminders were those which were coupled with regrets. Lucy had wanted her to play Matching Pairs on Thursday evening, and Sally had said no, she needed to cook supper. Lucy had demanded another chapter of the book they were reading at bedtime, an enormously dull chronicle of life among woodland folk, and had thrown a theatrical tantrum when Sally declined. Lucy had also wanted Michael to kiss her good night, but he had not been at home; she had not cried on that occasion, but her silence had been worse than her tears and screams. Lucy had wanted to bake gingerbread men the other day, Lucy had wanted the conjuring set from Woolworth's, Lucy this and Lucy that. Sally sat placidly at her desk and pretended to read a magazine while, all around her, the flat hummed with lost opportunities and reminders of her failure to be the mother that Lucy needed and deserved.

Suffering had a monotonous quality; Sally had never known that before. Only the phone broke into the tedium. Each time it rang, Sally willed it to herald news of Lucy; or, failing that, that it should be Michael. Yvonne answered all the calls. Sally held her breath, digging her fingernails into the palms of her hands, until it became clear that the caller was just a time-waster – or rather, worse than that, someone who might be preventing news of Lucy from reaching Sally.

'Mr and Mrs Appleyard aren't available for comment . . .'

Sally's fingernails left raw, red half-moons on her palms. Some of the calls were from friends but more were from journalists.

'I'm afraid they'll soon be camping on the doorstep.' Yvonne went to the window and looked down at the road below. 'Not a lot we can do about that except move you somewhere else.'

'Why are they so interested?' Sally made an enormous effort to be objective about what had happened. 'Thousands of children must vanish every year. They aren't news.'

'They are if their dad's in the CID and their mum's a vicar. Let's face it, love, that makes it a news story whether we like it or not.'

Michael did not ring. She wanted him very badly. What the hell was keeping him? Sally tried to prise information out of Yvonne but had no success: either the policewoman knew no more than Sally or had been forbidden to discuss the case.

By ten-thirty, there were three journalists outside the front of the block. Sally felt sorry for them: though they were well wrapped up against the weather, they looked pinched and cold. One of them tried to sneak into the service entrance at the rear and was indignantly shooed out of the communal garden by the owner of a ground-floor flat.

Sally tried to phone Carla, but there was no reply. Sally wondered how the child minder was feeling. Did she blame herself? Sally perversely wanted to monopolize the blame.

At eleven o'clock Sally made some coffee. By then she and Yvonne had stopped trying to talk to each other. Sally sat at her desk in front of the window, nursing the steaming mug between her hands, and waited for something to happen. In her mind, the pictures unfolded: she saw a pool of blood sinking into bare earth under trees; Lucy's broken body half-concealed under a pile of dead leaves; a man running. She heard laughter. Fire crackled; a bell tolled; there was snow, straw and excrement on the cobbles. Briefly she glimpsed the dream that had filled her mind just before waking. Had there been a woman screaming? In the dream or in reality? Another or herself?

'Do you do crosswords?' Yvonne asked.

Sally hauled herself out of the confusion. 'No – well, I used to, but I haven't had much time recently.'

Yvonne was working on the crossword in the *Daily Telegraph* and had already completed a respectable number of clues. 'It passes the time. Do you want a clue?'

Sally shook her head. She tried to read but it was impossible to concentrate. Her mind fluttered like a butterfly. She pushed her hand into her pocket and touched Lucy's sock, her talisman, her Jimmy.

Please God, may Lucy have her Jimmy. Please God, bring my darling back to me.

It was important to act normally, otherwise they might sedate her heavily or even put her in hospital. But what was normal now? Reality had lurched into unreality. The substantial was insubstantial, and vice versa. Sally felt that if she poked her forefinger at the surface of the pine table in front of her, the finger might pass straight through the wood and into the vacancy beyond. It was unreal to be sitting at home doing nothing; unreal not to be helping at the Brownies' jumble sale in St George's church hall; and most of all unreal not to know where Lucy was. Like a small hungry animal, Lucy's absence gnawed at Sally's stomach.

'Are you sure you wouldn't like a tablet?' Yvonne's voice was elaborately casual.

'No. No, thanks.'

There was shouting in the street outside. Sally looked down, and a second later Yvonne joined her at the window. A man was shouting at the journalists, waving his arms at them.

'Who's that?' Yvonne asked. 'Anyone you know?'

'It's Michael. My husband.'

Michael was very tired. When Sally hugged him, he leaned against her but otherwise he barely responded. His face was unshaven, his eyes bloodshot; he wore yesterday's clothes and smelled of sweat.

'The bastards won't tell me anything,' he muttered fiercely into her hair. 'And they won't let me do anything.'

Sally heard footsteps in the hallway. And the sound of voices, Yvonne's and a man's.

Michael raised his head. 'Oliver brought me home. Maxham phoned him up; someone told him we were friends. I want to do something, and all they can think of is to give me a fucking nanny.'

Oliver Rickford hesitated in the doorway. He was wearing a battered wax jacket over a guernsey and paint-stained jeans.

73

Yvonne bobbed up and down behind him. Yvonne was short, and in thirty years would be stout, whereas Oliver was tall and thin. Sally saw them both with the eyes of a stranger: they might have belonged to different species.

'I'm so sorry.' Oliver spread out his hands as if intending to examine his nails. 'Maxham really is doing everything he can.'

'And those bloody vultures outside,' Michael went on. 'I could kill them.'

'You need to rest,' Sally said.

Michael ignored her. 'If they're still there when I go down, I'm going to hit one of them. Tell them, Oliver. It's a fair warning.'

Sally stepped back and shook his arm. 'Why don't you have a bath and get into bed?'

Michael's eyes focused on hers. 'Don't be ridiculous. Sleep? Now? You must be out of your mind.' The hostility ebbed from his face. 'Sal, I'm sorry.' He put his hand on her arm. 'I don't know what I'm saying.'

'Sally's right.' Oliver had a hard face and a soft voice. 'You're practically asleep on your feet. You're no use to anyone like that.'

'Don't tell me what to do. I'm not one of your bloody minions.' Michael looked wildly from Oliver to Sally. His face crumpled. 'Oh shit.'

He stumbled out of the room and into the bathroom.

Oliver peeled off his jacket and dropped it on a chair. 'Can I help?'

She didn't answer, but he followed her into the bathroom. Michael was sitting on the side of the bath with his head resting on the rim of the basin. Sally turned on the taps. Between them, she and Oliver persuaded him through the bath, into pyjamas and into bed. Yvonne dispensed two sleeping pills from the supply the doctor had left behind. Sally sat with him until he went to sleep.

'When they get the man I'm going to kill him. I could kill Maxham, too. Devious little shit.' As time slipped by, Michael's words grew less distinct. Once he opened his eyes and looked straight at Sally. 'It shouldn't be like this, should it, Sal? It's all our fault.'

She bowed her head to hide the tears. Michael was being unreasonable and part of her feared that he was right.

He wasn't looking at her now but talking to himself. 'For Christ's sake. Lucy.'

He drifted into silence. His eyes closed, and after a while his breathing became slow and regular. Sally stood up. She tiptoed towards the door. As she touched the handle, the figure on the bed stirred.

'It's always happening,' Michael mumbled, or that was what it sounded like to her. 'It's not fair.'

She closed the bedroom door softly behind her. The living room was empty. She found Oliver Rickford stooping over the sink in the kitchen, scouring a saucepan.

'Where's Yvonne?'

'She went out to buy sandwiches.'

Sally automatically picked up a tea towel and began to dry a mug. 'You shouldn't be doing this.'

'Why not?'

'Shouldn't you be at work?'

'I'm on leave. How's Michael?'

'Sleeping.'

'This is very hard for him.' Oliver hesitated, perhaps guessing Sally wanted to yell, *And don't you think it's hard for me too?* 'I mean, even worse than it would be for many other fathers in the same position. As you know, he's worked on similar cases.'

Jealousy twisted through her. Sally busied herself with the drying up. Michael rarely talked about his work to her. It had been different for a few months around the time of their marriage. Then the barriers had gone up. Michael was made that way, she told herself fiercely; it wasn't her fault.

Not for the first time she had a depressing vision of her husband's life as a series of watertight compartments: herself, Lucy and the flat; his job and the friendships he shared with men like Oliver; and the past he shared with his godfather, David Byfield. Cutting like a sword across this line of thought came the fact of Lucy's absence. Sally turned away, pretending to put the mug in its cupboard. Her shoulders shook.

A moment later she heard Oliver say, 'I'm sorry. I shouldn't have said that.'

She turned round to him. The kitchen was so small that they were very close. 'It's not your fault. What's Michael been doing?'

'Getting in the way. Mounting his own private investigation. At one point he was hanging round the house where the child minder lives and trying to question neighbours.'

Sally wished he had come home instead. 'He had to do something.' It was a statement of fact, not an argument for the defence.

'Maxham was not amused.'

'What are we going to do?'

'There's not much we can do except wait. Maxham's said to be good. He gets results.'

Alert to nuances, Sally said, 'You don't like him, do you?'

'I don't know him. He's one of the old school. Must be coming up for retirement quite soon. The important thing is that he's good at his job.' Oliver hesitated, and she sensed that he was holding something back. 'They'll probably ask if you'd like psychological counselling,' Oliver went on. 'Might be sensible to say yes. Good idea to take all the help you're offered. No point in making life harder for yourselves.'

'You mean Michael needs help?'

'Anyone in your position needs help.'

They finished the washing and drying in silence. Oliver went to check on Michael. Meanwhile, desperate for the activity, Sally emptied the contents of the dirty-clothes basket into the washing machine. When she had switched it on, she realized that she hadn't bothered to sort the clothes, and that the machine was still set for the fast-coloured programme.

'He's asleep.' Oliver leaned against the jamb of the kitchen door. 'Sally?'

'What?'

'This isn't my case. I've got no jurisdiction.'

'What are you trying to say?'

'That I can't do much to help.'

'You're not doing badly so far.'

'I mean I can't tell you any more about what's in Maxham's head than Michael can.'

'Of course.'

Sally's voice sounded low and reasonable, which was all the more remarkable because simultaneously she was screaming to herself, *I don't give a fuck about Maxham: I just want Lucy*. Oliver stood aside to let her pass into the living room. *I am ordained. I must not use language like that even in my own mind*. As she passed him, she was aware of his height and of the way he held himself back to minimize the possibility of accidental contact between their bodies. In the living room she crossed to the window and looked down to the street.

Oliver picked up his jacket from the back of the armchair. 'Still there, are they?'

'I can see six of them, I think. Two of them are talking to the neighbours.' She moved back from the window. 'We're besieged.'

'You could go and stay with relations or friends.'

'But this is where Lucy would come. She knows the phone number and the address.'

'We could transfer the calls and leave someone here just in case Lucy turns up on the doorstep.' Oliver stared down at Sally, making her feel like a specimen on a dish. 'Think about it. This is just the beginning. If it goes on, there'll be more of them. Maybe radio and TV as well. The whole circus.'

She shrugged, accepting that he might have a point but unwilling to think about it.

'I'll phone this evening if that's OK.' He rubbed his nose, which was long and thin and with a slight kink to the right near the end. 'Shall I leave my number?'

As she passed him a pen and a pad, their eyes met. She wondered whether he was being diplomatic; whether he realized that Michael had erected an invisible barrier between his family and his friends. Sally knew that the Rickfords had bought a flat in Hornsey, but she had no idea of the address or the phone number.

'I'm on leave till the new year,' he said.

'You and Sharon aren't going away, then?'

'Sharon's already gone, actually.' Oliver rubbed a speck of paint on his jeans. 'Permanently. She moved out a couple of months ago. We decided it just wasn't working out.'

'I'm sorry.' She had stumbled on another of Michael's failures in communication. She was past feeling humiliated.

'She got a chance of a job with our old force – Somerset.' Perhaps Oliver sensed a need for a diversion, any diversion. 'It came up at just the right time.'

'It gave you a positive reason to separate as well as all the negative ones?'

He nodded. He was very easy to talk to, Sally thought – quick on the uptake, unthreatening. She was not surprised that Oliver and Sharon had separated. They had made an ill-assorted couple. Sharon had struck her as a tough, sharp-witted woman, very clear about what she wanted from life.

'We're still good friends.' Oliver's fingers twitched, enclosing the last two words with invisible inverted commas. 'But you don't want to hear about all this now. Is there anything I can do before I go?'

Sally shook her head. 'Thank you for bringing Michael back.'

The words sounded absurdly formal. Sally felt like a mother thanking a comparative stranger for bringing her child home after a party. A silence ambushed them as each waited for the other to speak. The sound of a key turning in the lock was a welcome distraction. They both turned as Yvonne came into the flat. She looked pale beneath her make-up.

'You haven't watched the news, have you?' she blurted out. 'Or had the radio on?'

Sally took a step towards her, swayed and clung to the back of a chair. 'What's happened?' she whispered.

Yvonne opened her mouth, revealing the prominent and expensively regular teeth. No sound came out.

'Come on,' Oliver snapped.

'It was those journalists, sir.' Yvonne blinked rapidly. 'They asked me if I'd heard.' She turned to Sally. 'Look, I'm sorry about this. They said someone found a child's hand this morning. Just a hand. It was lying on a gravestone in Kilburn Cemetery.'

4

'. . . we carry private and domestick enemies within, publick
and more hostile adversaries without.'

Religio Medici, II, 7

On the morning of Saturday the thirtieth of November, Angel
opened Eddie's bedroom door and stood framed like a picture
in the doorway.

'Are you awake?'

He sat up in bed, reaching for his glasses. Angel was wearing
the cotton robe, long, white and in appearance vaguely hieratic,
which she used as a dressing gown. As usual at this time of
day, her shining hair was confined to a snood. Eddie liked
seeing Angel without make-up. She was still beautiful, but
in a different way: her face had a softness which cosmetics
masked; he glimpsed the child within the adult.

'Just the two of us for breakfast today. We'll let Lucy sleep
in.'

'OK. Have you been down yet?' He had heard the stairs
creaking.

'You know I have. And yes, Lucy's fine. Sleeping like a baby.'

He felt relief, a lifting of guilt. 'I'll put the kettle on.'

A few moments later, Eddie trotted downstairs to the kitchen.
He filled the kettle and set the table while waiting for the water
to boil. The washing machine was already on, and through
the porthole he glimpsed something small and white, perhaps
Lucy's vest or tights. In the quieter phases of its cycle, he heard
Angel moving about in the bathroom. He had hardly slept

during the night and now felt light-headed. He did not know whether Angel had really forgiven him for acting on impulse the previous afternoon. But he could tell she was pleased to have Lucy safely in the basement. The latter, he hoped, would outweigh the former.

At length Angel came downstairs, carrying the receiving end of the intercom to the basement. She plugged it into one of the sockets over the worktop. The tiny loudspeaker emitted an electronic hum.

'I thought I'd do a load while Lucy's asleep,' Angel said. 'Lucy's things, mainly. That toy of hers stinks.'

'Jimmy?'

Angel stared at him. 'Who?'

'The doll thing.'

'Is that what she calls it? It's not what I call a doll.'

Eddie shrugged, disclaiming responsibility.

'It had to be washed sooner or later,' Angel went on, 'so it might as well be washed now. It's most unhygienic, you know, as well as being offensive.'

Eddie nodded and held his peace. Jimmy was a small cloth doll, no more than four or five inches high. Yesterday Lucy had told Eddie that her mother had made it for her. It was predominantly blue, though the head was made of faded pink material, and Sally Appleyard had stitched rudimentary features on the face and indicated the existence of hair. Eddie guessed that Jimmy was special, like his own Mrs Wump had been. (Mrs Wump was still in his chest of drawers upstairs, lying in state in a shoe box and kept snug with sheets made of handkerchiefs and blankets made of scraps of towelling.) The previous evening, Lucy had kept Jimmy in her hands the whole time, occasionally sniffing the doll while she sucked her fingers. She had not relaxed her grip even in sleep.

'Lucy looks rather like how I used to look at that age,' Angel told Eddie over breakfast. 'Much darker colouring, of course. But apart from that we're really surprisingly similar.'

'Can I see her this morning?'

'Perhaps.' Angel sipped her lemon verbena tea. 'It depends how she is. I expect she'll feel a little strange at first. We must give her a chance to get used to us.'

But it's me she knows, Eddie wanted to say: it was I who brought her home. 'She wants a conjuring set,' he said. 'You can get them at Woolworth's; they cost twelve ninety-nine, apparently. I thought I might try and buy it for her this morning. I have to go out for the shopping in any case.'

'I think she's like me in other ways.' Angel's voice was dreamy. 'In personality, I mean. Much more so than the others. She's our fourth, of course. I knew the fourth would be significant.'

'How do you mean?'

'Because –' Angel broke off. 'What was that about a conjuring set?'

'Lucy wants one. Perhaps I could buy it and give it to her this afternoon.'

Angel stared at him, her spoon poised halfway between the bowl and her mouth. 'Lucy isn't like the others. Do you understand me?'

'Yes.' He dropped his eyes: facing that blue glare was like looking at the sun. 'I think so.'

Eddie didn't understand: why wasn't Lucy like the others? She was no more attractive than Chantal or Katy, for example, and probably less intelligent, certainly less articulate, than Suki. And why should the fact that Lucy was their fourth visitor be significant?

As he spread a thin layer of low-fat sunflower margarine on his wholemeal toast, he thought that Angel resembled one of those rich archaeological sites which humans have occupied for thousands of years. You laboriously scraped away a layer only to find that there was another beneath, and another below that, and so the process went on. How could you expect to understand later developments if you did not also know the developments which had preceded them and shaped them?

Angel dabbed her mouth with her napkin. 'If you want to give Lucy a present, why don't you buy her a doll?'

'But she wants the conjuring set.'

'A doll might distract her from that little bundle of rags. What does she call it?'

'Jimmy.'

The intercom crackled softly.

Angel cocked her head. 'Hush.'
A cat-like wail drifted into the kitchen.

Jenny Wren had liked dolls, especially the sort which could be equipped with the glamorous accessories of a pseudo-adult lifestyle. Her real name was Jenny Reynolds but Eddie's father always called her Jenny Wren. She had been overweight, with dark hair, small features and a permanent look of surprise on her face.

Her father was a builder in a small way. He and his wife still lived in one of the council flats on the estate behind Rosington Road. The Reynoldses' balcony was visible above the trees from the garden of number 29. When Eddie discovered which flat was theirs, he realized that the woman on the balcony whom he and Alison had seen, the woman who stared at the sky over Carver's, must have been Mrs Reynolds.

Jenny Wren was their only child, about two years older than Eddie. She started to come to the Graces' house in the summer of 1971, the Alison summer, always bringing her favourite doll, who was called Sandy. Alison used to laugh at Jenny Wren and Eddie had joined in, to show solidarity.

Eddie did not know how Jenny Wren had come to his father's attention. Stanley did house-to-house collections for several charities and this helped to give him a wide acquaintance. Or Mr Reynolds might have done some work on the house, or his father might have advised the Reynoldses on financial matters. Stanley might even have stopped Jenny Wren on the street. Eddie had witnessed his father's technique at first hand.

'You've got a dolly, haven't you?' Stanley would say to the girl. 'What's her name?' Eventually the girl would tell him. 'That's a pretty name,' he would say. 'Did you know I make dolls' houses? Do you think your dolly would like to come and see them? We'd have to ask Mummy and Daddy, of course.'

If there were concerned parents in the picture, as with the Reynoldses, he took care to reassure them. 'Yes, Eddie likes a bit of company. He's our only one, you know, and it can get a bit lonely, eh? Tell you what, I'll get my wife to give you a ring and confirm a time, shall I? Around tea time, perhaps? I know Thelma likes an excuse to bake a cake.'

Thelma lent her authority to the invitations, though they sometimes made it necessary for her to talk to neighbours, an activity she detested. But she had as little as possible to do with the girls as soon as they had crossed the threshold of 29 Rosington Road. Among themselves, Stanley and Thelma referred to the girls as 'LVs', which stood for 'Little Visitors'.

The proceedings usually opened with tea around the kitchen table. This would be much more lavish than usual. There would be lemonade or Coca-Cola, chocolate biscuits and cake.

'Ah, tea.' Stanley would bunch up his pale cheeks in a smile. 'Splendid. I'm as hungry as a hunter.'

During the meal Thelma spoke only when necessary, though as usual she would eat greedily and rapidly. Afterwards Thelma and Eddie cleared away while Stanley took the LV down to the basement, closing the door behind them. Eddie and Thelma carried on with their lives as normal, as though Stanley and a little girl were not in the basement looking at a dolls' house. When it was time for the LV to go home, Thelma and Eddie often walked her back to her parents, usually in silence, leaving Stanley behind.

If all had gone well, there would be other visits. Then Stanley would introduce the subject of his second hobby, photography. As ever, he was meticulously careful in his handling of the parents. Would they mind if he took a few photographs of their daughter? She was very photogenic. There was a national competition coming up, and Stanley would like – with the parents' agreement, of course – to submit a photograph of her. Perhaps the parents would like copies of the photograph for themselves?

It was after Alison moved away that Stanley Grace first asked Eddie into the basement when one of the little visitors was there.

'I'd like a two-headed shot in the big chair,' he explained to the space between Thelma and Eddie. 'Could be rather effective, with one fair head and one dark.'

Eddie was excited; he was also pleased because he interpreted the invitation as a sign that he had somehow earned his father's approval. The LV in question was Jenny Wren.

He remembered that first afternoon with great clarity, though as so often with memories it was difficult to know whether the clarity was real or apparent. He and Jenny Wren had been too shy to talk much to each other, and in any case, the two-year age gap between them was at that time a significant barrier. His father posed them in the low Victorian armchair, which was large enough to hold both children, their bodies squeezed together from knee to shoulder. He arranged their limbs, deftly tweaking a leg here, draping an arm there. The camera was already mounted on its tripod.

'Now try and relax,' Stanley told them. 'Pretend you're brother and sister. Or *very* special friends. Lean your head on Jenny's shoulder, Eddie. That's it, Jenny Wren: give Eddie a nice big smile. Watch the birdie now.' His father squinted through the viewfinder. 'Smile.'

The shutter clicked. Jenny Wren's breath smelled sweetly of chocolate. Her dress had ridden up almost to the top of her thighs. The rough fabric of the upholstery rubbed against Eddie's bare skin and made him want to scratch. He remembered the musty smell of the chair, the essence of a long and weary life.

'And again, children.' *Click*. 'Very good. Now hitch your legs up a bit, Jenny Wren: lovely.' *Click*. 'Now, Eddie, let's pretend you're kissing Jenny Wren's cheek. No, not like that: look up at her, into her eyes.' *Click*. 'Now let's have some with just you, Jenny Wren. How about a chocolate first?'

It wasn't all photographs. Stanley encouraged them to examine the dolls' house. He allowed Jenny Wren to push her doll Sandy about the rooms and sit her in the chairs and lie her on the beds, even though Sandy was far too large for the house and Jenny Wren's movements were so poorly coordinated that the fragile furniture was constantly in danger. The children helped themselves from the large box of chocolates. Eddie ate so many that he felt sick. At last it was time for Jenny Wren to go home.

'You can come again next weekend, if you like.'

Jenny Wren nodded, with her mouth stuffed with chocolate and her eyes on the dolls' house.

'By that time I'll have developed the films. Tell Mummy and Daddy I'll give you some photos to take home for them.'

Next weekend the photographs were ready. There were

more chocolates, more posing, more games with the dolls' house. Stanley took some of his special artistic photographs, which involved the children taking off some of their clothes. Next weekend it was very warm, one of those early autumn days which until the evening mimic the heat of summer. At Stanley's suggestion the children took off all their clothes.

'All artists' models pose without their clothes. I expect you already knew that. And I dare say neither of you would say no to a little extra pocket money, eh? Well, famous artists always pay their models. So I suppose I shall have to pay you. But this is our secret, all right? That's very important. Our secret.'

After taking the photographs he suggested that they played a game until it was time to go home. It was so hot that he decided to take off his clothes himself.

'You won't mind, will you, Jenny Wren? I know Eddie won't. He's seen me in the buff enough times. All part of our secret, eh?'

So it continued, first with Jenny Wren and later with others. The children who excited Stanley's artistic sensibilities were always girls. Even as a child, Eddie was aware that he was of secondary importance. In the photographs and in the games his role was not much more significant than that of the Victorian armchair. His father's attention was always on the girl, never on him. As time went by, the invitations to the basement became rarer and rarer.

Once Eddie had reached puberty, his father did not want him there at all. On one occasion he plucked up his courage and knocked on the basement door. He was fourteen, and his father was about to photograph the latest LV, a girl called Rachel with light-brown hair, wary eyes and a freckled face. His father's feet clumped slowly up the stairs. The key turned in the lock and the door opened.

'Yes?'

'I wondered if I could –' Eddie looked past his father into the basement: the camera was on its tripod; Rachel was fiddling with the dolls' house. 'You know – like I used to.'

Stanley stared down at him, his face moon-like. 'Better not. Nothing personal. But for child photography you have to get the atmosphere just right.'

'Yes.' Eddie backed away, hot and ashamed. 'I see that.'

'Young children are more artistic.' Stanley rarely missed an opportunity to stress that his photography was driven by a high, aesthetic purpose. 'Ask any sculptor from the Classical world.' At this point he glanced behind him, down into the basement, as if expecting to see Phidias nodding approval from the Victorian armchair, or Praxiteles leaning on the workbench by the window and smiling encouragement. Instead, Stanley looked at Rachel, who was pretending to be absorbed in the dolls' house. 'Children are so *plastic*.'

As a very young child Eddie had admired Stanley and wanted to please him. Then his father had become a fact of life like the weather – neither good nor bad in itself, but liable to vary in its effects on Eddie. Then, with Stanley's lecture on the aesthetics of his hobby, came the moment of revelation: that Eddie hated his father, and had in fact done so for some time.

The strength of Eddie's hatred took him unawares and had a number of consequences. Some of these were trivial: he used to spit discreetly in his father's tea, for example, and once he took one of his father's shoes and pressed the heel into a dog turd on the pavement. Other consequences were more far-reaching, and affected Eddie rather than his father. It was Stanley's fault, in a manner of speaking, that Eddie became a teacher, and Eddie never forgave him for that.

In his final year at school, Eddie told his father that he thought he might like to be an archaeologist. This was a few months before Stanley retired from the Paladin.

'Don't be absurd,' said his father. 'There's no money in archaeology. I bet there aren't many jobs, either. Not real jobs.'

'But it interests me.'

'That's no good if it won't pay the mortgage, is it? Can't you do it as a hobby?'

'There *are* jobs for archaeologists.'

'For the favoured few, maybe. Top scholars. One in a million. You've got to be realistic. Why don't I arrange for you to have an interview at the Paladin? There's a chap I know in Personnel.'

The upshot of this conversation was that Eddie attempted to

lay the foundations for a career in archaeology by studying for a degree in history at a polytechnic on the outskirts of London. It was not a happy time. As a student he floundered: it was not so much that the work was too demanding; it was more that there seemed such a lot to do, and it was difficult to know what was important and what wasn't, and besides, his mind had a tendency to drift into daydreams. He lived at home, which distanced him from the other students. In the first summer vacation he spent a fortnight on an archaeological dig in Essex, where he began to grow a beard. It rained all the time and the work was hard and tedious. Eddie's interest in the subject never recovered.

He kept the beard, however, wispy and unsatisfactory though it was, primarily because it annoyed his father. ('Makes you look a scruffy little wretch. You'll have to shave it off if you want to find a proper job.') As a token of rebellion, the beard made a poor substitute for a career in archaeology, but it was better than nothing.

Stanley continued to badger Eddie about the Paladin, showering him with information about vacancies for graduates.

'I've already dropped a word in the right ear,' he said towards the end of Eddie's final year. 'Or rather ears. It's never a bad thing to have a few friends at court, is it? And naturally, anyone who's the son of a former employee is bound to have a head start. But you'd better get rid of that beard.'

With hindsight, Eddie agreed that a job at the Paladin might have suited both his talents and his needs. At the time, however, the source of the suggestion automatically tainted it. Desperate to find an alternative, he glanced round the room. His father had draped the *Evening Standard* over the arm of his chair, and one of the headlines caught Eddie's eye: TEACHERS IN NEW PAY TALKS. Beside it was a photograph of a group of teachers armed with placards. Several of the men had beards. That was the deciding factor.

'If my results are good enough, I'm going to be a teacher.'

His father's attention sharpened. 'Really? I hope you've got the sense to teach younger children. If what you hear nowadays is anything to go by, older children are becoming quite unmanageable.'

'Secondary education's much more interesting. Intellectually, I mean.' Eddie hoped this last remark would remind his father that he had left school at sixteen, and therefore lacked his son's qualifications.

'It's your life,' Stanley replied, apparently oblivious of his intellectual inferiority. 'People don't look up to teachers as much as they used to in my day. There's the long holidays, I suppose.'

'Teachers have to work in the holidays. It's not a cushy job.'

His father took his time over lighting a cigarette. 'Yes.' He blew out a cloud of smoke. 'Well – as I say, it's your life. I doubt if you'll be able to cope, but that's your affair.'

His mother had been in the room but contributed nothing to the conversation. Eddie still felt that if his parents had handled the situation more diplomatically, they could have helped him avoid the disasters which followed. Thanks to them, he forced himself to spend another year at college doing a postgraduate certificate of education. He was lucky – or perhaps unlucky – in his teaching practice: they sent him to a quiet, middle-class school where class sizes were small and his stumbling attempts to teach were carefully and even kindly supervised. At that stage, he had realized that he was not a natural teacher, but he had hoped that with luck and perseverance he might grow used to it.

Nothing had prepared Eddie for Dale Grove Comprehensive. It was a school in north-west London, not far from Kensal Vale, in an area which even then seemed to be slipping away from the control of the authorities. He applied for the job because the school was an easy tube journey from Rosington Road, and without discussing the matter both he and his parents assumed that for the time being it would be best if he continued to live at home.

Keeping order was by far the worst aspect of the job. His failure in this department affected his relationships with other teachers, who regarded him with a mixture of irritation and scorn. It was not unusual for Eddie to find himself trying to teach three or four children at the front, while in the rest of the room the remainder of the class split up into small noisy groups engaged in disruptive activities.

He was scared of the children, and they knew it. He thought them outlandish and disgusting, too, with their croaking voices, their shrill laughter, their burps, their farts, their blackheads, their acne, their strange clothes and stranger customs. The girls were worse than the boys: strapping, big-boned brutes; delighting in mockery and subtler in their methods; scenting weakness as sharks scent blood in the water. He had fallen among savages.

Matters came to a crisis towards the end of the summer term. There was no one he could talk to about it. There were problems at home, too: his father's health was worsening, and his mother was never easy to live with. In the circumstances was it any wonder that things went wrong?

Two girls orchestrated what amounted to a campaign of sexual harassment against him. Their names were Mandy and Sian. Both were taller than he was. Mandy was thin, with spots and lank red hair. Sian was overweight and unusually well-developed. They began with innuendo, with whispers at the back of the class. 'Do you think sir's sexy?' Gradually the campaign picked up momentum. 'Please, sir, there's a word in this book I don't understand. What does S-P-E-R-M mean?'

After each of Eddie's failures to control them, his torturers would take one small step further.

'I can't go to sleep without my teddy in my bed,' Mandy confided to the class.

'Me too,' Sian remarked. 'Mine's called Eddy-Teddy. He's so warm and cuddly.'

Eddie found repellent drawings on his table when he returned from the staff room. Mandy, something of a raconteur in her primitive way, told dirty jokes to anyone in the class who would listen, which was most of them.

As the weeks passed, Sian hitched her skirt higher and higher. She and Mandy fell into the habit of sitting at a table near the front of the class. They would pull their chairs out and sit facing the front with their legs apart, forcing Eddie to glimpse their underwear, some of which was most unsuitable for schoolgirls, or indeed for any woman who wasn't the next best thing to a prostitute. One day, early in July, Mandy sat in a pose which revealed beyond any possible doubt that she was wearing no knickers at all.

The crisis arrived late on a Friday afternoon. Eddie's guard was down because he thought the children had gone; he was alone in his classroom, sitting at his table, trying to plan the next week's lessons and feeling relieved that the teaching week was over.

Mandy, Sian and three other girls strolled nonchalantly into the room. Mandy and Sian came to stand beside him, one on each side. A third girl lingered by the door, keeping watch; the other two constituted an audience.

'Wouldn't you like to fuck me, sir?' whispered Mandy on the left. She put a hand on the back of his chair and leaned over him.

'No – me.' Sian undid the top two buttons of her shirt. 'I can give you a much better time. Honest, sir. Why don't I suck your cock?'

Eddie tried to push back his chair, but it wouldn't move because Mandy now had her foot behind one of the rear legs as well as her hand on the back.

The other girls were sniggering, and one of them said in a loud whisper: 'Look – he's getting a hard-on.'

Mandy was now unbuttoning her shirt too. 'Go on, sir. Lick my titties. They taste nicer than hers.'

Eddie found his voice at last. 'Stop this.' His voice rose. 'Stop this at once. Stop it. Stop it.'

'You don't mean that, sir. You like it. Go on, admit it.'

'Stop it. Stop it. I shall report you to –'

'If you report us we'll say you were interfering with us.'

'Mr Grace is a bloody pervert,' said Sian. 'We got witnesses to prove it.'

The latter's shirt was now entirely unbuttoned. She pushed up her breasts, encased in a formidable black bra, and poked them hard into his face. The lace was rough against his nose. There was a smell of stale sweat.

'Fuck me, darling,' she murmured.

Eddie leapt up, knocking over his chair. Mandy shrieked and groped at his crotch. Abandoning his briefcase, he ran for the door. Their hands clutched at him. He collided with the sentry in the doorway, pushing her against the wall. The girls' laughter pursued him down the corridor. As he ran across the school car park, scattering a knot of teenagers, the laughter drifted after him through the open windows. In a way it was a relief that the final humiliation had come at last. Failure had its compensations.

The following Monday morning Eddie phoned the school secretary and, having pleaded illness too often in the past, desperately invented a dying grandmother. The same day, he saw his GP, who listened to him for five minutes and gave him a prescription for tranquillizers. On Tuesday he wrote a letter of resignation to the head teacher.

'I'm not surprised,' Stanley said when Eddie told him the news. 'I saw that coming from the start. I told you, didn't I?'

'You don't understand. I've decided that I don't approve of the philosophy behind modern education.'

His father raised his eyebrows, miming the disbelief he did not need openly to express. 'What now? You've probably missed the boat with the Paladin, but if you like, I –'

'No.' *Stuff the Paladin*. 'I don't want to work there.'

'So what *are* you going to do?'

At the time Eddie could not answer the question, but over the years an answer had evolved as if by its own volition. First he had made a half-hearted attempt to see whether he could retrain as a primary-school teacher. But he could not whip up much enthusiasm even for teaching younger children. In any case, he guessed that the head teacher at Dale Grove would give him an unsatisfactory reference. Quite apart from the discipline problem, there was also the possibility that Mandy and Sian had circulated rumours of sexual harassment, with Eddie in the role of predator rather than victim.

Worse was to come that summer – the unpleasant business at Charleston Street swimming baths. As a schoolboy, Eddie had learned to swim there, though not very well. It was an old building, full of echoes, with an ineradicable smell of chlorine and unwashed feet. In the first few months after he left Dale Grove, Eddie paid several visits to Charleston Street, partly to give himself a reason to get out of the house and away from his father, now a semi-invalid.

He disliked the male changing room, where youths who reminded him of the pupils at Dale Grove indulged in loud horseplay. The pool, too, was often too crowded for his taste. Nor did he like taking off his clothes in front of strangers. He was very conscious of the soft flab which clung to his waist and the top of his thighs, of his lack of bodily hair, and of his small stature. But he enjoyed cooling down in the water and watching the younger children.

He clung to the side and watched girls swimming races and mothers teaching their children to swim. Some young children appeared to have no adults watching over them, even from the balcony overlooking the swimming pool. Latchkey children, Eddie supposed, abandoned by mothers going out to work. He felt sorry for them – his own mother had always been at home when he came back from school and during the holidays – and tried to keep a friendly eye on them.

Sometimes he became quite friendly with those deserted children and would play games with them. His favourite was throwing them up in the air above the water, catching them as they descended, and then tickling them until they squealed with laughter.

On one occasion Eddie was playing this game with a little girl called Josie. She was in the care of her older brother, a ten-year-old who for most of the time horsed about with his friends in the deep end. Eddie felt quite indignant on Josie's behalf: the little girl was so vulnerable – what could the mother be thinking of?

'You funny man,' she said. 'Your name's Mr Funny.'

He came back the following day to find Josie there.

'Hello, Mr Funny,' she called out.

They played together for a few minutes. As Eddie was preparing to throw Josie into the air for the fourth time, he noticed surprise spreading over her face. An instant later he felt a tap on his shoulder. He turned. Beside him, standing on the edge of the pool, was one of the lifeguards, accompanied by a thickset, older man in a tracksuit.

The latter said, 'All right. You're getting out now. Put the kid down.'

Eddie looked from one hostile face to the other. Another lifeguard was walking towards them with Josie's brother. It was unfair but Eddie did not argue, partly because he knew there was no point and partly because he was scared of the man in the tracksuit.

He climbed up the ladder. Eddie was conscious that other people were looking at him – the other two lifeguards on duty, and also some of the adults who were swimming. It seemed to him that everyone had stopped talking. The only sounds were the slapping of the water against the sides of the swimming pool and the rhythmic thudding of the distorted rock music coming over the public-address system. The two men escorted him back to the changing room.

'Get dressed,' ordered the older man.

One on either side, they waited while he struggled into his clothes. He did not dry himself. It was very embarrassing. Eddie hated people watching him while he was getting dressed. Gradually the other people in the changing room realized something was up. The volume of their conversations diminished until, by the time Eddie was strapping on his sandals, no one was talking at all.

'This way.' The older man opened the door. Eddie followed him down the corridor towards the reception area. The young lifeguard fell in step behind. Instead of leading him outside, the thickset man swung to the left, stopped and unlocked the door labelled MANAGER. He stood to one side and waved Eddie to precede him into the room. It was a small office, overcrowded with furniture, and with three people inside it was claustrophobic. The lifeguard, a burly youth with tight blond curls, shut the door and leant against it.

'Identification.' The manager held out his hand. 'Come on.'

Eddie found his wallet, extracted his driving licence and handed it over. The manager made a note of the details, breathing heavily and writing slowly, as if using a pen was not an activity that came naturally to him. Eddie trembled while he waited. Their silence unnerved him. He thought perhaps they were planning to beat him up.

At last the man tossed the driving licence back to Eddie, who missed it and had to kneel down to pick it up from the floor. The manager threw down his pen on the desk and came to stand very close to Eddie. The lifeguard gave a small, anticipatory sigh.

'We've been watching you. And we don't like what we see. There've been complaints, too. I'm not surprised.'

Eddie's voice stumbled into life. 'I've done nothing. Really.'

'Shut up. Stand against that wall.'

Eddie backed towards the wall. The man opened a drawer in the desk and took out a camera. He pointed it at Eddie, adjusted the focus and pressed the shutter. There was a flash.

'You're banned,' the manager said. 'And I'll be circulating your details around other pools. You want to keep away from children, mate. You're lucky we didn't call the police. If I had my way I'd castrate the fucking lot of you.'

It was so unfair. Eddie had been only playing with the children. He couldn't help touching them. They touched him, too. But only in play, only in play.

It frightened him that the people at the swimming pool had seen past what was happening and through into his mind, to what might have happened, what he wanted to happen. He had given himself away. In future he would have to be very careful. The conclusion was obvious: if he wanted to play games it would be far better to do it in private, where there were no grown-ups around to spoil the fun.

Summer slid into autumn. Goaded by his parents, Eddie applied for two clerical jobs but was offered neither. He also told them he was on the books of a tutorial agency, which was a lie. He looked into the future, and all he foresaw was boredom and desolation. He felt the weight of his parents' society pressing down on him like cold, dead earth. Yet he was afraid of going out in case he met people who knew him from Dale Grove or the Charleston Street swimming baths.

While the weather was warm, he would often leave Stanley and Thelma, encased in their old and evil-smelling carcasses, in front of the television and escape to the long, wild garden. He listened to the trains screaming and rattling on the line beyond Carver's. Sometimes he glimpsed Mrs Reynolds among the geraniums on the balcony of the Reynoldses' flat. Once he saw her talking earnestly with a large, fat woman who he guessed was Jenny Wren. The ugly duckling, Eddie told himself, had become an even uglier duck.

Over the years the tangle of trees and bushes at the far end of the Graces' garden had expanded both vertically and horizontally. The fence separating the back gardens of 27 and 29 Rosington Road had been repaired long before. But there was still a hole in the fence at the back: too small for Eddie's plump adult body, but obviously used by small animals – cats, perhaps, or even foxes.

Thelma said that Carver's was an eyesore. According to Stanley, the site of the bombed engineering works had not been redeveloped because its ownership was in dispute – a case of Dickensian complexity involving a family trust, missing heirs and a protracted court case.

'Someone's sitting on a gold mine there,' Stanley remarked on many occasions, for the older he became the more he repeated himself. 'You mark my words. A bloody gold mine. But probably the lawyers will get the lot.'

Time had on the whole been kind to Carver's, for creepers had softened the jagged brick walls and rusting corrugated iron; saplings had burst through the cracked concrete and grown into trees. Cow parsley, buddleia and rosebay willowherb brought splashes of white and purple and pink. It was a wonder, Eddie thought, that the ruins had not become a haven for crack-smoking delinquents from the council flats or Social Security parasites in search of somewhere to drink and sleep. Perhaps the ghosts kept them away. Not that it was easy to get into Carver's, except from the back gardens of Rosington Road. To the north was the railway, to the east and west were high walls built when bricks and labour were cheap. Access by road was down a narrow lane beside the infants' school which ended in high gates festooned with barbed wire and warning notices.

Eddie was safe from prying eyes at the bottom of the garden. He liked to kneel and stare through the hole into Carver's. The shed was still there, smaller and nearer than in memory, with two saplings of ash poking through its roof. One evening in September, he levered out the plank beside the hole and, his heart thudding, wriggled through the enlarged opening. Once inside he stood up and looked around. Birds sang in the distance.

Eddie picked his way towards the shed, skirting a large clump of nettles and a bald tyre. The shed's door had parted company with its hinges and fallen outwards. He edged inside. Much more of the roof had gone. Over half of the interior was now filled with the saplings and other vegetation. There were rags, two empty sherry bottles and a scattering of old cigarette ends on the floor; occasionally, it seemed, other people found their way into Carver's. He looked slowly around, hoping to see the paint tin that he and Alison had used for the Peeing Game, hoping for some correspondence between past and present.

Everything had changed. A sob wrenched its way out of his throat. He squeezed his eyes tightly shut. A tear rolled slowly down his left cheek. Here he was, he thought, a twenty-five-year-old failure. What had he been expecting to find? Alison with the pink ribbon in her hair, Alison twirling like a ballerina and smiling up at him?

Eddie stumbled outside. On his way back to the fence he looked up. To his horror, he saw through the branches of trees, high above the top of the wall, Mrs Reynolds on the balcony of her flat. Something flashed in her hands, a golden dazzle reflecting the setting sun. Eddie ran through the nettles to the fence and flung himself at the hole. A moment later he was back in the garden of 29 Rosington Road. His glasses had fallen off and he had torn a hole in his trousers.

When his breathing was calmer, Eddie forced himself to stroll to the house. At the door he glanced back. Mrs Reynolds was still on her balcony. She was staring over Carver's through what looked like a pair of field glasses. At least she wasn't looking at him. Not now. He shivered, and went inside.

Autumn became winter. After Christmas, Stanley caught a cold and the cold, as often happened with him, turned to bronchitis. No one noticed until it was too late that this time the bronchitis was pneumonia. He died early in February, aged seventy-two.

*   *   *

In recent years the trickle of LVs had died away. But until a few days before his death Stanley continued to visit the basement to work on the latest dolls' house.

Since his retirement he had slowed down, and the quality of his work had also deteriorated. But the last model was nearly complete, a tall Victorian terraced house looking foolish without its fellows on either side. He had been sewing the curtains at the time of his death.

Stanley died in hospital in the early hours of the morning. The following afternoon Eddie found the miniature curtains bundled into the sitting-room wastepaper basket, together with Stanley's needles and cottons. The discovery brought home to him the reality of his father's death more than anything else before or later, even the funeral.

This was a secular event. The Graces had never been church-goers. Eddie's experience of religion had been limited to the services at school, flat and meaningless affairs.

'He was an atheist,' Thelma said firmly when the funeral director tentatively raised the subject of the deceased's religious preferences. 'You can keep the vicars out of it, all right? And we don't want any of those humanists, either.'

His mother's reaction to Stanley's death took Eddie by surprise. She showed no outward sign of grief. She gave the impression that death was an irritation and an imposition because of the extra work it entailed. In many ways widowhood seemed to act as a tonic: she was brisker than she had been for years, both physically and mentally.

'If we can clear out some of your father's stuff,' Thelma said as they ate fish and chips in the kitchen on the evening after the funeral, 'perhaps we can find a lodger.'

Eddie put down his fork. 'But you wouldn't want a stranger in the house, would you?'

'If we want to stay here, we've no choice.'

'But the house is paid for. And haven't you got a pension from the Paladin?'

'Call it a pension? Don't make me laugh. I've already talked to them about it. I'll get a third of what your father got, and that wasn't much to begin with. It makes me sick. He worked there for over forty years, and you'd think by the way they used to go on that they couldn't do enough for their staff. They're sharks. Just like everyone else.'

'But surely we could manage?'

'We can't live on air.' She stared at him, pursing her lips. 'When you get another job, perhaps we can think again.'

When. The word hung between them. Eddie knew that his mother meant not *when* but *if.* Like his father, she had a low opinion of his capabilities. He thought that she could not have made the point more clearly if she had spoken the word *if* aloud.

'So we're agreed, then,' Thelma announced.

'I suppose so.'

She nodded at his plate, at half a portion of cod in greasy batter and a mound of pale, cold chips. 'Have you finished, then?'

'Yes.'

'Well, pass it here.' Thelma's appetite, always formidable for such a small person, had increased since she had stopped smoking the previous summer. 'Waste not, want not.'

'So we'll need to clear the back bedroom?'

'It won't clear itself, will it?' said Thelma through a mouthful of Eddie's supper. 'And while we're at it, we might as well sort out the basement. If we have a lodger we'll need the extra storage space.'

The next few days were very busy. His mother's haste seemed indecent. The back bedroom had been used as a boxroom for as long as Eddie could remember. Thelma wanted him to throw out most of the contents. She also packed up her husband's clothes and sent them to a charity shop. One morning she told Eddie to start clearing the basement. Most of the tools and photographic equipment could be sold, she said.

'It's not as if you're that way inclined, after all. You'd better get rid of the photos, too.'

'What about the dolls' house?'

'Leave that for now. But mind you change your trousers. Wear the old jeans, the ones with the hole in the knee.'

Eddie went through the photographs first – the artistic ones in the cupboard, not the ones on the open shelves. The padlock key had vanished. In the end Eddie levered off the hasp with a crowbar.

The photographs had been carefully mounted in albums. The negatives were there too, encased in transparent envelopes and filed in date order in a ring binder. Against each print his father had written a name and a date in his clear, upright hand. Usually he had added a title. 'Saucy!' 'Blowing Bubbles!' 'Having the Time of Her Life!'

Eddie leafed slowly through the albums, working backwards. Some of the photographs he thought were quite appealing, and he decided that he would put them to one side to look at more carefully in his bedroom. Most of the girls he recognized. He came across his younger self, too, but did not linger over those photographs. He found the Reynoldses' daughter, Jenny Wren, and was astonished to see how ugly she had been as a child; memory had been relatively kind to her. Then he found another face he knew, smiling up at him from a photograph with the caption 'What a Little Tease!' He stared at the face, his excitement ebbing, leaving a dull sadness behind.

It was Alison. There was no possible room for doubt. Stanley must have taken the photograph at some point during the same summer as the Peeing Game. When else could it have been? Children grew quickly at that age. In the photograph Alison was naked, and just as Eddie remembered her from their games in Carver's. He even remembered, or thought he did, the ribbon that she wore in her hair.

They had both betrayed him, his father and Alison. Why hadn't Alison told him? She had been his friend.

After lunch that day his mother sent him out to do some shopping. Eddie was glad of the excuse to escape from the house. He could not stop thinking of Alison. He had not seen her for nearly twenty years, yet her face seen in a photograph still had the power to haunt him.

On his way home, Eddie met Mr and Mrs Reynolds in Rosington Road. He turned the corner and there they were. He had no chance to avoid them. The Graces and the Reynoldses had been on speaking terms since Jenny Wren's visits to the dolls' house. Eddie glanced at Mrs Reynolds's sour, unsympathetic face, wondering whether she had seen him trespassing in Carver's the previous autumn.

'Sorry to hear about your dad,' Mr Reynolds said, his face creasing with concern. 'Still, at least it was quick: that must have been a blessing for all of you.'

'Yes. It was very sudden.'

'Always a good neighbour. Couldn't have asked for a nicer one.'

The words were intended to comfort, but made Eddie smile, an expression he concealed by turning away and blowing his nose vigorously, as though overwhelmed by the sorrow of the occasion. As he did so he noticed that Mrs Reynolds was staring at him. He dropped his eyes to her chest. He noticed on the lapel of her coat a small enamel badge from the Royal Society for the Protection of Birds.

Perhaps that was why she spent so much time staring over Carver's, why she had the field glasses. Mrs Reynolds was a bird-watcher, a *twitcher*. The word brought him dangerously close to a giggle.

'Let us know if we can help, won't you?' Mr Reynolds patted Eddie's arm. 'You know where to find us.'

The Reynoldses turned into the access road to the council estate, passing a line of garage doors daubed with swastikas and football slogans. Eddie scowled at their backs. A moment later, he let himself into number 29.

'Where have you been?' his mother called down from her room. 'There's tea in the pot, but don't blame me if it's stewed.'

The hall felt different from usual. There was more light. An unexpected draught brushed his face. Almost instantaneously Eddie realized that the door to the basement was standing wide open; Stanley's death was so recent an event that this in itself was remarkable. Eddie paused and looked through the doorway, down the uncarpeted stairs.

The dolls' house was still on the workbench. But it was no longer four storeys high. It had been reduced to a mound of splintered wood, torn fabric and flecks of paint. Beside it on the bench was the rusty hatchet which Alison had used to break through the fence between the Graces' garden and Carver's, and which Stanley had found lying under the trees at the end of the garden.

Eddie closed the basement door and went into the kitchen.

When she came downstairs, his mother did not mention the dolls' house and nor did he. That evening he piled what was left of it into a large cardboard box, carried it outside and left it beside the dustbin. He and his mother did not speak about it later because there was nothing they wanted to say.

5

'We do but learn to-day what our better advanced judgments
will unteach tomorrow . . .'

Religio Medici, II, 8

Oliver Rickford put down the phone. 'It's all right,' he said again.
'It's not Lucy's.'

Sally was sitting in the armchair. Her body was trembling.
Yvonne hovered behind the chair, her eyes on Oliver. He knelt
beside Sally, gripped her arm and shook it gently.

'Not Lucy's,' he repeated. 'Not Lucy's hand. I promise.'

Sally lifted her head. On the third try, she succeeded in saying,
'They can't be sure. They can't *know* it's not Lucy's.'

'They can in this case. The skin is black. Probably from a child
of about the same age.'

'Thank God.' Sally dabbed at her eyes with a paper handkerchief. 'What am I saying? It's someone else's child.' Still the
shameful Te Deum repeated itself in her mind: *Thank God it's not
Lucy, thank God, thank God.* 'Did they tell you anything else?'

Oliver hesitated. 'They haven't had time to look at the hand
properly. But it looks as if it was cut off with something like
an axe. It was very cold.' He paused again. 'In fact, they
think it may have been kept in a freezer. It was still defrosting.'

Yvonne sucked in her breath. 'Jesus.' She glanced at Sally.
'Sorry.'

Sally was still looking at Oliver. 'No link with Lucy? You're
sure?'

'Why should there be? The only possible connection was in the minds of those hacks downstairs.'

Sally clenched her hands, watching without interest as the knuckles turned white.

'Would it be a good idea to try to rest for a while?' Oliver suggested. 'There's nothing you can do at present.'

Sally was too tired to argue. Her strength had mysteriously evaporated. Clutching the box of paper handkerchiefs, she smiled mechanically at the two police officers and left the room. The door of the room she shared with Michael was closed. She did not want to disturb him, and if he woke up she would not know what to say. Instead she took a deep breath and went into Lucy's bedroom.

It was like a cell – small, and with a window placed high in the wall. They had intended to decorate before Lucy was born but had failed to find the time. After Lucy's birth there had been even less time. The wallpaper showed a trellis with a stylized clematis growing up it. In places the wallpaper was coming adrift from the wall, a process which Lucy had actively encouraged, revealing another wallpaper beneath, psychedelic swirls of orange and turquoise from the 1960s.

Sally had dreaded coming here. She had known that the room would smell of Lucy, that everywhere there would be reminders. But it had to be done, sooner or later; in the long run avoiding the room would be worse. She sat down heavily on the bed, which was covered with a duvet whose design showed teddy bears gorging themselves on honey and apparently oblivious of a squadron of enormous bees patrolling the air around their heads. The duvet had been Lucy's choice, the bribe which had persuaded her to move from her cot to a proper bed.

Automatically, Sally began to tidy the books and toys which were scattered on and around the bedside table. Were all four-year-olds like this? Was chaos their natural environment? Or was Lucy exceptional in this as in so much else?

The book they had been reading on Thursday evening was lying between the bed and the wall. Sally rescued it and marked the place they had reached with a scrap of paper. She ran out of energy and let herself fall back on the bed. She buried her face in the pillow. Why did children smell sweet?

She supposed that she should pray for Lucy. It was then that she realized that she had not read the Morning Office today, or indeed the Evening Office last night. Discipline and regular exercise were as necessary in prayer as in athletics. She closed her eyes and tried to bring her mind into focus.

Nothing happened. No one was there. It was dark and cold and God was absent. It was not that he no longer existed, Sally discovered: it was simply that it no longer mattered to her whether he existed or not. He had become an irrelevancy, something pushed beyond the margins of her life. She tried to say the Lord's Prayer, but the words dried up long before she had finished. Instead she thought of the severed hand. What sort of person would leave it on a gravestone? Was there a significance in the choice of grave? Perhaps it belonged to a relative of the owner of the hand.

She hoped the child had been dead when they cut off the hand. The idea that he or she had been chopped up, perhaps parcelled in clingfilm and deep-frozen, made it worse for two reasons: it added an illusion of domesticity to what had been done, and it suggested premeditation and a terrible patience. What could have been the motive for such an action? A desire to hurt the child's mother? Punishment for a theft, a perversion of the Islamic penal code? Sally tried to imagine a need grown so egocentric and powerful that it would stop at nothing, even the carefully calculated destruction of children.

She dug her hand into the pocket of her jeans and wrapped her fingers round Lucy's sock. She thought of herself and Michael, Lucy and the unknown child, the child's parents, the old woman gobbling pills in the bedsitter in Belmont Road, the diseased and the abused, the tortured and the dying. The human race never learned by its mistakes: it merely plunged deeper and deeper into a mire of its own making.

At that moment, lying on Lucy's bed, it became clear to Sally that a loving God would not permit such things. At theological college she had learned the arguments why he might allow suffering. She had even parroted them out for parishioners. Now the arguments were suddenly revealed as specious: at last God was unmasked and revealed as the shit he really was.

She heard voices in the sitting room, one of them a man's but neither Oliver's nor Michael's. She sat up on the bed and wiped away her tears and blew her nose. There was a tap on the door and Yvonne put her head into the room.

'Mr Maxham's here. He wondered if you'd be up to having a word with him.'

Sally nodded, and dragged herself to her feet. 'Has Oliver gone?'

'About ten minutes ago. He didn't want to disturb you. He left a note.'

Sally's body felt hot and heavy. In the bathroom she washed her face and dragged a comb through her hair. In the mirror her face confronted her: a haggard stranger, pale and puffy-eyed, no make-up, hair in a mess.

In the living room, Yvonne was standing by the window, her head bowed, an anxious smile on her face.

'This is Chief Inspector Maxham. Mrs Appleyard.'

A small, thin man was examining the photographs on the mantelpiece. He turned round, a fraction of a second later than one would have expected.

'Mrs Appleyard.' Maxham ambled towards her, hand outstretched. 'I hope we haven't disturbed you.'

'I wasn't asleep.' His handshake was dry, hard and cold. She noticed that the hands were a blue-purple colour; he probably suffered from poor circulation. 'Is there any news?'

'I'm afraid not. Not yet.' He gestured to a tall man standing by the door to the kitchen. 'This is Detective Sergeant Carlow.'

The sergeant nodded to her. He wore a chain-store suit, a dark grey pinstripe whose sleeves and trouser legs were a little too short for him. His skin, his hair and even his eyes looked etiolated, as if he spent too much of his waking life staring at a computer screen under artificial light. His jaw was so prominent that the lower part of his face was broader than the upper.

Maxham nodded to one of her chairs. 'Do sit down, Mrs Appleyard.'

She remained standing. 'Have you found anything, anything at all?'

'It's early days.' Maxham had a plump face, the skin criss-crossed with red veins. Behind black-rimmed glasses the eyes were pale islands, neither grey nor blue but somewhere between. The accent was Thames Estuary, very similar to Derek Cutter's. 'As far as we can tell, Lucy just walked out of the back door. She –'

'But she wouldn't do that. She's not a fool. She's been told time and time again –'

'It seems that she and Ms Vaughan had had a bit of a disagreement. Lucy wanted Ms Vaughan to buy her something, a Christmas present, and Ms Vaughan said no. Then Ms Vaughan went upstairs to the bathroom. She left Lucy sulking behind the sofa. Five minutes later, maybe ten, Ms Vaughan comes down again, hoping Lucy had calmed down. But she was gone. The other little girl and boy hadn't noticed her going – one was watching TV, the other was upstairs with Ms Vaughan. Lucy's coat's missing. And so's Ms Vaughan's purse. Big green thing – it was in her handbag on the kitchen table.'

The little madam, Sally thought: she's not getting away with that sort of behaviour; just wait till I get my hands on her. In an instant she lurched back to the reality of the situation. Her legs began to shake. She sat down suddenly. Maxham sat down, too. He looked expectantly at her. She found a tissue in her sleeve and blew her nose.

At length she said, 'I thought Carla always locked the doors, put the chain on.'

'So she says,' he agreed. 'But on the back door she's only got a couple of bolts and a Yale. We think Lucy may have pulled over a stool and climbed up. The bolts had been recently oiled and the catch might have been up on the Yale – Ms Vaughan said she went out in the yard to put something in the dustbin earlier that afternoon, and she wasn't sure she'd put the catch down when she came in.'

Sally clung to past certainties, hoping to use them to prove that this could not be happening. 'She couldn't have got out of the yard. The fence is far too high for her. And there's a drop on the other side – she doesn't like jumping down from a height. There's a gate, isn't there, into some alley? It's always locked. I remember Carla telling me.'

'The gate was unbolted when we got there, Mrs Appleyard.'

'It's a high bolt, isn't it?' Sally closed her eyes, trying to visualize the yard which she'd seen on a sunny afternoon in the autumn. Dead leaves, brown, yellow and orange, danced over the concrete and gathered in a drift between the two dustbins and the sandpit. 'Was the bolt stiff?'

'As it happens, yes. Would you say that Lucy is a physically strong child for her age?'

'Look at me, Mum.' Lucy was standing on the edge of her bed in her pyjamas, holding Jimmy up to the ceiling. 'I'm King Kong.'

'Not particularly. She's a little smaller than average for her age.'

Sergeant Carlow was sitting at the table and writing in his notebook. The cuffs of the trousers had risen halfway up his calves, exposing bands of pale and almost hairless skin above the drooping black socks.

A soft hiss filled the silence: Maxham had a habit of sucking in breath every moment or so as if trying to clear obstructions lodged between his teeth; and as he did so he pulled back his lips in the mockery of a smile. 'We've talked to the neighbours all along the street. We've talked to the people whose gardens back on to the alley. No one saw her. It was a filthy evening, yesterday. No one was out unless they had to be.'

Sally shouted, 'Are you saying that someone opened that gate from the outside?'

Maxham shrugged his wiry little body. The plump face looked all wrong on such a scraggy neck. 'I'm afraid we're not in a position to draw any conclusions yet, Mrs Appleyard. We're just investigating the possibilities, you understand. Gathering evidence. I'm sure you know what these things are like from your husband.'

The condescension in his voice made Sally yearn to slap him. He sat there smiling at her. He was going bald at the crown and the grey hair needed cutting. He wore an elderly tweed suit, baggy at the knees and shiny at the elbows, which gave him the incongruous appearance of a none-too-successful farmer on market day. She did not like what she saw, but that did not mean he was bad at his job. Once more he hissed. Now that she had noticed the habit, it irritated and distracted her. She thought of protective geese and hostile serpents.

'What about dogs?' she asked, her voice astonishingly calm.

'We tried that. No joy. Doesn't prove anything one way or the other. All that rain didn't help.'

'And how can I help you?'

Maxham's head nodded, perhaps as a sign of approval. He took off his glasses and began to polish them with a handkerchief from the top pocket of his jacket. 'There's a number of things, Mrs Appleyard. Most of them obvious. We'll need a good up-to-date photograph of Lucy. We'll need to talk to you about what she's like – not just her appearance, what she's like inside. We'd like to find out exactly what she's wearing. Everything.' He inserted a delicate little pause in the conversation. 'Also, any toys she may have had with her, that sort of thing. Ms Vaughan said she wanted them to go to Woolworth's and buy a conjuring set. Can you confirm that?'

'Yes. Lucy and I had an argument about it on the way to Carla's yesterday morning. My daughter can be very persistent. If she wants something, she's inclined to go on and on about it until she gets it. And if she doesn't get it, which is what often happens, she sometimes throws a tantrum.'

'So you'd agree that her going off all by herself in a huff like that wouldn't be untypical?'

'Of course it would be untypical. She's never done anything like that before.' Yes, she had, Sally thought: Lucy had tried to run off in shops several times: but surely this was different in kind as well as in degree? 'But she's very self-willed. Her trying to run off like that shocks me but it doesn't altogether surprise me.'

'Ah.' Maxham breathed on his glasses one last time, gave them another polish and settled them on the bridge of his nose. 'I have to say your husband sees Lucy a little differently. He insisted that she wouldn't run off of her own accord, that she's far too sensible.'

'Lucy likes being with her father.' Sally chose her words carefully, unwilling to point out that she saw about five times more of Lucy than Michael did, and that Michael spoiled her terribly. 'Perhaps she tends to be better behaved with him than she is with me. But I don't think that there's any doubt about the determination she can show. You can ask Carla. Or Margaret Cutter.' She rushed on, answering the question before Maxham had time to ask it. 'She's our vicar's wife. She runs a crèche at St George's.'

'Would you have any objection if we had a look round?'

'A look where?'

'All over the flat, if you don't mind. Lucy's room, especially, of course. It can help us get a feeling of the missing child, you understand. And if you'd come with us, perhaps you'll notice if there's anything missing.'

What did they expect to find, Sally wondered? Lucy's body under her bed? 'All right. But my husband's asleep at present.'

'Yes, your husband.' Maxham drew out the words until he was speaking almost in a drawl. He sucked in air. 'We wouldn't want to disturb him.'

'He needs to sleep.'

'He was up all night.' Maxham's voice was neutral, uninflected. 'I had to ask his friend Mr Rickford to come and collect him this morning. So he got home safely?'

'Yes.' Before she could stop herself, Sally added a plea on Michael's behalf: 'He was very upset, yesterday. Still is. He's not himself.'

'That's understandable.' The voice was still neutral, and the want of sympathy was in itself an accusation. 'I gather he's had a lot on his plate lately.'

'Obviously.' A doubt niggled in Sally's mind: had Michael had something else to worry about, something that had happened *before* Lucy's disappearance? But there was no time for that now. 'What do you think might have happened?' She was suddenly furious with Maxham. 'Come on – you must have some ideas. What are the main possibilities?'

'Three main scenarios,' he said briskly. 'One, she wandered off by herself, and hopefully found shelter. Two, a man or maybe some kids were passing by and thought they'd take her with them. It happens, Mrs Appleyard, I won't conceal it from you; but it happens less often than you'd believe, so try not to think too much about it.' His tone was still neutral, and she wondered whether kindness or insensitivity lay behind it. 'Three: a woman took her. That counts as a separate option because usually the motives are different. You know, mothers who've lost their babies and need a replacement. Girls who want a young child to play with, a sort of doll. If that's what's happened, we'll probably get her back safe and sound.'

'Safe and sound?' Sally whispered, so angry and so scared that her teeth wanted to chatter together.

'These things are relative, Mrs Appleyard. You must understand that.'

'Why do these women do it?' Sally was reluctant to consider the other options; she knew they would haunt her later.

'Sometimes it's someone who thinks her relationship's breaking up. It's a way to keep a man with her. Usually that's a baby, though. Or then you get a young girl with a history of parental neglect. Broken home – Dad's in jail, Mum's got a new man. You could say they need someone to love. Don't we all, eh? And then you get the mentally ill. Usually no previous history of delinquency. Generally a one-off case, committed while the woman's in an acute psychotic state.' Maxham glanced at her, assessing the effect his words were having. 'We'll just have to see what –'

Without warning, Michael shambled into the room and leant on the back of the sofa. He stared at them as if at a roomful of strangers. Sergeant Carlow stood up, snapping shut his notebook. Yvonne looked at Maxham, asking mutely for guidance. Maxham simply sat there, his hands clasped loosely on his lap.

Sally had left the door open when she came into the room. Had Michael been standing in the hallway and listening for long? He was in his pyjamas, and he looked terrible: the jacket unbuttoned, his hair tousled, his face unshaven, his body dazed by the sleeping pill.

'Find her, Maxham,' Michael whispered. 'Just find her. Stop talking and find her.'

Sally did not like Maxham, but she had to admit that he handled the situation shrewdly. He asked Sally to show himself and Carlow round the flat. He left Yvonne sitting at the table with Michael. Michael might have picked a quarrel if he had been left alone with either of the men. But he would not quarrel with a woman. He treated women he did not know well as if they were delicate beings, easily damaged by rough handling.

Sally heard Michael and Yvonne talking as she showed the two police officers round the flat. She could not hear what they

110

were saying, but their voices rose and fell, stopped and started, in a reassuringly normal pattern.

When they returned to the living room, however, Michael looked up at Maxham and Sally knew from Michael's face that nothing had changed.

'The odds are a man took her,' he said. 'You know that. Women tend to take babies.'

Maxham drew back his lips and hissed. 'We'll have to see.' He turned to Sally. 'Thank you for your help, Mrs Appleyard. We'll be in touch. And don't worry – we're doing everything we can.'

'Bastard,' Michael muttered audibly in the living room as Sally was showing the police officers out.

Michael shaved and showered. By now it was mid-afternoon. Sally made a pot of tea which only Yvonne wanted. The policewoman was doing her best, Sally thought, but it was like having a nanny on the premises. She sat by the phone, apparently engrossed in the last few clues of the *Daily Telegraph* crossword.

Michael pushed aside his mug. 'I'm sorry, Sal. I can't stay here. I feel like the walls are pressing in. I'm going to get some fresh air.'

She wanted to seize his hand. *Don't leave me alone*. Instead she said, 'Will you be long?'

He didn't answer the question. He found his jacket and dropped his wallet in one pocket and his keys in the other. It was a waxed jacket, which reminded her of Oliver.

'Should you phone Oliver at some point?' she asked.

'When I get back.' He bent down and kissed the top of her head. 'I love you,' he murmured, too low for Yvonne to hear. He straightened up. 'I won't be long.'

His hand touched Sally's shoulder for an instant. He nodded to Yvonne and left the room. The two women sat in silence. The front door opened and closed. They heard his footsteps moving steadily down the stairs. Sally hoped that he wouldn't get into a fight with the journalists. In a moment or two she relaxed because no one was shouting in the street.

That was the last she saw of Michael on Saturday. She spent

most of the next five hours near the phone. When the phone rang, Yvonne would answer it, shaking her head at Sally when it became clear that Michael wasn't the caller.

Sally thought of Michael getting himself arrested; of him wandering in tears through the streets of London in search of Lucy; of accident, madness and suicide. Even in her misery she knew that Lucy's absence was far more worrying than Michael's; the greater fear did not cast out the lesser, but it made it easier to bear. This did not stop her feeling angry with him.

'The bloody man!' she burst out after yet another phone call from someone she did not want to talk to.

'That's right, dear,' Yvonne said helpfully. 'Get it out of your system.'

'Does Maxham know that Michael's gone?'

Yvonne nodded. 'I had to tell him. I'm sorry.'

'It's not your fault.'

On the mantelpiece, Sally found the note from Oliver propped against the broken silver clock, the wedding present from David Byfield. *Michael and Sally: Please phone me if I can do anything. Oliver.* Underneath his name he had had the sense to put his phone number. A polite man, too. When Yvonne was making tea in the kitchen, Sally picked up the phone. Oliver answered at the second ring.

'It's me. Sally.'

'Any news?'

'No. Not really.' She told him about Michael. 'I – I wondered if he might be with you.'

'I wish he was. Actually, Maxham's already phoned. Shall I come over?'

'No.' She heard a clatter from the kitchen. 'I've got to go.'

'Phone me, Sally. Any time. All right?'

'All right.' She broke the connection as Yvonne came in with mugs of tea. 'Just checking with Oliver Rickford. Michael's not there, either.'

Sally sat down with the tea. What hurt, then and later, was the way Michael had locked her out. *For better or for worse*: didn't it mean anything to him? If it didn't mean anything, why did he bother getting married? He could have found someone else to screw. Maybe that's where he was

112

now: with a prostitute, paying for what his wife was too tired to give him.

Yvonne went to the lavatory. The phone began to ring. Sally flung herself at it, spilling uncomfortably hot tea over her leg. '*Shit*. Hello.'

'Is that the Reverend Appleyard speaking?' A man's voice; unfamiliar. 'Sally? This is Frank Howell. Remember me? I did that piece on St George's for the *Standard*.'

'I'm sorry. I've nothing to say.'

'I understand, Sally.' The voice was unctuous. 'I don't want to ask you anything. Truly.'

She remembered the man's face now: the balding cherub with red-rimmed eyes; Derek's friend. 'I'm going to put the phone down, Mr Howell.'

He began to gabble: 'Sooner or later you and Michael are going to have to deal with the press. Maybe I can help. You need someone who knows the ropes, someone on your side, someone who –'

'Goodbye.' She broke the connection.

'Who was that?' Yvonne asked, a moment later.

'A journalist named Frank Howell.'

'He's already rung twice before. Leave the phone to me.'

'I thought it might be Michael.' *Or Lucy*. Sally started to cry again.

Yvonne gave her a handful of paper handkerchiefs. 'Try not to worry, love. I'm sure there's some perfectly simple explanation. He'll be back. You'll see.'

Through her tears Sally snarled, 'I'm not sure I want him back.' *I want Lucy*.

Afterwards, Sally learned that Michael turned right into the main road, walking towards the tube station. He went into the saloon bar of the King of Prussia and ordered a pint of beer and a double whisky. He sat by himself at a table in the corner of the room. According to the barman he gave no trouble. He drank two more double whiskies and repelled an attempt to draw him into conversation.

He took the underground to King's Cross Station, where he bought a standard single to Cambridge. He had time to kill before catching the train so he killed it in a bar. From Cambridge railway station he walked slowly into the centre of the town and out the other side, stopping at two pubs on the way. He staggered up the Huntingdon Road. Just before eight-thirty he reached a small but ugly block of modern flats near Fitzwilliam College. He rang one of the bells and lay down on the wet grass to rest. Soon he was asleep.

A little later, the telephone rang in the Appleyards' living room in Hercules Road. Yvonne answered. She listened for a moment, pressed the mute button and looked across the room at Sally.

'It's someone called Father Byfield. Do you want to speak to him? He says your husband's with him.'

Sally was furious and relieved when she heard Uncle David's voice. Jealousy was there, too, and also a sense of failure. She should have realized that in times of trouble Michael would turn not to her but to his godfather.

6

'Therefore for Spirits, I am so far from denying their existence, that I could easily believe, that not onely whole Countries, but particular persons, have their Tutelary and Guardian Angels.'

Religio Medici, I, 33

'Mummy. Mummy, where are you?'

Over the intercom, Lucy's voice sounded mechanical, like a juvenile robot's. Without the intercom and with the doors closed, they would not have heard her because the basement was now so well soundproofed.

'Mummy.' The voice sharpened and rose to a wail. 'Where are you?'

Angel dropped her napkin on the table and stood up, stretching her long white arm towards the keys on the worktop. At the door she glanced back at Eddie.

'You sort things out in here. I'll deal with her.'

Lucy was crying now. Eddie imagined her standing by the door or curled up in bed. She was wearing the pyjamas he had bought especially for her at Selfridges; they had red stars against a deep yellow background and in normal circumstances would suit her colouring. Last night, however, Lucy had not been looking her best: by the low-wattage light of the bedside lamp, her face had been white, almost green, mouth a black, ragged hole, the puffy eyes squeezed into slits.

'Daddy. Mummy.'

The intercom emitted a series of crackles: Angel was unlocking and opening the door to the basement.

'*Mummy*. I want –'

'You'll see Mummy very soon.' Angel's voice was tinny and precise. There was a click as she closed the door behind her. 'Now, what are you doing out of bed without your slippers?'

'Where's Mummy? Where am I? Where's Daddy?'

'Mummy and Daddy had to go away for a night or two. Don't you remember? Eddie and I are looking after you.' There was a pause, but Lucy did not respond. 'I'm Angel.'

Lucy began to cry again. The intercom twisted and distorted her sorrow.

'That's enough, dear. I don't want to have to get cross. Think how sad Mummy would be if she heard you've been naughty.'

The crying grew louder.

'Lucy. You won't like it if I have to get cross. Naughty children have to be punished.'

The wails continued. There was a sharp report like the crack of a whip. The crying stopped abruptly.

'We don't allow cry babies here, dear. You're going to have to pull your socks up, aren't you?'

Eddie could bear it no longer. He switched off the intercom and listened to the silence seeping into the kitchen like water flowing into a pool.

Here we all were on this overcrowded planet, Eddie thought, all members of the same species and yet each of us a mystery to everyone else. Especially Angel, who, like Churchill's Russia, was a riddle wrapped in a mystery inside an enigma. For example, where did she come from? How old was she? Who was she? If she did not particularly like little girls, why did she spend so much time with them? Last but not least, why had Angel said that Lucy was special? What made Lucy different from the other three?

Nothing about Angel was straightforward. To all intents and purposes she might have been born adult less than six years before, on the March evening when Eddie met her. She came to the house in Rosington Road in answer to an advertisement which Eddie's mother had put in the *Evening Standard*. The advertisement gave the name of the road but not the Graces'

116

name or the number of the house. Eddie's mother said that you couldn't be too careful, what with all the strange people roaming round the streets today.

From the start, Thelma refused to consider male applicants. 'They're dirty beasts. Women are tidier and cleaner.' Eddie himself was excepted from this general view of the male sex, which confirmed his suspicion that his mother did not think him entirely masculine.

When Angel phoned, Eddie's mother gave her the number of the house almost immediately. She liked Angel's voice.

'At least she speaks the Queen's English. More than you can say for the rest of them. And she says she's got a job. I don't want one of those Social Security scroungers under my feet all day.'

There had been nine other calls before Angel's, but none of them had led to an invitation to see the room. Thelma disliked the Irish, West Indians, Asians and anyone with what she termed a 'lower class' accent.

When the doorbell rang, Eddie and his mother were watching television in the front room.

'She's on time,' Thelma commented, looking at her watch. 'I'll say that for her.'

Eddie went into the hall and peeped through the fish-eye lens at the person on the doorstep. He could see very little of her, because she had turned to stare at the traffic on the road; and in any case, she was wearing a long, pale mackintosh with a hood. As he opened the door she turned to face him.

She was beautiful. For an instant her perfection paralysed him. He had never seen anyone so beautiful in real life, only on television, in pictures and in films. She stared at him as though she were assessing his suitability rather than the other way round.

'Ah,' he said. 'Ah, Miss – ah – come in.'

There was an infinitesimal pause. Then, to his relief, she smiled and came out of the rain. Angel was about his own height, which was five feet six. She had a long, fine-boned face, the skin flawless as a child's. Thelma, pop-eyed with suspicion, escorted her upstairs to see the spare room. Eddie lurked in the hall, listening.

'How lovely,' he heard Angel say. 'And, if I may say so, how tastefully decorated.' Her voice was self-assured, the crisp enunciation hinting at a corresponding clarity of thought.

By the time they came downstairs again the two women were chatting almost like friends. To Eddie's amazement, he heard his mother offering hospitality.

'We generally have a glass of sherry at this time, Miss Wharton. Perhaps you'd care to join us?'

'That would be lovely.'

Thelma stared at Eddie, who after an awkward hiatus leapt to his feet and went to the kitchen to search for the bottle of sweet sherry which his father had opened the Christmas before last. When he returned with three assorted glasses on a tray, the women were discussing how soon Angel could move in.

'Subject to a month's deposit and suitable references, of course.'

'Naturally.' Angel opened her handbag. 'I have a reference here from Mrs Hawley-Minton. She's the lady who runs the agency I work for.'

'A nursing agency?'

'Nursery nursing, actually. Essentially it's an agency for nannies with nursing training.'

'Eddie,' Thelma prompted. 'The sherry.'

He handed round the glasses. Angel passed an envelope to Thelma, who extracted a sheet of headed paper and settled her reading glasses on her nose. Eddie and Angel sipped their sherry.

'I see that Mrs Hawley-Minton knew your parents,' Thelma said, her stately manner firmly to the fore.

'Oh, yes. That's why she took me on. She's very careful about that sort of thing.'

Thelma peered interrogatively over her reading glasses.

'An agency like hers is a great responsibility,' Angel explained. 'Particularly as children are concerned. She believes one can't be too careful.'

'Quite,' said Thelma; and after a pause she added, 'I do so agree.' She folded the letter and handed it back to Angel. 'Well, Miss Wharton, that seems quite satisfactory. When would you like to move in?'

*   *   *

In those days, Angel was always Miss Wharton. Thelma took refuge in obsolete formality. Eddie avoided calling Angel anything to her face, but sometimes at night he whispered her Christian name, Angela, trying it for size in his mouth, where it felt awkward and alien.

By and large, Angel kept to her room. She was allowed the use of the bathroom, of course, and she had her own latchkey. For a time she had all the virtues, even negative ones.

'I'm so glad she doesn't smoke,' said Thelma, who had converted her former pleasure into a vice. 'It would make the whole house smell, not just her room. But I suppose she wouldn't, being a nurse.'

Before Angel moved in, Thelma had worried a great deal about the telephone. She had visions of Angel making unauthorized calls to Australia, of the phone ringing endlessly (a woman who looked like that was bound to have an active social life), of long conversations with girlfriends and, even worse, boyfriends.

Angel soon calmed Thelma's fears. She rarely used the phone herself, and when she did she kept a meticulous record of the cost. Nor did she receive many incoming phone calls. Most of them were to do with her work – usually from Mrs Hawley-Minton's agency. As the weeks went by, Thelma developed a telephonic acquaintance with Mrs Hawley-Minton.

'They value Miss Wharton very highly,' she reported to Eddie. 'Mrs Hawley-Minton tells me that her clients are always asking to have her back. One of them was a real prince. His father was a king. Bulgaria, was it? He was deposed a long time ago, of course, but even so.'

Eddie envied Angel her job. He thought a good deal about her children and what she might do with them. Sometimes he tried to imagine that he was she, that he was in her clothes, in her skin, behind her eyes.

'She's working in Belgrave Square this week,' Thelma would say, telling Eddie for want of anyone better to talk to. 'He's a Peruvian millionaire, and she's something to do with the embassy.' And Eddie would see dark-haired children with solemn faces and huge eyes in an attic nursery with barred windows; he would see himself looking after them and playing with them, just as Angel did.

Thelma was curious about Angel's antecedents, and about her apparently non-existent social life. 'If you ask me, she's been unlucky in love. Don't tell me a girl like that hasn't had plenty of opportunities. I bet she has men chasing after her with their tongues hanging out every time she walks down the street.'

Thelma's coarseness surprised Eddie, even shocked him. She had never shown that side of herself when Stanley had been alive. He noticed that the hypothetical fiancé appealed greatly to her.

'I wonder if she was engaged, and then he was killed, and since then she's never looked at another man.' Thelma also had a strong sentimental streak, buried deep but liable to surface unexpectedly. 'Perhaps he was in the army. Miss Wharton's father was, you know.' It transpired that Mrs Hawley-Minton's late husband had been a brigadier, and he and Angel's father had served together in India during the war. 'I think both parents must be dead,' Thelma confided. 'She seems quite alone in the world.'

Thelma's curiosity about Angel extended to her possessions. Angel kept her room clean and made her own bed. But Thelma retained a key, and every now and then, when Angel was out, she would unlock the door of the back bedroom and cautiously investigate her lodger's private life.

'I'm not being nosy. But she's my responsibility in a way. And I have to make sure she's not burning holes in the bedspread or leaving the fire on when she goes out.'

Eddie watched his mother on one of these incursions. He stood in the doorway of the back bedroom – a landlady's dream: clean, tidy, smelling faintly of polish and Angel's perfume. Thelma moved slowly round the room in a clockwise direction. She opened doors and pulled out drawers. On top of the wardrobe was a large modern suitcase.

'Locked,' Thelma commented, curious but not annoyed.

In the cupboard by the bed was a japanned box, and that was locked, too. 'Probably keeps family papers in there, mementoes of her parents and her fiancé. Funny she doesn't have any photographs of them. There's plenty of room on the dressing table.'

'You haven't got any pictures of Dad,' Eddie pointed out.

'That's quite different,' Thelma wheezed, her attention elsewhere. 'She's got an awful lot of books, hasn't she? I wonder if she's actually read them.' She peered at the spines. 'You wouldn't have thought she was *religious*, would you?' His mother spoke the word 'religious' in a tone in which incredulity, pity and curiosity were finely balanced. 'You'd never have guessed.'

Eddie noticed a bible, a prayer book and a hymnal. He ran his eyes along the row of spines and other titles leapt out at him: G. K. Chesterton's biography of Thomas Aquinas; the *Religio Medici* of Sir Thomas Browne; *The Christian Faith*; *The Four Last Things*; *A Dictionary of Christian Theology*; *The Shield of Faith*; *Man, God and Prayer*.

'She doesn't go to church,' Thelma said, her voice doubtful. 'I'm sure we would have noticed.' She drifted over to the dressing table, picked up a small bottle of perfume and sniffed it. 'Very nice.' She put down the perfume. 'Mind you, it should be. That stuff isn't cheap. You could feed a family of four on the amount she spends on dolling herself up.'

Insignificant though it was, the remark lodged in Eddie's memory. It was the first sign of a rift developing between Thelma and Angel. His mother was by nature a critical person, always willing to find fault and never satisfied with anyone or anything for long. She pursued perfection all her life and would not have known what to do if she had caught up with it.

As a mild grey spring slipped into a mild grey summer, the carping gathered strength. Thelma fired criticisms like arrows – at first one or two, every now and then, but steadily increasing in number.

As with Stanley, so with Angel: Thelma did not try to get rid of her lodger any more than she had tried to get rid of her husband. Angel's unwillingness to take remarks in the spirit they'd been uttered infuriated Thelma. But there was nothing she could do about it – Angel wore her placidity like a suit of armour.

On a sunny morning in the middle of summer, Eddie took a cup of coffee into the garden. His mother was out of the house for once – every four weeks she went by taxi to the health centre where she had her blood pressure checked and collected

121

her monthly ration of pills and sprays – and he felt unusually relaxed. He wandered towards the trees at the far end.

The peaceful mood was shattered when he heard the back door opening behind him. He turned. Angel came towards him, picking her way between a weed-infested flowerbed and the long grass of the lawn. Her hair was loose, and she wore a short green dress and sandals. The sun was to her right and a little behind her, casting a golden glow over her hair and throwing her face into shadow.

'I'm not disturbing you?'

'No.' He shrank back towards the fence.

'It's such a lovely day. I couldn't resist coming outside.'

He sipped his coffee, scalding his tongue.

'Do you know, I saw a fox the other day.' Angel pointed down the garden towards Carver's. 'It went down there. Probably into the wasteland at the back.'

'There's a lot of wildlife there.'

'Shame it's such a mess.' She stopped beside him, and he caught a suggestion of her perfume. Her eyes swung towards the council flats. 'Still, better a jungle than something like that.'

Eddie nodded.

After a pause, Angel went on, 'Have you noticed the woman with the binoculars? She's often on the balcony with the geraniums.'

Only one balcony had geraniums. It stood out starkly from its neighbours partly because of this, and partly because of its tidiness, the fresh paint on the railing and the absence of a satellite dish. No one was standing there now.

'I think she watches birds,' Eddie said. 'Her name's Mrs Reynolds.'

'She was there just now. I was looking out of my bedroom window, and for a moment I thought she was watching you.'

'Are you sure? Why?'

'She was probably looking at the house. Or at next door. Perhaps there's a bird on the roof.' She smiled at him. 'In any case, even if she was looking at you, I wouldn't take it personally.'

'Oh no. Of course not.'

'Old women do strange things.' Angel glanced back at the house, and Eddie knew that Mrs Reynolds was not the only old woman she had in mind. 'But it's their problem, not ours.'

Over the summer, as Thelma's criticisms multiplied, Eddie found himself warming towards Angel. The process was gradual and subtle. She would smile at him as they passed in the hall, or ask him what he thought the weather was going to do this morning and listen to his answer as if his opinion really counted. When Thelma was being more than usually absurd, Angel would occasionally glance at Eddie; and when their eyes met there was the delicious sense of a shared secret, of shared amusement.

Eddie was flattered and alarmed by these hints. Women had never shown any interest in him before, especially not beautiful women like Angel. Not that he liked her specifically as a woman, he told himself, but as a person. And there was no doubt that her beauty affected the way he responded to her: it added significance to everything she said and did.

Then came the first Sunday in September. It was a fine late summer day, and after breakfast Eddie decided to walk up to the Heath. (Since his father's death he had lost his fear of going out.) He happened to glance back as he was walking up Haverstock Hill and noticed, some way behind him, Angel walking slowly in the same direction. Her presence irritated him. On his walks he liked to be among strangers. He quickened his pace and cut down the next side road. He looked back more than once but there was no sign of her. He thought that she had probably continued up Rosslyn Hill to Hampstead Village.

He spent a pleasant hour on the Heath. It was a place he avoided in the evenings because parts of it were rough and dangerous and, they said, haunted by men doing horrible things to each other. But in daytime at weekends and during the holidays the Heath was full of children, some with grown-ups, some without. Eventually he found a bench on Parliament Hill and watched irritable fathers flying kites for bored children. Below him stretched the city, brick and stone, glass and tarmac, blues and greys and greens, trembling like a live thing in the haze.

To Eddie's delight, two girls of about eight began to do gymnastics near his bench. They were of an age when they were still unselfconscious about their bodies, when competition came naturally to them. One was wearing jeans, but the other – a girl with a pale, serious face spotted with freckles – wore a sweatshirt over a skimpy dress. Eddie watched her covertly. He tried to decide whether she was consciously teasing him, as Alison used to do in that far-off summer when she swung higher and higher, revealing more and more, and pretending that she didn't know he was watching her. He stared at her, wondering how soft the skin would be above the bony knees.

Then, with an abruptness which made him gasp, this pleasant reverie was shattered.

'Aren't they sweet?' Angel sat down beside him. 'All that energy. Where do they get it from?'

Eddie stared wildly at her. Her sudden appearance would have shocked him in normal circumstances and brought about another attack of shyness. But this was worse. Had his face revealed something of his thoughts? Angel was a nanny. She would be alert for strange men who watched children.

'It's a lovely day for the Heath. The best part of summer.'

'Yes,' he managed to say. 'Very sunny.'

The breeze blew a strand of her hair towards him. She smoothed it back into place. For an instant her sleeve brushed his and he smelt her perfume. She was wearing a blue sweatshirt and jeans. Her left hand was now lying on her leg, long-fingered, smooth-skinned, the nails not quite oval but egg-shaped, with the narrow ends embedded in the fingers; she wore no rings.

He looked away, worried that she might think he was staring at her. To his relief the two girls were running down the hill, shrieking to someone below. He no longer had to worry about betraying his interest in them.

'Would you like one?' Bewildered, Eddie turned towards her, for a moment thinking she was referring to the girls. But Angel was holding out a packet of Polos to him, the foil at the end of the tube peeled back. He took one because a refusal might offend her. For a moment they sat in silence. The mint seemed unnaturally strong, and he coughed.

'I like coming here,' Angel said. 'So nice to see the children playing.'

Eddie bit hard on the Polo, and it disintegrated. Two boys on the fringe of puberty raced by on their bikes. One of them dropped a crisp packet as he passed.

'When they're older, they're not nearly so appealing. Don't you agree?' She seemed not to expect an answer. 'But I wouldn't like to have children around all the time. They can be very tiring. What about you?'

Hastily he swallowed the fragments of Polo, the sharp edges snagging against his throat. 'I'm sorry?'

She smiled at him. 'I wondered if you'd like children of your own. I know I wouldn't.'

'No.' The word came out much more vehemently than Eddie had intended. He thought of the boys on the bicycles, of Mandy and Sian at Dale Grove Comprehensive, and of all the children who grew up. He was frightened that he might have revealed too much, so he took refuge in a generality. 'I think there're far too many people in the world as it is. Five and a half billion, isn't it, and more being born every day.'

Angel nodded, her face serious. 'That's a very good point.' Her tone implied that she'd never considered the question from that angle before. 'Still, they are sweet when they're young, aren't they? That's what I like about my job. I get most of the fun, but none of the long-term responsibility.'

'That must be nice.'

They sat there for another five minutes, talking in spurts about the city below them and its history. Slowly Eddie relaxed. He was surprised to find that he was enjoying the conversation, or rather the novelty of having someone to talk to.

'By the way, how did our road get its name?' Angel asked. 'I asked your mother but she didn't know.'

'It's because back in the Middle Ages the land round there used to belong to the Bishop of Rosington.'

A cloud slid across the sun.

'I thought it might be that. It's getting cold.' Angel hugged herself, dramatizing the words. 'Shall we find a cup of coffee? There's a café on South End Green.'

Before Eddie knew what was happening, they were walking

125

down the hill together. He felt lighter than usual, floating like a spaceman. *This can't be happening to me.* Part of him would have liked to run away, but this was swamped by other feelings: running away would be a very rude thing to do; he was flattered to be in Angel's company, and even hoped that someone he knew would see them; and he also liked the sense, obscure but powerful, that by being together he and Angel were somehow fooling his mother. For once, Eddie was not alone; he was part of a couple, and two was company. Soon they were sitting at a table by themselves, with coffee sending up twin pillars of steam between them.

'This is nice.' Angel smiled at him. 'It's good to get out. I worry about your mother sometimes. She spends so much time in the house.'

'Oh, she likes being at home. She's always been like that, even when my father was alive.'

'As long as it makes her happy.'

'She's getting old,' Eddie said, meaning that he couldn't imagine how old people could be happy.

Angel answered the thought, not the words: 'Old age is very sad. I'd hate to be old.' For an instant, her face changed: she pressed her lips and frowned; wrinkles gouged their way across her skin, a glimpse of what might be to come. Then she smiled, and the years retreated. 'That's one of the things I like about children. It's impossible to imagine them ever being old.'

Eddie nodded. He thought of Alison again – at present she was in his mind a good deal – and wished with all his heart that she could have stayed for ever young in the summer when they'd played the Peeing Game, and that he could have been young with her. He smiled across the years at Alison.

'What's funny, Eddie?' Angel asked.

'What? Nothing.' He bent his head to hide his embarrassment. Steam from the coffee misted his glasses.

'You don't mind if I call you Eddie?'

He felt himself blushing. 'Of course not.'

'But don't call me Angela. Horrible name.'

He looked up. She was leaning towards him, her face blurred by the steam like the city by its smog. It seemed to him that her features were dissolving in the vapour. She said something he didn't catch.

'What was that?'

'My friends always call me Angel.'

Over the next four months it seemed natural to keep Thelma in the dark about what was happening, though there was no reason to be secretive about their growing friendship. Eddie derived great pleasure from pretending at home in front of his mother that he and Angel were still on the old footing of lodger and landlady's son. It amused Angel, too.

'Children enjoy make-believe,' she told him on one of their outings. 'I think I still do.'

They met in a succession of public places – cinemas, Primrose Hill, the National Portrait Gallery, a coffee shop attached to an Oxford Street store, a pub near the Heath where children played while their parents drank.

Being with Angel allowed Eddie to watch children without worrying about what adults might be thinking. After all, he and Angel were roughly the same age: they might be taken for a married couple; in any case, a man and a woman together were much less threatening than a single man.

Once, in the garden outside the Hampstead pub, a little girl fell off a swing and scraped her knee. Angel picked her up and calmed her down. Eventually the child managed to tell them that her mother was inside the pub.

'Then we shall go and find your mummy.' Angel picked up the child, who was no more than three, and handed her to Eddie. 'This nice man will give you a ride.'

The girl nestled in Eddie's arms. He could not help wondering whether Angel had known that carrying her would give him pleasure. The three of them went into the pub.

'Where's Mummy?' Angel asked the girl.

The mother found them first. She rushed in front of Angel and snatched her child from Eddie. She clung so tightly to the little girl that the latter, until then perfectly happy, began to cry.

The woman stared at Eddie, her face reddening. 'What happened? What –?'

Angel cut in with an explanation which was an implicit accusation, delivered in her clear, confident voice. The mother reacted with an unlovely mixture of gratitude, guilt and surliness. She was a squat little woman in a long, dusty skirt; she wore no make-up and her arms were tattooed; piggy eyes glinted behind gold-rimmed glasses. She was also quite young, Eddie realized, perhaps not much older than the girls he had taught at school.

'You can't be too careful. Not these days,' she said in an unconscious echo of Thelma. She backed away from them, swallowed the rest of her drink and towed the child outside.

Eddie and Angel queued at the bar.

'If I hadn't been with you,' Angel said casually, 'that wretched woman would probably have thought you were trying to steal her child.'

As autumn turned to winter, Thelma seemed to sense that the atmosphere in the house had changed, that the emotional balance had tilted away from her. She grumbled more about Angel to Eddie. She became suspicious, wanting to know exactly where he'd been. There was not an open quarrel between her and Angel, but the old cordiality was no more than a memory.

Eddie was cautious by nature. (It was this which had kept him away from the networks of people who shared his special interests; he knew they existed because he read about them in the newspapers.) He did not want a rift with his mother. Sometimes he tried to imagine what life would be like if he and Angel could afford a flat or even a small house together. But financially this was out of the question. He had nothing to live on except what the state and his mother doled out to him.

It was wiser to keep a foot in both camps, at least for the time being. This was why Eddie did not tell Angel about his mother's snooping. He did not want to run the risk of provoking a quarrel between them.

The policy worked well until midway through January. One evening Eddie ran downstairs. He was due to meet Angel in

Liberty's in Regent Street: they planned to see a film and then have a pizza before coming home.

'Eddie,' Thelma called from the kitchen. 'Come in here a moment.'

He glanced at his watch, irritated because he was already a little on the late side and he didn't like to keep Angel waiting. He hesitated in the kitchen doorway. His mother was sitting at the table, breathing heavily. Her colour was high and there were patches of sweat under her arms.

'I'm in a bit of a hurry.'

'Where are you off to?'

'Just out.'

'You're always going out these days.'

'Just a film.'

Thelma's face darkened still further. 'You're seeing that woman. Go on, admit it.'

Surprised by the sudden venom, Eddie took a step backwards into the hall. 'Of course not.' Even to himself, his voice lacked conviction.

'I can smell her on you. That perfume she wears.'

Powerless to move, he stared at her.

'I tell you one thing,' Thelma went on, 'she's paid up till the end of the week, but after that she's out on her ear.'

'No!' The word burst out of Eddie before he could stop himself. 'You can't do that. There's no reason to do that.'

'She fooled me at the start, I admit that. But I'm not alone in that. She's fooled everyone.' Thelma tapped a sturdy manila envelope which lay on the table before her. 'Wait till Mrs Hawley-Minton hears about this. Unless she's in it, too. It's fraud, I tell you, bare-faced fraud. It's a matter for the police, I shouldn't wonder.'

Eddie stared at her. 'What do you mean? Are you all right?'

His mother opened the envelope and took out a British passport. She flicked over the pages until she found the photograph. She pushed the passport across the table towards Eddie, pinning it open with grubby fingers.

Reluctantly he came into the room and peered at the photograph, which showed a thin-faced, short-haired woman he had never seen before.

'So? Who is it?'

'Are you blind?' his mother shouted. 'Look at the name, you fool.'

Eddie stooped, holding the glasses on the bridge of his nose. The name swam into focus.

Angela Mary Wharton.

Eddie's memories of the next few hours were vivid but patchy. This was, he supposed later, a symptom of shock. He remembered slamming the front door of 29 Rosington Road, a thing he'd never done before, but after that there were missing links in the chain of events.

He must have walked to Chalk Farm underground station and taken the Northern Line to Tottenham Court Road. He could not remember whether he had changed on to the Central Line for Oxford Circus or simply walked the rest of the way. But he had a clear picture of himself standing just inside the main entrance of Liberty's: the place was full of people and brightly coloured merchandise; a security guard stared curiously at him; he tried to find Angel, but she wasn't there, and he felt despair creeping over him, a sense that everything worthwhile was over.

Suddenly she touched his shoulder. 'Let's go outside. I've got you a present.'

Taking his arm, which was something she had never done before, she urged him outside. There, standing on the pavement in Great Marlborough Street, she gave him a small Liberty's bag.

'Go on, open it.' Angel was like a child, incapable of deferring pleasure. 'I knew I had to get it for you as soon as I saw it.'

People flowed steadily past them like a stream around a rock. Inside the bag was a silk tie, blue with thin green stripes running diagonally across it. Eddie stroked the soft material, his eyes filling with tears as he tried to find the right words.

'See,' she said. 'It picks out the blue in your eyes. It's perfect.'

Everything except himself and Angel receded, as though rushing away – the black-and-white frontage of Liberty's, the people eddying along the pavement, the snarling engines and the smell of fast food.

'Put it on.' Angel did not wait for him to respond but buttoned the collar of his shirt, which he was wearing without a tie. 'That shirt will do perfectly.' She turned up his collar, took the tie from his hand and put it round his neck. Deftly she tied the knot, making him feel like a child or even a doll. She stood back and looked assessingly at him. 'Yes, perfect.'

'Thank you. It's wonderful.'

Angel looked at her watch. 'We're going to miss the film if we're not careful.'

'I'm sorry I'm late. My mother . . .'

'What is it? Something's happened.'

'My mother's been in your room.'

'That's nothing new.'

Eddie snatched at the diversion, a temporary refuge. 'You knew?'

'She pokes her nose in there most days. I leave things so I can tell. Now, what is it?'

He felt hot and embarrassed: he hoped she did not know that he too had sometimes been in there. 'She found something in a tin box.'

Angel wrapped her hand around his arm and squeezed so hard that he yelped. She was pale under the make-up, and she pulled her lips back and the wrinkles appeared, just as they had done on Parliament Hill. 'It was locked.'

'She must have found the key. Or found one of her own that fitted. Or maybe for once it wasn't locked. I don't know.' He stared miserably up at her. 'She's got the passport. She's going to show it to your boss at the agency. And maybe the police.'

At this point there was another broken link in the memories. The next thing he knew they were deep in Soho, in Frith Street, and he was following Angel's shining head down a flight of stairs to a basement restaurant whose sounds and smells rose up around him like a tide. They sat at a table in an alcove, an island of stillness. A single candle stood between them in a wax-coated bottle. Eddie could not recall what they ate, but he remembered that Angel bought first one bottle of red wine and then another.

'Drink up,' she told him. 'Come along, you need it. You've had a shock.'

The wine tasted harsh and at first he found it hard to swallow. As glass succeeded glass, however, it became easier and easier.

'Can you keep a secret?' Angel asked when they had finished the starter. 'No one else knows the truth, but I want to tell you. Can I trust you?'

'Yes.' *Angel, you can always trust me.*

She stared into the candle flame. 'If my mother had lived, everything would have been different.'

Her mother, she told Eddie, had died when she was young, and her father had married again, to a wife who hated Angel.

'She was jealous, of course. Before she came along, my father and I had been very close. But she soon changed that. She made him hate me. Not just him, either – she worked on everyone we knew. In the end they all turned against me.'

Desperate to get away, Angel found work as an au pair, at first in Saudi Arabia and later in South America, mainly in Argentina. Then she became a nanny. Her employers had been delighted with her: she had stayed with one family for over five years. Finally, she had been overcome by a desire to come back to England.

'It gets to you sometimes: wanting to go back to your roots, to your past. Then I met Angie Wharton. She was English, but she had been born in Argentina. Her parents emigrated there after the war. Angie wanted to come home, too. Not that she'd ever been here before.'

'How could this be her home?' asked Eddie owlishly. 'If she hadn't been here, I mean?'

'Home is where the heart is, Eddie. Anyway, Angie was a nursery nurse – she'd trained in the States before her parents died. We thought we'd travel home together, share a flat and so on. It's thanks to Angie that I know Mrs Hawley-Minton. Poor darling Angie.'

'What happened to her?'

'It was terribly sad.' Angel's eyes shone, and an orange candle flame flickered in each pupil. 'It hurts to talk about it.' She turned away and dabbed her eyes with a napkin.

'I'm sorry,' Eddie said, drunk enough to feel that he was somehow responsible for her sorrow. 'Let's talk about something else.'

'No. One can't hide away from things. It was one of those awful, stupid tragedies. Our first night in London. We'd only been here a few hours. Oh, it was my fault. I shall always blame myself. You see, I knew that Angie was – well, to be blunt, she was a lovely person but she had a weakness for alcohol.' Angel topped up Eddie's glass. 'Not like this – a glass or two over a meal. She'd go on binges and wake up the next day not knowing what had happened, where she'd been. It was terrible.'

Eddie pushed away his plate. 'What was?'

'It was on our first evening here,' Angel said, her eyes huge over the rim of the wine glass. 'Life can be so unfair sometimes. She'd been drinking on the plane. One after the other. When we got here, we found a hotel in Earl's Court and then we had a meal. Wine with the meal, of course. And then she wanted to carry on. "I want to celebrate," she kept saying. "I've come home." Poor Angie. I just couldn't cope. I was fagged out. So I went back to our room and went to bed. Next thing I knew it was morning and the manager was knocking on the door.'

The waiter brought their main course and showed a disposition to linger and chat.

'That'll be all, thank you,' said Angel haughtily. When she and Eddie were alone again she went on, 'I hate men like that. So pushy. Where was I?'

'The manager knocking on the door.'

The irritation faded from Angel's face. 'He had a policewoman with him. Apparently Angie had gone up to the West End. Drinking steadily, of course. Somehow she managed to fall under a bus in Shaftesbury Avenue. There was a whole crowd coming out of a theatre, and people coming out of a pub, and a lot of pushing and shoving.' Angel sighed. 'She was killed outright.'

'How awful.' Eddie hesitated and then, feeling more was required, added, 'For you as much as her.'

'It's always harder for those who are left behind. No one else grieved for her. And then – well, I must admit I was tempted. I mean, who would it harm if I pretended to be Angie? Without a qualification I couldn't hope to get a decent job. It was so unfair – I knew more about the practical side of nursery nursing than she ever did, and I could easily read up the theory. And then she had this ready-made contact in Mrs Hawley-Minton, who'd never met her. So I told the police that Angie was me, and I pretended to be her.'

'But didn't they know her name? From her handbag, or something?' Sensing Angel's irritation at the interruption, he added weakly, 'I mean, they knew the hotel where she was staying.'

'She didn't have any identification on her – just cash, and a card with the name of the hotel.' Angel smiled sadly. 'She'd left her passport and so on with me, in case they got stolen.'

'Oh yes. I see now. But surely the passport photo –?'

'I had an old one in mine. And physically we weren't dissimilar.'

'There must have been an inquest.'

'Of course. I didn't tell any lies. I didn't want to. There was no need to.'

'Didn't they ask your father to identify the body?'

'He'd gone to work in America years before this happened. We'd lost touch completely. He simply couldn't be bothered with me.' Angel leant closer. 'The point is, Eddie, I know Angie would have wanted me to do what I did. Just as I would have wanted her to do the same if the positions had been reversed.'

'I think you were right.' Eddie's voice was thick and his tongue felt a little too large for his mouth. 'I mean, it didn't hurt anyone.'

Briefly she patted his hand. 'Exactly. In a way, quite the reverse: I like to think I take my job very seriously, that I've made a difference for a lot of children.'

'What was your real name, then?'

'It doesn't matter. I gave it to Angie, and it's buried with her. Look forward, that's my motto. Don't look back. After the funeral I just waited until the dust had settled, and then I wrote to Mrs Hawley-Minton. And from there everything's gone like a dream.' She broke off and rested her head in her hands. 'Until now.' Her voice was almost inaudible. 'It's such a shame – just as everything was going so well.'

'I'll talk to my mother. I'll make her see sense.'

'You're a darling. But I don't think you'll succeed.'

'Why not?' He was almost shouting now and heads turned towards him.

'Hush, keep your voice down.'

'She wouldn't like us both to go away. She'd be lonely.'

'She's jealous of us. Don't you see? I wish I were richer – then we could get somewhere together, just you and me. As friends, I mean, just good friends. Would you like that?'

'Yes. Oh God, yes.'

There was a long pause, filled with the noise from the rest of the restaurant.

Angel picked up the bottle. 'Let's talk about something else.'

Eddie said, elaborately casual, 'What sort of children do you look after? You could always bring them to the house if you wanted. For tea, I mean. Make a sort of treat for them.'

'They often want to see where I live. But I don't think the idea would go down very well with your mother.'

Another silence stretched between them, heavy with silent suggestions and questions. Angel refilled their glasses.

'Drink up.' She held up her glass and clinked it against his. 'This may be our last chance of a celebration, so we'd better make the most of it.'

They finished that bottle before they left. By now Eddie was very drunk. Angel had to support him up the stairs. In Frith Street the fresh air made his head spin and the light seemed very bright. He vomited partly into the gutter and partly on the bonnet of a parked car.

'There, there,' Angel said, patting his arm. 'Better out than in.' Later he heard her calling out in her patrician voice: 'Taxi! Taxi!'

Eddie remembered little more of the evening. Angel took him home. He could not remember seeing his mother – it was very late, so perhaps she was asleep.

'Come on,' she said when they got home. 'Up the wooden stairs to Bedfordshire.'

In his mind there was a picture of the palm of Angel's right hand extended towards him with three white tablets in the middle of it.

'Take these. Otherwise you're going to feel terrible in the morning.'

He must have managed to swallow them. After that he fell into a dark, silent pit. The first thing that made an impression on him, hours later, was the pain in his head. This was followed, after an immeasurable period of time, by the discovery that his bladder was extremely full. Later still, he realized that if anything the headache was worse. He dozed on, reluctant to leave the peace of the pit and physically unable to cope with the complicated business of getting out of bed.

The next time he woke the light on the other side of the curtains was much brighter, and the sight of it made his headache worse. Someone was shaking him.

'Eddie. Eddie.'

Shocked, he turned over. As far as he knew Angel had never been in his room before. What would his mother say when she found out?

Daylight poured through the open door. Angel shimmered so brightly that he could not look at her. She was wearing her long white robe and, though her face was immaculately made up, her hair was still confined to its snood. His eyelids began to droop.

'Eddie,' Angel called. 'Eddie, wake up.'

'... we are somewhat more than our selves in our sleeps, and the slumber of the body seems to be but the waking of the soul.'

Religio Medici, II, 11

Sally had not expected to sleep on Saturday night, the second since Lucy's disappearance. Part of her was determined to stay awake in case Lucy needed her. When David Byfield rang with the news that Michael was safe, however, tiredness dropped over her like a blanket.

Judith, the policewoman who had been on duty on Friday, and who had relieved Yvonne in the early evening, took advantage of this weakness. She persuaded Sally to go to bed, brought her a cup of cocoa and cajoled her into taking another sleeping tablet.

'It'll just send you to sleep,' Judith said, her Welsh voice rising and falling like a boat on a gentle swell. 'It's not one of these long-term ones that knock you out for ages. There's no point in you flogging yourself to keep awake.'

'But what if –?'

'If there's any news, I promise I'll fetch you straightaway.'

Sally took the tablet and drank her cocoa. Judith lingered for a moment, her eyes moving round the room.

'Do you want something to read? A magazine?'

'Could you pass me the books over there? The ones on the chest of drawers.'

Judith brought them to her. 'I'll look in a little later. See how you're doing.'

Sally nodded. The door closed behind Judith and she was at last alone. *Lucy.* Her eyes smarted with tears. She wanted to bang her head against the wall and scream and scream.

Miss Oliphant's books lay before her on the duvet: unfinished business that would normally have nagged Sally until she had dealt with it. She touched their covers one by one with the fingertips of her right hand. The Bible. The Prayer Book. The *Religio Medici.* The first two were bound in worn black leather, dry with age, their spines cracking and in places breaking away from the covers. Sally knew without looking that the paper would be so thin that it was almost invisible, and that the type would be so small that even someone with 20:20 vision would have an effort to read it. The *Religio Medici* had a larger typeface but the book was as battered as the others. All three smelled musty: tired, repulsive and unwashed. Sally shivered, reluctant to open any of them. Each book might be a miniature Pandora's Box full of unexpected evils.

'You mustn't blame yourself,' David Byfield had told her on the telephone.

'Then who else do you suggest? God?'

There was a silence at the other end. Then David said dryly, 'The person who took Lucy, perhaps.' He had overridden her attempt to interrupt. 'Concentrate on this: you mustn't worry about Michael. He'll sleep it off tonight and be with you tomorrow. You mustn't blame him, either, or yourself. Do you understand, Sally? It's most important. Nor must you stop hoping and praying.'

'I can't pray.'

'Of course you can.'

'Listen,' Sally began, 'I don't like –'

'Don't argue. Pray, go to bed and try to sleep. That is the best thing you can do.'

David Byfield's voice had sounded unexpectedly youthful over the phone. Like Derek Cutter, the old man had been in full pastoral mode, but his technique differed completely from Derek's: the former's had made her squirm; David's infuriated her. Talk about arrogant, Sally thought. What did he know about losing a child? The autocratic, patronizing bastard: who had given him the right to give her orders? She glowed with anger at the memory. Only then did it occur to her that David might have intended to achieve just that effect. He was a clever man, she conceded: an old fool, but still clever.

Her eyelids drooped, she slid down the bed. Endowed with a life of their own, her fingertips continued to stroke the binding of the three books. Audrey Oliphant, she thought sleepily: that's a strange name. Oliphant sounded like elephant. Had there once been a saint called Audrey? Then, as sudden and as violent as a flash of lightning, the knowledge that Lucy was not there slashed across Sally's mind. She sat up in bed and screamed. But the sound which came out of her mouth was no more than a whimper. She sank back against the pillows.

The movement had dislodged the books. The corner of a piece of card protruded from the *Religio Medici*. Sally pulled it out. It was a postcard of the west front of a great church, an old-fashioned colour photograph bleached with age. The building was familiar, but for the moment her mind refused to produce the name. She flipped the card over: Rosington Cathedral. There was writing, too. She squinted at the postmark. April 1963? 1968? It was addressed to 'Miss A. Oliphant, Tudor Cottage, The Green, Roth, Middlesex'. The name Roth was faintly familiar. Somewhere west of London? Near Heathrow Airport? She tried to decipher the message.

> Too many tourists and more like Feb. than April but choral
> evensong was super. Our mutual friend still remembered.
> Small world! See you on Tuesday.
> Love, Amy.

A glimpse of other lives, Sally thought, of a time when Audrey Oliphant had perhaps been happy. Why do we even bother to try?

The card slipped from Sally's hand, and she sank into sleep. Thanks to the tablets she lay there for what she afterwards discovered was almost seven hours. For much of the time she moved restlessly through the dark phantasmagoria of her dreams, searching for Lucy. *This must be hell.* When she awoke, she swam up from a great depth, painfully conscious of changing pressure and a desperate need to reach the surface.

139

Lucy.

Still with her eyes closed, she made an enormous effort and gathered together the pain, the fear and the anger. She made a ball of it in her mind and kneaded it like dough. The ball was streaked with colours: red, brown, green and black, the colours of the emotions. She picked it up and threw it over her shoulder. Then she found the strength to open her eyes.

The bedroom was in darkness, apart from a band of light from the streetlamp slipping between the curtains and the red digits glowing on the clock display. Her pulse was racing, her mouth was dry and her eyelids were swollen and sore.

No Lucy, she thought, and no news of her either: they would have woken me.

Something had driven her awake. She had fled to consciousness as if to a refuge. Had something *down there* been even worse than this waking knowledge of Lucy's absence?

It was six-fifteen. She switched on the bedside light. Judith must have come in to turn it off last night. Miss Oliphant's books were in a neat pile on the bedside table. Sally lay back on the pillows, fighting the despair that threatened to overwhelm her. She tried to pray: it was no use – the lines were down, the airwaves jammed, or perhaps no one was bothering to answer at the other end. Pray, David Byfield had told her; pray and hope. She could do neither.

Gradually, fragments of her dreams slipped into her conscious mind. She glimpsed Miss Oliphant, attired in episcopal robes, standing in front of the high altar of a great church, which Sally knew must be Rosington Cathedral. Miss Oliphant was reading the Service of Commination from the office for Ash Wednesday in the Book of Common Prayer. *Is that why they've taken Lucy, because we were cursed?* But there are no woman bishops, Sally remembered thinking in her dream, not in this country. Have they changed the rules and not told me? In the dream world this possibility had been far more unsettling than the sight of Miss Oliphant, last seen dead in a hospital bed, apparently alive and well.

Another fragment of another dream had concerned David Byfield. He had seen an angel flying low over Magdalene Bridge in Cambridge.

'Real feathers,' he insisted to Sally and Michael, 'rather like a buzzard's.'

'But Lucy's *missing*!' Sally shouted.

'This is far more important.'

In a different part of the same dream, she and Uncle David were in a police station that smelled like a public lavatory. Chief Inspector Maxham leaned across the counter towards them, sucking in his breath, the air hissing between his tongue and his teeth.

'Couldn't have been an angel, sir. Angels don't exist.'

Sally was embarrassed. Grown men did not believe in angels. David became very angry with Maxham.

'Don't be naive, Officer. You're not competent to make wild assertions like that.'

The chief inspector smiled, revealing Yvonne's perfect teeth. 'You were dreaming.'

'I was not.'

Uncle David raised his arms and spread them wide. To her horror, Sally saw that his dark clerical suit was sprouting two rows of silvery-white feathers, one for each arm, running down the sleeves from shoulder to cuff. Uncle David was growing wings.

By eight o'clock, Sally had showered, dressed and had breakfast, which in her case consisted of three cups of coffee. She and Judith sat at the table in the living room. Judith tried to entice Sally's appetite from its hiding place by filling the flat with the smell of toasting bread and boiling herself an egg.

'No news is good news.' Judith's face creased with anxiety, and Sally felt guilty for spurning all those good intentions. 'Why don't you have a spoonful of cereal – something light like cornflakes?'

Sally reached for the coffee pot. 'Perhaps I'll have something later.'

'I expect you'll want to go to church this morning. I'm sure Yvonne will drive you.'

Bugger church. 'I don't want to, thanks.' Sally glimpsed, or imagined, hurt surprise in Judith's eyes. *Bugger Judith*. But it wasn't that easy to slough off the habit of being considerate. She heard herself saying soothingly, as if Judith, not herself, were the victim: 'It's kind of you to think of it, but I want to be here when my husband comes home.' *With his slippers warming by the fire, the newspaper on the arm of his chair and fresh tea in the pot?* 'And of course there might be some news.'

'I do understand.' Some of Judith's creases vanished. 'Won't be long now, will it? It will be easier with the two of you.'

Sally nodded and sipped her coffee. She doubted if it would be easier when Michael came. Nothing could be easy without Lucy. In the second place, there wouldn't be just the two of them because David Byfield was coming up to London, too. In the third place, Michael, much as she loved him, was likely to create more problems than he solved. He habitually repressed his emotions, which meant when they did come to the surface they tended to be under great pressure and boiling hot.

'I wonder if the newspaper's come,' Sally said, her eyes meeting Judith's.

'I'll see, shall I?'

Before Sally could protest, Judith was on her feet and moving towards the door. A moment later she returned with the *Observer*.

'Would you like me to . . . ?'

Sally held out her hand for the newspaper. 'I'd rather find out myself.'

The story was confined to a few paragraphs on one of the inside pages. Lucy Appleyard, four, had disappeared from her child minder's; the police had not ruled out the possibility of foul play. Chief Inspector Maxham provided a guarded comment, which in effect said no more than that the police were investigating.

'The whole parish is praying for Lucy, Sally and Michael,' Derek Cutter had told the *Observer*'s reporter. 'Sally's a marvellous curate. She's already made her mark at St George's.'

Sally pushed the newspaper, open at the story, across the table. Judith read it quickly.

'Fair enough, I suppose,' she said brightly.

'I wonder what the tabloids are saying.' Sally winced. 'Perhaps it's better not to know.'

A key scraped in the lock of the door to the landing.

'That'll be Yvonne.' Judith gathered up her handbag, and risked a small joke. 'Just in time for the washing-up.'

The living-room door opened and Maxham came in. Yvonne's blonde head bobbed above his shoulder in the hallway behind him. Judith glanced at Sally and stiffened, ready to take action. Sally put her hand to her mouth and stared at Maxham.

'There's been a development, Mrs Appleyard.' Air hissed into his mouth. 'It may not be connected with Lucy, so don't get upset.'

Maxham came to a halt a few paces inside the room. Yvonne moved round Maxham and came to stand beside Sally. Judith edged closer. *My God, what are they? Wardresses?*

'Do you know a church called St Michael's?' he asked.

'Which one?' she snapped. 'There must be dozens.'

'In Beauclerk Place – west of Tottenham Court Road, near Charlotte Street.'

She shook her head, unable to speak.

'When the caretaker – churchwarden, would it be? – came to unlock this morning, he found a black bin-liner in the porch. I gather there are wrought-iron gates on the outer arch of the porch and a proper door inside. Someone must have slipped the bin-liner through the railings or maybe over the top.'

Get on with it. Sally watched Maxham's face, saw the pale eyes blinking behind the black-rimmed glasses and the muscles twitching at the corners of the mouth. With a shock she realized that he was stalling because he found this no easier to say than she did to hear.

Air hissed. 'The fact of the matter is, Mrs Appleyard, there were some clothes inside that bag. A pair of child's tights and a pair of boots. They seem to resemble the ones you described Lucy as wearing.'

'For Christ's sake – what about Lucy? Is she there, too?'

Maxham hesitated, greedily sucking in breath. 'Well,' he said slowly. 'Yes and no.'

St Michael's, Beauclerk Place, stood at the end of a cul-de-sac squeezed between higher, younger buildings to either side and behind it. It was a scruffy little building built of red brick, rectangular in design, with pinnacles at the corners and debased

143

perpendicular windows. The visible windows were protected with iron grilles and decades of grime. The church was like a child who has never had quite enough love or money devoted to it.

The uniformed policeman pulled aside the barrier to allow Maxham's unmarked Rover to drive into the cul-de-sac. The buildings on either side were post-war, with plate-glass windows and Venetian blinds: probably offices, empty on a Sunday. As yet, there were no sightseers, but the police were ready. The car slid to a halt near the church. Two police cars were parked nearby.

The porch had been tacked on to the south-west corner of the church. The police had screened off the entrance. On the left of the porch was a row of iron railings which ended in a matching gate.

Sergeant Carlow switched off the engine. He looked over his shoulder at Maxham, sitting in the back of the car with Sally. Maxham nodded. Carlow extracted his long body from the car and walked towards the screened-off porch. His hips were unusually wide for a man's, Sally registered automatically, and as he walked his bottom swayed like a woman's.

Maxham folded his hands in his lap. 'Just going to see what's what.'

For a few seconds, silence spread through the car. In the front passenger seat Yvonne stared fixedly through the windscreen. The inspector rubbed his fingers on his thigh. Carlow reappeared. He looked paler than ever.

Maxham turned his head towards Sally. 'You sure you're up to it? Still time to change your mind.'

'I'm quite sure.'

'We can wait till your husband –'

'No.' *My baby.* 'Can we get it over with?'

Maxham nodded. The three of them got out of the car. It was suddenly cold: the wind funnelled through the cul-de-sac and escaped into the dull, grey sky. Sally forced herself to look away from the porch. She noticed that the gap between the railings and the church had silted up with a thick mulch of empty lager cans and fast-food wrappings, and that the gate at the north-west corner guarded the entrance to a narrow alleyway between the north side of the church and the adjacent building.

According to a notice on the wall, the Anglicans now shared St Michael's with a Russian Orthodox congregation and a Methodist one. Otherwise it would probably have been made redundant long ago. Perhaps that would have been better than this unloved half-life.

Half a life, half a person?

Sally found herself staring at the porch. From what she could see above the screens, it was about six feet wide and nine feet deep; it was covered with a pitched roof of cracked pantiles streaked with lichen and moss.

Maxham put a hand under Sally's elbow. They walked towards the screen. Yvonne and Sergeant Carlow fell in behind. A one-legged pigeon with frayed feathers hopped across their path. *An amputee.* To those in fear, creation was nothing but a mass of portents. Sally pulled away from Maxham and thrust her hands deep into the pockets of her long navy-blue coat. They rounded the corner of the screen.

The light dazzled her. For a moment she stopped to blink and stare. Two floodlights gave the interior of the porch a hallucinogenic clarity. The outer gates were open. On either side were benches, with notice boards above. It should have been sheltered in there, but the notices fluttered and rustled in the wind. A photographer was shooting away seemingly at random, the shutter falling in a stammering rhythm like irregular rifle fire.

The little space was crowded. Beside the photographer, another scene-of-the-crime officer was dictating into a hand-held machine. A third was measuring the dimensions of the porch. A fourth man, with a bag next to him, was kneeling in the far left-hand corner. Sally glimpsed shiny black plastic.

'This is Dr Ferguson,' Maxham said. 'Mrs Appleyard.'

The kneeling man half-turned and nodded, acknowledging the introduction.

Sally swallowed. 'Where –?'

'Here, Mrs Appleyard.' The doctor rose to his feet in one supple movement. He was younger than Sally, fresh-faced, with a healthy tan and a Liverpool accent. His eyes slid to

Maxham, then back to Sally. 'Are you sure you want to see this?'

'Yes.' With an effort she kept her voice low, concealing the scream inside her head.

Ferguson nodded. 'Over here.'

He gestured not as Sally had expected towards the black plastic on the floor behind him, but to a plastic sheet on the bench on the left. Two L-shaped ridges showed underneath in relief, each about twenty inches long. Automatically Sally looked up, unable to keep her eyes on the two ridges. She examined the notice immediately above, noted with furious concentration the yellowing paper, the nearly illegible typed letters and the circular rust stains left by vanished drawing pins.

She was aware that Maxham and Yvonne had moved a step nearer and were now standing directly behind her. The other police officers had stopped what they had been doing. The doctor was watching her, too. All of them were in position, she realized, ready to catch her when she fainted. Ironically, the thought braced her.

'You're ready?'

Ferguson drew back the plastic sheet. Beneath was a transparent plastic bag with a neatly written tag. The bag contained a pair of small, white, woollen tights with ribbing on the legs. For an instant they looked as if they had been stuffed with kapok like cuddly toys. The tights were lying in a reddish-brown puddle of blood. Sally compressed her lips and swallowed. She thought of meat from a supermarket defrosting on its plastic tray. Blood need only be blood: nothing more, nothing less: largely composed of water, a means of supplying living tissues with nutrients and oxygen and of removing waste products. Once separated from the pumping heart, it was nothing but a reddish-brown liquid.

Drink ye all of this; for this is my blood.

'Mrs Appleyard?' Ferguson murmured. 'Steady, now.'

'I'm fine.'

The waist of the tights lay flat against the plastic. There was no kapok in there. The blood was thickest from the top of the thighs to the waist of the tights. You could no longer see the whiteness of the wool.

146

O Lamb of God –

Sally's eyes travelled down the length of the legs to the feet. The feet were wearing miniature red cowboy boots. They were dainty things, the leather supple, a delicate pattern stitched in black thread at the ankles. In the toe of the nearer one was a shallow cut about half an inch in length.

You naughty girl. Have you any idea how much those cost?

'The ankle boots are Italian.' As Sally paused, she heard a faint, collective sigh behind her. 'They're made by someone with a name like Rassi. I bought them at a shop in Covent Garden about two months ago.' The boots had been an extravagance that Sally had been unable to resist. She had put towards the cost the money that David Byfield had sent for Lucy's last birthday. Michael had been furious. 'I wrote Lucy's name on the back of the maker's label.' Not the sort of boots you could afford to lose, she had thought. 'As for the tights, I'm pretty sure she was wearing ones like that on Friday. It's hard to be absolutely certain because of the blood.'

Lucy's blood. Oh Christ – can't you stop this?

They had known what Lucy was wearing, down to the maker's name in the boots. But they needed to be sure. *Sure?* Gingerly, Sally stretched out her hand towards the two legs.

'Mrs Appleyard –' the doctor began.

Sally ignored him. She touched the leg very gently with the tip of the index finger of her right hand. 'It's *icy*.'

'It may have been deep-frozen until recently.' Maxham's voice was harsher than usual.

'Like the hand they found in Kilburn Cemetery?'

'Yes.'

What struck Sally now was the silence. Here they were in one of the world's great cities, in the middle of a pool of silence. There must have been at least a dozen police officers within thirty yards and they all seemed to be holding their breath.

Dear God, the pain. Had they had the decency to kill her first, and kill her swiftly?

Sally ran her fingertip delicately down the leg, following the curve of the knee, on down the shin to the top of the boot. She bowed her head.

'Mrs Appleyard?' Maxham sounded anxious, with just a hint

of exasperation. 'That's all we need, thank you. You've been very helpful. Very brave.'

Sally slipped the thumb and forefinger of her hand right round the ankle and squeezed it, through the plastic bag and the leather. She felt the hardness of the bone underneath.

'Mrs Appleyard,' said Ferguson, 'there's a possibility of post-mortem damage. That could give us problems at the autopsy.'

Yvonne put her hand on Sally's arm. Sally shook her off. Someone snarled like a dog deprived of a bone. *Me.* Puzzled, she ran her hand round the bend of the L and on to the foot itself. Maxham grabbed her other arm. She felt the toes. It wasn't possible. Yvonne and Maxham pulled her gently back.

'I'm sorry, Mrs Appleyard.' Maxham allowed his exasperation to show plainly. 'Now we'll get you home. Your husband will be back soon.'

I don't want my husband: I want Lucy.

Then Sally saw how the impossible might have happened. *Must* have happened.

'The legs are too long,' she said slowly. 'So they aren't Lucy's.'

Maxham allowed Sally to sit inside the church because he could not think of a valid reason to prevent her. Besides, she knew, he had assumed that she wanted to pray, a possibility which embarrassed him. His embarrassment was a weapon she could use against him.

It was very cold. The gratings set into the cheap red tiles suggested underfloor heating, but either the system didn't work or the people using the church could not afford to run it. The silence pressed down on her. The air smelt faintly of incense. The brass of the lectern was smudged and dull. She glanced up at the roof, plain pitch pine, full of darkness, shadows and spiders' webs.

Her eyes drifted along the line of the roof to the east wall. A large picture in a gilt frame hung above the altar. The light was poor and the paint was dingy. Maybe the Last Judgement, Sally thought, a cheap and nasty Victorian copy if the rest of the church was anything to go by. Christ in Glory in the centre of the picture, a river of fire spewing forth at his feet;

flanked by angels and apostles; and below them the souls of the righteous queueing for admission to paradise; and the archangel with the scales – Michael or Gabriel? – weighing the souls of the risen dead. A picture story for children afraid of the dark.

And Lucy? Was she afraid? Or already dead?

Sally let out her breath in a long, ragged sigh. *Don't think about that. Think about the good news.* The legs were not Lucy's, any more than the hand had been. They were the wrong shape, wrong size, wrong everything. Lucy's were thinner and less muscular, and her feet were much smaller than the feet which had been stuffed into Lucy's red Italian cowboy boots.

At first Maxham had not believed Sally. Even Yvonne and Dr Ferguson had been sceptical. They had all been suspicious of her certainty, willing to attribute it to wishful thinking.

I'm her mother, damn you. Of course I know.

Sally bowed her head. Once again she tried to pray, to thank God that the legs were not Lucy's, and that therefore Lucy might still be alive. But her mind swerved away from prayer like a horse refusing a jump. An invisible barrier hemmed her in, enclosing her in her private misery. It was as if the church itself had surrounded her with a wall of glass which cut off the lines of communication. For an instant she thought she glimpsed the building's personality: sour, malevolent, unhappy – a bricks-and-mortar equivalent of Audrey Oliphant, the woman who had cursed her.

What's happening to me? Churches don't have personalities.

Gratitude was in any case misplaced. The legs had belonged to another child. Should she thank God for the other child's death and mutilation? Beside that terrible fact, the goodness of God receded to invisibility.

Sally opened her eyes, desperate to find a distraction. On the wall nearest to her hung a board with the names of the incumbents inscribed in flaking gold letters, beginning with a Reverend Francis Youlgreave MA in 1891 and ending, seven names later, with the Reverend George Bagnall, who had left the parish in 1970. It was a big board and three-quarters of it was blank. No doubt Youlgreave and his immediate successors had imagined that the list of incumbents would stretch on

149

and on, and that the building would always be a place of worship.

Things could never get better, she thought bitterly, only worse. How those long-gone priests would have hated the thought of her, a woman in orders. And what was the purpose of it anyway? It now seemed absurd that she had fought so hard to be ordained, and that she should devote her life to playing a minor part in the affairs of a dying cult. So far the effect had been wholly evil: she had ruined her own life, damaged Michael's and abandoned Lucy. She was to blame. She was too angry with herself even to share the blame with God. Oh yes, he was still there. But he didn't matter any more. If the truth were told, he never had. He didn't care.

You mustn't blame yourself. David Byfield's words twisted in her memory and took on a bitter and no doubt intended irony. *He* blamed her. He always had blamed her, the woman who had committed the double sin of wanting to be a priest and taking away his Michael. She wondered yet again what bound the two men so tightly together. Whatever the reason, now she had her reward for breaking into their charmed relationship, and no doubt David was rejoicing.

Sally stared at the list of priests. The church's dedication was written in gothic capitals at the head of the board: ST MICHAEL AND ALL ANGELS. Her mind filled with a thrumming sound, as though a thousand birds had risen into the air and were flying across the mud flats of an estuary. Her husband's name was Michael, and the church was dedicated to Michael. Just a coincidence, surely. It was a common name. Only a paranoiac would think otherwise.

And yet –

This evil was beginning to take shape. It had been planned and executed over a long period. The brown-skinned hand in Kilburn Cemetery and the bleeding legs in the porch must be connected with each other because there were so many correspondences: both had been deep-frozen; both were parts of a child's anatomy; both had been left in places which were sacred; and they had been found within twenty-four hours of each other. It was theoretically possible that the two were separate incidents – that the story of the severed hand had inspired a copycat crime – but this seemed less likely. The boots and the tights left no doubt at all that Lucy was at the mercy of the same person. Had there been a message there?

Lucy's dismembered, too.

Whoever had taken her had not done so merely for sexual gratification or from emotional inadequacy; or if he had, that was only a part of it. What lay in the porch had been designed to shock. And the urge to shock had been so great that it had outweighed the risk of being seen.

The wings rustled and whirred. *Not just to shock: also to tease.*

Had Lucy been chosen not for herself but because she was a policeman's child? Sally remembered Frank Howell's feature on St George's in the *Evening Standard*. Perhaps someone had read it who had a grudge against the police in general or Michael in particular.

Then why not leave the remains outside a police station? Why the church today and the cemetery yesterday? Perhaps the hatred was aimed at God rather than the police. A further possibility struck her: that this might be a more extreme form of the loathing which had gripped Audrey Oliphant; and in that case it followed that Sally herself, by wanting to become a priest, could have been directly responsible for bringing down on Lucy's head the attention of whoever had taken her.

'I'm getting paranoid,' she told herself, her voice thin and childlike in the empty spaces of the cold church; she shocked herself, for she had not realized that she had spoken aloud. 'Stop it, stop it.'

The thoughts spurted through her mind – fragmented and disjointed. The noise of the wings grew louder until it obliterated all other sounds and swamped her ability to think. The thrumming was so loud that Sally hardly felt like Sally: she was merely the sound of the wings. She drowned in the sound, as if in the black mud of the estuary.

'No. No. Leave me alone.'

The thrumming grew even louder. It was dark. She could no longer breathe. She heard a great crack, so loud that for a moment it dominated the thrumming of the wings. Cold air swirled around her.

'That's quite enough.' The voice was furious and male. 'This must stop at once.'

Sally opened her eyes and turned her head. Through her tears she saw Michael's godfather, David Byfield, stalking down the aisle towards her.

8

'Do but extract from the corpulency of bodies, or resolve things beyond their first matter, and you discover the habitation of Angels . . .'

Religio Medici, I, 35

'Lucy's as good as gold with me.' Angel rinsed the soap from the back of Lucy's neck. 'Aren't you, poppet?'

Lucy did not reply. She looked very young and small in the bath, her body partly obscured by a shifting mound of foam. She was staring at a blue plastic boat containing two yellow ducks; the boat bobbed up and down in the triangular harbour created by her legs. Her wet hair, plastered to her skull, was as black as polished ebony.

'It's the first of December today,' Angel went on, briskly sponging Lucy's back. 'Did you know, if you say "White rabbits" on the first of the month and make a silent wish, then the wish will come true? Well, that's what some people say.'

Eddie thought that Lucy's lips might have trembled, and that perhaps she was saying 'White Rabbits' to herself and making a wish. *I want Mummy*. She had had very little to eat for over thirty-six hours and this was beginning to show in her appearance. Children, Eddie had noticed, reacted very quickly to such changes. Now it was Sunday morning, and Lucy's shoulders looked bonier than they had done on Friday evening, and her stomach was flat. She was still listless from the medication, and perhaps from the shock, too, otherwise Angel would not have risked taking her out of the soundproofed basement to give her a bath.

153

(This had been Angel's rule since the incident with Suki, a sly girl who acted as if butter wouldn't melt in her mouth until Angel went out to fetch a towel, leaving her alone with Eddie: as soon as the door closed, Suki had bitten Eddie's hand and screamed like a train. After that, Angel gave their little visitors regular doses of Phenergan syrup, which kept them nicely drowsy. If a visitor became seriously upset, Angel quietened her with a dose of diazepam, originally prescribed for Eddie's mother.)

'There's a good girl. Stand up now and Angel will dry you.' With Angel's help, Lucy struggled to her feet. Water and foam dripped down her body. Eddie stared at the pink, glistening skin and the cleft between her legs.

'Uncle Eddie will pass the towel.'

He hurried to obey. There had been an unmistakable note of irritation in Angel's voice, perhaps brought on by tiredness. He noticed dark smudges under her eyes. He knew she had gone out the previous evening and had not returned until well after midnight. Eddie had tried the door to the basement while she was out, only to find that it was locked.

Angel wrapped the large pink towel, warm from the radiator, around Lucy's body, lifted her out of the bath and sat her on her knee. Eddie thought they made a beautiful picture, a Pre-Raphaelite Virgin and child: Angel in her long white robe, her shining hair flowing free; and Lucy small, thin and sexless, swaddled in the towel, sitting on Angel's lap and enclosed by her arms. He turned away. His head hurt this morning, and his throat was dry.

The clothes they had bought for Lucy were waiting on the chair. Among them was a dark-green dress from Laura Ashley, with a white lace collar, a smocked front and ties at each side designed to form a bow at the back. Angel liked her girls to look properly feminine. Boys were boys, she once told Eddie, girls were girls, and it was both stupid and unnatural to pretend otherwise.

'Perhaps Lucy would like to play a game with me when she's dressed,' Eddie suggested.

The girl glanced at him, and a frown wrinkled her forehead.

'She might like to see the you-know-what.'

154

'The *what*?' Angel said.

Eddie shielded his mouth with his hand, leaned towards her and whispered, 'The conjuring set.'

He had bought it yesterday morning and he was longing to see Lucy's reaction: all children liked presents, and often they showed their gratitude in delightful ways.

Angel rubbed Lucy's hair gently. 'Another day, I think. Lucy's tired. Aren't you, my pet?'

Lucy looked up at her, blinking rapidly as her eyes slid in and out of focus. 'I want to go home. I want Mummy. I –'

'Mummy and Daddy had to go away. Not for long. I told you, they asked me to look after you.'

The frown deepened. For Lucy, Eddie guessed, Angel's certainty was the only fixed point among the confusion and the anxiety.

'Now, now, poppet. Let's see a nice big smile. We don't like children who live on Sulky Street, do we?'

'Perhaps if we played a game, it would take Lucy's mind off things.' Eddie removed his glasses and polished the lenses with the corner of a towel. 'It would be a distraction.'

'No.' Angel picked up the little vest. 'Lucy's not well enough for that at present. When we've finished in here, I'm going to make her a nice drink and sit her on my knee and read a nice book to her.'

To his horror, Eddie felt tears filling his eyes. It was so unfair. 'But with the others, we always –'

Angel coughed, stopping him in mid-sentence. It was one of her rules that they should never let a girl know that there had been others. But when Eddie looked at her he was surprised to see that she was smiling.

'Lucy isn't like the others,' she said, her eyes meeting Eddie's. 'We understand each other, she and I.' Her lips brushed the top of Lucy's head. 'Don't we, my poppet?'

What about me?

Eddie held his tongue. A moment later, Angel asked him to go down and warm some milk and turn up the heating. He went downstairs, the jealousy churning angrily and impotently inside him as pointlessly as an engine in neutral revving into the red. The two of them made such a beautiful

155

picture, he accepted that, the Virgin and child, beautiful and hurtful.

He altered the thermostat for the central heating and put the milk on the stove. His headache was worsening. He stared into the pan, at the shifting disc of white, and felt his eyes slipping out of focus.

Virgin and child: two was company in the Holy Family. Poor old Joseph, permanently on the sidelines, denied even the privilege of making the customary biological contribution to family life. The mother and child made a whole, self-contained and exclusive, Mary and the infant Jesus, the Madonna and newborn king, the Handmaiden of the Lord with the Christ Child.

Where did that leave number three? Somewhere in the crowd scene at the stable. Or leading the donkey. Negotiating with the innkeeper. No doubt paying the bills. Acting as a combination of courier and transport manager and meal ticket. No one ever said what happened to old Joseph. No one cared. Why should they? He didn't count.

What about me?

It seemed to Eddie that almost all his life he had been condemned to third place. Look at his parents, for example. They might not have liked each other, but their needs interlocked and they excluded Eddie. Even when his father allowed Eddie to join in the photographs, Stanley's interest was always focused on the little girl, and the little girl always paid more attention to Stanley than to Eddie; they treated him as part of the furniture, no more important than the smelly old armchair.

When Stanley died, the pattern continued. His mother hadn't wasted much time before deciding to find a lodger. But why? There had been enough money for them to continue living at Rosington Road by themselves. They could have managed on Thelma's widow's pension from the Paladin, her state pension, and what Eddie received from the DSS. They would have had to live frugally, but it would have been perfectly possible with just the two of them. But no. His mother had wanted someone else, not him. She found Angel and there was the irony: because Angel preferred Eddie, at least for a time.

Only Alison and Angel had ever taken him seriously. But

Alison had gone away and now Angel no longer needed him because she had Lucy instead. But what made Lucy so special?

Eddie's eyes widened. The milk was swelling. Its surface was pocked and pimpled like a lunar landscape. A white balloon pushed itself over the rim of the saucepan. The boiling milk spat and bubbled. He lunged at the handle of the saucepan and a smell of burning filled the air.

I blame you.

Mummy, Mum, Ma, Mother, Thelma. Eddie could not remember calling his mother by name, not to her face.

Angel had taken charge when Thelma died. Eddie had to admit that she had worked miracles. When he finally managed to drag himself downstairs on the morning of his mother's death, he had sat down at the kitchen table, in the heart of Thelma's domain, and laid his head on his arms. Still in the grip of an immense hangover, he hadn't wanted to think because thinking hurt too much.

He had heard Angel coming downstairs and into the room; he had smelled her perfume and heard water gushing from the tap.

'Eddie. Sit up, please.'

Wearily he obeyed.

She placed a glass of water in front of him. 'Lots of fluids.' She handed him a sachet of Alka-Seltzers which she had already opened to save him the trouble. 'Don't worry if you're sick. It usually helps to vomit.'

He dropped the tablets one by one into the water and watched the bubbles rising. 'What happened to her?'

'I suspect it was a heart attack. Just as she expected.'

'What?'

'You knew she had a heart condition, didn't you?'

A new pain penetrated Eddie's headache. 'She never told me.'

'Probably she didn't want to worry you. Either that or she thought you'd guessed.'

'But how could I?' Eddie wailed.

'Why do you think she gave up smoking? Doctor's orders, of course. And those tablets she took, not to mention her spray . . . Didn't you ever notice how breathless she got?'

'But she's been like that for years. Not so bad, perhaps, but –'

'And the colour she went sometimes? As soon as I saw that I knew there was a heart problem. Now drink up.'

He drank the mixture. At one point he thought he might have to make a run for the sink, but the moment passed.

'It's a pity she didn't change her diet and take more exercise,' Angel went on. 'But there. You can't teach an old dog new tricks, can you?'

'I wish – I wish I'd known.'

'Why? What could you have done? Given her a new set of coronary arteries?'

He tried to rid his mind of the figure on the bed in the front room upstairs. Never large, Thelma had shrunk still further in death. He glanced at Angel, who was making coffee. She was quite at home here, he thought, as if this were her own kitchen.

'What happened last night?'

She turned, spoon in hand. 'You don't remember? I'm not surprised. The wine had quite an effect on you, didn't it? I didn't realize you had such a weak head.'

He remembered the basement restaurant in Soho. Snatches of their conversation came back to him. The silk tie, blue with green stripes. Himself vomiting over the shiny bonnet of a parked car. Orange candle flames dancing in Angel's pupils. The three white tablets in the palm of her hand.

'Did you see my mother last night?'

'No.'

'So what happened when we got back?'

'Nothing. I imagine she must have been asleep. I took you upstairs and gave you some aspirin. You went out like a light. So I covered you up and went to bed myself.'

'You're sure?'

Angel stared at him. 'I'm not in the habit of lying, Eddie.'

He dropped his eyes. 'Sorry.'

'All right. I understand. It's never easy when a parent dies. One doesn't act rationally.'

She paused to pour water into a coffee pot which Eddie had never seen before. He sniffed. Real coffee, which meant that it

158

was Angel's. His mother had liked only instant coffee.

A moment later, Angel said in a slow, deliberate voice: 'We had a pleasant meal out last night. Your mother was asleep when we got home. We went to bed. When I got up this morning I was surprised that your mother wasn't up before me. So I tapped on her door to see if she was all right. There was no answer so I went in. And there she was, poor soul. I made sure she was dead. Then I woke you and phoned the doctor.'

Eddie rubbed his beard, which felt matted. 'When did it happen?'

'Who knows? She might have been dead when we got home. She was certainly very cold this morning.'

'You don't think . . . ?'

'What?'

'That what happened yesterday might have had something to do with it?'

'Don't be silly, Eddie.' Angel rested her hands on the table and stared down at him, her face calm and beautiful. 'Put that right out of your mind.'

'If I'd stayed with her, talked with her –'

'It wouldn't have done any good. Probably she would have made herself even more upset.'

'But –'

'Her death could have happened at any time. And don't forget, it's psychologically typical for survivors to blame themselves for the death of a loved one.'

'Shouldn't we mention it to the doctor? The fact she was . . . upset, I mean.'

'Why should we? What on earth would be the point? It's a complete irrelevance.' Angel turned away to pour the coffee. 'In fact, it's probably better *not* to mention it. It would just confuse the issue.'

The dreams came later, after Thelma's funeral, and continued until the following summer. (Oddly enough, Eddie had the last one just before the episode with Chantal.) They bore a family resemblance to one another: different versions of different parts of the same story.

In the simplest form, Thelma was lying in the single bed,

159

her small body almost invisible under the eiderdown and the blankets. Eddie was a disembodied presence near the ceiling just inside the doorway. He could not see his mother's face. The skull was heavy and the two pillows were soft and accommodating. The ends of the pillows rose like thick white horns on either side of the invisible face.

Sometimes it was dark, sometimes misty; sometimes Eddie had forgotten his glasses. Was another pillow taken from Stanley's bed and clamped on top of the others? Then what? The body twitching almost imperceptibly, hampered by the weight of the bedclothes and by its own weakness?

More questions followed, because the whole point of this series of dreams was that nothing could ever be known for certain. What chance would Thelma have had against the suffocating weight pressing down on her? Had she cried out? Almost certainly the words would have been smothered by the pillow. And if any sound seeped into the silent bedroom, who was there to hear it? Who, except Eddie?

There had not been an inquest. Thelma's doctor had no hesitation in signing the medical certificate of cause of death. His patient was an elderly widow with a history of heart problems. He had seen her less than a week before. According to her son and her lodger she had complained of chest pains during the day before her death. That night her heart had given up the unequal struggle. When he saw the body, she was still holding her glyceryl trinitrate spray, which suggested that she might have been awake when the attack began.

'Just popped off,' the doctor told Eddie. 'Could have happened any time. I doubt if she felt much and it was over very quickly. Not a bad way to go, all things considered – I wouldn't mind it myself.'

After Thelma had gone, 29 Rosington Road became a different house. On the morning after the funeral Angel and Eddie wandered through the rooms, taking stock and marvelling at the possibilities that had suddenly opened up. For Eddie, Thelma's departure had a magical effect: the rooms were larger; much of the furniture in the big front bedroom, robbed of the presence which had lent it significance, had become shabby and unnecessary; and his and Angel's footsteps on the stairs were brisk and resonant.

'I think I could do something with this,' Angel said as she examined the basement.

'Why?' Eddie glanced at the ceiling, at the rest of the house. 'We've got all that room upstairs.'

'It would be somewhere for me.' She laid her hand briefly on his arm. 'Don't misunderstand me, but I do like to be by myself sometimes. I'm a very solitary person.'

'You could have the back bedroom.'

'It's too small.' Angel stretched out her arms. 'I need space. It wouldn't be a problem, would it?'

'Oh no. Not at all. I just – I just wasn't quite clear what you wanted.'

There was a burst of muffled shouting. Eddie guessed that it emanated from the basement flat next door, which was occupied by a young married couple who conducted their relationship as if on the assumption that they were standing on either side of a large windy field, a situation for which each held the other to blame.

'Wouldn't this be too noisy for you?' he asked.

'Insulation: that's the answer. It would be a good idea to dry-line the walls in any case. Look at the damp over there.'

As they were speaking, she moved slowly around the basement, poking her head into the empty coal hole and the disused scullery, peering into cardboard boxes, rubbing a clear spot in the grime in the rear window, trying the handle of the sealed door to the garden. She paused by the old armchair and wiped away some of the dust with a tissue.

'That's nice. Late nineteenth century? It's been terribly mistreated, though. But look at the carving on the arms and legs. Beautiful, isn't it? I think it's rosewood.'

Eddie remembered the smell of the material and the feeling of a warm body pressed against his. 'I was thinking we should throw it out.'

'Definitely not. We'll have it reupholstered. Something plain – claret-coloured, perhaps.'

'Won't all this cost too much?'

'We'll manage.' Angel smiled at him. 'I've got a little money put by. It will be my way of contributing. We'll need to find a builder, of course. Do you know of anyone local?'

'There's Mr Reynolds.' Eddie thought of Jenny Wren. 'He lives in the council flats behind. The one with the geraniums.'

Angel wrinkled her nose. 'So his wife's the bird-watcher?'

'He's nicer than she is. But he may be retired by now.'

'I'd prefer an older man. Someone who would take a pride in the job.'

Angel decided that they should leave a decent interval – in this case a fortnight – between Thelma's death and contacting Mr Reynolds. She spent the time making detailed plans of what she wanted done. Eddie was surprised both by the depth of her knowledge and the extent of her plans.

'We'll put a freezer in the scullery. One of those big chest ones. It will pay for itself within a year or so. We can take advantage of all the bargains.'

She examined the little coal cellar next to the scullery with particular care, taking measurements and examining the floor, walls and ceiling. There was a hatch to the little forecourt in front of the house, but Stanley had sealed this by screwing two batons across the opening.

'This would make a lovely shower room. If we tile the floor and walls we needn't have a shower stall. We can have the shower fixed to the wall. I wonder if there's room for a lavatory, too.'

'Do we really need it?'

'It would be so much more convenient.'

At length Eddie phoned Mr Reynolds and asked if he would be interested in renovating the basement.

'I don't do much now,' Mr Reynolds said.

'Never mind. Is there anyone you'd recommend?'

'I didn't say I wouldn't do it. I like to keep my hand in, particularly when it's a question of obliging neighbours. Why don't I come round and have a shufti?'

Ten minutes later Mr Reynolds was on the doorstep. He seemed to have changed very little in all the years Eddie had known him. He found it hard to keep his eyes off Angel, whom he had not previously met. They took him down to the basement.

'We were thinking that we might let it as a self-contained flat,' Angel told him.

'Oh aye.'

'There's more that needs doing than meets the eye. That's the trouble with these older houses, isn't it?'

Mr Reynolds agreed. As time went by, Eddie realized that Mr Reynolds would have agreed to almost anything Angel said. Soon they were discussing insulation, dry-lining and replastering. Angel said that the tenants might be noisy so they decided to insulate the ceiling as well. They touched lightly on plumbing, wiring and decorating. Neither of them mentioned money. Within minutes of Mr Reynolds's arrival they both seemed to take it for granted that he would be doing the work.

'Don't you worry, Miss Wharton. This will be a Rolls-Royce job by the time we're done.'

'Please call me Angela.'

Mr Reynolds stared at his hands and changed the subject by suggesting that they start by hiring a skip. Neither then nor later would he call Angel anything but Miss Wharton. His was a form of love which took refuge in formality.

Mr Reynolds did most of the work himself, sub-contracting only the electrical and plumbing jobs. It took him over two months. During this time a friendship developed between the three of them, limited to the job which had brought them together but surprisingly intimate; narrow but deep. Mr Reynolds worked long hours and, when reminded, invoiced Eddie for small sums. Angel paid the balance with praise.

'I'm not sure I can bear to let this room, Mr Reynolds. You've made it such a little palace that I think I might use it as my study.'

Mr Reynolds grunted and turned away to search for something in his tool bag.

The weeks passed, and gradually the jobs were completed. First the new floor, then the ceiling, then the walls. A hardwood door was made to measure, as was the long, double-glazed window overlooking the back garden.

'Beginning to come together now, isn't it?' Mr Reynolds said, not once but many times, hungry for Angel's praise.

If Mr Reynolds was curious about the relationship between Angel and Eddie, he never allowed his curiosity to become obtrusive. Almost certainly he guessed that Eddie and Angel were not living together as man and wife. Nor did Angel behave like a lodger: she behaved like the mistress of the house. Eddie came to suspect that Mr Reynolds did not ask questions because he did not want to hear the answers. Mr Reynolds was never disloyal to his wife, but from hints dropped here and there it became clear that he did not enjoy being at home; he liked this job which kept him out of the wet, earned him money and allowed him to see Angel almost every day.

When he had finished, the basement was dry and as airless as a sealed tomb. The acoustics were strange: sounds had a deadened quality. It seemed to Eddie that the insulation absorbed and neutralized all the emotion in people's voices.

'It's perfect,' Angel told Mr Reynolds.

'Tell me if you need any more help.' The tips of his ears glowed. The three of them were sitting round the kitchen table with mugs of tea while Eddie wrote another cheque. 'By the way, what did happen to all those old dolls' houses?'

Eddie glanced up at him. 'My father used to raffle them at work for charity.'

'Which reminds me,' Angel said. 'Some of his tools are still in the cupboard downstairs. Would you have a use for any of them, Mr Reynolds?'

The flush spread to his face. 'Well – I'm not sure.'

'Do have a look. I know Eddie would like them to go to a good home.'

'I remember your dad making those dolls' houses,' Mr Reynolds said to Eddie. 'Your mum and dad used to ask our Jenny round to look at them. She loved it.' He chuckled, cracks appearing in the weathered skin around his eyes and mouth. 'Do you remember?'

'I remember. She used to bring her dolls to see the houses, too.'

'So she did. I'd forgotten that. And look at her now: three

children and a place of her own to look after. It's a shame about Kevin. But there – it's the modern way, I'm afraid.'

'Kevin?' Angel said.

Mr Reynolds took a deep breath. Angel smiled at him.

'Kevin – Jen's husband. Well, sort of husband.' He hesitated. 'It's not general knowledge, but he's a bad lot, I'm afraid. Still, he's gone now. Least said, soonest mended.'

'I'm so sorry. Children are such a worry, aren't they?'

'He ran off with another woman when she was expecting her third. What can you do? My wife doesn't like it known, by the way. You'll understand, I'm sure.'

'Of course.' Angel glanced at Eddie. 'You and Jenny were friends when you were children, weren't you?'

Eddie nodded. He'd given Angel an edited version of his relationship with Jenny, such as it had been.

'Your mum and dad were very kind to her,' Mr Reynolds went on, apparently without irony. 'And she wasn't the only one, they say. Maybe they'd have liked a little sister for you, eh?'

'Very likely,' Eddie agreed.

'And he took some lovely photographs, too,' said the little builder, still rambling down Memory Lane. 'He gave us one of Jenny: curled up in a big armchair, looking like butter wouldn't melt in her mouth. We had it framed. We've still got it in the display cabinet.'

'Photographs?' Angel said, turning to Eddie. 'I didn't know your father took photographs.'

Eddie pushed the cheque across the table to Mr Reynolds. 'Here you are.'

'Do you have some of them still?' Angel smiled impartially at the two men. 'I love looking at photographs.'

Angel questioned Eddie minutely about his past, which he found flattering because no one else had ever done so. The questions came by fits and starts and over a long period of time. Eddie discovered that telling Angel about the difficulties and unfairness he had suffered made the burden of them easier to bear. He mentioned this phenomenon.

'Nothing unusual about that, Eddie. That's why so many people find psychotherapy appealing. That's why confession has always been such a widespread practice among Catholics.'

Since his father's death, Eddie had kept the surviving photographs in a locked suitcase under his bed. Angel cajoled him into showing them to her. They sat at the kitchen table and he lifted them out, one by one. The photographs smelled of the past, tired and musty.

'How pretty,' Angel commented when she saw the first nude. 'Technically quite impressive.'

In the end she saw them all, even the ones with Eddie, even the one with Alison.

What a Little Tease!

'That one's Mr Reynolds's daughter,' Eddie said, pointing to another print, anxious to deflect Angel's attention from Alison.

Angel glanced at Jenny Wren. 'Not as photogenic as this one.' She tapped the photograph of Alison with a long fingernail. 'What was her name?'

Eddie told her. Angel patted his hand and said that children were so sweet at that age.

'Some people don't like that sort of game.' Eddie paused. 'Not with children.'

'That's silly. Children need love and security, that's all. Children like playing games with grown-ups. That's what growing up is all about.'

Eddie felt warm with relief. Then and later, he was amazed by Angel's sympathy and understanding. He even told her about his humiliating experiences as a teacher at Dale Grove Comprehensive School. She coaxed him into describing exactly what Mandy and Sian had done. The violence of her reaction surprised him. Her lips curled back against her teeth and wrinkles bit into the skin.

'We don't need people like that. They're no better than animals.'

'But what can you do with them? You can't just kill them, can you?'

Angel arched her immaculate eyebrows. 'I think one should execute them if they break certain laws. There's nothing wrong with capital punishment if the system is sensible and fair. As for the others, why don't we put them in work camps? We could make the amount of food and other privileges they get depend on the amount of work they produce. Then at least they wouldn't be such a total liability for society. You have to admit, it would be a much fairer way of doing things.'

'I suppose so.'

'There's no suppose about it. You have to be realistic.' Angel's face was serene again. 'One has to use other people – except one's friends, of course; they're different. Otherwise they abuse you. Obviously one tries to be constructive about how one uses them. But it's no use being sentimental. They'll just take advantage, like Mandy and Sian did. In the long run it's kinder to be firm with them right from the start.'

Angel furnished her little palace as a bed-sitting room. She and Eddie brought down the bed which had belonged to Stanley and installed it on the wall opposite the long window. The reupholstered Victorian chair stood by the window. Beside it was a hexagonal table which Angel had found in an antique shop. She scattered small rugs, vivid geometrical patterns from Eastern Anatolia, over the floor. There were no pictures on the severe white walls.

Eddie went down to the basement only by invitation. By tacit consent, the new shower room was reserved for Angel's use. If they needed something from the big freezer in the former scullery, it was always Angel who fetched it.

'I know where things are,' she explained. 'I've got my little system. I don't want you confusing it.'

She bought a small microwave and installed it on a shelf over the freezer.

'Wouldn't it be more convenient in the kitchen?' Eddie asked.

'It would take up too much space. Besides, we'll use it mainly for defrosting. And having it down there will be handy if I want to heat up a snack.'

Despite the bed, Angel did not usually sleep in the basement, but in Thelma's old room upstairs. There was not enough space for her clothes in the wardrobes which had belonged to Eddie's parents, so she asked Mr Reynolds to fit new ones with mirrored doors along one wall of the front bedroom.

One morning in early May while Mr Reynolds was working upstairs, there was a ring on the doorbell. Eddie answered it. Mrs Reynolds was on the step, both hands gripping the strap of her handbag. For a second she stared at Eddie. She had bright brown eyes behind heavy glasses, a snub nose and small lips like the puckered skin round an anus.

'I'd like a word with my husband, if you please.'

Eddie called Mr Reynolds and went back into the kitchen, closing the door behind him with relief. Sometimes, when he was washing up in the winter months, he looked through the kitchen window, through the screen of leafless branches, and glimpsed Mrs Reynolds with her binoculars on the balcony of the flat. Mr Reynolds had told Angel at great length about how he had bought a new and more powerful pair of binoculars as a surprise birthday present for his wife.

There was a tap on the kitchen door. Mr Reynolds edged into the room.

'Sorry – something's come up. I'll have to go now. I'll give you a ring in the morning, if that's OK?' He looked perfectly normal. It wasn't what he said but how he said it. His voice trembled, and his breathing was irregular. He sounded ten years older than he really was.

Eddie stood up. 'Is everything all right?' He knew that Angel would want to know why Mr Reynolds had left early.

'It's our Jenny,' said Mr Reynolds, retreating backwards out of the room as if withdrawing from royalty. 'There's been an accident.'

Poor Jenny Wren. Who better than Eddie to know that patterns repeated themselves? Sometimes he thought of his father and wondered what had happened to him when he was young; and so on with his father's father and his father's father's father; and back the line went through the centuries, opening a vertiginous prospect stretching to the birth of mankind.

Even as a child, Jenny Wren had been marked out as a failure. Fat, clumsy and desperate for love, she carried her self-consciousness around with her like a heavy suitcase handcuffed to her wrist. Her children, Eddie learned later from Mr Reynolds, had been taken into care. And after the third one was born,

Jenny Wren plunged into a post-natal depression from which she never really emerged.

She lived in Hackney, in a council flat on the fourth floor of a tower block. On that morning when her father was putting the finishing touches to Angel's fitted wardrobes, she took a basket of washing on to her balcony. Instead of hanging out the clothes, however, she leant over the waist-high wall and stared down at the ground. Then – according to a witness who was watching, powerless to intervene, from a window in the neighbouring block – she lifted first one leg and then the other off the ground and rolled clumsily over the wall.

Characteristically, the suicide attempt was a failure. Though she dived head first on top of her cerebral hemispheres, the fall was partly broken by a shrub. She did a good deal of damage to herself – a badly fractured skull and other broken bones – but unfortunately she survived. A week after the fall, Mr Reynolds returned to 29 Rosington Road to finish off the wardrobes.

'Jen's in a coma. May never wake up. If she does, there may be brain damage.'

Angel patted his hand and said how very, very sorry they were. She and Eddie had sent flowers to the hospital.

'How's Mrs Reynolds coping?'

'Not easy for her. The chaplain's been very kind.' The shock had made Mr Reynolds less talkative, and everything he said had a staccato delivery. 'Not that we're churchgoers, of course. Time and a place for everything.'

'Are you sure you want to carry on with the wardrobes?' Angel asked. 'I'm sure we could find someone else to finish off. You must have so much to do. We'd quite understand.'

'I'd rather keep busy, thanks all the same.'

Halfway through June, about six weeks after Jenny Wren's fall, the first little girl came to stay at 29 Rosington Road.

Chantal was the daughter of an English investment analyst and his French wife. The family lived in Knightsbridge, a long stone's throw from Harrods. Chantal was the third child and her parents did not pay her much attention, preferring to hire nannies and au pairs to provide it instead. Angel had first noticed her at a birthday party for one of Chantal's school friends; at the time, Angel had been acting as a relief nanny for the school friend's younger sister.

Despite frequent temptation, Angel never took one of her own charges. 'Only stupid people run unnecessary risks,' she told Eddie when they were preparing the basement for Chantal. 'And they're the ones who get caught.'

Chantal's father was black and she had inherited his pigmentation. (Angel despised people like Thelma who were racist.) They dressed her in white dresses, which set off her rich dark skin. She had a tendency to giggle when Eddie played games with her. Occasionally Angel acted – in Eddie's phrase – as Mistress of Ceremonies. But he did not think she enjoyed the games very much.

Human beings were such a mass of contradictions. Although Angel was wonderful at looking after children, and skilled at making them do as she wanted, she seemed not to like playing with them.

Eddie had a wonderful time for two weeks and three days. One morning he woke to find Angel beside his bed. She was carrying a cup of tea for him, a rare treat. He sat up and thanked her, his mind already running ahead to the treats planned for the day.

'Eddie.' Angel stood by the bed, adjusting the knot that secured her robe. 'Chantal's gone.'

'Where? What happened?'

'Nothing's wrong, don't worry. But I took her back home last night. Back to her mummy and daddy.'

He stared at her. 'Why didn't you tell me?'

'Because I knew you'd be upset. I knew you'd hate having to say goodbye to her.' She paused. 'And she wouldn't want to leave you.'

Eddie felt his eyes filling with tears. 'She could have stayed with us.'

'No, she couldn't. Not for ever and ever. There would have been all sorts of difficulties as she grew older.'

Eddie turned his face towards the wall and said nothing.

'Think about it.'

Eddie sniffed. Then a new problem occurred to him. 'What

happens if she tells her parents about us, and they tell the police?'

'What can she say? All she's seen is our faces. She doesn't know where the house is, or what the outside looks like. She only saw the basement. Besides, the police aren't going to try too hard. Chantal's back home, safe and sound. No harm done, is there?'

'I still wish I could have said goodbye.'

'It made sense to do it this way. We didn't want tears before bedtime, did we?'

'Maybe she could come and stay with us again?'

Angel sat down on the edge of the bed. 'No. That wouldn't be a good idea. But perhaps we can find someone else to come and stay.'

'Who?'

'I don't know yet. But no one who lives in Knightsbridge. The police look for patterns, you see. They try to pinpoint the recurring features.'

For Katy, they travelled up to Nottingham and rented a flat there for three months. Katy was an unwanted child who escaped from her foster parents at every opportunity and wandered the streets and in and out of shops.

'Looking for love,' Angel commented. 'It's so terribly sad.'

Suki, their third little girl, had a stud in her nose and a crucifix dangling from one ear; she belonged to some travellers camping in the Forest of Dean. Angel said that the mother was a drug addict; certainly Suki smelled terribly, and when they washed her for the first time the bath water turned almost black. (This was the occasion when Suki bit Eddie's hand and screamed like a train.)

'Some parents shouldn't be trusted with children,' Angel used to say. 'They need to be taught a lesson.'

She repeated this so often, in so many ways and with such force, that Eddie thought it might amount to part of a pattern, albeit one invisible to the police.

On Sunday the first of December, after Lucy's bath, Angel spent the rest of the morning reading to her in the basement. At least, that was what Angel said she was doing. Eddie was both hurt

171

and angry. Angel had never been possessive with the others: she and Eddie had shared the fun.

To make matters worse, he wasn't sure what Angel was really doing down there. The soundproofing made eavesdropping impossible. After a while, Eddie unlocked the back door and went into the garden.

It was much colder today. The damp, raw air hurt his throat. He could not be bothered to fetch a coat. He walked warily down to the long, double-glazed window of the basement. As he had feared, the curtains were drawn. The disappointment brought tears into his eyes. His skin was burning hot. He leant his forehead against the cool glass.

The movement brought his head closer to the side of the window. There was a half-inch gap between the frame and the side of the curtains.

Scarcely daring to breathe, he knelt down on the concrete path and peered through the gap. At first he saw nothing but carpet and bare, white wall. He shifted his position. Part of the Victorian armchair slid into his range of vision. Lucy was sitting there. All he could see was her feet and ankles, Mickey Mouse slippers and pale-green tights, projecting from the seat. She was not moving. He wondered if she were sleeping. She had seemed very tired in the bath, perhaps because of the medication.

At that moment Angel came into view, still wearing her white robe. Round her neck was a long, purple scarf, like a broad, shiny ribbon with tassels on the end. Her eyes were closed and her lips were moving. As Eddie watched, she raised her arms towards the ceiling. Eddie licked dry lips. What he could see through the gap, the cross section of the basement, seemed only marginally connected with reality; it belonged in a dream.

Angel moved out of sight. Eddie panicked. She might have seen him at the window. In a moment the back door would open and she would catch him peeping. *I just came out for a breath of fresh air.* He straightened up quickly and glanced around. There was enough wind to stir the trees at the bottom of the garden and in Carver's beyond. The leafless branches made a black tracery, through which he glimpsed Mrs Reynolds on her balcony. Eddie shivered as he walked back to the house.

172

Mrs Reynolds watches me, I watch Angel: who watches Mrs Reynolds? Must be God.

Eddie giggled, imagining God following Mrs Reynolds's movements through a pair of field glasses from some vantage point in the sky. According to Mr Reynolds, his wife had become a born-again Christian since Jenny Wren had sent herself into a coma.

'It's a comfort to her,' Mr Reynolds had said. 'Not really my cup of tea, but never mind.'

Eddie opened the back door and went inside. The warmth of the kitchen enveloped him but he could not stop shivering. He went into the hall. The basement door was still closed. He pressed his ear against one of the panels. All he heard was his own breathing, which seemed unnaturally loud.

Clinging to the banister, he climbed the stairs and rummaged in the bathroom cupboard until he found the thermometer. He perched uncomfortably on the side of the bath while he took his temperature. *It's not fair. Why won't she let me in the basement too?* He took the thermometer out of his mouth. His temperature was over 102 degrees. He felt strangely proud of this achievement: he must be really ill. He deserved special treatment.

He found some paracetamol in the cupboard, took two tablets out of the bottle and snapped them in half. He poured water into a green plastic beaker which he had had since he was a child. The flowing water so fascinated him that he let it flood over the rim of the beaker and trickle over his fingers. At last he swallowed the tablets and went into his bedroom to lie down.

Alternately hot and cold, he lay fully clothed under the duvet. He thought how nice it would be if Angel and Lucy brought him a hot-water bottle and a cooling drink. They could sit with him for a while, and perhaps Angel would read a story. *Nobody cares about me.* He stared at the picture of the little girl which his father had given his mother all those years ago. *Very nice, Stanley. If you like that sort of thing.* A little later he heard his parents talking: dead voices from the big front bedroom; perhaps they were not really dead after all – perhaps they were watching him now.

Eddie drifted in and out of sleep. Just before three in the afternoon he woke to find his mouth dry and his body wet with sweat. He dragged himself out of bed and stood swaying and shivering in the bedroom. *I need some tea, a nice cup of tea.*

He found his glasses and went slowly downstairs. To his surprise, he heard voices in the kitchen. He pushed open the door. Lucy was sitting at the table eating a boiled egg. Angel was now dressed in jeans and jersey; her hair was tied back in a ponytail. As Eddie staggered into the room, he heard Lucy saying, 'Mummy always cuts my toast into soldiers, but Daddy doesn't bother.'

She stopped talking as soon as she saw Eddie. Angel and Lucy stared at Eddie. *Two's company, three's none.*

'What are you doing in the kitchen?' Eddie said, his voice rising in pitch. 'It's against the rules.'

'The rules aren't written in stone. Circumstances alter cases.' Angel stroked Lucy's dark head. 'And this is a very special little circumstance.'

'But they never come in the kitchen.'

'That's enough, Eddie. How are you feeling?'

Thrown off balance, he stared at her.

'Cat got your tongue?'

'How did you know I'm ill?'

'You should try looking at yourself in the mirror,' Angel said, not unkindly.

'I think it's flu.'

'I doubt it: probably just a virus. You need paracetamol and lots of fluids.'

Eddie sat down at the table. Lucy looked at him, her spoon halfway to her mouth, and to his delight she smiled.

'Finish your egg, dear,' Angel said. 'It's getting cold.'

'I don't want any more.'

'Nonsense. You need some food in that little tummy. And don't forget your Ribena.'

Lucy dropped her spoon on the table. 'But I've had enough.'

'Come along: eat up.'

'I'm full.'

'You'll do as I say, Lucy. You must always finish what's on your plate.'

'Mummy doesn't make me when I'm full.' Lucy's eyes

174

brimmed with tears but her voice was loud so she sounded more angry than afraid. 'I want Mummy.'

'We're not at home to Miss Crosspatch,' Angel announced.

Eddie laughed. He would not usually have dared to laugh, but now the boundaries were shifting. After all, he was not entirely sure that this was really happening. It might be a dream. At any moment he might wake up and see, hanging on the wall by the door, the picture of the little girl which his father had given his mother. The girl like Lucy.

'You're really not yourself, Eddie.' Angel walked into the hall. 'I'm going to take your temperature.' Her footsteps ran lightly up the stairs.

Lucy pushed the toast aside with a violent movement of her right arm. The far side of the plate caught the plastic cup, which slid to the edge of the table. Ribena flooded across the floor.

For an instant, Eddie and Lucy looked at each other. Then Lucy slithered off her seat and ran for the door – not the door to the hall but the door to the garden. Eddie knew he should do something, if this were not a dream, but he wasn't sure he would be able to stand up. In any case, it wouldn't matter: they kept the back door locked when they had a little girl staying with them.

He watched Lucy twisting the handle and pulling. He watched the door opening and felt cold air against his skin. Only then, as Lucy ran into the garden, did he realize that she really was outside. He was aware, too, that this was his fault – that he had unlocked the door when he went out to look through the basement window at Angel and Lucy. Seeing Mrs Reynolds on her balcony had made him forget to relock it when he came in. Angel would blame him, which was unfair: it was Mrs Reynolds's fault. He stood up, propping himself on the table.

Angel took him by surprise. She ran across the kitchen from the hall, the ponytail bouncing behind her, and out of the back door. Eddie heard a crack like an exploding firework. There was another crack, then a pregnant silence, the peace before the storm. He let himself sink back on to his chair.

It was almost a relief when Lucy began to cry: jagged sobs, not far from hysteria. Angel dragged her inside, kicked the door shut and turned the key in the lock. Angel was pale and tight-lipped.

'Very well, madam.' Angel was holding Lucy by the ear, her nails biting in to the pink skin. 'Do you know what happens to naughty children? They go to hell.'

Eddie cleared his throat. 'In a way, it's not her fault. She's –'

'Of course it's her fault.'

Lucy pressed her hand against her left cheek. The sobbing mutated into a thin, high wail.

'Perhaps she's tired,' Eddie muttered. 'Perhaps she needs a rest.'

Angel pushed Lucy away. The girl fell against a chair and slid to the floor. She stayed there, half-sitting, half-sprawling, with an arm hooked round a chair leg and her head resting against the side of the seat. Ribena soaked into the skirt of her dress.

The crying stopped. Lucy's mouth hung open, the lips moist and loose. Fear makes children ugly.

'It's all right, Lucy.' Eddie sat down on the chair beside hers and patted Lucy's dark head. She jerked it away. 'You're a bit overexcited. That's all it is.'

'That's not all it is.' Angel tugged open the drawer where they kept the kitchen cutlery. 'She needs a lesson. They all need a lesson.'

Eddie rubbed his aching forehead. '*Who* need a lesson? I don't understand.'

Angel whirled round. In her hand was a pair of long scissors with orange plastic handles. She pointed them at Eddie, and the blades flashed. 'You'll never understand. You're too stupid.'

He looked at the table and noticed the swirl of the grain around a knot shaped like a snail. He wished he were dead.

'If they do wrong,' Angel shouted, 'they have to pay for it. How else can they make things right?'

Eddie examined the snail. He wanted to say: *But she only spilled some Ribena.*

'And if they don't want to, then I shall *make* them.' Angel's face was ablaze. 'We all have to suffer. So why shouldn't they?'

But who are 'they'? The four girls or –

'Come here, Lucy,' Angel said softly.

Lucy didn't move.

Angel sprang across the kitchen, the scissors raised in her right hand.

'No,' Eddie said, trying to get up. 'You mustn't.'

With her left hand, Angel seized Lucy by the hair and dragged her to her feet. Lucy screamed. Oddly detached, Eddie noticed that there were toast crumbs and a long stain of yolk on the green Laura Ashley dress.

Angel pulled Lucy by the hair. Lucy wrapped one arm round a table leg and screamed. Angel pulled harder. The table juddered a few inches over the kitchen floor.

'Angel, let her go. Someone might hear.'

Lucy squealed. Angel yanked the little girl away from the table. She towered over Lucy, holding the scissors high above the girl's head.

'No, Angel, no!' Eddie cried. 'Please, Angel, no.'

'But that those phantasms appear often, and do frequent Cæmeteries, Charnel-houses and Churches, it is because those are the dormitories of the dead . . .'

Religio Medici, I, 37

If you wanted a model for the devil, you could find worse than David Byfield. Not one of the coarser manifestations: Uncle David would be a sophisticated devil, the sort who charms or terrifies according to his whim.

'You're being very foolish.' The old priest's voice was quiet but carrying; Uncle David had learned to fill the empty spaces of churches in the days before public-address systems.

Wide-eyed, Sally stared up at him. St Michael's filled with a blessed silence. Her mind had cleared as if a fever had receded, leaving her weak but in control. She concentrated on David Byfield, glorying in his ordinariness; he was real, safe and sane. He was wearing a dark, threadbare overcoat with a navy-blue scarf wound loosely round his neck, and between the woollen folds Sally glimpsed the white of his dog collar and old, sagging skin. He was neatly shaved. In the years since she had met him he had developed a stoop: his bony face curved over her like a gargoyle on a church roof.

'At times like this,' he went on, 'you need company. You do not sit alone in dank churches.' With a speed that took her by surprise, he placed his right palm lightly but firmly over the fingers of her left hand. 'You're freezing. You've probably had next to no breakfast. Is it any wonder that you're seeing devils waving toasting forks?'

'Don't be ridiculous.' The echo of her thoughts unnerved her. 'I was just thinking. And in my situation it's not surprising I'm a little depressed.'

'You're doing more than thinking. You're leaving yourself defenceless.' He sat down in the pew in front of her and turned slowly towards her. 'Devils – I should have known that word would embarrass you.'

'I'm not embarrassed.'

He ignored her. 'It's simply a metaphor. Why should that be so hard for your generation to grasp? All language is metaphor. When did you last talk to a priest?'

Sally stared at her lap. 'Yesterday morning.'

'Who?'

'My vicar.' She shied away from her reasons for not wanting to talk to Derek. 'He's being very supportive. So's his wife – and so's the whole parish.'

'Derek Cutter.'

She looked up, surprised. 'You know him?'

'Only by reputation.' David inserted a small, chilly pause. 'Did you pray together?'

'It's none of your business.' She paused but he said nothing, so after a while she muttered, 'As it happens, no. There wasn't the time. But I expect I'll be seeing him later today.' She knew she should at least phone Derek; she felt guilty about rejecting his offers of help, guilty about not liking him.

'Do you talk to any other priest on a regular basis? Do you have a confessor?'

'I'm sorry, but I really don't see that this is any of your business.'

'It's not just a question of what you think.'

'Where's Michael?' Sally was suddenly desperate to see him. 'And what are you doing here?'

'He's talking to the policemen outside. They met us at King's Cross and brought us straight here.'

'You know what they've found?'

He hesitated. 'They told us on the way. You're sure the – the remains aren't Lucy's?'

'Yes.'

'I don't understand how you can be so sure.'

'That's because you're not Lucy's mother.'

To her surprise he nodded. 'You know your own flesh and blood.'

She turned her face away from him, appalled by the images his words conjured up. A door creaked. David looked up.

'Here's Michael,' he went on. 'We must get you home.'

'I don't want to go home. I want to do something useful.'

Michael's quick footsteps clattered down the aisle. He was pale, but he had shaved and his hair was brushed. His jacket was open and Sally did not recognize the shirt and jersey underneath; he must have borrowed them from David. She gripped the back of the pew in front and pulled herself to her feet. David Byfield stepped away from her and tactfully feigned an interest in the list of the church's incumbents.

'Sally.' Michael hugged her. 'I'm sorry.'

She clung to him. 'It's all right. It's all right.' She found that she was patting his back. 'It doesn't matter, not now you're here.'

Over Michael's shoulder she watched David walking eastwards. He stopped at the step before the chancel and bowed towards the high altar. Bowed, not genuflected: which in a priest of his type meant that the sacrament was not reserved here. He straightened up and stood there, apparently absorbed in contemplating the east window.

Michael pulled away from Sally. 'They're talking to someone, the landlord of the pub round the corner. He thinks he saw someone turning into Beauclerk Place last night when he was locking up.'

David turned round. 'Any description?'

'No – he wasn't paying much attention. Someone wearing a longish coat, he thought. Medium height, whatever that means.'

'Man or woman?'

'He couldn't tell.' Michael turned his back on his godfather and touched Sally's cheek. 'Shall we go?'

Sally allowed him to lead her into the little vestry, where there were mousetraps on the floor and dust on the table, and out by the side door into the alley beyond. Michael was saying something, but she neither knew nor cared what. In her mind she was concentrating on the shapeless figure in the long coat: sexless, of medium height, and possibly completely unconnected with the package in the vestry. But even a possibility was better than nothing: it was something to focus on, something to hate. *May God damn you and yours.* The words set up echoes in her memory. Audrey Oliphant had used them when she cursed her, Sally, in St George's: only three months ago, and already so remote that it might have happened to someone else.

May God damn you and yours.

'Steady,' David said behind her.

Michael slipped his hand under her elbow. 'Are you all right?'

She stared blankly at him. Why did people keep asking if she was all right? She was all wrong.

Maxham was waiting for them at the end of the alley, leaning against the tall spiked gate that separated it from Beauclerk Place. 'There's a car here for you. You're going back to Hercules Road?'

'Yes.' When Michael was level with Maxham, he stopped. 'This person the landlord saw. Which way down the street was he coming?'

Maxham hesitated long enough to show that he was seriously considering refusing to answer. 'From the north.'

'Fitzroy Square? Euston Road?'

'Maybe.'

'When?'

'Between eleven-forty-five and midnight. That's all we know, Sergeant. OK? And there may not even be a connection.'

The two men stared at each other. Antagonism flickered between them. Sally tugged at Michael's arm. He allowed her to pull him away.

They were to travel back to the flat in the car which had brought Sally. Sergeant Carlow was leaning against the wing, smoking. Yvonne Saunders raised her hand a few inches, a token wave, and opened one of the back doors.

'You go on without me,' David said.

Michael glanced back. 'You're very welcome. We'd *like* you to come.'

'I know.' The old man stopped and folded his arms. 'And I shall, later, if Sally doesn't mind.'

'But where will you go?' In other circumstances Michael's surprise would have been comical.

'Oh, don't worry about me. I shall go to church.'

As soon as the car turned into Hercules Road, it was obvious that news of the discovery at St Michael's had gone before them. There were more cars, more reporters and men with cameras. A uniformed policeman stood at the entrance to the Appleyards' block of flats.

'Drive on,' Michael said to Carlow. 'Drive past the house and out the other end of the road.'

Carlow accelerated. 'Where do you want to go? A hotel?'

Sally touched Michael's sleeve. 'But what happens if Lucy tries to —'

'Maxham has someone in the flat round the clock, hasn't he?'

Carlow nodded. As they passed the house, a reporter recognized someone in the car, probably Sally. She saw him pointing, his mouth opening in a soundless shout. The group on the pavement fragmented into scurrying individuals. Two men started to run after the car but gave up after a few yards.

Sally said, 'But we'd need clothes and things.'

Yvonne glanced back from the front passenger seat. 'If you give me a list I can fetch what you need and bring it to the hotel.'

'Don't forget your mobile,' Michael said. 'Which hotel?'

Sally folded her arms. 'I don't want to go to a hotel.'

'As you like.' Michael twisted his lips. 'Well, where then?'

'I don't know.'

The car turned out of Hercules Road and nosed into a stream of traffic. A horn sounded behind them. For a moment no one spoke.

Michael looked at Sally. 'What about David? We'll need to find somewhere for him.'

'I don't see why.'

'Because he asked if I'd like him to stay and I said yes. I thought we'd be at the flat —'

'At the flat? So where was he going to sleep?'

'He could have –' Michael stopped.

'No,' Sally said. 'We couldn't have put him in Lucy's room, could we?'

'Maybe not.'

'No.'

They were back in West End Lane now. Sergeant Carlow pulled over to the kerb.

'Where to, then? Have you decided?'

Michael glanced at Sally. 'Christ knows.'

In the end they went to stay with Oliver Rickford. It was Sally's idea. She thought it would be better for Michael and better for her. Besides, Oliver had invited them. Michael was not enthusiastic, but on this occasion she was prepared to be more obstinate than he was.

'If that's what you want,' he said a mild voice, 'that's what we'll do.'

Michael's habits were cracking and dissolving like ice in a thaw. Sally knew that he hated asking favours; he preferred to keep his family separate from his friendships; he hated betraying signs of personal weakness, and since Lucy had gone his behaviour had been one long confession of inadequacy.

Oliver lived in Hornsey, about half a mile south of Alexandra Park. There was little traffic and Sergeant Carlow drove fast, a man anxious to be rid of his awkward passengers. He took them south round the Heath and then north on Junction Road.

At first no one talked. Carlow and Yvonne, models of discretion, stared through the windscreen. Sally rested her hand on the back seat between her and Michael, but he appeared not to notice.

At last, as they were approaching Archway, she put her hand back on her knee and said: 'There's no real need for David to come to Oliver's too.'

'Why shouldn't he?' Michael turned and stared at her. 'He's expecting to stay with us.'

'Couldn't we find him a hotel or a bed-and-breakfast? I'm sure he'd be far more comfortable.'

Michael shook his head. 'Oliver says he's got two spare rooms, and it's no problem having David as well as us.'

Sally lowered her voice. 'But it's not as if David can do any good here. I'm not quite sure why he's come.'

'I told you: he came because he offered and I asked him to. All right?'

She glared at the necks of the two police officers in front of them. 'At present we've got enough to worry about. David's just one more problem.'

'David is not a problem.'

'He bloody well isn't a solution, either.'

Michael stared out of his window. Sally squeezed her fingers together on her lap and fought back tears. After Archway, they drove along Hornsey Lane, Crouch End Hill and Tottenham Lane.

Inkerman Street was a short road with a church at the far end. Two Victorian terraces, built of grey London brick, faced each other across a double file of parked cars. Most of the houses had been cut up into flats. Oliver's was one of the exceptions.

A FOR SALE sign stood in the little yard in front of the house. Oliver must have been watching for their arrival because his front door opened almost as soon as their car pulled up outside the gate.

Michael's fingers closed around Sally's hand. 'You go in. I'm going back into town.'

'Why?' Sally was conscious of the listening ears in the front of the car. 'There's nothing you can do.'

'At least I can try and make sure that Maxham does what he should be doing.'

'If you think it will help.'

'God knows if it will help. But I have to do something.'

Frowning with concentration, Oliver pushed down the plunger of the cafetière. 'Milk? Sugar?'

'No, thank you.' Then Sally changed her mind. 'I'd like some sugar.'

He nodded and went to fetch it. Sally huddled in the armchair, hugging herself. Sugar was good for shock, for the wounded, for invalids. The gas fire was on full but she felt freezing. They were in a room at the front of the house, narrow and high-ceilinged, with a bay window to the street. The three-piece suite was upholstered in synthetic green velvet, faded and much stained. The Anaglypta wallpaper was dingy, and, near the window, strips of it were beginning to peel away. You could see where a previous inhabitant had put pictures and furniture against the wall, including a large rectangular object which had probably been a piano. Only the television, the stereo and the video looked new. Even they were covered with a layer of dust. Stacked along one wall were a number of cardboard boxes fastened with parcel tape and neatly labelled. She wondered how long ago they had been packed.

Oliver returned with the sugar. He made a performance out of pouring the coffee, reminding Sally incongruously of an elderly housewife, a regular at St George's, who had invited Sally to tea. His neat, finicky movements contrasted with the chaos in what she'd seen of his home.

'Have you had the house on the market long?' she said brightly.

'Since Sharon left.' His voice was unemotional. 'We're dividing the spoils.'

Sally lost interest in Oliver's problems. She warmed her cold fingers on the steaming cup of coffee and stared into its black, gleaming surface. She wished she could see Lucy's image there, as in a crystal ball. The reality of her loss swamped her. It was all she could do not to howl.

'It's much too big for me,' Oliver was saying. 'We bought it when we thought we might have kids.' He paused, perhaps aware that children were not the best subject to mention. 'I suppose I could take lodgers, but I don't much fancy having strangers in the house.'

'I wouldn't, either.' Sally made an enormous effort to concentrate on what he was saying. 'So you'll look for a flat or something?'

'Got to sell this place first. It means there's lots of room for you and Michael, anyway. And for his uncle, or whoever he is.'

'Godfather.' She registered in passing another of Michael's failures in communication. 'His name's David Byfield.'

'As long as he doesn't mind roughing it. I can manage a bed

and a sleeping bag for him, but sheets and curtains are a bit awkward.'

'I'm sure it will be fine. It's very kind of you.'

Oliver stirred his coffee, the spoon scraping and tapping against the inside of the mug. The lull in the conversation rapidly became awkward. Oliver said all the right things, but his house was unwelcoming and she hardly knew him; and no doubt the Appleyards' invasion had ruined his plans for Christmas. She regretted their decision to come here. The old irrational doubt – that Lucy might not be able to find them if they weren't at home – resurfaced. She would look a fool if she changed her mind, but she no longer cared about that.

'I'm sorry,' she burst out, 'I think I'd better go back to Hercules Road.'

'I'll drive you, if you like. But would you rather wait until Michael comes back? He may be on his way already. And so may David.'

'I don't know what to do for the best.'

'It's not easy. But don't worry about Lucy coming back to Hercules Road and finding no one there. Maxham will make sure that won't happen. Why don't you have some more coffee before you decide?'

Automatically she passed her mug to him.

As he handed it back to her, he said, 'What exactly did they find at that church?'

She stared at him. 'No one told you?'

'Not in any detail. There wasn't time.' His lips twitched. 'Maybe everyone assumed that someone would do it. But perhaps it's too painful for you? I'm sorry – I shouldn't have asked.'

'It's all right.' In a brisk, unemotional voice she told him about the package in the porch of St Michael's. 'They're keeping the details to themselves at present. And there was something else: there's a pub round the corner, and the landlord thought he saw someone turning into Beauclerk Place just before midnight. Wearing a long coat – could have been a man or a woman.'

'Is he trustworthy?'

'How can you tell?'

'You can't. Or not easily. You get all sorts in an investigation like this: people so desperate to help that they invent things; people who want to feel important; even people who think it's all a bit of a joke to waste police time.' He smiled anxiously at her. 'You must think me very insensitive. But in the long run it's wise to be realistic, not pin your hopes on that sort of evidence.'

'What hopes?'

He ignored the question. 'There's also the point that even if there was someone there, he might have had nothing to do with the case.'

'Then who was it? Besides the church, I think there's only offices in Beauclerk Place. No one should have been there on a Saturday night.'

'As far as we know. People do work odd hours. Anyway, it could have been someone looking for somewhere to doss down. A drunk, a drug addict. One of the homeless, and God knows there are plenty of those. Or just someone who took a wrong turning.'

To her surprise and embarrassment, she found herself smiling. 'You're a great help.'

There was a glimmer of an answering smile. 'The landlord's vagueness is a good sign. It suggests he's not making it up. And it was only last night, so he's not likely to have got confused about the day. But where does that leave you? A man or a woman turning into Beauclerk Place.'

'It has to be a man. A woman wouldn't do that sort of thing, not to children.'

Oliver shook his head. 'What about the Moors Murders? Myra Hindley was in it just as much as Ian Brady.'

The weight of the suffering, past and present, oppressed her. Sally stood up and walked to the window. She was aware that Oliver was watching from his armchair. She stared at the rows of parked cars and the blank windows of the houses opposite. No journalists here, not yet.

'I'm sorry. I shouldn't have said all that.'

'I wanted to hear.' Sally turned back to the room. 'How common is it?'

'That women offer violence to children? It's much more widespread than you might think. Some of it you can almost understand: it's the product of circumstance.'

187

'Mothers trapped with a small child in a bedsitter – that sort of thing?'

'Exactly. Or under the influence of a man. But some of it isn't like that. It's willed.'

Willed. Someone had decided to take Lucy, decided to cut off the hand of another child, decided to chop off the legs of a third, decided to leave them where they would be found. How did you explain that? You couldn't justify it, Sally thought, any more than you could pardon it.

'Evil,' she said quietly.

'Evil? What do you mean?' Oliver said sharply. 'I don't mean to be rude, but that's the trouble with clergy. Anything nasty they can't understand – no problem, they just label it evil. The work of the devil. All part of the divine plan, eh? Ours is not to reason why.'

'Maybe you're right. Maybe we don't try hard enough to understand. But right now I don't want to try. I just want Lucy.'

'Sally – I'm sorry. I didn't mean to –'

'It doesn't matter.'

She sat down again and sipped her coffee. It was cold here, in this unloved room in an unloved house. For an instant she thought she heard the thrumming of wings. She caught herself glancing up at the ceiling, as if expecting to see a giant bird hovering above her head. *I must not go mad. Lucy needs me.* Oliver was still watching her. His concern irritated her.

'You're having a hell of a time at present,' he told her in a low, sympathetic voice which brought her to the verge of screaming at him. 'All this on top of Michael's problems.'

'Yes.' Sally's mind made an unexpected connection: Oliver's phone call two weeks ago on that disastrous Saturday when Uncle David had come to lunch. She looked down, afraid her eyes would betray her. Suddenly cunning, she murmured, 'Poor Michael.'

'Don't worry too much. Maybe they'll drop the complaint.'

'And if not?'

'Hard to tell.' This time he avoided her eyes. 'Michael's record is in his favour. And most people feel a lot of sympathy. We're all tempted.'

'But Michael didn't resist.' It was not quite a question: more an intelligent guess.

'Obviously he acted on impulse and under great provocation.' Oliver sounded like counsel for the defence. 'It's not as if he makes a habit of hitting people. And in the circumstances . . .' His voice trailed into silence. Then: 'I assumed he'd have told you.'

'I'm sorry,' Sally said. 'I shouldn't have tricked you. But will you tell me the rest? Who did he hit, and why?'

'A man he'd just arrested.'

'But *why*?'

'Why the arrest? Handling stolen goods. Possession of a firearm. But that wasn't why Michael hit him. This guy liked putting out cigarettes on a toddler's arm. His own daughter. And he was acting as if it made him some kind of hero. A hard man doing what hard men do. So Michael punched him in the mouth: to shut him up, Michael said.'

Sally sat there, her head bowed, and tried to pray.

'I'd have done the same.' Oliver leaned forward in his chair. 'It's possible that the man was trying to provoke Michael into taking a swing at him. The lawyers on both sides are hoping for a deal. That was what the meeting on Friday morning was about.'

She remembered finding Michael in the flat at lunch time on Friday when he should have been at work; he had been drinking lager, which he never did on duty. Those and other signs had been there. She should have asked questions.

'Don't blame him,' Oliver said. 'He probably didn't want to worry you.'

Sally shook her head. 'It's as much my fault as his.' *Now as then.* It was abruptly clear to her that the kidnapping did not release her from other responsibilities.

'It all seems irrelevant now,' he went on.

She did not want to talk about it with Oliver. 'Do you mind if I make a phone call? I ought to get in touch with my boss.'

Oliver took her to a room at the back of the house. The only furniture was a dark, ugly dining table and a set of matching chairs. On the table was a phone, a computer, files and books. She tapped in the number for St George's. With luck, Derek and

189

Margaret would still be in church. In her mind she composed a warmly impersonal message for the answering machine.

'St George's Vicarage. Derek Cutter speaking.'

'Derek – it's Sally.'

'My dear, how are you? I tried ringing the flat before church, but –'

'I – we had to go out.'

'Any news?'

Sally hesitated. 'Not really.'

'We prayed for you today.'

Then it didn't do much good. 'Thank you. It's a great comfort.'

'Now, is there anything we can do in other respects? Margaret was saying only at breakfast that you shouldn't be left to cope with all this by yourselves. Why don't you come and stay with us? At times like this friendship can be a very real blessing. Besides, on a purely practical level –'

'In fact, we've decided to stay with a friend of Michael's.' Knowing that she was accepting another's offer while rejecting Derek's made her feel even guiltier.

'Ah. Well, the offer's still open.'

'It's so kind of you.' Sally heard the insincerity in her voice and tried to banish it. 'Do thank Margaret. And – and give her my love.'

'Would you like a word with her? She's here.'

'I'd better not. I'm in rather a hurry. And we want to leave the line free.'

'Of course. But shall I take your phone number? Just in case something comes up at this end.'

Fortunately the number was on the base unit of the phone. Sally read it out to Derek.

'Shall I phone you this evening?' he suggested. 'Unless you'd rather phone me. Just for a chat.'

'I'm not sure.' Sally's good resolutions dissolved. 'We may be out. I'm afraid I have to go now.'

She said goodbye and put down the phone. It was much easier to think charitably about Derek when you weren't dealing directly with him. At least she hadn't actually lied. Her conscience prodded her: there are silent lies as well as spoken ones.

190

Thanks to Derek, Sally realized, or rather thanks to her dislike of Derek, she hadn't thought about Lucy for at least a moment. But now her mind was making up for lost time. Sally stumbled into the hall and followed the sound of rushing water into the kitchen.

The room was clean and tidy, the real heart of the house. It had been recently redecorated. Oliver was washing up the coffee mugs.

'Would you mind if I went out for a walk?' she heard herself saying. 'I've been cooped up ever since this happened. I feel I need some air.'

That wasn't the entire truth, either: she also needed to find a church, to try to put right what had gone wrong inside St Michael's.

Oliver fussed over her, establishing first that she wanted to go by herself, second that her coat was warm enough and third that she did not need a street map.

'What happens if you need to phone? You've got a mobile, haven't you?'

'Yes, but I left it at home. Besides, I'm only going out for a few minutes.'

Oliver was treating her like a child, she thought crossly: nanny knows best. Couldn't he understand that she wouldn't be long because there might be some news of Lucy?

At last he let her go. Outside the air was raw, the wind cutting at her exposed skin. She turned left without a backward glance, walking briskly down the street in the direction of the church, hands deep in the pocket of her jacket. The road was seedier than she had first thought: the cars were older, the gutters lined with litter; satellite dishes projected from crumbling brickwork, pointing in the same directions like flying saucers on parade; and the curtains in many of the windows were ragged and unmatching, always a giveaway.

A line of railings sealed the far end of the road. A gate, standing open, pierced the railings and on the other side was the churchyard. It was lunch time, so the morning's services would have finished. The door might well be locked, but with luck the key holder would live nearby.

The church itself was partly masked by a screen of yews and

hawthorns which ran parallel to the railings just inside them. The nave and choir were a single, brick-built oblong with an apse projecting from the east end. Early nineteenth century, Sally thought automatically, perhaps a little older. The base of the tower, a mass of weathered masonry at the west end, must have belonged to a previous church on the site; the upper storeys were Victorian gothic.

She slipped through the gateway and into the churchyard. Almost immediately she realized that she had made a mistake. She would find no consolation here. Most of the gravestones had been removed, though a few remained propped up against the wall of the church. Tiles were missing from the roof. Two of the windows near the east end were broken, despite the grilles which covered them. A network of tarmac paths criss-crossed the muddy grass, with black litter bins standing like sentinels at the junctions. Under the drab sky the only signs of vitality and warmth came from the brightly coloured crisp packets and chocolate wrappings that drifted among the dog turds.

Sally followed one of the paths round the east end of the church. On this side of the churchyard there were benches, more trees, more railings, beyond which was the main road, heavily used by traffic even on Sunday. She slowly walked the length of the church, deciding to make a circuit of it before returning to Oliver's.

The gates of the south porch had been boarded up and secured with two padlocks. In the angle between porch and nave she noticed a pile of what looked like human excrement. Adolescents had been active with their aerosol sprays, displaying their limited grasp of literacy with the usual obscenities and tribal slogans.

Were such people human like herself? And if they were, what about child molesters and child murderers? Or the nurse who killed the children in her charge, or the father who stubbed out cigarettes on his baby's arm? Or, worst of all, the person who had stolen Lucy to practise unknown obscenities on her mind and body. 'Christ knows,' Sally muttered aloud, knowing that old certainties had grown misty and insubstantial.

The path narrowed as it turned into the dark, urine-smelling ravine between the tower and the blank gable wall of the terrace of shops on the western boundary of the churchyard. *The shadow of death.* Sally accelerated. Just as she was about to emerge into the wider spaces of the churchyard beyond, a man stepped round the corner of the tower and blocked her path. She stopped, her heart thudding.

He was almost six feet tall, with dark hair, a broken nose set in the middle of a pale, lined face, and a long, thin body. Despite the cold, he was wearing a T-shirt, a pair of thin trousers, and muddy trainers. The T-shirt had once been white, but was now stained and torn at the neck. He dug his hand in his pocket.

Sally took a step backwards, nearer the dangerously enclosed space between the tower and the wall. With a speed that caught her unawares, the man moved to her right and then drew closer to her, forcing her back against the wall of the tower. She put her hand in her jacket pocket and felt for the money which Oliver had given her in case she needed to phone: two or three pounds in change.

He was very close to her now. His mouth hung open, revealing the rotting teeth within. For an instant she smelled his breath and thought of open graves. He stretched out his arm towards her. Suddenly she realized that the lips were pulled back into a smile.

'Do you believe in Jesus? Do you?'

'Yes.'

'You've got to really believe.' He looked in his forties, but was probably younger than she was. He had a Midlands accent and spoke in a near whisper, breathless as if he had been running. 'Listen, just saying you believe isn't enough.'

'No.'

'Are you sure? Remember, Jesus can see into your inner-most soul.'

'Yes. Do *you* believe?'

'He chose me. Look, he put his sign on me.'

The man pointed to the inner edge of his left forearm. Among the scars and goose pimples was a red cross in faded felt-tip, surrounded by a wavering wreath of letters which made up the words JESUS SAVES.

'He pulled me up from the gutter. He sent an angel to wash

away my sins in the water of life.' The man stretched his arms wide. 'Look – I'm clean. Like driven snow.'

'I can see that.'

'You must be clean, too. Otherwise you'll never enter the Kingdom of Heaven.'

Sally took a step to her left, trying to outflank him.

'You must pray with me. Now.'

'I must go. My husband –'

He came even closer. 'You haven't much time. The Kingdom of God is at hand. We must kneel.'

He touched her shoulder, trying to force her to her knees. Revulsion welled inside her and she reacted instinctively: she slapped his face with all the strength she could muster. His skin was rough with stubble, like flabby sandpaper.

The man gasped, his face a parody of dismay, and stepped backwards. Sally flung herself through the gap between his arm and the wall of the tower. His hand gripped her wrist. She screamed, a long howl of fear and anger, and dragged her arm free.

'Piss off, you shithead!' Sally heard herself shrieking.

She broke into a run, crouching low, and escaped. The churchyard stretched before her. She glimpsed the railings through the branches of the trees. The panic affected her vision: nothing was fixed any more; the path, the trees, the grass – everything pulsed with a dull, menacing life, as if visible reality were nothing more than the skin of an enormous, dozing monster.

At the gateway she glanced back. The man was not pursuing her. The churchyard was empty. She clung to a railing and tried to get her breathing back to normal. The monster slipped away. Her body felt limp, as if each muscle had been individually drained of energy. Now the crisis was past, she could hardly walk, let alone run.

'Sally –?'

She turned. Oliver was jogging down Inkerman Street towards her. She stared blankly at him. Her legs could barely support her weight. A moment later he was beside her, his face dark and angry.

'What happened?'

'There was a man . . .'

'Easy, now. It's all right.' He put his hand under her arm. 'A mugger?'

She shook her head and began to laugh with the irony of it. Once she started laughing, it was hard to stop.

'OK, Sally. Calm down. It's OK.'

Oliver had his arm round her now. He half-carried, half-dragged her towards a bench a few yards away. They sat down. Trembling, she hugged him.

'What happened?'

'This man – he tried to *convert* me.'

'Are you hurt?'

'No. Oliver, I swore at him. I hit him.' She started to cry.

His arm tightened around her. 'Listen. Your reactions are out of kilter at present. It's hardly surprising.'

For a moment she thought Oliver's lips were nuzzling her hair. She said angrily, 'He shouldn't have been on the streets. If we had a halfway decent society someone would be looking after him properly.'

'A mental patient? Pushed back into the community?'

'It's possible. There were knife scars on his arms. I should go and find him. He can't have got far. I –'

'No. You're in no fit state to go after anyone. In any case, we don't want to go too far from the house.'

'I failed him.' As she spoke the words, she realized that she did not believe what she was saying: what did that shambling apology for a human being matter beside the fact that Lucy was missing? But old habits took a long time to die. She heard herself mouthing words which were no longer true. 'People like him are part of my job.'

'If you like I'll phone the local nick, see what they can do.'

She allowed this to satisfy her. A moment passed. She looked up at Oliver. His face was very close to hers.

'What were you doing? Did you come after me?'

'I was worried. I don't know why.'

She tried to smile. 'My guardian angel?'

He kissed her decorously on the forehead. 'We should go home. You're cold.'

For an instant Sally did not want to move. For an instant she wanted to stay on that bench for ever with Oliver's arms, warm and strong, wrapped around her. For an instant she felt, faint but unmistakable, a stirring of desire.

10

'. . . we are what we all abhor, *Anthropophagi* and Cannibals, devourers not onely of men, but of our selves . . . for all this mass of flesh which we behold, came in at our mouths; . . . in brief, we have devour'd our selves.'

Religio Medici, I, 37

Eddie pulled the front door closed behind him and walked swiftly down Rosington Road, his fingers scrabbling through his pockets for the keys. He stopped by the van, which was parked a few doors down, and hammered the windscreen with his clenched fist. The keys were still in his bedroom, in the pocket of the jeans he had worn yesterday. All the keys – the keys of the house as well as the van's. He had also left his wallet behind, though he had a pound or two in loose change.

He thought he heard a door opening. Without looking back, he broke into a run. His coat flapped behind him. The cold air attacked his face, his neck and his hands, its sharpness making him gasp; in his mind he saw a curved, flexible knife with an icy blade.

The word *blade* reminded him of the scissors. Had the screaming stopped? He was not sure. He thought he could hear screams, but they might have no basis in reality now; they might simply be echoes trapped within his mind. But he was certain of one thing: he could not go back to the house.

While he was running, he risked a glance behind him. No one was there. Angel wasn't following him. He wasn't worth following.

Panting, he slowed to a walk and buttoned his coat with clumsy fingers. Even if she did come after him, it wouldn't matter. He would just walk on and on and on. It was a free country. She couldn't stop him. He crossed the access road leading to the council flats.

'You all right, then?'

Eddie stopped and stared. Mr Reynolds waved at him. The little builder was about to open his garage door, on which someone had recently sprayed an ornate obscenity.

Mr Reynolds hugged himself with exaggerated force, as if miming winter in a game of charades. 'It's bitter, isn't it?'

Eddie opened his mouth but could think of nothing to say. Panic rose in his throat.

'The odds are shortening for a white Christmas,' Mr Reynolds remarked. 'Heard it on the radio.'

The silence lengthened. Mr Reynolds's face grew puzzled. Eddie's limbs might be temporarily paralysed but his mind was working. First, Mr Reynolds would do anything for Angel. Second, why was he spending the coldest Sunday afternoon since last winter standing outside his garage? Conclusion: he was keeping his eyes open at Angel's request. He was spying on Eddie.

The paralysis dissolved. Eddie broke into a run again.

'Hey!' he heard Mr Reynolds calling behind him. 'Eddie, you OK?'

Eddie ran to the end of the road and turned right. He had no clear plan where he was going. The important thing was to get away. He did not want to be a part of what was happening behind that door. He did not want even to think about it. He wanted to walk and walk until tiredness overcame him.

He crossed a road. Two cars hooted at him, and one of the drivers rolled down his window and swore at him. He walked steadily on. Why was there so much traffic? It was Sunday, the day of rest. There hadn't been all those cars when he was a child. Even ten or fifteen years ago the roads would have been far quieter. Everything changed, nothing stood still. Soon the machines would outnumber the people.

'It doesn't matter,' he told himself. 'It really doesn't matter.'

The world was becoming less substantial, less well-defined.

A bus rumbled down the road, overtaking him. The red colour spilled out of its outline. The bus's shape was no longer fixed but swayed to and fro like water in a slowly swinging bucket. You could rely on nothing in this world, and what other world was there?

Eddie remembered that he had a temperature. He might be very ill. He might die. A great sadness washed over him. He had so much to give the world, if the world would only let him. If Angel would let him. His mind shied away from the thought of her.

He was surprised that he was managing to walk so far and so well. It was not that he felt weak, exactly. His legs were as strong as usual but they did not seem quite so firmly attached to the rest of his body as they normally were.

'It's just the flu,' he said aloud, and the words – in blue, lower-case letters, sans serif – seemed to hang in mid-air beside him; he watched the wind muddling up the letters and whipping them away. 'I'll feel better in the morning.'

What if he felt worse? What if there was never any getting better?

Eddie forced himself to walk faster, as though the faster he walked the further he left these unanswerable questions behind.

The important thing was to get away. It was some time before he noticed where he was going. He crossed Haverstock Hill and zigzagged his way up to Eton Avenue. On either side were large, prosperous houses occupied by large, prosperous people. At Swiss Cottage, he hesitated, wondering whether to take the tube into town. It was too much of a decision: instead he kept walking, impelled by the fear that Angel might, after all, pursue him and by the need to keep warm. He drifted up the Finchley Road to the overground station for the North London Line. He went into the station because his legs were becoming weary and because it was starting to rain – thin, cold drops, not far removed from sleet. A westbound train clattered into the station. Eddie ran down the steps to the platform. The train was almost empty. He got on, grateful for the warmth and the seat.

At first, all went well. He closed his eyes and tried to rest. But the memory of what he had left behind in Rosington

Road shouldered its way into his mind. Eddie tried to distract himself with the usual techniques – making his mind go blank; remembering Alison on the swing and in the shed at Carver's; imagining himself as Father Christmas in a big store, with a stream of little girls queueing for the honour of sitting on his knee, a long line of pretty faces, sugar and spice and all things nice.

Today, nothing worked. As the train drew into Brondesbury Station, Eddie opened his eyes. He fancied that some of the other passengers were staring at him. Had he been talking aloud?

He stared out of the window at rows of back gardens. He was almost sure that someone was whispering about him. The words hissed above the sound of the train. He thought the whispers were coming from behind him, but he couldn't be sure without turning his head, which would betray to the watchers that he was aware that they were watching him and that someone was talking about him.

They reached another station. The whispering stopped with the train. A handful of passengers left and another handful boarded. As soon as the train began to move, the whispering started. It was a female voice, he was sure; probably a teenage girl's. Now he knew what to look for, he quickly found evidence to support this theory: the smell of perfume masking, but not quite concealing, the smell of sweat; and a sound which might have been a high-pitched giggle. Mandy or Sian? Of course not. They were no longer teenagers at Dale Grove Comprehensive.

Eddie could bear it no longer. At the next station he tensed himself. A man boarded the train but no one left. At the last moment, Eddie leapt to his feet, opened the door and jumped on to the platform.

No one followed him. The train moved away. Eddie stared into the windows as they slipped past him. There were no teenage girls behind where he had been sitting: only an old man, his eyes closed. Of course it proved nothing. The girls – he was now convinced that there had been at least two – could have ducked down beneath the sills of the windows just to confuse him. It would not do to underestimate their cunning; that was a lesson he had learned from Mandy and Sian.

It was only then that he realized where he was: Kensal Vale. He did not find this surprising. His feet had guided him along a familiar path while his mind was otherwise engaged. He knew the station and the area around it well because of the research he had done in the months before Lucy came to stay with them at Rosington Road. He had often taken the train here.

Eddie went out of the station. It was still raining. Usually Kensal Vale made him uneasy. Its reputation for violence was enough to make anyone wary. Today, however, Eddie felt almost relaxed. Because of the weather, and because it was Sunday, there were fewer people on the streets than usual. The buildings were innocent: only their inhabitants were evil.

Automatically, he made his way towards the squat broach spire of St George's, walking quickly because of the cold. The church, the Vicarage and the church car park occupied a compact site surrounded on all sides by roads, a moat of wet tarmac. The car park, once the Vicarage garden, filled most of the space between the church and the Vicarage. High brick walls and iron railings gave St George's the air of a place under siege.

By now it was early afternoon and services were over, at least until the evening. Eddie read the notice board outside the west door of the church. Sally Appleyard's name leapt out at him. Rainwater streamed down from a leaking gutter. The church was crying.

A bus passed, travelling further west. Eddie was growing colder now that he was neither in the warmth of the train nor generating his own warmth by walking. He looked up at the church, whose details were fading against the darkening sky. He would have to make a decision soon. He couldn't stay here for ever. He walked slowly onwards. As he drew level with the door of the Vicarage, he noticed that it, like Mr Reynolds's garage, had been defaced by a graffito. He stared at the capitals marching across the gleaming paint of the door. The letters huddled in a dyslexic tangle. For a few seconds his mind was unable to decode them.

IS THERE LIFE BEFORE DEATH?

Eddie stared at the question, uncertain whether to laugh or to shiver. Well, he thought, is there? At that moment the door opened. Eddie walked quickly away.

He was unable to resist the temptation to glance back at the doorway. There were two men on the doorstep. The one on the left, Eddie recognized immediately from the photograph in the *Standard*: the vicar, Derek Cutter, so pale he was almost an albino; the man who looked like a ferret in a dog collar. The second man was older, smaller and plumper. He had rosy cheeks, regular features and wispy hair. He was laughing at something Cutter had said. Eddie felt an unexpected and unsettling kinship with the unknown man: it was as if he, Eddie, were looking not in a mirror, but at the reflection of himself in twenty years' time.

The man glanced towards Eddie, who walked hurriedly away. It had been stupid to come to St George's, and worse than stupid to run the risk of being noticed. The rain brushed against the skin of his face, a cruel reminder of the dry heat in his throat. He was very thirsty. Had he not known he had a temperature, he would have been convinced he was going mad. No one could blame him for going mad. Not with all he had to put up with. Of course, a temperature and madness were not incompatible with each other: there was no reason why a lunatic should not have flu.

He looked over his shoulder, desperate for a bus, desperate for anything that would carry him away from St George's, away from the man who looked like an elderly Eddie. There were patterns and correspondences everywhere; why did people so rarely notice them?

Three black men spilled out of a doorway as Eddie passed it, and his insides clenched with terror. But the men ignored him, climbed into a car and drove noisily away. *Perhaps I am invisible.* He walked a little further down the road. Every step took him nearer to the centre of London. He did not want to go there. He wanted peace and quiet.

A bus shelter loomed up ahead, of a type that in fact offered very little shelter, because the main purpose of the design was not to protect people from the elements but to discourage muggers and vandals. He leant against it. Now he had a headache, too. The wind and the rain lashed him. Would anyone notice if he collapsed here? Would anyone notice if he died?

On the other side of the road was the long, high wall of Kensal Green Cemetery, a city of the dead. He noticed a black cab drawing up at one of the entrances and a tall, thin woman emerging from it. She turned back to the cab, her bright red lips moving. The noise of the traffic masked what she was saying, but Eddie knew from her movements that she was angry with the taxi driver. Abruptly she left him, stalking towards the entrance of the cemetery. The taxi swung across both carriageways of the road. Its yellow For Hire light came on. Eddie raised his hand and the taxi pulled over beside the bus shelter. Eddie opened the door, climbed inside and sat down heavily on the seat. The cab smelled strongly of a perfume similar to Angel's, which was no doubt all part of the pattern. The driver looked expectantly at him. Eddie looked back.

'Where to, then?' the man demanded.

Eddie stared blankly at him, remembering suddenly that he had only a handful of change in his pocket, hardly enough for a cup of coffee.

The driver was frowning now. 'Well?'

'Rosington Road,' Eddie blurted out, because he had no other answer to give.

'Where's that?'

'NW5. Off Bishop's Road.'

The taxi pulled away. Eddie sat back on the seat.

'That bloody woman wanted me to wait for her while she visited the dear departed,' the man said through the open partition, tossing the words like grenades over his shoulder. 'Didn't want to pay for it, though. Oh no. "Look, lady," I said, "I'm not a fucking charity, all right?" Jesus *Christ*.'

The man continued to complain for the whole journey, the angry words running as a counterpoint to Eddie's thoughts. Questions without answers flowed through his mind. Everything would depend on how angry Angel was when he reached the house. He wondered whether to ask the driver to wait while he went inside to collect his wallet. But then where would he go?

All too soon the taxi turned into Rosington Road. Eddie pointed out number 29. They drew up outside the house. Eddie stared at its blank windows.

'You getting out, mate? Or are you going to stay there all afternoon?'

The front door opened. Angel ran out to the taxi and opened

the rear door. He smelled her perfume and it was identical to the perfume in the back of the taxi. Her hands stretched towards him.

'Eddie. Eddie, dearest. Are you all right?'

No one could be kind like Angel. She had the power to make you feel as if you were the centre of the universe. What she did was quite ordinary: she paid off the taxi and drew Eddie into the house; she made him sit on the sofa in the sitting room and covered him with a blanket; she brought him a cup of sweet, milky tea and a digestive biscuit; she felt his hands and told him that he had been foolish to go out with such a high temperature. She endowed all these trivial actions with enormous significance. Eddie knew he was honoured. He was very happy, all the more so because he realized that in the nature of things such happiness would not last.

'Ah – Lucy?' he asked, when he was safely tucked up on the sofa.

'What about her? She's fast asleep.'

'She's all right?'

'Why shouldn't she be?'

'She – she –'

'Her tantrum? That soon passed. She was as right as rain five minutes afterwards. Children are like that, Eddie.'

'But she was so upset.'

Angel smiled. 'If you'd dealt with as many overwrought children as I have, you'd know that sometimes you have to be firm. It's the only way. Believe me, if you give in to them, they turn into little monsters.'

'What's she doing now?'

'She's asleep. It was time for her medication. But what about you?' She paused for a moment, waiting for an answer which did not come, and then went on: 'I've been terribly worried. What did you think you were doing?'

Eddie turned his face towards the back of the sofa and smelled the ghost of his father's hair oil. 'I needed to get out,' he mumbled. 'I needed fresh air.'

There was a short silence. Then Angel sighed. 'Least said,

soonest mended. I think the best thing is we draw a veil over the whole unfortunate business.'

'She really is OK?'

'Of course she is.' A hint of irritation had entered Angel's voice. 'Don't be silly.'

Eddie closed his eyes. 'I think I might rest. I'm very tired.'

'I'm not surprised. Anyway, what were you doing in Kensal Vale?'

'I didn't mean to go there. It was an accident. I didn't know what I was doing.'

'There's no such thing as accident,' Angel said.

'I saw the vicar. I don't think he saw me. In any case, he wouldn't have recognized me, would he?'

'No. Now go to sleep.' She smiled at him and slipped out of the room, closing the door behind her with a soft click.

Eddie fell into a doze. He slipped in and out of an inconclusive dream in which he was playing hide and seek with Lucy in a darkened church which he knew was St George's. In the dream, he never caught her. Once, however, he came close to it when she ran round a pillar and found him unexpectedly blocking her path. In the past, he had only seen her back view. Now she was facing him. Except that she had no face: the dark hair had swung in front of it, covering it completely, so that the back of her head was identical to the front of her head.

While this was going on, Eddie was aware of sounds around him in the house – not from below, of course, because the soundproofing prevented that. He heard Angel's footsteps in the hall and on the stairs. He heard her putting out the rubbish for the dustmen, who came on Mondays. He heard water rushing into the bath and Angel's footsteps moving to and fro in her bedroom, and the sounds of drawers being opened and cupboards closed.

He dozed again. When he woke, the room was dark, apart from light from the streetlamps filtering through the gap between the curtains. Now the house was silent. He lay on the sofa, his muscles aching, and tried to summon up the energy to go to the lavatory. Then the doorbell rang.

Automatically, he got up to answer it. The sudden movement made him dizzy and he swayed like a drunk as he crossed the room. At the doorway, he switched on the light and immediately regretted it. He didn't want to see anyone. If it was urgent they could telephone or come back later. But now it was too late: by switching on the light he had revealed his presence. Not answering the door would seem strange. It was one of Angel's rules that when they had a little visitor in the house they should be especially careful not to act in any way abnormally.

He went into the hall and, supporting himself with one hand on the wall, reached the front door. He peered through the spyhole. There was a small woman outside, staring towards the road, presenting her back to him; she was wearing a dark coat and a hat like a squashed cake. A memory stirred. Eddie had first seen Angel through this lens and she, too, had been staring at the road. He opened the door.

The woman turned towards him and he saw the sour, shrivelled face of Mrs Reynolds. She was carrying a pile of magazines in the crook of her left arm.

'Hello, Eddie. I wondered if you'd like a copy of the parish magazine.' She edged towards him, and automatically he took a step backwards into the hall; now she was standing on the threshold, her sharp eyes sending darting glances over his shoulder. 'It's only twenty-five pence.'

'Yes, of course.'

It seemed a small price to pay for getting rid of Mrs Reynolds. Eddie turned back into the hall, wondering where to find some money. Almost immediately he realized his mistake. Mrs Reynolds advanced another step. Now she was actually in the house.

'Perhaps you'd like to take it regularly. It's once a month. I know you're not a churchgoer, but there's always something interesting in the magazine.'

'All right. Yes, thanks.'

Mrs Reynolds looked around, openly curious. 'You've changed the place quite a lot since your mum and dad were alive.'

'How much did you say?' Eddie rummaged desperately through the pockets of his coat, which was hanging in the hall. His wallet wasn't there.

'Twenty-five pence.'

The landing light was on. The door to the basement was shut. Perhaps Angel was still in the bath.

'Is Miss Wharton in?'

'I think so. I've been having a nap.'

'My husband saw you today. He wondered if you were all right.'

'I was in a bit of a hurry.' Eddie cast about in his mind for a diversion. 'How's Jenny?'

'No better, no worse.'

Eddie found some change in the pocket of his jeans. 'While there's life there's hope.'

'It's not life, Eddie. It's a living death. She's in a sort of limbo. And because of that we're all in limbo. Why did she do it? That's what I want to know. No one else seems to care.'

He thrust fifty pence towards her. 'I'm sorry.'

'So am I.' She took the money.

'Keep the change.'

She had shown no sign of wanting to give him any. 'Will you have children? You and Miss Wharton?'

'Oh no. It's not that sort of – she's a tenant, that's all.'

Mrs Reynolds stared up at him. 'It's your business, I suppose.' She wheeled round and marched outside. On the step, she turned, her head nodding towards him. 'Sometimes I wish she was dead. My own daughter. You know what, Eddie? I wish she'd died when she was a kiddie. When she was three or four. When she was a baby, even.'

Mrs Reynolds squeezed her lips together and glared at him. Without another word, she walked away.

That evening Lucy was drowsy. When she woke up from her long afternoon nap, she was thirsty and her eyes kept drifting out of focus.

Angel was very kind to both Lucy and Eddie. She invited Eddie down to the basement. Though he knew what to expect, he could not help being shocked by the sight of Lucy. Angel had cut off most of her hair. For an instant he thought that Lucy was a boy.

'It was getting in her way,' Angel explained. 'And she hated having it brushed, didn't you, pet?'

Eddie sat in the Victorian armchair and Angel put the little girl on his lap. She warmed a red beaker of milk in the microwave and allowed Eddie to feed Lucy.

Afterwards, Eddie read Lucy a story about a lion who had lost his roar, while Angel sat cross-legged on the bed and shortened a pair of trousers for him. They made a family. This was how life should have been, how it was, how it would be.

It was very warm in the basement. As Lucy became sleepier, her body seemed to become heavier. Eddie wondered whether she too had flu. He thought she had fallen asleep. Then she stirred.

'Jimmy,' she murmured. She smelled stale and sweet, what Eddie thought of as the perfume of innocence. 'Where's Jimmy?'

'Here.' Angel picked up the little rag doll, which had been on the pillow of the bed, and passed it to Eddie. He gave it to Lucy. She stuffed the first two fingers of her right hand into her mouth and with her left hand pressed Jimmy against the side of her nose. Eddie smiled down at the dark head.

Suddenly Lucy squirmed on his lap. She threw Jimmy on to the carpet.

'What are you doing?' Angel asked sharply. 'He'll only get dirty again.'

Lucy began to cry.

Eddie patted her thin shoulder. 'What's wrong?'

The sobbing stopped for an instant. 'Doesn't smell right.'

'I told you so,' Eddie hissed across the room to Angel. 'He smells wrong when he's clean. And she's probably not used to the smell of our soap powder.'

'I can't help that. He was absolutely filthy. It's a question of basic hygiene.'

Angel's voice was calm but firm. Hampered by Lucy's weight, Eddie wriggled forward on the seat of the chair and stood up.

'What are you doing?' Angel said.

'I just want to get something.'

He carried Lucy towards the bed, towards Angel, who held out her arms. Lucy struggled and pointed at the chair.

'You want to stay there?' Eddie was secretly delighted,

interpreting Lucy's choice as a sign of favour. He lowered her back into the Victorian armchair. 'I won't be long.'

He was aware of Angel looking strangely at him, but he ignored her. He went upstairs to his bedroom, slowly, because any form of movement made his headache worse. Mrs Wump was in her – his? its? – bed in the shoe box in the bottom drawer of his chest. He took her out and sniffed her. She smelt of cardboard, clean clothes and old newspapers. There was a hint of Angel's washing powder, but not too much. Mrs Wump had never been through the washing machine.

He carried her down the stairs, knelt by the chair and said to Lucy, 'Would you like to meet Mrs Wump?'

Lucy, curled into a foetal ball, was still sucking the fingers of her right hand with furious concentration. She stared suspiciously at Eddie and then held out her left hand. Eddie laid Mrs Wump carefully on Lucy's palm. She sniffed it.

'It's not the same,' she said.

'Of course she doesn't smell the same. She wouldn't smell like Jimmy – she's Mrs Wump.'

Still holding Mrs Wump, Lucy rested her head wearily against the back of the chair.

'Time for beddy-byes,' Angel said. 'And perhaps Lucy should have some more medication before she does her teeth.'

Lucy was so tired that Eddie had to carry her into the shower room. Her head flopped against Eddie while he brushed her small white teeth. Afterwards, Angel pushed Lucy's limbs into pyjamas, settled her into bed and turned off the overhead light.

The only light was now from a lamp with a low-wattage bulb on the table by the window. Angel gathered up the discarded clothes. She washed out the red beaker and filled it with water in case Lucy wanted a drink in the night. Meanwhile, Eddie sat down in the armchair, which was very near the head of the bed, and passed Mrs Wump and Jimmy to Lucy. She laid Jimmy on the pillow and held Mrs Wump against her face.

'Are you all right?' Eddie whispered.

'I'm scared.'

'What of?'

Lucy didn't answer. Now that her head was shorn, she looked

even smaller than before. Her eyes seemed larger, and shadows thrown by the lighting created the illusion that her cheeks were sunken. She reminded Eddie of photographs he had seen of concentration-camp victims.

'I'm going to make some supper.' Angel climbed the stairs. 'Are you coming?'

'I might stay here a little. Just till Lucy drops off.'

He dug his nails into the palms of his hands, waiting for Angel to veto the proposal. But her footsteps continued to climb the stairs. He heard her opening the door to the hall.

'All right,' she called down. 'But don't be too long. I think we could all do with an early night.'

The door closed, and Eddie was alone with Lucy. She stared at him with dark, wary eyes. The duvet had fallen forwards over the lower part of her face. He was suddenly terrified that she would suffocate in the night. Slowly, so as not to frighten her, he reached out his hand and tucked the edge of the duvet under her chin. The movement dislodged Jimmy, who fell to the floor. Eddie picked up the little cloth doll and returned him to his place on the pillow.

As he did so, Lucy's eyes closed. Eddie froze, his hand still resting on Jimmy, unwilling to move in case he jarred her back into full consciousness. He felt her breath, warm against his skin, ruffling the hairs on the back of his hand. He had trapped himself in an uncomfortable position. Soon the muscles of his right arm and lower back were complaining. Just a little longer, he told himself, until she's properly asleep.

He watched, fascinated, as Lucy's hand emerged like a small, shy animal from the shelter of the duvet. It moved slowly over the pillow, the fingers working like miniature legs, and touched Eddie's hand. Her eyes were still closed. She gripped his forefinger.

The minutes passed. His finger grew sticky with sweat. He remained there, craning over the bed, his eyes fixed on Lucy's small, white face, until her breathing became slow and regular, until her grip relaxed.

When Eddie woke up in the morning, it was still dark. He knew at once that the fever was back in full force. It had receded during the previous evening but he had slept badly during the night, aware of a headache, feeling hot, and needing a drink.

He felt his forehead and the skin seemed to burn his hand. He was more than ever certain that what he had was flu. He felt aggrieved that Angel was not looking after him properly. People could die from flu. He flung his feet out of the bed and felt for his slippers. The house was very warm. Since Lucy's arrival, Angel had taken to leaving the central heating on at night.

Movement made his head hurt. He struggled into his dressing gown, opened his door and padded on to the landing. Angel's door was closed. He tiptoed into the bathroom and had a long drink of water. The paracetamol seemed to have vanished from the bathroom cupboard. He tried to remember what had happened last night after leaving Lucy. He had gone to bed without any supper; he hadn't been able to face the idea of food. He rather thought that Angel had given him some paracetamol in the kitchen, in which case they were probably still down there.

Despite the warmth of the house, he shivered. But it was not the fever that made him shiver. He stared at himself in the bathroom mirror and silently mouthed the words that Lucy had used: 'I'm scared.'

There was no telling what would happen now. During the night, fragments of memory had mixed with his dreams, and the boundary between them was no longer clear. He had heard Lucy's screams again. He had seen the flashing blades of the scissors hacking into the dark hair. The points of the scissors had danced perilously close to Lucy's eyes. Lucy, struggling so violently in Angel's grip, could have half-blinded herself with one rash movement. He heard again what Angel had said to him when Lucy had been locked, sobbing, into the basement.

'Next time it won't be the hair.'

The face in the mirror was looking at him with Lucy's eyes. Eddie groaned, and backed away.

He went slowly down the stairs, clinging to the banister, and automatically trying to make as little noise as possible. Angel slept lightly, and she hated being disturbed. In the hall he paused, leaning on the newel post and listening.

There was a line of light underneath the kitchen door. All his efforts to be quiet had been in vain: Angel must be already up. Eddie padded along the hall, opened the kitchen door and poked his head into the room. It was empty. Frowning, he drifted over to the worktop where the paracetamol were. He swallowed two of them, washed down with a glass of water from the tap.

His parched throat cried out for a cup of tea. He wondered whether Angel would like some. Either she had returned upstairs to her room or she was in the basement, probably the latter. Somewhere inside him, excitement turned and twisted like a rope being uncoiled. It would be nice to see Lucy again. She was almost certainly asleep, but she might wake up. Offering Angel a cup of tea gave him a good excuse for going to the basement.

He put the kettle on and went back to the hall. As he had hoped, the basement door was unlocked. It opened silently; Angel had asked Eddie to oil all the hinges in the house.

A faint pink radiance filled the room, slightly brighter on the side nearer Lucy's bed. Angel had plugged in the night light and it was still burning. Eddie could just make out the tiny mound which was Lucy in the middle of the bed. There was no sign of Angel, but an oblong of light outlined one of the doors to the right, the door to the freezer room. He hesitated, wondering what to do. A soft, clear ping filled the basement. The sound was not loud but very clear and silvery, as if someone had tapped a small bell with a hammer. An instant later he recognized it for what it was: the microwave's announcement that it had reached the end of its programmed cycle. Angel must be defrosting something for lunch or supper.

He tiptoed down the stairs and crossed the carpet to the door of the freezer room. Unlike the door to the hall, this was not soundproofed. As Eddie drew closer, he heard Angel speaking, her voice muffled by the thickness of the wood. It was difficult to make out individual words. What she was saying had a rhythm, though, like footsteps in an empty street.

He drew nearer the door, stretching out his hand towards the handle. As he touched the knob, Angel's voice rose slightly in volume. He heard her say quite distinctly, 'My body.'

He had never heard her talking to herself before. But, as he knew only too well, you could do the most absurd things when you thought you were by yourself. His hand dropped to his side. Indecision gnawed at him. Should he disturb her, thereby running the risk of making her feel foolish, or slip silently back to the kitchen?

'Memory of me,' said Angel, her voice rising once again and then dropping back to an indistinct mumble.

Eddie backed away from the door. Better not to interrupt, he thought. The door was shut, after all. Angel liked to be alone sometimes. She had always made that clear.

As he backed away, his attention on the door to the freezer room, Eddie stumbled against the arm of the Victorian chair. He stopped, listening. The murmur behind the door continued. Lucy stirred in the bed. In the faint light he made out her dark head moving on the pillow.

'Mummy,' she whispered in a thin voice.

Eddie bent down. 'Hush now. It's not time to get up. Go back to sleep now.'

Lucy did not reply. Eddie counted to a hundred. Then he tiptoed up the stairs, slipped into the hall, and closed the basement door quietly behind him.

Memory of me. The words wriggled uneasily in his memory, defying his attempts to pin them down. What had Angel been talking about?

The kettle had boiled. Eddie made a pot of tea. While he waited for it to brew, he parted the kitchen curtains and stared into the absence of darkness beyond. London was never truly dark. When he pushed his face against the glass, he saw the trees at the bottom of the garden outlined against the yellow glow of the sodium lamps far to the north. The three blocks of council flats rose like black monoliths on the right of Carver's. There were plenty of lights in the flats, on the walkways and landings; over the front doors; at ground level. He wondered if one of the lights belonged to the Reynoldses' flat.

On impulse, he opened the window and let the cool air flow on to his face. He felt it blowing away the wisps of his fever and leaving clarity behind. He thought of his mind like an empty desert beneath a starlit sky. Happiness caught him unawares. In the distance a goods train rattled over points and a whistle blew.

'What on earth are you doing?' asked Angel.

He swung round, in his agitation knocking the dishcloth on to the floor. Angel was standing in the kitchen doorway, her face unsmiling, her eyebrows raised. She wore jeans and a jersey and had her hair scraped back from her face.

'I'd shut the window if I were you. The gas bill's going to be bad enough as it is.'

He turned away and wrestled with the catch of the window. He heard her coming into the room.

'You're early,' she said.

'I couldn't sleep properly. I've still got a temperature.'

'Have you taken some paracetamol?'

'Yes.'

'Oh good – you've made some tea.'

He looked away from the window to find her opening the refrigerator. She glanced up at him as she slipped a package wrapped in foil and cardboard on to the top shelf.

'I thought we'd have moussaka this evening. In this weather you need something warming.'

He poured them both some tea. They sat at the table to drink it.

'I need to go out for a while,' Angel said.

'Now? It's not even six.'

'I've got one or two things to see to.' She gave him no chance to ask further questions. 'I think you should go back to bed. This fever's really knocked you out, hasn't it? You're not yourself.'

As ever, her concern warmed him. 'I am quite tired still,' he admitted. 'I spent a lot of the night tossing and turning. It wasn't very restful.'

'You go back to bed with another cup of tea. Lucy will be fine – she'll sleep until nine, at least. I'll look in on you when I get back.'

His body was reluctant to move, so Eddie sat at the kitchen table, sipping tea, and wondering when the paracetamol would begin to work. He heard Angel moving about in the hall and upstairs. A moment later, she returned to the kitchen. She was wearing her long, pale raincoat. On her head she wore a black beret, into which she had piled her hair. The collar of her coat was turned up. She lifted her keys from the hook behind the

214

door. In her other hand she carried a buff-coloured padded envelope.

'You'll be all right by yourself?'

'Fine. I'll just get some more tea and I'll go upstairs.'

'Plenty of fluids.' Angel touched his arm on her way into the hall. 'Try to get some rest.'

He listened to her footsteps in the hall and heard the click of the front door closing behind her. He was alone. This won't do, he told himself. Must get moving. Move where? If he looked inwards, he seemed to be enclosed by infinite space. As space was infinite, movement of any kind seemed pointless. But Angel would be cross if she found him here when she returned.

Supporting himself on the table, Eddie struggled to his feet. Angel had told him to have some tea. The teapot and the milk were on the worktop near the kettle. He crossed the room with enormous caution, like a man walking on ice which might be too thin to bear his weight. Not bothering to boil the kettle again, he filled up his mug with lukewarm tea.

Angel was a stickler for tidiness, just as Thelma had been. Eddie closed the carton of milk and opened the refrigerator to put it away. In order to put the milk inside, he had to move the moussaka which Angel had brought up from the basement. It was a supermarket meal for two, in a flat foil container enclosed by a cardboard sleeve. Eddie noticed a red dot no bigger than a squashed ant on the side of the sleeve. He touched it with a fingertip. The red smeared against the pale-blue background of the cardboard. A speck of blood from the moussaka? Poor dead lamb. Or perhaps Angel had pricked her finger like the princess in the fairy story.

As he staggered upstairs, Eddie wondered why Angel had gone out so early. The Jiffy bag suggested she was going to the post office; a packet that size would need weighing. Wasn't there a twenty-four-hour post office in central London, somewhere near Leicester Square? But why the urgency? Why not wait until their local post office opened? Perhaps it was something to do with one of her clients. Eddie knew that Angel sometimes did extra jobs for them, little tasks that were paid in cash, that did not attract the commission from Mrs Hawley-Minton.

At six o'clock on a Monday morning?

Eddie shook his head, trying to clear simultaneously his headache and his confusion. It didn't matter. Angel was a very private person, who liked to keep the different compartments of her life separate from one another.

He reached the landing. His bed looked very inviting through the open door of his room. But he hesitated on the threshold. What would he do if Lucy woke up? It was all very well for Angel to say that Lucy would sleep through, but what if she didn't? Children were notoriously unpredictable. He should have thought of the possibility before Angel left. Angel should have thought of it.

Eddie crossed the landing and pushed open the door of Angel's room. Although he was doing it for the best of motives, going into her room seemed almost sacrilegious. He remembered Thelma, who had so much liked to pry among Angel's things: he wasn't like that.

The room smelled of Angel. As he had expected, everything was very tidy. The bed had been made. The horizontal surfaces were empty of clutter. The doors of Mr Reynolds's fitted wardrobes were closed.

The receiving unit of the intercom was plugged into the socket nearest to the single bed. Eddie pulled it out. He was sure that Angel would understand. Angel was scathing about adults who did not look after the children in their care.

Eddie turned to leave. At that instant it occurred to him that the intercom was useless. True, if Lucy woke up, he would hear her cries, but he would not be able to get into the basement to comfort her. Angel had the key. It was on the same ring as her keys to the van and the front door.

Eddie leant against the wall, grateful for its coolness against the warmth of his cheek. It was very worrying. If Lucy woke up, he could go downstairs and try to talk to her through the door. But the door was soundproofed, so communication would not be easy. Besides, what good would talking through a door do to a frightened child?

A possible solution occurred to him. Mr Reynolds had given Angel two keys when he fitted the five-lever lock on the basement door. As far as Eddie knew, she had taken only one of them with her.

He looked around the room, wondering where Angel would keep spare keys. She was the sort of person for whom everything has its place. It should be possible to work out the key's location from first principles.

At that moment he heard a vehicle drawing up outside the house. The engine sounded like the van's. He scuttled to the window and peered down to the street below. To his relief, it was the red Ford Escort belonging to the quarrelsome young couple next door. But the incident had shaken him, physically as well as emotionally. Angel might come back at any time. Her movements were unpredictable. It would be terrible if she caught him poking around in her room. His legs felt weak, partly because of the fever and partly at the thought of her reaction.

Eddie abandoned the search and went into his own room and plugged the intercom into one of the sockets. He wasn't well. He needed to sleep. It wasn't fair that when he was ill he should have so much to worry about. He half-lay and half-sat on the bed and sipped the tea, which by now was tepid. Angel had been kind to him this morning, which was such a relief after yesterday. He shied away from the memory of her lunging at Lucy with the scissors. He had never seen Angel like that before, even with naughty little Suki. *Lucy's special.*

He tried to distract himself by thinking of Christmas. It was not much more than three weeks away now. He hoped Lucy would still be with them for Christmas. It would be wonderful to share such an exciting day with her. He would make a list in his mind of the presents he might buy her.

It was true that none of the other children had stayed as long as that – a fortnight was the norm. *But Lucy's special.*

He lay back and closed his eyes. The intercom hissed and crackled, a comforting background noise, like the creaks and murmurs of a gas fire. Eddie drifted towards sleep. He was almost there when a wail emerged from the intercom.

'Mummy . . .'

Eddie swung his legs from under the duvet and stood up. He waited, holding his breath as though there were a danger of Lucy hearing him. Perhaps she would slip back asleep.

'Mummy . . . I'm thirsty.'

Eddie waited, hoping. But Lucy did not go back to sleep. Soon she began to cry. It was a little after seven-thirty.

The crying continued as Eddie pulled on his dressing gown and pushed his feet into his slippers. His breathing was fast and shallow. He went back to Angel's bedroom. In desperation, he pulled out drawers and opened wardrobe doors. Lucy's crying continued, more faintly because further away, and this made it worse. Distance lent a malign enchantment: it left more room for the imagination to play.

In the end it was not so very difficult to find the key. Angel hadn't hidden it at all. Why should she? This was her home. He found it, along with other duplicates, in the top left-hand drawer of the chest. The black japanned box was there, too, the one that had contained Angela Wharton's passport. The keys had been wedged between it and a bundle of letters.

Eddie lifted out the ring. It held a complete set of their keys – house, car, back bedroom, basement and a smaller one which he assumed belonged to the chest freezer.

The crying changed gear – it became louder, sharper, higher in pitch; the sobs increased in frequency, too, as if fuelled by panic. *Nobody wants me, nobody loves me, they'll leave me here all alone until I die.*

With the crying filling his head, Eddie stumbled down the stairs, at one point almost falling. His hand was shaking so much that he found it difficult to push the key into the lock.

'It's all right,' he called, fearing that Lucy would not be able to hear him. 'I'm coming.'

At last the door opened. The bed was empty. His heart seemed to lurch. The night light was so faint that he could hardly see a thing. He brushed his hand against the switch and the overhead light came on. Lucy was curled up in the Victorian armchair with Jimmy in one hand and Mrs Wump in the other. She wasn't crying now. His appearance had shocked her into silence. She stared up at him with huge eyes, which in this light and from this angle looked black.

'Now what's all this, Lucy?' Eddie clattered down the stairs, knelt by her chair and put his arms round the tiny body. 'It's all right now. I'm here.'

She burrowed into him. 'I want to go home. I want Mummy. I want –'

'Hush. Do you want a drink?'

'No,' Lucy wailed. 'I want to go home. I want –'

'Soon,' Eddie heard himself saying. 'You'll go home to Mummy soon. But you have to be a good girl.'

Lucy's breath smelt stale. Her eyes were partly gummed up with sleep. She yawned.

'Angel won't be pleased if she finds you out of bed.' Angel would be even less pleased, Eddie suspected, if she found him down here. 'Why don't you snuggle under your duvet again?'

'I don't want to. I'm not tired.'

Eddie lifted her up and laid her down in the bed. She did not resist and her body was still heavy and uncoordinated.

'Don't go. Don't leave me alone.'

'I won't.' Eddie sat down in the Victorian armchair and passed Mrs Wump and Jimmy to Lucy. 'Now, you go to sleep.'

To his surprise, she did. Within five minutes she was fast asleep again. The medication was still affecting her. Eddie waited for a moment, just to make sure, before standing up.

The chair creaked when he moved, and Lucy opened her eyes.

'I want a drink.'

It was a delaying tactic, Eddie thought. The red beaker was still beside the bed. He picked it up and discovered that it was empty.

'I'll fetch you some more water.'

'I want Ribena.'

'We'll see,' Eddie said weakly.

He opened the door of the freezer room. It smelled faintly of cooking. He found Ribena in the cupboard over the sink and refilled the mug. He took it back to Lucy, only to find that she had fallen asleep again.

He left the drink by the bed and returned to the freezer room to put back the Ribena bottle in the cupboard. Angel need never know that he had come down here. He noticed that there was a bowl on the draining board and a knife, fork and spoon in the rack. They had special cutlery for the children, but these were the normal adult size. For some reason, Angel must have eaten breakfast down here.

219

On the other hand, there was nothing for her to eat. Usually she had muesli for breakfast, or sometimes bread or toast. In any case, why had she needed a fork? The problem niggled at him. On impulse, he unlocked the freezer and opened the lid.

He hadn't seen inside the freezer since it was new and empty. There were three compartments, two of them filled with shop-bought frozen meals in bright packaging. The third compartment was full of uncooked meat, which surprised Eddie because Angel did not believe in wasting time in cooking and preferred convenience foods. The meat was packed in polythene freezer bags, some transparent, others white and opaque. The cuts varied considerably in size and shape. Some were large enough for a substantial Sunday joint. It was not easy to see exactly what the packages contained, because they were frosted with ice. Some of the cuts looked rather bony. Angel had labelled the packages. Eddie took out one of the smaller ones.

The label said, in Angel's small, neat writing, 'S – July '95'. The meat was in one of the transparent bags. Eddie held it in his hands and felt the cold seeping into his fingers. Sausages? Spare ribs?

I'm feverish. I'm dreaming.

The whiteness of bone gleamed at one end of the package. The ends looked sharp and jagged. S, Eddie thought: S for Suki. A shudder ran through his body. His fingers went limp. His hands fell to his sides. The other, smaller pair of hands fell back into the freezer.

11

'For there are certain tempers of body, which, matcht with an humorous depravity of mind, do hatch and produce vitiosities, whose newness and monstrosity of nature admits no name . . .'

Religio Medici, II, 7

Sally thought that Michael was going to hit the man. He accosted them early on Monday morning as they left Oliver's house on their way to Paradise Gardens.

'Now look,' said Frank Howell, smiling his battered-cherub smile. 'It's not like I'm a stranger, is it? You and Mrs Appleyard know me. And these things work both ways.'

Sally moved forward, inserting her body as a barrier between the journalist and Michael. 'We're in a hurry, Mr Howell. Perhaps we can talk later.'

'How did you know where to find us?' Michael demanded as he unlocked the driver's door of the Rover.

'Ways and means.' Howell tried the effect of a smile. 'Just doing my job.'

'It must have been Derek Cutter,' Sally said, her voice suddenly bitter. Howell's eyelashes flickered. 'I gave him the phone number when I talked to him yesterday.'

Michael threw himself into the car and started the engine. Sally climbed into the front passenger seat. Howell, the perfect gentleman, held the door for her.

'Remember, Mrs Appleyard, it's a two-way process. Maybe there's things I know that you don't.'

Michael let out the clutch and Howell hurriedly slammed the door.

'I'm sorry.' Sally sensed the blood rushing to her face.

'It's not your fault,' Michael said. 'Bloody ghoul.'

After that they drove in silence. Damn Michael for mentioning ghouls. Sally tried to persuade herself that she was being unreasonable. How could he be expected to know that in Muslim legend a ghoul was an evil demon that ate human bodies, particularly stolen corpses or children?

There had been an accident in Fortis Green Road and the traffic slowed to a standstill. As they waited in the queue, Michael fidgeted in his seat, his eyes darting from side to side, looking for non-existent side streets, searching for ways of escape.

'I'll call Maxham. Can I have the mobile?'

'I left it at Oliver's,' Sally lied, her muscles tensing at the thought of yet another confrontation between Michael and Maxham.

Michael glowered at her. Sally felt sick with guilt. She opened her mouth to confess the lie, but at that moment the traffic began to move. Neither of them spoke again until they reached the North Circular.

'We've had a purple Peugeot 205 on our tail since Muswell Hill.'

'It's following us?' asked Sally. 'You sure?'

'Of course I'm not sure. All I know is, it's been two or three cars behind us since then.'

Sally turned round and tried without success to see the driver's face. 'Do you think Maxham's got someone keeping an eye on us?'

'I doubt it. He must be stretched enough as it is.' Michael overtook a lorry and, fifty yards behind them, the Peugeot pulled out to overtake as well. 'Unless he still suspects that we did it. That I did it.'

'Michael. Please don't.'

'Get the number.'

Sally opened her handbag and took out an old envelope and a pen. Michael became increasingly irritable as she struggled to read the licence plate of the Peugeot, which promptly ducked, perhaps intentionally, behind the cover afforded by the vehicles between them. She managed it in the end and then wished that there was something else she could do other than listen to her thoughts. Any job was better than none.

To distract herself from the ghoul within, Sally took out the A-Z road atlas. She turned to the index. There were three Paradise Roads and one each of Paradise Gardens, Paradise Passage, Paradise Place, Paradise Street and Paradise Walk. Paradise Gardens was the only scrap of heaven in north-west London. She wondered who had chosen the names and why. Probably nothing more significant than someone's sales technique: buy one of these houses and have an earthly foretaste of the joys to come. Tears filled her eyes. It was a cruel place to choose, a typical refinement, all of a piece with yesterday's discovery at St Michael's, Beauclerk Place.

'What was the message, exactly?' she asked Michael.

'That Lucy Appleyard was in forty-three Paradise Gardens. The message was repeated once. It was received just before eight o'clock. They recorded it automatically. Maxham said they traced the call to a public telephone in Golders Green.'

'It wasn't much more than eight-forty-five when he phoned us.'

Michael changed gear unnecessarily. A moment later he said, 'The caller said one other thing: *Not just her tights this time.*'

'So?'

'So the call wasn't a hoax. They've not released the fact that Lucy's tights were found.'

Paradise Gardens was a little over a mile west of Kensal Vale, a long, curving road of red brick terraced houses, perhaps ninety years old. Many of the houses were boarded up. Two police cars and an unmarked van were parked at the far end of the road.

'It's not Lucy,' Michael said. 'Just remember that. While there's life, there's hope.'

Sally stared through her window at two children, perhaps ten, who should have been at school and who were instead sitting on the wing of a car and sharing a companionable cigarette. 'If there's life.'

'God help me, I sometimes find myself hoping that there isn't.'

'Just so it could be all over?'

He nodded. 'For her. For us, too.'

'It's awful. Everything's changing because of this. You. Me. Everything.'

She was about to tell him of her lie about the phone. But he gave her no chance.

'We have to face it,' he said. 'Nothing will ever be the same again. Whatever happens. You can never go back. I found that out a long time ago.'

'What do you mean?' Sally asked.

'When I was a kid I was mixed up in a murder case.'

'What?' The word emerged as a gasp, as though someone had punched her in the stomach. 'Why did you never tell me?'

Michael drew up behind a police car. One of the two uniformed policemen on the pavement moved towards them.

'Because of Uncle David,' Michael said. 'At the time I promised him . . . He and his family were involved much more than I was. And in the early days I wasn't sure how you'd react. Then I thought, least said, soonest mended. All this – what's happening to Lucy – it's like a punishment.'

'Darling.'

He looked at her, and she saw the tears in his eyes. He opened his mouth to speak, but it was too late – the constable had come round the car and was bending down to Michael's window. Michael turned away to speak to him, leaving Sally to grapple with unanswered questions. *David's family?*

''Morning, Sarge.' The policeman was young and very nervous; he stared at Sally and quickly looked away, as if he had done something naughty. 'Mr Maxham is in the house. You're to go right in. If you leave the key in the car, we'll take care of it.'

As Sally crossed the pavement, she was aware of twitching curtains and watching eyes in the neighbouring houses. Apart from the boys further down the street, nonchalantly smoking their cigarette, there were no bystanders; it was not that sort of area. In Paradise Gardens, as in Kensal Vale, the police brought trouble, not reassurance: they were not the protectors of society, but its agents of retribution.

The ground-floor window of number 43 had been boarded

up. One of the windows above was broken, and none of them had curtains. As they approached, the second constable tapped on the front door and it opened from within.

Inside was a narrow hallway, its ceiling and walls covered with a yellow, flaking plaster and its floor carpeted with circulars and old newspapers; it smelled strongly of damp and excrement. The plain-clothes man who had let them in gestured towards the stairs. Maxham was coming down, talking to someone invisible on the landing above. 'Get her to make a statement. Don't take no for an answer. I want to see it in black and white by lunch time if not before.' He turned to Sally and Michael and, without changing his tone, went on, 'You took your time. Come and have a look at what we've got. I'd take you outside, where the smell isn't so bad, but then there's the problem of spectators. One of the bastards has got a pair of binoculars. And the next-door neighbour's playing with his video camera.'

He led them into a room at the back of the house. There were two mattresses on the floor and fading posters of footballers on the walls. The window was boarded up, but someone had rigged up a powerful lamp. Maxham looked ghostly by its light, his plump face bleached of colour. He had not shaved yet this morning and his face looked as tired as his tweed suit. It occurred to Sally that even Maxham might have feelings, that even he might find this case harrowing.

The only person in the room was a uniformed policewoman. Beside her, a kitchen chair without a back did duty as a table. Its top had been covered with a sheet of paper, and on this rested a padded envelope which was almost as large as the seat of the chair.

'You can buy them in any stationer's or newsagent's.' Maxham hissed, sucking air between his teeth. 'It's brand new. No address, no nothing.'

'Too big to get through the letterbox,' Michael said.

'It was folded. You can see the line.' Maxham's finger bisected the envelope. 'It wasn't even sealed.'

He pulled on a pair of gloves and, holding the envelope near its opening, gingerly lifted it so that the closed end was resting on the seat of the chair.

'Look. Not you, Sergeant. Mrs Appleyard.'

The policewoman altered the angle of the light. Sally peered into the open mouth of the envelope. There was a mass of dark hair inside.

'Don't touch,' Maxham ordered. 'Strictly speaking, I shouldn't be doing this. But I need to know if that hair's Lucy's. The sooner the better.'

'How can I tell? Especially if you won't let me touch.'

'Smell it.'

Sally bent down. The unwashed smell of the house fought with the plastic and paper of the envelope. Beyond those smells was another, a hint of the sort of perfume which is meant to remind you of Scandinavian forests.

'Some sort of pine-scented bath essence? Shampoo?'

'Do you use something like that? Could Lucy's hair smell of it?'

'No, we don't.' She looked more closely, longing to touch the dark cloud that might have been part of Lucy. 'It could be hers.'

'Then whoever's got her has given her a bath, maybe washed her hair.' Michael sounded very weary all of a sudden. 'I suppose we should be thankful for that.'

Sally turned to Maxham. 'Could it be a good sign? That they're looking after her?'

The black-rimmed glasses flashed, catching the light. 'Yes. It could be.'

'We can't tell,' Michael said. 'And nor can you.'

Maxham ignored him. 'We'll know for certain in an hour or two, Mrs Appleyard. We picked up samples of Lucy's hair from your flat. It's a simple matter of comparison.'

'And then what?' Michael demanded.

Maxham hissed but didn't answer.

'Thank you for showing us,' Sally said to Maxham. 'And thank you for showing us here.'

'I thought it would be better all round.' Maxham's voice was harsh, but for an instant there might have been a gleam of kindness in his face.

'Any witnesses?' Michael said. 'Surely someone must have seen something?'

'Nothing to speak of.' Maxham moved into the hall. 'A

woman over the road thought she saw a light-coloured van pulling up outside around six-thirty. No idea of the make, or who was driving. We're taking a statement but it's the next best thing to worthless.'

The Appleyards followed him into the hall.

'You've not got someone watching us, have you?' Michael asked.

Maxham swung round. 'No. Why?'

'We had a purple Peugeot 205 behind us most of the way from Inkerman Street.'

'You got the number?'

'Here.' Sally opened her handbag and produced the envelope.

Maxham reached out a hand for it. 'I'll have it checked out and get back to you. You sure it was following you?'

'Probable,' Michael said. 'Not absolutely certain.'

The constable at the far end of the hall opened the door as they approached.

'I'll be in touch if there's anything more,' Maxham told them. 'And I'll let you know the results of the test as soon as I hear myself.'

Michael stared at him and said nothing.

Sally said, 'Thank you. Goodbye.'

The door closed behind them. The Rover was still where they had left it. The young constable gave them an embarrassed wave.

Michael drove slowly down Paradise Gardens.

'It's aimed at me, isn't it?' Sally said.

'Why do you think that?'

'All the religion.'

'You're assuming the three incidents are connected.'

'They must be.' Sally paused, but Michael did not disagree. 'First the hand in a cemetery,' she went on. 'Then the legs in Lucy's tights in a church porch. And now the hair in Paradise Gardens.' A bubble of laughter rose in her throat. She choked it back. 'He's playing with us, whoever he is. Don't you think so?'

'I don't know what to think.'

Michael joined the stream of traffic moving south-east down

the Harrow Road. For a few moments neither of them spoke. Somewhere over to the left was the stumpy spire of St George's, Kensal Vale.

'There's another kind of pattern,' Michael said abruptly. 'Geographical. Apart from Beauclerk Place, everywhere else is in north-west London. Within a few square miles.'

'But there's only two other places. Paradise Gardens and Kilburn Cemetery.'

'And St George's. It's roughly equidistant between Harlesden and Kilburn. Like Carla's house. And Hercules Road is just east of Kilburn.'

Sally wriggled in her seat. 'Would it make a shape on the map?'

'A symbol or something? I doubt it. But maybe it means that the person we want is living or working between the two – somewhere between Beauclerk Place and the cluster of other locations. I wonder if –'

'Where are we going?' Sally interrupted, suddenly realizing that Michael was not taking them back to Inkerman Street but towards the centre of the city.

'I want to see Uncle David.' Michael glanced at her, his face half-angry, half-sheepish. 'It won't take long. In some ways it's a faster route.'

Sally stared at him. 'But what about Oliver? And have you told Maxham where we'll be? And what happens if there's some news?'

'If you'd remembered your phone, there'd be no problem.' His voice rose. 'All right, I'll call them.'

Without warning, Michael swerved into the kerb and parked the car on a double yellow line; Michael, who was so meticulous about obeying the smaller rules and regulations in life. For a few seconds, Sally was too surprised to speak. There was a pair of phone boxes outside a parade of shops.

She fumbled at the catch of her handbag. 'Michael, there's no need, I've –'

Before she could finish he was out of the car. He slammed the door and strode to the phone box without looking back. To Sally's relief, it was neither occupied nor out of order. She watched him through the glass, noting with a mixture of

228

irritation and compassion that he chose to stand with his back to her. The knowledge that she had lied to him worked inside her like corrosive acid.

She was aware of a car drawing up behind theirs, and of a door closing, but paid no attention. Then there were footsteps on the pavement and she glanced over her shoulder. The purple Peugeot 205 was parked immediately behind them. Sally lunged for the door lock and pushed it down. Frank Howell's face bobbed down until it was level with hers. Reluctantly, she lowered the window.

'Mrs Appleyard? I don't want to bother you –'

'Then don't.'

'Look, I don't mean to pester you, but maybe I can help.'

'How?'

'I hear things.' The little eyes were bloodshot. 'I've got a contact who's on Maxham's team.'

'Good for you.'

'Maxham doesn't tell you everything, you know. He plays his cards very close to his chest.'

'Give me an example.'

'And in return –'

'That depends.' Somewhere Sally found the strength to haggle. 'Eventually, maybe a personal interview. But not yet. And not until you've shown what you can do.'

'It's not what you think,' Howell said awkwardly. 'All right, an interview would be nice but I really want to help. We all do. Derek was saying –'

'I've not got much time.' Sally wanted to trust him, but it was safer to take refuge in cynicism. 'So what can you tell me?'

'There's some good news. You know the disciplinary proceedings against your husband, for hitting a suspect?'

Sally nodded. That part of the story had not been released to the public so it supported Howell's claim that he had a source within the police.

'The solicitors are meeting today. The word is, it's just for show. They've already met informally and done a deal. Your husband's in the clear.'

Sally concealed the relief she felt, which might in any case be premature. 'Is that all?'

Howell's mouth tightened. 'What about the first atrocity? Do you know where the hand was found?'

'In Kilburn Cemetery. There's no secret about that.'

'Exactly where the hand was found? On which grave? The police haven't released that detail. But I know. I've got a photograph.'

He pulled out a print about six by four inches from an inner pocket of his waxed jacket. He slid it through the open window.

'Keep it if you like. When can we talk? Maybe you'd like to make an appeal to the kidnapper.'

'What the hell are you doing?' Michael loomed up outside the window.

The journalist moved away. Sally rolled the window further down and put her head out. Howell was retreating towards his car and Michael was glaring down at him.

'It's all right, Michael. Come on – we've got to get going. Mr Howell won't be following us.'

'I'll phone you later, then,' Howell said, keeping an eye on Michael. 'Good luck.'

He scuttled round to the driver's door of his car. By the time Michael had settled himself behind the wheel, the Peugeot was receding rapidly on the Harrow Road.

Michael started the engine. 'What does Howell think he's up to?'

'He says he'll be our man in the media in return for an exclusive interview.'

'If I see him again –'

'It's OK. I can handle him.'

Michael took his eyes off the road and glared at her. '*You* can?'

'Don't be so bloody patronizing.'

The line of traffic in front of them slowed and stopped for a red light.

Michael turned to look at her. 'So did Howell tell you anything interesting?'

'It looks like the solicitors are going to sort out your little disciplinary problems.'

The Rover stalled, jerking as if stung by a wasp. Michael restarted the engine. 'What do you know about that?'

'Oliver told me, yesterday. He assumed I'd already heard about it from you. And it's just as well he did tell me, or else I wouldn't have had the slightest idea what Howell was talking about.'

The light changed to green. Sally wondered whether the hurt in her voice had been as obvious to Michael as it was to her.

'I was going to tell you on Friday evening,' he said, which was as near to an apology as he was likely to get.

'It doesn't matter.' Of course it mattered, as did whatever horrors he had shared as a child with David Byfield and now guarded so jealously. In both cases what mattered most was the fact that he had not told her.

Michael cleared his throat. 'How did Howell know?'

'He's got a source in the police. I don't know who or where. He also gave me a photo of the gravestone in Kilburn Cemetery, the one where they found the hand. There's a sort of medallion at the top of it, all rather cod Jacobean, a skull and so on.'

'It was probably chosen at random. Or because it wasn't overlooked – something like that.'

'Not necessarily.' The longer the nightmare continued, the more certain Sally became that everything was potentially significant.

After a while, Michael said, 'I phoned David while I was in the call box. They're expecting us.'

'I lied to you,' Sally blurted out. 'I have got the mobile. It's in my bag.'

'Why? I don't understand.'

'I thought you'd just shout at Maxham.'

'You were probably right.'

She shook her head and said flatly, 'I was wrong.'

For the rest of the journey, she closed her eyes and tried to pray. In the darkness of her mind she recited the Lord's Prayer. The words fell like stones into the cool, green silence. The silence was still there but God was absent, his attention elsewhere. *Oh my God, why do you leave me when I need you most?*

Time slowed and stopped. It was very quiet. Miss Oliphant was dead, dead, dead: among the angels. Sally reached out her hands in the darkness, trying to find Lucy. Her fingers closed on emptiness and she sank down and down into the dark. Is

231

this what hell means, she wondered, this slow drowning in the black waters of your own mind? But if you are drowning, you seize anything which may help you float and breathe. So then, as before, Sally made herself say over and over again the words that no longer meant anything.

'Your will be done,' she said, or thought she said. 'Not mine.'

'It's the next left, I think,' Michael said. 'Or the one after that.'

Sally opened her eyes. They were in the northern half of Ladbroke Grove, travelling south towards the raised section of Westway. Michael had driven his godfather here yesterday evening; to Sally's relief, the old man had declined the offer of a bed at Oliver's.

'Who's David staying with?' Sally asked.

'Someone called Peter Hudson. He's a retired bishop. An old friend.'

'There was a Hudson who was Bishop of Rosington in the seventies.' Once a senior diocesan bishop, he had been one of the more articulate opponents of the ordination of women, just the sort of friend for David Byfield.

'Could be him. David was there for a while himself. But that was much earlier.'

Sally remembered the Rosington postcard she had found in Miss Oliphant's books. *Our mutual friend still remembered. Small world!* Not so small you couldn't have secrets.

She said, 'So David had a family? A wife? Children?'

'A wife and child.'

'What happened to them?'

'They died.' Michael pulled over to the side of the road. 'I'll tell you about it later, Sal, OK?'

Neither Hudson nor his home were quite as Sally expected. The bishop lived in a small flat at the top of a nondescript modern block set back from the road. There was nothing overtly episcopal, or even clerical, about him: he wore slippers, baggy corduroy trousers and a tweed jacket with frayed cuffs; he had a pipe in his mouth when he opened the door to the Appleyards, and the pipe was never far away from him until they left. He was pink, plump and small – in appearance the opposite of his guest; Uncle David looked far more like a bishop than his host.

Hudson showed them into the living room, with its view of the bleak little garden at the back of the flats and the endless muddle of the city beyond. The walls and the ceiling were painted white. There was little furniture, few books and no pictures. The only ornament was a large wooden crucifix on the shelf over the gas fire. A pile of blankets and pillows on the floor suggested that the small sofa had spent the night as Uncle David's bed.

Within a couple of moments of their arrival, Hudson produced a tray of weak, instant coffee with the milk already added, and a plate of sweet, slightly stale biscuits. He handed round the mugs and then sat down beside Sally.

'This is very terrible, my dear,' he said conversationally, a gambit which took her entirely by surprise. 'How on earth are you managing?'

'I'm not,' Sally muttered, and started to cry quietly.

Hudson produced a large, freshly ironed white handkerchief from his trouser pocket. Sally mentally gave him full marks for preparation. 'Carry on,' he said. 'I doubt if you've found much time to cry. And sometimes one can't, of course.'

Michael and David were talking by the window with their backs to the room. Neither of them appeared to have noticed that Sally was crying. The tears flowed in near silence for over a minute. Hudson sat with half-closed eyes; he did not attempt to touch her or to say anything else. Gradually Sally's tears subsided. She blew her nose and wiped her eyes.

Hudson put his pipe back in his mouth and reached for a box of matches. 'I don't know if you'd like to wash? It's the door at the end of the hall, if you want it. The one on the left.'

Sally went into an ascetic little bathroom and rinsed her face with cold water. Her face, red-eyed and ugly, stared accusingly at her from the mirror. She returned to the living room to find that nothing had changed in her absence: Michael and David were still talking by the window and Hudson was puffing his pipe in the armchair next to hers.

'Have Michael and David told you what's happening?' she asked.

Hudson nodded. 'As much as they can.'

'I feel it's my fault, all of it. What I've done, what I am, has attracted someone's hatred. And Lucy's paying the price.'

'My wife once told me that I had a terrible tendency to blame myself.' A match scraped, and Hudson held the flame dancing over the bowl of the pipe. '"Don't be so self-centred," she used to say. She was quite right.'

'But the longer this goes on, the more it seems that whoever is doing it is trying to get back at me.'

'At you, or his parents, or himself, or God – what does it matter? The point is this: that person is responsible for his actions, not you. You mustn't blame yourself. I know it's tempting, but you must resist.'

'Tempting?'

'Because, in general, feeling guilty when it's patently not your fault is a soft option.' He beamed at her. 'Let's have a biscuit.'

Sally was so confused that she took one. 'I hope they're all right,' Hudson went on. 'I keep them for visitors and I think the packet has been open for rather a long time.'

For an instant, the smaller problem elbowed aside the infinitely greater one. Should she be rude but honest, or dishonest and polite? Should she eat this horrible biscuit or not? How on earth could she avoid either distressing her host or lying to him?

'Have you got that photograph?' Michael said from the window. 'David would like to see it.'

Sally jettisoned the biscuit and delved into her handbag. All four of them looked at the photograph, passing it from hand to hand. It was a black-and-white shot of a small gravestone – a simple slab, originally upright, which over the years had listed a few degrees to the left. Two people, almost certainly male, were standing near it, one on each side. The camera had cut them off at waist level, and only parts of their legs were visible: pinstripe trousers, a little too short, to the right, and something indeterminate on the left. Only the legs, the stone and the grass immediately in front of it were in focus. Everything else was a grey blur.

'It's a very short depth of field,' Michael commented. 'Probably taken from one of the houses overlooking the cemetery with a long-distance lens.'

What caught the eye was the medallion at the top, raised in bas relief. It showed a cowled death's head with the blade of a scythe arching above it. The inscription was still clearly legible.

FREDERICK WILLIAM MESSENGER
Born April 19th, 1837
Died March 4th, 1884

'On the laconic side, don't you think?' Hudson cocked his head to one side, mirroring the listing of the gravestone. 'Perhaps he didn't want the orthodox pieties on his gravestone.'

'Are you sure this is where the hand was found?' David said suddenly. 'Absolutely sure?'

Michael shook his head. 'We've only got Howell's word for it. I –'

'We've got more than that,' Sally interrupted. 'I think those trousers on the left are a pepper-and-salt tweed like Maxham's. And Sergeant Carlow wears a pinstripe suit.'

'Why have the police kept this quiet?' David asked.

'For the same reason that they didn't release the news that Lucy's tights turned up yesterday,' Michael said. 'To give them a chance of winnowing out the hoaxes.' He rubbed his forehead and stared down at the photograph in Hudson's hand. 'It's macabre, isn't it?'

Hudson peered at the print. 'I don't suppose the chap's name has any significance?' As he spoke, he glanced up at David Byfield, who shrugged and turned away to light a cigarette.

'I don't understand,' Sally said.

'A messenger usually brings a message, that's all. So perhaps the hand should be interpreted as a message. Don't you agree, David?'

Byfield nodded, his eyes on the glowing tip of his cigarette.

'The Greek for "messenger" is "angelos", of course,' Hudson went on. 'Which is where our word "angel" comes from. The Angel of Death? I wonder if someone might be playing word games?'

David straightened up and turned round. 'The important thing is the skull and the scythe.' His face was no different from usual, but at the end of the sentence his voice trembled; for the first time since Sally had met him, he sounded as old as he was. He stabbed the cigarette in the direction of the photograph. 'There's a pattern which links that to St Michael's yesterday and Paradise Gardens today.' He sucked in smoke. 'Whoever is behind this is probably Catholic, or at least has a nodding acquaintance with Catholic theology.'

'But St Michael's is an Anglican church,' Michael said.

David waved the cigarette impatiently, and a coil of ash fell to the carpet. 'Catholic in the wider sense. Not necessarily Roman.' The cigarette tip swung between Sally and Michael, and for an instant she glimpsed what David Byfield must have been like as a teacher. 'Do you know what the Four Last Things are?'

Michael glanced at Sally and shook his head.

'Death and Judgement,' Sally said automatically, her mind on Lucy, 'Heaven and Hell. In the Roman Catholic catechism, they are "ever to be remembered".'

'Precisely,' murmured Hudson. 'The *res novissimae*. Pre-Tridentine, aren't they?'

David nodded. 'The theological basis is a passage in the Apocrypha – in *Ecclesiasticus*. But the division into four isn't a formal one: it's a matter of popular usage. Long established, though. You find it in the catechisms of St Peter Canisius, for example. But I think it goes back further than the sixteenth century to the Gallican church.'

'I'm sorry,' said Michael, looking so young and vulnerable that Sally wanted to hug him, 'but I don't see what this is about.'

'It's about a great evil,' David said slowly. 'A perversion.'

'We know that,' Michael snapped. 'But what's theology got to do with it?'

'Eschatology, to be exact.'

Hudson blew a perfect smoke ring. 'I always found that a very difficult subject to get to grips with.'

'On a superficial level eschatology is quite straightforward,' David said, as if addressing a recalcitrant seminar. 'Technically it's the branch of systematic theology dealing with the ultimate fate of the individual soul and of mankind in general.'

Hudson leaned forward. 'David?'

'What?'

'Would you get to the point, please?'

For a moment, the two old men stared at each other. Sally held her breath. She knew there was a struggle going on, though not why, and she sensed both the authority flowing from Peter Hudson and David's obstinate anger. And there was another, less predictable emotion present: David was scared.

At last David nodded slightly, an unconditional capitulation. 'As you say, the name Messenger suggests that the hand wasn't left on that particular gravestone at random,' he said quietly, no longer the lecturer. 'It's a hint to the effect that there's a message for us, that there is something to be read into the symbol, a transference of meaning. And the bas relief makes it quite clear what that meaning is: the grim reaper, Death.'

'There was the painting.' Sally needed to pause because it was suddenly hard to breathe. 'The one over the high altar in St Michael's. Did you see it?'

David turned towards her, and to her astonishment she saw that there were tears in his eyes. 'Yes. Rather an unpleasant version of the Last Judgement. After Giotto, I suppose.'

Sally nodded. 'A long way after.'

His face almost lightened into a smile, then became grim again. 'So St Michael's would give us Judgement.'

'Michael's name is in the church's dedication. There might be significance in that.'

'Come off it.' Michael scowled impartially at the three of them. 'Isn't that the logic of paranoia? Selecting the facts to suit the theory?'

'Perhaps.' David stubbed out his cigarette and immediately shook another from the packet. 'But I rather doubt it. Too many facts fit. There's another possible link between St Michael's and Judgement. While we were there I happened to notice that the first incumbent was a Reverend Francis Youlgreave.'

'Youlgreave?' interrupted Michael.

'Yes.'

'But they used to live in Roth, didn't they?'

'That's how I know the name.' David stared at Michael and then turned back to Sally. 'I was Vicar of Roth for a few years, before I went to America. I don't know whether Michael has ever mentioned the place. It's a village in Middlesex, a suburb, really.'

She stared blankly at him. Miss Oliphant had lived, or at least stayed, in Roth. *Small world?*

'Francis Youlgreave is actually buried in the church,' David was saying. 'In his spare time he was a minor poet, rather in the manner of his namesake, Francis Thompson. One of his poems occasionally turns up in anthologies. It's called "The Judgement of Strangers".'

Michael was frowning. 'But that's quite a coincidence, isn't it?'

He looked at David, and David looked back. The old jealousy twisted inside Sally: they excluded her automatically from their shared past.

'In my opinion, coincidence is a much overrated idea,' Hudson said. 'It often seems to be the norm rather than the exception.'

David's lighter flared. 'True enough. And then, of course, there's Paradise Gardens, which gives us Heaven, the third of the Last Things. What do you think?' He was looking at Hudson.

'It's plausible. But will the police agree? Will you tell them?'

'We can try,' Michael said. 'I can't guarantee that Maxham will listen, though.'

'He must,' David said. 'He *must*.'

At that moment the doorbell rang. None of them moved.

'And what about the fourth Last Thing?' Sally stood up, scattering biscuit crumbs. 'Have you thought what your precious theory means for Lucy?'

'Yes,' Sally said, her throat dry and her stomach fluttering. 'I'm quite sure.'

Sergeant Carlow rubbed his long, clean hands as though trying to warm them by friction. 'It was the crucifix, you see. That's what made Mr Maxham wonder.'

'I don't think many churchgoers would encourage a child to wear a crucifix in that way.'

They were standing in Bishop Hudson's hall – Carlow and DC Yvonne Saunders, Sally and Michael. The two old men had remained in the living room, and their voices rose and fell in the background. Michael's face had a green pallor. Carlow was

238

wearing the same pinstriped suit; the trousers were so short that when he moved Sally glimpsed pale, hairless skin above his black socks. A wave of dizziness hit her and for a moment she thought she was going to faint.

'And you can confirm that Lucy's ears weren't pierced?'

'Of course I can.' A thought occurred to her, driving away the dizziness: 'The ear couldn't have been pierced recently?' She held her breath, waiting for the answer.

'We think the piercing was done a long time ago, and not very well. There's what they call a keloid on the lobe, sort of raised scar tissue. The ear was probably pierced months ago, if not years.'

Sally let out her breath. Her heart was still pounding uncomfortably; news of the temporary reprieve had not yet reached it. She swallowed convulsively. Michael gave a dry sob.

Yvonne smiled nervously, exposing the flawless teeth, and patted Sally's arm. 'Do you want to sit down, love?'

Sally allowed herself to be guided towards a chair that stood beside the wall. 'Not Lucy. Not Lucy.'

'No, love,' said Yvonne with the bright sincerity of a housewife assessing a washing powder in a TV advertisement. '*Definitely* not.'

'I'm sorry this has been a shock,' Carlow said mechanically. 'But Mr Maxham thought that we'd better check with you right away.'

Underneath the mass of black hair – Lucy's hair? – the police had found another, much smaller package, shrouded in clingfilm, at the very bottom of the padded envelope. It contained a small ear, roughly severed from the head. From the lobe dangled an earring with a silver crucifix attached to it.

Michael touched Sally's shoulder. Sally raised her hand and clung to his.

'Could the ear have come from the same body as the legs or the hand?' Michael asked.

'Definitely not the hand.' Carlow was patently happier talking to a man. 'The skin's white. Don't know about the legs. But if I had to put money on it, I'd say not.'

'Why?'

Carlow shrugged. 'I don't know – the legs were sort of big and

239

clumsy – whereas the ear's rather delicate. Just a guess, but I'd say they come from different kids.'

'Had the ear been frozen too?'

'We don't know yet. Quite possibly.'

Three victims, Sally thought: one for Death, one for Judgement, one for Heaven. And for Hell –

'There was one other thing,' Carlow went on. 'You know the tights we found yesterday?'

Sally nodded, thinking that this must pass for tact: not mentioning that the tights were Lucy's or what they had contained.

'Forensic found a hair clinging to the wool. Natural blonde. We should know more by this afternoon.'

'Man or woman?' Michael asked, his fingers tightening on Sally's shoulder.

'At a guess, a woman's: it's about twelve inches long and it's fine hair, too.'

'I need to talk to Maxham.'

Carlow looked blankly at him. 'Oh yes?'

'For God's sake!' Michael shouted, moving away from Sally and towards Carlow. 'We've just found what might be a pattern. If we're right, time's running out.'

'OK, OK. What sort of pattern?'

'The one the killer's using.'

'Tell me.'

'I'd rather tell Maxham. It supports what we already thought, that there's a religious nutter behind this.'

Carlow clamped his lips together. A muscle twitched above his big jaw. 'If you insist.'

'Of course I insist. And I'll need to bring someone with me.'

Carlow glanced at Sally, raising his eyebrows.

'A priest,' Michael said. 'David Byfield – you met him yesterday. He can explain the technical side better than I can.'

'The technical side?' echoed Carlow. 'I'm sorry, I don't –'

'We'll all be sorry if we don't get moving.' Michael turned back to Sally. 'You could stay here if you want, or take the car back to Inkerman Street. Up to you.'

'I'll see. You'd better take the mobile. You can phone me here or at Oliver's.' Sally was upset that he did not want her to go with him, but was unwilling to insist; she could add nothing but emotional complications. Besides, she had an overwhelming urge to find somewhere private so that she could cry without interruption or well-meant sympathy.

Carlow tried again. 'I'm not sure there's any advantage in this. If you've got any information, I can pass it on, of course. But Mr Maxham may be too busy to actually –'

'I know,' Michael said in a voice that climbed in volume and wobbled towards the edge of hysteria. 'He's got a full-time job. It doesn't leave him much time for socializing. But let's see if we can persuade him to make an exception.'

In Inkerman Street, Sally carefully reversed the car into an empty space. Unfortunately, she forgot to brake. The back of the Rover collided with the front of the dark-blue Citroën. The engine stalled.

Sally rested her forehead against the top of the steering wheel. *Your will be done.* Could God really and truly want something as stupid as this to happen? The red oil lamp on the dashboard winked at her, red drops on a dark background, blood on a floor. She closed her eyes but the blood would not go away. More than anything, she would have liked to pray for Lucy. When she tried, her mind filled with her daughter – not with her name or her face, but with the essence of her. In Sally's mind, Lucy expanded to such huge proportions that there was no room for anything else, even God.

Gradually the image of Lucy contracted. Like a departing aeroplane, the image grew smaller and smaller until it was no longer visible but still there. *I am not worthy to be a priest. I have no room for God.*

The sound of tapping forced itself to her attention. Sally opened her eyes, resenting the intrusion. Oliver was standing in the road outside, bending down so that his face was level with hers, just as Frank Howell had done. She rolled down the window.

'Are you all right?'

Dumbly she shook her head.

'Come inside.' He put his hand into the car and unlocked the door. 'You've had news? Is it –?'

'No. They haven't found her.'

241

'Then she may still be alive. She may still be all right.' Oliver opened the door. 'Out you come.'

Moving like an old woman, she struggled out of the car and clung to Oliver's arm. With his free hand he turned off the ignition, took out the key, rolled up the window, shut the door and locked it.

Sally stared at the front of the Citroën. It was this year's model and the paintwork gleamed. Now there was a dent in the front and one of the headlights had lost its glass. It was surprising how much damage a little knock could do. She had not realized that cars were so vulnerable.

'Look what I've done.'

'It doesn't matter.'

'But the owner –'

'I'm the owner. You can drive into it as much as you like. It's only a car.'

Oliver led her towards the house. He took her into the kitchen and put the kettle on. Sally put down her handbag on the table. She picked up a tea towel and began to dry the mug on the draining board.

'There's no need,' Oliver said after a while.

'No need of what?'

'No need to dry that. It's been draining there since last night, and even if it were wet, you would have dried it four times over by now.'

Sally stared at the mug and the towel in her hands. 'I don't know what I'm doing.'

'That's not surprising. Why don't you sit down?'

She watched Oliver making tea. He poured two mugs and added three spoonfuls of sugar to hers. He gestured towards the kitchen table.

'We'll sit there.'

She sank into a chair, grateful to have the decision taken away from her. 'We must do something about your car. Shouldn't I ring the insurers? Or report it to the police?'

'I told you: forget the car. Do you want to tell me what's happened?'

In the midst of everything, she noted his technique: asking questions rather than advancing propositions or making

242

statements. In that respect, policemen were like priests and psychologists. She told him what Maxham had shown them in Paradise Gardens. Gradually, his questions prised out the rest: the meeting with Howell, David Byfield's theory and the arrival of Sergeant Carlow.

'So what does it add up to?' Oliver said at last. 'If I was Maxham, I'd be thinking that the blonde hair probably belongs to one of the victims. As for the rest, it's largely speculative, isn't it? But I suppose it supports the theory that there's a religious crank behind this.'

Sally wrapped her cold hands around the warm mug. 'It does more than that. We've got two patterns now. One's obvious – the geographical concentration in north-west London. The other's religious, not just vaguely anti-religion but specifically tied to the Four Last Things.'

Where hell is, there is Lucy.

Oliver went out of the room. A moment later he came back with a London street atlas. He turned to the index.

'Michael's already looked,' Sally said. 'There's a Hellings Street, but that's in Wapping.'

'Way out of your geographical frame.' Oliver's finger ran down the printed column. 'But that's the closest match to hell.'

'It wouldn't be that simple. The connection will probably be oblique, like using that church in Beauclerk Place to represent Judgement.' Sally looked across the table at Oliver. 'Michael's trying to make Maxham take it seriously.'

'You must admit, there's not much to go on.'

'What else have we got?' With sudden violence, she pushed aside the mug. Tea slopped on to the table. Neither of them moved. 'Time's running out. Can't you see the schedule? Friday, Lucy was taken. Saturday, the hand was found in Kilburn Cemetery. Sunday was St Michael's, today was Paradise Gardens. So tomorrow –'

'Why?' Oliver interrupted. 'What's the purpose of it all? Have you thought of that?'

There was a silence. Then Sally said, 'Revenge, of course. Against the Church, authority, parents – who knows? But I think there's something else as well.' She shook her head, trying to clear it. 'The Four Last Things – in theological terms they're meant to represent what will happen to us all: death, then whatever lies beyond. And if there are four victims, each representing one of the stages, one part of the possible destinations of an individual soul . . .' She looked at Oliver, trying to gauge his reaction.

'Someone who wanted to be a priest but was turned down?' he suggested. 'This could be a way of –'

'No, I don't mean that, though you may be right.' Sally sat up. 'It's as if the killer wants to die by proxy. His victims are dying for *him*.'

'But what would be the point of that?'

'To cheat death and be reborn? To have a second chance? To escape from a private hell?'

His face had turned in on itself, like a house with curtained windows. 'You may be right.'

'I'm not sure. I'm not sure of anything.' Sally shot another glance at him. 'Anything at all.'

Except that where hell is, there is Lucy.

Oliver sipped tea and said nothing.

In the silence high above her she felt rather than heard the sound of wings. It was vital not to stop talking to Oliver, and yet so tempting to surrender, to let the wings overwhelm her.

'Pain is very dreary, you know,' she said hurriedly. 'I never realized that before. It's like a desert. Nothing grows there.' She hesitated. 'You don't go to church, do you?'

'Not now. My mum and dad were chapel people. When I was sixteen, I decided all that wasn't for me. Not just the chapel. The whole lot.'

'Lucky you.'

'What?'

'It sounds so simple. So comfortable.' She saw the disbelief in his face. 'A lot of people think religion's a prop. It isn't. If you believe in God, it's as if you're facing a constant challenge. He's always wanting you to do things. You can never relax and get on with your own life.'

'And you still believe in him? Now?'

'Oh yes. After a fashion. Not that it helps. Not in the slightest.'

Oliver raised the teapot and held it out towards her. Sally shook her head.

'I have dreams, too,' she heard herself saying. 'Waking dreams, sometimes. I wish I didn't.'

'That's a common side-effect of stress,' Oliver said briskly, topping up his own mug. 'We know there's a relationship between stress and suggestibility. That's been clear since Pavlov. And there's also a link between stress and the seeing of visions. If you apply the appropriate stimuli to the appropriate bits of the brain, you get hallucinations.'

'And waking dreams?'

'OK, and waking dreams.' He shrugged, telling her without words that he personally did not see any distinction between a hallucination and a waking dream. 'Stress is just another stimulus. It can cause the sort of electrical activity in the temporal lobe that makes you see things. It's as simple as that. There's nothing mysterious about it.'

'Isn't there?'

He was instantly apologetic. 'It's a bit of a hobbyhorse, I'm afraid. Don't take any notice. I'm reacting against all those sermons I had to listen to when I was a child.'

'This is a watershed,' Sally said. 'Whatever happens, however it ends, this is a watershed. In Paradise Gardens, Michael said that nothing would ever be the same again, and he's right. There will always be a gap between before and afterwards. It's made a break in the pattern.'

Oliver nodded as if he understood, which of course he couldn't. But it was nice of him to go through the motions. She wasn't sure why she found him so comfortable to be with, to talk to. If she talked like this to Michael, either he wouldn't listen or, if he did, he would engage passionately with what she was saying, agreeing or disagreeing.

He glanced up at the window. 'Why don't we drive down to Hampstead Heath and have a walk, and then have a pub lunch?'

'Now? I couldn't.'

'Why not? It will do you a lot more good than moping around here.'

'But what happens if –?'

'I'll let Maxham know where we are, and I'll take my phone.'

'I don't know. I –'

'Come on, the exercise will do you good. It's a lovely day.'

She lifted her head and stared out of the window. 'It's not.'

'It's better than yesterday. It's not raining and the wind's dropped.'

'I don't call it lovely.'

He smiled, and for an instant the plainness of his face dissolved. 'All right. But I still think we should go out.'

She shrugged, suddenly tiring of the discussion; it was easier to give in, and safer to be with Oliver than by herself. It took her much longer than usual to get ready. Everything distracted her – not the fact of Lucy's loss but little, unnecessary things. Twice she counted the money in her purse, but she still could not remember how much she had. She hesitated over which of two jerseys to wear, her mind swinging restlessly between them, before realizing that it didn't matter because her coat would cover the jersey, and in any case, she wasn't trying to impress anyone.

At last she declared herself ready, not because she felt that she was but because she did not want to keep Oliver waiting any longer. He untangled the cars and they drove down to the Heath in the Citroën. They parked in Millfield Lane and walked south from Highgate Ponds towards Parliament Hill.

There were a few other people scurrying along the paths; the weather wasn't warm enough for sauntering. She eyed them warily as they passed, ready for hostility, ready to assume that they belonged to a different order of humanity from hers. In a world where they stole children, anything was possible.

She walked close to Oliver, partly because she was scared in this green wasteland and partly because she was terrified that they would not hear his mobile phone if and when it began to ring. At first they did not talk. Then Oliver said something which she had to ask him to repeat.

'I had a letter from Sharon this morning. She's met someone else.'

'Do you mind?' Sally heard herself saying.

'I feel relieved. I think we both felt guilty when we separated: guilty because the marriage hadn't worked. If she finds someone else, it means the marriage wasn't one of those permanent mistakes that can't be put right.'

Like the death of a child.

'So as soon as you find someone else, it will all be sorted out.'

'That's the theory. There's a lot to be said for being able to start again, for second chances. But I suppose you wouldn't condone that.'

'Why not?'

'Isn't marriage meant to be for eternity?'

'Yes. But you know very well that even committed Christians get divorced.'

'Even clergy?'

The question took her aback. For an instant, Oliver's meaning – or rather a possible implication of what he was saying – penetrated the fog of unhappiness and fear in Sally's mind. 'These days even Anglican clergy get divorced. Their bishop may not like it, but it happens.'

She glanced up at his face, and on the whole liked what she saw. He smiled down at her. It seemed bizarre and inappropriate that they should be having this conversation, that she should be thinking these thoughts at this time. *Your will be done.* It was too easy to drown in the mess of your own life. You had to cling to commitments, like spars, and hope they would keep you afloat.

'Sally,' Oliver said. 'Have you ever –?'

'Do you mind if we go back to Inkerman Street now?' she interrupted.

'What's wrong?'

The fear flooded back. Oliver loomed over her, his face wooden, the features suddenly seeming exaggerated to the point of horror, like a gargoyle's; she remembered thinking in that horrible little church in Beauclerk Place that David Byfield now looked like a gargoyle. David must have been a sexy man when he was younger. All her defences were down, she realized; she was vulnerable.

She shivered. 'We must get back. I think something's happened.'

12

'I believe many are saved, who to man seem reprobated . . .
There will appear at the Last day strange and unexpected
examples both of his Justice and his Mercy; and therefore
to define either, is folly in man, and insolency even in the
Devils.'

Religio Medici, I, 57

No time. No time to lose. No time to wonder about consequences.

Leaving Lucy asleep, Eddie ran upstairs to his bedroom and
pulled open the wardrobe door. In the bottom was a brown
canvas bag strengthened with imitation leather and fitted with
a zip and lock plated to look like brass. It had belonged to Eddie's
father; every year Stanley would take it away with him on the
Paladin camping holidays.

Eddie pulled out the bag, which had been squashed almost
flat under several pairs of shoes. He unzipped it and glanced
wildly round the room. He pulled a shirt from the wardrobe
and stuffed it into the bag. Socks and pants followed. He opened
the drawer where he kept his papers and riffled through the
contents. He couldn't find his cheque book so he pulled out the
entire drawer and upended it on his bed. His cheque book and
wallet joined the clothes in the bag. As an afterthought, he also
threw in his birth certificate and his building society passbook.
He returned to the wardrobe and rummaged around until he
found the thickest jersey he owned. All the time he listened for
the sound of the van pulling up outside.

On impulse, he took down the picture of the dark-haired girl from the wall, the picture his father had given his mother. He would have liked to have taken it but he knew it wouldn't be practical. He tossed it on to the pillow. His aim was bad; the picture slipped off the end of the bed and fell to the floor; there was a sharp crack as the glass shattered in the frame.

Eddie carried the bag into the bathroom and collected toothpaste, toothbrush and shaving things. His legs were so wobbly that he had to sit down on the side of the bath. It was so unfair that all this should have come together – that he should have to cope with this while he was ill. He would need a towel. His own was wet so he took Angel's, which smelled faintly of her perfume. The smell made him feel nauseous, so in the end he fetched a clean towel from the airing cupboard.

He went slowly downstairs and into the kitchen, where he opened cupboards at random. He might need food and drink. He added biscuits, two cans of Coke and a tin of baked beans to the contents of the bag. He checked his wallet and purse and, to his horror, discovered that he had only a few pence. He emptied out the jar of housekeeping money into the palm of his hand. There was less than five pounds, all in small change. He pushed the loose coins into the pocket of his jeans. He would need more than that, he was sure. He couldn't rely on being able to get to a bank or a building society.

He remembered Carla's green purse. It was in the basement, along with the Woolworth's bag containing the conjuring set he had bought for Lucy on Saturday and had still not given to her.

Eddie went into the hall and pulled on his coat. He stood hesitating by the open door to the basement. He had not wanted to go down there. He peered in. Lucy was still asleep. Both the conjuring set and the purse were on the top shelf of Angel's bookcase, far above Lucy's reach. Eddie tiptoed down the stairs. He reached the bottom safely and, still carrying the brown bag, crossed the room to the shelves. He had to stand on tiptoe to reach the top one.

'Eddie.'

In his surprise he dropped both the purse and the conjuring set. 'What?'

'Is it getting-up time?'

'Well,' said Eddie, answering a question of his own, 'I don't know.' He bent down, picked up the purse and glanced inside the wallet section. There were at least three ten-pound notes.

Lucy wriggled out of bed and stared at the purse. 'That's Carla's.'

'Yes.' Eddie scooped up the conjuring set. He slipped it and the purse into the brown bag.

'What are you doing?'

Eddie stared at her. She looked enchanting in those pyjamas with the red stars on the deep yellow background; except that now the red stars made him think of splashes of blood. Everything was spoiled.

'I have to go out for a bit.'

'Stay with me,' she wheedled.

Eddie smiled at her. 'I wish I could.'

'I don't want Angel. I like you.'

'Angel's not here,' Eddie said, and then realized that this might be a mistake. 'She'll be back in a moment. She's just popped out.'

'Don't leave me.' Her face crumpled. 'Want Mummy. Take me to Mummy and Daddy.'

Eddie's legs gave way and he sank down on the bed. Lucy put her hand on his leg. He felt her warmth through the material of his jeans. None of the other little visitors had been so trusting.

'Nice Eddie,' she murmured encouragingly.

He found that he was staring at the door to the room of the freezer and the microwave. If he left Lucy here, she wouldn't be warm for much longer. In a very short time she would probably be as cold as ice. He couldn't leave Lucy to Angel. Yet he could hardly take her back to her parents' flat in Hercules Road or drop her in at the nearest police station. 'Hello, my name's Eddie Grace and this is a little girl called Lucy I kidnapped four days ago.' There must be a way round the problem. But his head hurt too much for him to find it immediately. He and Lucy needed time. They needed a place where they could go and where they would be safe from Angel, safe from the police, safe from Lucy's parents, safe from the whole world.

'Don't like Angel,' Lucy confided. 'I like *you*.'

Automatically he patted her hand. 'And I like you.'

Angel might come back at any moment. There was no time to waste. Lucy, the little coquette, was peeping up at him through her eyelashes in a way that reminded him of Alison all those years ago in Carver's.

Alison in Carver's. That was it: that was the answer, at least for the short term.

'We've got to get you dressed quickly if we're going out.' Eddie opened the chest of drawers and began to pull out clothes at random: jeans, socks, pants, vests, jerseys. All of them were new, all of them bought over the last few months by himself and Angel. 'Quick, quick. It will be cold outside so leave your pyjamas on.'

Lucy's surprise at this unorthodox way of getting dressed lasted only a few seconds. Then she decided to treat it as an exciting new game. The only problem was that there were no shoes. Eddie could not find the red leather boots which Lucy had been wearing when she came home with him. He had rather liked those boots. Then he remembered that in the cupboard in the basement there was a pair of lace-up shoes which had belonged to Suki. He got them out and tried them on Lucy. Lucy squealed excitedly at the idea of new shoes, partly because these were blue and decorated with green crocodiles. They were two or three sizes too large for her but she appeared not to mind. Eddie made up the difference with extra pairs of socks which would help to keep her warm.

'Going away?' Lucy asked as he helped her put on the second jersey. 'Never coming back?'

'That's right.'

'Never see Angel again?'

'No.' Eddie hoped he was speaking the truth. He ruffled her hair.

'I'm hungry. What's for breakfast?'

'I've got some food in the bag. We'll have breakfast after we've left.'

Lucy's eyes widened with excitement. She needed a moment to assimilate the information. Then: 'Jimmy? Mrs Wump?'

'You want to take them? Put them in the bag.'

She squatted and pulled open the bag. When she saw the

251

conjuring set, she sucked in her breath. 'Look – for me, Eddie? For me?'

'Yes.' Eddie added a few more clothes for Lucy. By this time the bag was bulging. 'We must go.'

'From Father Christmas?'

'Yes. Come on.'

In the hall Eddie hesitated, wondering whether to bolt the front door. It was already locked, but Angel would have taken her keys. He struggled to think out the implications. His head was hurting. Angel would come round to the back if the front door were bolted. She would guess that something was wrong, but not what. What if he bolted the back door, too, and if he and Lucy stayed inside the house? Would Angel break a window? Or ask Mr Reynolds for help?

Bolting the doors wouldn't be any use: either Angel would succeed in getting in, and be furious; or the uproar would lead to neighbours, even the police, coming in and finding Eddie with Lucy.

Better to go at once, to leave the house deserted and the front door unlocked. To his consternation, he found himself giggling at the idea of Angel walking into the house and finding that, in her absence, 29 Rosington Road had become the *Mary Celeste* of north-west London.

'What's funny?' Lucy asked.

Eddie took her hand and towed her towards the kitchen. 'Nothing important.'

'Where we going?'

He opened the back door and the cool air flooded in. 'We're going to my secret place. We're going to hide from Angel.'

Lucy did not reply, but her eyes seemed to grow larger with excitement and she jiggled up and down. Perhaps the absence of her morning dose of medication had made her livelier. Certainly, Eddie could not remember seeing her so vital before, even on that first evening when he saw her in Carla's backyard.

'Coat,' Lucy said. 'I need my coat.'

'Where is it?'

Lucy pointed towards her feet. 'Down there.'

'Wait here.' Eddie dropped the bag on the kitchen floor and hurried back into the hall and down the basement stairs. The green quilted coat was at the bottom of the chest of drawers. It had a hood, which would be useful, and as he carried it upstairs he discovered that there were gloves in the pocket.

The kitchen was empty. Panic attacked him and he began to tremble. Lucy had run away. Lucy had tricked him. She, too, had betrayed him. In the same instant, his mind filled with an unbearably vivid picture of her running down Rosington Road, her legs a blur, towards a uniformed policeman.

Lucy appeared in the doorway to the back garden. 'I saw a bird. A robin?'

He lunged at her and grabbed her by the shoulders. 'Don't do that. I didn't know where you were.'

She stared up at him but said nothing. He wondered how many times her parents had said those words to her. He wasn't Lucy's parent – he was her friend. He helped her into the coat and did up the zip and the buttons. Hand in hand, they walked into the garden. Eddie glanced up at the balcony of the Reynoldses' flat. It was empty. They reached the belt of trees at the bottom of the garden. In the distance a train went by. It was very quiet.

Eddie had not been down here since the previous summer. A faint track wound its way between the saplings and bushes – perhaps made by the fox. At the fence, Eddie pulled aside the lid of a wooden packing case which he had leant against the hole, partially blocking it. On the other side of the hole was a piece of wood he had manoeuvred into position to conceal its presence from anyone in Carver's. He poked his foot through the fence and kicked the wood over.

'Funny forest,' said Lucy, very seriously.

Eddie had put on weight since his last visit over six years earlier. The hole would be too narrow for him now. Lucy watched, fascinated, while he enlarged it. The surrounding wood had rotted still further, the damp creeping up from the earth. By pushing and kicking he managed to snap off enough of the neighbouring planks to widen the gap sufficiently for him to wriggle through.

'Angel cross?' Lucy suggested.

Eddie grunted non-committally, not wanting to frighten her unnecessarily. He wasn't sure whether she meant that Angel would be cross when she discovered the hole, or that Angel was already cross for other reasons. He picked up the bag and swung it through into Carver's.

'I'll go first.'

He crawled through the hole, making the knees of his jeans muddy. On the other side he turned, crouched down and held out a hand through the hole to Lucy. Without a moment's hesitation, she put her hand in his and stepped through. Eddie tried to conceal the gap in the fence with the packing-case lid. With a little luck, Angel would think that he and Lucy had left by the front door.

'There's a nice little shed through there.' Eddie pointed through the undergrowth. 'You can see the corner of it. It's like a house, isn't it? Let's go and explore.'

The fresh air was making him feel a little better. With the bag in his free hand, Eddie towed Lucy between the brambles and leafless branches. The ground was damp and mud clung to the soles of Eddie's trainers. Once he had to lift her over a fallen tree, and she floated as light as a feather in his arms, her face smiling down at his; and in that instant Eddie was as happy as he had ever been. They drew nearer to the shed.

'Is it a house?' Lucy asked, her voice full of doubt.

'It can be our house.'

Eddie hesitated in the doorway. Past collided with present. In memory it was always summer and the shed was in much better condition; he remembered it not as he had last seen it, but as he had known it with Alison. Now it was winter and the shed showed all too clearly the effects of exposure to the elements for over fifty years. Only a third of the roof was now left. The two ash saplings towered above the walls like a pair of gangling adolescents. The floor was a sea of dead leaves. The window opening had lost not only its glass but its frame as well. There was rubbish, too – more than before, which suggested that people were regularly finding their way into Carver's. Eddie glared at the empty cans and bottles, at the crisp packets and cigarette ends; they were blemishes on his privacy.

Lucy poked her head inside the doorway and looked around. She said nothing.

'We must tidy it up,' Eddie told her. 'Make it more homely.'

He noticed two tins which had once contained cement at the back of the shed. 'Look, they can be our seats. We'll put them under the bit with a roof.'

He set to work violently – pushing most of the leaves and rubbish into a heap against the wall underneath the window opening; setting the tins upside down so they could be used as seats; turning a wooden drawer on its side to serve as a table; and removing the worst of the cobwebs from the roof.

At first Lucy stood there, watching and sucking her fingers. After a moment, the magic of playing house affected her and they worked as a team. She fussed over the placing of the tins and the drawer, adjusting them, standing back to observe the results from afar, and then readjusting them. All the time she was doing this she hummed to herself, a made-up tune which consisted of three notes, monotonously repeated. He glanced covertly at her, marvelling at her absorption.

Lucy found a jam jar in the pile of rubbish, emptied out the brown water it contained and set it with a flourish on the table.

'It's a vase,' she informed him. 'For flowers.'

She darted out of the shed. There was a spindly mallow bush growing by the wall; it still had some leaves and even a few shrivelled flowers whose pink had rotted into a dark, funereal purple. She broke off a spray, brought it into the shed and stuck it into the jam jar.

'Lovely,' Eddie said. 'Very pretty.'

Lucy sat down on one of the tins and looked from the jam jar to Eddie. 'Is it time for breakfast?'

He sat down on the other tin, lifted the bag on to his lap and unzipped it. The exertion had brought back his illness in full force: he felt very dizzy, his eyeballs too large for their sockets. He put the packet of biscuits and a can of Coca-Cola on the table.

Lucy stared at them. 'For breakfast?'

Eddie opened the biscuits and removed the ring pull from the can. He waved his hand in a lordly gesture. 'Help yourself.'

Lucy looked worried. 'Mummy doesn't let me drink Coke. It's bad for your teeth.'

'This is a special treat.'

'Like on holiday?'

Eddie nodded. While she ate, Eddie hugged himself and tried to keep warm. He knew that he should be using this time to make plans, to avoid the opposing dangers of Angel and the police. Lucy was such a complication. He couldn't leave her and he couldn't take her with him. He stared at her and she lifted her head. Little white milk teeth chewed the biscuit. She smiled at him and picked up the Coke.

He decided to explore the contents of the bag again. If he were by himself, and if the police weren't looking for him, everything would be straightforward. He had several thousand pounds in his bank account and his building society account. He had his driving licence. He could go anywhere in the country, even apply for a passport and go abroad, and Angel wouldn't be able to find him. He could hire a solicitor who would evict Angel from the house. His mind shied away from considering what she would do with the contents of the freezer in the basement; take them with her, presumably. If necessary he would leave the house and start a new life somewhere else. The prospect was unexpectedly attractive: a new Eddie, away from Rosington Road, away from Angel, away from all the memories; anything might be possible.

But not with Lucy. The police were looking for her. These days there were video cameras everywhere – in banks, building societies, shopping centres. He could not take her anywhere without the risk of being seen.

While he was thinking, his fingers dug restlessly into the contents of the bag. He came up with Carla's purse. He opened it to count the cash it contained. There were credit cards, too, but he couldn't use those. Carla was an untidy woman, he thought disapprovingly. The purse was full of things which needn't be there at all. There were old receipts and credit-card slips, some going back for months. There were books of stamps, now empty. There were library tickets and photographs of small children. There were scraps of paper with telephone numbers and addresses scribbled on them. The woman should have had the sense to buy an address book. He stared at one of the pieces of paper, smoothing it out, his mind elsewhere. Suddenly his eyes focused on the writing: *Sally Appleyard*. Underneath was the address in Hercules Road and the flat's phone number. There were three other phone numbers: one was Michael's at work, complete with an extension; the second was in Kensal Vale, judging by the three-digit preface, and the third was for a mobile phone.

'Eddie,' Lucy said. 'Is it Christmas yet?'

'Not for about three weeks. Why?'

'Have I got to wait till then? For the magic set?'

'No – not necessarily. Would you like it now?'

'Can I? Won't he mind?'

'Who?'

'Father Christmas.'

'No, he won't. It's OK for you to have it now.'

He handed her the conjuring set, an oblong cardboard box. On the outside of the box was a colour photograph of a small, fair-haired boy in a long black cape; smiling broadly, he was in the act of tapping an inverted top hat with a wand; what looked like a pink rabbit was peeping coyly out of the hat. Lucy's fingers tore impotently at the packaging.

'Let me.'

Reluctantly, she returned the set to him. The ends were held down with Sellotape, which he slit with his thumbnail. He eased the end out and handed the box back to Lucy. She did not thank him. He did not mind. He knew that her entire attention was focused on the conjuring set.

Lucy shook the contents on to the table. They looked much less impressive than in the picture on the box. There was a pink, long-haired toy rabbit about the size of a well-nourished mouse. The wand was cardboard and had a kink in the middle. There was a polythene bag full of oddments, chiefly made of cardboard and plastic. Among them Eddie noticed three miniature playing cards and a purple thimble. Finally there were the instructions, a small booklet with smudgy print on poor-quality paper. Lucy glanced at him and then back at the conjuring set. He guessed that she was trying desperately to preserve her excitement in the face of disappointment. How do you explain to a four-year-old that it is better to travel hopefully than to arrive?

'No hat,' she pointed out, her lips trembling.

'Perhaps we can borrow one.'

Eddie tried to think constructively about what to do next. He couldn't concentrate. He stared instead at Lucy's hands as they picked their way through the contents of the conjuring set. Her head was bowed. The strange rigidity of her position told its own story.

'Lucy. Shall I help?'

She looked up. Her face was bright and her eyes gleamed with tears. Wordlessly, she pushed the instruction booklet towards him. He picked it up and opened it at random. The words looked like little insects, flies perhaps. They were moving. Some of them took off from the page as if to attack his mind. Some of the words made phrases. *Astonish your friends*. Why should you want to do that? *Hold card in place with thumb so audience see nothing*. Eddie turned over a page and found more insects, swarming as if feeding from an open wound. *A simple but effective trick* . . .His eyes slid diagonally across the page. *It will be the Queen of Spades*.

'I want to do the card trick. Why is it so hard?'

'I don't know,' Eddie said, thinking that it was hard because things were always harder than you thought they were going to be. 'I'll see if I can find out how to do it.'

There were three cards provided, about a third of the size of normal playing cards; one of them was double-sided. Eddie struggled to match them up with the instructions and the accompanying diagram. The writer of the booklet seemed to be labouring under the delusion that there were five cards, not three. Nor was English the writer's first language. While Eddie was working on the card trick, another part of his mind was wondering what he was going to do. His hands were growing colder. They couldn't stay here indefinitely. It was winter.

'Hurry up,' urged Lucy.

She must have had a vision of herself as a magician, looking like the boy on the box and effortlessly astonishing her friends and relations. How could the reality ever measure up to the anticipation? Perhaps it would have been wiser to have made her wait.

'I think you do it like this.' Eddie fanned out the three cards in his hand, their faces towards Lucy. 'You see – the Queen of Spades is the one in the middle.'

She looked blankly at him and he realized belatedly that she did not know what the Queen of Spades was. He laid the cards on the table and explained what each one was called. She nodded, frowning. Then he made up a version of the trick. You showed your audience the three cards and then hid them under the box. Then you waved your wand and said *Abracadabra*. Next you asked the audience to tell you which of the concealed cards was the Queen of Spades – the card on the right, the card on the left or the card in the middle. The audience thought they knew – but you fooled them, because the Queen of Spades was a double-sided card, and you had cunningly turned it over as you slid it under the box. On the other side of the Queen of Spades was the Two of Hearts and you showed them that instead. You made them think that the Queen of Spades had disappeared.

'Is that all?' Lucy asked when Eddie had finished explaining.

'Yes.'

She said nothing.

'You don't like it?'

She wriggled on the tin. 'It's all right. Where's the toilet?'

'There isn't one.'

The wriggling became more pronounced. 'But I need to go.'

'You'll have to do it outside.'

Lucy stared at him, her face shocked, but did not object. He led her outside, and with Eddie's help she managed to relieve herself in the angle between the mallow bush and the shed. He worried continuously – that she would wet herself, that she would catch cold, that someone would see them. Because it was winter, there was less cover than he had expected.

When Lucy had finished, he hurried her back into the shed and then helped her to dress herself again. It was the hurrying rather than having to pee outside that upset her. She began to cry. Eddie gave her Mrs Wump and Jimmy and sat her on his knee and put his arms around her. He felt her trembling gradually subside. The only sound was the soft *click-click* as she sucked her fingers. He rested his chin gently on the top of Lucy's head.

'Lucy? What do you want?'

There was a long silence – so long that he wondered whether she had not heard. Then she said, very clearly, 'Mummy.'

'Yes. All right.'

'I can go home?' The joy in her face was almost more than he could bear. 'Now? To Mummy and Daddy?' She slid off his knee and stood up. The playing cards fluttered to the cracked concrete floor. 'Shall we get a bus?'

He took her hands in his and shook them gently. 'It's not quite as easy as that.' He could see what to do now – not a perfect plan, by any means, but the least of the available evils. 'I need to go and phone her. I'll ask her to come here.' Lucy's hands were cold too, even colder than his. 'Will you be all right here while I go and phone?'

'I want to come with you.'

'It's not possible. You have to stay here.'

He could not risk being seen with her in the street. She stared at him, her lip quivering, but said nothing. She did not ask for reasons. She heard the finality in his voice and accepted it. He stood up and took off his coat.

'You must stay in the shed while I'm gone.' He made her sit down and wrapped the coat around her.

'And them.' Lucy held up Jimmy and Mrs Wump.

Eddie tucked an arm of the coat around the two toys. Lucy lifted them both to her face, pushed two fingers into her mouth and shut her eyes. He picked up Carla's purse; the phone numbers were there, and also change and even a phone card. 'I won't be long – I promise.' He bent down and kissed the top of her head.

He left her, small and forlorn, in the shed. His problems began immediately. If he went back through the hole in the fence, there was a danger that Angel might have returned and he would walk into a trap. In any case, he could not use the phone in the house. The police would probably be able to trace the call. The wisest course would be to find another way out of Carver's and use a public telephone box.

He moved slowly westwards, keeping the fences of the Rosington Road gardens on his left. It would have been difficult at the best of times. The further into the site, the more overgrown it became. Nature had partly masked the hazards of brick, concrete and rusting iron. Brambles slashed at his clothes and tore the skin on the back of his hands. He missed his coat. It

260

began to rain, fine drops of moisture which drifted like powder from the dense grey sky. As he walked, he searched in vain for a gap in the fence on the left.

After what seemed like hours he stumbled on the main gates, which were in the south-west corner of the site. They were surprisingly narrow – two sheets of metal mounted on a cast-iron frame, surmounted by rows and rows of barbed wire. On either side were brick pillars topped with spikes. There was a wicket in the left-hand leaf of the gates, secured by bolts and a large padlock.

Eddie wondered what to do. Nowadays there was no other way into Carver's. They had torn up the railway tracks inside the works and fenced off the lines to the north. The place was like a fortress or a prison. He ran his eyes along the western boundary of the site: this was a high brick wall, similar to the one that divided the eastern side of the site from the council flats but in less good condition. It might be possible to climb it. But on the other side was a terrace of shops on Bishop's Road. Presumably there would be yards behind the shops. Even if he managed to get over the wall, he would then have the problem of getting from a yard to the road.

His eyes on the top of the wall, he stumbled on a loose brick and almost fell. His head swimming, he bent down and worked the brick out of the mud into which it was impacted. There was a colony of woodlice underneath. His skin crawled. He dropped the brick and most of the woodlice clinging to it fell off. He scraped the remainder away with a stick. Perhaps brute force was the answer.

Eddie carried the brick carefully towards the gates. It felt cold, hard and heavy, and its jagged edges hurt the skin of his hands.

He stopped beside the wicket. If there was no one on the other side, it might be all right. The sound of banging during the day was not in itself suspicious. He raised the brick in both hands and brought it down on the padlock. There was a dull clang. The brick twisted painfully out of his hands and fell to the ground. Just in time, he jumped backwards before it dropped on his feet. Flecks of blood oozed from a graze on the side of his left thumb. The padlock was hardly marked.

Steeling himself against the pain, Eddie picked up the brick and tried again, this time more cautiously. The brick did not fall. Once again, the padlock was undamaged. But the rusting staple to which it was attached was now bent at a slight angle. He hit the padlock again and again, building up to a rhythm. Air laboured in and out of his lungs and the pain seared his hands like flames.

Finally the staple gave way. The padlock fell to the ground; apart from a few scratches, it showed no signs of the ordeal to which it had been subjected. Eddie opened the hasp and then worked the bolts to and fro until they too moved back. He lifted the latch and the wicket gate opened.

He stepped warily into the alley beyond, half-expecting to find a squad of policemen waiting for him. He closed the wicket behind him and walked away. Both his hands were bleeding now so he stuffed them in his pockets. Brick walls reared up on either side – to the right was the yard belonging to the end shop of the terrace in Bishop's Road; and to the left was the playground of the infants' school on the corner of Rosington Road and Bishop's Road.

The mouth of the alley was on Bishop's Road. Eddie hesitated on the corner, feeling extraordinarily conspicuous. The pavement was crowded. Cars, vans and lorries rumbled up and down the road. He feared that everyone was looking at him.

He took a deep breath and began to hurry along the pavement after the bus. Ahead of him the road rose towards the railway bridge. There were two public telephone boxes beside the bridge. As he walked, Eddie kept his face turned towards the windows of the shops in case Angel passed by in the van. The cold made his eyes water.

At last he reached the telephone boxes. One was in use but the other was empty. He hurried inside, relieved to have some shelter from the wind, relieved not to be exposed to the curious eyes on the street. The box took phone cards, so he fed Carla's into the slot. He dialled the Hercules Road number first.

The phone was answered on the second ring. 'Hello.'

Eddie said nothing. He wasn't sure, but he didn't think that the voice belonged to Sally Appleyard: it sounded higher-pitched.

'Hello. Who's speaking, please?'

It definitely wasn't Sally's. There was a hint of a Welsh accent. He put the phone down hastily. A friend? A police officer? He tapped in the Kensal Vale number.

'St George's Vicarage. Derek Cutter speaking.'

Once again, Eddie broke the connection. He felt foolish. Of course Lucy's mother wouldn't be at work at a time like this. He wanted to cry. Why were they making it so hard for him to help Lucy? Why was it so difficult to do a kind action? If there were a God, you would think he'd make it easy to be good.

Slowly he pushed the buttons for the mobile's number. While it was ringing, he allowed himself to think for the first time what would happen if he could not get through to Sally Appleyard. The problems multiplied. Then the phone was answered.

'Appleyard.'

Michael Appleyard, not his wife. Eddie said, 'Is Sally there?' Panic made his voice sound even higher-pitched than usual. 'I want to speak to *her*.'

'I can take a message. Who is this?'

Suddenly the future seemed inevitable: it swept down on Eddie like a tidal wave. 'I know where Lucy is.'

'Where?'

'It's all a mistake,' Eddie heard himself saying. 'Lucy mustn't be hurt.'

'Why should I believe you? How do I know this isn't just a hoax?'

The injustice took Eddie's breath away for a moment. He was only trying to help. 'She's wearing the dark-green quilted coat she was wearing at Carla's. I found this number in Carla's purse.' His voice sounded petulant. 'Now do you believe me?'

'I believe you. Is she all right?'

'She's fine, I promise.'

'When did you last see her?'

'Ten minutes ago? Fifteen? I left her playing with a conjuring set.'

There was a sound on the other end of the line which at first Eddie couldn't identify; a second later, he wondered if it might have been a sob.

'You can come and get her,' Eddie said. 'But don't tell the police. Don't bring them. Promise?'

'I promise.'

'If you do,' Eddie said as menacingly as he could manage, 'you'll regret it. Lucy will regret it. No police. Not if you want to see her alive.'

'All right. But where is she?'

'Do you know Bishop's Road in Kentish Town?'

'I'll find it.'

'There's a school just south of the railway. Beside the school, there's a lane leading to an old engineering works. It's called Carver's. She's in there.'

With a surge of optimism, Eddie slung the handset back on its rest. *I've done it. Everything's going to be all right.* The phone card emerged like a tongue from its slot. As he pulled it out he noticed that it was smeared with his blood. *Whose blood on the moussaka packet?* He would walk down to the bus stop, climb on the next bus and let other people sort out the mess that Angel had made. He was sorry that he would never see Lucy again, but this way was best for everyone.

He pushed open the door of the telephone box. The cold air hit him. With it came the realization that he had miscalculated.

Eddie ran all the way back to Carver's. As he ducked into the mouth of the alley, Mr Reynolds's van passed him, signalling left for the turning beyond the school into Rosington Road.

He didn't see me. Please God he didn't see me.

Eddie reached Carver's gates. Relief washed over him as he pulled the wicket closed behind him. Carver's felt safe. He took a few steps towards the shed and then stopped. He leant against the fence, bent over and retched unproductively. The stitch dug deep into his side. He was panting so hard that for a moment he thought his heart would pack up, just as his mother's had. The nausea came in waves. His head hurt. Entwined with the physical distress was the urgency of panic. He felt his forehead: so hot you could cook an egg on it.

He picked his way through the wilderness towards the shed. He hadn't been thinking straight. He couldn't walk away from Lucy and leave her in Carver's: not without the brown bag, not with Lucy just a few yards from the fence leading to 29 Rosington Road, not without his money.

With luck there should be enough time to do what he needed to do before Michael Appleyard arrived. Eddie planned to take Lucy and the bag away from the shed and lead her by a roundabout route to the gates. He would leave her there, just inside, with Jimmy and the rest of her things. She would come to no harm: her father would soon reach her. There was, of course, the risk that Lucy would be able to lead the police to the back garden of Rosington Road. It was a risk that had to be run. The more he confused her about the geography of Carver's, the safer he would be. In any case, if the worst came to the worst, and the police raided 29 Rosington Road, then they would find Angel there, Angel and the contents of her freezer. He would be far away. Once he was better, once his temperature was normal and he had regained his strength – that would be the time to consider what to do for the best.

The journey back seemed shorter than the journey out had been. Eddie saw the silhouette of the shed looming. He glanced upwards, and for a moment he thought he saw movement on the balcony of the Reynoldses' flat. *I'm imagining things.* That was the trouble with a fever: the boundary between the world within your head and the world outside was not as effective as usual; it was still there, but it was porous. An event inside could become an event outside, and vice versa. Eddie tripped over a root and fell flat on his face. *Must concentrate. Must concentrate.*

Eddie picked himself up and hurried on. He was dimly aware that his clothes were wet and muddy. He wanted someone to look after him. Into his mind flashed a picture: someone large, kind and faceless urging him into a warm bath, making him a drink, slipping a hot-water bottle into a bed with Mrs Wump on the pillow.

The shed was very close now. Eddie heard a high-pitched wail. For an instant, he thought the wail was inside his mind – a sound of disappointment, because the bath, the hot-water bottle and the bed weren't real after all.

Lucy was crying. Eddie put on a spurt of speed. Tripping over tree roots, skidding in the mud, he flung himself towards the shed. The crying continued. The grief of children was unconditional, fuelled by the implicit belief that it would last for ever; for a child, grief was not grief unless it was eternal.

He stopped in the doorway of the shed. Lucy was sitting where he had left her, clutching herself, hunched over the makeshift table. Her tears fell on the conjuring set. The vase had fallen to the floor. Her face was white, tinged with green. It seemed rounder than usual, the features less well-formed, the eyes smaller. That was another effect of grief on children: it made them a little less human.

'Lucy, darling.'

He picked her up, sat down on the other cement tin and held her on his lap. Her arms clung to his neck. She rammed her face painfully against his cheek. The sobbing continued, violent surges of emotion that rippled through her whole body. He patted her back and mumbled endearments.

Gradually the sobbing grew quieter. As the crying diminished, Lucy went through a stage of making mewing noises like a kitten. Then the sounds turned to words.

'Mummy. I want Mummy. Daddy.'

After a while, Eddie said, 'I've just talked to your daddy on the phone. He's –'

'You left me alone.' Lucy let out another wail. 'I thought you weren't coming back.'

'Of course I was coming back.'

'Don't leave me. Don't leave me.'

'I won't, I promise.' He had spoken without thinking. Of course he would have to leave her. 'Your daddy's coming to collect you. He'll take you home to Mummy.'

'Don't leave me.' Lucy seemed not to have understood what he had said – either that or she had automatically dismissed it as meaningless. 'I'm cold.'

Still holding her, Eddie leant forward and picked up his coat, which had fallen on the floor. With his free hand he wrapped it clumsily round her shoulders. Automatically he rocked her to and fro, to and fro. Lucy's breath was warm on his cheek.

'I must go.' Eddie felt the arms tighten round his neck. 'We must go.'

Lucy shook her head violently. 'Want a drink.'

Eddie leant down and picked up the can of Coca-Cola from

the floor. Judging by the weight, it was well over half-full. He handed it to her. Leaving one arm round his neck, she pulled away from him a little. She drank greedily, her eyes glancing at him every few seconds, as if she feared he might try to take the can away. He stroked her back.

Time trickled away. Eddie's head hurt. Part of his mind rose above the pain and the fear and surveyed his situation from a lordly elevation. Every moment that passed increased the risk he was running. But how could he leave Lucy before she was ready? She needed him. What would it be like if the worst happened and the police arrested him and he was eventually sent to jail? He knew that prisons were foul and overcrowded, and that sex offenders were traditionally picked on by the other prisoners; and that those whose offences had involved children were the most hated of all and were subjected to unimaginable brutalities.

'Eddie?' Lucy held out the can to him. 'There's some for you.'

He disliked Coca-Cola but on impulse he nodded and took the can from her. She rewarded him with a smile. For an instant the roles were reversed: she was looking after him. He drank, and the fizzy liquid ran down his throat and refreshed him unexpectedly. He lowered the can from his lips.

'Drink,' Lucy commanded. 'For you.'

He smiled at her and obeyed. When the can was empty, he rested it against his cheek and the cool of the metal soothed him. Lucy slithered off his knee and picked up the wand from the conjuring set.

'Let's do more magic.'

Eddie stood up suddenly. The dizziness returned. He leant against the wall to support himself. 'There's no time. We must go.'

'To Daddy?'

Eddie nodded. He bent down and pushed their belongings into the bag.

'And Mummy?'

'Yes.' He straightened up, his head swimming, with the bag in one hand. 'Come on.'

Lucy refused to be parted from Jimmy, Mrs Wump and the

conjuring set. She clasped them in her arms and allowed him to push her gently towards the doorway. But as she reached it, she gave a whimper. Instantly she backed away. Eddie heard footsteps among the dead leaves. A branch cracked. Then he saw what she had seen.

'No,' Lucy whispered, retreating to the corner of the shed furthest from the door. 'No, no, no.'

'We'll go in a minute,' Eddie said to her. 'See if you can find the magic wand and learn another trick.'

He stood in the doorway. Angel had stopped just outside the shed. She was wearing her long white raincoat with the hood. Her lips were drawn back and her face was lined and old.

'And where are you thinking of going?' she asked, her voice soft.

'I – I'm taking Lucy away.' The words came out in a trembling whisper. 'She's going home.'

'I don't think so.'

Eddie stared at Angel, desperately wishing to do as she wanted. 'She's going home. No one need know.'

'About what?'

Eddie gestured towards the house. 'About all this.'

'You're a fool. Mr Reynolds saw you in Bishop's Road. He said you were coming out of a phone box. Who were you phoning?'

Eddie felt sweat break out all over his body. 'No one.'

'Don't be absurd. If you didn't phone from the house, it means you didn't want the call traced. So you were phoning the police.'

'I wasn't.'

'You're lying.'

Angel turned her body slightly. The full skirt of her raincoat had concealed her right hand. Now Eddie saw not only the hand but what it was holding: the hatchet, the one that his mother had used on Stanley's last dolls' house. He had not seen it for years. Most of the blade was dull and flecked with rust, as it had been before. But not the cutting edge. This was now a streak of silver. He thought of the joints of meat in the freezer and of the three lives, cut into pieces, wrecked beyond repair like the dolls' house.

Behind him, Eddie heard Lucy murmur, 'Abracadabra. Now you're a prince.'

'What have you told them?' Angel said, swinging the hatchet to and fro.

'Nothing. I haven't phoned the police. I promise. I just want Lucy to go home so I tried to phone her mother but she wasn't in.'

Angel hit him on the collarbone with the hatchet. He heard the bone snap. He heard himself scream, too. Then she hit him again, this time on the side of the head. He fell against the jamb of the doorway and slid slowly to the ground.

He wanted to turn to Lucy and say, 'It's OK. Your daddy's coming.'

Angel lifted the hatchet once more. Warm liquid trickled down Eddie's left cheek. There was a great deal of pain, which swamped the headache completely. Men were shouting in his mind. Were they cheering or condemning him? He heard cracking and rustling, the sounds of fire devouring wood. He burned. Angel was no longer beautiful, but an old, foul woman, a witch, an avenging fury. The blade was descending. There was blood now on the silver edge.

Two men were running towards Angel. It was all just a dream. When you had a fever, you had terrible dreams. A man was screaming and screaming. Eddie wished the man would stop. The sound might frighten Lucy. She had been frightened enough already.

A thunderbolt hit him. The force drove his body deep into the ground, into a lake of fire with flames streaking across the surface. There was a bubbling sound. He could not breathe. Someone hung a piece of red gauze across his eyes.

Finally, the flames died, the sun went down, and the grown-ups switched off the light.

13

'This is the day whose memory hath onely power to make us honest in the dark, and to be vertuous without a witness.'

Religio Medici, I, 47

'Do you think Michael's already there?' Sally asked. 'Oh God, I hope he is.'

Oliver turned into Bishop's Road. He was driving far too fast and the Citroën tilted dangerously towards the near side. 'Could be. Depends on the traffic.'

Michael had used the mobile to call Inkerman Street. He had phoned just after Sally and Oliver returned from Hampstead Heath; Oliver had taken the call. Michael had been in Ladbroke Grove with David and Bishop Hudson when the kidnapper phoned, because Maxham had sent him away with a flea in his ear.

'But Michael hasn't got a car,' Sally wailed.

'Hudson lent them his.' As Oliver drove, his eyes flicked from side to side of the road. 'It must be here. There's nowhere else.'

He swung the wheel round and the Citroën cut across the stream of oncoming traffic. A horn squealed. The car surged into the little alley. Sally registered the frightened face of a woman they had nearly knocked down. The woman's shopping bag lay on the pavement, disgorging tins and packets.

The car rocked and jolted in and out of ruts and potholes. Sally saw a school on the corner, its playground empty. Next came high brick walls on either side. The alley curved round a corner. Oliver braked hard.

Immediately in front of them was a small, white car, parked at an angle across the alley, the driver's door hanging open. Beyond the car was a pair of high metal gates between tall brick posts.

Oliver pulled up alongside the other vehicle. Sally leapt out, pushing her door so vigorously that it collided with the open door of the white car. She noticed in passing that the keys were still in the car's ignition, and that on the back seat there was a black umbrella and a copy of the *Church Times*. She broke into a run.

'Where's Maxham?' said Oliver behind her. 'He should have got the local boys here by now.'

There was still a notice on one of the gateposts.

JW & TB CARVER & Co LTD.
RAILWAY ENGINEERING
ALL VISITORS MUST REPORT TO THE OFFICE

She raised the latch of the wicket gate. It swung outwards.

'Sally – let me go first.'

Ignoring him, she stepped through the opening into the wilderness beyond. Even in winter, the predominant colour was green. The remains of the buildings were barely visible. For the time being, nature had the upper hand.

'It's huge,' Oliver said behind her. 'We'd better try shouting.'

'No.' Sally pointed to the ground. There were footprints in the mud leading away from the gates on a course roughly parallel with the fence to the right. 'They're fresh.'

'Padlock's smashed. From the inside.'

Sally was studying the mud. 'There's such a jumble here.' Her voice rose. 'I can't tell if any of them belongs to a child.'

Oliver joined her. 'Looks like three people. One in trainers.' He pointed. Then his finger moved. 'Trainers go both ways, to and from the gate. Another pair of shoes with smooth soles. Size eight or nine.'

'David's? That one's Michael's, I think.' She too pointed, at a single footprint from a moulded sole, as crisp and unblemished as a plaster cast. 'See? So maybe the trainers belong to the man who phoned Michael.'

271

'He said it might have been a woman.' Oliver straightened up. 'Or a man trying to pitch his voice high. They're small enough for a woman's.'

As they talked, they were moving, casting about, trying to find more footprints. They kept their voices low, almost at the level of a whisper.

'Here.' Oliver set off at a run.

Sally followed. She stumbled several times, and once she fell, bruising her shoulder against an abandoned oil drum. She was praying, too, if you could call the word 'please', repeated over and over again, a prayer.

They crossed a patch of open ground. For a moment Sally could see ahead. She glimpsed a high wall and beyond it grey blocks of flats, faced with weather-mottled concrete. A woman was standing on one of the balconies and Sally clearly saw binoculars in her hand. *A ghoul.* The woman was looking at something below her at a point roughly midway on a line between herself and Sally. Then the wall, the flats and the woman were gone.

Sally plunged after Oliver into a thicket of brambles and saplings. Thorns tore at her clothes, her hands and her face. Oliver tripped over a fallen branch and fell head first into a clump of nettles. He swore. Sally overtook him and struggled out of the embrace of the thicket.

She found herself on what once might have been a path. Crumbling concrete was visible among the mud and the puddles; so too were more footprints, including those of the trainers. In the distance was a small brick building, almost roofless. Sally ran towards it. She was almost there when she heard Michael's voice say, 'Drop it, please. Drop it on the ground.'

She put on a final rush of speed and burst round the corner of the building. Her first impression was of a bright, vivid redness.

Michael and David were five yards away. They did not look at Sally. Their eyes were on the woman in the doorway.

For an instant Sally thought that it was Miss Oliphant, the woman who had cursed Sally and later killed herself; whom Sally had last seen on her deathbed.

But only for an instant. Then a form of reality took over,

and that was even worse because this woman was so clearly a part of a recognizable world. Like Miss Oliphant, this woman wore a long raincoat and a black beret, but there were few other similarities. Sally had never seen her before. She was tall and slender, with long, pale hair. Her face was pinched, the skin glowing with angry red blotches, the teeth and the eyes unnaturally prominent. In her hand she carried a sort of axe with a tall blade which at the end curved into a hook.

Around the woman was a pool of blood. There was so much of it. Pints and pints and pints. It had sprayed over the wall of the shed, the jamb of the doorway and the long skirt and arms of the woman's raincoat. Those were not blotches on her face, but splashes of blood.

Sally had not known there could be so much blood in this world, let alone in one person. Frozen with shock, she stared at the scene in front of her. It took her a moment to realize that a man was lying on his back in the pool.

He was at the woman's feet, one arm almost touching her left shoe, his legs across the threshold of the doorway and his body along the base of the wall. Sally's eyes travelled up the body. The man's head no longer fitted on his shoulders.

The blood had come from the side of his neck. It was still flowing, but only just: pumping out sluggishly over the ground. Carotid artery, Sally thought automatically. Far too late to do anything. Not that she really cared about the man on the ground or the woman in the doorway or even Michael and David.

'Where's Lucy?'

The woman, who had been staring as if fascinated at Michael and David, glanced at her.

'Sssh,' the woman whispered. 'She mustn't see.' She waved the hatchet in the direction of the body. 'It would inflict terrible psychological damage. With a child that age, the scar would remain for life. Surely you know that?'

'If you put down the hatchet,' Michael suggested, sounding unbelievably calm and relaxed, 'we could cover it with my coat.'

Oliver stumbled round the corner of the shed. Sally put a hand on his arm.

'I had to kill him,' the woman said. 'He was going to kill the

273

little girl, you know. It was the only way to stop him. He's done terrible things to little girls in the past. Terrible,' she repeated, in a slower, deeper voice like a clock running down, 'terrible, terrible.'

'How do you know?' Michael asked.

'I rent a room in his house.' The voice was middle class, rather musical. 'His name's Edward Grace. I've been there for five or six years. But until today I hadn't the faintest idea what he was up to.'

Sally knew that the woman was lying, that she was talking not to convince them but to gain time. 'May I see Lucy now?'

The head of the hatchet swung in Sally's direction. 'In a moment.' Her eyes slid down to what lay at her feet. 'The pervert – do you think he's dead yet?'

The blood was no longer flowing.

'Almost certainly,' Michael said. 'And if he isn't, he soon will be. Now – if you put the hatchet on the ground –'

'You.' The woman pointed the hatchet at David Byfield. 'You can see her if you want. Come here.'

For the first time Sally looked at David. His face was extraordinarily pale.

'Yes,' the woman said to him in a flat voice. 'I want *you* to see her.'

He looked steadily at her but did not move. The pair of them reminded Sally of wrestlers studying each other in the few seconds before the fight began. And when the bell rang, the false stillness would vanish and everything would change.

God does not change. But we do.

The words came from nowhere. Time once again was paralysed. The silence was total. As time could not move, all time was present. This is where it began, Sally thought, with Miss Oliphant in St George's; and in the beginning was this end.

She saw David's face and saw behind it to the pain and the guilt beyond. Why all that guilt? What had he done to deserve it? She saw the woman's face and saw that it was almost a mirror image of David's, except that there was no guilt within her, only pain streaked with anger, and more pain beyond, dark, dense, impacted like a seam of coal.

'Your will be done,' Sally said, or thought she said. 'Not mine.'

As if the words were a signal, time began to flow once more.

'*Mummy*.'

The tableau broke into pieces. Lucy was standing at the far corner of the shed, on the woman's right. In her hand she held three minuscule playing cards.

'Lucy,' the woman snapped, 'did you climb through the window?'

Lucy stared open-mouthed at the stern face.

'I thought I told you to stay inside. Naughty girls have to be smacked.'

Sally thought: *Lucy mustn't see that man on the ground*. The desperate importance of that overrode everything else: all the blood and that horrible body – it wasn't something for a child to see.

She flung herself at Lucy. Somehow she found the time to hope that the woman herself would be a barrier between Lucy's eyes and that terrible, ghastly mess on the ground.

She was aware, too, of a flurry of movement behind her. Oliver, Michael and David were converging on the woman in the doorway of the shed.

The woman lifted the axe and swung it towards Sally. There was all the time in the world to notice the lazy arc of the blade. The shortest route to Lucy would take Sally within a yard of the woman, well within her reach. The need to be with Lucy was more important than the need to avoid a blow.

The hatchet slammed into Sally's left arm halfway between the shoulder and the elbow. She gasped, but as a moving target she missed the worst of the force of the blow. She swept her daughter into her arms. Lucy cried out as the air was driven out of her.

Sally threw her round the corner of the shed. Lucy lay on her back, her arms and legs wide, in a pose that mimicked the dead man's. Sally flung herself on top of her daughter.

'It's all right. It's all right. I'm here now.' Sally burst into tears. Between sobs the words continued to stagger out of her mouth as though by their own volition. 'It's all right, darling, it's all right. Mummy's here. It's all right . . .'

Lucy lay very still and said nothing. One of the playing cards, a Two of Hearts, had fallen beside her head. People were shouting and crying, but they did not matter. Lucy smelled different from before, impregnated with the aromas of strange people and places. For an instant Sally was on the edge of despair: perhaps all this had been in vain; perhaps she had saved not Lucy but some other child.

After a while, the shouting and the screaming stopped. For a few seconds the world was quiet. The tears ran down Sally's face and splashed on to the shorn, dark hair.

At last Lucy stirred. She looked up at her mother and said, 'Mummy. I can do magic.'

EPILOGUE

'There are wonders in true affection: it is a body of *Enigma*'s,
mysteries and riddles . . .'

Religio Medici, II, 6

The chapel was little more than a room full of chairs with a
crucifix on the far wall. The Reverend David Byfield lowered
himself slowly on to one of the red, plastic seats. The chaplain
sat down nearby, angling her chair so she was at right angles
to him.

'There's no change.' She touched the pectoral cross she wore.
'She spends most of her free time either praying or reading
the Bible.'

'How does she behave with the others?'

'She has as little to do with them as possible. It's not that she's
rude or difficult about it. She simply ignores them. Some of them
call her "Lady Muck". But not to her face.'

'I suppose the question is whether the repentance is sincere.'

'It's very difficult to tell, Father.' The chaplain was meticulously courteous. 'The psychiatrist isn't convinced. As you know,
there's a history of manipulation, and he feels that this may be
one more example of it.'

'He's probably right.' David stared at his hands, knotted
together on his lap, the fingers like a tangle of roots. 'But we
have to bear in mind the possibility that she means it.'

'Of course. Another point that concerns him is that she still
won't use her own name. She insists on being called Angel. By
everyone.'

The silence between them lengthened. It was restful, not uncomfortable. David thought that the woman was probably praying. She was in her fifties, he guessed, short and stout, swathed in shapeless clothes. Before ordination, she had run one of the larger children's charities.

At length, he stirred and asked the question he had wanted to ask on previous visits. 'Does she ever mention me?'

'Not that I know. She mentions no one from the past. It's as if her life began when she came here.' The woman leant forward. 'Would you like us to pray?'

'No.' David looked up. 'Don't think me rude. Perhaps after I've seen her.'

The chaplain nodded.

After a moment, David said, 'Sally tells me that you and she were ordinands together at Westcott House.'

'Yes, though I didn't know her well. How is she? And the rest of the family?'

'Things have calmed down a little.'

'And Lucy?'

'It will take time. She's changed.'

'We can pray for healing, but not to turn the clock back.'

'Just so.' David shrugged. 'When Lucy prays at night, she wants to pray for the man Grace. She adds him to the list, along with Mummy and Daddy.' He paused. 'And Father Christmas.'

'Why does she pray for him?'

'She liked him. He gave her a conjuring set and some sort of cuddly toy. She's still got them. She's very attached to them.'

'It must be hard for Sally and Michael to accept.'

'That and the uncertainty. No one really knows what was happening in that house. No one knows how it's going to end. Michael's leaving the police. Did you know?'

She nodded.

'It's his own choice.' He knew he must sound defensive and was mildly surprised to discover that he did not care. 'There's no question of his being forced to resign.'

'What's he going to do?'

'He hasn't made up his mind. Sally's still on leave. But they can't go on like this for ever. They're in limbo.'

'At least they have Lucy.'

David was tempted to pass on the news he had heard the previous evening: that Sally was pregnant. But it wasn't his news, and in any case, it was a long step between conception and birth. For a few moments neither of them spoke.

'It's almost time,' the chaplain said at last.

David followed her out of the chapel and along a corridor that seemed to stretch for miles. The place smelled like a school. Summer sunlight streamed through high windows. The security was omnipresent, though unobtrusive. The chaplain led him to the interview room they had used before. She conferred with the warder on duty.

The warder stared blankly at David. 'You can see her now.'

Angel was sitting at the table, examining her hands, which lay palms downwards on the metal surface. She looked up as David came in. He thought she might have put on weight. She wore no make-up. Her face was pink and unlined.

With sudden clarity he saw the child she had once been. In his mind he saw her running down the path towards the garden door into the house, saw her looking up at his face as he stood waiting in the doorway.

'Hello, Father,' she said, and smiled.

THE JUDGEMENT
OF STRANGERS

'Cursed is he that perverteth the judgement of the stranger, the fatherless, and widow.'

> from the Service of Commination, in the office for
> Ash Wednesday in *The Book of Common Prayer*.

'The Manor of Roth is not mentioned in the Domesday Book . . .'

> Audrey Oliphant, *The History of Roth*
> (Richmond, privately printed 1969), p.1.

Then darkness descended; and whispers defiled
The judgement of stranger, and widow, and child . . .

. . . . .

With flames to the flesh, with brands to the burning,
As incense to heav'n the soul is returning

> from 'The Judgement of Strangers' by
> the Reverend Francis St. J. Youlgreave in *The Four Last Things*
> (Gasset & Lode, London, 1896)

For Val and Bill

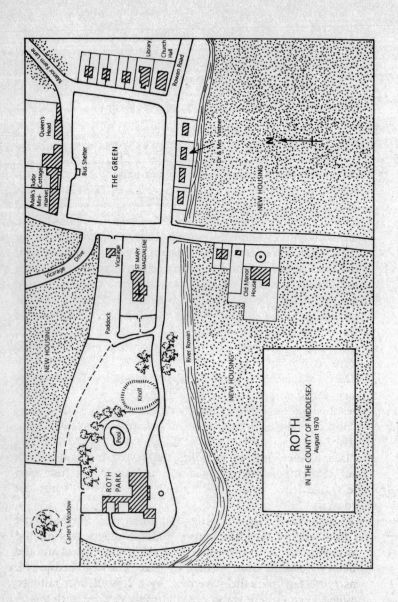

ROTH
IN THE COUNTY OF MIDDLESEX
August 1970

Manor Farm Lane

Library

Church Hall

Rowan Road

Queen's Head

Tudor Cottage

Malik's Mini-market

Bus Shelter

THE GREEN

Dr & Mrs Vintner

NEW HOUSING

Vicarage Drive

Vicarage

St Mary Magdalene

Paddock

Old Manor House

NEW HOUSING

River Rowan

NEW HOUSING

Knoll

Pool

ROTH PARK

Carter's Meadow

N

1

We found the mutilated corpse of Lord Peter in the early evening of Thursday the 13th August, 1970. He was the first victim of a train of events which began towards the end of the previous summer when I met Vanessa Forde – or even before that, with Audrey Oliphant and *The History of Roth*.

Every parish has its Audrey Oliphant – often several of them; their lives revolve around the parish church, and in one sense the Church of England revolves around them. It was inevitable that she should be a regular visitor at the Vicarage, and it shamed me that I did not always welcome her as warmly as I should have done. It also irritated me that the Tudor Cottage cat treated the Vicarage as his second home, braving the traffic on the main road to get there.

'Miss Oliphant practically lives here,' said my daughter Rosemary at the end of one particularly lengthy visit. 'And if she doesn't come herself she sends her cat instead.'

'She does an awful lot for us,' I pointed out. 'And for the parish.'

'Dear Father. You try and find the best in everyone, don't you?' Rosemary looked up at me and smiled. 'I just wish she would leave us alone. It's much nicer when it's just the two of us.'

Audrey was in her late forties and unmarried. She had lived in Roth all her life. Her house, Tudor Cottage, was on the green – on the north side between Malik's Minimarket and the Queen's Head. Its front garden, the size of a large bedspread, was protected from the pavement by a row of iron railings. Beside the gate there was a notice, freshly painted each year:

YE OLDE TUDOR TEA ROOM
(Est. 1931)
PROPRIETOR: MISS A. M. OLIPHANT
Telephone: Roth 6269
Morning Coffee – Light Meals – Cream Teas
Parties By Appointment

I had known the place for ten years, and in that time trade, though never brisk, had steadily diminished. This gave Audrey ample opportunity to read enormous quantities of detective novels and to throw herself into the affairs of the parish.

One evening in the spring of 1969, she appeared without warning on my doorstep.

'I've just had the most wonderful idea.'

'Really?'

'I'm not interrupting anything, am I?' she asked, initiating a ritual exchange of courtesies, a secular versicle and response.

'Not at all.'

'Are you sure?'

'Nothing that can't wait.' I owed her this polite fiction. 'I was about to have a break.'

I took her into the sitting room and, making a virtue from necessity, offered sherry. Audrey was a small woman, rather plump, with a face whose features seemed squashed; it was as though her skull, while still malleable, had been compressed in a vice – thus the face would have been splendidly in proportion if the eyes and the cheekbones and the corners of the mouth had not been quite so close together.

She took a sip of sherry, allowing the wine to linger in her mouth before she swallowed it. 'I was in the library this afternoon and some schoolchildren came in to ask Mrs Finch if she had any books on local history. And it turns out that there's a certain amount on neighbouring towns and villages. But very little on Roth itself.'

She paused for another sip. I lit a cigarette, guessing what was coming.

'Then it came to me in a flash.' Her heavy jowls quivered with excitement. 'Why not write a history of Roth? I'm sure lots of people would like to read one. And nowadays so many people are living here who have no idea what the *real* Roth is like.'

'What an interesting idea. You must let me know if there is anything I can do. The parish records, perhaps? I wonder if Lady Youlgreave might have some useful material. She –'

'I'm so glad,' Audrey interrupted. 'I hoped you'd want to help. Actually, a collaboration was what I had in mind. It seemed to me that we would be ideally suited.'

'I wouldn't say –'

'Besides,' she rushed on, 'the history of the village can't be separated from the history of the church and the parish. We could even have a chapter on famous inhabitants of the past. Francis Youlgreave, for example. What do you think?'

'I'm not sure how much use I'd be. After all, you're the one with the local knowledge. Then there's the question of time . . .'

I watched the excitement draining from Audrey's face like water from a bath. I felt ashamed of myself and also irritated with her. Why did she insist on calling Roth a village? It was a suburb of London, similar in all essentials to a dozen others. Most of its inhabitants had their real lives elsewhere. In Roth they merely serviced their bodily needs, watched television and on Sundays played golf or cleaned their Ford Cortinas.

'I quite understand.' Audrey stared at her empty glass. 'Just an idea.'

'I wonder,' I went on, trying to lessen the guilt that crept over me, 'would it be a help if I were to glance through your first draft?'

She looked up, her face glowing. 'Yes, please.'

The decision was made. If Audrey had not decided to write her history of Roth, none of what followed might have happened. It is tempting to blame her – to blame anyone but myself. But fate has a way of finding its agents: if Audrey had not volunteered to be the handmaid of Providence, then someone else would have come forward.

Audrey completed her little book early in August 1969. In a flutter of excitement, she brought me the manuscript, which was written almost illegibly in pencil. It was mercifully short, largely because Roth had relatively little history. Since the Middle Ages, the parish had been overshadowed by its larger neighbours. It was too far from the Thames, and later too far from the railway.

Still, to judge from the old photographs which Audrey had found, Roth had been a pretty place, and remarkably unspoilt, despite the fact that it was only thirteen miles from Charing Cross. All that had changed in the 1930s, when the Jubilee Reservoir was built: seven hundred acres of the parish, including the northern part of the village itself, were drowned beneath seven billion gallons of water, sacrificed to assuage the endless thirst of the inhabitants of London.

I soon discovered that Audrey's spelling and grammar were shaky. The text consisted of a patchwork of speculations – *Who knows? Perhaps Henry VIII stayed at the Old Manor House on his way to Hampton Court* – and quotations lifted, often inaccurately, from books she had found in the library. I persuaded her to have the manuscript typed, and managed – diplomatically, I hoped – to arrange for the typist quietly to incorporate some of my corrections. I then went through the typed draft with Audrey and revised it once more. By now it was early September.

'We must find a publisher,' Audrey said.

'Perhaps you could have it privately printed?'

'But I am sure it would interest readers all over the country,' she said. 'In many ways the story of Roth is the story of England.'

'In a sense, yes, but –'

'And, David,' she interrupted. 'I want all the royalties to go to the restoration fund. Every last penny. So we must find a proper publisher who will pay us lots of money. Why don't you come to supper tomorrow and we'll discuss it? I'd like to cook you a meal to say thank you for all the work you've done.' She tapped me playfully on the arm. 'You look as if you need a good feed.'

'Unfortunately I can't manage tomorrow. The Trasks have asked me to dinner. Some other time, perhaps.'

'Some other time,' she echoed.

I was relieved that the Trasks had given me such an impregnable excuse. As a consequence of my accepting their invitation, two people died, a third went to prison, and a fourth was admitted to a hospital for the insane.

2

The Trasks lived in a rambling Victorian rectory cheek by jowl with a rambling Victorian church. I knew from past visits that both the church and the house were warm and welcoming. Ronald did a very good job. His congregations were considerably larger than average.

I parked on the gravelled forecourt in front of the house. Two other cars were already there: an Austin Cambridge and a dark-green Daimler. The front door opened before I had reached it. Ronald beamed at me. I was wearing my clerical suit and a dog collar, but he was in mufti – rather a good dark suit, which made him look slimmer than he was, and a striped tie. He was shorter than me but much broader, and he gave the impression of never walking when he could trot. This evening, everything about him sparkled, from his black shoes to his fair hair. Aftershave wafted out to meet me.

'David!' He clapped me on the shoulder and drew me into the house. 'Good to see you. Come and meet the others.'

The hall was full of flowers and smelled strongly of polish. Ronald led me into the drawing room, which was at the back of the house. It was a warm evening. The French windows were open and a knot of people was standing on the terrace beyond.

Cynthia Trask came forward to greet me. She was square and trim, like her brother, and she wore a severe blue dress like a uniform. While Ronald fetched me a glass of sherry, she steered me towards the other guests.

I knew one of the couples – Victor and Mary Thurston. Thurston had made a great deal of money selling cabin cruisers for use on the river, and now he and his wife 'served the community' as they liked to put it, which meant sitting on a variety of committees; she preferred philanthropic causes and he concentrated on political ones. Thurston was a councillor and, now he was on the Planning Committee, wielded considerable power.

I had not met the other couple before – they turned out to be the headmaster of one of the local grammar schools and his wife; she was one of Ronald's churchwardens.

The first thing I noticed about the fifth guest was her hair, which was curly and the colour of glossy chestnuts. As she turned towards me, the evening sun swung behind her, giving her head a nimbus of flame. She was wearing a long dress of thin cotton, with full sleeves and a ruffled neck. For an instant, the setting sun made her dress almost transparent. Her body darkened. I saw the inside of her legs up to her crotch. The dress might as well have been invisible.

'Here we are, David.' Ronald was at my elbow with a glass of sherry. 'Vanessa, I don't think you know David Byfield. David, this is Vanessa Forde.'

We shook hands. I was momentarily unnerved by the sudden lust I felt. This was a familiar problem. Over the years I had learned to ride the feeling as a surfer rides a wave, until its force diminished. One way to avoid wallowing in sensation was to concentrate on observation. In a few seconds I had noticed that Vanessa had a pleasant face, attractive rather than beautiful, with a high colour and curving nose.

'Let me get you another drink.' Ronald snatched the empty glass from Vanessa's hand. 'Gin and lemon?'

She nodded, smiling. Ronald darted towards the drinks trolley, which was just inside the drawing room. There was something very boyish about him that evening. At times I glimpsed the adolescent he must once have been; and if I am honest, I should add that I preferred what I glimpsed to the senior churchman he had now become.

I offered Vanessa a cigarette. She accepted, bending forward to receive a light. I saw that she wore a wedding ring. For an instant, I smelt her perfume. It reminded me of one my wife used to wear. We spoke simultaneously, diving into the conversation like swimmers at the start of a race.

'Do you live locally?'

'Do you have a parish – ?'

We smiled at each other and any awkwardness dissolved.

'After you, Mrs Forde.'

'Vanessa, please. To answer your question, I live in Richmond.'

I noticed that she had said I rather than we. 'And to answer yours, I'm the vicar of Roth.'

'Oh yes.'

'Do you know Roth, then?'

'A little.' She stared up at me and smiled. 'Does that surprise you?'

I smiled back. 'Its identity tends to get swamped by its neighbours. A lot of people think the name is familiar but have no idea where it is.'

'I went there a few years ago to see the church. Rather an interesting one. You've got that medieval panel painting over the chancel, haven't you? The Last Judgement?'

'That's right. With scenes from the life of Christ underneath.'

'One gin and lemon coming up,' said Ronald, materializing at Vanessa's elbow and handing her the glass with a flourish. He had a similar glass in his own hand, which he raised. 'Chin-chin.' He beamed at me. 'David, I know Cynthia wanted to have a word with you about Rosemary.'

'My daughter,' I explained to Vanessa.

'Our niece dropped in last week,' Ronald went on. 'She left school at the end of last term and she brought over a trunk of stuff for us to dispose of. Clothes, I suppose. I think there's a lacrosse stick, too. Cynthia wondered if anything might come in useful for Rosemary.'

I smiled and thanked him. There was a time when I would have objected to being on the receiving end of the Trasks' philanthropy. Now I knew better. Pride is a luxury and children become increasingly expensive as they grow older. At this moment Cynthia reached us, bearing bowls of peanuts and olives.

'Did I hear Rosemary's name?' she asked. 'Such a delightful girl. How's she liking school now?'

'Much better, I think.' I turned to Vanessa. 'When Rosemary first went away, she disliked it very much.' In fact, she had twice tried to run away. 'But she seems to have settled down in the last year.'

'She will be taking her A levels next summer,' said Cynthia, with a hint of interrogation in her voice, indicating that this was an inspired guess rather than a statement of fact.

She detached me from Vanessa and Ronald and talked to me for a moment or two about Rosemary. We decided – or rather Cynthia decided – that she would send Ronald over with the trunk during the next week or so. Anything we did not want for Rosemary could go to our next jumble sale. Having settled the matter, she steered me away from Vanessa and Ronald, who were talking together at the far end of the terrace, and skilfully inserted me into a conversation between Victor Thurston and the headmaster's wife.

I did not get another opportunity to talk to Vanessa for some time. While we were on the terrace I glanced once or twice in the direction of her and Ronald, still talking, their faces intent. At one point I noticed her shaking her head.

Eventually we went through to the dining room, and Cynthia steered us to our places at the round table. Vanessa was diametrically opposite me. There was a substantial flower arrangement in the middle of the table, so I caught only the occasional glimpse of her. I was sitting between Cynthia and the headmaster's wife.

Ronald said grace. The meal which followed was uncharacteristically elaborate. Melon with Parma ham gave way to *coq au vin*. Ronald, usually the most careful of hosts, kept refilling our glasses with an unfortunate Portuguese rosé. The headmaster's wife tried delicately to interrogate me about Ronald. It soon became clear that she knew the Trasks rather better than I did. At last she gave up and spoke across me to Cynthia.

'My dear, this is wonderful. How on earth do you manage to prepare a meal like this and go out to work?'

'I only work in the mornings. I find there's ample time if one is sufficiently organized.'

'I didn't know you had a job,' I said.

'I work for Vanessa. I'm her secretary, really. Jolly interesting.'

I wondered whether that explained the special effort the Trasks were making. Was Cynthia hoping for promotion?

'I suppose you spend most of your time dealing with authors and so on,' said the headmaster's wife. 'It must be marvellous. Do you have lots of bestsellers?'

Cynthia shook her head. 'We tend to do fairly specialized non-fiction titles. Actually, I think Royston and Forde's out-and-out bestseller was something called *Great Engines of the 1920s.*'

Ronald and Thurston talked to Vanessa for much of the meal. When we left the table, Mary Thurston seized her husband's arm as if to re-establish her claim to him. Ronald went to the kitchen to make coffee.

'Ronald bought a machine when he was in Italy last year,' Cynthia explained to the rest of us. 'He does like to use it when we have guests. Too complicated for me, I'm afraid.' She added as an afterthought, 'Super coffee.'

We went back to the drawing room to wait for it. Vanessa came over to me.

'I don't suppose you could give me another cigarette, could you? I've mislaid mine. So silly.' She smiled up at me. Even then I think I knew that Vanessa was never silly. She was many things, but not that. She sat down on the sofa and waved to me to join her.

'Are you in Ronald's – whatever it is? – area?'

'He's my archdeacon, yes. So in a sense he's my immediate boss.'

I did not want to talk about Ronald. He and I did not get on badly – not then – but we had little in common, and both of us knew it.

'Cynthia tells me you're a publisher.'

She squeezed her eyes together for an instant, as though smoke had irritated them. 'By default.'

'I'm sorry?'

'It was my husband's firm.' She stared down at her cigarette. 'He founded it with a friend from Oxford. It never made much money for either of them, but he loved it.'

'I didn't realize. I'm sorry.'

'I – I assumed Ronald might have mentioned it to you. No reason why you should know. Charles died three years ago. A brain tumour. One of those ghastly things that come out of a clear blue sky. I've taken over his part in the business. Needs must, really. I needed a job.'

'Do you enjoy it?'

She nodded. 'I'd always helped Charles on the editorial side. Now I'm learning a great deal about production.' She smiled towards Cynthia, who was embroiled with the headmaster's wife. 'Cynthia keeps me in order.'

'At dinner Cynthia said she thought *Great Engines of the 1920s* was your bestselling book.'

'She's perfectly right. Though I have my hopes of *The English Cottage Garden*. It's been selling very steadily since it came out last year.' She drew on her cigarette. 'In fact, our real bestseller in terms of copies sold is probably one of our town guides. The Oxford one. We do quite a lot of that sort of thing – that's where the bread and butter comes from.'

At that moment, Ronald appeared in the doorway bearing a large silver tray. 'Coffee, everybody,' he announced in a voice like a fanfare. 'Sorry to keep you waiting.' He advanced into the room, his eyes searching for Vanessa.

'One of my parishioners has written a book,' I said to her.

Vanessa looked warily at me. 'What sort of book?'

'It's a history of the parish. Not really a book. I'd say it's about ten thousand words.'

'How interesting.'

She glanced at me again, and I think a spark of shared amusement passed between us. She knew how to say one thing and mean another.

'She's looking for a publisher.'

'Sugar, Vanessa?' boomed Ronald. 'Cream?'

'In my experience, most authors are.' She smiled up at Ronald. 'Just a dash of cream, please, Ronnie.'

Ronnie?

'She believes it might appeal to readers all over the country,' I continued. 'Not just to those who know Roth.'

'The happy few?'

I smiled. It was a novelty to have someone talk to me as a person rather than as a priest. 'Could you recommend a publisher she could send it to?' I stared at the curve of her arm and noticed the almost invisible golden hairs that grew on the skin. 'Someone who would have a look at the book and give a professional opinion. I imagine you haven't got the time to look at stray typescripts yourself.'

'Vanessa's always looking at stray typescripts,' Ronald said, and laughed. 'Or looking *for* them.'

'I might be able to spare five minutes,' she said to me, her voice deadpan.

Once again, she glanced at me, and once again the spark of amusement danced between us.

'Brandy, anyone?' Ronald enquired. 'Or what about a liqueur?'

For the rest of the evening Vanessa talked mainly to Ronald, Cynthia and Victor Thurston. I was the first to leave.

3

The following Monday, I looked up Royston and Forde in the directory and phoned Vanessa at her office. Cynthia Trask answered the phone. Oddly enough this took me by surprise. I had completely forgotten that she worked there.

'Good morning, Cynthia. This is David Byfield.'

'Hello, David.'

After a short pause I said, 'Thank you so much for Friday.'

'Not at all. Ronald and I enjoyed it.'

I wondered if I should have sent flowers or something. 'I don't know if Vanessa mentioned it, but one of my parishioners has written a book. She volunteered to have a look at it.'

'I'll see if she's engaged,' Cynthia said.

A moment later, Vanessa came on the line. She was brisk with me, her voice sounding much sharper on the telephone. She was busy most of the day, she was afraid, but might I be free for lunch? Ninety minutes later, we were sitting opposite each other in a café near Richmond Bridge.

The long, clinging dress she had worn at the Trasks' on Friday had given her a voluptuous appearance. Now she was another woman, dressed in a dark suit, and with her hair pulled back: slimmer, sharper and harder.

The typescript of *The History of Roth* was in a large, brown envelope on the table between us. I had picked it up from Audrey on my way to Richmond. ('So kind of you, David. I'm so grateful.')

Vanessa did not touch the envelope. She picked at her sandwich. A silence lay between us, and as it grew longer I felt increasingly desolate. The friendly intimacy that had flourished so briefly between us on Friday evening was gone. I found it all too easy, on the other hand, to think of her as a desirable woman. I had been a fool to come here. I was wasting her time and mine. I should have sent the typescript in the post.

'Do you visit many churches?' I asked, to make conversation. 'You mentioned our panel paintings on Friday.'

Vanessa fiddled with one of the crumbs on her plate. 'Not really. I wanted to see Roth because of the connection with Francis Youlgreave.'

'The poet?' My voice sounded unnaturally loud. 'He's buried in the vault under the chancel.'

'He deserves a few paragraphs in here.' Vanessa tapped the envelope containing the typescript. 'Quite a sensational character, by all accounts.'

'Audrey does mention him, but she's very circumspect about what she says.'

'Why?'

'There's a member of the family still living in Roth. I think her husband was the poet's great-nephew. Audrey didn't want to give people the wrong idea about him.'

'Defile their judgement, as it were.' Vanessa smiled across the table at me. Then she quoted two lines from the poem that had found its way into several anthologies. It was usually the only poem of his that anyone had read.

> 'Then darkness descended; and whispers defiled
> The judgement of stranger, and widow, and child.'

'Just so.'

'Does anyone remember him in the village?'

'Roth isn't that sort of place. There aren't that many people left who lived there before the last war. And Francis Youlgreave died before the First World War. Have you a particular reason for asking?'

She shrugged. 'I read quite a lot of his verse when I was up at Oxford. Not a very good poet, to be frank – all those jog-trot rhythms can be rather wearing. But he was interesting more for what he was and for who he knew than for what he wrote.'

'Not a very nice man, by all accounts. Unbalanced.'

'Yes, but rather fascinating.' She looked at her watch. 'I'm awfully sorry, David, but I've got to rush.'

I concealed my disappointment. I paid the bill and walked with her back to the office where I had left my car.

'Would you like to telephone me tomorrow?' she asked. 'I should have had time to look at the book by then.'

'Of course. At the office?'

'I'll probably read it at home, actually.'

'What time would suit you?'

'About seven?'

She gave me her number. We said goodbye and I drove back to Roth, feeling profoundly dissatisfied. I had made a fool of myself in more ways than one. I had expected more, much more, from my lunch with Vanessa – though quite what, I did not know. I was aware, too, that there was something absurd in a middle-aged widower acting in the way that I was doing. It was clear that she saw me as an acquaintance and that by looking at the typescript she was merely doing me – and Audrey – a good turn from the kindness of her heart.

Still, I thought, at least I had a reason to telephone Vanessa tomorrow evening.

In the event, however, I did not telephone Vanessa on Tuesday evening. This was because on Tuesday afternoon I received an unexpected and unpleasant visit from Cynthia Trask.

4

Cynthia arrived without warning in the late afternoon.

'I hope I'm not disturbing you,' she said briskly. 'But I happened to be passing, and I thought this might be a good opportunity to drop in those odds and ends from my niece.'

In the back of her Mini Traveller were two suitcases and a faded army kitbag containing the lacrosse stick and other sporting impedimenta. I carried them into the house and called Rosemary, who was reading in her room. She did not appear to hear.

'I won't disturb her, if you don't mind,' I said. 'She's working quite hard this holiday. Would you like some tea?' It would have been churlish not to offer Cynthia tea but I was mildly surprised that she so readily accepted. She followed me into the kitchen which, like the rest of the house, was cramped, characterless and modern.

'Anything I can do to help?'

'Everything's under control, thank you.'

'This is the first time I've been inside the new vicarage. You must be so relieved.'

'It's certainly easier to keep warm and clean than the old one was.'

It was partly due to Ronald's influence that the old vicarage – a large, gracious and completely impractical Queen Anne house – had been demolished last year. The new vicarage was a four-bedroomed, centrally heated box. Its garden occupied the site of the old tennis court and vegetable garden. The rest of the old garden and the site of the old house itself now contained a curving cul-de-sac and six more boxes, each rather more spacious than the new vicarage.

'Of course, you didn't really need all that space. You and Rosemary must have felt you were camping in a barrack.'

'Rather an elegant barrack,' I said. 'Do you take sugar?'

I carried the tea tray into the sitting room. Having a stranger in your home makes you see it with fresh eyes, and the result is rarely reassuring. I imagined that Cynthia was taking in the shabby furniture, the cobwebs in the corner of the ceiling and the unswept grate.

'Much cosier,' Cynthia said approvingly, as though she herself were responsible for this. 'Do you have someone who comes in to do for you?'

I nodded, resenting the catechism. 'One of my parishioners acts as a sort of housekeeper.' I handed Cynthia a cup of tea. 'Your house is pretty big,' I said, trying to change the subject, 'but it always seems very homely.'

She smiled wistfully. 'Yes, I've enjoyed living there.'

'Are you moving?'

'Almost certainly.'

'How wonderful.' I felt a sudden stab of envy. 'You must be very proud of Ronald.'

Cynthia frowned. 'Proud?'

'I assumed you meant he's been offered preferment. Well deserved, I'm sure.'

Cynthia flushed. She was sitting, pink and foursquare in my own armchair. 'No, I didn't mean preferment. I meant that, when Ronald marries, I shall naturally move out. It will be time to make a home of my own. It wouldn't be fair to any of us if I stayed.'

'I didn't realize that he *was* getting married.' I guessed that Cynthia and her brother had shared a house for nearly twenty years, for I remembered hearing that Ronald's first wife had died soon after their marriage. I wondered how Cynthia felt at the prospect of being uprooted from her home. 'I hope they will be very happy.'

'There hasn't been a formal announcement yet. They haven't sorted out the timing. I know Ronald nearly said something on Friday evening, but they decided it would be better to wait.'

A suspicion mushroomed in my mind. Suddenly everything began to make sense.

'They are ideally suited,' Cynthia was saying, talking rapidly. 'And Vanessa has been so lost since Charles died. She's the sort of woman who really needs a husband.'

'Yes. Yes, of course.'

Cynthia put down her cup and saucer and looked at her watch. 'Heavens, is that the time? I really must be going.'

I took Cynthia out to her car. I think I said the right things about the charitable donation she had brought. I asked whether she would like me to return the suitcases, though I cannot remember what she replied.

At last she drove away. I trudged back into the house and took the tea tray into the kitchen. I was being childish, I told myself. I had not even realized that I was entertaining foolish hopes about Vanessa Forde until Cynthia had made it so clear that my prospects were hopeless. I had been celibate now for ten years – at first from necessity and later by choice – and there was no reason why I should not remain celibate for the rest of my life.

That afternoon some very unworthy thoughts passed through my mind. Jealousy and frustrated lust are an unsettling combination. I respected Ronald Trask, or rather I respected some of his achievements. One day he would probably be a bishop. I did not find that easy to accept. It was a shock to discover that I found even less palatable the thought that he and Vanessa would soon be married.

Sex apart, I had liked what I had seen of Vanessa. Ronald was a bore. A worthy bore, but still a bore. Vanessa deserved someone better. But of course there was nothing I could do about it. In any case, if Ronald and Vanessa chose to marry, it was nothing to do with me.

It was one thing to frame these rational arguments; it was quite another to accept them emotionally. I went into my study and tried to write a letter to my godson, Michael Appleyard. That proved too difficult. I turned to the parish accounts, which were even worse. Always, in the back of my mind, were the interlocking figures of Ronald and Vanessa. Physically interlocking, I mean. It was as if I were trapped in a cinema with a film I did not want to see on the screen.

Time crept on. Rosemary was still working in her room. At

six-thirty I decided to go over to the church and say the Evening Office. Then I would ring Vanessa about Audrey's book. I went into the hall.

'Rosemary?'

She did not answer. I went upstairs and tapped on the door of her room. Her room was uncluttered. Even as a young child she had had a formidable ability to organize her surroundings. She was sitting at her table with a pile of books in front of her and a pen in her hand. She glanced at me, her eyes vague.

'Is it supper time already?'

'No – not yet. I'm going over to church for a while. Not for long.'

'OK.'

'You'll be all right, my dear?'

She gave me a condescending smile, which said, *Of course I'll be all right. I'm not a baby.* 'I'll start supper in about fifteen minutes.'

'Thank you.'

Rosemary let her eyes drift back to her book. I envied her serenity. I wanted to say something to her but, as so often, I could not find the words. Instead I closed the door softly behind me, went downstairs and let myself out of the house and into the evening sunlight.

The Vicarage was next to the churchyard, separated from it by a high wall of crumbling eighteenth-century brick. I walked through the little garden to our private gate, a relic of the old house, which gave access from the grounds of the Vicarage to the churchyard. As I opened the gate the church was suddenly revealed, framed in the archway.

Most of the exterior of the St Mary Magdalene was of brick, and in this light it looked particularly lovely: the older bricks of the sixteenth-century rebuilding had weathered to a mauve colour, while the eighteenth-century work was a contrasting russet; and together the colours made the church glow and gently vibrate against the blue of the sky. Housemartins darted round the tower.

I closed the gate behind me. Traffic rumbled a few yards to the left on the main road and there was a powerful smell of diesel fumes in the air. I caught sight of a shadow flickering through the grass near the gate to the road. I was just in time to see Audrey's cat slipping behind a gravestone.

I walked slowly round the east end to the south door on the other side. On my way I passed the steps leading down to the Youlgreave vault beneath the chancel. The iron gate was rusting and the steps were cracked and overgrown with weeds. No one had been interred there for almost fifty years. The last Youlgreave to die, Sir George, had been killed in the Pacific in 1944, and his body had been buried at sea. I noticed there were grey feathers scattered on the bottom step, immediately in front of the iron gate, where no weeds grew. I wondered if Audrey's cat was in the habit of dismembering his kills there.

I went into the porch. The door was unlocked – I left the church open during the day, though after two robberies I now locked it at night. Inside, the air smelled of polish, flowers and – very faintly – of incense, which I used two or three times a year. The church was small, almost cosy, with a two-bay nave and a low chancel. Above the chancel arch were the panel paintings, their colours murky; the pictures looked as if they were wreathed in smoke. I walked slowly to my stall in the choir. I sat down and began to say the Evening Office.

Usually the building itself had a calming effect on me, but not this evening. At times I found my mind drifting away from the words of the office and had to force myself to concentrate. Afterwards I simply sat there and stared at the memorial tablets on the wall opposite me. It was as though my will had abdicated.

Vanessa and Ronald, I thought over and over again. I wondered if I would be invited to the wedding and, if so, whether I should accept. By that time, perhaps it would no longer matter. I was aware, of course, that I was making too much of this. On the basis of two short meetings, I could hardly claim to have become deeply attached to Vanessa. The real problem was that, quite unintentionally, she had aroused my own long-suppressed needs. At the bottom of my unhappiness was a feeling of profound dissatisfaction with myself.

Time passed. Slowly the light slipped away from the interior of the church. It was by no means dark – merely less bright than it had been before. The memorial tablets were made of pale marble that gleamed among the shadows. Gradually there crept up on me the feeling that I was being watched.

I stared with increasing concentration at the tablet directly in front of me, which belonged to Francis Youlgreave, the poor, mad poet-priest. Everything led back to Vanessa. How odd that she should be interested in him. I remembered the lines that she had quoted to me at lunch time. I could not recall the words exactly, something about darkness, I thought, and about whispers that defiled the judgement.

Defiled. It suddenly seemed to me that I was irredeemably defiled, not just by the events of the last few days, but by the active choice of someone or something outside me.

At that moment, I heard laughter.

It was a high, faint sound, like the rustle of paper or a whistle without a tune. I thought of wind among the leaves, of beating wings and long beaks, of geese I had seen as a boy flying high above Essex mudflats. Sadness swept over me. I fought it, but it turned to desolation and then to something darker.

'No. Stop. Please stop.'

I was on my feet. The paralysis had dissolved. I stumbled down the church. The sound followed me. I put my hands over my ears but I could not block it out. The church was no longer a place of peace. I had turned it into a mockery of its former self. *Defiled*. I had defiled the church even as I had defiled myself.

I struggled with the latch of the south door. I was in such a state that it seemed to me that someone on the other side was holding it down. At last I wrenched it up and pulled at the door. I almost fell into the porch beyond.

Something moved on my right. Audrey's cat, I thought for a split second, her wretched, bloody cat. Then I realized that I was wrong: that a person was sitting on the bench in the corner by the church notice board. I had a confused impression of pale clothing and a golden blur like a halo at the head. Then the figure stood up.

'Hello, Father,' said my daughter Rosemary. Her voice changed, filling with concern. 'What's wrong?'

305

5

At half past nine the following morning there was a ring on the doorbell. I was alone in the house. Rosemary had caught the bus to Staines to go shopping. I had managed to shave, but the only breakfast I had been able to face was a cigarette and a cup of coffee.

I found Audrey hovering on the doorstep, her body poised as if ready to dart into the hall at the slightest encouragement. I kept my hand on the door and tried to twist my mouth into a smile.

'Sorry to disturb you, David. I just wondered what the verdict was.'

'What verdict?'

'You're teasing me,' she said in an arch voice. 'The verdict on the book, of course.'

'I'm so sorry.' Indeed I was, though not for the reasons Audrey assumed. 'I've not been able to talk to Mrs Forde about it yet.'

She stuck out her lower lip, which was already pinched and protuberant, and increased her resemblance to a disappointed child. 'I thought you were going to phone her yesterday evening.'

'Yes, I'd hoped to, but – but there was a difficulty.'

'Oh. I see.'

'I'll try to talk to her today.' I smiled, trying to soften the effect of my words. 'I'll phone you as soon as I hear something, shall I?'

'Yes, please.' She turned to go. She had taken only a couple of steps towards the road when she stopped and turned back to me. 'David?'

'Yes?'

'Thank you for all you're doing.'

My conscience twisted uncomfortably. Audrey smiled and walked away. I went back to my study and stared at the papers on my desk. Concentration demanded too much effort. I had slept badly, with dreams that hovered near the frontier of nightmare but did not actually cross it. One of them had been set in a version of Rosington, where Rosemary and I had lived before we came to Roth – when my wife Janet was still alive. I had not dreamed of Rosington for years. Vanessa had unsettled me, breached the defences I had built up so laboriously. (And I had been all too willing to have them breached.)

Audrey's visit reminded me that I still had the problem of contacting Vanessa. I should have phoned her, as arranged, the previous evening, but I had spent much longer in the church than I had intended. By the time I had returned to the Vicarage the last thing I had wanted to do was talk to anyone, let alone Vanessa. I had persuaded myself without much trouble that it was too late to phone.

On the other hand, I could not run away from Vanessa for ever, or at least not until I had sorted out the business of Audrey's wretched book. I did not want to phone her at the office, however, because that would mean having to run the gauntlet of Cynthia. I remembered that Cynthia worked only in the mornings. In that case, I thought, I would phone Vanessa this afternoon.

Now that I had made the decision, I felt slightly happier. I returned to the accounts I had abandoned the previous evening. But I had not got very far when there was another ring at the doorbell. I swore under my breath as I went into the hall. I opened the door. There was Vanessa herself.

I stared at her, fighting a rising tide of disbelief. She was wearing her dark suit and she had the envelope containing Audrey's typescript clamped to her chest.

'Hello, David.'

'Vanessa – do come in.'

'I'm not interrupting anything, am I?'

'Only the accounts. And I was about to make some coffee, in

any case. But I hope you haven't come all this way to bring me back the book?'

She shook her head. 'I had to visit a bookshop in Staines this morning. I'm on my way back.'

She followed me into the hall, and I led her through to the sitting room.

'I'm sorry I didn't phone yesterday evening.'

'That's all right.' She looked out of the window, not at me. 'I didn't expect you to phone me back so late.'

'I'm sorry?'

She turned from the window and looked at me. 'Didn't you get my message?'

'What message?'

'I phoned last night. I had another phone call, and I – I thought you might not have been able to get through. I left a message saying I'd phoned.'

'I didn't receive it.' I thought of Rosemary waiting for me in the porch of the church. 'You must have spoken to my daughter. I expect it slipped her mind.'

She smiled. 'Young people have more important things to think about than relaying phone messages.'

'Yes.' I did not know what to say next. I knew I should make the coffee, but I did not want to leave Vanessa. I cleared my throat. 'I saw Cynthia yesterday afternoon. She brought those things round for Rosemary.'

'I know. She told me . . . I think she may have misled you about something.'

I stared at her. We were still standing in the middle of the room.

Vanessa picked at a piece of fluff on her sleeve. 'I believe she gave you to understand that Ronnie and I are engaged.'

I nodded.

'Well, that's not true. Not exactly.'

I patted the pockets of my jacket, looking for the cigarettes I had left in the study. 'There's no need to tell me this. It's none of my business.'

'Cynthia and Ronnie were very good to me when Charles died.'

'I'm sure they were.'

308

'You don't understand. When something like that happens you feel empty. And you can become very dependent on those who help you. Emotionally, I mean.'

'I do understand,' I said. 'Only too well.'

'I'm sorry.' She bit her lip. 'Ronnie told me about your wife.'

'It's all right. It was a long time ago.'

'One gets so wrapped up in oneself.'

'I know.'

'Listen, two weeks ago, Ronnie asked me to marry him. I didn't say yes, but I didn't say no, either. I said I needed time. But he thought I was eventually going to say yes. To be perfectly honest, *I* thought I was going to say yes. In a way I felt that he deserved it. And I'm fond of him . . . Besides, I don't like living on my own.'

'I see. Won't you sit down?'

I was not sure whether she was talking to me as a man or as a priest – a not uncommon problem in the Anglican Church. When we sat down, somehow we both chose the sofa. This had a low seat – uncomfortably low for me. It caused Vanessa's skirt to ride up several inches above the knees. The sight was distracting. She snapped open her handbag and produced a packet of cigarettes, which she offered to me. I found some matches in my pocket. Lighting the cigarettes brought us very close together. There was now no doubt about it: as far as I was concerned, the man was well in ascendancy over the priest.

'Ronnie hoped to announce our engagement on Friday evening,' she continued. 'I think that's why he wanted the dinner party – to show me off. I didn't want that.' She blew out a plume of smoke like an angry dragon. 'I didn't *like* it, either. It made me feel like a trophy or something. And then this morning, Cynthia told me she'd been to see you, told me what she'd said. I was furious. I'm *not* engaged to Ronnie. In any case, it's nothing to do with her.'

'No doubt she meant well,' I said, automatically clinging to the saving grace of good intentions.

'We all mean well,' Vanessa snapped back. 'Sometimes that's not enough.'

We smoked in silence for a moment. I glanced at her stock-inged legs, dark and gleaming, and quickly looked away. She fiddled with her cigarette, rolling it between finger and thumb.

'The book,' I said, my voice a little hoarse. 'What did you think of it?'

'Yes.' She seized the envelope as if it were a life belt. 'There's a good deal of interesting material in it. Particularly if you know Roth well. But I'm afraid it's not really suitable for us.'

'Is it worth our trying elsewhere?'

'Frankly, no. I don't think any trade publisher would want it. It's not a book for the general market.'

'Too short,' I said slowly, 'and too specialized. And not exactly scholarly, either.'

She smiled. 'Not exactly. If the author wants to see it in print, she'll probably have to pay for the privilege.'

'I thought you might say that.'

'She'll probably blame my lack of acumen,' Vanessa went on cheerfully. 'A lot of authors appear to believe that there are no bad books, only bad publishers.'

'So what would you advise?'

'There's no point in raising her hopes. Just say that I don't think it's a commercial proposition, and that I advised investigating the cost of having it privately printed. She could sell it in the church, in local shops. Perhaps there's a local history society which would contribute towards the costs.'

'Is there a printer you could recommend?'

'You could try us, if you like. We have our own printing works. We could certainly give you a quotation.'

'Really? That would be very kind.'

Simultaneously we turned to look at one another. At that moment there was a sudden movement at the window. Both our heads jerked towards it as if tugged by invisible strings, as if we were both conscious of having done something wrong. I felt a spurt of anger against the intruder who had broken in on our privacy. Audrey's cat was on the sill, butting his nose against the glass.

Vanessa said, 'Is that – is that *yours*?'

'No – he belongs to Audrey, in fact – the person who wrote the book.'

'Oh.' She looked relieved. 'My mother was afraid of cats. She was always going on about how insanitary they were. How they brought germs into the house, as well as the things they caught.' She glanced sideways at me. 'Do you think these things can be hereditary?'

'Phobias?'

'Oh, it's not a phobia. I just don't particularly like them. In fact, that one's rather dapper. It looks as though he's wearing evening dress.'

She was right. The cat was black, except for a triangular patch of white at the throat and more white on the paws. As we watched, he opened his mouth, a pink-and-white cavern, and miaowed, the sound reaching us through the open fanlight of the window.

'He's called Lord Peter,' I said.

'Why?'

'As in Dorothy L. Sayers. Audrey reads a lot of detective stories. His predecessor was called Poirot. And before him, there were two others – before my time: one was called Brown after Father Brown, and the first of the line was Sherlock.'

'I can't say I have much time for detective stories.'

'Nor do I.'

I repressed the uncharitable memory of the time that Audrey had lent me Sayers's *The Nine Tailors*, on the grounds that it was not only great literature but also contained a wonderfully convincing portrait of a vicar. I stood up, went to the window and waved at Lord Peter, trying to shoo him away. I did not dislike cats in general, but I disliked this one. His constant intrusions irritated me, and I blamed him for the strong feline stench in my garage. Ignoring my wave, he miaowed once more. It occurred to me that I felt about Lord Peter as I often felt about Audrey: that she was ceaselessly trying to encroach on our privacy at the Vicarage.

'David?'

I turned back to Vanessa, ripe and lovely, looking up at me from the sofa. 'What is it?'

'To go back to – to Ronnie. It's just – it's just that I'm not sure I'm the right person to marry a clergyman.'

'Why?'

'I'm not a regular churchgoer. I don't even know if I believe in God.'

'It doesn't matter,' I said, knowing that it did, though not perhaps in the way she thought. 'In any case, belief in God comes in many forms.'

'But his parish, the bishop –'

'I am sure Ronald thought of all that. I don't mean to pry, but surely it came up when he asked you to marry him?'

She nodded. 'He said that God would find a way.'

There was a silence. Lord Peter rubbed his furry body against the glass and I wanted to throw the ashtray at him. I felt a rush of anger towards Ronald, joining the other emotions which were swirling round the sitting room. If I stayed here, they would suck me down.

I moved to the door. 'I'll make the coffee. I won't be a moment.'

I slipped out of the room without giving her time to answer. In the hall I discovered that my forehead was damp with sweat. The house seemed airless, a red brick coffin with too few windows. I went into the kitchen and opened the back door. While I was waiting for the kettle to boil I stared at my shrunken garden.

It was then that the idea slithered like a snake into my mind, showing itself openly for the first time: if anyone was going to marry Vanessa Forde, why shouldn't it be me?

6

Vanessa did not linger over coffee. It was as if she were suddenly desperate to leave. We made no arrangement to see each other again. During the afternoon, I called at Tudor Cottage and relayed her opinion of *The History of Roth* to its author. Audrey's reaction surprised me.

'But what do *you* think, David?'

'I think Vanessa's opinion is worth taking seriously. After all, it's her job. And it's true that *The History of Roth* is rather short for a book.'

'Perhaps she's right. Perhaps it would be simpler to have it privately printed. And then we wouldn't have to share the profits with the publisher. I wonder how much it would cost?'

'I don't know.'

'Would you mind asking Mrs Forde on my behalf? I'd feel a little awkward doing it myself. I haven't even met her.'

Audrey continued to play the unwitting Cupid. After discussing the pros and cons exhaustively with me, she entrusted Royston and Forde with the job of printing *The History of Roth*. Audrey asked me to – in her words – 'see it through the press' for her. The typescript provided a reason for Vanessa and me to see each other without commitment on the one hand or guilt on the other; she was doing her job and I was helping a friend. We spent several evenings editing the book, and several more proofreading it. Usually we worked at her flat.

Vanessa cooked me meals on two occasions. Once I took her out to a restaurant in Richmond to repay her hospitality. I remember a candle in a wax-covered Chianti bottle, its flame doubled and dancing in her eyes, a red-and-white checked tablecloth and plates of gently steaming spaghetti bolognese.

'It's a shame there's not more material about Francis Youlgreave,' she said on that evening. 'And why's Audrey so keen to avoid giving offence?'

Because she's a prude and a snob. I said, 'When she was growing up, the Youlgreaves were the local grandees.'

'So you had to treat even their black sheep with respect? That may have been true once, but does she need to be so coy now?'

I shrugged. 'It's her book, I suppose.'

'I've been rereading Francis's poems. He'd be an interesting subject for a PhD. Or even a biography. Now that *would* be commercial.'

'Warts and all?'

Vanessa grinned across the table. 'If you took away the warts, you wouldn't have much left. Nothing interesting, anyway.'

There was no element of deception about our meetings. Vanessa never mentioned Ronald, and nor did I. I assumed that an engagement was no longer on the cards. The Trasks knew that Vanessa and I were working together on *The History of Roth*. What Cynthia thought about it, I did not know; but Ronald took it in his stride.

'And how's the book coming along?' he asked me at one of the committee meetings he so frequently convened. He smiled, and his white teeth twinkled at me. 'Vanessa's told me all about it. I'm grateful, actually. She's seeing another clergyman in a secular context, as it were. It's so easy for lay people to assume we're all dog collars and pious sentiments.'

When two people work together towards a shared goal, it can create a powerful sense of intimacy. Vanessa and I did not hurry, and at least the little book benefited from the attention we lavished on it. It was a happy time because we discovered that many of our tastes coincided – books, paintings, humour. Being a parish priest can be a lonely job, and her friendship became precious to me. Two months later, by the middle of November 1969, I decided to ask Vanessa to marry me.

It was not a decision I reached hastily, or rashly. It seemed to me that there was a host of reasons in favour. Vanessa was an intelligent and cultivated woman, a pleasure to be with. I was lonely. Rosemary would benefit from having an older woman in the family. The Vicarage needed the warmth Vanessa could bring to it. The wife of a parish priest can act as her husband's eyes and ears. Last but not least, I urgently wanted to go to bed with Vanessa.

I was very calm. How things had altered, I thought smugly, since I had last considered marriage. Before proposing to Vanessa, I discussed my intentions with my spiritual director, Peter Hudson. He was an old friend who had helped me cope in those dark days after I left Rosington.

Peter was a few years older than I and was now a suffragan bishop in the neighbouring diocese of Oxford. At that time, he lived in Reading, which meant I could easily drive over and see him.

The Hudsons had a modern house on an estate. Peter's wife June welcomed me with a kiss, gave each of us a cup of coffee and shooed us upstairs to his little study. The atmosphere was foggy with pipe smoke.

'You're looking well,' he said to me. 'Better than I've seen you for some time.'

'I'm feeling better.'

'What do you want to talk about?'

'I'm thinking of getting married again.'

Peter was in the act of lighting his pipe. He cocked an eye at me through the smoke. 'I see.'

'Her name's Vanessa Forde. She's a widow, and a partner in a small publishing company in Richmond. She's thirty-nine.'

Smoke billowed from the pipe, but Peter said nothing. He was a small, sturdily built man who carried too much surplus fat. His plump face was soft-skinned and relatively unlined, with heavy eyebrows sprouting anarchically like twin tangles of barbed wire. He was the only person in the world who knew how ill suited I was to celibacy.

'Tell me more.'

I told him how I had met Vanessa and how working on *The History of Roth* had brought us together. I outlined my reasons for asking her to marry me.

'I realize it must seem selfish of me,' I said, 'but I know

315

she doesn't want to marry Ronald. And I honestly think I could make her happy. And she could make me happy, for that matter.'

'Do you love her?'

'Of course I do. I'm not pretending it's a grand passion – I'm middle-aged, for heaven's sake. But there's love, nonetheless, and liking, shared interests, affection –'

'And sexual attraction, at least on your side.'

'Yes – and why not? Surely that's one of the purposes of marriage?'

'You're not allowing that to warp your judgement? Ten years is a long time. The pressure can build up.'

I thought of Peter's comfortable wife and wondered briefly if the pressure had ever built up in their marriage. 'I'm making allowances for that.'

We sat in silence for a moment. The sound of the television filtered up the stairs.

'Other things worry me,' he said at last. 'It seems that there's a very real danger that this will cause trouble between you and Ronald Trask.'

'She and Ronald were never engaged.'

'That's not the point, David.'

'He misunderstood the situation completely. One could even argue that he took advantage of her emotional vulnerability after Charles's death. Unconsciously, of course.'

'Unlike you?'

'I'm not proposing to take advantage of her. Any more than she'd be taking advantage of me. Besides, Vanessa's husband died three years ago. Plenty of time to get back on to an even keel.'

'Your wife died more than ten years ago. Do you feel you were on an even keel after three years?'

'That was different.'

'I see.'

'Ronald will understand,' I said with an optimism I did not feel. 'I'll make every effort to talk to him. I wouldn't want to let the problem fester, naturally.'

'Do you think it's possible to build happiness on the unhappiness of others?'

316

'Is that worse than making all three of us unhappy?'

Peter nodded, not conceding the point but merely passing on to the next difficulty. 'And there's the consideration that if a priest marries, he should choose someone who shares his beliefs. Otherwise it can put an intolerable strain on the marriage.'

'Vanessa was confirmed in her teens. She's not an atheist or anything like that. She's simply not a committed churchgoer.' I drew in a deep breath. 'Quite apart from anything else, I think that this may be a way of bringing her back to the Church.'

'I shall pray that you're right.'

'You don't sound very hopeful.'

'It's merely that, if I were you, I'd tread very carefully. In my experience, a priest should be a husband to his wife. If he tries to be a priest as well, it can cause difficulties. It's like a doctor treating his own family. There are two sets of priorities, and they can conflict.'

'I take your point. I wouldn't be heavy-handed about it. But Vanessa's the sort of person who might well appreciate the more intellectual side of post-war theology. Tillich, Bultmann, Bonhoeffer – people like that. They could offer her a way back. I doubt if she's even read *Honest to God*. I know you and I don't altogether see eye to eye with –'

'David?'

'Sorry. I'm rambling, aren't I?'

'Have you discussed the idea with Rosemary?'

'Not yet.' I hesitated, knowing Peter was waiting for more. 'All right. I suppose I'm putting it off. I could have mentioned it when she was home at half-term.'

'You've obviously made up your mind that you're going to ask Vanessa to marry you,' he said slowly. 'Very well. But in that case, I think you should tell Rosemary as soon as possible. She's bound to feel upset. And if she hears the news from somebody else, think how much more damaging it will be.'

'You're right, of course.'

'You may even find Rosemary's jealous.'

I smiled. 'Surely not.'

Even as I spoke I remembered the evening in September when I experienced that unpleasant, dreamlike state in church: the sense of being defiled; the wings of geese flying over the mudflats of an estuary. On the same evening Vanessa had phoned the Vicarage and left a message for me with Rosemary. I had never discovered why Rosemary had failed to pass on the message. I wondered now if she really had forgotten. But what other reason could there be?

The following evening I went to Vanessa's flat in Richmond. She led me into the living room. A parcel was lying on the coffee table.

'The book's ready,' she told me. 'I've brought advance copies for you and Audrey.'

'Damn the book,' I said. 'Will you marry me?'

She frowned, staring up at me. 'I don't know.'

'You don't want to?'

'It's not that. But I'm not sure I'd be right for you.'

'You would. I'm sure.'

'But I'd be no good as a vicar's wife. I just don't have the credentials. I don't *want* to have them.'

'I don't want to marry a potential vicar's wife.' I touched her arm and saw her eyes flicker, as if I had given her a tiny electric shock. But she did not move away. 'I want to marry *you*.'

We stood there for a moment. She shivered. I slipped my arm round her and kissed her cheek. I felt as clumsy as a teenager with his first girl. She pulled away. Hands on hips, she glared at me with mock anger.

'If I'd known this wretched book would lead to . . .'

'Will you marry me? Will you?'

'All right.' Her face broke into a smile. 'As long as I don't have to be a vicar's wife. I ought to get that in writing.'

I put my arms around her and we kissed. My body reacted with predictable enthusiasm. I wondered how on earth I could restrain myself from going further until we were married.

Afterwards, Vanessa brought out a bottle of Cognac, and we drank a toast to our future. Like teenagers, we sat side by side on the sofa, holding hands and talking almost in whispers, as though there were a danger that someone might overhear and envy our happiness.

'I can't believe you've agreed,' I said.

'*I* can't understand how you've managed to stay single for so long. You're far too good-looking to be a clergyman, let alone an unmarried one.' She stared at me, then giggled. 'You're blushing.'

'I'm not used to receiving compliments from beautiful women.'

Simultaneously we picked up our glasses. I think we were both a little embarrassed. The small talk of lovers is difficult when you're out of practice.

Vanessa cradled the glass in her hand. 'You've made me realize how lonely I've been,' she said slowly. 'I've had more fun with you in the last two months than I've had in the last three years put together.'

'Fun?'

Her fingers tightened on mine. 'When you're living on your own, there doesn't seem much point in having fun. Or a sense of humour. Or going out for a meal. Didn't you find that?'

Didn't, not *don't*. 'Yes. But surely Ronald –'

'Ronnie's kind. He's a good man. I like him. I trust him. I'm grateful to him. I almost married him. But he isn't much fun.'

'I don't know if I am, either,' I felt obliged to say. 'Not on a day-to-day basis.'

'We'll see about that.' She turned her head to look at me. 'You know what I really love about you? You make me feel it's possible to *change*.'

My inclination was to announce our engagement at once. It gave me great joy, and I wanted to share it. Vanessa, however, thought we should keep it to ourselves until we had told Ronald and Rosemary.

Her delay in telling Ronald almost drove me frantic. I could not feel that she was truly engaged to me until she had made it clear to Ronald that she would never be engaged to him. She did not tell him until ten days after she had agreed to marry me. They went out to lunch, in the Italian restaurant where we had talked about the warts of Francis Youlgreave.

Vanessa did not tell me what they said to each other and I did not ask. But the next time I saw Ronald, which was at a diocesan meeting, he was cool to the point of frostiness. He did not mention Vanessa and nor did I. I had told Peter that I would talk to Ronald, but when it came to the point I could not think of anything to say. He was businesslike and polite, but I sensed that any friendship he had felt for me had evaporated.

His sister Cynthia was less restrained. I had been up to London one afternoon, and I met her by chance at Waterloo Station on my way back home. We saw each other at the same time. We were walking across the station concourse and our paths were due to converge in a few seconds. Her chin went up and her mouth snapped shut. She veered away. After a few paces, she changed her mind and swung back towards me.

'Good afternoon, Cynthia. How are you?'

She put her face close to mine. Her cheeks had flushed a dark red. 'I think what you did was despicable. Taking advantage.' There were tears in her eyes. 'I hope you pay for it.'

She turned away and, head down, ploughed into a crowd of commuters and vanished from my sight. I told myself that she was being unreasonable: that the fact of the matter was that Vanessa had chosen to marry me of her own free will; and there was no element of deception about it.

7

The round of parish work continued. Normally I would have welcomed much of this. Week by week, the rhythm of the church services made a familiar context for my life, a public counterpart to my private prayers. Weddings, baptisms and funerals punctuated the pattern.

There was satisfaction in the sense that one was carrying on a tradition that had developed over nearly two thousand years; that, through the rituals of the church, one was building a bridge between now and eternity. Less satisfying was the pastoral side of parish work – the schools and old people's homes, visiting the sick, sitting on the innumerable committees that a parish priest cannot avoid.

At that time Roth Park, once the big house of the village, was still an old people's home. The Bramleys, who owned it, were running it down, which meant that their guests were growing older, fewer and more decrepit. Their policy had an indirect effect on me. There was a run of deaths at Roth Park in those winter months of 1969–70, which became cumulatively depressing. Sometimes, when I walked or drove up to the house, I felt as though I were being sucked towards a dark vacuum, a sort of spiritual black hole.

Rosemary came back from school for the Christmas holidays. She had changed once again. Boarding school had that effect: each time she came home she was a stranger. I was biased, of course, but to me it seemed that she was becoming increasingly good-looking, developing into one of those classic English beauties, with fair hair, blue eyes, a high brow and regular features.

On her first evening home, I told her about Vanessa while we were washing up after supper. While I was speaking I could not see her face because her head was bent over the cutlery drawer. Afterwards she said nothing. She stacked the spoons neatly in the drawer, one inside the other.

'Well?' I said.

'I hope . . .' She paused. 'I hope you'll be happy.'

'Thank you, my dear.'

Her words were formal, even stilted, but they were better than I had feared.

'When will you get married?'

'After Easter. Before you go back to school. Talking of which, Vanessa and I were wondering if you would like to transfer to somewhere nearer for your last year in the sixth form. So you could be a day girl.'

'*No.*'

'It's entirely up to you. You may well feel it would be less upheaval to stay where you are. Where you are used to your teachers, among your own friends, and so on.'

Rosemary gathered a pile of plates and crouched beside a cupboard. One by one, with metronomic regularity, she put them away. I still could not see her face.

'Rosie,' I said. 'I know this isn't easy for you. It's been just the two of us for a very long time, hasn't it?'

She said nothing.

'But Vanessa's not going to be some sort of wicked step-mother. Nothing's going to change between you and me. Really, darling.'

Still she did not speak. I crouched beside her and put a hand on her shoulder. 'So?' I prompted. 'What do you think?'

At last she looked at me. To my horror, I saw that her eyes had filled with tears. Her face was red. For a moment she was ugly. The tea towel slipped from her hands and fell to the floor.

'What does it matter?' she said. 'We'll end up doing what you want. We always do.'

Christmas came and went. Vanessa and I announced our engagement, causing a flurry of smiles and whispers among my congregation. We also agreed a date for our wedding –

the first Saturday after Easter, shortly before Rosemary would be due to return to school for the summer term.

'Couldn't we make it sooner?' I said to Vanessa when we were discussing the timing.

'I think we're rushing things as it is.'

I ran my eyes over her. Desire can produce a sensation like hunger, an emptiness that cries out to be filled. 'I wish we didn't have to wait. I'd like to feast on you. Does that sound absurd?'

She smiled at me and touched my hand. 'By the way, I had a chat with Rosemary. It was fine – she seemed very pleased for us.'

'I'm so glad.'

'"I do hope you and Father will be very happy." That's what she said.' Vanessa frowned. 'Does she always call you "Father"? It sounds so formal.'

'Her choice, as far as I remember. She always did, right from the start.'

'Is it because you're a priest? She's very interested in the trappings of religion, isn't she?'

'It must be because of growing up in the odour of sanctity.'

Vanessa laughed. 'I thought clergymen weren't meant to make jokes about religion.'

'Why not? God gave us a sense of humour.'

'To go back to Rosemary: she's agreed to be maid of honour.'

The wedding was going to be in Richmond, and Peter Hudson had agreed to officiate. The only other people we invited were two of Vanessa's Oxford friends and a couple called the Appleyards, whom I had known since my days at Rosington. Early in the New Year, Vanessa and I spent a day with the Appleyards.

'They seemed quite normal,' she said to me as I drove her back to Richmond. 'Not a dog collar in sight. Have you known them long?'

'For years. Henry rented a room from us when we were living in Rosington.'

'So they knew Janet?'

'Yes.'

We drove in silence for a moment. I had told Vanessa about Janet, my first wife. Not everything, of course, but everything that mattered to Vanessa and me.

'Michael's nice,' she went on. 'How old is he?'

'Coming up to eleven, I think.'

'You're fond of him, aren't you?'

'Yes.' After a pause I added, 'He's my godson,' though that did not explain why I liked him. Michael and I rarely had much to say to each other, but we had been comfortable in each other's company ever since he was a toddler.

'Do they ever come to Roth?'

'Occasionally.'

'We must ask them to stay.'

I glanced at her and smiled. 'I'd like that.'

She smiled back. 'It's odd, isn't it? It's not just us getting married. It's our friends and relations as well.'

In January, Rosemary went back to school. Vanessa spent the following Saturday with me. Now we had the house to ourselves, we wanted to plan what changes would have to be made when Vanessa moved in; we had thought it would be tactless to do this while Rosemary was there. After lunch, the doorbell rang. I was not surprised to find Audrey Oliphant on the doorstep.

She wore a heavy tweed suit, rather too small for her, and a semi-transparent plastic mac, which gave her an ill-defined, almost ghostly appearance.

'So sorry to disturb you,' she said. 'I wondered if you'd seen Lord Peter recently.'

Vanessa came out of the kitchen and said hello.

'Lord Peter – my cat,' Audrey explained to her. 'Such a worry. He treats the Vicarage as his second home.'

I leant nonchalantly against the door, preventing her from stepping into the hall. 'I'm afraid we haven't seen him.'

'The kettle's on,' Vanessa said. 'Would you like a cup?'

Audrey slipped past me and followed her into the kitchen. 'Lord Peter has to cross the main road to get here. The traffic's getting worse and worse, especially since they started work on the motorway.'

'Cats are very good at looking after themselves,' Vanessa said.

'I hope I'm not disturbing you.' No doubt accidentally, Audrey tried to insinuate a hint of indecency, the faintest wiggle of the eyebrows, into this possibility. 'I'm sure you were in the middle of something.'

'Nothing that wasn't going to wait until after tea,' Vanessa said. 'How's the book selling?'

'Splendidly, thank you. We sold sixty-three copies over Christmas. I knew people would like it.'

'Why don't you take Audrey's coat?' Vanessa suggested to me.

'People like to know about their own village,' Audrey continued, allowing me to peel her plastic mac away from her. 'I know there have been changes, but Roth really is a village still.'

Changes? A village? I thought of the huge reservoir to the north, of the projected motorway through the southern part of the parish, and of the sea of suburban houses that lapped around the green. I carried the tea tray into the sitting room.

'There's not much of it left,' Vanessa said. 'The village, I mean.'

Audrey stared at Vanessa. 'Oh, you're quite wrong. Let me show you.' She beckoned Vanessa towards the window, which looked out over the drive, the road and the green. '*That's* the village.' She nodded to her left, towards the houses of Vicarage Drive. 'Here and on the left: the Vicarage and its garden. And then on our right is St Mary Magdalene, and beyond that the gates to Roth Park and the river. If you cross the stone bridge and carry on down the road, we'll come to the Old Manor House, where Lady Youlgreave lives.'

'I must take you to meet Lady Youlgreave,' I said to Vanessa, attempting to divert the flow. 'In a sense she's my employer.'

It was no use. Audrey had now turned towards the green and was pointing at Malik's Minimarket, which stood just beside the main road at the western end of the north side of the green.

'That was the village forge when I was a girl.' She laughed, a high and irritating sound. Her voice acquired a faint sing-song cadence. 'Of course, it's changed a bit since then, but haven't we all? And beside it is my little home, Tudor Cottage. (I was born there, you know, on the second floor. The window on the left.) Then there's the Queen's Head. I think part of their cellars are even older than Tudor Cottage.'

We all stared at the Queen's Head, a building that had been modernized so many times in the last hundred years that it had lost all trace of its original character. The pub now had a restaurant which served steaks, chips and cheap wine. At the weekend, the disco in the basement attracted young people from miles around, and there were regular complaints – usually from Audrey – about the noise.

'The bus shelter wasn't there when I was a girl,' Audrey went on. 'We had a much nicer one, with a thatched roof.'

The bus shelter stood on the green itself, opposite the pub. It was a malodorous cavern, whose main use was as the wet-weather headquarters of the teenagers who lived on the Manor Farm council estate.

'And of course Manor Farm Lane has seen one or two changes as well.' Audrey pointed at the road to the council estate which went off at the north-east corner of the green and winced theatrically. 'We used to have picnics by the stream beyond the barn,' she murmured in a confidential voice. 'Just over there. Wonderful wild flowers in the spring.'

The barn was long gone, and the stream had been culverted over. Yet she gave the impression that for her they were still vivid, in a way that the council estate was not. For her the past inhabited the present and gave it meaning.

The finger moved on to the east side of the green, to a nondescript row of villas from the 1930s, defiantly suburban, to the library and the ramshackle church hall. 'There was a lovely line of sixteenth- and seventeenth-century cottages over there.'

Vanessa's eyes met mine. I opened my mouth, but I was too late. Audrey's head had swivelled round to the south side, to the four detached Edwardian houses whose gardens ran down to the Rowan behind them. Two of them had been cut up into flats; one was leased as offices; and the fourth was where Dr Vintner lived with his family and had his surgery.

'A retired colonel in the Bengal Lancers used to live in the one at the far end. There was a nice solicitor in Number Two.

326

And the lady in Number Three was some sort of cousin of the Youlgreaves.'

Black fur streaked along the windowsill. A paw tapped the glass. Lord Peter had come to join us.

'Oh look!' Audrey said. 'Isn't he clever?' She bent down, bringing her head level with Lord Peter's. 'You knew Mummy was coming to look for you, didn't you? So you came to find Mummy instead.'

8

In February, Lady Youlgreave demanded to see Vanessa. She invited us to have a glass of sherry with her after church on Sunday.

When I told Vanessa, her face brightened. 'Oh good.'

'I wish she'd chosen some other time.' Sunday was my busiest day.

'Do you want to see if we can rearrange it?'

'It would be diplomatic to go,' I said. 'No sense in upsetting her.'

'I'll take you out to lunch afterwards. As a reward.'

'Why are you so keen to meet her?'

'Not exactly keen. Just interested.'

'Because of the connection with Francis Youlgreave?'

Vanessa nodded. 'It's not every day you have a chance to meet the surviving family of a dead poet.' She glanced at me, her face mischievous. 'Or for that matter the man responsible for the care of his earthly remains.'

'No doubt that was the only reason you wanted to marry me?'

'Beggars can't be choosers. Anyway, I want to meet Lady Youlgreave for her own sake. Isn't she your boss?'

The old woman was the patron of the living, which meant that on the departure of one incumbent she had the right to nominate the next. The practice was a quaint survival from the days when such patronage had been a convenient way to provide financially for younger sons. In practice, such private patrons usually delegated the choice to the bishop. But Lady Youlgreave had chosen to exercise the right when she nominated me. An ancient possessiveness lingered. Though she rarely came to church, I had heard her refer to me on more than one occasion as 'my vicar'.

On Sunday, swathed in coats, Vanessa and I left the Vicarage. We walked arm in arm past the railings of the church and crossed the mouth of the drive to Roth Park. The big wrought-iron gates had stood open for as long as anyone could remember. Each gate contained the letter Y within an oval frame. On the top of the left-hand gatepost was a stone fist brandishing a dagger, the crest of the Youlgreaves. On the right-hand gatepost there was nothing but an iron spike.

'What happened to the other dagger?' Vanessa asked.

'According to Audrey, some teddy boys pulled it down on New Year's Eve. Before my time.'

Vanessa stopped, staring up the drive, a broad strip of grass and weeds separating two ruts of mud and gravel, running into a tunnel of trees which needed pollarding. The house could not be seen from the road.

'It looks so mournful,' she said.

'The Bramleys haven't spent much money on the place. I'm told they're trying to sell it.'

'Is there much land left?'

'Just the strip along the drive, plus a bit near the house. Most of it was sold off for housing.'

'Sometimes it all seems so pointless. Spending all that time and money on a place like that.'

I glanced at the gates. 'How old are they, do you think?'

'Turn of the century? Obviously made to last for generations.'

'Designed to impress. And the implication was that the house and the park would be in your descendants' hands for ever and ever.'

'That's what's so sad,' Vanessa said. 'They were building for eternity, and seventy years later eternity came to an end.'

'Eternity was even shorter than that. The Youlgreaves had to sell up in the nineteen-thirties.'

'I remember. It was in Audrey's book. And they hadn't been here for very long, had they? Not in dynastic terms.'

We walked across the bridge. A lorry travelling north from

the gravel pits splashed mud on my overcoat. Vanessa peered down at the muddy waters beneath. The Rowan was no more than a stream, but at this point, though shallow, it was relatively wide.

We came to the Old Manor House, a long low building separated from the road by a line of posts linked by chains. This side of the house had a two-storey frontage with six bays. The windows were large and Georgian. At some point the façade had been rendered and painted a pale greeny-blue, now fading and flaking with age. There were darker stains on the walls where rainwater had cascaded out of the broken guttering.

Between the posts and the house was a circular lawn, around which ran the drive. The grass was long and lank, and there were drifts of leaves against the house. Weeds sprouted through the cracks of the tarmac. In the middle of the lawn was a wooden bird table, beneath which sat Lord Peter, waiting. Hearing our footsteps, the cat glanced towards us and moved away without hurrying. He slithered through the bars of the gate at the side of the house and slid out of sight behind the dustbins.

'That cat's everywhere,' Vanessa said. 'Don't you find it sinister?'

I glanced at her. 'No. Why?'

'No reason.' She looked away. 'Is that someone waving from the window? The one at the end?'

An arm was waving slowly behind the ground-floor window to the far left. We walked towards the front door.

'How do you feel about dogs, by the way?'

'Fine. Why?'

'Lady Youlgreave has two of them.'

I tried the handle of the front door. It was locked. There was a burst of barking from the other side. I felt Vanessa recoil.

'It's all right. They're tied up. We'll have to go round to the back.'

We walked down the side of the house, past the dustbins and into the yard at the rear. There was no sign of Lord Peter. The spare key was hidden under an upturned flowerpot beside the door.

'A little obvious, isn't it?' Vanessa said. 'It's the first place anyone would look.'

We let ourselves into a scullery which led through an evil-smelling kitchen towards the sound of barking in the hall.

Beauty and Beast were attached by their leads to the newel post at the foot of the stairs. Beauty was an Alsatian, so old she could hardly stand up, and almost blind. Beast was a dachshund, even older, though she retained more of her faculties. She, too, had her problems in the shape of a sausage-shaped tumour that dangled from her belly almost to the floor. When she waddled along, it was as though she had five legs. When I had first come to Roth, the dogs and their owner had been much more active, and one often met the three of them marching along the footpaths that criss-crossed what was left of Roth Park. Now their lives had contracted. The dogs were no longer capable of guarding or attacking. They ate, slept, defecated and barked.

'This way,' I said to Vanessa, raising my voice to make her hear above the din.

She wrinkled her nose and mouthed, 'Does it always smell this bad?'

I nodded. Doris Potter, who was one of my regular communicants, came in twice a day during the week, and an agency nurse covered the weekends. But they were unable to do much more than look after Lady Youlgreave herself.

The hall was T-shaped, with the stairs at the rear. I led the way into the right-hand arm of the T. I tapped on a door at the end of the corridor.

'Come in, David.' The voice was high-pitched like a child's.

The room had once been a dining room. When I had first come to Roth, Lady Youlgreave had asked me to dinner, and we had eaten by candlelight, facing each other across the huge mahogany table. Then as now, most of the furniture was Victorian, and designed for a larger room. We had eaten food which came out of tins and we drank a bottle of claret which should have been opened five years earlier.

For an instant, I saw the room afresh, as if through Vanessa's eyes. I noticed the thick grey cobwebs around the cornices, a bird's nest among the ashes in the grate, and the dust on every horizontal surface. Time had drained most of the colour and substance from the Turkish carpet, leaving a ghostly presence on the floor. The walls were crowded with oil paintings, none of them particularly old and most of them worth less than their heavy gilt frames. The exception was the Sargent over the fireplace: it showed a large, red-faced man in tweeds, Lady Youlgreave's father-in-law, standing beside the Rowan with his large red house in the background and a springer spaniel at his feet.

Our hostess was sitting in an easy chair beside the window. This was where she usually passed her days. She spent her nights in the room next door, which had once been her husband's study; she no longer used the upstairs. She had a blanket draped over her lap and a side table beside the chair. A Zimmer frame stood within arm's reach. There were books on the side table, and also a lined pad on a clipboard. On a low stool within reach of the chair was a metal box with its lid open.

For a moment, Lady Youlgreave stared at us as we hesitated in the doorway. It was as though she had forgotten what we were doing here. The dogs were still barking behind us, but with less conviction than before.

'Shut the door and take off your coats,' she said. 'Put them down. Doesn't matter where.'

Lady Youlgreave had been a small woman to begin with, and now old age had made her even smaller. Dark eyes peered up at us from deep sockets. She was wearing a dress of some stiff material with a high collar; the dress was too large for her now, and her head poked out of the folds of the collar like a tortoise's from its shell.

'Well,' she said. 'This is a surprise.'

'I'd like to introduce Vanessa Forde, my fiancée. Vanessa, this is Lady Youlgreave.'

'How do you do. Pull up one of those chairs and sit down where I can see you.'

I arranged two of the dining chairs for Vanessa and myself. The three of us sat in a little semi-circle in front of the window. Vanessa was nearest the box, and I noticed her glancing into its open mouth.

Lady Youlgreave studied Vanessa with unabashed curiosity. 'So. If you ask me, David's luckier than he deserves.'

Vanessa smiled and politely shook her head.

'My cleaning woman tells me you're a publisher.'

'Yes – by accident really.'

'I dare say you'll be giving it up when you marry.'

'No.' Vanessa glanced at me. 'It's my job. In any case, the income will be important.'

Lady Youlgreave squeezed her lips together. Then she relaxed them and said, 'In my day, a husband supported a wife.'

'I suppose I've grown used to supporting myself.'

'And a wife supported her husband in other ways. Made a home for him.' Unexpectedly, she laughed, a bubbling hiss from the back of her throat. 'And in the case of a vicar's wife, she usually ran the parish as well. You'll have plenty to do here without going out to work.'

'It's up to Vanessa, of course,' I said. 'By the way, how are you feeling?'

'Awful. That damned doctor keeps giving me new medicines, but all they do is bung me up and give me bad dreams.' She waved a brown, twisted hand at the box on the stool. 'I dreamt about that last night. I dreamt I found a dead bird inside. A goose. Told the girl I wanted it roasted for lunch. Then I saw it was crawling with maggots.' There was another laugh. 'That'll teach me to go rummaging through the past.'

'Is that what you've been doing?' Vanessa asked. 'In there?'

'I have to do something. I never realized you can be tired and in pain and bored – all at the same time. The girl told me that the Oliphant woman had written a history of Roth. So I made her buy me a copy. Not as bad as I thought it was going to be.' She glared at me. 'I suppose you had a hand in it.'

'Vanessa and I edited it, yes, and Vanessa saw it through the press.'

'Thought so. Anyway, it made me curious. I knew there was a lot of rubbish up in the attic. Papers, and so on. George had them put up there when we moved from the other house. Said he was going to write the family history. God knows why. Literature wasn't his line at all. Didn't know one end of a pen from another. Anyway, he never had the opportunity. So all the rubbish just stayed up there.'

Vanessa leant forwards. 'Do you think you might write something yourself?'

Lady Youlgreave held up her right hand. 'With fingers like

this?' She let the hand drop on her lap. 'Besides, what does it matter? It's all over with. They're all dead and buried. Who cares what they did or why they did it?'

She stared out of the window at the bird table. I wondered if the morphine were affecting her mind. James Vintner had told me that he had increased the dose recently. Like the house and the dogs, their owner was sliding into decay.

I said, 'Vanessa's read quite a lot of Francis Youlgreave's verse.'

'I've got a copy of *The Four Last Things*,' Vanessa said. 'The one with "The Judgement of Strangers" in it.'

Lady Youlgreave stared at her for a moment. 'There were two other collections, *The Tongues of Angels* and *Last Poems*. He published *Last Poems* when he was still up at Oxford. Silly man. So pretentious.' Her eyes moved to me. 'Pass me that book,' she demanded. 'The black one on the corner of the table.'

I handed her a quarto-sized hardback notebook. The seconds ticked by while she opened it and tried to find the page she wanted. Vanessa and I looked at each other. Inside the notebook I saw yellowing paper, unlined and flecked with damp, covered with erratic lines of handwriting in brown ink.

'There,' Lady Youlgreave said at last, placing the open notebook on her side table and turning it so it was the right way up for Vanessa and me. 'Read that.'

The handwriting was a mass of blots and corrections. Two lines leapt out at me, however, because they were the only ones which had no alterations or blemishes:

> *Then darkness descended; and whispers defiled*
> *The judgement of stranger, and widow, and child.*

'Is that *his* writing?' Vanessa asked, her voice strained.

Lady Youlgreave nodded. 'This is a volume of his journal. March eighteen-ninety-four, while he was still in London.' The lips twisted. 'He was the vicar of St Michael's in Beauclerk Place. I think this was the first draft.' She looked up at us, at our eager faces, then slowly closed the book. 'According to this journal, it was a command performance.'

Vanessa raised her eyebrows. 'I don't understand.'

Lady Youlgreave drew the book towards her and clasped it on her lap. 'He wrote the first half of the first draft in a frenzy of inspiration in the early hours of the morning. He had just had an angelic visitation. He believed that the angel had told him to write the poem.' Once more her lips curled and she looked from me to Vanessa. 'He was intoxicated at the time, of course. He had been smoking opium earlier that evening. He used to patronize an establishment in Leicester Square.' Her head swayed on her neck. 'An establishment which seems to have catered for a variety of tastes.'

'Are there many of his journals?' asked Vanessa. 'Or manuscripts of his poems? Or letters?'

'Quite a few. I've not had time to go through everything yet.'

'As you know, I'm a publisher. I can't help wondering if you might have the material for a biography of Francis Youlgreave there.'

'Very likely. For example, his journal gives a very different view of the Rosington scandal. From the horse's mouth, as it were.' Her lips twisted and she made a hissing sound. 'The trouble is, this particular horse isn't always a reliable witness. George's father used to say – but I mustn't keep you waiting like this. You haven't had any sherry yet. I'm sure we've got some somewhere.'

'It doesn't matter,' I said.

'The girl will know. She's late. She should be bringing me my lunch.'

The heavy eyelids, like dough-coloured rubber, drooped over the eyes. The fingers twitched, but did not relax their hold of Francis Youlgreave's journal.

'I think perhaps we'd better be going,' I said. 'Leave you to your lunch.'

'You can give me my medicine first.' The eyes were fully open again and suddenly alert. 'It's the bottle on the mantelpiece.'

I hesitated. 'Are you sure it's the right time?'

'I always have it before lunch,' she snapped. 'That's what Dr Vintner said. It's before lunch, isn't it? And the girl's late. She's supposed to be bringing me my lunch.'

There was a clean glass and a spoon beside the bottle on the mantelpiece. I measured out a dose and gave her the glass. She clasped it in both hands and drank it at once. She sat back, still cradling the glass. A dribble of liquid ran down her chin.

'I'll leave a note,' I said. 'Just to say that you've had your medicine.'

'But there's no need to write a note. I'll tell Doris myself.'

'It won't be Doris,' I said. 'It's the weekend, so it's the nurse who'll come in.'

'Silly woman. Thinks I'm deaf. Thinks I'm senile. Anyway, I told you: I'll tell her myself.'

I could be obstinate, too. I scribbled a few words in pencil on a page torn from my diary and left it under the bottle for the nurse. Lady Youlgreave barely acknowledged us when we said goodbye. But when we were almost at the door, she stirred.

'Come and see me again soon,' she commanded. 'Both of you. Perhaps you'd like to look at some of Uncle Francis's things. He was very interested in sex, you know.' She made a hissing noise again, her way of expressing mirth. 'Just like you, David.'

9

Vanessa and I were married on a rainy Saturday in April. Henry Appleyard was my best man. Michael gave us a present, a battered but beautiful seventeenth-century French edition of *Ecclesiasticus*; according to the bookplate it had once been part of the library of Rosington Theological College.

'It was his own idea,' his mother whispered to me. 'His own money, too. Quite a coincidence – Rosington, I mean.'

'I hope it wasn't expensive.'

'Five shillings. He found it in a junk shop.'

'We've been very lucky with presents,' Vanessa said. 'Rosemary gave us a gorgeous coffee pot. Denbigh ware.'

It was only then that I realized Rosemary was listening intently to the conversation. Later I noticed her examining the book, flicking through the pages as if they irritated her.

Vanessa and I flew to Italy the same afternoon. She had arranged it all, including the *pensione* in Florence where we were to stay. I had assumed that if we had a honeymoon at all it would be in England. But Florence had been Vanessa's idea, and she was so excited about it that I did not have the heart to try to change her mind. Her plan had support from an unexpected quarter: when I told Peter Hudson, he said, 'She's right. Get right away from everything. You owe it to each other.'

It was raining in Florence, too. Not that it mattered. I wouldn't have cared if the city had been buried beneath a pall of snow.

We had dinner in a little restaurant. Vanessa was looking alluring in a dark dress which set off her hair. We talked more about Rosemary than ourselves. I found myself glancing surreptitiously at my watch. I did not eat much, though I drank more than my fair share of the wine.

While we talked, I allowed my imagination to run free for the first time in ten years. I felt like a schoolboy at the end of term, or a convict coming to the end of his sentence.

As the meal progressed, we talked less. An awkwardness settled between us. My thoughts scurried to and fro as though I were running a fever. Once or twice, Vanessa looked at me and seemed about to say something.

The waiter asked if we would like coffee. I wanted to go back to our room, but Vanessa ordered coffee, with brandies to go with it. When the drinks came, she drank half her brandy in a few seconds.

'David, I have to admit I feel a bit nervous.'

I leaned forward to light her cigarette. 'Why?'

'About tonight.'

For a moment, neither of us spoke.

'We'll get used to it,' I said. 'I dare say we'll both find it strange.' The urgency was building up inside me. I touched Vanessa's hand. 'Dearest – you know, there's no reason why it needn't be enjoyable as well.'

She ran her finger around the rim of her glass. 'Charles didn't seem – he didn't want it very much. I don't know why. Of course, it happened quite a lot when we were first married, but then it tailed off.'

'You don't have to tell me this.'

'I want to explain. Charles used to stay up reading until all hours and often I was asleep when he came to bed. There just never seemed to be much opportunity.'

'Darling,' I said, 'don't worry.'

Her mouth twitched. 'It'll be all right on the night, will it?'

'It will be. And then it will get better and better. Shall I get the bill?'

We walked back – sedately, arm in arm – to our *pensione*. There was a part of me that wanted to make love to her there and then: to pull her into an alley, push her up against a wall and tear my way into her clothes; and all the while the rain would patter on our heads and shoulders, the lamplight would glitter in the puddles, and the snarls and honks of the traffic would make a savage, distant music.

At the *pensione*, we collected our key and went upstairs. I locked the door behind us. I turned to find her standing in the middle of the room with her arms by her side.

'Vanessa.' My voice sounded like a stranger's. 'You're lovely.'

I took off my jacket and dropped it on a chair. I went to her, put my hands on her shoulders, stooped and kissed her gently on the lips. Her lips moved beneath mine. I took off her coat and let it fall to the floor. I nibbled the side of her neck. My fingers found the fastening of her dress. I peeled it away from her. She stood there in her underwear, revealed and vulnerable. Her arms tightened round my neck.

'I'm cold. Can we get into bed?'

I was a little disappointed: I had looked forward for months to slowly removing her clothes, to touching as much of her body as I could with my mouth. But all that could wait. She allowed me to help her quickly out of the rest of her clothes. She scrambled into bed and watched me as I quickly undressed. My excitement was obvious.

'My handbag. I've got a cap.'

'I've got a condom.' I dropped my wallet on the bedside table and slithered into bed beside her.

There was goose flesh on her arm. It was hard to move much because she was holding me so tightly. The restraint somehow increased my excitement. I kissed her hair frantically.

'I want you,' I muttered. 'Let me come in.'

She released her hold. I rolled over and found the condom in my wallet. My fingers were twice as clumsy as usual. At last I extracted the condom from its foil wrapper and rolled it over my penis. Vanessa was lying on her back, her legs slightly apart, watching me. There was a noise like surf in my ears.

'Now, darling,' I said. 'Now, now.'

I climbed on top of her, using my knees to spread her legs wider. I abandoned all attempts at subtlety. I wanted one thing and I wanted it now. Vanessa stared up at me and put her hands on my shoulders. Her face was very serious. I lowered myself and thrust hard into her. She gasped and tried to writhe away but now my hands were on her shoulders and she could not move. I cried out, a groan that had been building up inside me for ten years. And then, with embarrassing rapidity, it was all over.

Trembling, I lay like a dead weight on top of her. In a moment, my trembling turned to sobs.

Once again her arms tightened around me. 'Hush now. It's all right. It's over.'

It wasn't over, not for either of us, and it wasn't all right. Two hours later, I wanted her again. We were still awake, talking about the future. Vanessa agreed with me that it would obviously take time before we were sexually in tune with each other. That was to be expected. The second time everything happened more slowly. She lay there while I explored the hollows and curves of her body with my mouth. She let me do whatever I wanted, and I did.

'Dearest David,' she murmured, not once but many times.

After I had come again, I asked if there was anything I could do for her, and she said no, not this time. She went into the little bathroom. I lit a cigarette and listened to the rustle of running water. When she came back, she was wearing her nightdress and her face was pink and scrubbed. Soon we turned out the light and settled down for sleep. I rested my arm over her. I felt her hand take mine.

'How was it?' I asked. 'Was it very painful?'

'I'm a little sore.'

'I'm sorry. I should have –'

'It doesn't matter. I want to make you happy.'

'You do.'

We were in Florence for seven days. We looked at pictures, listened to music and sat in cafés. And we made love. Each night she lay there and allowed me to do whatever I wanted; and I did. On the seventh night I found her crying in the bathroom.

'Darling, what's wrong?'

She lifted her tear-stained face to me, a sight which I found curiously erotic. 'It's nothing. I'm tired, that's all.'

'Tell me.'

'It's a little painful. Sore.'

I smiled. 'So am I, as a matter of fact. Not used to the exercise.

I dare say we'll soon toughen up. It's like walking without shoes. One needs practice.'

She tried to smile, but it didn't quite come off. 'And my breasts are rather painful too. I think my period is due.'

'We needn't do anything tonight,' I said, my disappointment temporarily swamped by my desire to be kind.

We sat in bed reading. She was the first to turn out the light. The evening felt incomplete. I lay on my back and stared up into the darkness.

'Vanessa?' I said softly. 'Are you awake?'

'Yes.'

'How do you feel about making love when you have a period?' It had suddenly occurred to me that it might be several days before we had an opportunity to do it again. 'I should say that I don't mind it, myself.'

'Actually, it's very painful for me. I have heavy periods. I'm sorry.'

'Not to worry,' I said; I turned and put my arm around her. 'It doesn't matter. Sleep well. God bless.'

As usual, her hand gripped mine. I lay there, my penis as erect as a guardsman on parade, listening to the sound of her breathing.

10

After our return from Italy, Vanessa and I slipped into the new routine of our shared lives. We were even happy, in a fragmentary fashion, as humans are happy. Though what was in store was rooted in ourselves – in our personalities and our histories – we had no inkling of what was coming. As humans do, we kept secrets from ourselves, and from each other.

Towards the end of May, Peter and June Hudson came to supper. They were our first real guests. The meal was something of a celebration. Peter had been offered preferment. Though there had been no official announcement, he was to be the next Bishop of Rosington.

'It's a terrifying prospect,' June said placidly. 'No more lurking in the background for me. No more communing with the kitchen sink. I shall have to be a proper Mrs Bishop and shake hands with the County.'

'You could be a Mrs Proudie,' Vanessa suggested. 'Rule your husband's diocese with a rod of iron.'

'It sounds quite attractive.' She smiled at her husband. 'I'm sure Peter wouldn't mind. It would give the little woman something to do.'

The news unsettled me. I was not jealous of Peter's preferment, though in the past I might have been. But inevitably the prospect of his going to Rosington awakened memories.

After the meal, June and Vanessa took their coffee into the sitting room while Peter and I washed up.

'When will you go to Rosington?' I asked.

'In the autumn. October, probably. I shall take a month off in August and try to prepare myself.'

I squirted a Z of washing-up liquid into a baking dish. 'I'll miss you. And June.'

'You and Vanessa must come and visit. At least there'll be plenty of space.'

'I don't know. Going back isn't always such a good idea.'

'Sometimes staying away is a worse one.'

'Damn it, Peter. You don't make it easy, do you?'

He dried a glass with the precision he brought to everything. We worked in silence for a moment. It was a muggy evening and suddenly I felt desperate for air. I opened the back door to put out the rubbish. Lord Peter streaked into the kitchen.

Had I been by myself, I would have shouted at him. But I did not want Peter – my friend, not the cat – to think me more unbalanced than he already did. When I returned from the dustbin, I found that the two Peters had formed a mutual admiration society.

'I didn't know you liked cats.'

'Oh yes. Is this one yours?'

'It belongs to one of my parishioners.'

The cat purred. Peter, who was crouching beside it with a pipe in his mouth, glanced up at me. 'You don't like either of them very much?'

'She's a good woman. A churchwarden.'

'Is that an answer?'

'It's all you're going to get.'

'I shall miss our regular meetings.'

'So shall I.'

'When I go to Rosington, you'll need a new spiritual director.'

'I suppose so.'

'A change will do you good.' Peter's voice was suddenly stern, and the cat wriggled away from him. 'Perhaps we know each other too well. A new spiritual director may be more useful to you.'

'I'd rather continue with you.'

'It just wouldn't be practical. We shall be too far away from each other. You need to see someone regularly. Don't you agree?'

'Yes. If you say so.' My voice sounded sullen, almost petulant.

'I do say so. Like one of those high-performance engines, you need constant tuning.' He smiled at me. 'Otherwise you break down.'

11

If it hadn't been for sex, or rather the lack of it, Vanessa and I would probably still be married. There was real friendship between us, and much tenderness. We filled some of the empty corners in each other's lives. A semi-detached marriage? Perhaps. If so, the arrangement suited us both. Vanessa had her job, I had mine.

One of the things I loved most was her sense of humour, which was so dry that at times I barely noticed it. On one occasion she almost reduced Audrey to tears – of rage – by suggesting that we invited the pop group that played on Saturday nights at the Queen's Head to perform at Evensong. 'It would encourage young people to come to church, don't you think?'

On another occasion, one afternoon early in August, Vanessa and I were in our little library on the green. Vanessa took her books to the issue desk, to be stamped by Mrs Finch, the librarian. Audrey was hovering like a buzzard poised to strike in front of the section devoted to detective stories.

'I'd also like to make a reservation for a book that's coming out in the autumn,' Vanessa said in a clear, carrying voice. '*The Female Eunuch* by Germaine Greer.'

I glanced up in time to see a look of outrage flash between Mrs Finch and Audrey.

Mrs Finch closed the last of Vanessa's library books, placed it on top of the others and pushed the pile across the issue desk. She jabbed the book cards into the tickets; the cardboard buckled and creased under the strain. She directed her venom at inanimate objects because by and large she was too timid to direct it at people.

While Vanessa was filling in the reservation card, I joined her at the issue desk to have my own books stamped. Audrey swooped on us; today her colour was high, perhaps because of the heat. 'So glad I caught you,' she said, her eyes flicking from me to Vanessa. 'I wanted a word about the fete.'

I did not dare look at Vanessa. The annual church fete was a delicate subject. It was held in my garden on the last Saturday in August. Audrey had organized it for the past nine years. Although she would almost certainly have resisted any attempt to relieve her of the responsibility, she felt organizing the church fete was properly the job of the vicar's wife. She had made this quite clear to both Vanessa and me in a number of indirect ways in the past few weeks.

Vanessa, on the other hand, was determined not to act as my unpaid curate in this capacity or in any other, and I respected her for the decision. We had agreed this before our marriage. She had a demanding and full-time job of her own, and had little enough spare time as it was: I could not expect her suddenly to take on more work, even if she had wanted to.

This year we had another problem to deal with. This was the suburbs, so many of our patrons came in cars. In recent years, the Bramleys had allowed us to use their paddock, a field which lay immediately behind the church and the Vicarage, as a car park. Unfortunately, they had suddenly left Roth Park at the beginning of June. They had sold the house and grounds without telling anyone. Bills had not been paid. There were rumours – relayed by Audrey – that litigation was pending.

The new owner of Roth Park had not yet moved in, so we had not been able to ask whether we could have the paddock. It would not be easy to find an alternative.

'Time's beginning to gallop,' Audrey told us. 'We really must put our thinking caps on.'

'Perhaps they could park in Manor Farm Lane,' I suggested.

'But they'd have to walk miles. Besides, it's not a very safe place to leave cars. We have to face it: without the paddock, we're hamstrung. I even rang the estate agents. But they were most unhelpful.'

'We've still got several weeks. And if the worst comes to the worst, perhaps we can do without a car park.'

'Quite impossible,' Audrey snapped. 'If people can't park their cars, they simply won't come.'

It wasn't what she said – it was the way in which she said it. Her tone was almost vindictive. In the silence, Audrey looked from Vanessa to me. Audrey's face was moist and pink. Mrs Finch studied us all from her ringside seat from behind the issue desk. The library was very quiet. A wasp with a long yellow-and-black tail flew through the open doors into the library and settled on the edge of the metal rubbish bin. Lorries ground their way down the main road. The heat was oppressive.

Audrey snorted, making a sound like steam squirting from a valve, relieving the pressure of her invisible boiler. She turned and dropped the novels she was carrying on to the trolley for returned books.

'I've got a headache,' she said. 'Not that any of you need concern yourselves about it. I shall go home and rest.'

Mrs Finch and Vanessa began to speak at once.

'My mother always said that a cold flannel and a darkened room . . .' began Mrs Finch.

Vanessa said, 'I'm so sorry. Is there anything we . . . ?'

Both women stopped talking in mid-sentence because Audrey clearly wasn't listening, and had no intention of listening. She walked very quickly out of the library. I noticed that her dress was stained with sweat under the armpits. In a moment, the doorway was empty. I stared through it at the green beyond, at the main road, the tower of the church and the oaks of Roth Park. I heard the faint but unmistakable sound of a wolf whistle. I wondered if one of the youths were baiting Audrey as she scurried round the green to the sanctuary of Tudor Cottage.

'That'll be one shilling, Mrs Byfield.' Mrs Finch held out her hand for the reservation card. 'Five pence. We'll do our best, of course, but I can't guarantee anything. The stock editor decides which books we buy. He may not think this is suitable.'

Vanessa smiled at Mrs Finch and gallantly resisted the temptation to reply. A moment later, she and I walked back along the south side of the green towards the Vicarage.

'Is Audrey often like that?' she asked.

'She gets very involved with the fete.' I felt I had to explain

347

Audrey to Vanessa, even to apologize for her. 'It's the high point of the year for her.'

'I wonder why.' Vanessa glanced up at me. 'Tell me, is she normally so irritable?'

I felt uncomfortable. 'She did seem a little tetchy.'

'I wonder how old she is. Getting on for fifty? Do you think she might be going through the menopause?'

'I suppose it's possible. Why?'

'It would explain a great deal.'

'Yes.' I was in fact unclear what the change of life could mean for a woman. I put on speed, as if trying to walk away from this faintly unsavoury topic. 'But was she really acting so unusually? She did say she had a headache.'

'David.' Vanessa put a hand on my arm, forcing me to stop and look at her. 'You've known Audrey for so long that I don't think you realize how odd she is.'

'Surely not.'

We moved on to the main road. We waited for a gap in the traffic.

'I'd better look in on her this evening,' I said. 'See how she is.'

'I wouldn't. Fuel to feed the flame.'

'Flame? Don't be silly.'

In silence, we crossed the road and went into the drive of the Vicarage.

'It's not that I *want* to see her this evening,' I went on, wondering if Vanessa might conceivably be jealous. 'People like Audrey are part of my job.'

Vanessa thrust her key into the lock of the front door. 'You sometimes sound such a *prig*.'

I stared at her. This was the nearest we had ever come to a quarrel. It was the first time that either of us had spoken critically to the other.

Vanessa pushed open the door. The telephone was ringing in the study. When I picked up the receiver, the news I heard pushed both Audrey's problems and my squabble with Vanessa into the background.

12

When I was a child I had a jigsaw with nearly a thousand pieces, intricately shaped. Some of them had been cut into the shapes of objects which were entirely unrelated to the subject of the picture.

I remember a cocktail glass lying on its side in the blue of the sky, and a stork standing upside down in the foliage of an oak tree. A rifle with a telescopic sight was concealed in a door. Not that I knew that it was a door at the outset, or that the stork was in an oak tree. The point about the jigsaw was that a picture had not been supplied with it. Only by assembling the pieces could one discover what the subject was. Since much of the picture consisted of sky, trees, grass and road, it was not until a relatively late stage in the assembly that you realized that the jigsaw showed a Pickwickian stagecoach drawing up outside a country inn with a thatched roof.

The analogy may seem laboured, but something very similar happened in Roth during 1970. One by one, the pieces dropped into place. My marriage to Vanessa, for example. *The History of Roth*. The preparations for the fete. The sudden departure of the Bramleys from Roth Park. Peter Hudson's preferment. Lord Peter's inability to stay away from the Vicarage. Lady Youlgreave's belated interest in her husband's relations. Vanessa's long-standing interest in the poetry of Francis Youlgreave.

All these and more. Slowly the picture – or rather its components – came together. And one of the pieces was my godson Michael.

The telephone call on that August afternoon was from Henry

Appleyard. He had been offered the chance of a lucrative four-week lecture tour in the United States, filling in for a speaker who had cancelled at the last moment.

'I'm flying out the day after tomorrow, from Heathrow,' he said. 'I wondered if I could look in for lunch?'

'Of course you can. When's your flight?'

'In the evening.'

'Are all of you coming?'

'Just me, I'm afraid.'

The organizers had offered to pay his wife's travel expenses as well, I gathered, but she had to stay to look after Michael.

'Can't you leave him with someone?'

'It's such short notice. His school friends are all on holiday, too.'

'He could stay with us. If he wouldn't find us too dull.'

'It's too much of an imposition.'

'Why? He's my godson. But would he be lonely?'

'I wouldn't worry about that. He's quite a self-contained boy.'

'Rosemary will be home in a few days, so at least he'd have someone nearer his own age. And our doctor has a boy of eleven.'

'It still seems too much to ask.'

'Why don't I have a word with Vanessa and phone you back?'

Henry agreed. I put down the phone and went into the kitchen to talk to Vanessa. She listened in silence, but when I had finished she smiled.

'That's a wonderful idea.'

'I'm glad you like it. But why the enthusiasm?'

'It'll make it easier when Rosemary comes home. For her as well as me.' She touched my arm, and I knew our squabble was over. 'Besides, you'd like it, wouldn't you?'

Two days later the Appleyards arrived for lunch.

'I'm sorry this is such short notice,' Henry said as we were smoking a cigarette in the drive.

'It doesn't matter. Michael's welcome. I'm glad Vanessa's here. For his sake, I mean.'

Henry started to say something but stopped, because the

front door opened and Michael himself came out to join us. The boy was now eleven years old, fair-haired and slim. He stood close to Henry. They didn't know what to say to each other.

At that moment a dark-blue car drove slowly down the main road towards the bridge over the Rowan. It had a long bonnet and a small cockpit. It looked more like a spacecraft than a car. The windows were of tinted glass and I could make out only the vague shape of two people inside. It slowed, signalled right and turned into the drive of Roth Park.

'Cor,' said Michael, his face showing animation for the first time since he had arrived. 'An E-type Jaguar.'

Another piece of the jigsaw had arrived.

That evening I telephoned Audrey to see if she was all right. I had not seen her since her outburst in the library. When she answered the phone, her voice sounded weak.

'Just a headache,' she said. 'I'll be fine in a day or two. Rest is the best medicine. That's what Dr Vintner said.'

'You've been to see him?'

'He came to me, actually. I wasn't up to going out.'

I felt guilty, as perhaps she had intended me to feel. 'Is there anything we can do?'

'No. I'll be fine. Well, actually there is one thing. Apparently the new people have moved into Roth Park. You could go and ask them about the paddock. I'd feel so much happier if that were settled. It'd be a weight off my mind.'

I remembered the Jaguar. 'When did they move in?'

'Today at some point. Mr Malik told Charlene when he brought the groceries round this afternoon. They've opened an account with him. Their name is Clifford.'

'Are they a family?'

'Mr Malik's only met a young man so far. Perhaps he's the son.'

I promised I would go to see them in the morning. A moment later, I rang off and went to join the others in the sitting room. Michael had lost that frozen look his face had worn since his parents left. He was talking to Vanessa about his school. They both looked up as I came in. I allowed myself to be drawn into

351

a game of Hearts with them. I hadn't played cards for years. To my surprise I enjoyed it.

The next morning I walked up to Roth Park. Vanessa was at work, and we had arranged for Michael to spend the day with the doctor's son, Brian. I had not been to Roth Park since May, when the last of the Bramleys' patients had moved to another nursing home. Privately I had never had much time for Mr and Mrs Bramley, a red-faced and loud-voiced couple who, I suspected, bullied their patients.

It was another fine day. With a copy of the parish magazine under my arm, I strolled down the road, past the church. The traffic was still heavy. In the last thirty or forty years, houses had mushroomed like a fungus along the highways and byways of Roth. The fungus had spread away from the highways and byways and devoured the fields between them. All the occupants of these new houses appeared to own at least one car.

I turned into the drive. On the right was the south wall of the churchyard. To the left, the turbid waters of the Rowan were visible through a screen of branches, nettles and leaves. It was mid-morning and already very warm. It was too hot to hurry.

I was not in the best of moods. I had wanted to make love the previous evening, but when I came to bed Vanessa was asleep. Or rather – I uncharitably wondered – she was pretending to be asleep.

After about sixty yards, the drive dived into a belt of oak trees. It was cooler here, and I lingered. At the time this felt an indulgence. Now, when I look back, it seems as though I were clinging to my state of innocence. A track went off to the right, following the west side of the churchyard; it passed through the paddock behind the Vicarage garden, which we hoped to use as our fete car park, and ran north-west towards the drowned farmlands beneath the Jubilee Reservoir.

I walked on. Once past the oaks, the park opened out. To the south was the Rowan, now a silver streak, lent enchantment by distance. Beyond it, housing estates covered what had once been pastureland south of the river. On the right were the roofs of another housing estate south of the reservoir, encroaching on the grounds from the north.

The drive, which had been moving away from the river, changed direction and swung towards it in a long, leisurely leftward loop around the base of a small hill. There, sheltered by the hill and facing south, was Roth Park itself.

Looked at with an unbiased eye, the house was not a pretty sight. Thanks to Audrey's book, I now knew that the great fire of 1874 had destroyed most of a late-seventeenth-century mansion. The owner of the estate, Alfred Youlgreave, had built a plain, ugly, red brick box on the same site with an incongruous Italianate tower attached to the west end.

As the house came into view, two things happened. First, I had the sensation, rightly or wrongly, that I was being watched, that behind one of the many blank windows was a face. I had an impression of stealth, even malice. I knew, of course, that it was more than possible that I was entirely mistaken about this – that the sensation had no external correlation whatsoever; that I was merely projecting my inner difficulties on to the outside world. That did not make the experience less unpleasant.

The other feeling was, if anything, even more powerful. I wanted to run away. I wanted to turn and scurry down the drive as fast as I could. It was not, strictly speaking, a premonition. It was in no sense a warning. I was simply scared. I did not know why. All I knew was that I wanted to run away.

But I did not. I had spent most of my life learning how to restrain my feelings. Besides, I remember thinking, think how odd it would look if there were a watcher: if he or she saw a middle-aged clergyman in a linen jacket hesitating in front of the house and then leaving at a gallop. Our dignity is very precious to almost all of us; and fear of losing face is a more powerful source of motivation than many people imagine.

I walked towards the house. There was an overgrown shrubbery on the right. Outside the house, marooned in a sea of weed-strewn gravel, was a large stone urn stained with yellow lichen. On the plinth – again, according to Audrey – was a plaque commemorating a visit that Queen Adelaide had paid to the Youlgreaves' predecessors in 1839. I paused by the urn, pretending to examine the worn lettering. I really wanted a chance to look more closely at the house.

I could see no one at any of the windows, but that proved

nothing. The building was not as imposing as it looked from a distance. Several slates were missing from the roof at the eastern end. A length of guttering had detached itself and was hanging at an angle. There was a large canopy sheltering the front door, a wrought-iron porte-cochère supported by rusting cast-iron pillars, which gave the house the appearance of a provincial railway station.

Parked beneath the canopy was the Cliffords' E-type Jaguar, the car which had aroused Michael's admiration. I marched up the shallow steps to the front door and tugged the bell pull. It was impossible to tell what effect, if any, this had. I noted with irritation that my fingers had left smudges of sweat on the pale-blue cover of the parish magazine.

No one answered the door. I rang the bell again. I waited. Still, nothing happened. I did not know whether to be relieved or irritated. I moved away from the door and walked a few paces down the drive. It felt like a retreat. I didn't like the idea that I might be running away from something. Then I heard music.

I stopped to listen. It was faint enough to make it difficult to hear. Some sort of pop music, I thought; and suddenly I guessed where the Cliffords were. It was a fine morning, their first in their new home. They were probably in the garden.

I was familiar with the layout of the place from my years of visiting the Bramleys and their patients. I followed a path that led through the shrubbery at the side of the house to the croquet lawn below the terrace on the east front. The lawn was now a mass of knee-high grass and weeds. On the terrace, some four feet above it, were two people in deckchairs, with a small, blue transistor radio between them. A male voice was croaking against a background of discordant, rhythmic music. I walked on to the lawn and raised my Panama hat.

'Good morning. I hope I'm not disturbing you. My name is David Byfield.'

Two faces, blank as masks, turned towards me; astonishment wipes away much of a person's outward individuality. If the Demon King had appeared before them in a puff of smoke, the effect would have been much the same.

The moment of astonishment dissolved. A young man switched off the radio and stood up. He was skinny, his figure emphasized by the fitted denim shirt and the hip-hugging bell-bottomed jeans. He had a beaky nose and bright, pale-blue eyes. His hair was thick and fair, with more than a hint of ginger, and it curled down to his shoulders. A hippy, I thought, or the next best thing. But I had to admit that the long hair suited him.

'Good morning. What can we do for you?'

I took a step forward. 'First, I'd like to welcome you to Roth. I'm the vicar.'

The man dropped the cigarette he was holding into the bush of lavender which sprawled out of an urn at the edge of the terrace. 'The church at the gates?' He came down the steps to the lawn and held out his hand. 'I'm Toby Clifford. How do you do?'

We shook hands. I realized that he was a little older than I had thought at first – perhaps in his middle or late twenties.

'This is my sister Joanna.' Toby turned back to her. 'Jo, come and say hello to the vicar.'

I looked up at the terrace. There was a flurry of limbs in the other deckchair. A young woman stood up. She wore a baggy T-shirt which came halfway down her thighs and – I could hardly help noticing as she scrambled out of the deckchair – green knickers. Short hair framed a triangular face.

'The vicar,' she said and giggled. 'Sorry. Shouldn't laugh. Not funny.'

I held out my hand. 'It's the dog collar. It often has that effect on people.'

Her eyes widened with surprise. I guessed she was a year or two younger than her brother.

'Would you like some coffee?' Toby said. 'We were just going to make some.'

'Thank you. If it's not too much trouble.'

Toby tapped Joanna's shoulder. She trailed through the French windows into the house. Toby settled me in one of the deckchairs and went to fetch a third. He sat down cautiously.

'I don't trust these chairs,' he said. 'We found them in the old stables. They look as if they came out of the ark.'

'I brought you a parish magazine.'

'Thank you. You must put us down for a regular copy.'

We chatted for a few minutes. Toby's appearance was misleading, I decided: he had decent manners and knew how to keep a conversation going – indeed, he was rather better at it than me. While we talked, I wondered how best to introduce the subject of his parents. Did they or did they not exist?

'Who'd have thought it could be so quiet on the edge of London?' Toby said. At that moment, a jet roared low across the sky towards Heathrow Airport. He snorted with amusement. 'Some of the time, anyway.'

'What are your plans for the house?' I asked. 'By modern standards, it's pretty big.'

He looked at me, a swift, assessing glance that was at variance with his earlier smiles, his light conversation and the way he sprawled so casually in the deckchair. 'In the long run, I'm not sure. But in the short term, Jo and I need somewhere to live. And we both like having lots of space.' He leant towards me and lowered his voice. 'Between ourselves, Jo needs a little peace and quiet. She's not been well.'

I abandoned subtlety. 'So it's just the two of you?'

Toby nodded.

At that moment Joanna returned, carrying a tray with three mugs of coffee, a half-used bottle of milk and a packet of sugar. She was still wearing the T-shirt, but she had pulled on a pair of jeans. Soon the three of us were sitting in a row facing the overgrown lawn, each with a mug in one hand and a cigarette in the other.

'God, I'm hot,' Joanna said.

'It'll be better when we've got the swimming pool fixed,' Toby said. 'A man's coming round tomorrow.'

'Will it be difficult?' I asked. 'I don't think the Bramleys have used it for years.'

'I can't swim,' Jo said.

Toby waved his cigarette impatiently. 'You'll soon learn. Having a pool in your back garden makes all the difference.'

'Talking of your back garden,' I said, 'I have a favour to ask.'

Toby smiled but said nothing.

'It's the church fete. The Bramleys used to let us borrow your paddock as our car park. I wondered if you might be kind enough to do the same.'

'A paddock?' Joanna giggled. 'We've got a *paddock*?'

'I've never known horses to be kept there,' I said. 'I imagine the name goes back to a time before the Bramleys. It's the field beside the churchyard.'

Toby nodded. 'When is this fete?'

'The last Saturday in August.'

'I don't see why you shouldn't. It'd be a pleasure. Wouldn't it, Jo?'

His sister said nothing.

Soon afterwards, I levered myself out of the deckchair and said goodbye. Toby ushered me through the shrubbery and back to the drive. On the fringe of the shrubbery, though, I turned back, intending to wave at Joanna. She was still sitting in her deckchair. She was staring at me with great concentration, her face not so much sullen as serious. She did not wave at me and I did not wave at her.

I had taken only a few steps down the drive when I realized that my Panama hat was still beside the deckchair I had been sitting in. I went back through the shrubbery. Toby was speaking in a soft, pleasant voice. I could only just make out what he was saying.

'You've got to pull yourself together, Jo. We want the natives to like us.'

She said something inaudible in reply.

'You'll do as I say,' he said. 'You're not in fucking Chelsea now.'

13

I could have telephoned Audrey with the good news about the paddock, but I decided that it would be better to go and see her. I could spare twenty minutes. I tended to forget that she was a person and treat her as a convenience.

The front door of Tudor Cottage stood open. Inside was a square hall several feet below the ground level outside. The place was cool, even on a warm day in August. The smell of damp lingered beneath the scent of the potpourri in the bowl on the oak table. The ground floor of the cottage was almost entirely given over to the café. The long room on the left of the hall, which stretched the depth of the house, was the tea room itself. The kitchen was at the back of the house, overlooking the walled garden where, on fine days, they put out tables and chairs. On the right was the small panelled room which Audrey used as an office.

I looked into the tea room. At the table in the window, two women with three toddlers in tow were talking in shrill voices. Judging by the bags around them, they had done their shopping at Malik's Minimarket. Charlene Potter was sitting by the till, listlessly polishing a selection of the numerous horse brasses which hung around the fireplace and dangled from the beams. She was a fat girl, with wiry yellow hair, a spotty complexion, and a mouthful of grey fillings. She looked up as I came in and smiled. She had one of the warmest smiles I had ever known, the sort that makes you feel that the person smiling is actually pleased to see you. The two women and the three toddlers stopped talking and stared at me.

'If you want Miss Oliphant,' Charlene said, 'she's in the office.'

'Thank you. By the way, how's your father?'

Again, the smile flashed out. 'He's got himself a job. Working down the gravel pits. Like a new man.'

'Give him and your mother my best wishes.'

Charlene's mother Doris was a regular communicant, which was one reason why Audrey had offered her this job. The other reason was that Charlene's mother helped to look after Lady Youlgreave. The family lived on the council estate and Audrey had entertained grave doubts about Charlene's suitability. But her mother's piety, the Youlgreave connection and the absence of other candidates had tipped the scales in her favour.

I tapped on the office door and Audrey called me to come in. She was sitting at a roll-top desk and turning the pages of a red exercise book. When she saw me, her face coloured. With sudden violence, she shut the book, snatched off her glasses, pushed back her chair.

'David – how nice. I'll get Charlene to bring coffee.'

'Not on my account, please. I've just had some with the Cliffords.'

'What are they like?'

'Very pleasant; and they say we can use the paddock.'

Audrey wanted more than this. I told her what I knew. She would like Toby, I guessed, despite his louche appearance, but I was less sure how she would react to Joanna.

'It's a very respectable surname,' she remarked when I had finished.

I wondered if Audrey were fantasizing aristocratic connections for the new inhabitants of Roth Park.

'Roth Park – a private house again,' she went on. 'I can hardly believe it. It really could make a difference to the village. To the whole feel of the place.'

The two women and their children were leaving, and the sounds of their voices penetrated from the hall.

Audrey winced. 'There'll be crumbs all over the floor. And the last time those two were in, I found jam all over one of the chairs.' A wistful expression settled on her face. 'It would be so pleasant to have some *nice* customers.'

'Are you feeling all right now?'

She put her hand to her forehead. 'A slight migraine. I don't think this heat agrees with me. And then there were the louts last night.'

'The louts?'

'A whole gang of them in the bus shelter. I could see them quite plainly from my sitting-room window. Smoking and drinking. They had a girl in there, too. I closed the windows, but I could still hear them. And then . . .' Her voice trailed away, her cheeks were pinker than before. 'I hardly like to mention it. I – I noticed a puddle spreading across the floor. It looked black in the streetlamp.' The flush deepened in colour. 'And suddenly, I realized that one of them must be urinating.'

'They hadn't spilt their drink?'

'Oh no. Sometimes that bus shelter smells like a public lavatory. Anyway, I telephoned the police and frankly they weren't very helpful. They said they'd send someone down, but if they did, I didn't see them. Sometimes I despair at this place. I just don't know what the village is coming to.'

I stayed with Audrey for a few minutes, trying to calm her down. At one point I thought I caught a whiff of alcohol on her breath, which surprised me. I knew she sometimes had a sherry before lunch, but it was not yet midday. I tried to distract her by steering her thoughts towards the church fete. James Vintner had offered to do a barbecue for us. Audrey was instinctively against innovation, but James had persuaded her into agreeing on principle. By the time I left her, she was in a happier frame of mind.

Charlene intercepted me in the hall.

'Do you think she's all right?' she asked.

'Why?'

Charlene led the way outside and said in a low voice, 'Seems a bit hot and bothered, I suppose. Them kids last night upset her. And Lord Peter wasn't in for breakfast, and that always upsets her.'

'He'll be all right. That cat always lands on his feet.'

'I'm not worried about the cat,' Charlene said. 'I'm worried about Miss Oliphant.'

14

In the late afternoon, my daughter Rosemary came home. Since the end of term she had been staying on the Isle of Wight with the family of a school friend.

Vanessa was still at work, but Michael had returned from the Vintners', so I took him with me to meet Rosemary. He and Brian seemed to have enjoyed each other's company – they had arranged to go to the cinema tomorrow afternoon. I had a vague hope that Michael and Rosemary would entertain each other. I should have realized that there might not be much common ground between a seventeen-year-old girl and an eleven-year-old boy. Especially, perhaps, between this girl and this boy.

There was little conversation on the drive back from the station. Rosemary sat beside me; she was grave-faced and beautiful, and she answered my questions with a series of monosyllables. She was not rude: it was merely that she had withdrawn into a private place inside herself. I knew that because I was inclined to do the same thing myself when under stress. I thought that I knew the reason: her A level results were due in a few days' time.

Michael was sitting in the back. Every now and then I glanced at him in the rear-view mirror. He was always staring out of the window.

Rosemary was beside me in the front of the car. She opened her bag, produced a small mirror and examined her face. Her absorption excluded me – excluded everyone but herself. I glanced in the rear-view mirror at Michael's face, as rapt as Rosemary's. For them both, I was no more than a mechanical contrivance driving the car. Each of them might have been alone in the world.

We reached Roth and parked in the drive of the Vicarage. Vanessa's car was not there – she had promised to leave work early, in honour of Rosemary's return, but she was unlikely to reach Roth before 6.30 p.m. Rosemary glided into the house. A moment later, I heard the bathroom door closing. Michael helped me carry in the luggage. The boy looked at a loose end so I suggested he put the kettle on.

I went back outside to lock the car. My heart lurched when I saw a familiar figure waving vigorously at me from the other side of the stream of traffic. Audrey darted across the road and scurried into the Vicarage drive.

'I've got them,' she announced. 'I really have.'

'Who have you got?'

'Those louts, those wretched louts. Someone had to blow the whistle. Give them half a chance and they would try to get away with murder.'

My mind filled with an improbable image of one of those overgrown children running berserk waving an axe. 'But what have they been doing?'

'What they always do.' Audrey's face was now a dark red verging on purple. 'They're no better than animals. When the Queen's Head closed at lunch time, a whole group of them trooped into the bus shelter. I knew what they were up to. Filthy, degenerate beasts.'

'Audrey, why don't you come inside and sit down? We were just about to make some tea.'

'I won't tell you what I found in there this morning. Too horrible. They're no better than animals.'

I wondered what she meant. A contraceptive? Excrement?

'Anyway, they were in there this afternoon, and I happened to see a police car turn into Vicarage Drive. Aha, I thought, I'll settle your hash. So I popped out there and made the two policemen come with me to the bus shelter. You should have seen the faces of those hooligans. There were five of them. Two of them were girls, would you believe? I told the police I wanted to have them prosecuted to the full rigour of the law.'

'But what were they doing?'

Audrey waved her hand. 'Smoking. Drinking. You could tell where it was going. That sort of person is only interested in one thing.' Audrey's face suddenly changed, as though an invisible sponge had wiped away the anger and the agitation. 'Why, Rosemary. How lovely to see you. I didn't realize you were coming home today.'

When I went to lock the church that evening, I found a surprise waiting for me. It was not late – a little after seven o'clock. I had left Vanessa preparing supper in the kitchen, with Michael sitting at the table peeling potatoes. Rosemary was having a bath, and had been for some time.

I let myself into the churchyard by the garden gate. The sky was grey, and a breeze ruffled the long grass among the graves. I walked round the east end of the church to the south door. Before locking it, I went inside to check that the church was empty.

It was as well that I did. A figure was standing in the chancel.

I cleared my throat. 'Good evening.'

The figure turned and I saw that it was Joanna Clifford. I walked up the church to join her. Her arms were folded across her breasts as though she felt cold. She was looking at the floor.

'It's all right,' she mumbled, 'me coming in here?'

'Of course it is. This is your church.'

'I must be going. Toby will be wondering where I am.'

I remembered what Toby had said about Joanna having been ill. I walked with her to the door. When I had met her this morning, I had taken away an impression of sullenness. Now I thought she was more likely to be shy than sullen. I opened the door for her and followed her into the porch.

'Where were you living before?'

'We had a flat just off the King's Road.' Joanna watched me locking the door. 'It's so quiet here.'

I turned to face her, and for the first time I noticed her eyes. I was standing quite close to her, in the archway dividing the porch from the churchyard. For an instant her eyes reminded me of sunlit seawater trapped in a rock pool. They were not large but their colour was unusual: a mottled greeny-brown, their vividness accentuated by small pupils, and by a black rim which separated the irises from the whites. She was smaller than Vanessa, the top of her head barely above my shoulders.

'I must get back,' she said.

'You must have a lot to do.'

She looked up at me, her eyes startled. 'What do you mean?'

'It's always a busy time, isn't it? Moving into a new home.'

'Oh – that. Yes. Well, goodbye.'

She darted away from me towards the small gate in the west wall of the churchyard, which led directly into the grounds of Roth Park. I watched her go. What an awkward child, I thought – except she wasn't a child at all: she was probably well into her twenties.

I walked slowly home. All evening, the memory of Joanna Clifford stuck on the back of my mind like a burr on the back of my jacket.

At Vanessa's suggestion, we tried to make Rosemary's first meal at home something of a celebration: we ate Coronation Chicken and drank a bottle of white Burgundy. Michael had half a glass of wine and became sufficiently relaxed to tell us an interminable joke involving an Englishman, a Scotsman and an Irishman.

Part way through the meal, Vanessa said, 'You'll never guess who phoned me today.'

Michael and I looked expectantly at her. Rosemary stared at her plate.

'Lady Youlgreave's cleaner. Mrs Potter, isn't it? She phoned the office this morning. Lady Youlgreave wants me to go and see her.'

'Why?' I asked.

'To talk about Francis Youlgreave. She said something about wanting to get the family papers catalogued. And she wondered if I was serious about wanting to publish a biography of Great-Uncle Francis.'

'Are you?'

'Oh yes. As long as there really is new material. That notebook she showed us looked promising. If I could find the time, I wouldn't mind writing it myself.'

'Who would want to read about him?' Rosemary said. 'Most

people have never heard of him.' She stared challengingly around the table. 'It's not as if he was a real poet, after all.'

'I've heard of him,' Michael said.

We all looked at him, and he blushed.

'What have you heard?' Vanessa asked.

'He was mad. He preached a sermon about how there should be women priests. And he used to cut up animals and things.'

'You *are* well informed,' Vanessa said. 'How did you learn all that?'

'Dad told me. There was something in the paper about the Methodists having women ministers, and Dad said it would soon be the Church of England's turn. And Mum laughed, and said it was just like Francis Youlgreave said it should be. So I asked who Francis Youlgreave was.'

'He used to cut up animals?' Rosemary said. 'I never knew that. Did he do it here?'

'Mainly in Rosington,' I said abruptly. 'He was a very sick man. He had delusions. This business about women priests was one of them. Another was some sort of mumbo jumbo about blood sacrifices.'

'Plenty of classical precedents,' Vanessa said. 'And Old Testament ones, too, for that matter.'

'Why?' Michael said. 'What were blood sacrifices *for*?'

'In those days, people thought the gods liked them – they were sort of presents to the gods, I suppose.' I did not want to get too involved in this subject. 'The idea was that if the gods liked your present, they'd be nice to you.'

'Or they'd be nasty to your enemies,' Rosemary added. 'Which came to much the same thing.'

'But that was the Old Testament,' Michael said. 'Francis Youlgreave was quite modern.'

'He was mentally ill,' I said. 'He was –'

'Mad,' Rosemary interrupted. 'Or maybe a genius. "Great wits are sure to madness near alli'd",' she added smugly. 'Dryden. *Absalom and Achitophel.*'

There was a stunned silence. And into that silence came the ringing of the telephone.

'Oh *no*,' said Vanessa to me. 'I wish they'd leave you alone. Just for an evening.'

I pushed back my chair and went into the study. Perhaps the wine had loosened Vanessa's tongue, as it had Michael's. I picked up the phone.

It was Audrey Oliphant and she stumbled over her words as though someone were shaking her as she was speaking. Lord Peter still had not come home and someone had thrown a stone through the window of her office at Tudor Cottage.

15

The next morning there was a postcard from Peter and June Hudson. They were looking at ruins in Crete, eating olives, and swimming every day. 'Rosington,' Peter wrote, 'seems very far away. See you on the 9th September.' That was the date for me to meet my new spiritual director, an Anglican monk who lived in Ascot. ('Absolutely ruthless,' Peter had told me on the telephone. 'Just what you need.')

Vanessa had arranged to see Lady Youlgreave in the morning. I asked if she would mind my coming with her.

'Why do you want to see her?'

'No particular reason. I like to pop in from time to time, and I thought it would be nice if we could do it together.'

Vanessa said nothing. I caught a sudden glimpse of the darkness that lay beneath the friendly harmony between us. Perhaps Peter had been right: I had taken advantage of her vulnerability. Need and love are so curiously and inextricably entwined.

When we reached the Old Manor House, there was a Harrods van parked outside the front door. Lady Youlgreave never shopped at Malik's Minimarket. She had everything she needed, from lavatory paper to sherry, sent down by weekly delivery from Harrods. If Doris wasn't there, the driver let himself in with the key hidden near the back door.

Today the front door stood open. Beauty and Beast barked at us, but more half-heartedly than usual, perhaps because the man from Harrods had already exhausted them. Before I could ring the bell, Doris, Charlene's mother, came into the hall with the delivery man. She was a small woman with a gentle face and

367

an overweight body encased in a shiny, pale-blue nylon overall. She came to the Old Manor House twice a day, morning and evening, trying to care for an obstinate old woman who should have been in a nursing home and a decaying house the size of a small hotel.

'Hello, Vicar. Mrs Byfield. Wasn't expecting you both.'

'It's not inconvenient?' I asked.

'Oh no. The more the merrier. Could you find your own way? I'm up to my ears this morning. It'd be wonderful if you could keep her occupied for a while.'

The dogs were quiet now. Beast even wagged her tail as we passed her. Vanessa and I went along the corridor to the dining room. Lady Youlgreave was in her usual chair, her head bowed over an old letter. She seemed to have aged by as many years in the few weeks since I had last seen her.

'Ah, David.' She gave the impression she'd last seen me five minutes earlier. 'And who's this?'

'Vanessa Byfield,' Vanessa said. 'Do you remember? You asked Doris to ring me at work yesterday, to talk about Francis Youlgreave.'

Lady Youlgreave's fingers plucked at the blanket over her legs. 'Silly man. Thought he'd raised the dead. Thought he talked to them, and they talked to him.'

'Who did he talk to?' I asked.

She gave no sign that she had heard me. 'Sometimes they told him to write his poems, like the angels did. One of them made him preach that sermon, the one about the women priests. Then afterwards they hounded him out of his job – not the dead, of course, the living; though they're all dead now. So's he. He came back here to die.'

'Here?' Vanessa said. 'In this house?'

Lady Youlgreave shook her head. 'No. Roth Park. He had the room at the top of the tower.'

'How did he die?'

'Jumped out of his window. Thought he could fly.' The old woman's hand gestured feebly towards the black metal box beside her chair. 'There's something in there about it. The last entry in his journal. An angel had come for him and was going to carry him up to God.' Her mouth twisted into a grin. 'In a manner of speaking, I suppose that's exactly what happened.'

'But he went down rather than up,' Vanessa said.

Lady Youlgreave stared at her. Then she grasped the joke and cackled. I pulled up the chairs we had used last time. Vanessa and I sat down. The medicine bottle was still on the mantelpiece. Outside the window two blackbirds were pecking at something on the bird table. The front door slammed and the blackbirds flew away. The delivery man's shoes crunched across the gravel. A moment later, the Harrods van pulled into the main road.

Vanessa leaned forward. 'Do you still want me to look at his papers?'

The old woman nodded.

'If you like, I could catalogue them for you, and then you could decide what you'd like done with them. If there's enough material for a biography, I'm sure we could find a suitable author.'

Lady Youlgreave snorted. 'How my father-in-law would have hated it. A book about Uncle Francis.' She threw a glance at the Sargent over the fireplace. 'Such a conventional man. He wouldn't have minded if Francis had been a bishop. But a mad poet – that was quite different.'

'So you'd like me to go ahead?'

The old woman stared at the bird table. 'If you like.'

Vanessa moistened her lips. 'There's no time like the present.' She looked at me. 'I'm sure David wouldn't mind bringing the car round. We could take the box away now.'

'Oh no.' Lady Youlgreave huddled more deeply into her chair, as if trying to retract into herself. 'The papers must stay here. Everything must stay here. I may want to look at them. You must read them here. In this room. Where I can see you.'

There was a silence. Outside, the blackbirds had returned to the bird table; one of them pecked and the other gave off a thread of melody.

I said, 'Are you sure you wouldn't find that rather a disturbance? You could let Vanessa take away just one or two things at a time. I'm sure she'd take the greatest care of them and she could tell you exactly what she finds in them, too.'

'Yes, of course.' Vanessa sat back, smiling, but her hands

were knotted together on her lap. 'That's the best way to do it, isn't it?'

There was a look of yearning on my wife's face, a look that was almost sexual in its intensity.

'If you want to read them, you must do it here.'

The wizened face settled into a barely human mask. Nothing moved in the hot, stuffy room with its smell of old age. It was as if all three of us were holding our breath. Even the blackbird was silent. The bird table was empty.

'I'm tired now. David, I want you to give me my medicine. It's on the mantelpiece, with a spoon.'

Lady Youlgreave agreed to let Vanessa begin looking through the papers on Saturday morning; and Vanessa had to be content with that. We left soon afterwards – Vanessa to go to her office in Richmond, and I to carry on with my work.

'I suppose she wants the company,' Vanessa said as we walked back to the Vicarage. 'But it's going to be very inconvenient.'

In the afternoon, Lord Peter turned up. He appeared on the windowsill of the Vicarage sitting room. I was not at home at the time. Rosemary was, however, and she phoned Audrey with the good news. Audrey came over at once with the cat basket. Lord Peter, who had been lured into the sitting room with the help of a saucer of cream, protested violently when Audrey put him in his cat basket. He left two parallel scratches on her left forearm.

I knew about the scratches because Audrey showed them to me. They were in some way meritorious – a sign of Lord Peter's intrepid personality, perhaps, or of Audrey's willingness to suffer torments, if necessary, for the wellbeing of her pet.

The incident had an unexpected consequence. Audrey was fulsomely grateful to Rosemary. To hear Audrey speak, you would think Rosemary had saved Lord Peter, at considerable personal cost, from a terrible fate. She asked Rosemary to tea the following afternoon, ostensibly to see how well Lord Peter had recovered from his trying experience. To my surprise, Rosemary accepted. She appeared to enjoy the experience. A few days later, she went over to Tudor Cottage again for coffee.

I was pleased. In the past, Rosemary had considered Audrey

as an irritation. But now a sort of friendship seemed to be developing between the two of them. Vanessa said they would be company for each other; she thought Rosemary was trying to develop emotional independence from me, on the whole a healthy sign. Vanessa had a weakness for amateur psychology.

Gradually, the four of us at the Vicarage fell into a routine. Vanessa went into the office every day, but somehow managed to find time to buy the ingredients for and to prepare our evening meal. Rosemary and I usually organized something at lunchtime – sandwiches, perhaps, or soup.

Rosemary retreated to her bedroom for hours at a time, where she worked and listened to music that jarred on me. After the summer she was going back to school for one more term to sit the Oxford entrance exam. In the evenings we sometimes talked about her reading, and I helped her with her Latin. I enjoyed these sessions – intellectually our minds worked in a remarkably similar way.

'I wish you could coach me for Oxford,' she said on one occasion when we were alone in the sitting room. 'I'm sure I'd do much better than at school.'

'I wish I could, too.'

'I wish –' she began.

Then the door opened, and Michael and Vanessa came in.

'He *did* do something here,' Michael announced.

Bewildered, I looked at him. 'Who did?'

'Francis Youlgreave.'

'I was just telling Michael,' Vanessa explained. 'Lady Youlgreave showed me a letter.'

'It was a cat.' Like many small boys, Michael took an uncomplicated pleasure in past bloodshed. 'He cut it up. But they didn't put him in prison for it. I suppose it was just an animal, so it didn't matter too much.'

'The family hushed it up,' Vanessa said. 'It was just before he died. It happened in Carter's Meadow, wherever that is. I imagine it's covered with houses by now.'

'Carter's Meadow?' Rosemary stood and began to gather up her books. 'No, it's still there. It's a field on the other side of Roth Park.'

'We came to see if you wanted to play cards,' Vanessa said.

Rosemary raised her eyebrows. 'Cards? I'm afraid I haven't got time for things like that.'

She went upstairs to her room. Vanessa, Michael and I played Hearts.

Later, in our bedroom, I whispered to Vanessa during one of our nightly conferences, 'Was it wise to tell Michael about the cat?'

'Meat and drink to him. Small boys like that sort of thing.' She looked at me. 'He's having a surprisingly good time here, isn't he?'

'Thanks to Brian Vintner. A friend of his own age makes all the difference.'

'And he's much more relaxed with us than he was.'

'But not with Rosemary. And she's not very pleasant to him. Do you think I should have a word with her?'

'I wouldn't.'

'Why not?'

'Rosemary's having an awful time. I don't think you realize. She's had you to herself all these years, and now I've come along and pinched you. Added to that, she's worried about her exams. And on top of everything else, we've got Michael in the house. It's obvious you're fond of him, and he's fond of you. So he gets treated as the baby of the family, and we can't even spoil Rosemary.'

'That doesn't make sense –'

'It's not a matter of logic,' Vanessa hissed. 'We're talking about people. You expect everyone to be too rational.'

'Do you mind?'

'Mind what? You expecting others to be rational?'

'All these people in the house. The lack of privacy.'

Vanessa stared at me. She was sitting up in bed, with her auburn hair brushed down on to the shoulders of her cotton nightdress. She looked very attractive.

'Me?' she said at last. 'At present, I'm just trying to keep the peace, and trying to survive.'

I wanted her to expand on this, but she wouldn't. Instead, she said she was tired and turned out her light.

During this time I kept out of Audrey's way as much as possible.

I had no wish to be drawn into the arrangements for the fete. Besides, I told myself, I was so busy that I had to be careful how I used my time.

To my relief, her feud with the adolescents of the council estate seemed to have died a natural death. No prosecutions resulted from the raid on the bus shelter; the police let the youths off with a caution. Audrey had the broken glass in her window replaced and assumed a martyred expression whenever the incident was mentioned.

All this was a lull. But the storm – or rather the series of storms – was about to break over our heads. The lull ended on Thursday the 13th August, the day of Vanessa's party.

It was Vanessa's party in the sense that it was her idea. She felt that it would be polite to welcome the Cliffords to Roth, and to return the hospitality they had given me the previous week. It would also be a way of signalling our gratitude for the loan of the paddock. We invited Audrey, so we could discuss the practicalities of the fete with them, and several other parishioners, including the Vintners. James and Mary were involved in the fete, and Brian would be company for Michael.

We asked Rosemary if there was anyone she would like to invite, but she said that there wasn't. I remember her coiling a strand of blonde hair around her finger and saying, 'But I don't know anyone in Roth.'

Vanessa had another reason for wanting to get to know the Cliffords: 'I'll want to have a good look over the house at some point,' she told me as we were going to bed on Wednesday night. 'There are lots of references to it in the Youlgreave papers. And to the grounds. I'd especially like to see Francis's room in the tower.'

'Isn't that rather morbid?'

'Not at all.'

'But what would you do in his room? Look for scratches on the windowsill?'

She stared at me, ready to snap. 'Listen, the more I see of those papers, the more I want to do the biography myself. Francis really was interesting. He came from an Establishment background, and yet he lived on the margins of society. He did all the things the Victorians weren't meant to do. And even this business about women priests strikes a modern chord. Perhaps Rosemary was right – perhaps in some ways he wasn't as mad as people thought.'

'The ordination of women is theologically unsound. It was then, and it is now, whatever the Methodists think.'

She shrugged away my interruption. 'If only the old lady would let me take away the papers and look at them properly.'

'When are you going there next?'

'Tomorrow afternoon. I'm taking the afternoon off work because of the party. If you do some of the shopping, I should be able to fit in an hour or two with the papers after lunch.' She picked up a pencil and a notepad from the bedside table. 'I'd better make a list of what we need to get.'

Vanessa's party on the 13th August: that was the day when we passed the point of no return, though we did not realize it at the time.

16

Thursday started badly.

After breakfast, Rosemary went to the study to phone the school. It was the day her results were due. She was so long that eventually I went into the hall and eavesdropped at the study door. There was nothing to hear except the ticking of the clock on the wall and the rumble of traffic. I knocked and opened the door.

Rosemary was sitting at my desk, staring at the bookcase on the opposite wall. Her eyes flicked towards me and then back to the bookcase. Her face was pale.

'Are you all right?'

She nodded.

'Did you get through to the school?'

Another nod.

'Have the results come?'

She moistened her lips. 'Yes.'

'And?'

She said nothing. I put my arm around her shoulders. She pulled away.

'What did you get?'

'Bs in Latin and History. An A in English.'

'That's marvellous.' I kissed the top of her head. 'I'm very proud of you.'

She pushed me away and stood up. 'There must have been a mistake. There should have been three As.'

'But you don't need them. Your results are excellent. You –'

'I wanted three As,' she said. 'I *deserved* three As.'

'But, Rosie –'

'*Don't* call me that.'

She walked quickly out of the room. The front door slammed.

Rosemary returned before midday. To my relief she seemed to have come to terms with her results. I gave her a cheque as a present, and Vanessa gave her another when she arrived at lunch time.

'Please don't tell people unless they ask,' Rosemary said as we were eating. 'I don't want everyone to make a fuss.'

After lunch we separated. Vanessa walked down to the Old Manor House. Rosemary went up to her room. Michael went to the library. I drove into Staines to do the shopping.

In the off-licence, I bumped into Victor Thurston; I had not seen him since that evening nearly a year ago when we had dined together at the Trasks' and I had met Vanessa for the first time. Because of the fondness for committees he shared with his wife, he was often mentioned in the local paper. I came up to the counter with two bottles of sherry, one of gin and one of lemonade to find him in the process of ordering three cases of Moët & Chandon. He turned and saw me. He had a rubbery face with features always on the move.

'Hello,' he said. 'We've met, haven't we?' He raised his eyebrows in a combative way, as though I had denied this.

'Yes, it was –'

'I remember. At Ronnie and Cynthia Trasks' last year.'

'That's it. September.'

'And how are you and Vanessa getting on?' If I hadn't been wearing a dog collar, I think Thurston would have dug me in the ribs. 'She's adjusted to the life of the manse, has she? Ha ha.'

I smiled dutifully. I tried and failed to remember the name of his wife. For a moment we had a laboured conversation about the Trasks.

Then Thurston said, 'You live at Roth, don't you? I gather there are changes in the air.'

'What do you mean?'

'I was talking to a chap who was thinking of buying a house there. Off the record, as it were. It was only a few weeks ago. Young fellow.'

'Toby Clifford?'

'That's the one. Bit too hairy for my liking, but seemed a nice enough young chap under the thatch.'

'He and his sister have moved into Roth Park – that's the big house behind the church.'

'So I dare say you've heard his plans,' Thurston said. 'Could bring a few changes.'

I nodded.

Thurston went on, 'Of course, schemes like that need a good deal of money. Many a slip between cup and lip, eh? And then there's the Planning Committee. He was only sounding me out on an informal basis. At first sight I couldn't see any objection myself. But the planning officer may think otherwise, and you can never be quite sure which way some members of the committee are going to jump.'

Neither of us wanted to prolong the conversation – we had little to say to each other. But as I drove home, I puzzled over his remarks about Roth Park. Toby had given me to understand that he and Joanna intended to treat the house as their home. He had not mentioned any development of the site. But from what Thurston had said, Toby had been investigating the possibility before they even moved in. Perhaps he was merely looking to the future. Thurston had made it clear that Toby had not made a formal application for planning permission.

When I got back to the Vicarage, Michael was hoovering the sitting room. Vanessa, who had cut short her researches at the Old Manor House, was assembling cocktail snacks in the kitchen.

She pecked me on the cheek. 'Mary Vintner phoned. They've cried off. James's got to cover for his partner this evening, and she's got a stinking cold.'

'It solves the problem of not having enough armchairs.'

'Could you check there's ice in the fridge? And we may need to get some more tonic from Malik's.'

'How was Lady Youlgreave?'

'Slightly more loopy than usual, I'm afraid. I wonder how long she's going to last. There aren't any children, are there?'

I was refilling the ice tray at the sink. 'No.'

'So who will inherit the papers when she does die?'

'I've no idea.'

'It's a worry. Do you know, I found a letter from Oscar Wilde today. It's so frustrating. And I was just about to look at another packet of letters when Lady Youlgreave got worried about the bird table.'

'The bird table?'

'The one she can see from her window. There were a couple of crows on it who were frightening away the smaller birds. She'd got out a pair of opera glasses, trying to work out what was interesting them. She wanted me to go and find out. But when I did go out, there wasn't much left. Looked like a bit of bone or something. Quite fresh – there was blood as well.'

'On the bird table? Isn't that a bit odd?'

Vanessa shook her head. 'I imagine one of the birds brought it. Or perhaps Doris put it out. The trouble was, by the time I'd done that, Lady Youlgreave had had enough. The poor thing finds it very tiring having me there. All she really wants is her medicine and some peace and quiet. That and no pain.' She glanced at me, the knife in her hand poised over a slab of Cheddar. 'I wish we didn't have to get old. It's so dreary.'

I put the ice tray into the freezing compartment of the refrigerator and closed the door. 'Where's Rosemary?'

'She went to see Audrey.'

'Heaven knows what they find to talk about.'

At that moment, the phone began to ring yet again.

'I'm sometimes tempted to cut the wires,' Vanessa said. 'Don't people realize that you occasionally need five minutes' peace?'

It was the secretary of the Parochial Church Council. His wife had gone down with flu so they would be unable to come this evening. I went back to the kitchen to tell Vanessa.

'Oh well,' she said. 'In some ways, the fewer the better. It will give us more chance to get to know the Cliffords.'

'Audrey will be there.'

'I'm sure she will. She'll be waiting on the doorstep on the stroke of half past six.'

As it happened, though, Vanessa was wrong. Rosemary returned home at tea time with the news that Lord Peter was missing again. Audrey was very worried and had set off on a tour of the neighbourhood in search of him. She had asked

Rosemary to warn us that she might be late, and to apologize on her behalf.

Neither Vanessa nor I was disposed to take this latest disappearance very seriously. Vanessa murmured that she could quite understand the cat's wanting an occasional break from his mistress's company.

At a quarter to seven, the E-type bringing our sole surviving guests pulled up outside the front door of the Vicarage. I heard Vanessa suck in her breath as Toby got out of the car. He was wearing very tight bell-bottomed trousers and a white shirt without a collar. Joanna climbed awkwardly out of the passenger seat, exposing almost all of her bare legs. She wore a short, crumpled green dress which looked as if it were made of silk. We went out to meet them.

'If I hadn't known better,' Toby told Vanessa as they shook hands, 'I'd have said that you and Rosemary were sisters.'

The tips of Vanessa's ears went pink, the way they did when someone paid her a compliment. Then it was Rosemary's turn. I heard him asking which university she went to. We went into the house. Michael was hesitating in the hall. I introduced him to the Cliffords. Michael's eyes drifted out towards the E-type in the drive.

'You can look inside her, if you want,' Toby said, following the direction of his gaze. 'It's not locked.'

'Really? Thanks.'

'You should try the driving seat. It's fantastically well designed.'

I wished that Michael would look at me as he looked at Toby. We left the boy with the car and went into the sitting room, where I poured drinks. Toby chatted with Vanessa and Rosemary. Joanna sat down in an armchair and asked for gin and tonic. As I gave it to her, she leant forward and the neck of her dress gaped open. I could not help noticing that she was not wearing a bra.

'Thank you,' she said, looking up at me.

Her face distracted me. She looked pinched and worried; and the whites of her eyes were bloodshot.

'Are you feeling all right?' I murmured, too low for the others to hear.

'It's OK,' she said equally softly. 'It's OK here.'

379

Her eyes met mine. I was about to say something when Toby appeared at Joanna's shoulder. 'Have you got your cigarettes, Jo? I must have left mine at home.'

She delved into her bag, a gaudy object made of leather patches and fastened with a drawstring, and produced a packet of Rothmans.

'I bumped into Victor Thurston this afternoon,' I said to Toby.

For an instant the skin tightened at the corners of his eyes, as though a bright light had unexpectedly shone into them. 'Oh yes. Nice chap. I've only met him the once. I went to see him just before we exchanged contracts on this place. The estate agent thought it might be a good idea.'

'He seemed to think you were considering developing the place.'

Toby played it exactly right – relaxed, smiling, with every appearance of frankness: 'Well, in the long term, anything's possible. Just a case of knowing what one's options are. As I say, the estate agent practically bullied me into it.'

'If you did develop Roth Park, what might you do?'

'I did wonder about turning it into a hotel. There's lots of room. And it's not a bad location, either. Heathrow Airport only a few miles away. There'll soon be two motorways within easy reach. And of course London's on the doorstep.'

'The house and grounds might appeal to the Americans,' Vanessa suggested. 'Feed their fantasies about the English aristocracy. And you could offer culture, too.'

'Francis Youlgreave?'

She smiled at him, and he smiled back; it was like watching an evenly matched game of tennis. 'You've obviously done your research,' she said.

'I bought a copy of *The History of Roth* from Mr Malik.'

'To go back to Francis Youlgreave: I'm researching his life at present. I wondered if you'd mind me looking over the house some time. I've never seen it.'

Toby spread out his hands. 'Whenever you want. In fact, Jo and I were thinking about holding a little housewarming party after the fete. Do you think that's a good idea? You could have the Grand Tour while you're there, if you liked. We should be more or less straight by then. At present we're rather at sixes and sevens.'

The conversation moved on to the fete and the proposed party. Time passed quickly, and I was aware that I was drinking more than I usually did.

At a quarter to eight, Toby glanced at his watch. 'Is that the time? We'd better get going.'

'Michael's still in your car,' Vanessa said, peering out of the window. 'He's sitting behind the wheel and looking very serious. Having a whale of a time, I think.'

'You could take him for a drive, Toby,' Joanna suggested suddenly. 'I'll walk home. It's not exactly far.'

Toby glanced at her and then at Vanessa and me. 'I'd be happy to – if it wouldn't upset your plans for the evening.'

'I'm sure Michael would love it,' Vanessa said. 'But can you spare the time?'

'Oh, we wouldn't be long. Twenty minutes or so. Would that be OK?'

By now we had all moved into the hall. I opened the front door. A diversion was approaching in the shape of Audrey, who was walking very quickly over the gravel. Her face was pink and shiny; she was not wearing a hat, and her hair hung raggedly down over her left ear.

'Hello,' I said. 'Has Lord Peter turned up?'

She shook her head. 'I've looked everywhere. But I found this.'

She held up a thin green strap with a small brass medallion attached to it.

'What is it?' Vanessa asked.

Audrey took a deep breath. Her chest was pumping up and down. 'It's Lord Peter's collar,' she said between gasps. 'It was in the bus shelter. I phoned the police but – but they weren't very helpful.'

The evening broke up quickly after that. Vanessa and Rosemary took Audrey into the sitting room. Rosemary sat with her while Vanessa made her some tea. Meanwhile, Toby took Michael for a drive, as originally arranged; it seemed the best thing for all concerned.

'Will you be all right?' Toby asked Joanna before he left.

'Of course I shall. It's only a few hundred yards.'

'You'll cut off quite a bit if you go through the gate in the garden and then through the churchyard,' I said. 'I'll show you.'

My motives were mixed. To be frank, I was glad of the chance to leave Audrey with Vanessa and Rosemary. And common politeness required that I show Joanna the way to the gate. I took her down the path at the side of the house and into the garden at the back. We walked in silence across the lawn to the gate in the wall of the churchyard. I opened it for her.

'If you follow the path round the church, go past the south door, then you come to the little gate in the paddock. The one you used the other day.'

Joanna stopped under the archway and looked up at me. I looked into the shifting green depths of her eyes and thought how beautiful they were; and another part of my mind smugly congratulated myself on the fact that my appreciation was purely aesthetic.

'Can I talk to you?' she said suddenly.

'Of course you can.' I had been half expecting this. 'That's what I'm here for.'

Unexpectedly, she giggled. 'A sort of agony uncle?'

I smiled back. 'Sort of.'

'Will you walk with me a little way?'

I followed her into the churchyard and shut the gate behind us.

'It's strange here,' she said. 'I miss the noise of the city. There were always people around where we lived – day or night. But here, apart from the main road and the planes, most of the time it's dead.'

We passed the east end of the church and the flight of steps leading down to the vault under the chancel.

'It's not town,' she went on, 'and it's not country, either. It's not *real*.'

'That's the trouble with suburbs,' I said. 'They feel like the middle of nowhere. But one gets used to them.'

She glanced at me, and for the first time I saw her smile. She stopped suddenly. We were beside the south porch. It was quiet, as if the churchyard had slipped away from the suburbs and returned to the country it had left behind. I distinctly remember hearing a bee in the rosebush that grew in the south-west angle between the porch and the church.

'Do you believe in ghosts?' She looked up at me and then past me. Suddenly her eyes widened. Her expression changed as completely as though a mask had been dropped over her face. She clutched my arm.

'What is it?'

'Look. In the porch.' She had difficulty forcing the words out. 'Beside the door.'

I stepped under the archway into the porch. Immediately before me was the heavy door into the nave of the church, great oak planks bleached with age. To the left of this was the board we used for parish notices.

Someone had given it a new use. Dangling in front of it was a ragged mass of black fur. I stared at it and felt my stomach churning in disgust. There were patches of white and red among the black.

I remembered Joanna. I swung round. She was still staring at the obscenity in the porch. I put my arm over her shoulder and she pushed her head into my chest. She was shaking. I tightened my grip around her. She was trying to say something.

'What?'

She lifted her head and said, 'Why would someone do a thing like that?'

She pushed her head into my chest again. Absently, I lowered my head to smell her hair. Dear God, I even felt, on some level, a stirring of sexual excitement. It was too long since Vanessa and I had made love.

Joanna's question remained unanswered, and terrible in its implications. Why would anyone want to slaughter Lord Peter and display his body at the door of my church?

17

It seemed to me that the younger of the two policemen was
looking at Vanessa with an interest that went some way beyond
the purely professional. His name was Franklyn. He was a thin,
sallow-skinned constable with thick eyebrows; he seemed barely
old enough to have left school. I guessed that Vanessa was aware
of his gaze because she turned slightly in her chair and crossed
her legs, impeding his view.

'So,' Sergeant Clough said wearily to Audrey. 'Let me see if
I've got this right.'

We were in the living room amid the debris of our little party.
The two policemen had arrived in their patrol car forty-five
minutes after Vanessa had first dialled 999. Sergeant Clough had
a tanned, knobbly skull which made me think of an unwashed
potato. He asked most of the questions while Franklyn took
notes. Audrey was sitting opposite Clough in the big armchair
by the fireplace, hunched like a frightened child over her second
glass of brandy. Her face was sheet-white and her hair was still
awry; she had resisted Vanessa's suggestion that she have a rest
upstairs.

'The last time you saw your cat was yesterday evening?' the
sergeant went on.

Audrey's face crumpled. 'I do try to keep him in at night, but
it's so difficult, especially in summer.'

Clough cleared his throat. 'No need to blame yourself, miss.
Now, when exactly did you last see him?'

'He had his supper, a nice bit of fish, about seven-thirty. I saw
him dozing in the chair at about half past eight. He must have
slipped out of the kitchen window downstairs. It could have

been any time after then. You could ask Mr and Mrs Malik, of course, and see if they –'

'Yes, Miss Oliphant, and you realized he was missing this morning, when he didn't come back for breakfast?'

'I wasn't worried at first, or not that worried. He often went off on his own. He was such an adventurous cat. It was such a worry because of the road. There's always a lot of cars on it, and vans and lorries, even at night. I started looking seriously for him at about five o'clock. I went all over the village, calling him. I was just about to come over to the Vicarage – Mr and Mrs Byfield had asked me over – when I had a brainwave. The bus shelter.'

She looked triumphantly at the sergeant, who stared back.

'I should have thought of it at once,' she went on. 'Don't you see? It's obvious. They blamed me for calling out the police the other week.'

'Who did?'

'The vandals. They even threw that stone through my window. I phoned the police station and told you all about it. Surely you remember?'

Clough said, 'I think one of my colleagues handled the case. So you looked in the bus shelter, because the kids go there, and you thought they might have taken your cat out of revenge. Is that it?'

'The bus shelter was empty,' Audrey said, ignoring his question. 'They were all guzzling beer in the pub. And on the floor, under the bench, I found that.' With a dramatic gesture, she pointed at the thin, green leather strap on the coffee table in front of the sofa. 'Proof positive, Sergeant.'

Franklyn scribbled briefly in his notebook and glanced at Vanessa. Clough scratched his left kneecap.

'How could they?' Audrey burst out. 'Lord Peter never harmed a soul.'

Clough blinked. 'Who, miss?'

'My cat,' she snapped. A flush rose in her cheeks. 'It makes me feel quite ill.'

Vanessa leant forward and put her hand on the arm of Audrey's chair. 'He may have died in a road accident. Perhaps someone found the body.'

'The postmortem will tell us,' Audrey said. 'I hope that's what happened. He wouldn't have felt as much pain. And he wouldn't have been so upset – he always trusted people, you see.' She stared at Clough. 'How soon will you hold the postmortem?'

'Ah – we don't usually hold postmortems on animals, Miss Oliphant. I tell you what, though. We'll take him down for you. Then you can bury him, nice and decent – in your back garden, perhaps.'

'But I want to find out how he died.'

The sergeant gently rubbed a finger over his knee, as if caressing an itch. 'I suppose you could ask a vet to have a look at him.'

'But it's *evidence*, Sergeant. It may well be important to your investigation to know how Lord Peter died.'

'I think if you want a postmortem, miss, a vet is your best bet.' He glanced out of the window. 'Look, if we're going to get him down, I suggest we do it now, rather than later. I mean, anyone might see him. Could give some old lady a nasty shock, eh?' He stood up and stretched. 'Mr Byfield – would you happen to have a cardboard box or something of that sort we could use?'

I went into the kitchen. Rosemary was sitting at the table eating a strawberry yoghurt and apparently absorbed in Sartre's *Nausea*, in a French edition. She looked up as I came in.

'How's it going in there?'

'Audrey's still in quite a state. Understandably enough. They want a cardboard box to put the cat in.'

Rosemary pushed back her chair. 'There are some in the garage.'

She went through the utility room and opened the connecting door to the garage. As she was rummaging in there, Vanessa came into the kitchen.

'I'll put the kettle on. We could all do with a cup of tea.'

'Have you got something we could wrap the body in?' I asked.

'What?'

'To use as a shroud.'

Vanessa blinked. 'There's an old pillow case under the sink. I was going to cut it up for dusters.' She filled the kettle and plugged it in. 'You make it sound as if Lord Peter's going to have a state funeral.' Her voice wobbled. 'Is there a section in the Prayer Book to meet the contingency? "The Order for the Burial of Murdered Pets"?'

I put my arm round her. She leant against me, only to pull sharply away when Rosemary returned with a box that had once contained tins of cocoa.

'The coffin,' Rosemary announced.

I found the pillow case under the sink and took it and the box into the sitting room. Audrey and the two policemen seemed not to have moved since I left.

Clough stood up quickly. 'Right. We'll go and sort it out. Frankie, you can carry the box.'

Franklyn scrambled up and took the box and pillow case from me.

Clough turned to Audrey. 'I'd be inclined to go home now, if I were you. Maybe Mrs Byfield will take you over.'

'I can't do that. Not until Lord Peter –'

'I'm afraid there's nothing you can do now. The best thing is to go home, have a nice sweet cup of tea, get into bed and have a nice sleep. Have you got any sleeping tablets or something like that?'

Audrey shook her head violently.

'Maybe you should ring your GP. Or perhaps Mrs Byfield could do it for you. You've had a shock, you know.'

'I don't want a doctor.' Audrey scowled at him and then remembered her manners. 'Thank you.'

'It's up to you.'

'I want the culprits caught.'

'Culprits? So there's more than one, you think.'

'Those louts always go round in gangs.'

Clough sighed. 'We don't know it was them.'

'Who else could it have been?'

He shrugged and said nothing. An uncomfortable silence hung in the air. Franklyn cast a longing glance at the door. Vanessa came back into the room.

'How many for tea?'

Franklyn and Clough declined. Audrey said she wouldn't mind another glass of brandy, but was persuaded to try tea instead. Clough asked if he could have a word with me on the way out. We went into the drive, where Franklyn collected a torch and a pair of rubber gloves from the car. While we were walking round to the gate to the churchyard, Clough stuck a briar pipe in his mouth and lit it with a gas lighter whose flame was like a flare.

'Has anything like this happened before, sir?'

'Mutilated cats?'

'Not just that. Every now and then we get someone who's been reading too many Dennis Wheatley novels.'

'Satanism?'

'Whatever you want to call it. Witchcraft. Mumbo jumbo. Raising the devil. Usually it's just an excuse for naughty sex in fancy dress. Sometimes it gets nasty, though.'

'No. To the best of my knowledge, there's been nothing like this before. Not here.'

'Sure?'

'Quite sure. I think I would have noticed.'

'Did you have a good look at the cat?'

'No.' I had not wanted to. 'Enough to see it had been cut open.'

'More than that. Its head's missing.'

'*What?*'

'Let me know if you come across it, eh?' Clough clicked his lighter and a tongue of flame licked the bowl of his pipe. 'Do you lock the church?'

'Only at night.'

'It might be wise to consider locking it during the day as well. There's some sick people around these days.'

'There always have been.'

'I wouldn't take it personally,' he went on. 'Probably any old church would have done.' He tapped his head. 'Just another passing nutter, eh? Oh – by the way: who was the young lady you were with when you found the cat?'

'Her name's Joanna Clifford. Do you need to talk to her? She lives near here.'

'Where?'

'She and her brother have just moved into Roth Park. You know it? The big house behind the church. They had been having a drink with us and I had been showing her a short cut home through the churchyard.'

'Her brother? Would that be Toby Clifford?'

'That's right. Do you know him?'

Clough paused to relight his pipe. 'Oh – someone mentioned there were new people up at Roth Park.'

We walked on to the south porch. The light was fading fast. The bricks in the porch glowed palely in the dusk.

'You get it down, Frankie,' Clough said. 'I'll hold the torch.'

'Oh, *Sarge*.'

'Get on with it, lad.' In a stage whisper, he added to me, 'Privilege of rank, eh?'

Franklyn gave Clough the torch and pulled on the gloves. The beam leapt into the porch, a stripe of light across the stone floor, and slid up to the notice board on the left of the door. Lord Peter was no longer there. Clough puffed smoke into the evening air.

'We've only been gone half an hour,' Franklyn said, his voice aggrieved, as if Lord Peter's absence were a personal insult.

Clough let the torch beam drop to the floor. He gave a whistle of relief. There was a huddle of black fur in the corner, partly concealed by a cast-iron umbrella stand.

'Thought we'd lost him for a moment,' he said. 'That would have been a turn-up for the books.'

'The case of the vanishing pussy,' Franklyn suggested, as he stepped forward with the box and the pillow case. 'Whoops.'

'How did he fall?' I said.

Clough stepped into the porch. The beam zigzagged across the notice board, then down to the cat. Franklyn bent down and lifted the tail. A piece of string was still attached to it.

'Simple enough.' Clough let the torch slide up the wall to the hook from which the notice board hung. 'One end of the string was tied to the hook, and the other to the cat. Obviously they weren't very good at knots.'

'Probably not a boy scout, then?' Franklyn said.

'Aren't you going to photograph it?' I asked. 'Or at least examine it?'

'We've seen all we need to see, sir,' Clough said. 'There's a limit to what we can do in cases like this. It's a question of resources.'

I shrugged, knowing from his tone of voice that I had irritated him. We watched Franklyn stuffing the body into the pillow case and dropping shroud and corpse into the box. He closed the flaps with a flourish.

'You'd better have a look here in the morning, sir,' he said to me. 'There may be a bit of blood or something. I dare say you'll want to clean up.'

The police drove away soon afterwards. Vanessa and I took Audrey back to Tudor Cottage. The brandy and the shock were having their effect: we had to support her, one on each side. She would not let Vanessa help her into bed, but she accepted one of my sleeping tablets.

'What have you done with Lord Peter?' she asked me.

'He's in the garage.'

'I shall bury him in the garden. After the postmortem.'

'I'm not sure the police –'

'I'll pay to have it done. Then they'll see I'm right. Why are the police so *stupid*?' She put her hand to her temple. 'My head hurts.'

Vanessa and I walked back to the Vicarage. Laughter and music poured through the open doors of the Queen's Head, and the river of traffic still flowed on the main road.

'Do you think she's serious about the postmortem idea?' Vanessa asked.

'Audrey's always serious.'

A light shone in the window of the spare bedroom. Michael was still awake. We found Rosemary in the sitting room, still reading *Nausea*.

'How is she?'

'Audrey?' Vanessa said. 'Still in a state. Understandably.'

'It's horrible.' Rosemary looked at me. 'I just don't understand why people do things like that.'

I touched her shoulder. 'None of us does. Not really.'

While Vanessa was making tea, I went up to see Michael. He was already in bed, sitting in blue-and-white striped pyjamas, with his hair neatly brushed, reading a book. He glanced up at me but said nothing. I thought he looked worried.

'What are you reading?'

He held up the book, a paperback in the green-and-white

390

Penguin crime livery. '*The Adventures of Sherlock Holmes*. It was in the bookcase.'

'You must be finding it rather dull here.'

Michael smiled at me and shook his head.

'And I'm afraid this evening can't have been much fun. Did you manage to get something to eat?'

'Aunt Vanessa made me a sandwich.'

'Good. This business with the cat – you mustn't let it upset you.'

'It's not upsetting,' Michael said. 'It's interesting.'

Vanessa and I did not get a chance to talk privately until we were in bed.

'So what do you think?' Vanessa whispered. 'Is it personal?'

'The police seem to think it's most likely someone mentally unbalanced. Probably any church would have done. St Mary Magdalene just happened to be the first they noticed.'

'And any cat? It's perfectly possible that Audrey's right. She's really upset some of those kids from the council estate.'

'I hope you're wrong.'

She snorted in exasperation. 'You have to at least consider the possibility that I'm not. And there's two other things you ought to think about. The first one is Francis Youlgreave.'

I picked a feather out of the eiderdown. 'Surely what he did isn't common knowledge?'

'You'd be surprised. It's the sort of thing that people remember if they remember nothing else about a person. After all, you remembered it.'

'But it doesn't really narrow the field much,' I pointed out. 'And I don't think it's enough to establish a connection.'

'And then there's the other thing. Do you remember I told you about the crows pecking something on Lady Youlgreave's bird table?'

I stared at her. 'Surely not. You're not implying – ?'

'Why not? The cat's head had to go somewhere. What if someone put it on the bird table? It would be one way of ramming home a connection with Francis Youlgreave.'

'But why?'

'How should I know?' Vanessa picked up her book. 'Isn't that more your province than mine?'

I glanced at her, trying to tell if she was being serious. Her sense of humour could be so very dry. She settled her glasses on her nose and opened the book, her own copy of Youlgreave's *The Four Last Things*. It struck me that I was only beginning to discover the real Vanessa. I was like one of those nineteenth-century explorers travelling up a river into the heart of an unknown continent and glimpsing a vast, uncharted interior, more mysterious with every passing mile.

'I don't follow,' I said at last. 'What's my province?'

'Evil, of course, what did you think I meant?'

18

The next problem came from an unexpected direction. I was working in the study the following afternoon when the telephone rang.

'David, it's Ronald Trask.' The voice was abrupt to the point of rudeness. 'What's this Cynthia tells me about an outbreak of Satanism at St Mary Magdalene?'

He used the word *Satanism* like a cudgel. I took a deep breath and tried to persuade myself that Ronald was only doing his duty. An archdeacon used to be known as the bishop's eye. Such matters came within his province.

'We don't know it's Satanism. I think it's unwise to jump to conclusions. It may just have been a teenage prank which got out of hand.'

'A prank? A cat beheaded in your own parish church?'

'It wasn't beheaded in the church. We found the body hanging from a hook in the porch.'

'That's not the point, in any case.'

'Then what is?'

'That this could be a public relations disaster.' Ronald lowered his voice, as if he were afraid of being overheard. 'Not just for the church. For you personally.'

There was a pause. Vanessa had gone into the office this morning. She must have mentioned the events of last night to Cynthia, who had evidently lost no time in relaying the news to her brother. Anger stirred inside me. Ronald might have a right to interfere, but not in this heavy-handed way.

'There's just a chance we can nip this in the bud,' he went on. 'I think the best thing to do is to ring Victor Thurston.'

393

'I don't see any need to bring Thurston into this. It's nothing to do with him. In any case, I think I'd prefer to handle it in my own way.'

Ronald sighed, expressing irritation rather than recording sorrow. 'Let me spell it out for you. This is just the sort of story that the more sensational elements of the press will leap at. First, it's August, the silly season. They're hungry for material. Secondly, anything that smacks of devil worship sells newspapers. It's regrettable, but it's a fact of life. Third, Cynthia tells me there's local colour in the shape of that damned poet, the priest who dabbled in Satanism. Youlgreave – the one Vanessa's so keen on. And finally, once the hacks start digging, heaven knows what they might come up with. How will you feel if they connect you with that business in Rosington? How will Vanessa feel?'

I was so surprised that for an instant I forgot to breathe. I sucked in a mouthful of air. I had not even realized that Ronald knew about Rosington. He had never mentioned it. In that same instant there rushed over me the crushing knowledge of my own naivety. Of course he knew. Probably every active Christian in this part of the diocese fancied that they knew all about it. One of the less desirable qualities of the Church of England is that it is a nest of gossip.

'Listen to me, David.' His voice was gentler now, almost pleading. 'You'll get an army of journalists on your doorstep. You'll probably have coachloads of sightseers coming to gawp at the church. You may even get copycat incidents.'

I said nothing. It was true that devil-worshippers tended to be unimaginative. By and large, evil is banal; imagination is not a quality it nurtures, so repetition is common. Into my mind came an image of grey mudflats, silver streaks of water and a grey sky; and far above me I heard the sound of wings. The hand holding the telephone receiver was slippery with sweat, and my armpits prickled. Evil causes led to evil effects which themselves became causes of further evil. Could you ever hope to end the consequences, or would they stretch through the centuries from past and future?

I tried to focus on Ronald, sensible and safe. I imagined him sitting at his polished desk, surrounded by serried ranks of dusted books; I gave him a silver vase full of white rosebuds; no clutter on the desk, just a blotter, a notepad and perhaps a file containing letters to be answered. And there was Ronald, impeccable in his suit and clerical collar, the very picture of a senior clergyman in waiting for a bishopric.

It wasn't good enough. The beating of the wings was growing gradually louder. My mouth was parched.

The wall, I thought, the wall beside his desk. No bookshelves there. A crucifix. A plain wooden crucifix. No body on it, but there would be a rush cross, left over from Palm Sunday, tucked behind the crossbar. I thought so hard about the crucifix that I could visualize the colour of the varnish and the grain of the wood.

'David? I'm trying to *help*.'

Ronald was sane, I told myself. Ronald was good. Recognizing that was hard, too. He was doing his best to do his Christian duty, according to his lights. I had stolen the woman he had thought of as his future wife. He had every reason to dislike me, even hate me. Yet he was going out of his way to help me – or perhaps Vanessa. I might not enjoy his assumption of authority and superior knowledge, but that was a relatively minor matter.

'Are you still there, David?'

'Yes. I was thinking. Why should all this reach the papers in the first place?'

'Through the local rag, of course. They'll be in regular contact with the police. Fortunately, Victor Thurston's on the board of the *Courier* group. I'll have a word with him tonight.' Ronald sounded cheerful now, delighted to have his hands on the reins. 'He has some useful contacts with the police, too, through the Masons. Don't worry. We'll do our best to smooth things over.'

There was another pause in our conversation. There was only one thing to say and in the end I made myself say it. 'Thank you.'

The trick with Lady Youlgreave was to catch her at her lucid times. Her body was a battlefield: old age, pain, decay, a cocktail of medicines and an almost wilful reluctance to die fought each other, changing sides frequently, forming shifting alliances.

The morphine encouraged her mind to drift. Often she was confused about the day of the week, occasionally the year and, on at least one occasion, the century. Time is a slippery notion, a set of assumptions she found it increasingly difficult to grasp.

She was at her best in the late mornings and the early evenings. I left the Vicarage at 5 p.m. on Friday, shortly after the phone call from Ronald Trask. I was restless, tired of my own company. Doing anything was better than doing nothing.

I called upstairs to Rosemary but there was no answer. I went into the garden. Michael was playing patience on the grass in the shade of an old apple tree that had survived Ronald's restless desire to modernize my house and garden. There was a deckchair on the lawn, with *Nausea* on the seat. The afternoon had been sunny, but now the sky was beginning to cloud over, and there was a clinging dampness in the air that presaged rain.

'I'm just going out for a while,' I told Michael. 'I shouldn't be more than half an hour. Will you be all right on your own? I'm sure the Vintners wouldn't mind if –'

'No. I'll be fine.'

'I'll be at the Old Manor House if anyone needs me.'

'OK.'

'Is Rosemary upstairs?'

'I think she went for a walk. She was here until about five minutes ago.'

'Aunt Vanessa should be home between half past five and six.'

'OK.'

He smiled at me and returned to his game. I walked down the road, over the bridge and turned into the forecourt in front of the Old Manor House. The bird table stood at a slight angle from the perpendicular at the centre of the scrubby lawn. I went over to it. It was a simple affair – a small wooden tray nailed to a stake, obviously home-made. The surface of the wood was cracked and covered with a patina of dirt from the weather and traffic. I found no trace of the blood and bone which Vanessa had seen, and which had so excited the crows.

I bent down and looked at the grass below the table. I felt ridiculous, like a schoolboy looking for clues, for cigarette ash or strands of hair. I abandoned the search, walked on to the door and rang the bell. The dogs barked. Doris answered the door.

'Hello, Vicar.'

'Is Lady Youlgreave well enough for visitors?'

'She'll be glad to see you. Just had her tea and that always gives her a bit of a lift. Which means she wants to talk. And I just don't have time to listen.'

I followed her into the gloom of the hall. Beauty was tethered to the newel post and did not bother to get up. She thumped her tail on the floor. Beast, trailing her tumour, waddled towards me and sniffed my shoes.

'You should have more help,' I said to Doris. 'Either that or Lady Youlgreave should go into a home.'

Doris shook her head. 'She doesn't like strangers in the house. And if you talk to her about going into a home, she starts crying.'

'It's not fair to you.'

'I cope. Dr Vintner is in and out, and that helps. And then there's the nurse from the Fishguard Agency at weekends. Not that they're much use.'

'Even so –'

'She wants to die in her own home,' Doris interrupted. 'So why shouldn't she?'

There wasn't any answer to that, or rather, none that Doris would accept. I wondered how much Lady Youlgreave paid her.

'I hear your husband has a new job.' I wished I could remember the man's name.

'About time, too,' she said. 'If there was an Olympic gold medal for sitting on your backside in front of the telly, Ted would be in the running for it.'

Beast slobbered over my shoe. She looked up at me with imploring eyes. What did she want? Everything to be all right again? For herself and Beauty and her mistress to be young?

'You go and see her, then,' Doris said, deciding it was time to dismiss me. 'I'll go and make her bed again. Can you find your own way? Otherwise I'll get caught as well.'

Lady Youlgreave was nodding over a book when I went in. She looked up with a start.

'David? Is that you?'

'Yes. How are you today?'

'The same as always. Where's the girl? It's time for my medicine.'

'Soon. Doris will be here soon.'

I wasn't sure if she had heard me. She closed the book slowly – a thin volume bound in green leather with gilt lettering on the spine. Then she said, 'She's late. She's always late. If she doesn't get her skates on, I'll sack her.'

I knew better than to argue. 'Doris is making your bed.'

'How odd.'

'Why?'

'Beds are made in the morning. Everyone knows that. Is it the morning?'

'No.' I looked at my watch. 'It's a quarter past five in the evening. Friday evening.' I noticed that Lady Youlgreave was still looking expectantly at me, a worried frown on her face. 'Friday, August the fourteenth.' She was still frowning, so I added, 'Nineteen-seventy.'

'Oh. Where's your wife? Not been in today. Or has she?'

'No. Vanessa's at work.'

'Never thought you'd get married again. Poor old Oliphant. Bet it made her squirm.' Lady Youlgreave paused, and her lips moved as though she were chewing something. A thread of saliva ran from the corner of her mouth, as though marking the passage of a tiny snail. 'Could have liked you myself, once. Silly business, don't you think?'

'What is?'

'Sex. Best thing about growing old: not having to worry about sex.' The little eyes peered at me and looked away. 'You should stop Vanessa wasting her time on Uncle Francis.'

'I can't do that. I'm not her master.'

'You should put your foot down.'

I could imagine Vanessa's response if I tried to do such a foolish thing. 'What's wrong with Francis, anyway? I thought you wanted Vanessa to go through the papers.'

'I didn't realize what he was like. Not then.' Lady Youlgreave tapped the book on her lap. 'Nasty mind. And getting worse. Do you know why he started killing those animals?'

I said nothing.

'I think you do.' She sighed. 'This was his last book.'

'*The Voice of Angels*?'

'More like devils. There's one poem called "The Children of Heracles". Disgusting. He must have had an evil mind to make up something like that.'

I would have liked to take the book and glance at the poem, but her fingers had locked themselves around the covers. 'It's part of a Greek myth.'

'So Heracles really did kill his children? He really chopped them up?'

'As far as I can remember, Zeus's wife, Hera, hated Heracles, and one night she put a spell on him. In his sleep, he lashed out with his sword, dreaming that he was killing imaginary enemies. Then he woke up and he saw that he'd killed his own children.'

'And chopped them up.' Lady Youlgreave snuffled, a sound that might have expressed mirth. '*He* did that, too.'

'Francis?' I smiled. 'Not children, though.'

'How do you know?' She stared up at me. 'There's a lot you don't know.'

She opened the book and seemed to become absorbed in a poem. I waited for a moment. Vanessa had warned me that these mood swings were becoming more frequent and more pronounced.

I cleared my throat. 'Vanessa told me about your bird table. About the meat or whatever it was that the crows were pecking at. I don't suppose you got a good look at it, did you? With your opera glasses?'

She raised her head once more and I realized at once that I was not forgiven or forgotten. 'I said there's a lot you don't know, David. Even about your own family.'

'What do you mean?'

'I saw the whole thing. I'm not blind.' The irises of her eyes were mud-brown pools, the pupils almost invisible. 'It was in a paper bag.'

'What was?'

'Whatever it was. A little head?'

'So you saw who put it there?'

'I told you. I'm not blind.' She sniffed. Her eyes misted with tears. 'I don't understand. Why don't I understand? Is it late? My watch has stopped. What's the time?'

The door opened and Doris came in. 'How about a nice drink before bed, love? A nice cup of cocoa?'

'Medicine.' Lady Youlgreave brightened. 'It's time for my medicine.'

'Not quite, dear. I've put it all out on your bedside table, like usual. You can have the first one when you get into bed.' Doris looked at me. 'You'll want to be getting home, I expect, Vicar. I saw Mrs Byfield's car go by.'

19

She rushed out of the drive of Roth Park, her arms outstretched towards me.

'Father! Wait!'

I stopped. Rain was drifting from a grey sky. Rosemary propped herself against one of the gateposts. She was out of breath and bursting with life. Even when wearing jeans and a white shirt which had once belonged to me, she somehow contrived to look elegant.

'I found something. You'd better come and see.'

'What is it?'

She shook her head. 'Come with me.' She seized my arm and gave it a little tug. 'Please.'

I allowed her to draw me into the drive. 'Why all the mystery?'

'Not a mystery.'

She led me past the churchyard and into the grove of oaks. Instead of continuing down the drive towards the house, she turned right on to the footpath which led into the paddock we hoped to use for the fete's car park. It was raining harder, now, and I suggested going back for an umbrella. But Rosemary urged me on.

On the far side of the paddock, the footpath split into two – one branch continuing north towards a cluster of council houses and the Jubilee Reservoir, the other cutting westwards across a patch of waste ground in a direction roughly parallel to the drive. The land had been part of the demesne of Roth Park, and was owned by the Cliffords.

'Where are we going?' I asked.

She looked back, her eyes gleaming and her face full of colour. 'Carter's Meadow. Look – there's the way in.'

We followed the path to a five-bar gate made of rusting tubular steel, wired permanently closed. Rosemary and I climbed over. Nowadays Carter's Meadow was a no man's land sandwiched between the ruined formal gardens of Roth Park and the housing estate. Like so many places on the fringes of cities, it was permanently dirty: even the weeds were grubby.

Rosemary led me past an abandoned car to a small spinney, a self-seeded clump of straggly trees and saplings. A track zigzagged through ash and birch, brambles and nettles. She plunged into it. I wondered what she had been doing here. Smoking? Meeting a boy? The air smelled rank, as though the spinney were a large animal beginning to decay. We came out on the far side of it.

She stopped abruptly, wiping rain from her face. 'There.' She pointed to the ground beside a dead elder tree on the edge of the spinney. 'Look at that.'

I followed the direction of her finger. An empty bottle leaned against the tree. The grass at the foot of the tree was stained a rusty brown.

'*Look*,' she repeated, stabbing the air with her finger. 'Don't you see what must have happened here?'

I hitched my trousers and crouched down. The grass was dry. The bottle had contained a cider called Autumn Gold. The label was fresh. The bottle might have been left there yesterday. Cigarette ends lay in various stages of decay between the blades of grass. There was sadness in this place.

'It's blood,' Rosemary said. 'Father, it's blood, isn't it?'

'I think so.'

I picked up the bottle between finger and thumb. Underneath was a tuft of black hair.

'This is where they did it,' Rosemary said. 'You can buy that cider in Malik's Minimarket. Did you know?'

I wished she had not found this. It meant nothing but trouble. We could not be sure that the stain was dried blood, let alone that it and the fur came from Lord Peter. But I would have to tell the police, who would not want to hear. I would also have to tell Audrey, and the discovery would feed her forensic fantasies – and incidentally serve to confirm her belief that the youths from the council estate were responsible. And why did Rosemary have to be the one to find it?

'What were you doing here?' My voice was sharper than I had intended.

'I wanted a walk.'

'Here?'

'If you follow the path you get to the river. It's pretty.'

Pretty? I had not been this way for years. I had a vague memory of a tangle of trees on boggy ground, through which meandered the Rowan, scarcely more than a stream. But teenagers had different standards of beauty from adults. I looked at Rosemary and suddenly remembered my adolescent self finding a perverse satisfaction from reading Auden in the shell of a burned-out house: I had sat on a pile of rubble bright with rosebay willowherb and smoked illicit cigarettes.

I stood up. The rain was falling more heavily now. The trees gave us partial shelter but I did not want to stay here any longer than necessary. There was poison in this place, and I felt it seeping into me.

'Do you think they cut up Lord Peter here?' Rosemary asked.

'It's possible. But we mustn't jump to conclusions.'

'This is where Francis Youlgreave cut up a cat, isn't it?'

'So they say. Come on.'

'But we'll get soaked.'

I glanced at her. Her eyes met mine. Her face was calm and beautiful. *My daughter*. I wanted to believe that truth was beauty, and beauty truth. But what if Keats was wrong and beauty did not have a moral dimension? What if beauty told lies? Rosemary had told lies in the past. But she had been too young to know better. Children only gradually become moral beings. I pushed aside the memory.

I walked quickly away from the shelter of the trees. I felt better in the open. Rosemary followed me. Did she not feel the atmosphere of the place? There was a growl of thunder. The rain sluiced out of the sky. Water ran down my neck and soaked through the shoulders of my jacket. *Wash me clean*. Would it wash away the evidence – and, if so, was that a good thing, for fear of what the evidence might reveal?

Rosemary took my arm again – unusual for her, because she tended not to touch me very much. 'Are you OK?'

'Fine. We'd better go home and get dry.'

'You'll ring the police?'

'Yes.'

She nuzzled against me, as if trying to push me into action. 'If we cut through the Cliffords' garden we can get up to the drive. It'll be quicker than going back the way we came.'

I followed her. It was easier than arguing about whether or not we should trespass. In a way I was grateful that she had taken charge. I was not usually indecisive. Indeed, I tend to go the other way, sometimes to the point of arrogance. But at that moment I could no more make a choice than I could play a note on a violin with slackened strings. The poison under the trees was working at me, sapping my will.

The poison had other effects. Rosemary led the way – she seemed to know it, and I did not. We walked along the line of a straggling hedgerow towards a dark-green mass of trees and shrubs. The rain plastered her hair to her head and her clothes to her body. I could not see her face – just her figure, and the lilting sway of her bottom as she walked. I felt a stirring of desire, just as I had when I put my arms round Joanna the previous evening. But this was far worse. Rosemary was my daughter. *What is happening to me?* Nausea mingled with my desire. I stared at the ground. It was so long since Vanessa and I had made love.

'Lord have mercy,' I muttered. 'Lord have mercy.'

She could not have heard me, but she turned. 'I'm *soaking*,' she said happily.

We came to a barbed-wire fence which separated the strip of wasteland from the belt of trees and bushes. The wire was rusting and some of the posts were either missing or leaning.

Rosemary picked up one of the posts, leaving a gap nearly three feet high between the ground and the lowest strand of wire. 'I'll hold it for you.'

I crawled underneath. It was clear that people had been through the fence at this point before, and I suspected that Rosemary had been one of them. I felt ridiculous: a middle-aged clergyman dragged back to adolescence. Rosemary scrambled after me. I had never been here before, but I guessed that we were in what had once been part of the garden of Roth Park. The belt of trees was dominated by a big copper beech. Among the tangle of seedlings were other, older plants – rhododendrons and laurels; the remains of a yew hedge; and the long carcass of a fallen Douglas fir.

'This way,' Rosemary urged, the rainwater streaming down her cheeks. She smiled brilliantly. 'Follow me.'

We picked our way through the undergrowth and passed under the canopy of the copper beech. Despite the cover from the branches, the rain was still pounding down. Suddenly the trees thinned and the rain increased in intensity. I caught sight of the chimneys and upper windows of the house. I realized where we were.

A few paces ahead of me, Rosemary stopped. She turned back to me. The rain poured over her. 'Oh *no*,' she hissed. 'How embarrassing.'

The ground shelved. Before us was what had once been a sunken rose garden surrounded by stone walls. Now it contained a kidney-shaped depression made of concrete, filled not with water but with dead leaves. A springboard still arched over what had once been the deep end, its coconut matting slimy with rain. A pavement of stone flags ran round the pool. There were benches set at intervals in the wall, and halfway down one of the longer sides was a wooden structure with a pitched roof and a little verandah running along the front. Sitting in a director's chair on the verandah was Toby Clifford, smoking a long, white cigarette.

He saw us a few seconds after we saw him. He waved. 'Come and get out of the rain,' he called.

We picked our way round the edge of the pool towards the building, a combination of changing room and summer house. Toby was wearing jeans and a loose cotton top with embroidery around the neck, and his feet were bare; he looked more like a hippy than ever. He stubbed out his cigarette, even though it was only partly smoked, and threw it into the bushes. There was another chair on the verandah. He unfolded it with a flourish. Rosemary was first up the steps. He bowed from the waist, waving her into the chair.

'I'm sorry,' I began. 'We were walking across Carter's Meadow, and it began to rain hard.'

'So you thought you'd look for shelter. Jolly good idea. Have a seat.'

'I'm afraid we're trespassing –'

'You're welcome.' Toby perched on the rail. 'I'll run up to the house and get an umbrella and a couple of towels.'

'There's no need.'

'You mustn't catch cold.'

Rosemary said, 'I'm not cold. I'm *boiling*.'

We both looked at her – sitting back in the chair, smiling – almost laughing – at us. She was bedraggled but as beautiful as ever, almost as if the rain had colluded with her and brought out another aspect of her beauty: nature meant her to be drenched and glistening. Her shirt was plastered to her body, marking the outlines of her thin bra, through which poked the outlines of her erect nipples. Now my emotions shifted to another mode, and I wanted to cover her up, to shield her body from the eyes of a strange man. There was a half smile on Toby's face.

'You mustn't let us put you to any trouble,' I said. 'When the rain slackens off, we'll be on our way.'

'It's no trouble. Nice to have an opportunity to return your hospitality. How's Miss – Miss Oliphant, is it? Jo told me about the business with the cat.'

'She's taking it –'

'That's why we came out,' Rosemary interrupted. 'We found some blood.'

'Blood?' He stared at her. 'Where?'

'In Carter's Meadow. You know, the field beyond your garden. It's part of the park, isn't it?'

'Not exactly – but what do you mean, some blood?'

'There's a place under one of the trees . . . Father found some fur as well.'

Toby whistled.

'It may be where they cut off the cat's head,' Rosemary said, her voice prim. 'We shall have to tell the police.'

'You can phone from here, if you like.' Toby was talking to Rosemary, not me. 'It's nearer. And then I could run you home in the car.'

She nodded. 'Thank you.'

'Do you think the police will do anything about it?'

'I don't know. But one has to try. Poor Audrey.'

I noticed that at some point in the last few days Rosemary had stopped calling Audrey 'Miss Oliphant'.

Toby stood up. 'You stay there. I'll fetch the umbrella.'

'There's no point,' Rosemary said. 'We're both soaked as it is.'

Toby stared at her again, and they exchanged smiles. 'OK. We'll run through the rain instead.' Then he remembered me. 'But I can bring back the umbrella for you, David.'

'No need, thanks. But I may not run. Walking's more my style, these days.'

The two of them ran ahead – darting up the steps behind the pavilion and tearing ragged tracks through the long grass of the croquet lawn. I followed them up to the terrace where I had had coffee with Toby and Joanna. Sexual desire had sensitized me to the presence of desire in others. It was quite clear that Rosemary was attracted to Toby, and that he was attracted to her.

The two of them entered the house through one of the French windows that opened on to the terrace. 'Jo!' I heard Toby call. 'Visitors!'

I went after them. The room beyond was large, light and well proportioned, a double cube at least twenty-five feet long. As well as two pairs of French windows on to the terrace, there were two tall windows looking out on the drive. In the Bramleys' time this had been the residents' lounge.

'I'm afraid it's still a bit of a mess.' Toby grinned at Rosemary. 'Any time you want a job as a housekeeper, you have only to ask.'

I hesitated just inside the door, aware that a puddle was rapidly forming around my feet.

'Come on in,' Toby said. 'A little water won't hurt the place.'

The size of the room dwarfed its contents – G-Plan furniture, two easy chairs, a mattress, several tea chests and a roll of carpet. Beside the empty fireplace was a record player – a series of expensive-looking boxes linked by wires – and several cartons of long-playing records. Ghostly traces of the Bramleys remained

407

– pale patches marking the sites of pictures and furniture. There were cigarettes and whisky on the mantelpiece. Propped against the wall behind them was a large mirror with an ornate gilded frame and a long crack running diagonally down the glass. Our footsteps were loud on the bare floor and left trails of wet prints across the boards.

Toby was at the door. 'Let's find some towels, shall we? This way.'

He led us into a short corridor which ran down to the central hall by the front door. I had been here often enough in the Bramleys' day, but now the place felt and looked like a different house. The clutter of wheelchairs had gone from the foot of the stairs. The carpets, pictures, and shabby furniture had departed, and so had the smell of powder, perfume, disinfectant and old age. I was aware of empty rooms around and above us, of the cellars beneath our feet, of silent, enclosed spaces, of damp, musty smells.

In the hall, the emptiness stretched up to a skylight like a glass tent on the roof of the house. The panes were cracked and stained with bird droppings. To our right, a pitch-pine staircase divided in two at mezzanine level and ran up to a galleried landing.

'Damn,' Toby said. 'There's a leak. I'm not surprised.'

A puddle had already gathered on the black-and-white tiles of the floor. *Plop – plop – plop.* I watched a silver drop describe what looked like a curving path from skylight to floor, where it shattered.

'Jo,' Toby called, and his voice bounced up the stairwell. 'Jo, where are you?'

I heard feet pattering along the landing above our heads. Not pattering: bare feet thudding on bare boards. Suddenly the footsteps stopped and Joanna's pale face appeared twenty feet above us, hanging over the rail of the banisters.

'What is it?' She sounded out of breath.

'We need towels,' Toby said. 'David and Rosemary were caught in the storm, and so was I. There are clean ones in that room by the bathroom. Inside the blue trunk.'

The head vanished. A moment later Joanna came down the stairs with an armful of towels. She was wearing a dark-blue halter-neck T-shirt, which clung to her body, and a long wrap-around skirt. Her feet were grubby, and the toenails were decorated with green nail varnish, much chipped. She handed round the towels. When she came to me, she raised her head. Our eyes met, and I saw that her eyelids were puffy.

Toby towelled himself vigorously. 'I'm sure that Jo could find something for Rosemary to change into. As for you, David, I could see what –'

'There's no need,' Rosemary interrupted. 'Thank you. I'm quite warm. I'll soon dry out.'

'I'm all right as well,' I said to Toby.

He grinned. 'To be perfectly honest, I'm not sure I've got anything that would fit you.'

'Hadn't you better ring the police, Father?' Rosemary suggested.

'The police?' Joanna's face was stiff like a mask, the green eyes murky. 'What's happened?'

'We found some fur and something that might be blood on the waste ground near your garden,' I said. 'We think it may have something to do with that business last night.'

'The cat?' She hugged herself and, still staring up at me, murmured, 'That's horrible.'

'There's a phone along here, David,' Toby said from the other side of the hall.

I smiled in what I hoped was a reassuring fashion at Joanna and followed Toby into a small room facing the front of the house. The Bramleys had used it as an office. It was furnished with a scarred dining table, a pair of kitchen chairs and a row of empty shelves screwed to the wall. On the table was an ashtray and a telephone.

Toby left me alone. I rang the operator, who put me through to the police station. I asked for Sergeant Clough, and after a few minutes he came on the line. I told him what Rosemary and I had discovered.

'Well, that's very interesting.' There was a pause, filled with a click followed by a hissing noise: Clough was lighting his pipe. 'I'll make a note of it. No sign of the cat's head, I suppose?'

'No.' I wondered whether to tell him about Vanessa's theory but decided against. It was a safe bet that Clough would not be interested in speculations about Lady Youlgreave's bird table. 'Aren't you going to send someone out to look at the place?'

'In an ideal world, yes. But we're very stretched at present, Mr Byfield, very stretched.' Another pause, another click, another hiss. 'We have to allocate resources as we think best. We do have one or two slightly more important cases than this business with the cat. And – if you don't mind me speaking plainly – we can't even be sure that what you and your daughter found has any bearing on it. I can't help feeling my inspector would say it was all a bit of a wild-goose chase. I'm sorry, sir, but you know how it is.'

I agreed that I knew how it was, though of course I didn't. I didn't much like Clough, but I had to admit, if only to myself, that the man probably knew what he was talking about.

'But let us know if anything else turns up, Mr Byfield. No harm in it, is there, and you never know.'

We said goodbye politely and I went to find the others. They were waiting in the big room with the French windows. Rosemary and Toby were kneeling on the floor and leafing through a box of long-playing records. Joanna was by the fireplace with a cigarette in her hand, staring in the mirror at my reflection in the doorway.

'Are the police coming?' she asked.

'No.'

Rosemary looked up, her face flushed. 'Why ever not?'

'They don't think it sufficiently important.'

She stood up. 'That's terrible. Of course it's important.' She turned her head sharply to look at Toby, and her hair lifted from her shoulders. 'Don't you agree?'

'Policemen aren't like other people,' he said. 'Their minds are mysterious.'

'But it could be a vital clue,' Rosemary persisted, talking not to me but to Toby. 'Did you know that Audrey is going to pay the vet to do a postmortem?'

He shook his head. 'You said there was a tuft of fur?'

Rosemary nodded.

'If they put that under a microscope,' he went on, 'they'd be able to match it up with the hair of the cat. Well, I expect they could, anyway.' His eyebrows shot up. 'Modern science is wonderful. I suppose we'd better go and fetch it.'

'Now?' Rosemary said.

'The sooner the better.' He flashed a glance at me and then a smile at Rosemary. 'Otherwise we'll dry out and then get wet again. And if we leave it, anything might happen. The rain could wash it away. Or . . .' He paused and licked his lips. 'Or the person who did it might come back to tidy up.'

'We must go. It's only fair to Audrey.' Rosemary looked at me. 'Don't you agree?'

Before I could answer, Toby said, 'It can do no harm, at least, can it? And who knows, it might actually do some good.'

I looked at the mirror, but Joanna had turned her head so I could no longer see the reflection of her face. 'Surely you'll wait until the rain has stopped, at least?'

'Better not,' Toby said. 'Anyway, Rosemary and I can take an umbrella. Why don't you stay and have some tea with Joanna?'

Rosemary pushed a strand of damp hair from her cheek like a cat grooming her face with a paw. 'No point in us all getting wet.'

The two of them were already at the door. I sensed Rosemary's excitement. I had never seen her like this before. Her body was taut, and in every movement there was an awareness of its possible effect on Toby.

He threw a glance at his sister. 'You'll be OK?'

It seemed a strange question. Why should she not be all right in her own home in the company of a middle-aged priest?

Jo nodded, dropping her cigarette end in the empty grate.

'On second thoughts,' Toby went on, 'it's a bit late for tea – must be after six. Why don't you see if David would like a drink?'

Then he and Rosemary were gone. I heard their footsteps in the corridor. Toby said something and Rosemary laughed in reply, a quick, high, gasping laugh. A door slammed in the distance. The big room filled with silence. The only sound was the patter of the rain. Joanna stared down at her hands and flexed her fingers. Automatically, I fumbled in my pocket for cigarettes. The packet was damp but the contents were dry.

'What would you like to drink?' Joanna said, without looking at me.

'Nothing just now, thanks.'

She looked up at me and smiled, which transformed her face, filling it with warmth and charm. 'You won't mind watching me, will you?'

I shook my head, smiling, and lit a cigarette. She fetched a glass from the cupboard by the fireplace and poured herself an inch of whisky from the bottle on the mantelpiece. And I watched.

'Let's sit down,' she suggested.

She led the way to the nearer French window, the one we had not used when we came in from the terrace. Two armchairs faced each other on either side, standing on bare floorboards. An upturned tea chest between them served as a table. Joanna sat down and, holding the glass in both hands, sipped. Colour filled her face. The skirt parted. I watched as the triangular gap extended, riding up her legs to an inch above the knee. I looked away; I remembered who I was and where I was; I remembered Vanessa.

I sat smoking, staring outside at the rain pounding down on the flagstones of the terrace, sending up a fine, grey spray. Beyond the terrace, the long grass of the lawn swayed and bowed beneath the onslaught; and the trees of the garden rustled and trembled in agitation.

'Can I have a cigarette?' she asked. 'I've finished mine.'

I gave her a Players No 6. When I bent down to light it for her, for a moment our faces were very close. Her eyes were outlined in kohl, and she wore a faint but insistent perfume which made me think of Oriental spices. There was a fine, fair down on her cheek; and I knew that if I touched it it would be softer than anything in the world. I hastily straightened up and blew out the match.

'Do you believe in ghosts?' she said.

Joanna had a talent for catching me off guard. I stared at the hissing curtain of rain and wondered if the question had anything to do with our truncated conversation the previous evening, when she had hinted at difficulties just before we found Lord Peter's body.

'I don't know about ghosts,' I said at last, 'but I certainly believe that there are phenomena which don't fit into the accepted scheme of things.'

She leant forward in her chair. 'Like what?'

'Any parish priest comes across odd events which can't be explained. People tend to call us out when there's a hint of the supernatural.'

'Like plumbers? To deal with spiritual leaks?'

'In a way.'

'Can *you* explain them?'

I shook my head. 'It's not like that. It's perfectly possible that there are rational explanations for everything we now class as paranormal. But we simply haven't stumbled on them yet. In the meantime, the church can sometimes help people come to terms with their existence, if only because theology at least recognizes the existence of the supernatural. And the average scientist doesn't. It's a curious truth that modern materialism is far more dogmatic about its beliefs than modern theology . . .'

I broke off, aware that I was beginning to lecture Joanna. The truth was that she was making me nervous, and I was taking refuge in my classroom manner – just as I had with every woman who had ever attracted me; it is chillingly easy to repeat our mistakes. I glanced at her sitting opposite me, hunched over the glass in her hands, with a cigarette smouldering between her fingers. The harsh grey light revealed every detail of her without flattery; and I liked what I saw.

'I'm wasting your time,' she said abruptly. 'But I don't know who else to talk to about it.'

'Of course you're not wasting my time. Do you believe you've seen a ghost?'

Joanna half shrugged, half shivered; her body moved fluidly as water flexes to contain a ripple. 'Not *seen*, exactly. But I've heard things.'

'Has Toby, too?'

She shook her head. 'It was the night before last. I – I don't sleep well. You know the tower at the end of the house? My room's there, the one below the top. I was going to have the top one but I didn't like the atmosphere, and Toby thought it smelled of dry rot. Anyway, I was lying in bed and I heard a

413

man walking. At least, I think I heard him. A man in the room above me. To and fro, to and fro.'

'What did you do?'

'Nothing. I locked the door and covered my head with the bedclothes. After a while the noise stopped. Or maybe I dozed off . . . You'll think I'm a coward. I suppose I am.'

'It's not cowardly to be afraid. Did you tell Toby in the morning?'

She stubbed out her cigarette, stabbing it in the ashtray. 'He said I was imagining things.' She bit her lip. 'I don't know – maybe I was. I made him fetch the key and we went upstairs together, to the top room. There was nothing there, of course. Just an empty room.'

I waited, looking at the rain.

'You don't believe me,' she burst out. 'You're just like Toby.'

'I believe you.'

She stared hard at me, as though trying to read in my face whether or not to trust me. At length she said, 'Do you think rooms can have emotions? That they can be happy or sad?'

I remembered my uncomfortable experience in the chancel of St Mary Magdalene the previous summer, the evening when Rosemary had failed to pass on a message for me from Vanessa. 'I'm not sure whether places have atmospheres or whether we project our emotions on to them and create an atmosphere.'

She looked disappointed. 'The room was unhappy,' she said flatly. 'I don't know – maybe someone had been unhappy there. Toby said that poet used to sleep there – Vanessa told him. Or maybe it was me: maybe it was me who was unhappy.'

I waited for a moment, listening to the rain and looking at Joanna, whose head was bowed over her lap. Her neck and shoulders were bare and I would have liked to stroke them, for stroking is the simplest and the oldest way to bring comfort.

'Joanna,' I said slowly. 'Would it help if –'

There was a rapping on the window. Joanna and I both looked up sharply. For an instant I felt a shaft of shame, as though I had been surprised in a guilty secret.

Standing on the terrace on the other side of the window were Toby and Rosemary, both of them streaked with rain, despite the umbrella which Toby carried. In his other hand was a nylon shopping bag containing what looked like a bottle. Rosemary, her blue eyes glowing, was even wetter than she had been before, her hair dark with water, plastered in tendrils over her skull. She held up what looked like a tobacco tin, tapped it with her finger and mouthed through the glass: 'We've got it.'

Joanna smiled at Toby and made as if to open the window. He shook his head and pointed along the terrace: it was as clear as if he had spoken the words that he did not want to come in by the French windows because they were too wet. Then he and Rosemary had gone, and all we could see through the French windows was the grey sky and the green, rainswept garden.

'I was beginning to think they'd got lost,' I said to Joanna.

In the distance, a door slammed and Rosemary laughed. Joanna looked up. There was no trace of a smile left on her face.

'*Please*, David,' she whispered. 'I need to talk to you without Toby knowing.'

20

Rain sluiced down the windscreen and thrummed on the long bonnet of the Jaguar. The car rolled over the gravel of the Vicarage drive and pulled up outside the front door. There were lights in some of the windows, earlier than usual because of the gloom.

'Have you got time for a drink?' Rosemary asked from the tiny back seat, sounding a good ten years older than she really was, apart from a quiver on the last word.

'That's very kind.' Toby turned, including me in the conversation. 'Are you sure I wouldn't be in the way?'

'Not at all,' I said, as I had to say.

The three of us struggled out of the car. Toby produced a black umbrella and held it over Rosemary and myself as we stumbled to the front door: it was a courteous gesture, but not one that kept much rain from us. I unlocked the front door and the three of us fell into the hall. Vanessa opened the kitchen door. Michael was behind her, sitting at the table with a plate in front of him.

'I was about to send out a search party,' she said, smiling. 'Hello, Toby. Have you rescued them?'

'Yes, he has,' said Rosemary, still aspiring to a precarious adult dignity. 'And now we're going to reward him with a drink.'

Vanessa's eyes sought mine and found no objection there. 'Of course. Come into the sitting room. David, you and Rosemary look as if you need a change of clothes.'

Rosemary began to say something and then stopped. 'Back in a moment,' she said and then, flushing, she galloped upstairs with uncharacteristic clumsiness.

'You'd better have this,' Toby said to me, holding out the nylon shopping bag which contained the tobacco tin and the empty cider bottle.

'What's that?' Vanessa asked.

Toby grinned at her. 'Clues.'

I explained briefly to Vanessa and then went upstairs. While I was changing, I heard a Niagara of rushing water from the bathroom. I went downstairs and poked my head in the kitchen. Michael was working his way through an enormous bowl of apple crumble.

'Everything all right?'

The boy's mouth was full, so he nodded.

'We'll be in the sitting room. Come and join us if you like.'

Michael swallowed. 'Thank you.' He loaded his spoon with another mouthful of crumble. I shut the kitchen door. How did one talk to children? Something about Michael encouraged one to treat him as more grown-up than in fact he was: his stillness, perhaps, his wary eyes and his slow, grave smile.

I went into the sitting room. Vanessa was laughing at something that Toby had said, genuine, unforced amusement with her head thrown back. It was a long time since I had seen her so eager to be pleased.

'We're having gin and tonic,' she said to me, 'so I poured you one, too.'

I sat down and took a long swallow of my drink.

'Vanessa's been telling me about her book,' Toby said. 'Wonderful stuff. I can't wait for my signed copy.'

Vanessa flushed. 'There's a long way to go before that happens.'

There were footsteps on the stairs and Rosemary came in. In her short time upstairs she had managed to transform herself. It looked as if she had bathed and washed her hair. She had changed into a short turquoise needlecord skirt and a tight, long-sleeved T-shirt. On her wrist were silver bangles, and she brought in a powerful cloud of perfume.

'I could murder a gin and tonic,' she said in an airy voice.

'I beg your pardon –' I began.

Vanessa was already on her feet. 'I'll get it, shall I?' she said to no one in particular. As she turned towards the drinks trolley,

417

her face averted from everyone in the room except me, she glared, wordlessly telling me not to interfere.

'I like your bracelets,' Toby said. 'Jo's looking for some like that.'

'It's a Moroccan *semaine*,' Rosemary explained. 'One bangle for each day of the week.'

While she was speaking, I watched Vanessa pour a teaspoonful of gin into a long glass and top it up with tonic water. She gave the glass to Rosemary, who raised it and said, 'Cheers.' If I had not known better, I would have thought Rosemary was already a little tipsy. But people can intoxicate you as well as alcohol.

Vanessa sat down beside me on the sofa. 'By the way, there was a message for you while you were out. Doris phoned.'

'But I saw her this evening at Lady Youlgreave's.'

'This was after you left. The old lady wants you to come and see her on Monday morning.'

'It sounds like an order,' I said, trying to make a joke of it, though Lady Youlgreave's occasional outbreaks of imperiousness irritated me profoundly. 'Did Doris say why?'

Vanessa hesitated. 'It's about the bird table, apparently. Lady Youlgreave wants to tell you – ah – who was feeding the birds.'

It was clear what Vanessa meant. She was a discreet and diplomatic woman, in many ways an ideal clergyman's wife – ironically enough. Rosemary was asking Toby a question about the fuel consumption of his Jaguar, no mean achievement considering she had never shown any interest in cars before.

'Has she told Doris who it was?' I murmured.

Vanessa shook her head. 'Doris sounded quite put out.'

'I've no idea how much juice she uses.' Toby wrinkled his eyebrows in a way that I suspected women might find attractive. 'I just like driving the thing. What goes on under the bonnet is an enormous mystery to me.' Turning to Vanessa, he went on, 'Talking of mysteries, I wanted to ask you something about our poet. I feel quite possessive about him, you know – because he lived in the house.'

'And died,' Rosemary pointed out in a cool voice.

'And died.' Toby flashed a grin at her, then turned back to

Vanessa. 'Jo found a copy of that poem of his – "The Judgement of Strangers" – in an anthology she's got. I read it last night and I just couldn't make head or tail of it. What's it meant to be about? What does the title mean?'

'No one's quite sure,' Vanessa said. 'I hope to find out when Lady Youlgreave lets me examine the relevant part of the journals. It's generally taken to be a medieval trial scene. With a woman in the dock who's being accused of everything from heresy to murder. And finally she's condemned and burned at the stake.'

'A bit like Shaw's *St Joan*?' said Toby, sounding like a bright undergraduate in a tutorial.

'In a way. But it's a narrative poem, remember, rather than drama. Like Keats's "Eve of St Agnes" or Browning's "Abt Vogler". Youlgreave goes all mystical at the drop of a hat, and there's a rather unpleasant theme of defilement running through it. The idea that when judgement is perverted, then everything falls apart. But it's hard to know for certain. Francis is almost wilfully obscure.'

'He probably found the title in *The Book of Common Prayer*,' I said.

Vanessa's face sharpened; she was a scholar *manqué*, a sort of intellectual terrier – wasted as a provincial publisher. 'Where?'

'I think it's in the Service of Commination. I'll see if I can find it.'

I went to the study to fetch a Prayer Book. When I came back, a moment later, Rosemary was on her feet. She emptied her glass and put it down on the table. 'I'll leave you to it,' she said. 'I'd better go and do some work.' She slipped out, shutting the door behind her.

'She's working very hard at present,' Vanessa said, as if apologizing for the abruptness of Rosemary's departure. 'Oxbridge entrance, next term. But you wouldn't think this was her summer holiday, would you?'

'Here it is, "A COMMINATION OR DENOUNCING OF GOD'S ANGER AND JUDGEMENTS AGAINST SINNERS". There's a list of curses. Rather like the Ten Commandments. "Cursed is he that perverteth the judgement of the stranger, the fatherless, and widow."'

'Where does it actually come from?' Vanessa asked.

'It might be from one of the Ash Wednesday services of the Middle Ages. But originally it probably comes from the Old Testament. I can look it up, if you like.'

'Please.' Vanessa smiled at Toby. 'You must find this rather tedious.'

'Not at all,' he said politely. 'But do remember to tell me what the poem means when you find out.'

'I'm looking forward to seeing the house, too – especially Francis Youlgreave's room. How are you getting on with the swimming pool?'

'They could have it ready by next week.' Toby glanced out of the window. 'All we need is the weather for it.'

He finished his drink. Vanessa offered him another, but he shook his head. 'I really should be going, thank you. I don't like leaving Joanna alone for too long.' Despite his words, he stayed in his chair, looking from Vanessa to me. 'Actually, there's something I wanted to tell you,' he said slowly. 'And this might be a good moment. You remember that I mentioned that Joanna hasn't been well? Well, in fact, the trouble was mainly psychological. Our mother died – it was an overdose, actually – and poor Jo was the one who found the body.'

'I'm so sorry,' Vanessa said, 'for you both.'

He smiled at her. 'Afterwards, she had a sort of nervous breakdown.' He hesitated. 'Obviously, it's not something she generally likes known. But I thought I'd better mention it. If only in case she sometimes acts a little strangely. So you'll know why.' He looked at his watch. 'I really must go.'

Vanessa and I saw him out. In the hall, I called upstairs to tell Rosemary that Toby was leaving but there was no answer.

Behind Toby's back, Vanessa mouthed a single word: *sulking*.

'Don't bother,' Toby said. 'I don't want to break her concentration.'

We watched him skipping like a dancer through the rain to the shelter of the E-type. The Jaguar's engine roared. As the car slipped out of our drive, Vanessa said, 'It's not a car, is it? It's a phallic symbol on wheels.'

21

As the evening progressed, the storm slackened to a steady downpour. It was surprisingly cold for August.

After Toby had driven away, I went into the study and, without turning on the light, dialled the familiar number of Tudor Cottage. The phone rang on and on. I stared out at the village green. There was less traffic than usual and hardly any pedestrians. The car park of the Queen's Head was almost empty.

The tea room would have closed several hours ago. Audrey must be out. I wondered idly what could have taken her away from the warmth and shelter of her home on a night like this. It did not occur to me to worry about her. In the end, I replaced the receiver. The news about Rosemary's unpleasant discovery this afternoon could wait.

The next day, Saturday, the doorbell rang while we were still having breakfast. Vanessa raised her eyes to the ceiling. Rosemary pushed back her chair and went to answer the door. I heard an excited voice and footsteps; then Audrey burst into the kitchen. She seemed somehow larger and pinker than before, as though she were on the verge of erupting from her clothes like a chick from its shell.

'Well!' she announced, stopping in the kitchen doorway. 'I was right.'

Vanessa gave me what old-fashioned novelists used to call a speaking look. This one said, loud and clear: *Can't your bloody parishioners leave us alone even at breakfast time?*

I abandoned my toast and stood up. 'Shall we go in the study? Perhaps a cup of coffee – ?'

Rosemary's face, bright and feverish, appeared at Audrey's shoulder. 'What do you mean? How were you right?'

'I saw the vet last night. He confirmed what I've said all along.' Audrey sniffed. 'Lord Peter was beheaded. The good news is that the poor darling was . . . was dead before those terrible things were done to him. The vet said his spine was broken, almost certainly by a car going over him, and that's probably what killed him. He may not even have known what was happening.' Audrey's voice faltered. 'If only that was all that had happened. I think I could have accepted that.'

Michael was staring in fascination at Audrey. I took a step towards her, hoping to shoo her into the study. She stood her ground.

'He was beheaded some time after death,' Audrey went on, her voice sounding unexpectedly triumphant. 'It was no accident, Mr Giles was sure of that. It was almost certainly some sort of saw, definitely something with a serrated edge, like a hacksaw. I do so wish I knew what had happened to the head.'

I dared not look at Vanessa. 'Audrey –'

'And then he was left for us to find at the church door.' She swallowed and her eyes filmed with tears. 'Hanging by his tail.'

Michael gave a strangled giggle. I could not blame him. Audrey was one of those unfortunate people whose tragedies are tinged with farce.

'David,' she hissed. 'You do realize how *diabolical* this is? Every detail so carefully thought out.'

I nodded.

'It's a sort of blasphemy,' Rosemary muttered.

'Yes, dear. Exactly.' Audrey smiled at her. 'And the police may be content to pretend it never happened, but I'm not. Why, this is the next best thing to murder. I'm simply not prepared to hide my head in the sand. If the police won't do their job, I shall just have to do it for them.'

'Like Miss Marple,' Rosemary suggested. 'In a manner of speaking.'

'Precisely. Though I say it myself, I do have *some* knowledge of human nature.'

I made another attempt to sweep Audrey into the study. She wouldn't move. She wanted an audience.

'Don't you think this sort of thing is best left to the police?' I said.

'Fat lot of good they'll be. If I leave it to them, nothing will happen.'

'Sometimes it's wiser to try to put something like this behind one.'

'I'm not putting Lord Peter behind me. Not until I've got to the bottom of how he died.'

'We found something yesterday afternoon,' Rosemary said. 'I think it's a clue. It was in Carter's Meadow.'

Audrey spun round, still blocking the doorway. 'What?'

Rosemary had the Golden Virginia tobacco tin, which had spent the night on the hall table, in her hand. She opened it and showed Audrey what it contained.

'What is it?'

'We think it may be a piece of Lord Peter's fur. And that browny stuff – see? – I think that may be blood.'

Audrey seized the tin. While she examined its contents, her mouth worked uncontrollably.

'Toby – that's Toby Clifford, I mean – he was with me when we collected it. It's his tin, actually. Toby thought perhaps you could compare the hairs with Lord Peter's. Perhaps the vet –'

'If it can be done, then Mr Giles will do it. I'll make sure of that.' Audrey raised a pink, shiny face. 'Thank you, my dear. This is a start. Now, tell me exactly where you found it.'

Prodded by Audrey's questions, Rosemary described what had happened yesterday afternoon. When it transpired that I had seen the fur in its original position, Audrey was delighted.

'You'll make an ideal witness, David. People trust what a clergyman says.'

That had not always been my experience.

'There was also an empty bottle of cider nearby,' Rosemary was saying. 'Toby says glass is very good for fingerprints, so we brought that away.'

'What sort of cider, dear?'

'Autumn Gold.'

'I knew it.' Audrey vibrated with excitement. 'I've seen them drinking it in the bus shelter. They leave the empty bottles there –'

'It's in Daddy's study if you need it. Toby says that it could be important if the fur turns out to be Lord Peter's.'

'How very thoughtful of him,' Audrey said. 'He sounds a very nice young man.'

'Yes,' said Rosemary; and paragraphs were compressed into that monosyllable.

Vanessa cast a longing glance at the coffee pot. 'Well, now that's settled, should we – ?'

'The evidence is beginning to build up,' Audrey announced. 'I've been approaching the case from another angle. And I've managed to uncover another piece of evidence.' She paused for an instant, as if expecting a round of applause. 'I happened to be in Malik's Minimarket this morning, and Doris Potter was there. A very good sort of woman . . . She was asking me about Lord Peter. People are so kind. Even Mr Malik expressed his sympathy, and being Muslim – or is it Hindu? – he can't really be expected to appreciate how terrible it all is. But at least he tried. Where was I? Doris. Yes, she actually popped into church on Thursday afternoon. Heaven knows why – it's not her week for the flowers and she's not on the cleaning rota at all.' The possibility that Doris might have some other purpose in going to church had eluded Audrey. 'She was on her way to Lady Youlgreave's. So she thinks it must have been about four. The point is, she's absolutely sure that Lord Peter wasn't in the porch then. She remembers looking at one of the notices, the one about South Africa, when she came out. So – that's useful, isn't it? Slowly we're building up a picture. I know we still have an awful lot to learn. But at least we know that Lord Peter was brought to church sometime between four o'clock and seven o'clock on Thursday evening.' She beamed at Rosemary, revealing teeth to which clung small yellow specks, perhaps corn flakes. 'And if we put that information together with what you've found out, dear, it's possible that whoever did it came into the churchyard by the gate into Roth Park rather than from the road.' Once again she hesitated. Then she added, with a devastating lack of subtlety, 'What time exactly did the Cliffords arrive here in the evening?'

*   *   *

424

The rest of the weekend was quiet. On Saturday afternoon I drafted a sermon which after tea I redrafted because on reading it seemed abstruse and pompous. I had planned to spend some of the evening tracking down the origin of the phrase which presumably had given Francis Youlgreave the title of his poem: *Cursed is he that perverteth the judgement of the stranger, the fatherless, and widow.* In the event, however, I spent most of the evening at the bedside of a man who eventually died shortly after midnight. Neither he nor his wife was a churchgoer, which led later to a heated argument with Rosemary, who could not understand why these people were as much my responsibility as Audrey Oliphant or Doris Potter.

On Sunday, I celebrated Communion twice in the morning, dozed after lunch and conducted Evensong. I went to bed early.

Externally the pattern was familiar and comforting. But my mind was less placid than I would have liked. I thought a great deal about the Cliffords. Where had their money come from? Who had their parents been? Was their father alive? I found that I could visualize the faces of both Toby and Joanna with unusual clarity – Toby's with its bony features, its frizzy curls, and the nostrils permanently flared, which gave him an apparently misleading effect of perpetual disdain. And Joanna – what I remembered most clearly about her was the down on the curve of her cheek and the green eyes with a dark edge to the iris, and the green dappled like a pond under trees on a sunny day. Most of all, I wondered about the relationship between them, whether Toby was all he seemed, and whether Joanna's apparent fear of him was due to calculation, paranoia, or a simple and entirely rational response to a genuine threat. There was Rosemary to consider, too: she seemed to be attracted to Toby.

I tried to talk about some of this with Vanessa on Sunday evening as we were going to bed.

'Puppy love,' she said briskly. 'Rosemary's too young for him. Nothing to worry about – he seems a perfectly sensible young man so it will probably die a natural death. As for Joanna, from what Toby said, she's had some sort of nervous breakdown. But she'll get over it, I'm sure, with Toby's help. I wish I could warm to her more, though. She's rather off-putting, don't you think?'

I wasn't sure what I thought about Joanna Clifford. What I needed very badly was to talk to my spiritual director about the Cliffords in general and Joanna in particular. But Peter Hudson was out of the country and I had not yet met his successor. To make matters worse, I wasn't sure whether I thought of Peter's absence as a problem or as a stroke of good fortune. I did not really want to talk about the Cliffords with anyone – not with Peter and certainly not with a priest I did not know well. By arranging for Peter's absence at this juncture, it was as if Providence had allowed me to stray briefly into limbo.

'No, Rosemary will be all right,' Vanessa went on. 'But I'm not so sure about Audrey.'

'The Miss Marple business?'

'It's absurd, isn't it?'

'She's so obstinate it's almost magnificent.'

Vanessa clicked her tongue against the roof of her mouth. 'She's a grown woman, David. There's nothing magnificent in having absolute faith in the forensic wisdom in the novels of Agatha Christie.' She glanced at me and her eyelids fluttered. 'If you ask me, it's unwise to have absolute faith in *anything*.'

I smiled at her. 'Are you sure?'

She laughed. 'Now you're trying to make a fool of me.' That was how matters stood on the morning of Monday, the 17th August. Vanessa and I were in the kitchen preparing breakfast and listening to the eight o'clock news on the radio. Michael was doing his teeth in the bathroom, clearly audible in the kitchen below. Rosemary was still in bed; recently she had taken to sleeping late. The telephone rang.

'I don't think I can stand much more of this,' Vanessa hissed at me. Her face had reddened. 'They never leave you alone. Can't you let it ring? Just this once.'

I already had my hand on the door. 'No – I'm afraid I can't.'

'But this is an utterly ridiculous time,' she snapped, her voice rising. 'Tell them you'll ring back.'

She glared at me and, God help me, I glared back. I went into the hall, closing the door rather more loudly than I should have done. In a cloud of childish indignation I stormed into the study and picked up the telephone receiver. Outside in the main road, the dustcart had drawn up outside the Vicarage. A dustman dropped the lid of our bin on the ground with a clatter and hoisted the bin itself on to his back.

'The Vicarage.'

There was a strangled sound on the other end of the line, which after a moment I identified as sobbing.

I tried to make my voice gentler. 'Who is this, please?'

The dustcart drove away. Someone was whistling. On the other end of the line, the sob mutated into a snuffle.

'It's me. Doris.'

'What's wrong?'

'She's dead. The old lady's dead.' There was a fresh burst of sobbing.

'Doris, I'm so sorry.'

The sobbing continued. I had not realized that Doris was quite so attached to her employer; nor would I have said that she was an hysterical woman – quite the reverse. But death is a great revealer.

'You've just found her, I imagine?' There was no reply, except sobbing, but I persevered. 'My dear, she was an old lady. It had to happen. Probably sooner rather than later.' The familiar platitudes slipped out of my mouth automatically. 'She was in a great deal of pain, and there was nothing to look forward to, either.' Platitudes have the outstanding advantage of being true. 'And think how she would have hated having to go into a home or a hospital. At least she died in her own bed.'

'But she didn't,' Doris wailed.

'She'd managed to get up in the night, had she?' Perhaps she had wanted her commode. 'After the nurse had –'

'I could kill her.'

'Who?'

'That nurse. The bloody woman didn't turn up. The old lady's been lying there for days.' The voice rose into a wail again, but the words, though distorted, were clear enough. 'And the dogs have been eating her.'

22

Ronald Trask loved committees the way other men love football or train-spotting. He was in his element, especially when he was in the chair. He had the knack of driving his way through the agenda, achieving his own aims while preserving the appearance of democracy. He had become archdeacon two years before; and since then he had invited me to more meetings than his predecessor had done in the previous eight years.

One of Ronald's little gatherings was scheduled for half past ten on the morning of Monday the 17th August. The weather was cool and cloudy. Six of us sat at the round table in the Trasks' dining room. We could see our faces in the polished surface. There were flowers, a carafe of water, glasses, pristine ashtrays and in front of each of us a neatly typed agenda, the work of Cynthia. The details stuck in my mind like pins in a pin cushion – hard, sharp particles of reality embedded in a sponge of uncertainty; I concentrated on them because they left less room for what I had seen an hour earlier at the Old Manor House.

'We are not so much a committee,' Ronald informed us, 'as a working party.'

He and the others murmured soothingly in the background. Our purpose was to examine ways of halting the decline of Sunday School attendance. On two occasions Ronald tried to draw me into the discussion but without marked success. Afterwards, as the others were leaving, he asked me to stay behind for a word. He took me into his study.

'Are you all right, David? I thought you looked a little out of sorts in the meeting.'

'I'm sorry – I do have a headache.' I couldn't face telling him the details about Lady Youlgreave so I merely added, 'Two of my parishioners died over the weekend.'

'It's always a bit of a shock, isn't it? Even when the death's expected. Do sit down.' Ronald waved me to a chair in front of his desk and hurried on. 'Tell me, have you seen any more of the Cliffords?'

'In a manner of speaking, we're neighbours. They're very kindly lending us their paddock for our fete on Saturday week.'

'Ah.'

'What is it?'

'Don't worry, there's nothing wrong,' he said, eyeing me curiously. He settled himself behind the desk, and his fingertips stroked the leather cover of his diary – tenderly, as though it were a woman's skin. 'Just grounds for caution.'

'What on earth do you mean?'

'We had lunch with the Thurstons yesterday. Victor had been at some Masonic do the night before, and he'd been talking to one of his policeman friends. I thought I'd pass on what he'd told me. Word to the wise, eh?'

'What's wrong with the Cliffords?'

'Nothing's wrong with the children – not as far as I know, nothing for certain, though the boy seems to have some unsavoury friends. No, the problem is the parents. Ever heard of Derek Clifford?'

I shook my head.

'Nor had I until yesterday,' Ronald went on. 'Not the name he was born with, by the way – his parents came from Poland. Apparently, he owned a chain of clubs in London. Little nightclubs, I gather. Most of them had a short life. Nothing was ever proved, but the police were absolutely certain that Clifford was running them as a front for all sorts of other activities – gambling, prostitution, even receiving stolen goods.'

'But nothing was proved?'

'Not in a way that would stand up in a court of law. But I understand that there was no real doubt about it.'

'Is the father alive?'

'He died last year. The mother died in the spring. There was an inquest.' Ronald interlaced his fingers and stared at the ceiling, as if praying, as perhaps he was. 'The poor woman was an alcoholic, and on the night in question she'd taken some sleeping pills. She choked on her own vomit. There was some question about the death – whether it was suicide or accident.'

I thought of Joanna finding her mother's body.

'And then there's the question of money,' Ronald was saying. 'I don't know what those young people paid for Roth Park, but presumably the money ultimately came from their father. The odds are, it wasn't honestly come by.'

'You can't blame them for that.'

'It depends, doesn't it?'

'What do you mean?'

Ronald leant forward, his elbows resting on the desk, and smiled at me. 'It depends on whether the children were involved with their father's activities. Thurston's asked his policeman friend to have a word with a few colleagues in London. Just in case there's something there.'

'I don't like it.' I stood up. 'I'm sorry, Ronald, but it seems as though the Cliffords are being condemned because of hearsay evidence about what their father might or might not have done.'

'Condemned?' Ronald stood up as well. 'Of course not. My fault – I can't have made myself clear. All I'm saying is that it's wise to take elementary precautions. Especially in our position. Don't you agree?'

'If you say so.' I didn't bother to keep the anger from my voice. 'Is there anything else?'

'No, not at present.' He followed me into the hall. 'I'll keep you informed.'

We said goodbye. I wondered whether Ronald was doing his job, or using the Cliffords as a way to make my life a little uncomfortable. Or perhaps both – motives are often muddled. As I drove back to Roth, I thought about my reasons for taking an interest in the young Cliffords. I had no right to condemn Ronald or anyone else for mixed motives.

Vanessa was at work so there were three of us for lunch in the Vicarage kitchen. No one was hungry. We nibbled at cold ham and elderly salad.

430

Afterwards, while we were washing up, Rosemary said, 'You know this thing about perverting the judgement of strangers – did you have time to look it up?'

'Not yet. It's Old Testament. I'm almost certain it's from Deuteronomy.'

'Does it mean muddling strangers?' Michael asked suddenly. 'Making visitors confused?'

'No.' I smiled at him. 'It was about legal disputes in Israel. Widows and orphans and strangers were the vulnerable people in a community.'

This seemed to satisfy the curiosity of Rosemary and Michael, but it stimulated mine – and reminded me that I had promised Vanessa to look into the origins of the phrase. After washing up, I took my coffee into the study.

I found the relevant verse in Deuteronomy, Chapter 27, Verse 19. Both the Authorized Version and the Revised Version had an almost identical translation to that in the Prayer Book. I looked out my copy of the Vulgate to check the Latin translation: *Maledictus qui pervertit iudicium advenae pupilli et viduae*. The most recent translation I had on my shelves was the Jerusalem Bible. 'A curse on him who tampers with the rights of the stranger, the orphan, and the widow.' The notes in the commentary referred me to parallel texts in an earlier chapter of Deuteronomy and to a much earlier one in Exodus, Chapter 23:

> Thou shalt neither vex a stranger, nor oppress him: for ye were strangers in the land of Egypt. Ye shall not afflict any widow, or fatherless child. If thou afflict them in any wise, and they cry at all unto me, I will surely hear their cry; and my wrath shall wax hot, and I will kill you with the sword; and your wives shall be widows, and your children fatherless.

I opened a drawer and took out a pad of paper, thinking that I should write a few notes for Vanessa. I knew, of course, that I was trying to distract myself from the thought of Lady Youlgreave and the implications of her death. This sort of work was a luxury for me; scholarship could be a snare just as surely as the more traditional temptations. It occurred to me as I was uncapping my fountain pen that I was not the only one looking for distractions. Why else had Rosemary raised the subject of 'The Judgement of Strangers' at lunch? Why had none of us mentioned the subject of Lady Youlgreave?

I pushed aside the questions and made notes. The Deuteronomic legislation of the seventh century BC had been comparable to the Reformation and Counter-Reformation in Europe over two thousand years later: a determined attempt to reform the national religion. The compilers of the book were intolerant of dissent, but their moral teaching was remarkably humane. The fact that the phrase 'perverting justice' was so well established in the Old Testament suggested that such abuse was a long-running problem.

I turned to the original Hebrew and to the Septuagint, the most influential of the Greek translations of the Old Testament. The word I wanted to check, the crucial word in the passage, was *stranger*. In Hebrew the word was *gêr*, which meant 'protected stranger' – in other words, a stranger who lived under the protection of a family or tribe to which he did not belong. (The Arabs had a similar word for the protected stranger, the *jâr*.) The life of a *gêr* could be hard – I made a note about Jacob's complaint concerning his treatment by Laban in Genesis 31. A whole clan or family might be *gerim*. The same distinction was preserved in the Greek of the Septuagint. 'Stranger' was not translated by the obvious word, *xenos*, but by *proselutos*, which meant a licensed foreign resident. Was the implication, I wondered, that complete strangers were unprotected, that they were the legitimate prey of those whose territory they strayed into?

As I was making a note of these points for Vanessa, I heard a car pulling off the main road into the Vicarage drive. I glanced out of the window and saw an Austin Maxi drawing up. The passenger door opened and Sergeant Clough climbed out, pipe in mouth. Franklyn wriggled out of the driver's side. My tranquillity evaporated. I reached the front door before they did.

'Good afternoon, sir.' Clough rubbed his bald head and stared past me into the hall. 'Mind if we come in? Just for a quick word.'

I took them into the study, and settled them in hard chairs in front of my desk.

'Mrs Byfield not in? She works, doesn't she?' Clough made the idea sound slightly indecent.

'How can I help you?'

'It's Lady Youlgreave, this time, not the cat.' He raised his eyebrows, perhaps signalling that he was making a mild joke; the rest of his face remained serious. 'Sad business.'

'Indeed.'

Franklyn took out his notebook and a pencil.

'Don't mind Frankie taking notes, sir. Just for the record.'

'I'm not sure I see how I can help you. I didn't actually find the body – Doris Potter did that. And Dr Vintner can tell you more about Lady Youlgreave's injuries – he must have arrived about fifteen minutes after I did.'

'Oh, we have to look down every avenue, sir. It may be a cul-de-sac, so to speak, but we have to check. You wouldn't believe how much of Frankie's time is spent taking notes that turn out to be absolutely useless. But you never know, do you? You can't take anything for granted.'

Clough in his role as homespun philosopher was irritating me. 'What exactly do you want to know?'

'I wish I knew, sir – in a manner of speaking, that is. Something and nothing. In cases like this – sad death of old lady, who is already very ill – bound to have happened sooner or later, probably sooner – well, usually there's no problem. Not as far as we're concerned. And there may not be a problem in this case, either. But Dr Vintner thought that he should have a word with the coroner's officer, and he thought we should have a word with you. In view of the circumstances, you see.'

'Which circumstances?'

'Well, first of all: the last person to see the old lady was apparently her cleaning woman, Mrs Potter. And that was at about seven o'clock on Friday evening. But the body wasn't found till Monday morning. Now that's –'

'One minute,' I interrupted. 'Why didn't the nurse from the Fishguard Agency go in over the weekend? Mrs Potter goes in – went in – during the week, Mondays to Fridays. But the agency nurse came in on Saturday and Sunday. Twice a day – morning and early evening.'

'But not this weekend, Mr Byfield.' Clough was watching me closely. 'Curious, eh? Apparently, Lady Youlgreave phoned the agency on Friday evening – must have been about seven-thirty, they reckon – and said some relations had come to stay for the weekend, and they'd look after her.'

'I wasn't aware that Lady Youlgreave had any close relations. But I do know that she didn't like using the telephone.'

Clough struck a match and held it over his pipe. The pipe made a gurgling sound. 'Why did you go and see the old lady on Friday, sir?'

I did not want to involve myself in explanations concerning the bird table. I could imagine Clough's reaction. Lord Peter had already made me ridiculous enough in the eyes of the police. I took the morally dubious course of avoiding the question while seeming to answer it. 'I regularly visited her, Sergeant. It's part of my job to visit the old and infirm.'

He nodded, and I had an uneasy sense that I might not have misled him. 'How did she seem? In good spirits?'

'As well as could be expected. Dr Vintner can fill you in on her state of health, if he hasn't already. But she was declining rapidly. She was also in a great deal of pain. But yes, we had a chat, and I left at about half past five.'

'How mobile was she? In general, I mean.'

'It rather depended how she felt.' I could not see where these questions were tending. 'She spent most of her time in her bed or in her chair. But she could move about with the help of a Zimmer frame.'

'Could you describe to us exactly what happened this morning? What you saw at the Old Manor House?'

'Everything? I don't understand.'

'It was unfortunate, sir. After you and the doctor had been, Mrs Potter was by herself in the house for upwards of an hour. No doubt the poor lady was in a state of shock. Anyway, she started tidying up. Moved the old lady into her chair. Covered her up. Hoovered. When she opened the door to us, she had a duster in her hand.'

'Perhaps she didn't realize that she shouldn't move anything.'

'The doctor said he'd told her.'

'Then,' I said, 'as you say, it must have been the shock. But why is this so important? Does the coroner think that Lady Youlgreave's death was suspicious?'

'We have to tie up the loose ends.' He veered away on a tangent. 'Talking of which, how did people get in if they called at the house when Mrs Potter wasn't there?'

'There's a key hidden at the back of the house. It's been there for years.'

'Who knew about it?'

'Anyone who needed to, I imagine. I think Mrs Potter has her own key, but there are a number of other people who went in regularly, and they would use the key in the kitchen yard if Mrs Potter wasn't there to let them in. It's under the flowerpot by the door.' I paused, assembling the possibilities. 'I knew about it, and so did Dr Vintner and the Fishguard Agency. There's a weekly delivery from Harrods, and I know the man sometimes let himself in when Mrs Potter wasn't there. And there may well have been others. Do you think that Lady Youlgreave had another visitor after Doris Potter left on Friday evening?'

'I don't know what to think yet, sir. I'm just working out the possibilities. Would Mrs Byfield know about the key?'

'Yes, she did.'

Clough looked at me, waiting for more.

'My wife has been working on Lady Youlgreave's family papers during the last few weeks. She used to sit with Lady Youlgreave in the dining room, and work on them there.'

'What about the dogs? How do they react to visitors?'

'They bark if they have the energy.' I swallowed. 'Too old to do anything else except eat and sleep.'

'So if a stranger turned up, they wouldn't have seen him off the premises?'

'I doubt it. They might have barked, but no one outside the house would have heard.'

Clough nodded. 'And now, could you tell us what happened this morning?'

I leant back in my chair. 'We were having breakfast in the

kitchen when Mrs Potter phoned. It was a little after eight o'clock. She was very upset. But I understood from her that Lady Youlgreave was dead. She said something about the dogs, too, but . . .' I swallowed. 'But I thought the shock had made her confused – even hysterical. I phoned Dr Vintner and then went round to the Old Manor House at once. The dogs were in the back garden. There's an iron gate at the side of the house and they were poking their noses through the bars and barking at the dustmen.'

'Did the dustmen know what was happening?'

'Not as far as I know. Their lorry was parked on the road. One of them had just collected the bin by the gate.' He had been a grimy little man who had not wanted to meet my eyes. I had said, 'Good morning,' automatically, but he walked past me as though I were somewhere else; and all the time he whistled 'Waltzing Matilda' at a tempo suitable for a funeral.

'And where was Mrs Potter?'

'She opened the front door before I rang the bell.' *Pink-rimmed eyes but no tears. Cheeks pale and lined like crumpled handkerchiefs.* 'She took me along to the dining room straightaway and showed me Lady Youlgreave.'

Clough was turning his pipe round and round in his hands. 'Take your time, sir. Take your time. Tell us exactly what you saw, what the room was like, where the old lady was.'

I swallowed again. 'She was lying face down on the carpet near the window. Roughly midway between her chair and the fireplace. Her head was by the corner of the fender. The Zimmer frame was on the hearthrug, lying on its side.'

I paused and reached for a cigarette. The room had smelled of faeces and urine, human and canine. I saw the telephone on the table and the tin trunk on the floor. Lady Youlgreave's father-in-law glowered down on us from his vantage point above the fireplace.

'She was in her night clothes.' *A nightdress, bed socks up to the knee, a dressing gown. Her head lying on its side on the hearthrug, eyes open wide as if in astonishment, and mouth open wide, too, as though snapping at a fly. Bare pink gums. I had never seen Lady Youlgreave without her teeth.* 'The nightdress had ridden up, or perhaps the dogs had pushed it up. Up to the waist.' *Pale, wrinkled legs; not much strength in them and not much nourishment either. Brown stains, and in those parts which were relatively fleshy, the sight of raw meat.* 'The dogs had obviously been starving,' I went on slowly. 'I suppose that's why James Vintner had to get in touch with the coroner's officer . . . You know what dogs are like when they get old, Sergeant? Often their training begins to slip away from them. Their taboos no longer have the same force. Like humans, really. They had tried to eat her –'

I broke off. Clough stared blandly across the desk at me. Franklyn wrote in his notebook.

'Damn it,' I burst out, surprising myself as much as the two policemen. 'What have you done with the dogs?'

'Don't you worry about that, sir,' Clough said. 'We'll look after them for the time being. Now, to go back to this morning: tell me about the rest of the room.'

'It was much as usual.' Apart from a pile of dogs' excrement beside Lady Youlgreave's armchair.

'Were the curtains drawn across the window?'

'No.'

'The table by the chair: was there anything on that?'

'I think there was a book.' A slim volume in a green leather binding: *The Voice of Angels.* 'I suppose she must have got up after Mrs Potter left her in bed. Her bedroom's next to the dining room. She probably went in there and read for a bit. And then she stood up and tripped, I imagine.'

'Suppose you're right,' Clough said. 'She stands up. Why should she move towards the fireplace?'

'Her medicine was there.'

'Ah. The medicine.' Clough scratched the sparse tuft of hair above his right ear. 'Now that's interesting. It's in a bottle, right? You know what it looks like?'

I nodded.

'And did you notice it this morning?'

'No. I had other things on my mind.' I remembered Lady Youlgreave's hunger for her medicine. 'I suppose she was going to give herself a dose, and as she walked towards it, she stumbled on something. The edge of the hearthrug, perhaps.'

437

There was a silence. Something was wrong, and I couldn't put my finger on it. Franklyn yawned. Clough stared over my shoulder and out of the window, his face sad.

'Wait a moment,' I said slowly. 'When I was there on Friday, Doris said something about leaving her medicine out in the bedroom.'

'She did. In three separate glasses to cover the period until the nurse turned up on Saturday morning. But they'd been knocked over.'

'So that would explain her going into the dining room?'

Clough did not answer. 'Tell me, Mr Byfield, have you known Mrs Potter long?'

'A good ten years.'

'Reliable, is she?'

'Extremely reliable. She's a regular churchgoer so I know her well. And she's done a great deal for Lady Youlgreave.'

'Surely she was paid for that?'

'I don't think the money was particularly important. Lady Youlgreave and Mrs Potter had known each other for years.'

I pulled myself up short, knowing that I was on the verge of becoming angry. In their own way, the two women had been friends; and Doris had given far more than she had ever received. Clough's questions were like a cynical chisel, chipping away at Doris's kindness.

'So Mrs Potter and the old lady got on well?'

'Very well.'

Clough sighed. 'We have to ask these questions, sir. I know it must seem tiresome, but there it is.'

'Will there be an inquest?'

'Not for me to say, sir. It depends on what the coroner thinks.'

I allowed my eyes to stray back to the notes I'd been making for Vanessa. 'Is there anything else?'

'No, not at present.' Clough stood up and extended his hand to me. 'Thank you for your time.'

We shook hands and I came round the desk to show them out. As I stood up, I caught movement in the corner of my eye – movement on the other side of the window. I looked out and was just in time to see Michael running to the side of the house. Had he been eavesdropping? The window was open. Clough and Franklyn seemed to have noticed nothing.

I followed them into the hall. 'Sergeant?'

Clough turned back. 'Yes, sir?'

'Just a couple of points about Miss Oliphant's cat.'

'Ah. This won't take long, will it?'

'No. But I thought I should let you know that there was something on Lady Youlgreave's bird table the other day. She told my wife and me that she thought it was a head.'

'A *head*?'

'A small one, badly pecked by birds. We wondered if it might have been the cat's.'

'Did you have a look?'

'Yes, but by the time I did, there was no trace of it.' I paused, then added: 'She said someone brought it there in a paper bag.'

There was a snuffling sound from Franklyn: barely concealed laughter.

'So who did she say put it there?' Clough said.

'She couldn't or wouldn't say.'

'I see.' He put his hand on the door handle. 'And did you say there was something else?'

'You remember I phoned you about the place where the cat might have been cut up?'

Clough nodded.

'It's called Carter's Meadow. Our local poet, Francis Youlgreave, is said to have cut up a cat in the same place.'

After another pause, Clough said, 'Thank you, sir. All a bit speculative, if you don't mind me saying so, a bit vague. But I'll bear it in mind.' He opened the front door. On the threshold, however, he stopped and turned back to me. 'Oh – by the way. You know those young people up at Roth Park? The Cliffords?'

I felt myself tense. 'Yes.'

'Do you know if they ever met Lady Youlgreave?'

'Not to my knowledge. They've not been living here that long.'

'Thank you, sir.'

Clough put his hands in his pockets and sauntered towards the car, where Franklyn was unlocking the driver's door. Franklyn was still snuffling happily.

'Why?' I called after him. *First Trask, now Clough.*

'Just wondered,' he said over his shoulder. 'After all, they were neighbours.'

23

Shortly after the police left, I went to visit the widow of the man who had died over the weekend. She lived in one of the council houses on Manor Farm Lane, not far from the Potters'. The house was full of relations, and the television was on all the time I was there. I did what I could and left as soon as was decently possible; now the man was dead and the funeral was arranged, I was no longer wanted.

I walked back along the north side of the green. As I was passing the bus shelter, I heard a voice call my name. Audrey was leaning from the window of her first-floor sitting room.

'Can you spare a moment?' Her face was bright and alert. 'One or two points about our fete.'

She came down to meet me in the hall. The tea room had just closed, and Charlene Potter was clearing the tables. She gave me a smile as I passed. I followed Audrey upstairs. She settled me in the wing armchair that had been her father's. ('It's a chair meant for a man, don't you think? I never sit in it myself.') She opened the door of her sideboard and took out glasses and a bottle.

'You'll join me in a glass of sherry, won't you?'

'Thank you.'

She was already pouring sherry into the glasses. 'Such terribly sad news about Lady Youlgreave. Of course, she was very old and I suppose it could have happened at any time – living by herself in that wreck of a house with only those dogs for company.' She handed me a brimming glass. 'I wonder who will inherit. I believe there are Youlgreave cousins in Herefordshire somewhere, but I don't think they were in touch. And some of them emigrated. New Zealand, was it?' She settled herself in the chair by the window, sighed with satisfaction, and raised her glass. 'Chin-chin. She should have gone into a home years ago. She would have had to if Doris hadn't been there. I told Charlene, "Your mother may think she's doing Lady Youlgreave a kindness," I said, "but the poor dear would be much better off in a proper nursing home." Still, some people just won't be told.'

I sipped my sherry.

'Do smoke. It's Liberty Hall here!' Audrey jumped up to fetch me an ashtray. 'Charlene tells me you were actually *there*.'

'Doris phoned me when she found the body.'

'It must have been frightful,' Audrey said with relish. 'Of course, the police have got it wrong as usual. Typical. I'm not surprised after the way they handled Lord Peter's death.'

'What have they got wrong?'

'Apparently they think that Lady Youlgreave was trying to reach her medicine on the mantelpiece, and she tripped. But it can't have happened like that. Charlene was quite upset about it. She thinks the police are trying to blame her mother – for leaving the medicine out on the mantelpiece. But that's nonsense. The whole point of leaving it on the mantelpiece was because Lady Youlgreave couldn't reach it there.'

Startled, I said, 'But the mantelpiece isn't that high.'

'You obviously hadn't seen Lady Youlgreave walk lately.' Audrey wagged a finger at me in playful reproof. 'She was bent almost double, apparently – because of the crumbling of the spine or something. And she couldn't raise her arms above her shoulders. That's why they chose the mantelpiece: for the simple reason she couldn't reach it. You know how confused these poor old dears can get about whether or not they've had their medicine.'

I had found a cigarette and was patting my pockets, searching for matches. Audrey leapt up again to bring me a light. While she was on her feet, she topped up our sherry glasses.

'And then there's the fact that she cancelled the nurse from the Fishguard Agency: *very* puzzling.' Audrey sank down again in her chair, sitting more heavily than before, and sipped her sherry. 'She didn't like having a nurse, of course. She was only really happy with Doris. But Dr Vintner made her, for Doris's sake.'

'You mentioned something about the fete –'

Audrey was still speaking. 'There's also the point that she didn't like using the telephone . . .'

She half closed her eyes and stared out of the window. It was an unnatural pose, as rigid as a waxwork's – and, also like a waxwork, a pose designed with the viewer in mind. I realized suddenly that what I was seeing was the great detective at work: Roth's answer to Miss Marple.

'To my mind, there are two alternatives,' Audrey went on. 'Either Lady Youlgreave cancelled the nurse, intentionally intending to commit suicide over the weekend. Or she cancelled the nurse simply because she didn't like her. We have to remember that she was very confused. What with the pain and the morphine she was hardly human any more, was she?'

'We shall all grow old,' I said. 'Or most of us will. Does that make us any less human?'

Already pink, Audrey's face darkened to red. 'Just a figure of speech. I'm as sad as anyone that Lady Youlgreave has passed on. It's the end of an era. The last Youlgreave in Roth. She was so striking as a young woman, too. So dashing. She used to have wonderful parties before the war . . . I was telling Rosemary how she seemed to us children only the other day – Rosemary could hardly believe me.'

I stubbed out my cigarette carefully in the ashtray. 'It's good of you to let Rosemary spend so much time with you.'

'It's a pleasure,' Audrey cooed, allowing herself to be diverted from Lady Youlgreave. 'Between you and me, I think she's rather lonely. If Vanessa were at home in the week, it would be a different story – but Vanessa is a working woman.' She giggled. 'So am I: I have always been a career woman and proud of it. But you see, I work at home, and I can choose my own hours. It's been a real pleasure to see more of her this holiday. Such a lovely girl. More sherry?'

'No, thank you.' I glanced at my watch. 'I really should be –'

'I think I might have a teensy little one.' Audrey reached out for the bottle. 'Dr Vintner says that a glass or two of sherry is just the thing to help one unwind after the day's work.' The neck of the bottle trembled against the rim of Audrey's glass and a drop of sherry snaked down the curves of glass and stem, slid across the base and formed a miniature puddle on the gleaming surface of the wine table. 'She's been terribly useful in my investigation.'

'Rosemary has? What's she been doing exactly?'

Audrey dabbed at the puddle of sherry with a lace-trimmed handkerchief. 'Nothing to worry about, I promise you. No, she's made one or two useful suggestions about lines of approach. It was her idea that I asked Mr Malik about who buys his cider. You remember you found a bottle of Autumn Gold with the fur and the blood?'

'I expect dozens of people buy that particular brand of cider.'

'Perhaps. But I felt one name was especially significant.' She lowered her voice to a hiss: 'Kevin Jones – he's Charlene's boyfriend.'

'I really think you must be very careful.'

'Oh, but I am. I lock up very carefully and I take the poker upstairs with me.'

'That's not what I mean. We don't know that the cider bottle had anything to do with what happened to Lord Peter. There's no proof whatsoever. And even if there were, there's no proof that Charlene's young man bought the bottle. And even if he did, it wouldn't follow that he played a part in what happened to Lord Peter.'

Audrey waved her glass and the little liquid it contained slopped dangerously near the brim. 'I've seen him in the bus shelter. He's one of that gang of louts. He wasn't there when I called the police. But he might have been. And the others were his friends. I hate to say it, but I have to consider the possibility that' – once again she lowered her voice to a conspirator's whisper – 'there's a traitor in the camp. Lord Peter trusted Charlene completely. He would have gone anywhere with her.'

'Audrey,' I snapped. 'You must stop this.'

She flung herself against the back of her chair, flinching as though I had hit her. 'But –'

'I'm serious. For your own sake. Saying this sort of thing without evidence constitutes slander. If you repeat it in public, you might end up in court.' I watched her lips tremble and tried to soften my tone. 'I don't know Kevin, but Charlene seems the last person to become involved with a business like this.'

'Slander? I suppose you're right.' She had her face under control once more. 'I should have thought of that. It's so infuriating, the difference between knowledge and proof. But those louts must have been involved. Lord Peter's collar was in the bus shelter. You can't get away from that.'

I looked at my watch, more openly this time. 'Dear me.' I pantomimed mild shock. 'Time's getting on. Now, what did you want to discuss about the fete?'

Audrey swallowed and for a moment I thought she would take the change of subject as a reproof. Instead she smiled. 'Dear Rosemary. A wise head on young shoulders. I would never have thought of it. It's the car parking.'

'I thought we'd sorted that out.'

'Rosemary reminded me that last year we had a number of people who parked on the double yellow lines round the green. Do you remember? The police were rather annoyed. Nowadays, every Tom, Dick and Harry has his own car. None of them walks anywhere at all, as far as I can see. Rosemary wondered whether the Cliffords would let us use the verge of their drive as an overflow car park once the paddock's filled up. I know we asked the Bramleys one year, and they said no, because they felt it would upset their residents. (They always said that when they didn't want to do something.) But the Cliffords are quite a different kettle of fish. Rosemary said she was quite friendly with them so she would ask them. I said, how splendid, naturally – I didn't want to hurt her pride. But I did wonder if the request might come better from you.'

I put down my empty glass very carefully on the table. 'I'll see if I can have a word with them.'

'That would be marvellous. And do you think you could also manage to see how many cars might fit? I know it can only be an estimate, but it would be a help. I've already added "Car Parking" to next week's advertisement in the paper.'

I promised I would see what I could do. Audrey had always been inclined to fuss about the details of the fete, but this year she was fussing even more than usual.

445

I stood up, determined to leave. She took me downstairs, chattering brightly about James Vintner's barbecue ('I hope it won't encourage the wrong sort of people') and the enormous quantity of home-made cakes which had been promised for the cake stall. As we reached the hall, the kitchen door opened and Charlene came out with a handbag draped over her arm. She had taken off her overall.

'Are you off home?' Audrey asked. 'Already?'

'It's after half past six,' said Charlene. 'Everything's cleared. The tea towels are soaking in the sink.'

'I see,' Audrey said darkly, and paused as if searching for some flaw or omission in this. 'Good. Well, see you tomorrow. Are you and your young man going out tonight?'

Charlene shot her a wary glance. 'Maybe.'

'Well, be careful,' Audrey said enigmatically. 'That's all I ask.'

I stood aside to let Charlene go first.

Audrey brought her head close to my ear. I could smell sweat on her body and sherry on her breath. 'Such a coarse girl,' she hissed. 'And quite untrainable. My poor mother would be turning in her grave.'

'Thank you so much for the sherry,' I said. 'I'll let you know about the car parking as soon as I can.'

We said goodbye. Audrey waved from the doorway as I walked through the little front garden and up the steps to the wrought-iron gate. Only when I was on the pavement did the door close at last.

Charlene was standing outside Malik's Minimarket, apparently studying the window display. As the door closed, she looked at me.

'Mr Byfield? Could you spare a minute?'

I smiled at her. 'Of course.' I wondered if I would ever get home that evening. 'What is it?'

'Would you – would you mind coming over here?' She beckoned me towards where she was standing. When we were both in front of the shop window, she went on, 'It's only that Miss Oliphant will see us standing outside her gate, and she'll wonder what we're talking about.'

'Would that be awkward?'

'She'd badger me tomorrow until I'd told her what it was about.'

We stood side by side, staring at an array of cereal packets. Neither of us said anything, but it was not an uncomfortable silence. She snapped open her bag, took out a packet of cigarettes. 'Do you mind?'

'No.' I shook my head when she offered me the packet.

'She doesn't let me smoke on the premises.' Charlene grinned up at me, suddenly wicked. 'It's not ladylike. Nor's smoking in public.'

I nodded, and waited.

'Don't get me wrong,' Charlene told the cereal packets. 'She's been good to me, really. Her bark's worse than her bite.'

Like Beauty and Beast?

'The thing is, I'm worried about her. I told Mum about it last night, and she said the best thing to do was have a word with you.' Charlene shot off on a tangent. 'Poor Mum. She's really knocked sideways.'

Doris was someone else I should see. In a sense she was the one most affected by Lady Youlgreave's death: the principal mourner. Those who care for dependent persons become themselves dependent. And Doris and Lady Youlgreave had been friends, though perhaps neither would have used the word in relation to the other.

'Miss Oliphant's always had her little ways. You know, going on about how things have changed since she was a little girl. And – and things like that.' Charlene glanced up at me to see how I was taking this. 'But these last few months she's been different. Now she's always up and down. Right up and right down. And since her cat went, it's got even worse. She talks to herself, you know – she never used to do that. And once or twice she's shouted at me, really screamed. I don't think she's eating much, either. And she gets these ideas in her head – like she thinks the kids are after her.'

'And are they?'

Charlene looked startled. 'They've got better things to do. Mind you, she's not their favourite person. But that's neither here nor there. What worries me is, she really seems to think she's some sort of detective. Like in them books she reads.'

Charlene's voice slid into high-pitched, genteel mimicry. 'It was the butler did it in the library. With the lead piping. And – Mr Byfield – don't think I'm talking out of turn, but I don't think Rosemary's helping. She's sort of encouraging her.'

'What do you mean?' I knew I must have spoken sharply by the expression on Charlene's face. 'How?'

'You know,' she mumbled. 'Looking for clues. Stuff like that.'

'Clues about what happened to Lord Peter?'

Charlene nodded.

'Yes, I know something about that,' I said. 'Don't worry. I'll have a word with Rosemary, and we'll all keep an eye on Miss Oliphant.'

A moment later, I said goodbye and walked home. I was aware that I had not handled the interview well. I liked Charlene, but I thought it likely she was exaggerating. In every parish there tends to be at least one unmarried, churchgoing middle-aged lady who occasionally acts oddly; there are men, too, for that matter; and the older they get, the more oddly they tend to behave. But in ninety-nine cases out of a hundred, it was nothing more than harmless eccentricity. Why should Audrey be any different?

Vanessa's car was in the Vicarage drive. I let myself into the house. Michael was watching television in the sitting room.

'Hello. Where is everyone?'

'Rosemary's out still,' he said. 'Aunt Vanessa's upstairs.'

I was about to leave when a thought delayed me. 'Michael?'

He dragged his eyes away from the grey figures flickering on the screen. I had intended to ask him if he had been listening to my conversation with Clough and Franklyn earlier this afternoon. Suddenly I no longer wanted to. It would be tantamount to making an accusation. The boy had probably just been playing a game. Nor was it likely that he would have heard much, even if he had been eavesdropping. Clough and I were both relatively soft-spoken.

The phone rang, giving me the excuse I needed.

'Nothing.' I smiled at him and went into the study. It was James Vintner, sounding harassed.

'Have you heard?' he said.

'Heard what?'

'There's going to be an inquest.'

'When?'

'Wednesday, probably. Waste of an entire afternoon.'

'Do you know if I'm likely to be called as a witness?'

'I doubt it. If they wanted you, I think they would have been in touch by now. But I thought I'd better warn you.'

'You don't think – ?'

'I don't think anything. In normal circumstances I'd have certified the death without another thought. Old lady, I'd seen her in the morning of the day she died. Terminally ill. Has a fall, and off she goes: all very sad, but just like dozens of other old ladies. Nothing suspicious about it.'

'So why aren't these normal circumstances?'

'Ask your Mrs Potter. It's all her fault. Her and those damned dogs.' He hesitated. 'Sorry to sound off like this. It's been a long day. And I don't like it when my patients die.' He cleared his throat, perhaps aware that for once he had openly admitted that he cared about his job. He added hurriedly, 'Especially the private ones. Like gold dust, these days.'

A moment later we said goodbye. I went upstairs. Vanessa was in our room, sitting on the bed and staring grimly into space.

'That was James,' I said. 'There's going to be an inquest on Lady Youlgreave.'

She nodded but did not reply.

'What is it?'

She turned her head to look at me. 'Nothing, really. I suppose it's her dying. It seems strange that I won't be able to go and sit in her dining room any more.'

'I suppose it may cause problems with the book.'

'It's not just that.'

'Then what is it?'

Vanessa glared at me. She said, 'Oh God,' and began to cry quietly. I sat down beside her on the bed and put my arms around her. She leant against me. I hugged her, feeling her warmth. Desire stirred inside me and began to uncoil. Gradually she relaxed, and the tears stopped.

I stroked her back, running my fingertips down the knobs of her spine. How many weeks was it since we last made love?

'Vanessa?'

She pulled herself gently away from me. 'I need to blow my nose,' she said. 'And then I really must do something about supper.'

24

On Tuesday morning, I waited until I had the house to myself.

Vanessa went to work. Half an hour later, Rosemary left to catch a bus – she was going into London to spend the day with a school friend. Michael had already gone to spend the day with the Vintners. He and Brian had an ambitious project to build a tree house in the back garden. I had two hours before my first engagement of the day, a routine meeting with the diocesan surveyor.

When I was alone, I went into the study, shut the door and telephoned Roth Park. I wondered if I had a temperature. I felt unlike myself – excited, and almost furtive. I let the phone ring on. I was on the verge of hanging up when Joanna answered.

I apologized for disturbing her and asked if we could use the drive as an overflow car park at the fete.

'Of course you can. You can park anywhere you like.' It was almost ten o'clock yet she sounded half asleep. 'It's not exactly going to harm the lawn or damage the flowers.'

'Should I check with Toby that it's all right for us to park in the drive?'

'Toby's not here. Anyway, it's nothing to do with him.'

'I beg your pardon?'

'It's my house,' Joanna said, her voice suddenly distorted as though she were yawning. 'My land. Nothing to do with Toby.'

'I see. I wonder – would it be convenient for me to walk up the drive and estimate how many cars there'd be room for. Audrey Oliphant feels it's important to have a good idea.'

'Now?'

'If it's not inconvenient.'

'You know the oak trees near the paddock?' she asked. 'I'll be there in about ten minutes.'

I hesitated too long. 'There's no need for you to come.'

'I'd like some air. Besides, I – I need to see where the parking will be. Just in case there's a problem.'

We said goodbye and I put down the phone. I observed my own symptoms with a proper scholarly detachment: with perfect propriety, I was making arrangements for the church fete; yet I felt guilty: almost as though I had arranged a furtive assignation.

It was a sunny morning, a relatively rare occurrence in that dreary August. I strolled through the churchyard and into Roth Park. A moment later I reached the oaks. I leant against a tree trunk and smoked a cigarette. From where I was standing I could see the rutted drive; I followed it with my eye as it curved round the hillock which concealed the house. It was very peaceful. Such moments of leisure were a rarity in my life. The only things moving were the smoke from my cigarette and a few wispy, almost transparent shreds of cloud high in the blue sky. In the real country, there would have been birds, and there would not have been the omnipresent rumble of traffic. But for the time being this would do very well.

Then I saw Joanna on the drive. She raised her hand in greeting and I waved back. I threw away my cigarette and watched her approaching. She wore a thin cotton dress which came down almost to her ankles. Her hair was loose. As she drew closer, I saw that her feet were bare. Closer still, I saw that she wore no make-up and her eyes were smudged with tiredness. She looked up at me with those green eyes with their dark rims and their fragmented depths, shifting like a kaleidoscope. For a moment I did not know what to say. All I knew was that I should not have come. I was in danger. Joanna was in danger, too.

'Can I scrounge a fag?'

I gave her a cigarette and lit it for her. She touched my hand, quite unself-consciously, to steady the flame. That was good, I told myself: if she had been aware of what I was feeling, she would have avoided touching me.

'I must get some more from Malik's,' she said. 'Typical Toby.

Drove off this morning with the last packet of cigarettes in the house.'

'Where's he gone?'

She shrugged, then yawned. 'Sorry. Can't stop yawning this morning.'

'Didn't you sleep well?'

She smiled, slyly. 'I tried not to sleep at all.'

'Why?'

'I wanted to find out if the ghost would come back. You remember? The footsteps? So I took something to help me stay awake and I waited. But nothing happened. Except I grew more and more scared.' She turned aside to stub out the half-smoked cigarette on the bark of a tree. 'I didn't see anything, or hear anything. But I felt something.' She swung back to face me. 'Something waiting. Silly, isn't it?'

'Fear isn't silly. It's frightening.'

She nodded.

'What about Toby?'

'What about him? As far as I know he slept all night. I heard the car start up a little after nine. Off he went. No note, no cigarettes.'

'Did he know you were staying awake?'

'He'd have laughed at me. Especially after the fuss I made the other night.'

I wasn't sure whether she liked or disliked her brother. 'Perhaps the other night was a bad dream. Sometimes one can have these dreams between sleeping and waking.'

She shook her head vigorously. 'David – could you do something about it? Say some special prayers. What do you call it? Exorcism?'

'I could come and say some prayers, if you wanted.'

'Would you? It can't do any harm.'

I felt my hackles rising. 'It can only do good.'

'Oh God – I'm sorry. And I didn't mean to say that, either.' She looked so contrite standing there in the dappled shade of the trees. 'Double sorry.'

'It's all right. Do you want to do it now?'

'Don't you need equipment?'

'The candle, book and bell?' I smiled at her. 'We save those for special occasions. To be honest, I don't know much about exorcisms. I think the diocese might have an official exorcist, who goes where the bishop tells him. But full-dress exorcisms are very rare these days. Something less formal will often do the trick just as well.'

She giggled. 'You make it sound so normal.'

'In a sense it is.'

We walked up the drive to the house. Joanna speculated about the number of cars they could fit in. 'At least another fifty if we use the bit outside the front door.' While she was talking, I told myself that I was only doing my duty: my duty as a priest. We reached the dry fountain commemorating the visit of Queen Adelaide. Joanna stopped and leaned against the worn stone of the basin. She stared up at the façade of the house.

'Ugly place, isn't it?'

'Why did you buy it, then?'

'Toby wanted to.' She glanced up at me through long lashes, as if assessing the effect of her words. 'He can be very persuasive. He said it would be a good investment. He said I needed to get away from London.' Suddenly her voice rose, and she turned to face me. 'He's told you, hasn't he?'

'He told me that your mother committed suicide,' I said. 'And that you found the body.'

For a long moment we stared at each other. Then she dropped her eyes.

'Did he tell you that after that I was ill?'

'Yes.'

'It's not true. I wasn't ill. He likes to tell people I've had a nervous breakdown. He likes to hint I'm mad. I bet he's done it with you.' She paused, but I said nothing. She went on, speaking slowly and carefully: 'He gives the impression that he's looking after me out of the kindness of his heart. That without him I'd just fall apart. That I'm something fragile that he has to treat very carefully.'

'And you're not?'

'Do I look fragile?' she demanded.

I shook my head. *Yet you hear ghosts.* 'Then why does he do it?'

'I told you. He likes to. It makes him feel good.' She shivered. 'Let's go inside and get this over with.'

We walked towards the front door, our footsteps loud on the gravel. The door closed behind us with a dull boom like distant thunder. The house was cool and silent.

Joanna said, 'Should I offer you coffee or something?'

'No. This isn't a social call.'

She looked at me again – why did she keep on looking at me? – and I hoped that she could not see too far. There's no fool like a middle-aged fool: old enough to know better, and young enough to do something about it.

I followed her upstairs, watching her dress frothing and whispering above her ankles. At the mezzanine level there was a window, and as Joanna walked past it, with the light beyond her, her body was outlined through the dress, just as Vanessa's had been all those months ago at the Trasks' party. History has a habit of almost repeating itself, like the pattern in a hand-woven carpet.

'It's quite a long walk,' Joanna said over her shoulder. 'I'm glad I wasn't a maid in those days. It must have been sheer hell.'

'I've never been upstairs before.' I wanted to bite the words back. They seemed loaded with hidden meanings.

We reached the main landing. A long corridor stretched into the heart of the house, its boards uncarpeted, the plaster bulging and cracking on walls like a relief map of the desert.

'It's less posh than downstairs,' Joanna said. 'I reckon the Youlgreaves ran out of money.' We walked together down the corridor, our footsteps setting up a drumming in the silence. 'I don't know why they needed a house this big. It's stupid. I'd much rather live somewhere smaller.'

'Why don't you?'

She shrugged.

I wanted to ask: *Has Toby some way of keeping you here? Why did you buy this house for him?* But of course I did not.

'Mind the hole,' Joanna said, steering me round it. 'Toby put his foot through there the other morning. Woodworm.'

'Are you going to start renovating soon?'

'We need more money. Toby wants to find an investor.' She glanced at me. 'When Dad died, the money was left in trust to Toby and me. Mum had the use of it while she was alive. But Toby borrowed against it; he had this company which was importing stuff from India. But it didn't work out. When Mum died, he had to use his share to pay off his debts.'

I felt rather embarrassed. Englishmen do not like talking about money. Joanna stopped at a door near the end of the corridor. 'We're in the tower bit now.' She opened the door and we went into a large square room with windows on three sides. 'I always wanted to live in a tower.' She led the way to another door in the corner. Beyond it was a spiral staircase with uncarpeted wooden treads. The stairs were lit by narrow windows like anachronistic arrow slits designed with dwarfs in mind. 'I'm on the floor above. And the floor above that is the top room. Francis Youlgreave's room.'

'Who told you that?'

'Toby.' She was already climbing the stairs and her voice floated down to me. 'He mentioned it again last night.'

To scare her?

We came to an open door. My first impression was that emptiness and light lay beyond it. The room was square, with a round-headed sash window in each wall. The wallpaper – stylized golden tulips on a faded blue background, perhaps as old as the house – was beginning to part company from the walls. In the opposite corner from the door was a plain, cast-iron fireplace, the grate littered with cigarette ends and ash. A carpet designed for a suburban sitting room filled about a third of the floor; the rest was bare boards. On the carpet, as if on a castaway's raft, were Joanna's belongings – a mattress, the radio I had seen her with on the terrace, a green trunk, a pair of suitcases, an archipelago of discarded clothes, an ornate walnut-veneered dressing table with a tall mirror attached to it. The top of the dressing table was littered with cosmetics, paperbacks and an overflowing ashtray. The room smelled of a powerful, crude perfume, which overlaid another smell, sweet and spicy, reminding me of Indian food.

'It's a bit of a tip, I'm afraid.' Joanna gave me a crooked smile – one corner of her mouth turned up and the other turned down. 'If I'd known you were coming, I'd have done something about it.'

'It doesn't matter.'

The bedroom was like a glimpse behind a drawn curtain. Rosemary and Vanessa were both tidy people. Their bedrooms showed only that they disliked clutter and knew how to control it. Joanna's made a present of her personality to a visitor, and I was touched. For a moment I felt young and full of daring. For a moment it amused me to imagine what Audrey Oliphant or Cynthia Trask would make of my situation.

I walked to the window and looked down on the drive, on the roof of the canopy over the front door with its slipped slates and its outcrops of moss like green pimples. The knowledge of my indiscretion sank in: a middle-aged clergyman alone with an attractive young woman in her bedroom. I turned back, eager to finish what had been started. Joanna was still standing just inside the doorway, watching me.

'What will you do?' she asked.

'Just say a prayer.'

'OK.'

I fancied that she looked disappointed, as if she had been hoping for something more dramatic. She bowed her head and I prayed for the room to be filled with God's peace. Then I invited Joanna to join me in the Lord's Prayer. Her voice stumbled softly after mine, like a distant echo.

When it was over, she said, 'Is that all?'

'Yes. Shall we go upstairs?'

She nodded, and without a word slipped out of the room. I followed her up the spiral staircase. Our footsteps thudded on the bare wood. I kept my eyes on Joanna's ankles, pale and flickering before me. At the top was a tiny landing, barely large enough for one person, and a closed door. It seemed colder to me here than it had been on the floor below.

Joanna twisted the handle and pushed open the door. The room was a copy of hers – the same dimensions, the same round-headed sash windows, the same cast-iron fireplace. One of the windows was slightly open – the one overlooking the canopy and the fountain; and I had the foolish thought that this must have been the one from which Francis Youlgreave jumped into the arms of his angel. The wallpaper was modern – flowers once more, but psychedelic daisies in turquoise and orange.

I moved slowly into the centre of the room. It was empty – no furniture, no carpet, no dust on the bare boards. Francis Youlgreave had left behind him a vacuum, waiting to be filled.

'Well?' Joanna was standing by the fireplace, the fingers of her right hand kneading the flesh of her left forearm. 'What do you think? Can you feel anything?'

'No.' The room was merely a room, somehow incomplete like all unused rooms, but nothing more than that. 'Can you?'

'I don't know what I feel any more.'

Suddenly I wanted to be gone – away from this house and away from Joanna. In a brisk voice, I repeated the prayer asking for God's peace. Once again I said the Lord's Prayer, galloping through the familiar words with Joanna's voice stumbling after mine. I wondered whether to say another prayer, one specifically for Francis Youlgreave. I glanced at Joanna. She was still clutching her arm, but the fingers were still. Her eyes met mine. She stared at me as if I were a stranger – or, for that matter, a ghost.

'Did you hear that?' she asked.

'What?'

She took a step towards me, stopped and looked over her shoulder. 'I thought I heard someone crying. A child.' She held up a hand, and for thirty seconds we listened to the silence. Then she shook her head. 'It's stopped.' She took a step towards me, and then another, and another; her feet faltered; as if each footstep required a separate decision, and as if sometimes the decisions were unwelcome. She stopped a few feet away from me and raised her face to mine. 'Do you think I imagined it?'

'I don't know.' I wished she would look away from me. 'Perhaps.'

'Do you think I'm mad?'

'Of course you're not.' I took a step backwards. 'Now –'

'David,' she interrupted.

I looked at her. Once, years ago, driving late on a winter night across the Fens to Rosington, I almost ran over a young badger who was playing in the middle of the road. The car went into a skid but stopped in time. For a long moment the badger did not move: he stared into the beam of my headlights.

'It's so strange . . .' Joanna whispered.

Another silence grew between us, and I did not know how long it went on for. What was so strange? This house? The crying child? Francis Youlgreave? Or even the two of us alone in this room?

We did not move. There was a hair on Joanna's cheek, and I wanted desperately to brush it away. Then I heard, or thought I heard, the beating of distant wings on the edge of my hearing. In my mind I saw the badger abruptly recollecting himself and stumbling into the darkness of the verge.

'I must go. Goodbye.'

Without another word, I scuttled out of the room and almost ran down the stairs.

25

The inquest was at 2.30 p.m. on Wednesday the 19th August. I myself was not called as a witness, but I drove Doris Potter there.

The proceedings did not take long. The coroner was an elderly doctor named Chilbert, a sharp man who kept glancing at his watch as if impatient to be gone. There was a jury of seven men and three women – two in their twenties, two in their sixties, and the remainder scattered between; the only thing they had in common was an expression of wary self-consciousness, but even that wore off as the proceedings continued.

Dr Vintner was the first witness to be called. He gave evidence of Lady Youlgreave's identity. Then Chilbert took him through her recent medical history. James had seen a good deal of her because she had a terminal malignancy – breast cancer. It was clear that he thought she could have died at any time in the last few months. He described how he had tried and failed to persuade her to move into a nursing home. Her mind had been increasingly confused, he said, because of the morphine. It was true that osteoarthritis of the shoulders had made it impossible for her to raise her arms. But she had been quite capable of forgetting that she could not reach the bottle on the mantelpiece.

Beside me, Doris sucked in her breath.

The pathologist's report confirmed what James had said. He said that Lady Youlgreave had fractured her skull when she fell, probably on the corner of the hearth. There was a laceration with swelling and bruising around it. Her injuries were entirely consistent with her having tripped on the hearthrug. Finally, he briefly described the postmortem damage inflicted by Beauty and Beast – but in technically obscure vocabulary designed, I suspected, to confuse the two journalists in the public gallery.

The coroner nodded with monotonous regularity while James and the pathologist were speaking. But he stopped nodding when he questioned Doris, the next witness to be called. She was trembling and her voice shook. But she insisted that Lady Youlgreave, however confused about other matters, knew that she could not reach her medicine. She also mentioned her employer's dislike of using the phone.

Chilbert screwed up his lips and then said, 'In general, no doubt you're right, Mrs Potter. But we have just heard from Dr Vintner how muddled Lady Youlgreave had become.' He glanced at James as if drawing support from a colleague. 'It's a sad truth, but people in her condition do deteriorate. So I find it hard to believe that her behaviour was still predictable by normal standards. In fact –'

'But, sir, I –'

'This is a medical question, Mrs Potter, and we should leave it to those competent to answer it.' Chilbert raised a heavy eyebrow. 'You're not a doctor of medicine, I take it?'

'But why would she want to say her cousins were coming?'

'Who knows? She may have dreamed that they were. But we're not here to speculate. Now, perhaps you would like to tell us why you moved Lady Youlgreave's body and tidied the room before the police arrived?'

She shrugged. 'I just did it. It seemed right. She would have liked to be decent.'

'You should have left everything as it was.'

'Left the dogs in there with her, do you mean? Left her all uncovered for all those men to see? She wouldn't have wanted them to see her like that.'

Chilbert looked at Doris's flushed face and – showing more wisdom than I had credited him with – told her she could stand down. Next he talked to the teenager who had taken Lady Youlgreave's call cancelling the nurse. The teenager's mother ran the Fishguard Agency, but she had been away. The boy, younger than Rosemary, was quite definite about the time of the call.

'What did the caller sound like?' Chilbert asked.

'I don't know. An old lady, I suppose. She said she was Lady Youlgreave.'

'What exactly did she say to you?'

'Her cousins had come down for the weekend. Out of the blue, like. And they were going to look after her so she didn't need the nurse to call until the weekend afterwards.'

'So what did you do?'

'I phoned the nurse and cancelled her.' Stolid as a suet pudding, the boy stared up at Chilbert. 'I knew what to do. I often look after the phone when Mum's out, and there's always people ringing up to change things.'

Sergeant Clough confirmed that there had been a call from the Old Manor House to the agency number at that time on Friday evening. His bald scalp gleaming in the striplight above his head, he emphasized that there had been no sign of a break-in.

The coroner reminded the jury that the probable time of death was Friday evening: the agency nurse had been due at 7.45 a.m. on Saturday morning so, even if she had come, she could not have prevented Lady Youlgreave's death. The jury, suitably instructed, returned a verdict of accidental death.

Afterwards, Doris and I walked back to the car.

'I don't believe it,' she said. 'She wouldn't have phoned the agency.'

'But she must have done. They traced the call.'

'Anyone could have got in. Everyone knew where the key was.'

'I know it's hard to accept,' I said, 'but I have to say that I think the verdict is probably right. People do odd things. Especially when they're old and confused. And there was nothing to suggest otherwise, was there?'

She screwed up her mouth like an obstinate child, but said nothing.

'I know it was ghastly,' I went on, unlocking the door of the car, 'and the fact you found her like that was even worse.' I held open the door for her. 'Wretched animals.'

Doris scrambled inelegantly into the passenger seat. 'What's going to happen to them?'

'The dogs? I imagine they'll be put down.'

'No.' Doris's head snapped up, and she looked at me, her face outraged as though I had hit her. 'They mustn't be put down. Can't I have them?'

'But, Doris – look, they should have been put down years ago.'

'I'd like them. They'd be all right with me.'

'I'm sure they would. But have you considered – ?'

'They know me. I remember Beaut when she was a puppy.'

'They need a great deal of care. Then there's vets' bills as well. And really, wouldn't it be kinder to them if they were put down?'

'How do you know? Most people don't want to die, even when they're old and ill. Why should animals be any different?'

I looked down at her and remembered the high moral tone I had taken when Audrey was a little less than charitable about old people. 'You must do what you think best. And let me know if there's anything I can do to help.'

'How do I set about getting them?'

'Lady Youlgreave's solicitor is the person to ask about that.'

'Mr Deakin.'

'He'll know. In theory I suppose the dogs now belong to Lady Youlgreave's heirs. But I can't believe they'd object to your having them.'

Doris nodded. 'Thank you.'

We drove back to Roth. I turned into Manor Farm Lane and drew up outside the little house she shared with her husband, and with Charlene and Charlene's two younger brothers. I tried and failed to imagine what effect the addition of Beauty and Beast to their ménage would have. Doris did not get out. I fumbled for my own door handle, intending to walk round and open the passenger door for her.

'Vicar?'

'Yes?'

Doris was sitting upright in the seat, her fingers gripping the strap of her handbag. 'There's something I maybe should have told them.'

'Told whom?'

'The police. That coroner.'

I stared at her, alarm creeping over me. 'What do you mean? Something to do with Lady Youlgreave?'

'On Friday – as I was going – she wanted me to put some stuff in the dustbin. I always move the dustbin just before I go, you see, put it by the gate. It's not something the nurse would want to do, and sometimes the dustmen come early on Monday, before I get there.'

'So why was this any different?'

She turned to look at me. 'It was some stuff from the tin box. You know, the one Mrs Byfield's been looking at. Not all of it – just a few of them notebooks and letters and things.'

'But they were family papers, Doris. They might have been important.'

She shook her head. 'Lady Youlgreave said this was stuff no one wanted.'

'I don't think she was necessarily the best judge.'

'But she wanted me to throw them away so badly. Said it was nasty.' Doris's face was miserable. 'She was crying, Vicar. Like a child. And when all's said and done, what did they matter? She was all upset, and they were only papers.'

'You could have taken them away,' I suggested, trying to speak gently. 'And then perhaps discussed what to do with –'

'She made me promise I'd do it. It was the only way to stop her crying.' Doris stared defiantly at me. 'I don't break promises.'

There was a silence in the car. I bowed my head.

'No,' I said at last. 'Of course you don't.'

'But should I have told the police? Or should I tell them now?'

I thought for a moment. 'I don't think so.' It would only complicate matters. The information would not have affected the verdict: it merely confirmed Lady Youlgreave's confused mental state. 'Perhaps I should have a word with my wife. She may be able to tell if anything significant is missing. If necessary we can mention what happened to the solicitor.'

'All right.' Doris opened the car door. 'Thanks for the lift.' Before she shut the door she turned back to me and added, 'She did it for the best, you know. It wouldn't have been nice for the Youlgreaves, she said, and she didn't want your wife to see. Not *suitable*. That's what she said, Vicar. Not *suitable*.'

Doris slammed the door. I watched her walking with a suggestion of a waddle up the concrete path to her front door. I wondered which of Francis's shabby little scandals Lady Youlgreave had wanted to conceal.

I drove home. As I had expected, there was no one at the Vicarage. Vanessa was still at work. Michael was out with Brian Vintner. Rosemary had announced at breakfast that she was going up to London again, with the same school friend. I was relieved. I was not used to sharing a house with three people, and the longer the summer went on, the more the attractions of solitude increased.

I took off my jacket and tie and dropped them on a chair in the study. I put the kettle on and went to the lavatory. In mid-performance, the doorbell rang. I swore. Hastily buttoning myself up, I rinsed my hands and went to answer the door. It was Audrey. Some people have a talent for arriving inconveniently which amounts to genius.

Pink and quivering, she advanced towards me, forcing me to step back. A moment later, she was in the hall beside me. She was wearing a dress of some synthetic, shiny material – a loud check in turquoise and yellow. The dress clung to her like a second skin. I noticed smears of mud on her stockings. Her jowls trembled.

'I'm sorry, David. I've come to complain.'

I blinked. 'What about?'

'That boy. Michael. I know he's your godson. I know his parents are great friends of yours. But I just can't put up with it.'

'But what's he been doing?'

'Spying on me. I was walking in the park yesterday afternoon and there he was. I kept seeing his face peering at me round trees or through bushes.' She hesitated, her jaws moving as though she were chewing over the insult. 'And this afternoon he's been doing the same thing.'

'In Roth Park?'

She flushed. 'I'd been taking a little exercise after lunch. I've not been sleeping well lately.'

I wondered if the unaccustomed exercise had something to do with her detective work. 'The footpaths are public rights of way, Audrey. Perhaps Michael was playing there. There's no reason why he shouldn't have been there as well as you.'

'He was snooping. Him and that nasty Brian Vintner. I won't put up with it.'

I felt a rush of anger. 'I don't think Michael's the sort of boy who would snoop.'

She glared up at me. 'Are you saying I'm a liar?'

'Of course not.' I stared at her, realizing how close I had come to losing my temper and realizing how inappropriate my behaviour was. 'I'm sorry. I shouldn't have spoken like that.'

She grunted. To my dismay, I saw her eyes were glistening.

'The fact is,' I hurried on, 'I'm just back from Lady Youlgreave's inquest.'

'The inquest?' The jowls wobbled once more. 'I was thinking of going myself, actually. I had hoped you might be able to give me a lift. But nobody answered when I phoned.'

'We've all been out for most of the day.'

'What happened?'

'What you'd expect.' I was puzzled by Audrey's change of tack. 'They decided it was an accident.'

Audrey sniffed. At that moment, the whistle on the kettle began to squeal, higher and louder.

'I was about to make some tea,' I said reluctantly. 'Would you like a cup?'

Audrey allowed herself to be mollified. She followed me into the kitchen and talked while I made the tea. I promised I would have a word with Michael, and she promised she would say no more about it. Audrey stayed for half an hour. While I tried not to think of the work I should be doing, she talked about Lady Youlgreave in a manner which suggested she had been to Roth what the Queen Mother had been to the country. She also talked, at length, about her determination to bring to justice whoever was responsible for Lord Peter's mutilation. Finally, she talked about the fete. I am afraid I did not listen very carefully.

At last she went. I returned to the kitchen to wash up the tea things. Afterwards, I was crossing the hall on my way back to the study when I heard a key in the lock of the front door.

Rosemary burst into the house. She was dressed in denim,

jeans and a shirt with studded poppers which I had not seen before. Around her neck was a silk scarf, also new. The colours were dark green and bronze: they would have suited Vanessa. I registered all this automatically. What I really saw was her face: red and tear-stained, framed by dishevelled blonde hair.

'Rosemary – whatever's happened?'

Her face working, she stared at me. Then, without a word, she ran up the stairs and into the bathroom. I heard the bolt on the door click home.

The Vicarage walls and floors were thin. A moment later, I heard the sound of vomiting.

26

On Wednesday evening I went reluctantly to St Mary Magdalene. The reluctance had been growing on me over the last year. I had always tended to anthropomorphize churches, to endow the buildings with personalities: as with humans, some personalities were more attractive than others. For most of my time at Roth I had liked St Mary Magdalene. If I had had to find a human equivalent to it, I would have chosen Doris Potter.

In the past twelve months, however – ever since that odd experience just after Vanessa and I had met – I had no longer felt the same about the place. The feeling was almost impossible to pin down. It was like the faint blush of damp spreading almost imperceptibly on a whitewashed wall. I knew it was there. I could not see it, but I thought I could feel it. I felt as though the church were no longer entirely mine, as though something or someone were trying with gradual success to take it over. On one level, I knew very well that I was imagining things. As a man and as a priest, I was prone to see shadows where there were none.

I came out to lock the church before supper. After a grey day, it was a fine evening, though there were dark clouds over much of the sky. The churchyard was bathed in strong, metallic light: it looked like a stage set. I left Vanessa cooking supper. Michael was spending the evening at the Vintners'. Rosemary was resting in her room; she had told me that she had an upset stomach – something she had eaten at lunch must have disagreed with her. I did not know whether or not to believe her.

Before I locked up, I went inside the church to make sure everything was all right. The ladies had been in recently, and the place smelled of flowers and polish. The sombre colours of the Last Judgement painting glowed above the chancel arch. I walked slowly up to my stall in the choir, intending to pray. My footsteps sounded louder than usual, as though I were walking on the skin of a drum.

As I passed under the chancel arch, a movement caught my eye – to the left and above my head. I looked up. I was directly beneath the marble tablet commemorating Francis Youlgreave. Nothing was moving. Sometimes, I told myself, the flutter of your own eyelash can give you the impression of movement beyond yourself.

In my mind, Francis's tablet coalesced with the idea that I was walking on a drum. If this was a drum, then inside the drum, the home of its resonance, was the vault beneath the chancel where the Youlgreaves lay. Not that there were very many Youlgreaves in there. I had not been down there for years, but I remembered a small, dusty chamber laid out rather like a wine cellar with deep shelves on either side; there had been only three coffins, one of them presumably belonging to Francis Youlgreave. There was ample room for at least a dozen more.

The vault must have been built in another time for other families, but there was no sign of them now. The first of the Youlgreaves had wanted to make the place his own, and now only Youlgreaves waited there for the Second Coming. I assumed that the vault would need to be reopened for Lady Youlgreave.

Suddenly I did not want to pray. I told myself I was in the wrong frame of mind. I shivered as I walked back to the south door. I did not know why but I was frightened. I felt like a weary swimmer, alone, out of his depth and too far from land.

I left the church, locking the door behind me. As I came out of the porch the full force of the sunlight hit me. On the right, beside the path which led to the private gate from the churchyard to Roth Park, there was a wooden bench, donated by Audrey in memory of her parents. A figure was sprawling on it, arms outstretched along the back of the seat, a silhouette against the blinding light of the sun. For an instant my heart lurched. I thought it was Joanna.

'Hello, David,' Toby said. 'Lovely evening.'

I blinked in the light. He sat up and moved along the bench, as if making room for me to sit. He looked particularly androgynous this evening in red trousers and a deeper red T-shirt whose low neck and long flared sleeves gave him a faintly medieval air. His feet were bare and he was smoking a cigarette.

'Was there something you wanted?' I asked.

'Yes and no.' He laughed. 'I didn't realize you were in there, actually, but now we've met, there is something.'

With sudden, irrational terror, I wondered if Toby knew: that I had seen his sister without his knowledge: that she had taken me to her room, that she had talked to me about him. I realized how vulnerable I was. Toby was speaking and I had to ask him to repeat what he had said.

'How was the inquest?'

'They decided the death was an accident.'

Toby laughed again, a shrill squirt of sound. 'Which everyone knew already. Our legal system has a genius for stating the obvious, hasn't it?'

'I suppose they have to make sure.'

Toby bent forward and carefully stubbed out his cigarette in the grass. 'I wanted a word about the fete actually. I wondered if you have a fortune-teller.'

'Not as far as I know. I don't think we've ever had one.'

'I thought it might add to the fun. If you've no objection, of course.'

'As long as it's suitably light-hearted, I don't think there'd be a problem. But I wouldn't want anyone to take it seriously.'

'Oh no,' said Toby.

'Who had you in mind?'

'Actually, I thought I could do it myself. I did it at school once. Just for a joke, at a sort of show we had. I wore a wig, and a long dark robe covered in stars.' The fingers of his left hand fluttered as though miming the flowing folds of the robe. 'Just a bit of fun.'

I thought about it for a moment. The idea was attractive. I had felt for some years that under Audrey's hand the fete was becoming rather a dull affair, with the same stalls and the same sideshows coming round monotonously every year.

'There's an old tent in the stables up at the house,' Toby went

470

on. 'It looks sound enough. I could use it as my booth.'

'What sort of fortune-telling?'

Toby shrugged. 'I'm not choosy. Palmistry, the cards, astrology, the I Ching. Whatever the customer wants.'

'I'm sure people would enjoy it. And it's very kind of you, too. But I'd better have a word with Audrey first. She's doing most of the organizing.'

'I shall have to think of a name.' He grinned up at me. 'The Princess of Prophecy: something like that.'

I glanced at my watch. 'I must be going. Vanessa will have supper on the table soon.'

Toby stood up. 'How's the research going, by the way?'

'Lady Youlgreave's death is a complication. We're a little concerned about what will happen to the papers.'

'It all depends on who the heir is, I suppose. No news on that?'

I shook my head.

'The solicitor must know,' Toby went on, half to himself. 'There must be a solicitor.'

I nodded but said nothing. I had never met Mr Deakin, though Lady Youlgreave had mentioned him once or twice. I wondered if he'd been at the inquest, one of the anonymous men in dark suits.

Toby took a step away from me, then stopped, as if something had occurred to him. 'Why doesn't Vanessa come and see Francis's room on Sunday afternoon? I know we were going to wait till the party after the fete, but it would be much better to do it in daylight. Besides, you know what parties are like. Full of distractions.'

'That would be very kind, but –'

'It's no problem,' he rushed on. 'Tell you what, why don't you all come? And if any of you would like a swim, you can bring your costumes. The pool should be sorted out by then.'

I thanked him, and said that Vanessa or I would phone later in the evening.

'Do come,' he said. Then he smiled and loped away – not along the path but among the graves. The cuffs of his T-shirt and of his trousers swayed as he walked. He looked like a blood-red pixie.

* * *

Later that evening, Vanessa and I had another whispered conference in our bedroom. It was a warm evening and we sat propped up against pillows on top of the bed, I in my pyjamas and she in her nightdress. The nightdress was dark-blue with cream piping around the neck and the cuffs. I dared not look at her too much because it made me want to make love.

'What on earth's wrong with Rosemary?' she hissed. 'She's been very subdued all evening.'

'She's got an upset stomach.'

Vanessa shook her head vigorously. 'I don't believe it for a moment.'

'She was sick when she came home. I heard her.'

'Perhaps she was. But no one with an upset stomach eats the supper she did. No, if you ask me, it's something else. Maybe something shocked her.' She paused. 'Who is this mysterious school friend?'

'I think she's called Clarissa. Or Camilla. Something like that.'

'Are you sure she exists?'

Startled, I turned and looked at Vanessa. Her hair floated on her shoulders. Her face was very close to mine. The neck of her nightdress was open and I could see her left breast. I longed to be old – to reach an age where sexuality was no longer a distraction and a temptation.

'Why shouldn't the friend be real?' I said, clinging to the safety of words.

Vanessa picked up an emery board from the bedside table and began to buff her nails. 'I may be maligning her,' she said thoughtfully, 'but it's a classic tactic – the old school friend, going shopping, that sort of thing.' She smiled at me. 'We used to use it when I was young. I suspect my parents knew perfectly well what I was up to, but they chose to turn a blind eye.'

'But I thought she was interested in Toby Clifford.'

'She is. I wouldn't be at all surprised if he's the mysterious school friend.'

'But –' I stopped. But what? *But he's years older than she is. But he's a hippy, or at least he dresses like one. But I was talking to him only a few hours ago. But I don't like to think of my daughter with a man like that, perhaps with any man.*

'Just a thought,' Vanessa said. 'He might have tried something on. That might account for her being so upset.'

'So upset it made her sick?'

'It happens.'

'What does?'

She glanced at me, then away. 'Sudden physical revulsion. In some ways, Rosemary's very young for her age.'

'You really think he may have made advances to her? Physical advances?'

'I don't know,' Vanessa said. 'I'm just saying it might have happened that way: if Rosemary had her head stuffed full of romantic dreams about Toby, and he misinterpreted how she was responding to him, he might have made a pass at her, and she might have found the whole thing totally revolting. Men and women look at these things very differently.'

After all, you and I look at these things differently. The words lay between us. There was no need to speak them aloud.

'Rosemary said she didn't want to come on Sunday,' I said haltingly, as though in a language I did not fully understand. We had discussed Toby's invitation over supper.

'Exactly. Yesterday nothing would have kept her away from Roth Park. Still, maybe it's all for the best. He's very charming, but really too old for her. And I'm not altogether sure I trust him.'

We sat there in silence for a moment. Traffic grumbled in the main road.

'Audrey came round this afternoon to complain about Michael,' I said.

'Hush.' She darted a glance at me. 'They'll hear if you're not careful. What's he been doing?'

'She claimed that he and Brian Vintner had been spying on her.'

'Where?'

'In Roth Park somewhere. I suspect she's been out looking for clues. I had a word with Michael but he denied it. He did say that they had seen her in the park this afternoon.'

'Audrey will always find something to complain about.'

'She's having a difficult time.'

'So are we all,' Vanessa snapped, forgetting to lower her voice.

'The woman's a cow and that's all there is to it. A menopausal cow at that.'

'You may be right. But she's a victim as well. What happened to Lord Peter would have been a terrible shock for anyone.'

Vanessa glared at me.

'By the way,' I said before she had time to reply, 'there's something we need to discuss. It's about the Youlgreave papers.'

'You're trying to change the subject.'

'Yes, but we still need to talk about this. And I'm not sure there's much more we can usefully say about Audrey.'

She held up her hand and examined her nails. 'All right. What's this about the papers?'

'After the inquest, Doris told me something. I think we should treat it as confidential. She knows I'm going to mention it to you, though. It seems that on Friday evening, Lady Youlgreave asked her to throw away some of the papers. They went out with the rubbish on Monday morning.'

Vanessa stared at me. The colour in her cheeks receded, and suddenly there were freckles where I had noticed none before. 'Oh my God – the ones in the box? Which ones?'

I passed on what Doris had told me. Vanessa rested her head on her hand.

'I could *kill* her,' she said slowly. 'If only Doris had had the sense to *pretend* to throw them away.'

'She's not that sort of person.'

'Then I wish she was. I wonder what we've lost. The old lady was very cagey about letting me see some of the stuff.'

'About Francis's time in Rosington and afterwards?'

'Yes.' Her eyebrows wrinkled. 'How did you guess?'

'That seems to have been the most controversial period in his life.'

'There's no hope we could get them back, is there?'

'By now they'll be yards deep in rubbish in some landfill.'

'Is the box still at the house?'

'I don't know. Doris said that someone from the solicitors came to take away any easily portable valuables. Just in case. Would you be able to know what was missing?'

Vanessa shook her head. 'Lady Youlgreave never let me catalogue the entire contents of the box. She doled things out to me as she saw fit.' Unexpectedly she put her hand on top of mine, which was lying palm down on the bedspread. 'You are very patient with me, David. All this must seem rather unimportant.'

I twisted my hand so I could grip hers. 'It's important to you so it's important to me. But part of me thinks Lady Youlgreave was right. Perhaps the least said about Francis Youlgreave the better.'

She drew away. 'I never knew you felt like that.'

'I don't want to put it too strongly. But maybe in the long run this is a blessing in disguise.'

She said nothing. I turned on my side, facing her, and ran the fingers of my right hand lightly down her arm from the shoulder to the hand. I brought my head closer and kissed her on the lips.

'David,' she said softly. 'I'm sorry. I just don't feel like it.'

I drew back. 'Not to worry. It doesn't matter.'

'I know you're disappointed in me,' she went on, 'but sometimes I wish we could just leave sex out of it. Just for the time being. I've tried and tried. But at present it just won't work. It's not that I don't love you. I just don't want to show it like *that*. Not now. Perhaps later, when I've had time to get used to the idea.'

'Vanessa —'

'You were celibate for ten years. You must have got used to it. Couldn't you get used to it again? Just for a little while. What I'd like to do is live together, like brother and sister almost.' She paused. 'Like Toby and Joanna.'

475

27

The secretary spoke with an upper-class drawl of the type that takes generations to perfect. She telephoned me from Lincoln's Inn on Thursday morning to arrange a meeting with Lady Youlgreave's solicitor. Mr Deakin, she said, was going to be at the Old Manor House for most of the day and he wondered if we might be able to discuss the arrangements for the funeral. I had a busy day in front of me, but I knew that I would be free at some point in the early afternoon, so I suggested that I call at the Old Manor House between two and three.

The sunshine of yesterday evening had given way to dull, clammy weather, neither hot nor cold. It mirrored my mood. When I reached the Old Manor House, it was about a quarter past two. I had been there less than a week ago, on the day that Lady Youlgreave died, but already the shabby house looked even shabbier.

I rang the doorbell. A moment later, the door was opened by a thin-faced, ginger-haired youth with long sideburns and a tweed suit with a mustard-yellow-and-black check.

'Afternoon, Reverend,' he said, extending a hand. 'Good of you to pop round. I'm Nick Deakin.'

We shook hands, and he took me into a little room at the back of the hall which was furnished as a study; I'd never been in there before. I had been expecting a different sort of solicitor – a pinstriped family lawyer, a man to match the secretary, overbred and pompous.

'Afraid the whole place stinks,' Deakin said. 'Those dogs, I suppose. Let's sit down and make ourselves comfortable. Would you like a coffee or something?'

'No, thank you.'

The room was very dirty, every horizontal surface covered with a layer of gritty dust. Deakin had flung open the window, which overlooked the tangled garden at the back of the house. The furniture was old and heavy; like that in the dining room, it had been designed for larger rooms in a larger house. There were two armchairs near the window, upholstered with brown leather, dry and cracked. Deakin waved me towards the nearer one.

'I gave them a good dust.' He grinned, revealing projecting front teeth which gave him the appearance of a friendly red squirrel. 'Poor old Mrs Potter, eh? Must have been a hell of a job trying to keep this house clean as well as keep the old lady on the straight and narrow.' He sat down and offered me a cigarette. 'You know Mrs Potter?' he went on.

'Very well.'

Deakin clicked an enormous gold lighter under my nose. 'She says she wants the dogs.'

'She told me that, too.'

'I don't think anyone else would mind. They're practically dead on their feet, eh? Besides, after what happened, you'd think they'd be better off in the Great Kennel in the Sky. Still, none of my business. But she knows what she's doing, does she? I thought I'd better check before we made any decisions.'

'Oh yes,' I said. 'More than most people.'

We went on to talk about the arrangements for the funeral. Deakin had already discussed possible times with the undertaker, and we soon agreed on Monday, at 2 p.m.

'Burial or cremation?' I asked.

Deakin opened his briefcase and took out a sheet of paper. 'Cremation – she specified it in her will. There's another point: she doesn't want to go in the family vault. She's left quite detailed instructions about the headstone, et cetera, but that needn't concern you.'

Relief washed over me, surprising me with its intensity. I had not wanted to go into that vault under the chancel of St Mary Magdalene. I felt reprieved. I also wondered why Lady Youlgreave had not wanted her mortal remains to wait for the Last Judgement beside Francis Youlgreave's. Perhaps she had known too much about him to feel comfortable in his company, dead or alive.

'Will any of Lady Youlgreave's relations be there?'

Deakin shrugged. 'Almost certainly not. There's no close family. But we'll put a notice in *The Times* and the *Telegraph*. Maybe the odd friend will turn up.'

'Some local people may want to come as well. I'll pass the news around the parish. What about afterwards?'

'Eh?'

'People often expect something. If only a cup of tea.'

'Oh, I see. What do you suggest?'

'We could use the church hall. It's on the green, next to the library. One of our churchwardens has a tea room – if you like, I could ask her to provide tea and biscuits. It shouldn't be expensive.'

'Sounds OK to me. Can't exactly have it here, can we?' He leant forward and stubbed out his cigarette in a discoloured brass ashtray embedded in what looked like the foot of an elephant. 'Not unless we have the place fumigated first.'

'What will happen to the house?'

He hesitated, then grinned at me. 'No reason why you shouldn't know. Under the terms of her husband's will, Lady Youlgreave only had a life interest in most of the estate. It'll go to some of his relations – second cousins, once removed; something like that. They live in South Africa now, so I doubt if they'll be at the funeral.'

'My wife was working on some Youlgreave family papers. I don't know if you've heard of Francis Youlgreave?'

Deakin shook his head.

'He was a minor poet at the turn of the century. My wife was going to write a biography of him – with Lady Youlgreave's approval. But what's the position now?'

'She'll need to discuss that with the heir. Why don't you suggest she writes to them? We can forward a letter, if you'd like. There are one or two bequests from Lady Youlgreave's personal estate, but Youlgreave family papers won't come into that.'

Shortly afterwards, Deakin saw me out. We shook hands on the doorstep.

'She was a game old bird,' he said cheerfully. 'You know, in a funny way I'll miss her.'

We said goodbye. It was not until I was crossing the bridge over the Rowan that the obvious question occurred to me. How had Nick Deakin known Lady Youlgreave? Deakin could not have been qualified for very long – he looked in his mid-twenties, at the most. He must have seen her recently. I wondered why.

As I was passing the entry into the drive of Roth Park, I glanced across the green and noticed Audrey coming out of Tudor Cottage. I waved to her, but she appeared not to see me. There was a sudden gap in the traffic so, on impulse, I crossed the road to the green. She too had crossed the road outside her house and was now on the green as well. She would need to know about the arrangements for Lady Youlgreave's funeral, and about the tea and biscuits afterwards. Now was as good a time to tell her as any. If I intercepted her on the green, I thought, there was less chance of her delaying me.

Audrey still had not seen me. She veered towards the bus shelter. I began to walk more quickly across the grass. I heard her talking but could not see her, because the bus shelter was between us. Her voice rose higher and higher. I swore under my breath and broke into a clumsy run.

She was standing just outside the bus shelter haranguing the people inside – three hairy youths in T-shirts and jeans, and a fat girl with dyed blonde hair and a short pink dress.

'Parasites,' she was saying. 'You ruin the village for everyone. If I had my way, I'd bring back the birch. And which of you did those horrible things to my cat?'

'Audrey,' I said, laying a hand on her shoulder, 'let's go back to the cottage.'

She whirled round. Her cheeks wobbled – by now she was gobbling like a turkey, making half-articulate sounds. Her breath smelt of sweet sherry. I took her arm, but she tore it away from me. She swung back to the young people in the bus shelter. Before I could stop her, she darted towards the tallest of the youths, a strapping boy with several days' growth of beard on his face.

'You're scum,' she shrieked. And she spat in his face.

I seized Audrey's arm again and tried to drag her away. Simultaneously the girl in the pink dress slapped Audrey's face. Audrey screamed, a high animal sound.

'Shut up, you dried-up old bitch,' the girl yelled, bringing her face very close to Audrey's. 'What the fuck do you think you're doing, swanning around pretending to be Lady Muck? Don't you know everyone laughs at you?'

There were running footsteps behind me. Charlene appeared beside me in the doorway.

'You can shut that big mouth of yours, Judy.' Charlene took Audrey's other arm and pulled her gently outside. 'Come along, Miss Oliphant.'

Judy, the girl in pink, took a step after Audrey but stopped when Charlene glared at her.

'Kevin,' Charlene said to one of the other boys. 'Aren't you meant to be at work?'

He stared at his shuffling feet and said he was just going.

Charlene and I helped Audrey across the road and into Tudor Cottage. Fortunately there were no customers in the tea room. We took Audrey upstairs and into the sitting room, where she sank into the armchair by the window. She was still trembling, but less violently than before and her face was pale where it had previously been red. I glanced out of the window. The bus shelter appeared to be empty.

'I'm going to fetch her a cup of tea,' Charlene told me. 'And one of those pills Dr Vintner left. Can you stay with her? I won't be long.'

Charlene left us alone.

'Do sit down,' Audrey said faintly. 'I always think that chair needs a man. There's a clean ashtray over there . . .'

The effort to act normally seemed to exhaust her still more. For a moment she said nothing. I noticed on the little table beside her chair an empty glass and a red exercise book, probably the one I had seen in her office the other day.

Audrey peered out of the window, down at the empty bus shelter. 'I was sitting here after lunch, writing my journal, when I saw them,' she said quietly, looking not at me but the bus shelter. 'I knew they were up to no good. They had been in the pub. The three of them with that dreadful girl. No better than she should be ... And they were laughing and giggling, and I knew they were laughing at me and Lord Peter. I had to say something. No one else will. It's not right that evil should go unpunished.' She stared at me. 'And if no one else will punish evil, then we must do it ourselves. You do agree with me, David, don't you? David?'

On Friday evening, after Evensong, Doris Potter was waiting for me on the bench by the south porch.

'Can you spare a moment, Vicar?'

I went and sat beside her on the bench. I had noticed her in church but thought nothing of it. I said Evensong on Tuesdays and Fridays, and she usually tried to come to at least one of them. I was in no particular hurry to get home. I knew we were having a cold supper. Besides, since our conversation on Wednesday evening, Vanessa and I had not had a great deal to say to each other.

'I saw that solicitor the other day,' Doris said.

'Mr Deakin?'

She nodded. 'He's asked me to stay on at the house for a while – try and clean it up a bit.' She stared down at her rough, red hands. 'He says the old lady left me something in her will.'

'I'm not surprised – after all you did for her.'

She shrugged impatiently. 'There's a bit of money which will come in handy, I don't mind admitting. There's something else too. She added it to her will a few months before she died. A – a – what's it called?'

'A codicil?'

'That's it. She got me to ring Mr Deakin and he came to the house a couple of times. I knew it was about her will, but she didn't tell me what it was. But Mr Deakin did. She's gone and left me some land. Carter's Meadow. You know – that bit of land in Roth Park – between the garden and the housing estate near the reservoir.' She glanced at me, her grey eyes calm and serious. 'Where you and Rosemary found the blood and Lord Peter's fur.'

'But doesn't that belong to the Cliffords?'

Doris shook her head. 'It wasn't sold with the rest of the land. The Bramleys didn't own it. And it's not Youlgreave land either, not family – it doesn't go with the Old Manor House. It was Lady Youlgreave's.'

From what Doris told me, Carter's Meadow was an anomaly. According to Lady Youlgreave, it had once belonged to a large farm in the northern part of the parish, the part which was now underwater. For many years it had been leased to the Youlgreaves, but the owner had refused to sell it to them outright and had even tried to break the lease.

'There was bad blood between him and the family,' Doris said, watching me carefully. 'Something to do with Francis, she thought.'

Because Francis killed a cat in Carter's Meadow?

In the nineteen-thirties, Doris went on, when they built the Jubilee Reservoir, Carter's Meadow had at last come on the open market and Lady Youlgreave had bought it, intending to give it to her husband as a present. But the sale of Roth Park and then the war and her husband's death prevented this; because the land belonged directly to Lady Youlgreave, it had not been sold with the rest of the estate.

'I think she'd forgotten all about it until that man came to call,' Doris said. 'He wanted to buy it, you see, but she took against him.'

'Which man?'

'Toby Clifford. He tried to push her into selling it, but she wouldn't budge. You know what she was like – she could be so obstinate. Then he tried to get me to do his dirty work for him.' Doris frowned. 'Bare-faced cheek. We were in the hall and I was showing him out, and he pulled out a wallet. Said maybe we could come to an arrangement.' She snorted. 'I told him he and his money weren't wanted.'

'Why did he want the land?'

'Something to do with his plans for Roth Park. He thinks big, that one. Eyes bigger than his stomach.' Her face creased into a smile full of mischief. 'The only reason she took against him was because he looked like a girl with all that hair. The thing is, now she's gone and left *me* that land. The Clifford boy's still interested in buying it – Mr Deakin told me. But I don't know what to do for the best. *She* wouldn't have liked me to sell Carter's Meadow to him.'

'I don't think you should worry about that,' I said. 'You can do whatever you like with the land, unless Lady Youlgreave laid down any conditions in the will.'

'So do you think I should let him have it? If he offers a fair price, that is.'

I thought of Toby and Joanna, camping like a pair of waifs in that tumbledown house. And I thought of the hints I'd heard about Toby. I thought of the things that Toby had told me about Joanna, and Joanna had told me about Toby.

Toby was a determined young man, and if Carter's Meadow was essential for his plans for Roth Park, then the timing of Lady Youlgreave's death must have been convenient for him. I glimpsed melodramatic possibilities: a visit to a vulnerable old woman when the house was empty; another refusal countered by a quick push; a disguised voice on the telephone; knocking over the medicine in the bedroom to suggest a reason why Lady Youlgreave might have tripped on the hearthrug. I shook my head, trying to clear it of these fancies. But a residue of doubt remained.

'If I were you,' I said to Doris, 'I'd hang on to the land for a while. Wait and see.'

28

At lunch time on Sunday, Rosemary said that she could not possibly spare the time to come to Roth Park: she had to work. We did not press her. Michael wanted to go because of the swimming pool. Vanessa wanted to go in order to see Francis Youlgreave's room. Even though her access to the family papers was now in doubt, and some of the papers had been destroyed, she was still determined to write the biography – far more so than she had been when Lady Youlgreave was alive. It was as if the Youlgreaves had infected her with a bacillus, and the disease would have to run its course.

'There must be other materials,' she said over lunch. 'Just because nobody's found them yet, it doesn't mean they're not around if one only looks in the right place. Perhaps I should go to Rosington.'

'I doubt if you'll find much there.'

'How do you know?'

'I'm sure there's some public record of him,' I said carefully, aware that Rosemary and Michael were listening to us. 'The dates of his appointments, where he lived and so on.'

'Yes – but did people talk about him when you lived in Rosington?'

'Occasionally. Gossip, mainly. But that's not really what you want, is it?'

'It all helps.' She looked at me across the table, and I had the feeling that she saw me properly for the first time since our conversation on Wednesday evening. 'I'm going to write this book, David, I really am.'

We finished the meal in silence. I wanted to go to Roth Park because I would see Joanna. I didn't want to go for the same reason. Every night since Wednesday I'd dreamed about her. Try as I might to forget her, the image of her lingered in my waking hours as well.

At half past three, Vanessa, Michael and I walked slowly up the drive of Roth Park. Michael had his bathing costume and a towel, Vanessa carried a notebook and I had a bunch of roses from the Vicarage garden. Vanessa had insisted that we take the roses.

It was a warm afternoon, still sultry, but sunnier than it had been in the past few days. The house came into view. The E-type Jaguar was parked beside the empty fountain. I felt uneasy, as if some primitive part of me sensed that we were being watched, as if we might be walking into an ambush. I glanced up at the tower at the far end of the house. My eyes found the windows belonging to Joanna's room, the one under Francis Youlgreave's.

Vanessa said, 'It's quite a drop, isn't it? I wonder if he was killed instantly. I must try the local papers. They must have something in their back files about it.'

'I imagine the Youlgreaves tried to hush it up.'

'Yes, but there'll be something. But of course the big question is what is – or was – in the journals. There may have been a suicide note or something.' She hugged her notebook. 'It's so frustrating.'

Michael watched us as we talked, his eyes flicking from one to the other. He spent most of that summer watching us.

'Hello.' Toby was standing in the path through the shrubbery at the corner of the house. 'Come through this way. I've got chairs down by the pool.'

He was wearing a pair of shorts – cut-off jeans – and nothing else. Even his feet were bare. His hair flowed on either side of his central parting, twin waterfalls of ginger curls. The bones of the shoulders and the ribcage stood out clearly. His body was slighter than I had expected and almost hairless. I remembered then what he usually made it so easy to forget: how young he was.

'Rosemary not with you?'

'She felt she had to work,' Vanessa replied. 'She's got a holiday reading list as long as my arm.'

'Shame.' Toby led us into the shrubbery. 'Joanna sends her apologies, by the way. She's lying down. She woke up with a foul headache, and it's been growing steadily worse.'

Lying down in the room below Francis Youlgreave's. I was both frustrated and relieved. *Thank God she's not here.* Yet while I thought this, my nails were digging into the palms of my hands because I had wanted to see her so badly.

We reached the path beside the terrace. Someone had cut back the grass to an uneven stubble. To our left, the east façade of the house reared up to the sky. We picked our way across the ragged lawn.

'I'm beginning to think we're making a difference here at last,' Toby said. 'I hope we'll be playing croquet by this time next year.'

I doubted it. Among the stubble were molehills and stumps of thistles. Brambles had colonized the former flowerbed beneath the terrace and in places were spreading into the lawn. It struck me then with renewed force what an insanely difficult job Toby had taken on. Surely he was too intelligent not to realize that Roth Park needed an ocean of money poured over it? Or was his belief in his own powers so strong that he had drifted into fantasy? Or was it simply that age had not yet blunted his ambitions, that the never-ending compromises that come with maturity had not yet hit him?

'Gosh,' Michael said, and whistled.

He was a few paces ahead of us and had seen the swimming pool first. Freshly painted, it glowed in its stone-lined hollow. It seemed much larger than it had in its derelict state. The water was clear and blue. The flagstones around the pool had been weeded and swept. The little changing hut with the verandah, where Rosemary and I had sheltered on the afternoon of the storm, gleamed a fresh, clean white in the sunshine. The springboard had either been replaced or re-covered.

'Not bad, eh?' Toby said. 'Take care of the luxuries and the essentials will take care of themselves.'

Near the changing hut was a row of four deckchairs. Beside one of them was the radio, a heavy cut-glass ashtray and a paperback novel.

Vanessa and I made appropriate noises of admiration. Toby

smiled and stretched his arms above his head, reminding me suddenly and incongruously of Lord Peter when he was well fed and pleased with life.

'How would you like to do this?' Toby asked Vanessa. 'Would you like to see the room first or have a swim? Or you might like a cup of tea?'

'I'd like to see the room, please.'

Toby smiled at her. 'I'm afraid there's not much to see. Not unless you're psychic and can decode the vibrations, or whatever psychics do.' He turned to Michael and me. 'Would you like to come?'

I didn't want to see the room again. I did not want to remember my last visit. Besides, if I went up to Francis's room, there was a very real risk that I would bump into Joanna. I could not say that I had seen the room before, because Toby did not know of that visit to Roth Park and my conversation with Joanna. Nor for that matter did Vanessa. I glanced at Michael: he was staring wistfully at the water and that gave me my cue.

'I'll stay here with Michael,' I said. 'Watch him swim.'

Vanessa looked sharply at me.

'It's up to you,' Toby said. 'There're towels in the hut. Are you sure you'll be all right?'

Toby seemed excited, in a hurry to be gone. I even wondered if for some reason he wanted to be alone with Vanessa; but that was ridiculous. The two of them walked towards the house. Michael went into the hut to get changed. I moved one of the deckchairs, the one nearest the pool, into a patch of shade. There was a wet footprint on the slab that had been under the deckchair: a small, bare foot – too small for Toby's so it was almost certainly Joanna's. Presumably she had been out here until a few moments ago. Had she suddenly felt unable to cope with us? Or unable to cope with me?

Michael came out of the hut, suddenly shy in a pair of black swimming trunks. I smiled at him and he darted towards the water. There was a great splash. His head appeared, the hair plastered against his skull.

'What's it like?' I shouted.

'Freezing. It's wonderful.'

He looked younger in the water, less guarded, less self-conscious. He turned away from me and began to swim towards the shallow end of the pool, using a primitive crawl that made a lot of noise for very little return. Watching Michael, I stepped forward to the side of the pool. I heard a noise behind me, half concealed by the splashing. I turned.

Joanna was sitting in the deckchair I had moved from the edge of the pool.

For a second I could not speak. I knew I must look a fool, standing there open-mouthed. Joanna wore a white wrap that came down to her ankles. It was made of fine cotton, or perhaps silk, and there were long splits in the material from the armpits down to the thighs. Underneath the wrap was a green bikini, still damp to judge by the marks on the wrap. She smiled up at me. It was the sort of smile that hints at shared secrets.

'Toby said you were lying down. Is your headache better?'

'I haven't got a headache.' She spread her arms wide, a gesture which made the wrap fall open, revealing the bikini, revealing the high, firm breasts. 'He thought I wasn't in a fit state to receive visitors.'

'Well, I'm glad you're not ill.'

'Come and sit down.'

I glanced back at the pool. Michael had reached the far end and was swimming back to us. Joanna waved to him. There could be no harm in talking to Joanna, I told myself. Michael was our chaperone. Not that we would need one, of course. I sat down beside Joanna and tried not to stare at her. Her voice was slightly slurred and the whites of her eyes were bloodshot. I wondered if she might be on drugs. That might explain why Toby did not want her to meet us.

Her eyes slid towards me and away. 'So Rosemary didn't come?'

'She had to work, I'm afraid. Oxbridge entrance coming up, and she's very tense about that.'

'I think she didn't want to see Toby.'

I didn't say anything. In a sense, I did not want to hear any more.

'I think they had a quarrel,' Joanna went on. 'They were both up here, in the house.'

There was a silence. Then I moistened my lips and said, 'When?'

'On Wednesday. He drove her up to London the day before. But on Wednesday they came here.' The green eyes slid towards me again and this time they did not slide away.

I heard myself saying, 'You don't have to tell me this.'

'I do. I saw her running down the drive afterwards. She was crying.' She bit her lip. 'I don't know. I'm just trying to do what's best. I thought you should know.'

I was not sure whether to believe her. Wild accusations might be no more than a symptom of psychological disturbance. On the other hand, what she had said fitted neatly with what had happened on Wednesday afternoon, and with Vanessa's speculations about why Rosemary had been upset.

'Don't tell Toby I told you.' Joanna's voice was urgent now. 'He'd take it out on me.'

For a few minutes we watched Michael swimming up the pool towards us. He clambered out and ran on to the springboard. He turned to make sure we were watching him and plunged in with an even greater splash than before.

'I'm not like Rosemary.'

Startled, I looked at Joanna. 'I'm sorry. I don't follow.'

She ran a fingernail down her bare forearm. Suddenly she stretched out her hand and touched mine. As if stung, I jerked away from her. We stared at each other.

'Do you understand what I'm saying, David?'

I looked at Michael. He was swimming underwater. I turned back to her. She made no further attempt to touch me, but she leant a little towards me. She was smiling. I wanted to touch her face, her neck, her breasts.

'No,' I muttered.

But she was no longer looking at me. She was looking past me, towards the house.

Vanessa and Toby were walking across the lawn towards us. Vanessa was laughing at something Toby had said. At a distance, they looked much of an age. As a couple she and Toby were far better matched than she and I were.

They came down the steps from the lawn. I stood up. It suddenly occurred to me that we might have been visible from one of the windows of the house. Toby or Vanessa might have seen Joanna touch my hand.

'You sure this is wise?' Toby said to Joanna as he came down the steps from the lawn. 'The sunshine won't do your head much good.'

'I'm feeling much better now.' She sat back in her deckchair, as though resisting any attempt to prise her away from it. She asked Vanessa: 'What did you think of Francis Youlgreave's room?'

'A very lonely place,' Vanessa said.

'With a very long drop from the window,' Toby added dryly. 'What about some tea?'

We drank tea from cracked mugs and ate digestive biscuits from the packet. Michael swam on and on. He gave us all something to look at, a useful activity to fill the silences. There were many silences. The urge to look at Joanna was almost overpowering.

At last it was time for us to go – I was due to take Evensong, at which I would be lucky to have a congregation of more than three people. The Cliffords both came out to the drive to see us off.

'Oh, by the way,' I said to Toby, 'I had a word with Audrey Oliphant after church this morning. She'd be delighted if you could do some fortune-telling at the fete.'

'Madam Mysterioso. Your fate is in her hands.' He grinned. 'And indeed your fete, if you'll excuse the pun.'

Michael got the joke and burst out laughing.

'She'll have a word with you about the details during the week,' I said. 'It's very kind of you.'

Joanna was standing just behind her brother and I could not help seeing her face when I said the word 'kind'. Her eyebrows lifted. It was as if she had whispered in my ear: *Kind? You must be joking.*

We said goodbye and walked down the drive.

'Was it worth it?' I asked Vanessa. 'Have you learnt anything?'

'Nothing concrete. But it's odd. Being in that room, looking out of those windows – it was as if I was suddenly much closer to him. As if I knew him slightly before and now knew him much better. I know that sounds fanciful, but that's how I feel.'

'I understand.' I felt rather the same about Joanna.

'What was the water like?' Vanessa asked Michael; and for the rest of the way we talked about the swimming pool.

When I opened the front door of the Vicarage, the first thing that greeted me was the smell of alcohol. We went into the sitting room. Rosemary was dozing on the sofa with the television on at a deafening volume. On the table beside her was a bottle of sweet sherry, almost empty.

The following day was Monday the 24th August. Lady Youlgreave's funeral was in the afternoon. Doris Potter was there, of course, and so were Audrey Oliphant and Nick Deakin. There were half a dozen others – all female, all elderly, some of whom I did not know. There is nothing like a funeral for flushing out unfamiliar faces. Apart from Deakin, no one came to represent the family.

No one, that is, apart from the dogs. Doris had asked me if she might bring Beauty and Beast into the church. It was a bizarre request and, had someone else made it, I would probably have refused. They sprawled on the floor at the west end of the church, at the foot of the font. Doris sat beside them. Beauty snored occasionally, but apart from that I would not have known they were there. Afterwards, the only sign of their presence was a large puddle where they had lain. Doris's husband loaded them into his car and drove them away, back to their new home in the little house on Manor Farm Lane.

Doris, Deakin and I went with the coffin to the crematorium. Audrey conducted the other mourners over the road to the church hall. When we joined them later, we found them sipping tea and talking in whispers. It was one of the quietest, saddest funerals I could remember taking.

After it was over, Audrey wanted to complain to me about the behaviour of the dogs in the church. I managed to escape from her. I felt I needed air, as though I were suffocating. On my way home I met Mary Vintner. She wanted to ask me about the funeral but I muttered an excuse and brushed past her.

I knew I should go back to the Vicarage. I had letters to write, phone calls to make, and Audrey had been pestering me for my monthly contribution to the parish magazine. Over the last week or so, I had allowed work to pile up. The business of running a parish seemed unbearably tedious. There was nothing new in that. What was new was my inability to ignore the tedium and get down to the job.

On impulse, I turned into the gates of Roth Park. Once I was past the church, I turned right, following the route that Rosemary had taken me on the day that she had found the fur and the blood in Carter's Meadow. I had the curious sensation that everything was out of my hands now, that it was too late for me to intervene in the course of events.

It was almost with relief that, a moment later, I saw Joanna coming towards me down the path from Carter's Meadow. She was wearing the green dress I had seen her in before, and sandals. When she saw me, she broke into a run. I held out my arms and she walked into them, as naturally as if she had been doing so for years. Her body was firm and warm. She slipped her arms around my waist.

For a while we stood there, not moving. A devil within me said, *It's all right, there's nothing sexual in this, you are comforting a friend, a parishioner*. If I allowed the situation to develop, yes, I would move towards mortal sin and I would no longer be fit to be a priest. But that would not happen. There was nothing to worry about. Joanna's feeling for me must be purely filial, the orphan's desire to replace a lost father. It would be sheer vanity on my part to suppose otherwise. My friendly devil obligingly pointed out: *How can anything so sweet be bad?*

'David, look at me.'

I looked down into Joanna's eyes, green and dark-rimmed. I opened my mouth to say something but she shook her head.

'Kiss me,' she said. '*Please.*'

I bent my head and obeyed.

29

There was a kind of madness in the air that summer, spreading like a disease, infecting first one person and then another, until the final weekend in August. That does not excuse what I did. Out of all of us, I was the one who should have known better. I was the one who could have prevented it.

The first time I kissed Joanna was late in the afternoon of Monday, 24th August – the day of Lady Youlgreave's funeral; the church fete was the following Saturday. After the kiss, we stood there, neither moving nor speaking for at least a minute. Suddenly she pushed me away from her. Her nipples were erect under the thin material of her dress. And she had had an effect on my body, too.

'I'm sorry,' I blurted out. 'I should never –'

'It's not that,' she whispered. 'Someone's coming.'

She was looking behind me. I turned. There were two small figures among the oak trees near the drive. Michael and Brian Vintner had their backs to us. Michael seemed to be pointing to something down by the river.

'They didn't see us,' Joanna said. 'I'm sure.'

'I must go.'

She stared at me. 'I don't want you to go.'

'I'm a married man, a priest.' My tongue stumbled. 'It's out of the question. I should never have –'

'I've wanted to touch you for ages. Almost since we met. It wasn't the first time, when you came to the house to talk about the fete. I didn't know what to make of you then. It was the time after that – do you remember?'

I remembered.

'I was in the church,' she went on. 'Everything was so quiet, I thought I was going to go mad. And I had this feeling someone was watching me, someone nasty. And then you came in, and everything was all right.'

'But everything isn't all right. I must go now.'

'I wish you wouldn't. I've never met anyone like you.'

'I must go.' But I did not move away.

The boys were walking away from us, towards the river. A moment later, they were out of sight.

'I need your help,' she said.

'Why?'

'Because of Toby. Because – oh *hell*. There's someone else coming.'

She was looking in the opposite direction – towards the path to Carter's Meadow. The remains of a hedge ran along what had been the eastern boundary of the meadow. Someone was walking along behind it – slowly, head bowed, as if looking for something. It was Audrey.

'Please,' Joanna said. 'I need to talk to you.'

Without warning, she darted away, aiming for the drive at a point nearer the house than the oak trees. I glanced back at Audrey. She still had not seen me – or so I hoped. I began to walk – almost to run – towards the gate from Roth Park into the churchyard.

I slipped inside the church. It still smelled of the funeral – of flowers and recently extinguished candles. I walked up to the chancel and sat down in my stall in the choir. I lifted my eyes, trying to pray, and instead saw the memorial tablet of Francis Youlgreave. His mortal remains lay somewhere beneath my feet. But for an instant it was as if he were with me in the church, a dark shape leaning against the whitewashed wall beneath his own memorial. I thought he was laughing at me.

'Is this your fault?' I heard myself saying.

There was no answer. How could there be? I was the only person in the church. There was nothing and no one beneath the tablet, not even a shadow. *Is this your fault?* A faint, mocking echo of the words floated in the still air. The question twisted like a snake that bites its tail: and for an instant I thought someone else had spoken the words – *Is this your fault?* – and that the question was directed at me.

'Not me,' I said aloud. *'Francis?'*

Francis Youlgreave was the thread, almost invisible, that bound us. I came to Roth, all those years ago, because of him. Vanessa's original interest in me was sparked by the fact that I lived in the place where Francis Youlgreave had died. Lady Youlgreave had provided fuel to feed the fire. Now Lady Youlgreave was dead, gnawed by her pets. Francis Youlgreave had mutilated animals, and Audrey's Lord Peter had been mutilated in his turn. Vanessa was increasingly determined to write his biography. And I – there was no point in trying to fool myself – was in love with a young woman who lived in Francis Youlgreave's family home and thought she heard his footsteps in the room above hers at night.

Sitting there in the empty church, I felt a coldness creeping over me. There was no pattern in this, or none that I could discern. Where were we going? Where would this end? On the edge of my range of vision, the marble tablet stared down like a blank white face.

I was not going mad, I told myself. True, I was under considerable stress. There was a great deal to worry about. But I was not going mad. What I needed now was a little peace in which to pray for guidance, to work out how best to deal with the situation. I closed my eyes and tried to focus inwardly.

There was a crack of metal on metal followed by a long creak. Someone was at the south door. Hastily I stood up. I picked up a hymnal and pretended to leaf through it.

Audrey came into the church. She had changed from the black dress she had worn for Lady Youlgreave's funeral, and was now wearing a blouse and skirt. She saw me and advanced up the nave.

'I thought I might find you here. I'm not interrupting, I hope?'

I tried to smile. I was terrified that she had seen me with Joanna.

'I felt I had to show you this right away. I was walking in the park just now and I happened to be near where Rosemary found the fur and the blood. And I saw something in the hedge.'

She held out what looked like a piece of rust-stained rag. I reached out to take it but she pulled her hand back. 'Better not. The police may need to send it for analysis.'

'What is it?'

'It's a handkerchief,' Audrey said. 'And it's stained with blood. A pound to a penny it's Lord Peter's blood. The vet should be able to tell us.' She looked up at me, and suddenly her eyes were wary. 'But first there's something you should know. Look.'

Once again she held out the handkerchief. She took one of the hems in both hands and pulled it apart so the material became flat. The rusty stains could easily be blood. There were other stains, grass, perhaps, and mud. Audrey clicked her tongue against the roof of her mouth as she ran the hem of the handkerchief through her fingers. She was looking for something. Then she found it.

She held up the handkerchief to me, closer and closer until it was a few inches from my eyes. I took a step backwards to bring it into focus. A tape had been sewn to the hem. Scarlet capitals trembled, then steadied into a name: M. D. H. APPLEYARD.

'If you don't talk to Rosemary,' Vanessa said, 'I will. Someone's got to.'

'You don't think we should let sleeping dogs lie?' I suggested. 'She's already paid the price.'

'If you drink more than half a bottle of sherry, of course you're going to feel awful. But only for a few hours. The thing is, we need to have a word with her so she understands very clearly that we don't approve of that sort of behaviour.'

'There must be a reason for it.'

'I'm sure there is. Probably this wretched squabble with Toby Clifford. Or perhaps it's the A level results not being quite as brilliant as she would have liked. But that's neither here nor there. In any event, we need to say something. And you're her father, so you're the best person to do it.'

'All right. You've made your point.'

Then the silence grew between us again. We were in the kitchen, just the two of us, washing up after supper. Michael had gone to bed, and Rosemary was in her bedroom, technically working. She seemed none the worse for drinking herself into a stupor yesterday afternoon.

Afterwards I went wearily upstairs. Michael was reading in bed and we waved to one another through the open door of his room. It had taken me more than half an hour to persuade Audrey that the bloodstained handkerchief was not incontrovertible evidence of his guilt. She was still determined to consult the vet, to see if he could identify the stain as cat's blood, compatible with Lord Peter's; I could not change her mind about that.

Everything was irritating me this evening. Vanessa had spent most of supper talking about her intention of writing to Lady Youlgreave's heir to see if she could continue her researches into the family papers. I wished that Doris Potter had thrown the lot away.

All I wanted to do was lie down and close my eyes. Not to find refuge in sleep: I knew I would see Joanna's face, and I knew that I would relive what had happened this afternoon in Roth Park. I had to remember what had happened, I told myself, if only to decide what to do about it. I was lying to myself – I wanted to remember because to do so brought me a blend of pain and pleasure that I could not do without.

I tapped on the door of Rosemary's room. There was no answer.

'Rosemary?' I murmured, keeping my voice low because of Michael. 'May I come in?'

There were footsteps on the other side of the door, destroying my hope that she might be asleep. The key turned in the lock and the door opened. Her hair was pulled back from her scrubbed face and she wore a long dressing gown.

'What is it?'

'May I come in?' I said again. 'I'd like a word. We can't talk on the landing.'

Rosemary hesitated for a second and then opened the door more widely. The room was very neat and, apart from the books, impersonal, as though in a hotel. She sat down on the bed, her back straight, her knees close together. I took the chair in front of the table by the window.

The window was open and there was enough light to see

across the garden to the trees of Roth Park. It was much quieter than at the front of the house where Vanessa and I slept. I looked at the trees and thought: *Beyond the oaks is the little hill, and beyond the little hill is the house, and at the far end of the house is the tower, and in the tower is Joanna. I love you.* I wanted to fire the thought like an arrow through her window.

I turned back to look at Rosemary. Her face was as blank as Francis Youlgreave's marble tablet. She wasn't looking at me but at the cover of a book that lay beside her on the bed. It looked familiar; and a second later I recognized it: Vanessa's copy of *The Four Last Things*, the collection of poems which included 'The Judgement of Strangers'. I wondered if Vanessa knew that Rosemary had borrowed it.

'It's about yesterday,' I said.

Rosemary gave no sign that she had heard.

'When we came back from the Cliffords', you were flat-out on the sofa with a bottle of sherry beside you. Or what was left of it.'

Still she said nothing.

'I presume you'd drunk quite a lot of it, and that's why you fell asleep.' I waited, but she neither confirmed nor denied what I had said. 'It's not that we mind you having the occasional drink but –'

'*We*. I wish you wouldn't keep saying *we*.'

'Vanessa's your stepmother. She cares about you very much, as do I. I don't know if you drank all that sherry because you were unhappy, but take it from me that alcohol doesn't dissolve unhappiness.'

That at least earned a reaction. Rosemary raised her head and stared directly at me, her eyes brilliant. 'Audrey thinks it does,' she said. 'When I saw her the other evening' – Rosemary paused for effect – 'she was as pissed as a newt.'

I stared at her. 'I don't like you speaking like that about anyone, let alone a friend such as Audrey.'

'She's not a friend of yours. You hate her. You take everything she gives you, all the help with the church, but really you think she's an embarrassment.'

'Don't be silly.' But there was enough truth in what Rosemary said to make me feel even more uncomfortable than I already

498

was. I wondered too if she really had seen Audrey drunk. Audrey had always liked her glass of sherry, but recently she had been drinking rather more than usual.

'You laugh at her,' Rosemary said softly. 'As if she's just a bad joke.'

'That's absurd. In any case, I've not come here to talk about Audrey. I've come here to talk about you.'

'But I don't want to talk about me. There's nothing to say.'

'Darling, I know life seems hard sometimes. But it will get better. I know your results weren't quite as good as you wanted, but it doesn't really matter.'

She turned her head away from me.

'Your results are more than adequate. Anyway, as far as Oxford is concerned, it's the entrance exam that counts. That and the interview.'

Her head was lowered. With a fingertip she traced an invisible spiral on the cover of The Four Last Things.

I wondered whether to mention Toby. Better not – Rosemary wouldn't thank me for breaching her privacy. I persevered for a few more minutes, trying to encourage her to respond to me, but got nowhere. She needed help, I knew, but I could not find a way to give it to her. Another failure; and the fact that this failure concerned my own daughter made it worse. When I left I kissed the top of her head. She opened the book and began to read.

I closed the door softly and went across the landing to Michael's room. Rosemary and I had kept our voices low automatically – as one had to in this house – but I wondered if he'd heard anything. He was still sitting up in bed.

'Good book?'

'Yes.' He marked his place with a finger. 'Agatha Christie. Five Little Pigs. But I think I know who did it, and I'm only a third of the way through.'

I perched on the end of the bed and for a few minutes we talked about Agatha Christie. 'By the way,' I said as I was leaving, 'Miss Oliphant found one of your handkerchiefs this afternoon.'

'Where?'

'In the park.'

'I expect it was down by the river. We usually go there.'

'No – it was on the other side. Between the Cliffords' garden and the council estate.'

Michael looked sharply at me. 'In Carter's Meadow? Where Rosemary found the fur and blood?'

I nodded.

'Well, I don't know what it was doing there,' he said carefully.

'Not to worry. Anyway, I expect Miss Oliphant will give it back to you soon.' I cast around for a reason for the delay. 'I wouldn't be surprised if she wants to wash it first.'

Michael smiled politely at me. He looked vulnerable in his pyjamas, and younger than he was. I would have liked to give him a hug, as I used to do when he was much younger, but I was afraid of embarrassing him.

I said good night and went downstairs to report my failure with Rosemary to Vanessa. On the way down, I thought that a bloodstained handkerchief was just the sort of clue you would expect to find in an Agatha Christie novel. But if Agatha Christie presented you with a handkerchief marked with the name of the suspect, you knew it was probably a false clue. And you also knew that when you had found the person who had planted the false clue, you had almost certainly found the criminal.

30

After breakfast on Tuesday, I went across the road to buy cigarettes at Malik's Minimarket. Audrey and two other women were talking to Mr Malik, their heads nodding together over the counter. When I came in there was a lull in the conversation.

'David!' Audrey cried. 'And how are you this morning? Bright and breezy?'

'Fine, thank you.' I noticed that the other women had turned aside to study a poster advertising a new brand of instant coffee. 'And how are you?'

Audrey smiled bravely. 'As well as can be expected. Now – you go first.' She opened her handbag and peered inside. 'I'm looking for my shopping list.'

I asked for a packet of Players No 6.

'So Mrs Potter is now a landowner.' Mr Malik grinned at me as he gave me my change. 'To be sure, I shall be treating her very respectfully in future.'

'Carter's Meadow,' Audrey said at my elbow. 'At least two acres. It does seem a little odd. After all, when all's said and done, Doris was only the charwoman. Still, Lady Youlgreave wasn't really herself in the last few years, was she? When I think what she was like before the war . . . Of course, I'm sure we're all delighted for Doris, but I wouldn't be surprised if she finds it a bit of a white elephant.'

I smiled and said goodbye. To my dismay, Audrey followed me out of the shop.

'You'd think she'd have had the decency to leave something to the church, wouldn't you? After all, she was the patron of the living.'

'We'll survive without it.'

'And singling out Doris in that way – really most peculiar. And have you heard that she's taken in those dreadful dogs? After what they did to Lady Youlgreave! I was never so shocked in my life. Not a very *sensitive* thing to do.'

I looked at my watch. 'You must excuse me.'

Audrey laid a hand on my sleeve. 'Just one more thing. No, I tell a lie – two. I phoned the vet, but unfortunately he's on holiday. So we'll have to wait until next week until he can run the tests.'

'Do you really think it's necessary? I had a word with Michael last night, and I'm sure he had nothing to do with Lord Peter.'

Audrey looked at me, and her look said, *You would think that, wouldn't you?* She rushed on, 'The other thing, of course, is the fete. Toby Clifford rang up this morning. So nice and friendly. We're going to add fortune-telling to our advertisement in the paper. And if you agree, we thought we'd put his tent beyond the books and the home-made cakes and jam. Right in the corner of the garden. I think there'll be enough room if we move the white elephants along a little. Rather a squeeze, perhaps, but I'm sure we all agree that Toby's well worth a little inconvenience.'

'I'm sure he'll be wonderful –'

'I must fly. Such a lot to do. If I'm not there to chivvy her, Charlene works at a snail's pace.'

With a wave of her hand, and a whiff of cologne and body odour, Audrey was gone. I turned to cross the road. I was just in time to see Joanna emerging from the drive of Roth Park.

At that moment, a heavily laden gravel lorry rumbled slowly down the main road, shielding Joanna from me. I waited outside Malik's Minimarket. Thoughts chased across my mind at breakneck speed during the tiny patch of time while the lorry blocked my view of her. Perhaps she would not be there when the lorry had passed. Perhaps I wanted to see her so badly that I had imagined her. Or I had projected her appearance on to some other young woman. Or Joanna had been real; but she would have glimpsed me and, embarrassed and mortified by the memory of what had happened yesterday, she would have ducked back into the drive to avoid meeting me or even seeing me. And, of course, it was quite out of the question that I should talk to her or have anything to do with her at all. A lover's logic is as elaborately fantastic as a schizophrenic's.

The lorry rolled over the bridge. Joanna was still standing in the mouth of the drive. She waved to me. No, she *beckoned* me.

At that moment there was a gap in the traffic and she darted over the road to the green. I crossed to the green myself and we walked slowly towards each other over the scrubby, litter-strewn grass. Her hair bounced on her shoulders as if endowed with separate life. I wanted to break into a run and put my arms around her. When only two or three yards were between us, we both stopped.

'I hoped you'd be here,' she said. 'I hoped you'd be early. I couldn't stop thinking of you.'

'We mustn't – someone might see.'

'What is there to see?' She smiled at me. 'We're neighbours.' The smile twisted and slipped away. 'We *mingle* with each other socially.'

'The family at the Vicarage and the family at the big house,' I said wildly. 'Just like a Jane Austen novel.'

'I want to kiss you again.'

'Joanna –'

'And we need to talk.'

I felt as though she were older than I. Not that it really mattered, in one sense. When you are in love, your respective ages shrivel into irrelevance.

'I'm worried,' she murmured. 'Not just about us. It's Toby.'

'What's he been doing?'

'Cooee!'

I turned round. Audrey was standing at the gate of Tudor Cottage. She waved vigorously at us.

'Cooee! Miss Clifford! Can you spare a moment? It's about the parking for the fete.'

'Coming,' Joanna called. In a lower voice, she said to me, 'I'll come out for a walk at about eight this evening. No, let's make it nine – it'll be beginning to get dark. I'll be on the drive, or near it, or perhaps in the churchyard. Please come if you can.' She lifted her face, full of pleading, towards mine. '*David*.'

She waved casually at me and set off across the green towards Audrey. I remembered to wave to Audrey. My hand was trembling.

I walked back to the Vicarage, narrowly escaping a collision with a speeding Ford Capri, and went into my study. I sat down and put my head in my hands.

There was a dreadful irony about all this. I had married Vanessa for the comforts of friendship and sex. Especially sex. But sex with Vanessa had become like the jam in *Through the Looking-Glass*, perpetually retreating into the past and the future. Now something far worse had happened: I wanted to make love with a woman who was young enough to be my daughter. I could cope, after a fashion, with that – after all, I had had plenty of practice at suppressing that particular urge in the last decade.

Sex was not the real problem. When I married Vanessa, I had thought in my arrogance that love in the adolescent sense – as a romantic prelude to the biological necessities of mating and procreation – belonged to a stage of my life which I had left behind in Rosington. So Providence had sent Joanna Clifford into my life.

Providence had decided I should fall in love with her. And what did Providence intend me to do about it?

'Wonderful news.' Vanessa had just returned from work, and was leaning against the jamb of the study doorway. 'I went to see Nick Deakin today, and really he couldn't have been nicer.'

'You talked about the papers?'

She came into the room and dropped her briefcase on a chair.

'Apparently old Mr Youlgreave phoned from Cape Town, about something completely different. But Nick mentioned that I was working on the family papers, and asked if he would mind me continuing. And Mr Youlgreave – his name's Frank, by the way; I wonder if Francis is a family name? – said I was welcome to carry on if Mr Deakin could vouch for me, which of course he did, bless him. He – Frank Youlgreave, I mean – wants me to send him a sort of *catalogue raisonné* of what's there, and then we'll talk about what we do next.'

Vanessa's face was pink, the flush spreading to the roots of her hair; and the excitement bubbled almost visibly out of her. I thought, without particular sadness, if only I could have made her do that; not that it mattered now.

'And I've actually got them here. I've got the tin box in the boot of the car. I can't believe it. Nick said it was a bit irregular, but seeing as the new owner had given me permission, and seeing that I was a vicar's wife, he thought it would be all right. Such a sweetie.'

'Do you know what's missing yet?'

She shook her head. 'I've not had time to have a proper look. Would you mind if we ate early this evening? I'd like to make a start after supper.'

Of course I didn't mind. That is another thing that love can do: it turns its victims into conspirators.

'On my way home I went to the Central Library. Did you know they've got a back file of the *Courier*? All the way back to eighteen-eighty-six.' She stared at her hands. 'My fingers are filthy.'

'The report on the inquest?'

She nodded. 'Took me ages to find it. Officially it was an accident. During the night Francis fell from the window of his room. He landed near the fountain.'

'So it must have been the east window?'

'I suppose so. It was a very hot night, and he hadn't been well. A maid found the body in the morning. The coroner sent his condolences to the family and warned about the danger of leaning too far out of the window. Not a hint of suicide.'

No hint of angels, either?

'"The distinguished poet," the *Courier* called him. "Formerly a Canon of Rosington until ill health forced him to retire."' Vanessa picked up her briefcase. 'Supper in about half an hour?'

She left me alone with the ghost of Joanna. I smoked and looked out of the window. Ronald Trask phoned to ask if I had finished compiling my parish statistics, which were several weeks overdue. I told him I was working on them. He wanted to discuss how I intended to implement his latest brainchild, the Diocesan Ecumenical Initiative, but I put him off by leading him to believe that I had a visitor with me. Indeed I had: the ghost of Joanna.

Eventually Michael came to tell me that supper was ready. The four of us had a hurried meal of baked beans, toast and cheese. I seemed to have mislaid my appetite. Michael and I washed up while Rosemary made coffee.

Everyone made it easy for me. Vanessa wanted to examine the Youlgreave papers. Rosemary went upstairs to work in her bedroom. Michael asked if he might listen to a programme on Radio Luxembourg while he wrote to his parents.

At ten to eight I went into the sitting room. Vanessa was at her desk with the black box on a little table by her chair. She was working her way through a bundle of letters and making notes on a sheet of foolscap.

'I'll lock the church,' I said, trying to make my voice sound casual. 'Then I might make one or two parish calls.'

The pen continued to travel over the paper. 'OK.'

'I'm not quite sure how long I'll be.'

Vanessa unfolded another sheet of paper. 'I'll expect you when I see you.' Suddenly she looked up. 'You don't mind me doing this, do you?'

'Of course not.' I forced a smile. 'Have fun.'

'I've already found a holograph poem that's not in any of the collections. It's called "The Office of the Dead" – undated but middle-to-late period, I think; probably Rosington.'

'You're really enjoying this, aren't you? I'm so glad.'

She reached out and touched my hand. 'You are good to me. I know we don't get much time together. I feel guilty.'

'But you mustn't feel guilty. Please don't.'

Guilt was my prerogative, not hers. Besides, I wanted Vanessa to be happy. And I also wanted Joanna. I said goodbye and left the house. Feeling like a truant sneaking out of school, I walked through the garden and through the gate to the churchyard. I followed the path that skirted the east end of the church. Absurdly superstitious, I averted my eyes from the steps leading down to the Youlgreave vault.

What if Francis is down there, watching me?

I let myself into the church by the south door. I made a circuit of the inside of the building rather more quickly than usual. I found that I did not want to let my eyes linger on certain objects – on the cross on the high altar, for example, on the smoky colours and swirling shapes of the Last Judgement panel painting, and on the moonface of Francis Youlgreave's memorial tablet.

As I returned to the south door, I thought, quite dispassionately, that my behaviour was abnormal; I might well be on the verge of a nervous breakdown. I should go and see somebody about it, preferably Peter Hudson when he returned from Crete. Not yet, though; I was not ready to share my possible nervous breakdown with anyone except Joanna. But should Joanna be considered as its cause or its effect?

I locked the door behind me and walked slowly through the churchyard. I looked at my watch. It was ten past eight. I was fifty minutes early. I did not mind. There was pleasure even in being alone and being able to think of her.

I passed through the gate from the churchyard into the grounds of Roth Park. It was cool under the oaks and noticeably darker than in the churchyard. The sky was cloudy. I stopped for a moment and waited, looking around. This was, after all, a public place. People walked their dogs along the footpaths. Children played here. Adolescents found other pleasures. For all I knew, Audrey had chosen this evening to mount another detective expedition into the grounds of Roth Park. The need to be furtive heightened my pleasure.

I looked at my watch again. Another forty-five minutes, assuming Joanna was on time. I knew nothing about her, I realized – not even whether she was the sort of woman who was usually early or late. I patted the pockets of my jacket, looking for cigarettes.

At that moment, Joanna slipped from behind the trunk of an oak tree fifty yards away from me. She wore a long, pale-coloured dress which swayed as she walked and glowed against the greens of the leaves and the grass and the brown of the trees. She saw me and began to walk towards me. Faster and faster she came. I held out my hands to her and, at long last, I felt the touch of her fingers on mine.

31

Love is a form of haunting, and Joanna was my ghost.

I knew the terrible danger I was in – both socially and, far more importantly, spiritually. I ran the risk of hurting all those I loved. I was wantonly endangering the happiness of Vanessa and Rosemary. The feelings that Joanna and I shared had no future. We had very little in common.

I also knew that, even if I had the power to rewrite the immediate past and to prevent what was happening now, I would not choose to exercise it.

Joanna and I packed a great deal into that week, into a handful of meetings.

'You're early,' she said on Tuesday evening, still holding my hands in hers.

I was so happy I could not stop smiling. 'So are you.'

'Toby's out.'

'When will he be back?'

She glanced to her right, towards the drive. 'I don't know. He didn't say.' Her fingers tightened on mine. 'I think someone's coming.'

We snatched our hands apart. For a moment we listened. I heard traffic on the road and a distant burst of laughter, perhaps from one of the televisions in Vicarage Drive.

'It's no one,' I said.

'Come into the garden.'

'But if Toby –'

'We'll hear the car on the drive.' She smiled at me. 'Trust me.'

She led me through the oaks and up the drive towards the

house. We cut through the shrubbery on to the lawn. As we came on to the grass, she took my hand.

'We can go into the house if you like.'

I felt a shiver running through me. Fear and desire, inextricably mingled. 'We'd better not.'

'Then let's go down to the pool.'

Hand in hand, we walked quickly across the lawn. The pool was a good choice. It was masked by trees and set lower than the surrounding garden. We could hear and not be seen. If need be, if someone came from the house, I could slip away through the fence into Carter's Meadow. Conspirators plan ahead.

We sat on one of the benches recessed into the stone wall around the pool. The stone was warm to the touch. The evening sun slanted across the swaying waters of the pool, creating shifting black stains of shadow against the clear blue of the water. A passenger jet flew overhead and Joanna covered her ears with her hands and pushed her face against my shoulder. Slowly the sound diminished and silence flooded back. She reached up, cupped the back of my head with her hand, and pulled my face towards hers. With my free hand I stroked her arm. Without moving her mouth, she took my hand and placed it over her breast.

I pulled away from her. I was trembling like a man with a fever. 'I can't do this.'

Her face was flushed and smiling. Suddenly she kissed me again. This time her tongue darted into my mouth and flicked to and fro like the tail of a landed fish. Despite myself I responded.

Afterwards she said, 'I've wanted to do that since I met you in church.'

'You were in there when I came to lock up. You said you couldn't get used to the quiet here.'

At that moment another aeroplane went over our heads. We looked at each other and started to laugh.

'Do you remember when we found that cat?' she asked. 'You put your arms around me.'

'I remember.'

Joanna's hands were under my jacket now, exploring and stroking my body like two small animals. Suddenly the hands stopped moving. She pulled her face away and looked up at me.

'We mustn't let Toby find out.'

'We mustn't let anyone find out.'

'No, you don't understand. If Toby finds out, he'll use the knowledge.'

'How?' I tried to smile. 'Blackmail?'

I had intended the suggestion as a joke. But Joanna nodded.

'He'll be out of luck,' I said. 'I haven't any money.'

'He'd find something else you could give him. Or do for him.'

'You make him sound like a monster.'

Joanna said nothing. She looked away from me and stared into the dappled surface of the pool.

'Joanna,' I whispered; even saying her name was a pleasure, intensified because the pleasure was touched with pain.

'He's my brother.' She spoke to my chest; she would not look at me. 'I've known him all my life. But I don't know *why* he's like he is. All I know is *what* he is.' She swallowed. 'How do you think he got that car? His precious bloody Jaguar?'

A rich boy's toy. 'Tell me.'

'He was dealing. Not dope, or acid, or even speed. I could have handled that. He was dealing heroin. He was going out with a girl called Annabel. Poor little rich girl. Her dad gave her everything, including the E-type. Toby got her into heroin, I'm sure of that. Then he started using her as his front for the dealing. She had a flat at the back of Harrods. He was very clever. When the police began prowling around, everything led to her not him. They busted her. They could have done her for dealing, but the father could afford a good barrister. Toby's name just didn't come into it. In the end they did her for possession, instead, and now she's in a nursing home in Switzerland. She worshipped Toby, you know. Still does, I expect. She told him he could use the car while she was gone.'

'And you?'

She stirred in my arms and looked up at me. 'What?'

'Do you use drugs?'

'Nothing you need worry about.'

'What about you and Toby? Why are you together? Why did

you buy this house with him?' I hesitated and added a further question, one that bubbled up unexpectedly, surprising me perhaps more than her. 'And why are you so scared of him?'

Joanna did not reply. My lips brushed her hair. She was breathing rapidly and shallowly. A small black ant scurried along the stone bench and climbed rapidly up to the top of my left thigh. It ran down to my left knee. It stared over the swimming pool like stout Cortez over the Pacific. Suddenly it turned through 360 degrees as if searching for its fellows. Finally it plunged over my kneecap and ran down the shin to the unknown territory of my foot and the paving slabs beyond. Like myself, the ant had gone too far to turn back.

'Joanna? Why?'

I wanted to say that I loved her so much that I had a right to know, but I felt that that would be putting unfair pressure on her. She raised her head and stared at me with those green-brown eyes, wide and innocent. Her lips parted but, instead of speaking, she pulled my mouth down on hers.

While we were kissing, we heard the dark throb of the Jaguar's engine on the drive.

For the rest of the week, time behaved capriciously, sprinting and crawling by turns. Joanna and I managed to meet every day, usually in the evening. On Wednesday, we went to the cinema in Richmond. I cannot remember what the film was. We bought tickets separately and met in the darkness. We sat side by side, unable to speak, our fingers exploring each other. Afterwards we left separately, just before the lights came on. I had parked in a side road near the green and Joanna joined me in the car. While we were kissing, I thought how easy it would be for a policeman to pass by and shine a torch into the car; how easy for a colleague or parishioner to recognize the car and come over to talk to me.

Joanna pulled slightly away from me. 'I want all of you. I want you inside me.'

'No. That's impossible.'

'I'm not a virgin, you know. Not since I was sixteen.'

I wanted to ask about those nameless lovers she had known before.

'I wish you were my first,' she went on. 'I've never felt like that before.'

I kissed her again.

A few minutes later she returned to the subject: 'So why don't we make love properly?'

Why not indeed? 'Not yet,' I managed to say.

'But why? You want me.' Her hand was working between my legs and I could hardly deny what my body made so clear. 'I don't care where. We can do it here if you like. Now.'

'No.'

'Why not?'

'Because . . .' For me, I knew, penetration would be the final step, the point of no return. I had surrendered so much else but I was not – illogically but powerfully – prepared to surrender that. 'I'm not ready. Just give me a little time.'

'That's the one thing we don't have.'

'One of several things we don't have, actually.'

Joanna giggled. 'I love you.' Her hand began more vigorous operations. 'Still –'

'Yes,' I said faintly. 'There are other possibilities.'

She lowered her head over me. I stroked her hair.

All this should have been squalid, even ridiculous. Many people would have used worse words, and perhaps they would have been right. There are few defences left for a married, middle-aged clergyman who furtively exchanges sexual favours with a vulnerable young woman in a variety of undignified and uncomfortable situations.

I thirsted for Joanna as, at other times, I had thirsted for God. Discomfort, guilt, fear of discovery, lack of time – everything fed whatever emotion bound us together. It was not merely lust, because lust is straightforward and this was not; and lust can be satisfied, at least briefly, and this never was. Obsession? No, because that is entirely selfish and neither of us wished solely to take from the other – we also wished to give. What else was left? Only love, that vague and much-maligned word: a love that embraced lust and obsession.

During that month, I skimped and neglected the religious framework of my life, the framework that had sustained me for so long. I was afraid of God. I felt as though I were in the

Garden of Eden but had no right to be there, and at any moment the order for my expulsion would come. Nor did I have time for Him. There was no longer enough room in my life.

There was little room for anything except Joanna. My in-tray filled up with unanswered letters and unpaid bills. The pad by the telephone filled with messages asking me to phone people I did not want to phone.

On Thursday I invented an attack of flu to avoid a diocesan meeting, a lie which gave us five whole hours in the afternoon and early evening. Joanna and I drove down to Hampshire, parked the car in a lay-by and followed a footpath into a wood. We left the footpath and followed tracks made by small animals until we came to a little clearing in a hollow. I laid out the rug from the car. Then, for the first time, I saw Joanna naked.

Despite everything that happened later, that afternoon glows in my mind. Sunlight trickled down through the leaves, casting shifting patterns on our bodies. I had never known such pleasure, such excitement, such happiness. Morally, I knew, avoiding penetration was a mere quibble – my guilt was already absolute. But I clung to the quibble as if it meant something, like a man holding a life belt in the face of a tidal wave.

What happened did not feel squalid: it felt inevitable, sad, guilt-ridden and wonderful. We knew that there would be a price to pay; and there was. But neither of us could have known how high that price would be.

32

Even Vanessa, at work during the day and immersed in the
Youlgreave papers during the evening, noticed that something
had changed.

'Did you have a good meeting?' she asked, as I got into bed
on Thursday evening.

'The usual sort of thing.'

She smiled at me. 'Except that it went on for even longer than
usual. Still, you seem quite cheerful about it.'

'I've known worse.' I was appalled by my automatic hypocrisy,
by my careful choice of words designed to avoid an actual lie.

'I forgot to tell you: Mary Vintner phoned. James wants to do
the barbecue on the paved bit outside our kitchen window. Is
that all right?'

'Do you mind?'

'Not if I don't have to do it. She said they'll bring everything,
including food to cook, and she'll make sure he clears up
afterwards.' She sniffed. 'You smell nice.'

'I rather overdid the talcum powder, I'm afraid.' It had worried
me that Vanessa might smell Joanna on me so I had taken
precautions.

'I like it. You've been very busy this week. We've hardly seen
each other.'

'Sometimes it's like that. Parish life tends to be unpredictable.
You've been fairly busy yourself. How's it going?'

'With Francis?' Vanessa sat down at the dressing table and
began to brush her hair; once I had loved watching her at
this nightly ritual. 'Rather well, actually. I've nearly finished
cataloguing what's there.'

'Have you read everything?'

'Not really. Just enough to get an idea of the contents. His handwriting was appalling, and as he grew older it got worse. You remember that poem I found?'

'"The Office of the Dead"?'

'Yes – I've still not been able to decipher it all. And there's another complication – the spirit regularly moved him to write when he wasn't exactly sober. Laudanum, brandy and sodas, opium – you name it, he liked it. Plus, there's a lot of semi-coded references whose meaning I haven't worked out.'

'What about the papers that Doris threw away?'

Vanessa frowned at the mirror. 'Honestly, I know she's a nice woman, but sometimes I could strangle her. I think two volumes of the journal went, and quite a lot of letters and things. As far as I can see, Lady Youlgreave wanted to weed out anything that dealt with that Rosington episode. So frustrating.'

I shivered.

'Are you cold?' her reflection asked me.

'It is beginning to get cooler at night, don't you think? A hint of autumn.'

'How depressing. It's been such a rotten summer.' She put down the brush and got into bed. 'Are you – are you very disappointed?'

'About what?'

'About me?'

'Of course not.'

'You are good to me. I don't think many husbands would be so – so *gracious* about having to share me with Francis.'

'I can understand the fascination,' I said. 'Anyway, it's important.'

'Francis?'

'Discovering the truth. Separating fact from speculation. You should have been an academic.'

She stroked my arm, then let her hand rest on mine. 'And you?'

'I told you – at one time I thought I wanted to be an academic, but then being a priest seemed more important.'

'So we're two of a kind. I wanted to do research, but I married Charles instead and turned into a publisher.' She shifted beside me in the bed, moving a little closer. 'Why couldn't you combine being a priest with being an academic?'

'I tried. But it didn't work out.' I turned my head and smiled at her. 'But it's all right. Everything's worked out for the best.'

If I hadn't become Vicar of Roth, how could I have met Joanna?

'I want you to be happy,' Vanessa said. 'I feel I'm failing you.'

'You're not failing me.' I patted Vanessa's hand and thought of Joanna. 'And I'm very happy.'

On Friday, Audrey temporarily delegated control of Ye Olde Tudor Tea Room to Charlene, moved her headquarters into the Vicarage and presided over the preparations for the fete. This year she seemed to take it even more seriously than usual. She camped in the dining room, the room we used least. Rosemary acted as her aide-de-camp.

The dining room filled up with smaller items of jumble, and the garage served as a dump for the larger pieces and for a heterogeneous collection of wallpaper-pasting tables, chairs and home-made signs. Toby phoned me and asked if it would be all right if he and Joanna brought the tent in the afternoon and put it up in the garden.

'You've come to see what we've been up to,' Audrey informed me when I took some coffee to her and Rosemary in the middle of the morning.

'You're doing wonders.' I edged towards the doorway. 'Let me know if there's anything I can do.'

'Let us pray for fine weather,' Audrey said, eyeing me in a way that suggested she had earmarked this responsibility for me. 'People always enjoy themselves more when the sun's out, and then they spend more.'

Vanessa was at work, but Michael was recruited to help with the preparations as well as Rosemary. He helped willingly, excited by the break in routine.

During the day a steady trickle of people arrived at the Vicarage. Some came to help, some brought items for selling, some came simply to gossip. There would be more in the morning. I sometimes thought that the real importance of the fete was not the money it made, never very much in comparison

516

with the effort that went into it, but the way it brought people together.

All day I found it hard to concentrate. I did not know when Joanna would come. Or even whether she would come. We had not been able to arrange another meeting for today – I was fully occupied until the evening, and we might not be able to see each other alone later on. My love for her was like an itch: the more I scratched it, the worse it became.

As the day went on, frustration and uncertainty made me increasingly irritable. I snapped at Michael when he dropped a fork while laying the table for lunch. During lunch itself Rosemary said nothing: she sat with her head bowed so that her hair fell to either side of her face, effectively curtaining it. When I tried to make conversation, she answered in monosyllables.

'For heaven's sake,' I burst out at last. 'Must you be quite so gloomy?'

Rosemary made a sound that might have been a sob, scraped back her chair and left the room. Michael stared at his plate, flushing with embarrassment. I went up to Rosemary's room afterwards, intending to apologize. I'd hardly begun when she interrupted me.

'You don't care about me. You never have.'

'Of course I do. You're my daughter.'

She lowered her head once more, retiring behind her golden curtain. 'I wish I lived anywhere but here. Anywhere in the world.'

'My dear –'

'It's all changed since you married Vanessa. You never have any time for me. You talk to *Michael* more than me.'

I sat down on the bed beside her and tried to take her hand, but she stood up at once and moved to the window. 'That's simply not true. I love you very much and I always will.'

'I don't believe you.' She looked out into the garden, towards the trees of Roth Park. 'I don't want to talk about it. There's no point.'

'Rosie, you really –'

'*Don't* call me that.'

The doorbell rang. My first thought was that it might be Joanna and Toby.

'Go on, answer it,' Rosemary told me. 'It might be someone important.'

'We'll talk later,' I said, trying to retrieve something from my failure.

She shrugged. I went downstairs and opened the door.

'It's only little me,' said Audrey. Something in my face must have alerted her, for she added almost at once, 'Is there anything wrong?'

'Nothing at all, thank you.' I stood back to let her into the house. She surged past me, trailing clouds of perfume and perspiration.

'I've a feeling,' she said gaily, 'this is going to be our best fete yet.'

'I hope you're right. Now, if you'll excuse me –'

She was between me and the study door, cutting off my obvious line of escape. 'All the stalls are very well stocked, and we've got a really good band of helpers this year. And I think that Toby Clifford's fortune-telling tent is going to make all the difference. Even the Vintners' barbecue.'

'Good.'

'I wanted to ask you – what time do you think we should announce the result of the Guess-the-Weight Competition? Last time we left it until the end, and I'm not sure that was a good idea – a lot of people had already left, including the winner, in fact. Do you remember? It was Mrs Smiley, that woman with the poodle who lives in Rowan Road.'

'You must do whatever you think best.' I edged towards the study door, but Audrey held her ground.

'I thought perhaps we should announce the winner just before tea – at about ten to four. I mean, let's face it, if anyone's going to guess the weight, they're going to do it in the first two hours, aren't they? Doris told me that they took most of the guesses in the first hour.'

'I'm sure that'll be fine, then.'

'There was one other thing – the cups and saucers. Last year several of them got broken. The Church Hall Committee were rather upset. If you're happy with it, I'll say at the outset that we'll replace any breakages from our profits so there's no doubt about the matter.'

'Audrey,' I said desperately, 'I'm sure you'll make all the arrangements marvellously. You've already made the decisions. You do not need me to rubber-stamp them for you.'

It wasn't so much what I said as the way that I said it. I watched the colour flooding into her face. I saw her mouth trembling and her eyes screwing up. It was as if her features were disintegrating. And it was my fault.

'I'm so sorry.' In my agitation, I laid a hand on her arm. 'I didn't mean to snap. You're doing a wonderful –'

To my horror she came even closer to me until her body was nudging against mine.

'Oh, David,' she said between sobs. 'I hate it when you're like that.'

I tried to back away from her but succeeded only in backing into the wall. 'Now there's nothing to worry about. Why don't I make us some tea?'

'Everything's changed,' she wailed. 'You never used to be like this.'

'There, there.' I patted the doughy flesh of her bare forearm. 'Everything's all right. Now, there's a great deal to do before tomorrow.'

By now I was sandwiched between Audrey and the wall. It was a ridiculous situation. I could have stamped my feet with rage, irritation and embarrassment. Each of us has a child inside him, and mine was very near the surface and on the verge of having a tantrum.

'It's Vanessa,' Audrey whimpered, her voice rising higher and louder. 'It's all her fault.'

At that moment the doorbell rang once again. Relieved at the interruption, I turned towards the door. As I did so, I realized that Audrey and I were not alone and might not have been for some time.

Rosemary was standing at the head of the stairs, with the light from the window behind her outlining her body and streaming through her blonde hair. In that instant, she looked as beautiful, and as implacable, as an angel.

The tent was contained in a great canvas bundle, the foot of which rested on the floor in front of the front passenger seat of the Jaguar. The top of the bundle poked through the sun roof. When I followed Toby into the drive, leaving Audrey to compose herself in the dining room, Joanna was disentangling her body from the tiny back seats. The despair and frustration I had felt a moment earlier dropped away from me. In her absence, I imagined Joanna so intensely that the reality was almost more than I could cope with: she was, literally, a dream come true.

She clambered out of the car by the driver's door, said hello to me in an offhand manner, and walked round the long bonnet to the passenger door.

'Joanna was once in the Girl Guides,' Toby told me. 'So she'll be able to tell us how to put up the tent.'

'You're a liar,' she said over the roof of the car. 'I was never in the Guides any more than you were.'

'It makes a good story, though. And you'd have looked very fetching in the uniform.'

Joanna ignored him. She opened the passenger door and tried to lift the base of the bundle on to the seat. Toby and I went to help her. The nearer I came to her the more unsettled I felt.

'How's the family?' Toby asked me.

'Fine, thank you.'

'And Vanessa's research?'

'Quite well, I think.' I was aware, as lovers are aware, that Joanna was listening. 'It takes up most of her spare time, though.'

'Odd to think of a dead poet coming between man and wife,' Toby said with a smile. 'And Rosemary's still working hard?'

I nodded. 'You'll probably see her. She's here. She's acting as Audrey's right-hand woman.'

Toby edged Joanna out of the way. He bent down and hoisted the bundle on to the seat. 'If I push it upwards, could you sort of guide it out of the sun roof? It's not as heavy as it looks.'

We extracted the tent from the car and carried it round to the garden, with Joanna following. I glanced up at Rosemary's window, but I could not see if she were watching us. I explained where Audrey wanted the tent to go – in the corner of the garden where the churchyard wall joined the boundary wall of Roth

Park. I offered to help but Toby said he was better off by himself, at least at first.

'I'll let you know, though, when I need a second pair of hands.'

'I'll go and put the kettle on.'

'Is there anything I can do?' Joanna said, looking at me. 'For the fete, I mean.'

'I'm not sure.' I hesitated. 'We could ask Audrey. She's in the dining room.'

The dining room overlooked the back of the house, and I guessed that Audrey was monitoring developments in the garden. Joanna and I walked sedately across the lawn to the back door, keeping a safe distance apart from each other. We went into the house. The door from the kitchen to the hall was closed. Keeping well back from the window and to one side of it, I turned to Joanna. She put her hands on my shoulders, stared at me for a moment and then kissed me slowly and gently.

'I feel like a bee,' she said, 'sucking honey from a flower. Does that sound stupid?'

'No.' If she had said that the moon was made of solid silver, that would not have sounded stupid either. She smelt of mown grass and cigarettes. We kissed again, keeping our bodies apart.

At last she drew away from me. 'You'd better put the kettle on. And I suppose I'd better go and find Miss Oliphant.'

'Don't go.'

'No, not yet.' She watched me filling the kettle and putting it on the ring. 'David?'

'Mm?'

'I can't bear this. Not being with you all the time. Not even making love properly.'

'I know.' I thought of what the future might contain: leaving the priesthood, divorcing Vanessa, finding some other job – and in that instant all that seemed as irrelevant as an old skin seems to a snake. What did it matter, as long as Joanna and I could be together?

'I'm scared,' she said.

I reached for her hand.

'I want everything from you,' she said slowly. 'I want your

children. That's why we have to make love before it's too late.'

'Too late?'

'You know what I mean. Just in case . . .'

I played with her fingers. *Make love now, just in case we have no future?* But we would have a future. Of course we would. *But just in case?*

'All right.' My voice was hoarse.

'You mean you will? Properly?'

I cleared my throat. 'Yes.'

'This evening?'

'We've got the Vintners coming round.'

'Tomorrow, then?'

'There's the fete. I'll have to be on parade for that. And afterwards there'll be your party. Won't you be very busy with that?'

She shook her head. 'Toby's ordered stacks of booze and crisps and things. He's hiring glasses. It's not as if there's any point in our cleaning the house. So there's nothing to do. We'll just let people get on with it.'

'It'll be getting dark by then.'

Her eyes gleamed; they looked greener and deeper than ever. 'And if it's fine we'll be in the garden as well as the house. I'm sure we can slip away. And if we don't manage then, we'll manage afterwards.'

I nodded. I wanted her now.

'We'll have to be careful about Toby, though,' she said. 'He's so sharp, especially where something like this is concerned.'

I felt a spurt of anger: something like what? Did his sister often have clandestine affairs with married men?

'He can be very malicious,' Joanna went on.

'Then why do you stay with him?'

My voice was suddenly harsh. I was not angry with her. I was jealous of past lovers, furious with Toby for making his sister afraid, and desperate to have more of Joanna than at present I could.

She moved away from me. 'There are reasons.' It was as if a light had gone out behind her face. 'I will tell you. But not now.'

'Why not?'

'This isn't the right time.'

'But you would leave him, wouldn't you? You would leave him to come with me?'

She smiled at me and ran her fingers through her hair. 'Yes. If you still wanted me.'

'Is it that bad?'

She did not speak.

'Joanna. Please tell me.'

She looked up at me and I saw the tears in her eyes.

'I love you,' I said.

'David –'

The door opened and Audrey came into the kitchen. Apart from a reluctance to meet my eyes, she betrayed no sign of the last conversation that we had had.

'Hello, Joanna. Come to help? Are you any good at lettering notices? Oh jolly good! You've put the kettle on. I'm dying for a cup of tea.'

33

When I woke on Saturday morning, rain was rattling on the windowpane. I drew back the curtains. Black clouds hung low over the green and spread out to the eastern horizon, threatening London. Traffic threw up a fine spray as it passed up and down the main road, and puddles dotted the gravel of the Vicarage drive.

At breakfast, Vanessa said cheerfully, 'So it looks like the church hall, doesn't it?'

I stared out of the window at the back garden. Toby's tent stood forlornly in the far corner, its canvas stained with damp. The church hall was Audrey's contingency plan for wet weather. Some of our attractions, such as the barbecue, would have to be abandoned. There would not be room for many members of the public, either, even if they felt like trekking through the rain across the green from the paddock of Roth Park to the church hall.

The telephone rang. It was Audrey.

'We shall just have to pray for a miracle,' she said, her voice shrill. 'I simply can't *believe* this wretched weather.'

Whether Audrey prayed or not, the miracle duly appeared: by half past nine, it had stopped raining; and by ten o'clock, the dark clouds were receding over London, while blue sky was coming in from the west. By half past ten, the Vicarage felt as crowded as a railway terminal in the rush hour.

The sun had broken through the clouds and the grass was steaming. Stalls were going up all over the lawn, according to Audrey's directions. After a while, I realized that I was redundant – in fact, that my presence was actually impeding people because they felt they had to consult me or merely make conversation. I retired to the study, where I angled my chair so I could see out of the window. Joanna and Toby were not due to arrive until after lunch, but there was always the possibility that they might change their plans.

The room felt alien to me. Joanna had that effect. She had cut me adrift in my old life, made me a foreigner in a country which had once been my home. I looked at the shabby cloak hanging on the back of the door, at the books – rows and rows of theology, at the stack of parish magazines on the windowsill and finally at the crucifix on the wall. All these things belonged to another person in another life; they were no longer familiar.

Towards lunch time, Vanessa stormed into the study. I felt a stab of guilt that she had caught me doing nothing. Not that she noticed. She was carrying the tin box in her arms and her face was flushed.

'I'm going upstairs to our bedroom,' she told me. 'And I do not want to be disturbed for anything short of an earthquake.'

'What's up?'

'I've been trying to work in the sitting room, but people keep coming in and asking me for things. If it isn't Audrey, it's James; and if it isn't him, it's Ted Potter. I may be your wife, but I'm not a parish amenity.' She grinned at me. 'I feel better for getting that off my chest. You know where I am if you want me.'

I heard her footsteps on the stairs. I knew that people like Audrey thought that Vanessa was an unsuitable wife for a parish priest. What would they think of Joanna? My mind filled with the memory of her on Thursday afternoon – naked in the wood, sprawling on the blanket, smiling wantonly up at me. My body began to respond to the memory. This would never do. I got up and went to the kitchen to make myself some coffee.

James Vintner poked his head through the open window. 'Got any paraffin?'

'I'm afraid not.'

'I can't get this damn charcoal to light. Want to have a look?'

I went outside. 'I've never used a barbecue.'

'Needs to burn well for an hour or so before you can cook on it.' James sniffed appreciatively, his mind leaping ahead. 'Nothing like meat barbecued in the open. Irresistible.'

'Perhaps Audrey has some paraffin.'

He clapped his hands. 'I don't see why petrol shouldn't work. I've got a can in the car.'

He fetched the can and poured some of the petrol over the charcoal. There was a whoosh of flame when he lit the match. For an instant, tongues of fire danced over his hair.

'Bloody hell!' He slapped his head vigorously and glared at me. 'No harm done.'

At least the charcoal seemed well alight. James asked Rosemary to put the can in the garage in case he needed it again. Audrey pounced on me and towed me away to look at the book stall – at the centre of which was a carefully arranged pyramid of *The History of Roth*, donated by its author.

'I've put out thirty-six copies,' Audrey said. 'Do you think that will be enough? I've got some more under the table.'

'I'm sure that will be enough. It's very generous of you.'

Audrey simpered. 'Every little bit helps. And it's all in a good cause.' Her eyes slipped past me towards the tent in the corner of the garden. 'No sign of Toby?'

'He's not due till after lunch. Do you need him for something?'

'I'd just like to have more of an idea of what he's going to do. After all, this is a *church* fete. One wouldn't want anything *inappropriate*.'

As she was speaking, she walked towards the tent. She opened the flap and we looked into its cool green interior. Despite the rain in the night, it was perfectly dry. In the middle of the tent was a card table covered with a blue chenille cloth. Two kitchen chairs faced each other across the table.

'It might be wise if you were his first customer,' Audrey suggested. 'If you wouldn't mind, that is.'

'Why?'

'Well, you could make sure that what he's doing is all right. And also, if you go and see him, it'll encourage everyone else.' She giggled. 'In fact, I almost think I might try him myself. I've never had my fortune told.' She looked up at me. 'Of course, I know it's complete nonsense – just a bit of fun.' She giggled once more. 'Still, I suppose one never knows.'

*   *   *

526

At first, the only problem was that there was no sign of Toby Clifford – or of Joanna.

The fete began at two o'clock. The sun shone down from a cloudless sky. Ted Potter directed the cars in the paddock and along the drive of Roth Park. Rosemary sat at a table just inside the Vicarage gates taking the entrance money and bestowing smiles in return. Audrey even persuaded Vanessa to accept a roving commission to sell raffle tickets.

'Many hands make light work,' Audrey told her.

Vanessa glanced at me, her eyebrows lifting and her mouth twitching. 'I thought that too many cooks spoiled the broth.'

I managed not to laugh. 'Audrey – are those books quite safe? Couldn't someone knock the pile over?'

In the first five minutes, two visitors bought copies of *The History of Roth*. The barbecue settled down to a steady glow. James, whose face was glowing too, added more and more charcoal.

'We could roast a pig on this,' he told me. 'Maybe I should have been a chef.'

At twenty past two, Mary Vintner and I were trying to guess the weight of the cake, an activity which took place at the side of the house, in full view of the drive. A group of young people had just paid their entrance fee. Among them was Charlene's friend Kevin Jones. They had spent lunchtime in the Queen's Head, and they were in a cheerful mood. Behind them I glimpsed a woman – dark flowing hair, a long dark dress and some sort of brightly coloured headscarf.

I heard Rosemary say, 'Excuse me. You haven't paid.'

For the first time I saw the woman's face, dominated by sunglasses with mirrored lenses and a bright-red slash of lipstick across the mouth.

'Oh no,' the woman squealed. 'Madam Mysterioso never pays. Cross my palm with silver, dearie, and we'll see if we can find you a handsome young man lurking in your future.'

Rosemary had recognized Toby and even before he began to speak her embarrassment was obvious, at least to me. She stood back, waving him in.

'Vanessa,' Toby called, declining to be waved in, 'come and vouch for me. We madams must stick together.'

Several people laughed, including Mary. He had a gift for making people laugh when he wanted to, even when what he said was not intrinsically funny. Vanessa came into view with her roll of raffle tickets. Smiling, their heads close together, she and Toby followed the path down the side of the house towards Mary and me. Rosemary looked after them, her face pink and tight.

'Sorry I'm a bit late,' Toby said to me. 'I started to drive down, but some idiot had blocked the drive, so I had to reverse back up to the house and then walk. And walking in a skirt is an art I haven't entirely mastered.'

'It's a splendid costume.' What I wanted to say was, *Leave my daughter alone*, and, *Where's Joanna?*

'I'll get started, shall I? Is there a queue?'

As it happened, there was. When we reached the tent, Kevin and his friends were clamouring for Madam Mysterioso.

'Ah,' cried Toby in his falsetto. 'The price of fame. My public needs me. Hello, children! Just give me a moment to powder my nose.'

He winked at Vanessa and went alone into the tent.

Audrey sidled up to me. 'Shouldn't you go first?' she hissed.

At this moment there was a diversion.

'Fire!' shouted Brian.

Almost everyone in the garden turned towards the barbecue. His face purple, James was jumping up and down on a flaming tea towel. His wife took in the situation at a glance. She darted into the kitchen, lifted the washing-up bowl from the sink, returned outside and deposited several pints of dirty sudsy water over the tea towel and over her husband's trousers and shoes. James swore. Then he looked up and realized that he was the centre of attention.

'Almost ready to take your orders, ladies and gentlemen,' he called, taking advantage of his audience. 'Beefburgers, sausages, fried onions, rolls, mustard, tomato ketchup – we have everything you could possibly want to eat.' He added, in a slightly lower voice, 'Damn it, Mary, you'll have to send Brian home for my shorts and sandals. I wish you wouldn't panic like that.'

By the time I returned to Madam Mysterioso, Kevin was already inside the tent, laughing hysterically.

I spent the rest of the afternoon in a daze. I wandered around the fete and talked to people. After all, as Vanessa pointed out to me during a lull in the proceedings, it was my party and I was expected to circulate. The weather was wonderful, attendance was as good as we had ever had, if not better, and both the barbecue and Madam Mysterioso were doing excellent trade.

But all I could think of was Joanna. Why wasn't she here? Had she changed her mind about me? Had Toby found out and somehow prevented her from coming? In the end, I could stand it no longer. I slipped into the house and went into the study. I dialled the number of Roth Park and waited.

The phone rang on and on. While it rang, I looked out of the window at Rosemary sitting at her table by the gate, staring out at the main road and the green beyond. I wondered if Joanna had had an accident, if she were lying in a coma at the foot of the stairs. Or she might have slipped, cracked her head and fallen into the swimming pool. I was about to give up when there was a click at the other end of the line and Joanna's sleepy voice said hello.

'It's me.'

'David. Dear David. What time is it?'

'About a quarter to four. Are you coming down to the fete? I thought –'

The study door opened. Vanessa came in with a cup of tea in each hand.

'No,' I said swiftly. 'I'm afraid you've got a wrong number. Goodbye.' I put down the phone.

'I thought we could have tea in peace and quiet,' Vanessa said. 'It's like a Roman circus out there. With Audrey as the principal lion.' She sat down opposite me and took a cigarette from the packet on the desk. 'A wrong number? I didn't hear the phone ring.'

'It had hardly started when I picked the phone up,' I said. 'Thanks for the tea. It's thirsty work.'

'I visited Madam Mysterioso,' Vanessa said. 'She foresaw an outstanding literary success in my life. You should give Toby a try – he's really rather good.'

I was scared that Joanna might phone me back. I gulped my tea and went outside with Vanessa. The fete was beginning to wind down. James beamed at us as he dropped the last sausages on to the grill.

'Have a hot dog. Vanessa? David?'

The smell of burning meat reached my nostrils.

'*With flames to the flesh*,' Vanessa quoted, '*with brands to the burning*. Yes, please.'

'Not for me, thanks,' I said.

The smell made me queasy. Trust Francis Youlgreave to be both ambiguous and disgusting. *As incense to heav'n the soul is returning* . . . It had never occurred to me before that a burning heretic must have smelled of roasting meat, and that the smell must have titillated the taste buds of the spectators, especially those with empty bellies. A missionary who had talked to me when I was an ordinand had told me that roasted human flesh smelled and tasted like pork.

'Pork sausages,' James said. 'Can't beat them. Much nicer flavour than beef.'

Four more copies of *The History of Roth* had been sold and there was no longer a queue outside Madam Mysterioso's tent. The flap was open. Toby beckoned me in. He held out his right hand, palm upwards.

'Cross me palm with silver,' he squeaked, his voice sounding hoarser than it had at the beginning of the afternoon.

I laid a ten-shilling note in his hand.

'That's right, my dear. Generosity shall have its reward. Shut the flap and we can be nice and private.'

When the flap was closed, the tent became another place – cool, green and shadowed. A joss stick smouldered in a brass holder, filling the air with a heavy scent. Toby, hunched over the table, in his black wig, his long black dress and his shawl, seemed in no hurry to begin. He had added a silk scarf, worn as a headband, and a large necklace of imitation diamonds to his attire. On the table between us were some of the tools of his trade: a pack of tarot cards, a crystal ball, and the *Prophecies* of Paracelsus.

'Isn't this cosy?' he said. 'Now, what can I do for you? A little palmistry, perhaps?'

Examining my hand with a large magnifying glass, Toby launched into an entertaining survey of my hypothetical future.

Soon I would be a bishop. In a year or two I would have my own television show. Meanwhile (he threw in for good measure), my wife would become a world-famous author.

'I usually end by consulting my crystal ball,' he informed me in a voice that was now reduced to an imperious wheeze. 'In it I see a vision of the future, a picture that encapsulates what is to come. Frequently its meaning is symbolic. I like my clients to take away this picture and meditate upon it, if possible for years to come.'

He grinned at me across the table. 'Stare into the crystal,' he commanded.

The two of us placed our elbows on the table and peered into its glassy depths. All I could see was a distorted image of myself and the walls of the tent. Seconds passed.

'I can see a little girl,' Toby said in his normal voice. He looked up at me, his eyes wide and surprised. 'She's sitting on a bed, and she's got dark hair.' He frowned. 'And she's *crying*.'

34

A sign consisting of a ragged sheet of cardboard attached to a wooden baton had been pushed into the soft verge beside the drive: PARTY, it said in red letters, and underneath was an arrow pointing to the path through the shrubbery. Pop music pulsed steadily through the warm evening air.

Audrey made a face. 'Oh dear. That jingly-jangly music. If music's the word I want.'

She had walked with us up the drive, joining us as we came through the gate from the churchyard – her timing was so perfect that I suspected that she had been watching out for us.

It was a little before seven o'clock. The evening sun was directly in our eyes. It slanted across the façade of the house, creating black bars of shadow. The Vintners' Rover was among the cars in front of the house in the shadow of the tower. Brian ran across the gravel and annexed Michael. The two boys darted into the shrubbery.

'Hello, Vicar,' said Ted Potter, coming up behind us with Doris. He beamed at Vanessa and Rosemary and sidled closer to me. His breath smelled of beer. 'Never thought we'd be coming up *here* for a party. Times change, eh?'

Toby had been generous with his invitations. A stream of people, some on foot and some in cars, were making their way up the drive towards the house. Kevin and Charlene walked self-consciously arm in arm, followed by Judy, the fat girl in the bus shelter who had sworn at Audrey.

We followed the boys through the shrubbery to the ragged lawn on the other side of the bushes. The French windows were open. People were chatting and drinking on the terrace, on the lawn and down by the swimming pool. There were many faces I did not recognize.

'I wonder where our host and hostess are,' Audrey said, her nose wrinkling.

There was a loud splash from the direction of the pool. For a moment we hesitated, feeling the awkwardness of those who have arrived at a gathering but have not yet been assimilated by it.

There was no sign of Joanna.

Kevin and Charlene emerged giggling from the shrubbery, with Judy trailing behind.

'David! Vanessa!'

James Vintner waved from the terrace. Somewhere in the room behind him came the familiar bray of Mary's laughter. The music stopped abruptly.

'Thank heavens for that,' muttered Audrey.

'Come and get yourself a drink,' James called. 'Toby's made me deputy barman for the evening.'

We trooped up to the terrace and into the long sitting room. A group of teenagers clustered round the record player. A trestle table had been set up as a makeshift bar at one end.

'Gin, whisky, vodka?' James waved his arm to and fro, pointing out what was on offer. 'Beer, cider, red wine, white wine, Coca-Cola, orange squash, sherry – and of course punch. Come on, David, why not push the boat out? I see you've come in mufti so you can let your hair down. What about a large gin?'

We all asked for gin, even Rosemary, because it was the easiest thing to do.

'Where are the Cliffords?' Vanessa asked as James was rummaging in the ice bucket.

'Toby took a jug of punch down to the pool. I wouldn't advise trying it – absolutely lethal. At least a bottle of brandy went into it, and heaven knows what else . . . Jo's around somewhere – I saw her a moment ago.'

Jealousy kicked me. I didn't like James calling her 'Jo'.

'There you are. You know where to come for refills.' James leered at Charlene and Doris. 'And what can I get you, my dears?'

We drifted by stages on to the terrace and down to the lawn. Rosemary was soon in conversation with two young men I did not know and to whom she did not introduce me. The three of them followed us across the lawn. Michael and Brian zigzagged like swallows around the garden. Audrey was hailed by our librarian, Mrs Finch, who was with her husband.

'I don't think I've ever seen ground elder quite so well established as this,' the husband said in a voice like a satisfied whinny. 'I mean, they'll be having it growing inside the house if they're not careful.'

Vanessa and I moved away.

'I'll be glad when this is over,' she murmured. 'Can we leave early?'

'It's been a long day,' I said, not wanting to commit myself. 'It's always a relief when the fete is out of the way for another year.'

'I'm dead on my feet.'

'I may have to stay for a while. I feel I'm partly on duty.' I added, as casually as I could manage, 'But there's no reason why you shouldn't slip off whenever you want.'

'I might do that. I'd like to do a little reading tonight.' She paused to sip her drink, and made a face. 'James's made this awfully strong.'

We went down the steps into the paved area around the swimming pool. Several teenagers were swimming or splashing each other. Toby was at the centre of a knot of people in front of the white changing hut where Rosemary and I had sheltered with him from the rain. He saw us and waved. We walked round the pool to join him. He stood out from everyone else because he was in white – a collarless shirt and tight, flared trousers.

'You're looking very festive,' he said to Vanessa, who was in fact wearing the dress that she had worn at the Trasks' dinner party almost a year ago, on the occasion of our first meeting.

Vanessa laughed and said, 'Go on with you, Toby.'

He leant forward unexpectedly and kissed her on the cheek. 'Welcome to the party, anyway. If David doesn't mind, you can be our official Belle of the Ball. By the way, I've got something to show you.'

'Really? What?'

'It's a surprise.' She looked at him in a way that was almost flirtatious. Which *was* flirtatious. It suddenly struck me that Vanessa was not averse to flirtation when it was divorced from any possibility of leading to sexual activity.

Toby looked past us. 'And Rosemary – how are you?'

My daughter was standing with the two youths only a few yards away. She ignored him.

'Why are you being so mysterious?' asked Vanessa.

'I like surprises,' Toby said. 'Don't you? I'll give you a clue: it's something to do with Francis Youlgreave.'

'I see.' Vanessa's voice did not change, but her features sharpened as if the skin of her face had tightened over the bones beneath: suddenly she looked hungry. 'And when is the secret going to be revealed?'

'Soon. Give me a moment.' He smiled impartially at both of us. 'I need to collect my thoughts and discharge my hostly duties.' He turned and in one swift movement picked up a dish that had been resting on the step of the little wooden verandah behind him. 'Have some cheese.'

He held out a large, chipped serving plate designed for a joint of meat. At present it held a mound of cheese diced roughly into cubes. On one side of the plate was the kitchen knife he had been using to cut up the cheese, and on the other was the remains of a hunk of Cheddar.

'We should have got some of those little cocktail sticks. But I hope you won't mind using your fingers.' Toby looked up at the house. 'Clouds coming up from the west. I think we're going to get rain, so we might as well enjoy the garden and the pool while we can.'

Nibbling the cheese, I stared at the sky. I caught sight of Rosemary, still only a few yards away, flanked by escorts. But she wasn't listening to them. She was looking at us. I smiled at her but she appeared not to see me.

Toby popped two cubes of cheese into his mouth. 'Let's go up to the house and I'll put you out of your misery,' he said indistinctly. 'Have you seen Joanna yet?'

'No.' Vanessa glanced at me. 'Was she at the fete? I didn't see her.'

'She decided she'd do a few things for the party,' Toby said. 'At least, that was her story. My theory is, she didn't want to run the risk of being pointed out as the sister of Madam Mysterioso.'

'Audrey tells me that you and the barbecue were our top-earning attractions,' I said.

'That's a comfort.' Toby waved at the red brick bulk of the house. 'So if my career as a hotelier falls through, at least I can make a new life as a professional prophet.'

Toby picked up the jug of punch and the three of us walked slowly back to the house, pausing every now and then to allow Toby to fulfil his hostly duties. I wondered whether the glance Vanessa had given me was significant, whether she suspected that there might be something between Joanna and me. Hindsight always colours memory; but even at that moment I felt there were strange emotions abroad, an uneasiness which affected the way that people mixed with each other.

A burst of rock music came to meet us from the sitting room. A few couples were dancing on the terrace. In the room beyond, James was explaining how to make champagne cocktails to a ravishingly beautiful Asian girl. Mary was dancing with a large young man in a leather jacket. The drinks table was surrounded by a crowd of people who had evidently decided that it was simpler to serve themselves rather than wait to be served by the deputy barman.

Mary and her partner lurched a few paces to the right. Suddenly I saw Joanna. She was standing by the fireplace talking to Audrey.

Audrey had seen us, too. 'I was just asking Joanna if we could turn the music down a little,' she shouted, crossing the room towards us. 'It's absolutely deafening. In fact, it's so loud I'm not sure she can hear what I was saying.'

'Oh, you have to have loud music at parties,' Vanessa said. 'Otherwise it wouldn't be a proper party.'

Audrey stared at her. It was an undiplomatic remark, and Vanessa was not usually undiplomatic. Either she wanted to offend Audrey, I thought, or her mind was on other things – on Toby's surprise connected with Francis Youlgreave.

'Of course we can turn it down,' Toby said, smiling at Audrey.

He walked over to the record player, but it was too late. Audrey had wheeled round on Vanessa. At that moment Toby turned the volume down. He must have turned the knob too far because suddenly there was no music at all.

'I've had enough of you,' Audrey shrieked in the sudden silence. 'You're quite intolerable. Why do you have to interfere? You don't belong here.'

She flung a startled glance round the room, at the blank faces staring at hers. She gave a high, wordless cry and stumbled through the nearest French window on to the terrace. Simultaneously, Toby turned up the music. Audrey ran across the flags, down the steps and on to the lawn. A moment later she vanished among the bushes of the shrubbery between the lawn and the drive.

I had begun to follow her. I reached the French window. Vanessa came up behind me and laid a restraining hand on my arm.

'Better leave her,' she said. 'It'll be kinder in the long run.'

'Are you OK?'

'Of course.' She smiled, cool and faintly amused.

James abandoned his Asian beauty and came over to the two of us. He looked from one to the other of us.

'Flew off the handle, eh?'

'You heard what happened,' Vanessa said, though James could not possibly have heard what she had said to spark off Audrey's outburst.

He shrugged. 'Time of life. Takes some people harder than others. How are your glasses? You can't go round with half-empty glasses. This is a party.'

The buzz of conversation resumed.

'I feel responsible,' Toby said, every inch the concerned host.

'There's nothing you could have done,' James pointed out. 'Best forget about it. Kindest thing all round. Don't let it spoil the party.'

Toby turned to Vanessa. 'Are you ready for the secret?'

'Where is it?'

'It *was* in the old stables. I found it when I was digging out that tent, but I didn't have a proper look till this evening.'

In her eagerness, Vanessa laid a hand on his arm. 'Yes, but what *is* it? It had better be good after all this build-up.'

He stared at her, obviously wondering whether to prolong the tease. 'All right. It's a box – a dusty old pine box full of dusty old books. Three or four dozen of them. I've not been through them, but most of them look like theology. And the ones I did look at had "F. St. J. Youlgreave" on the flyleaf. I've moved them into the office.'

As he was talking, he and Vanessa were edging towards the door to the hall. They did not ask me to accompany them and I did not want to go. As soon as they had left the room, I strolled over to the fireplace. Joanna looked up at me. The music cocooned us in a bubble of privacy.

'Look,' she said; I half heard her and half saw her lips move. Her eyes showed me where to look – behind me, towards the terrace.

I was just in time to see Rosemary turning away. As I watched, she stepped down to the lawn and rejoined the youths she had been with at the pool.

'She's in a state,' Joanna said. Then only her lips moved without any accompanying sound: '*I love you.*'

'Come outside?' I mouthed back.

She nodded, picked up her glass from the mantelpiece and led the way on to the terrace. It was noticeably darker and cooler than it had been even a few minutes before. We walked down the steps, away from the dancers and the drinkers. There was no sign of Rosemary or her escorts.

'I missed you. Why weren't you at the fete?'

'Because I wouldn't have had a chance to be with you. What happened when you tried to phone?'

'Vanessa came into the study.'

'I want to be alone with you. I *have* to be.'

We met Doris and Ted Potter at that moment. I heard myself congratulating them on their contribution to the fete and telling them how much money we had made this year – a record. I even asked about Beauty and Beast. And then, as if in a dream, they were no longer there; and Joanna and I were alone on the edge of the lawn.

'There're too many people,' she whispered, turning so she could see if anyone was coming towards us. 'They're all over the place. Some of the younger ones aren't going to go for hours and hours. Not until the booze runs out. And Toby's really gone to town on that.' She looked at me over the brim of her glass. 'He's trying to make everyone like him. Have you noticed?'

I shrugged. At that moment I was not particularly interested in Toby.

'He wants to get the locals on his side for the hotel scheme, you see.' She reverted abruptly to what we'd been talking about before. 'It's too dangerous outside. I thought it would be easy, once it began to get dark, but people are everywhere.'

'Then what can we do?'

'Go inside the house. Up to my room.'

'But – but what if someone comes?'

'We can lock the door.' She waved her free hand around the garden. 'We can't lock the door here. It's such a big place that no one will think it odd if they can't find us.'

I ached to touch her. We had so few choices. It took me only a moment to convince myself that if we wanted to be alone, then her room was the safest place.

She knew me well enough to take my agreement for granted. 'We'd better go there separately. You remember the way?'

I nodded.

'I'll go first,' she said. 'You can follow in a couple of minutes. Use the main stairs. Toby's put a sign to the lavatory on the landing. Everyone will assume you're going up there.'

She smiled up at me and mouthed the words *I love you*. Then she slipped away across the grass. She was wearing a short dress which buttoned up the front; it was made of a soft material the colour of claret. On the terrace, she paused for a moment to say something to the man in the leather jacket who had been dancing with Mary Vintner. I heard her laugh. Then she disappeared into the house. I felt sick with desire, sick with shame.

Drink in hand, I walked slowly down to the swimming pool.

'Uncle David?'

Startled, I looked up. Two small white faces loomed against the dark-red foliage of the copper beech. Michael and Brian were ten feet above my head.

'It's a great climbing tree once you get up to the first main branch.'

'I'm sure it is.' I wanted to add, *Do be careful*, but managed to restrain myself.

He grinned down at me. 'We can see everyone. But they can't see us.'

'Let's hope they all behave themselves, then. See you later.'

I walked round the swimming pool, arriving in time to see another fully clothed youth falling into the water accidentally on purpose. I looked down at my glass and saw to my surprise that it was empty. Surely I need not wait any longer? I sauntered back to the house.

'Have a refill,' James called as I went inside.

I allowed him to give me one, because it was the simplest thing to do. I drifted across the room, smiling at faces I knew, and slipped out into the hallway. To my relief, there was no sign of Rosemary, Audrey or – most importantly of all – Vanessa. I walked down the corridor to the main hall at the front of the house.

No one had turned on the lights. The office door was closed, but there was a line of light between the bottom of the door and the threshold. I assumed that Vanessa and Toby were still inside, still examining the books which might have belonged to Francis Youlgreave. Suspicion stirred – was I not a conspirator myself? Surely they had been in there a very long time? I glanced at my watch. It seemed hours since Toby and Vanessa had left, but in fact it was no more than ten or fifteen minutes. I pushed the pair of them out of my mind.

As I went up the stairs, I glanced upwards through the gloom towards the great lantern skylight on the roof. This was a monochrome world, a place of shadows.

I reached the landing. A few yards away from me, a lavatory flushed. Simultaneously I noticed the light under a door on my left.

Abandoning dignity, I scuttled along the landing. A large cupboard, stretching from floor to ceiling, stood against the wall of the corridor. I ducked beside it and pressed my back against the wall so the bulk of the cupboard was between me and the lavatory door and the head of the stairs.

A bolt shot back. There were footsteps on the bare boards,

footsteps clattering down the stairs. I waited until all was silent and then continued along the corridor.

The door to the room beneath Joanna's was ajar. Despite the gathering dusk, it was lighter here than on the landing. One of the windows faced west and part of the sky was dark with rain clouds. For a moment, I hesitated. I thought I heard a faint rhythmic rustle, like the beating of distant wings.

Francis Youlgreave's angel?

There was a pattering sound in the fireplace. I went over to it and peered down at the flecks of soot which had fallen into the grate. Nothing to worry about. Just the wind in the chimney.

I crossed the room to the spiral staircase, whose door was also ajar. I went up the uncarpeted stairs as quietly as I could manage. It was suddenly much darker again, because the only light in this enclosed space came from the tiny arrow slits set low in the walls. Joanna's door was shut. Beyond it, the stairs carried on upwards through the darkness to Francis Youlgreave's room. I tapped on her door.

What if she isn't here?

I barely had time to formulate the thought before the handle turned. Joanna smiled up at me. She held the door open and I slipped inside. I turned to see her closing the door and turning the key in the lock. She faced me and leant back against the door. I saw that she was shivering.

'What is it?'

'I thought you wouldn't come.'

I put my arms around her. It was very quiet. One of the windows was open and I could hear the faint sound of music, of chinking glasses and laughter; but the sounds were so far away that they emphasized the silence rather than broke it. The big room was much as I had seen it before – the mattress on the carpet, an island on a sea of bare boards – except that it was tidier.

Gradually Joanna stopped trembling. Her fingers ran down my spine, up and down, up and down, as though she were playing a musical instrument. Then she stirred, pulled herself a little away from me and smiled. Slowly she undid the buttons of her dress and let it drop to the floor. She stepped out of it and took my hand.

'Toby –' I began.

She put her finger to my lips. 'Not now. Just you. Just me.'

I drew her towards me. We kissed. I ran my fingertips over her breasts. She pulled at the knot of my tie. When we were both naked, I led her to the mattress.

Gradually the light ebbed from the room. Detail seeped away. The four windows became round-headed oblongs in varying shades of grey. At times, it seemed to me that the tower was rocking gently. I heard the wind moaning, almost obscuring the faint sound of beating wings. Into my mind slipped an incongruous image of Francis Youlgreave's angel carrying him up to heaven.

Afterwards we lay in a warm huddle of naked limbs under a single sheet. *Now I have done the unforgivable*, I thought; and joy welled like a fountain inside me. Joanna nestled against me, her hand slowly stroking my chest. I could hardly breathe for happiness.

'I want it all over again,' she whispered, so quietly I could barely hear; her breath teased the hairs of my chest.

'And again,' I said.

'And again.'

It wasn't funny but we laughed. Vanessa and I had never laughed after making love. Joanna reached over me for cigarettes and lighter. Still entwined, we struggled into a sitting position, leaning against the wall. She pushed a cigarette in my mouth and lit it.

'Do you think they're missing us?' she asked.

'Probably. It doesn't matter.'

She twitched. 'It might if Toby notices.'

'Forget Toby.'

Joanna drew on her cigarette and her features acquired an infernal glow. 'We should go downstairs.' But she did not move.

I touched her cheek. 'Why do you stay with him? Why are you afraid of him?'

She said nothing. Her face was a pale oval in the gloom. I heard her breathing, rapid and irregular.

'Is it true that this house is yours?' I persisted, my voice becoming harsh because I was anxious. 'Did you tell me the truth?'

Joanna sucked in her breath. 'I've never lied to you. Not really . . . I never will. We must go.' She made a half-hearted attempt to scramble off the mattress, but our bodies were too entangled for her to be able to move without my cooperation. 'I'm sorry. I'm not worth it, you know.'

'You're worth everything. I love you.'

'Really?' She stubbed out her cigarette, her head bowed over the ashtray. 'It's not just sex?'

'No. Though I'm not pretending that's not important. But I love you – I want to marry you. Will you?' There was a silence. My stomach felt as though I were falling. *Falling from a high window into the arms of an angel.*

'You can't.' She made a sound that was half a giggle and half a sob. 'You're already married.'

'There's such a thing as divorce.'

'But you wouldn't be able to. You're a clergyman.'

'There are other ways of making a living.'

She kissed me. Then she rested her head against my shoulder. 'Anyway, there's Toby.'

'What's he got to do with it? I don't want to marry *him*.' A monstrous suspicion sprouted in my mind. 'You and Toby – surely you're not – ?'

Joanna laughed, a sharp, nervy sound like a shower of stones against a windowpane. 'Toby and I aren't lovers, if that's what you're worried about.'

'Then what is it?'

'I told you about the heroin. I didn't lie to you. But I didn't tell you everything.'

I waited. The evening air cooled my bare skin. Ash fell from my cigarette to the sheet. I brushed it off and dropped the cigarette end in the ashtray.

'You remember Annabel? Toby's friend?' She pulled herself away from me and sat up on the mattress, her arms round her knees. 'Well, he used the same technique on me as he did on her.'

'Heroin.' My hand slipped on to Joanna's thigh, as if I needed to reassure myself that she was still there, to feel the flesh and blood of her. 'Are you – you're addicted to heroin?'

'Yes.'

'But you're not –'

'I'm not a half-starved junkie living in a basement room in Notting Hill? I'm not selling my body to pay for my habit? I'm not covered in sores. I'm not subhuman.'

I put my arms around her and hugged her.

'It doesn't have to be like that, you know. If you've got a regular supply of it, you can lead a perfectly normal life.'

'But there was no sign of it.'

'I don't use a syringe. I smoke it. That's how Toby got me started.' Her voice was low and the flow stumbled. 'We used to smoke dope together. Cannabis, pot – whatever you want to call it. Everyone did. All our friends. And why not? As far as I can see, it's perfectly harmless. But Toby began rolling me joints with a little something added. My special joints, he called them.' Her shoulders twitched. 'And after a while, I couldn't do without them. So what could I do? I didn't know anyone else who could get me heroin. Only Toby. *Keep it in the family*: that's what he said. And as long as I do what Toby wants, there's no problem there.'

'There are doctors. A GP could refer you to a – ?'

'But I *like* it. Besides, I'm scared.'

'Why are you scared?'

'Because if I try to stop using heroin, Toby won't be able to rely on me to do what he wants.'

'But that's the whole point of it, surely?'

'He'll do something. He'll try and get me back on it. And if he can't manage that, he might do *anything*. It's very easy to overdose, you see. Especially with Chinese heroin. And his stuff's all Chinese. It comes in from Hong Kong, and you never really know how strong it is or what they've cut it with. It's not pure, like the stuff you get on the NHS. Not that there's much of that around these days. But if a dealer gets annoyed with a customer, he'll sometimes give him a shot of unusually pure heroin. There's a word for it in the trade. It's called a hotshot. And it kills you.'

'But what good would that do him? You said he hasn't any money of his own. Wouldn't he be killing the golden goose?'

'If I made a will, you mean? Left what I've got to someone else. I'm not sure it would work. When we bought this house, he made me sign something. A sort of option clause. It gives him the right to buy it at a nominal sum unless he agrees to the sale.' By now it was almost entirely dark and Joanna's voice had sunk to a whisper. 'He'd probably kill me anyway. There'd be no danger for him, because everyone would say I was just another addict who had taken an overdose. He likes to feel in control, you see. That's important in itself.'

'But *killing* you?'

She twisted in my arms. 'Believe me. You must believe me. He's my brother, I know him.'

She reached for the cigarettes again. For a moment we smoked in silence.

'Have I made you hate me? Despise me?'

'Of course you haven't. We'll go away together. Then I can look after you, help you with the treatment. We'll find you a lawyer, too. Toby won't be able to find you. That's the important thing.'

'I can't do that. I can't ruin your life.'

'You don't want to come with me?'

'You know I do. But if we go away together, I'll ruin you – one way or another. And I love you – so how can I do that to you?'

'You must let me decide that. I know what I'm letting myself in for.'

'You don't, not really. You don't know what living with an addict is like. You don't even know me very well.' She stroked my neck, tracing the outline of the Adam's apple. 'We must go. They'll be wondering where we are.'

'They don't matter.'

'They do. You know they do.'

It was then, as if on cue, that we heard footsteps slowly crossing the bare boards of the room below. There was a faint creak.

'That's the door to the stairs,' Joanna whispered. 'He's coming up.'

'The door's locked.'

'Yes, but the key's in the lock. If they bend down and look . . .'

We clung together like babes in the wood. The footsteps were slow but not heavy. They could have belonged to a man or a woman. They slowed as they approached our door, and then stopped. Joanna squeezed my hand.

There was a faint tapping. I held my breath. Someone wanting to be quiet – why? Not wanting to disturb Joanna if she were asleep? Or afraid of a third party hearing the knock? At length – I had lost track of time – the footsteps began again.

'They're going *up*,' Joanna murmured.

Enclosed in darkness, we listened to the sounds and tried to decode them. The higher the footsteps climbed, the more muffled they became. Suddenly they were louder and more crisply defined.

Joanna stirred against me. 'He's in the room above.' Her breath tickled my ear. 'You don't think . . . ?'

'No. It's not Francis Youlgreave. You can be quite sure of that.' As I spoke I wondered if I were right.

The footsteps crossed the ceiling above our heads. I thought they led to the window overlooking the drive, the one from which Francis Youlgreave had jumped to the gravel below.

Silence settled around us again. When at last the footsteps began again, I felt Joanna letting out her breath. A sigh of relief? *He hasn't jumped, this time*.

The steps stopped. What was he – or she – doing now? Staring out of another window? Then the movement began again – more rapid now, almost a run, and much louder. The steps tapped across the floor and clattered down the stairs, not pausing at Joanna's door. Somewhere below us another door slammed.

Joanna slithered away from me, rolled off the mattress and scrambled to her feet. Her naked body was a dark blur, as beautiful in the semi-darkness as it was in the light. I struggled up myself – far more slowly, for my limbs were less supple, and I was not used to scrambling up from mattresses. She tiptoed across the room to the north-facing window. Her body darkened into a silhouette in front of the paler grey of the glass.

'David – look.'

I padded across the floor. The room was full of draughts, slipping through the windows, under the door, through the cracks in the floorboards. The warmth from our lovemaking

546

had gone and I felt cold. When I reached the window, Joanna leant against me and drew my arm over her shoulder and down between her breasts.

'See.' She pointed with her free hand. 'Over there – beyond the pool, beyond the trees.'

On the far side of the trees, just beyond the garden boundary, flames flickered red and orange in Carter's Meadow. They had climbed high and were still climbing higher. Because of the screen of leaves and branches between us and the fire, the flames were an impressionistic jumble of sparks. The window was open a little at the top, and for an instant I thought I could even hear the crackle of the fire and perhaps a cry of pain and terror.

> *With flames to the flesh, with brands to the burning,*
> *As incense to heav'n the soul is returning . . .*

35

'Someone's having a bonfire.' The calmness of my voice amazed me. 'Teenagers, perhaps. After all, it's Saturday night.'

Joanna did not reply. She began to search for her clothes in the semi-darkness. I did the same. I felt ungainly, unclean and furtive. Joanna finished dressing before me. While I was still knotting my shoelaces, she was unlocking the door.

'It's a good time to go,' she said. 'They'll have seen the fire. It'll be a diversion.'

I straightened up. 'I wish we could stay.'

'So do I.'

'There's so much we need to talk about. The future.'

'I don't belong in your future.'

'You do.'

She reached up and kissed me. 'I so much want to believe you.' Her arms tightened round my neck. 'If I could sort out Toby somehow, could we really be together?'

'Of course we could. We can in any case.'

'I've got an idea.'

'What?'

'I don't want to tell you yet. I don't know if I'm brave enough to do it. I don't know if it would work.'

I started to ask a question, but she covered my mouth, first with her fingers and then with her lips. A moment later, she turned the key and opened the door . . .

'Give me your hand,' she murmured. 'We'd better not use the light, and I know the way.'

'You sound as if you're talking in parables.'

She stopped so suddenly that I bumped into her, and again

she reached up and kissed me. Without another word she led me down the stairs, across the room below and along the landing which ran the length of the house.

The music had stopped. The light was on at the head of the stairs. People were talking somewhere in the distance. Their voices echoed up from the hall, sounds chasing each other through the house to the lantern in the roof. Among the voices I thought I recognized James's and perhaps Vanessa's.

Joanna tugged me into a passage on the left, leading towards the back of the house. There was still enough light for me to be able to make out broad outlines and variations of light and shade; but all detail had gone. We went up and down short flights of stairs and across bare rooms smelling of dust. In one room we heard the scuttling of a startled animal, probably a rat. Joanna shied away from the sound and for an instant nestled against me.

She opened a door. 'The backstairs,' she whispered. 'I'll go first and check there's no one in the kitchen.'

A moment later, I joined her in the kitchen, a large, untidy room which smelled of damp and stale milk, and which looked in the gloom as though little had changed there since the Youlgreaves left in the 1930s.

'We'd better separate,' Joanna said. 'If you go through that door and carry straight on, you'll reach the hall. You could say you were looking for a lavatory. I'll go round the back.'

'Where?'

'There's a kitchen yard outside, and then the stables. I can get round into the garden, near the swimming pool.'

She gave me a gentle push towards the door to the hall. She herself moved away in the opposite direction. When I reached the door I stopped and looked back at her.

She, too, was looking at me. 'I love you,' she said softly but very distinctly. 'Whatever happens, remember that.'

She opened the door and was gone. Sadness swept over me like a fog. I stumbled blindly through the house.

There were lights in the hall. I forced myself towards the glare. I saw no one. The door to the office was still shut. I heard voices on my left, presumably coming from the sitting room with the bar. I could not make out the words, but the voices were no longer making party sounds: they sounded urgent and confused.

I pushed my fingers through my hair and straightened my tie. If only I could find a mirror – I was suddenly afraid that my appearance must in some way proclaim not only that I loved Joanna but that we had spent much of the evening making love. I looked at my watch. It was after nine o'clock. It felt much later.

I peered down the corridor. The door to the sitting room was open. Someone had left a half-filled glass on the hall floor. On impulse I picked it up. A partygoer has a drink in his hand; the possession of a drink helped to create an illusion of my innocence.

The sitting room was full of people. Many of them were clustered round the makeshift bar. I could not see Vanessa or Toby.

James's voice rose above the others: 'Softly, softly, eh? No point in letting it spoil the party.' He spotted me and waved me towards him. 'Have you seen Toby?'

'He might be outside.'

'He went off somewhere. Thought he might have been looking for you.'

I shook my head.

'Someone's lit a bonfire in that field by the council estate.'

'So I gather.'

'Just a bit of fun, probably.'

There were footsteps outside and suddenly Vanessa was in the room. Her face was flushed and she looked very happy – almost as though she had come from meeting a lover. She came towards me.

'I was wondering where you were,' she said. 'What's happening?'

'There's a bonfire on Carter's Meadow.'

'That fire's on our land,' interrupted Ted Potter, waving a beer bottle belligerently. The bottle was not empty and some of the contents trickled on to his face and shoulders. 'Bloody trespassers, Vicar, if you don't mind me saying so. We're going to turf them out.'

'It's not your land, Ted,' Doris said, grabbing his arm. 'It's mine. And now you've got beer all over your jacket.'

'Oh Doris,' he crooned. He held the bottle up to the light and saw that it was now empty. He lunged towards the bar table and beamed at James. 'It's my round, Doc. What's everyone having?'

Doris looked at me. 'I'm sorry. It's only once or twice a year he gets like that. Doesn't touch the stuff the rest of the time. I just wish he wouldn't do it in public.'

I smiled at her. 'At least he's enjoying himself. And he's worked very hard today.'

'So have we all. That's no excuse.'

'What have you got there, Vicar?' Ted called. 'Gin, is it?'

I covered the stolen glass with my hand and shook my head. Suddenly the memory of Joanna pushed its way to the forefront of my mind and I wanted to laugh with happiness.

'Wonderful, isn't it?' Vanessa was saying. 'Such a piece of luck.'

I spilled a few drops of my drink. 'I'm sorry – what is?'

'The books. Toby says I can take them home.'

'So they did belong to Francis?'

'Yes. There must be about thirty of them. Mainly theology, but there are some oddities as well. There's a copy of *The Tongues of Angels* with the pages uncut. And a mid-Victorian housewives' manual on meat.'

'On *what*?'

Vanessa stared up at me with a half smile on her face. Implacable as fate, she knew exactly what she was telling me. 'Meat. Everything the housewife needed to know. How to buy it, prepare it, cook it, serve it, dress it, carve it, use up the leftovers.' She paused. 'How to cut it up. There was a little textbook of human anatomy, too. Some of the passages had been marked.'

I sipped my drink, discovering that it was neat gin.

'I'm not going to sanitize Francis Youlgreave. I want to know the *truth*.'

Ted Potter stumbled between us and sat down heavily in one of the armchairs. 'To be perfectly honest, it's past my bedtime,' he confided to the glass in his hand. He nodded, as though at something the glass had replied. 'Yes, tomorrow is another day.'

551

His eyelids closed. The glass wavered. Doris removed it and stared down at her husband. Charlene came to join her. A moment later, Ted began to snore gently.

'Kevin'll have to give us a hand with him,' Doris said.

Charlene shook her head. 'Kevin's flat on his back. Miss Oliphant tripped over him and he didn't even notice.'

'Just leave them where they are,' Vanessa suggested. 'Why should getting them home be your responsibility?'

'Toby!' James roared at my shoulder. 'How's the Great Fire of Carter's Meadow?'

Toby was at the nearer French window. 'Seems to be dying down. I don't think anyone's out there. I'm going to have a look at it now. Anyone want to come?' He turned to me. 'David?'

'David'll soon sort them out,' James said, and laughed loudly. 'The church militant.'

Vanessa followed me on to the terrace. From this angle, you could not see the fire. Audrey was standing by the steps leading down to the lawn.

'Is Rosemary all right?' Vanessa asked.

'I expect so. I haven't seen her recently.'

'David?' Audrey called from the shadows at the edge of the lawn. 'I'd like a word.'

I could tell by her voice that she was upset. 'Could it wait a moment? I gather there's a little problem in Carter's Meadow.'

'The fire? I bet you anything it's those wretched boys.'

'The ones from the bus shelter?'

'No – Michael and Brian Vintner.' She walked slowly towards us. 'They've been behaving like barbarians all evening. I'm sorry to have to tell you this, but Michael barged into me by the pool and then rushed off without apologizing. And he and Brian were playing in the trees near the fence and making a terrible racket. I think they deserve a severe punishment.'

'Audrey,' Vanessa interrupted. 'Thank you for telling us, but I really think you should leave Michael to us.'

'I'm sorry, Mrs Byfield.' Audrey spat out Vanessa's married name as if it were a curse. 'It's just not good enough.'

'May we talk about this later?' I said.

'Leave it to me,' Vanessa said, her voice grim. 'I'll talk to Audrey. You and Toby go and sort out the fire.'

Coward that I was, I was glad to take the easy way out. I had no wish to become involved in yet another of Audrey's outbursts. Not that I was particularly keen to go with Toby, either. The irony was that while Audrey was merely an irritation, Toby – if what Joanna had told me was true – was capable of real evil. Yet Toby was intelligent and had good manners, and he didn't make scenes; so in one way he was the more attractive choice of companion. It is always simpler to judge by externals, even when there is no excuse for doing so.

Toby and I walked across the lawn, the beam of his torch snaking before us. Few people were out here now. A young couple were embracing on one of the benches beside the swimming pool. When they saw us they hastily sat up and straightened their clothes. It was too dark to recognize their faces. Toby and I walked round the pool and I heard the couple scurrying into the night like the startled rat Joanna and I had disturbed upstairs.

'You can't see the fire from here,' I said.

'I only noticed it because I went up the tower to see if Jo was there. Have you seen her lately, by the way?'

'Not recently. I've not seen Michael or Rosemary, either.'

'Michael and Brian have been having the time of their lives. But I'm afraid Audrey hasn't.'

'Perhaps we should have taken the boys home.'

'Why? It's their party, too. I like parties where you have all sorts, all ages.'

He led me towards the path through the bushes, the one Rosemary and I had taken in the opposite direction on the afternoon when Rosemary found the blood and the fur in Carter's Meadow. There was a pattering on the leaves above our heads.

'It's starting to rain,' Toby said. 'It's been trying to all evening.'

'At least it'll help put out the fire.'

The path had swung round to the left, and we could see the fire quite clearly on the far side of the fence. A few minutes later, we scrambled through into Carter's Meadow. We set off across the rough grass towards the little spinney of self-seeded trees.

'It's at the same place we found the fur,' Toby said. 'Exactly the same. How odd.'

I glanced at him, but the darkness hid his face. 'It may be a coincidence.'

We walked on towards the clump of trees. The dead elder stood on one side, apart from the others. Its wood must have dried out still further over the summer. It was a tree of fire, burning with one last glow of artificial life. By now the flames were dying down, but many of the branches and twigs still gleamed red. Two of the neighbouring trees had blackened leaves, but fortunately the flames had not spread.

Toby panned the torch beam to and fro. No one was there. Nothing moved apart from the dying flames and the rain, which was growing steadily heavier. Trapped in the beam, the raindrops looked like needles showering from the sky.

'Phew,' he said. 'You can feel the heat from here.'

'Lucky the wind wasn't in the other direction. The other trees would have gone, too.'

The beam of the torch raced across the grass to the base of the tree. 'What's that?'

Picked out in the torchlight was a black oblong with a red glow along the top. Something else lay half concealed on the ground immediately behind it – something red, I thought, though it was hard to be sure because the colour might simply be a reflection of the flames.

Toby stopped a few yards away from the tree; the heat made it uncomfortable to go nearer. He played the beam on the ground.

'It's a sort of box. And that might be a petrol can behind it.'

'So the fire was started deliberately?'

'Probably CHBs.'

'What?'

Toby turned his head towards me and the reflections of the flames danced like snakes among his ginger curls. 'Council house brats.' He threw back his head and laughed.

The words shocked me – not merely because of their grotesque snobbery, but because Toby had assumed I would share his amusement. Was that how I appeared to him?

He turned back to the fire. 'It'll burn itself out in an hour or so, and I don't think it's going to do any damage to anything else. But it's a bit close to the garden for comfort.'

'We'd better report it to the police.'

'If this were my land, the first thing I'd do is rebuild the fences.'

I was only half listening to him. I edged across the grass towards the tree. The heat was unpleasant but not unbearable. Beside the box, the petrol can lay on its side, its cap off.

'Do you think Mrs Potter might sell the field to me eventually? It would round off the garden rather nicely.'

I picked up a long twig, one end charred from the fire. I used it to touch the blackened side of the box. The two came together with a faint *clunk*, which suggested that the box was made of metal.

Dear God – not CHBs. Much closer to home.

'David – what are you doing? Mind out – that branch is going to come down.'

I ignored him. Shielding my face with my free arm against the heat, I took another two paces closer to the box. This must have been where the fire had started. I poked one end of the stick inside. A rectangular shape emerged from the debris, scattering ashes and sparks.

'David – ?'

The object slithered down the stick and settled on the base of the box again, sending up another puff of ash. I retreated quickly to Toby.

'What is it? What did you find?'

In the space of a few seconds, the possibilities chased through my mind. I could say I did not know what it was. I could let someone else make the connection. I could say nothing to Toby but go and find Vanessa. Or I could say nothing to Toby or Vanessa, but instead phone the police. Or I could go back to the Vicarage and see if there was any damage there. Most of all, I wished that it was not I who had to deal with this.

'I'm pretty sure that's the tin box that contained the Youlgreave papers. It was in our house. If I'm right, someone must have broken in and stolen it. James left a can of petrol in the garage this afternoon, and I think they must have stolen that as well.'

Toby whistled. 'Vanessa – what's she going to say?'

'It depends if the papers were still in the box.'

'No point if they weren't. Anyway, *something* was inside. What a mess.'

He was right. Less than half an hour earlier, Joanna and I had been in bed together, and everything had seemed so simple. Not easy, but simple. Now, standing beside a burning tree with rain falling steadily on my head and shoulders, I felt as though nothing would ever be simple and straightforward again.

'We'd better phone the police.'

'Come this way.' Toby pointed the torch beam across the field to another part of the fence between it and the garden. 'We can go through the stables. Less chance of meeting people, and we'll get less wet.'

He took me through the darkened stables and into a yard in the shadow of the back of the house. Soon we were in the kitchen where I had last seen Joanna. He led me along the corridor to the office by the front door. The room was empty. On the table was a wooden box, with its lid open. I saw books inside, neatly stacked. Toby shut the door behind us and put the torch on the table.

'You'd better phone. They'll take more notice of you.'

He found me the number of the police station. When I got through, I talked to a desk sergeant who was reluctant to believe that anything was seriously amiss. We argued to and fro for several minutes.

'Look,' the man said at last. 'It's Saturday night and we're already overstretched. From what you've told me, it sounds like a bit of fun that got out of hand. But there's no real damage done, is there? Still, I'll make sure someone's round first thing in the morning.'

'Isn't burglary and the destruction of property serious any longer?'

'Of course they are, sir.' The policeman's good humour seemed unruffled. 'I tell you what: why don't you go home and see if there's any evidence of a break-in? Maybe it wasn't your box, after all. No harm in checking. If you have had a break-in, of course, you give us a ring. I'll make a note of your call.'

That was the end of my attempt to fetch the police. Toby, who had been leaning against the door smoking a cigarette, straightened up and smiled at me.

'The boys in blue not being too helpful?'

'You probably gathered what they said.'

'I'll drive you down to the Vicarage if you want.'

'I'd better have a word with Vanessa first. Break the news.'
I hesitated. 'Perhaps we shouldn't mention the box to anyone
else until we've told her.'

We left the office and walked along the corridor towards the
sitting room. Little had changed in our absence. The Potter
women were still beside the head of the family, as he snored
quietly in the armchair. James and Mary, supported by a dedicated band of helpers, were working their way methodically
through the remaining contents of the bar. Rosemary had
returned and was surrounded by three youths who were vying
for her attention by the fireplace. Joanna wasn't there; nor were
Vanessa and Audrey.

'Seen Vanessa?' Toby asked.

'Thought she went out with you and David,' James said. 'Did
you catch our arsonist?'

'No sign of anyone. Just a burning tree.'

'Sounds like your province, David. Isn't there something in
the Bible about a burning bush and the angel of the Lord?'

'Exodus. Chapter three.'

I went to the nearest French window, with Toby behind me.
The rain was no longer a shower but a downpour. Reflected light
from the sitting room sparkled in the puddles on the terrace.

'Maybe she's sheltering by the pool,' Toby suggested. 'Shall I
fetch an umbrella? There's one in the Jag.'

'One of the boys will get it,' James said. 'Brian! Toby's got a
job for you.'

Brian slipped through the crowd. For once Michael was not
with him. I felt a stirring of unease. If he was still outside, he
would be soaked.

Toby gave Brian the car key. 'The car's just outside the
front door, under the canopy. There's a brolly on the back
seat.'

The boy ran off, glad to have a job to do, wanting to show
off his speed and efficiency. Too late, I wished I had asked him
where Michael was.

'Vanessa?' I called. 'Vanessa?'

I waited for an answer. Beside me, Toby was silent. I stared across the lawn, a pale-grey smudge in the darkness.

Suddenly Brian was in the doorway of the sitting room. 'There are two men outside,' he gasped. 'They've broken into your car.'

There was a moment's silence.

Then Toby said, '*Shit!*' and ran past Brian, pushing him out of the way. Brian and I followed, with at least a dozen others trailing behind us. Rosemary was just behind me.

'Are you all right?' I asked in a low voice.

She did not answer. The current of people carried us side by side down the corridor into the hall. The front door was standing open. Rain gusted into the house, and a pool of water covered the tiles near the door. Framed in the doorway were two men in sodden raincoats, their bare heads wet with rain. Behind them was Toby's car under the shelter of the canopy. The driver's door was hanging open, and the panel shielding the door and window mechanisms had been removed.

'Mr Clifford?' said the taller of the two, a man with a broad face and eyes that slanted down at the outer corners. 'Mr Toby Clifford?'

'Yes,' Toby said. 'Who are you?'

'Police.' For an instant the man held out what might have been a warrant card. 'I'm Detective Sergeant Field, and this is Detective Constable Ingram. We'd like to ask you some questions, sir.'

'What are you doing with my car? Have you broken into it?'

'It was unlocked. We –'

'You're lying. It was locked.'

'Perhaps in the circumstances it would be better if you accompanied us to the station, sir. We wouldn't want to upset your guests, would we?'

Toby didn't answer. He was staring at the other man, who was holding what looked like a small brown parcel.

'I should tell you that you're not obliged to say anything unless you wish to do so,' Field was saying, 'but what you say may be put into writing and given in evidence.'

Someone behind me gasped.

Toby swung round, turning his back on the police officers. His face was so pale it was almost green. His eyes searched the little crowd of his guests.

'You,' he said, pointing at Rosemary. 'You tight-arsed, screwed-up little bitch, you frigid little fucked-up cow.'

He lunged at her. Automatically I stepped in front of Rosemary and he cannoned against me. Then the two policemen grabbed his arms from behind.

'Party's over,' Field said.

But it was not over. Toby was handcuffed and led to the car. While Field radioed for assistance, Ingram began to take our names and addresses. He began with me. When he realized I was a clergyman, his eyebrows rose, making me feel like a naughty child caught out.

'What about Miss Clifford?' he asked me. 'Where's she?'

'I don't know.'

He moved on to James, who was looking almost sober again. I glanced round the crowded hall. Almost everyone was there, apart from the Potters, Joanna, Audrey, Vanessa and Michael.

And Rosemary, too, I suddenly realized: she had been there a moment ago, but now she had slipped away.

There was a light under the office door. Perhaps Vanessa had returned to pore over Francis Youlgreave's books, oblivious of the commotion. I opened the door. No one was there. The books and the torch were still on the table. So was the telephone.

'Officer?' I called to Ingram. 'Do you mind if I try phoning the Vicarage to see if my family's gone back home?'

Ingram nodded, and went back to Mary Vintner, who was still nursing a large gin.

I dialled the Vicarage number. The phone rang on and on.

'I bet they're all down at the pool,' James said at my shoulder. 'Probably sheltering in that little hut. I expect Joanna's there as well.'

'We'd better go and see. If the police let us.'

Ingram raised no objection, so James and I walked back to the sitting room; James brought the torch. We went out on the terrace.

'Vanessa?' I shouted. 'Audrey? Michael?'

'Joanna!' yelled James a few inches away from my left ear.

There was no reply. Just the steady rustle of the rain.

'Damn it,' James said. 'We'll have to go down there and get soaked.'

Then someone began to scream.

It was a high, gasping sound in two parts, with the stress on the first. It sounded completely inhuman, like the cry of a seabird. But the screams made a word, repeated over and over again.

David. David. David.

I ran down the steps to the lawn towards the source of the scream. James flicked on the torch and followed. We pounded in the direction of the pool. My feet skidded on the wet grass. Rain ran down my cheeks and filled my eyes. The beam danced like a will-o'-the-wisp in front of us. I stumbled and almost fell down the short flight of steps from the lawn.

Rain speckled the surface of the water. The torchlight swooped from one side of the pool to another. It picked out Audrey in the shallow end, her hair hanging wet and loose on her shoulders, and the skirt of her dress floating around her on the water. She was standing with her arms upraised, her mouth wide open and her head thrown back as if she were addressing a deity only she could see.

David. David. David.

The beam danced on. It showed a woman in Vanessa's dress, lying on her belly in the water, with Vanessa's hair floating like black seaweed beside Audrey's ballooning skirt.

The light skipped onwards. The water was no longer merely blue: reds and pinks swirled like clouds on a dawn sky. Its surface was pockmarked with a shifting pattern of raindrops.

David. David. David.

The wind soughed in the branches of the trees beyond the pool, and the leaves of the copper beech rustled. The beam danced back, light as a feather, first to Audrey and then to Vanessa. All the while the baying continued.

David. David. David.

36

Only one thing could have been worse than Vanessa dead.

I had few memories of the rest of the night after we found her floating in the swimming pool, and they were little better than a succession of snapshots. Even their sequence was uncertain. In my mind I shuffled them to and fro, trying to put them into order, trying to make sense out of nonsense. Coherence is a weapon against chaos, against fear, against evil. I made myself believe that.

First in the sequence came the stench of chlorine filling my nostrils. The water was cold, almost icy. It slapped and patted me like a hostile masseuse. It did not want me to reach Vanessa.

David. David. David.

I was aware of an obstacle, of something clinging to me, hindering me from reaching Vanessa. I made an effort and threw it aside. Did I hit it? Not *it*: her. Audrey.

Vanessa lay in the water like a log – a thing not a person. I pawed at her, trying to get a grip. Her dress ripped. Tendrils of hair coiled around my wrist. I thought again: yes, *how like seaweed*. I hooked my arms under her armpits and pulled the top half of her body out of the water. Even with the water partly supporting her lower half, she was so heavy I could hardly raise her. She might have been made of iron. *A dead weight.*

I hauled her up. Her head lolled against my shoulder. I held her, squeezing her against my chest as, less than an hour earlier, I had held Joanna. Slowly I staggered towards the side of the pool. It was as if I were fighting my way through chilly treacle. A torch flashed like a spotlight across my face. A man was shouting but I did not have the energy to listen to the words.

David. David. David.

There was a splash. The water rocked in the pool and drops of it spattered on my face. James was beside me.

'Give her to me,' he ordered.

I shook my head. She was my burden.

He took no notice. He prised one of my arms free and between us we half carried, half dragged Vanessa towards the ladder at the shallow end.

A little later, she lay on her back beside the pool and around her spread dark stains of blood and water. James crouched over her like an animal over its prey. Was he hitting her? Kissing her? I tried to stop him but someone held me back. Later still, perhaps, James issued orders. Blankets, bandages, hot-water bottles, ambulances. He sent people here, demanded things from there. How odd, I thought – a moment ago he was drunk, but now he seems perfectly sober.

Around us in the darkness people gathered. I heard a siren. I saw a flashing light, barely visible through the bushes of the shrubbery.

'No, no, no,' someone was saying; and I did not realize it was myself until Mary Vintner wrapped a blanket round my shoulders and told me to be quiet.

'The boys,' I muttered to her. 'The boys mustn't see this. Where are they?'

'Don't worry,' Mary said. 'They're safe. We'll look after them.'

'And Rosemary?'

'Don't worry.'

There were police cars in the drive as well as an ambulance. In the ambulance, they made me lie down. I could not see what they were doing to Vanessa. The ride was very bumpy.

'Drive more carefully,' I said. 'You mustn't shake her up.'

Nobody heard me; I was not even sure that I had spoken aloud.

At the hospital, they put me in a chair. Somebody gave me a cup of tea. People talked to me and I talked back to them. What I remember most clearly, however, was a cracked tile above a washbasin in a room where they took Vanessa. The crack had a curve to it. I stared at it for what seemed like hours. The longer I stared, the more I was convinced that the line the crack

562

described was identical to the curve of Joanna's cheek from eye socket to chin. It was clearly a sign. But I could not interpret its significance.

I saw two hands before me: one palm upwards, holding two white tablets, and the other with a glass of water between forefinger and thumb.

'Not heroin,' I said, perhaps aloud. 'Not heroin.'

'These will help you relax,' a woman's voice said with such authority that I knew that she was telling the truth. 'Swallow them.'

There was also a policeman. Before or afterwards? Or both? He wore a uniform. As he talked, he turned his cap round and round in his hands. His fingernails were chewed to the quick, and there were bright orange nicotine stains on the fingers. His voice was ugly. I did not hear what he said.

I must have slept because I remember waking. When I woke, it was as though I had climbed out of a pit of darkness into a world I had never seen before, into a bleak, featureless landscape which stretched, flat as a table, all around for as far as I could see; and above my head was the vast hemisphere of the sky; a Fen landscape, such as had surrounded me at Rosington. It was silent, apart from a faint beating of wings which might have been no more than the pulsing of my own heart.

Janet – oh Janet. Something was wrong, worse than wrong. *Not Janet. Wrong place, wrong time, wrong woman. Vanessa? Joanna?*

I remembered the pills on the woman's hand – barbiturates? – before I remembered what had happened to Vanessa. I turned my head on the pillow. The first thing I saw was another uniformed policeman. This one had the face of a child. His scared eyes met mine. Why was he afraid of me? I stared at him.

'How – how are you feeling?'

He didn't wait for an answer. He stood up, opened the door and murmured something to a person I could not see.

'My wife,' I said; my voice sounded weak and strained. 'How is she?'

'Detective Inspector Jeevons will be here in a moment,' the constable said. 'He'll probably be able to tell you.'

'Surely you know?'

'Me? No one tells me anything.'

'But is she alive?'

'I'm sorry, sir,' he said, his hand on the door, eager to be gone. 'I just don't know.'

It was nearly an hour before I saw the inspector. In the meantime a nurse brought me tea.

'My wife?'

'Still unconscious. But she's pulled through the night.'

While I drank the tea, I sat in a pair of borrowed pyjamas in an armchair by the window, looking down on a hospital car park where people with sad, intent faces passed to and fro. I assumed that someone had taken away the clothes I had been wearing last night to dry them – and possibly for examination, as well. I found blood encrusted under my fingernails and washed my hands over and over again. I tried to pray but I could not find words. After a while I simply sat there and watched the car park. At last there was a tap on the door.

Sergeant Clough sidled into the room after Detective Inspector Jeevons. Clough was more subdued than I had seen him before. He kept his brown, bald head bowed and did not speak unless Jeevons asked him to. Jeevons was younger – a man in his early forties with a dark, cadaverous face, coarse skin and black hair; he had long sideburns that reached to the bottom of his ears.

'My wife. How is she?'

'She's alive, sir,' Jeevons said. 'But her condition's very serious.'

'I can't remember properly. What happened to her? How was she hurt?'

'She was stabbed in the left shoulder and hit over the head, probably with an ashtray. Then she fell or was pushed into the swimming pool at Roth Park. By that time she was probably unconscious.'

A woman in Vanessa's dress, lying on her belly in the water, with Vanessa's hair floating black and glistening around the head . . .

'But she was face downwards. She wouldn't have been able to breathe.' I swallowed. 'Will she live?'

'I don't know. The *doctors* don't know. I'm sorry, sir – but there it is.' He looked peeved, as though the uncertainty irritated him. 'We've arrested her attacker.'

My eyes were open but they saw only the swimming pool, the dark stains on the clear water. *Pink clouds in a dawn sky. Red in the morning, shepherd's warning.*

'Are you well enough for a little chat?'

I nodded. Clough had already opened his notebook.

'I understand there'd been bad feeling between your wife and Audrey Oliphant for some time?'

'I knew they didn't get on. But surely you're not implying –'

'Just asking a few questions, sir. Sorry to have to trouble you at a time like this, but it has to be done. Now – several witnesses have told us that Mrs Byfield and Miss Oliphant were having words near the swimming pool just before the attack. Heated words, it seems. There had been another exchange of views, too, but that was in the house, and much earlier in the evening. This one was while you and Mr Clifford were looking at the fire. Do you remember the fire?'

'The burning bush – tree, I mean?'

He frowned at me. 'The one on that bit of waste ground near the garden.'

'I rang the police.'

'That's right. You were going to see if there had been a break-in at the Vicarage. Remember?'

'Yes. But then –'

'Your daughter says she saw Miss Oliphant starting the fire. I gather she was burning some valuable papers which belonged to your wife. Or rather which had been loaned to her.'

'*Audrey* did that?'

'So it seems. Dr Vintner tells me that Audrey Oliphant is going through the menopause. Women can do funny things at that stage in their lives. Spiteful. A little unbalanced, even.' Jeevons stared out of the window. 'We've seen her diary.'

I thought of the red exercise book I had seen in Audrey's sitting room.

'Did you realize that Audrey Oliphant was in love with you, sir?'

'Surely that's putting it a bit strongly, Inspector? She's a devout churchgoer and I suppose as her priest I –'

'She wasn't interested in you just as a priest, sir. Take it from me. We got something else from that diary. She thought your wife was responsible for cutting up her cat.'

'But that's absolutely ridiculous.'

'So it seems,' he said again, baring his teeth in an unpleasant smile. 'But people do make themselves believe ridiculous things. It's human nature.' He sighed. 'And then they go and act out the consequences.'

'Are you suggesting that Audrey Oliphant attacked my wife?'

'Mr Clifford tells us there was a knife down there. He'd been cutting up cheese earlier in the evening in that little changing hut. We found the knife in the bottom of the pool. There was an ashtray in there as well – a heavy, cut-glass thing, with sharp corners. According to Mr Clifford, it was on the verandah of the changing hut. No prints on either of them, I'm afraid.'

'You're telling me that Miss Oliphant went for my wife with a knife and an ashtray? In a homicidal frenzy?'

'For what it's worth, I think she was trying to help your wife afterwards. So it seems. We think she was trying to pull her out. I dare say they'll take that into account.'

My mind grappled with his words. 'Who will?'

'The court. Miss Oliphant's in custody, now. She'll be charged later this morning.'

'It – it doesn't seem possible.'

'It never does, sir, until it happens. But there's very little doubt about it. You see, your daughter saw them fighting on the edge of the pool. She saw Miss Oliphant with the knife. And then she scooped something up from the verandah.'

The room was silent. Engines revved in the car park below.

'Where is my daughter?'

Jeevons glanced at his notebook. 'She's with friends. Mr and Mrs Potter. We had a word with her earlier this morning.'

'And Michael? My godson – what's happened to him?'

'He spent the night with Dr and Mrs Vintner. We've not talked to him yet. I'm told he's been asking after you.'

'I must see Vanessa.' I said Vanessa's name but I saw Joanna's face in my mind: it was as if a screen slid back in my memory: Joanna reminded me of Toby, his attack on Rosemary and the two men dripping in the doorway of Roth Park. 'What happened about the drugs?'

Jeevons stared down his long nose at me. 'What do you mean, exactly?'

'There were two plain-clothes policemen already at the house,' I went on, trying to conceal my irritation. 'They had found something – drugs? – in Toby Clifford's car. They were arresting him.'

'It's a separate enquiry,' said Jeevons, his voice suddenly formal and precise as though he were in a witness box. 'The officers were from the drug squad. They discovered a considerable amount of heroin concealed in Mr Clifford's car, and also some cannabis in the house.'

'Someone must have told them where to look.'

Jeevons said nothing.

'Toby accused Rosemary – my daughter.'

'So I understand, sir.'

It was typical of Toby to store his heroin in the Jaguar, typical of him to allow Michael to play in the car. But the fact that Toby had accused Rosemary could only mean that she knew about the location of the cache. Had he tried to introduce her to heroin, as he had introduced others? I remembered the day Rosemary had run upstairs into the bathroom.

'Can heroin make you sick? Physically vomit, I mean?'

Jeevons frowned. 'Why do you ask?'

'Because there was one time that Rosemary came back in quite a state after seeing Toby. She acted very oddly. She was sick.'

'First-time users often are sick.'

'So that's how she knew where he kept the stuff.' I stared at Jeevons, and suddenly I knew that I was only partly right. 'But it wasn't Rosemary who tipped you off, was it? It was Joanna Clifford.'

'I'm afraid I can't comment on that.'

He didn't need to comment. His face confirmed what I had thought. Joanna must have phoned the police soon after we parted. Probably she had also unlocked the car to make it easy for the police. Joy stabbed me, just for an instant, and I winced with the pain of it: the pain of knowing that she did care for me, that she had been prepared to fight her addiction and face up to her brother; the pain of knowing that she believed we might have a future.

'What's happened to her? Joanna, I mean?'

Jeevons looked at me, and I sensed that he was puzzled. 'Miss Clifford? She's gone to London to stay with an aunt. We drove her there last night. Why?'

'I – I'm glad she's with her family. This must be a very terrible time for her.'

He was still staring at me. 'Quite so.'

'I must see my wife. And then I must see the children.'

'That's all right, sir. We'll need to talk to you again, later. We've got a suitcase with some clothes for you in the car. Your daughter packed it.'

'My daughter . . .' I echoed.

Jeevons stood up. 'I'll make sure someone brings up the case. Then you can see your wife and go home. We'll give you a lift back to Roth.'

I stood up as well. *I don't want to see my wife, I don't want to go home. All I want is Joanna, you stupid man.* Aloud I said, 'Thank you, Inspector.'

37

Vanessa was still unconscious when I left the hospital early in the afternoon. Before I saw her, I had an interview with the consultant.

'She's still in a coma,' he said. 'But that's hardly surprising. You have to remember that your wife's survived a drowning, and that's more than most people do.'

'Surely she should have come out of the coma by now?'

'It's early days yet. We're hoping she'll wake up soon. Could be any time.'

'But if she does wake up, will there be brain damage?'

He looked at me, his face professionally wary. 'I'm afraid we couldn't possibly say. Not at this point.'

As the car drew up in the Vicarage drive, the front door opened and Rosemary ran out. I kissed her, and she clung to me in a way she had not done since she was a little girl.

'How's Michael?'

She pulled herself away from me. 'He's still at the Vintners'. He spent the night there.'

'They told me.'

'I stayed with the Potters. Mrs Potter's here now.'

I looked past Rosemary. Doris was standing in the doorway. She had an expression on her face which I had never seen before. Concern? Shock? Sadness? It was none of those things. As I was walking towards her I realized suddenly what it was: Doris was scared.

Later that afternoon, I went to collect Michael from the Vintners. James was working. Mary asked us all to supper, but I declined.

Brian and Michael were playing Monopoly in the sitting room and barely seemed to notice my arrival.

'He can stay if he likes,' Mary murmured. 'He's no trouble.'

Perhaps Michael heard. He looked up at me. 'Are we going now?'

'You can stay here with the Vintners if you want. They've very kindly invited you.'

He got to his feet and hauled up his jeans, which had slithered down his narrow hips. 'I'll come with you, if that's OK.' He looked at Mary, his face serious. 'Thank you for having me.'

When he and I were walking back to the Vicarage, I tried to talk to him but he answered in monosyllables. We crossed the main road and came to the gate to the churchyard. A few yards further on would bring us to the Vicarage.

'Uncle David?'

I stopped. 'What?'

Michael looked up at me and began to speak. Then three lorries trundled by, nose to tail, their engines so loud I could not hear what he was saying. I took him by the arm and led him into the churchyard. We walked round to the bench by the south porch. I sat down and Michael followed suit. It was only then that I remembered that Audrey had presented the church with this bench in memory of her parents. I wanted to stand up and run away from it, but I could not for Michael's sake.

'I haven't told the police,' he said in a voice so low I could hardly hear. 'I thought I should tell you first.'

'Tell me what?'

'I was playing near the garden fence. The fence near Carter's Meadow. Brian had gone to the lavatory . . . I saw her, when she lit the match and dropped it in the box. There was a huge flame . . . I saw her face.'

'Whose face?'

He stared up at me and there were tears in his eyes. 'Rose-mary's.'

I said nothing. The tears were rolling down his cheeks now and his lips trembled. I put my arm round his shoulders, which seemed very small and fragile.

'I looked for you,' he went on. 'But you weren't there.'

I was with Joanna. I touched Michael's hand, which was gripping the edge of the seat. 'I'm sorry.'

'There's more. Worse.'

'Go on.'

He began to shiver. 'I didn't see what happened to Aunt Vanessa. But I heard it. I heard her falling in.' He had stopped crying now, but his whole body was trembling.

I felt a spasm of pure anger – directed at myself, at God – that Michael should have had to witness this. I said, 'Where were you?'

'Near the pool – behind that little hut thing. We were playing detectives, you see. Shadowing people. Brian was following you and Toby. I was watching Miss Oliphant.'

'*Miss Oliphant.* Where was she?'

'Under the copper beech. It was raining. I think everyone else was inside. She – she was . . . sort of snuffling.'

'Crying?'

'I don't know.' He wriggled: the idea of adults crying made him uncomfortable in a way that arson and assault did not. 'Maybe. I didn't dare move or she'd see me. And then Aunt Vanessa came out of the house with an umbrella. She came down to the pool and started calling Audrey's name. Miss Oliphant went all quiet. I think Aunt Vanessa went to look for her in the hut. I couldn't see. But then Rosemary came running over the lawn and down the steps to the pool.'

I gave him my handkerchief. He blew his nose.

'Michael?' My voice emerged as a whisper. 'What happened next? Did you see?'

'No. I *heard.*'

For a moment we sat in silence. I did not want him to go on. The church clock began to chime. It was six o'clock.

'There were voices near the pool,' Michael said slowly. 'No, just one. Aunt Vanessa's. "No, don't be so stupid." That's what she said. And then there was a sort of gasp, and a splash.'

'But Audrey –'

'I *told* you – *she* was under the tree. I couldn't see her well, but I know it was her. And then she ran off *towards* the swimming pool.'

'After the splash? After you heard the voices near the pool? Are you sure?'

'Yes.'

'And you?'

'I – I went off.' His face was chalk-white, except for his eyes, which were red-rimmed and huge. 'She started screaming . . . I – I thought I'd look for you. I went down to Carter's Meadow but you weren't there.'

'Toby and I had come back to the house a different way.'

'And then . . . she was still screaming. And you came with Brian's dad.'

'You did well.'

With the arm which was around his small body, I pulled him gently towards me and he laid his head against my chest. He started to cry again.

Not for long, though. For a while, we sat there side by side on the bench, not moving, not speaking; and I stared into the porch at the notice board to the left of the door where Rosemary had displayed the mutilated corpse of Lord Peter.

EPILOGUE

On the night Vanessa died, the world turned white outside the hospital window. I sat and prayed until it was light enough to see the broad lawn and the black tangle of the trees along the main road. I looked out of the window at the view that Vanessa had never seen: at a landscape that belonged in a fairy tale. I was still there when Peter Hudson came to fetch me.

The sister understood hierarchy and enjoyed having a bishop on the premises. She fluttered around him, trying to antici-pate wishes which did not exist. When at last she left us alone with Vanessa, Peter patted my shoulder. The ameth-yst in his episcopal ring caught the light: a stab of purple fire.

'Are you all right?'

'I don't know.'

'Pneumonia?'

I nodded. 'It was always the danger. If you're in a coma you can't cough, you see, you can't get rid of the phlegm. Apparently that's what usually carries them off. Broncho-pneumonia.'

All meaningless. Words to ward off the evil spirits. How could I tell Peter what really mattered? That Vanessa's breath had rattled and wheezed. That it sounded like a mechanical contrivance, not human at all: like a clockwork toy winding down almost imperceptibly.

'The sister tells me you've been here for nearly forty-eight hours.'

'She lasted longer than everyone thought she would.' My eyes filled with tears and shamefully they were for myself. 'Do you know, I thought perhaps she might wake up before she died?

Say something. Or even just move. But she didn't, of course. She just stopped breathing.'

Suddenly there had been the shock of silence. The machine had stopped. What mattered most of all was the emptiness: the sense of departure. While Vanessa had been in a coma, I had thought of her as being effectively dead; but now I knew that I had been wrong.

Peter turned and stared at the figure on the bed. His lips moved. Neither of us spoke for a moment. Her skin was pale and waxen. Her mouth was open. I hoped desperately that part of her somewhere, somehow, was still alive.

'Come along,' he said. 'It's time to leave now. Say goodbye.'

I stooped and kissed my wife's forehead.

The hotel was a Tudor mansion near Egham. At the end of its truncated garden, the ground rose to a snow-covered ramp. Beyond the ramp was a motorway, the one which cut through my former parish a few miles to the east.

In the dining room, we had a table by the window overlooking the garden. Because of the snow, the room was lit by a clear light, so cool it was almost blue. Peter ordered cooked breakfast for both of us.

'I'm not hungry,' I said when the waitress had gone.

'I am. Coffee?'

When the food came I ate ravenously. I had not eaten a proper meal since the day before yesterday. We did not talk. Afterwards the waitress cleared the table and brought more coffee.

'What next?' Peter said.

'The funeral. I must see to the funeral. She –'

'After the funeral. What will you do then?'

'I can't think about that now.'

'I think you can. It's time to begin letting go.'

There was a silence. Peter struck a match and held it over his pipe. In the light reflected off the snow, the flame was drained of colour, almost invisible. No secrets in this light. No place for darkness.

'While she was dying,' I said, 'I couldn't stop thinking of Joanna.'

Peter dropped the match in the ashtray.

'It seems so unfair to Vanessa. As if I can't even mourn her properly.'

'You've been mourning her for nearly eighteen months.'

'No, I haven't. For all that time it was as if she wasn't a real person. As if I'd cheated her even of that.'

'You did what you could.'

'It wasn't enough. After all, what happened was my fault.'

He shook his head. 'Sloppy thinking. Not like you. *You* didn't attack Vanessa and put her in a coma. Rosemary did. Just as she cut up that poor cat and killed Lady Youlgreave to shut her mouth. Just as she tried to blame Michael and the teenagers for what happened to the cat, and Audrey for what she did to Vanessa. *Rosemary*. Not you.'

'I made Rosemary what she is.'

'Don't be so arrogant,' Peter said. 'She's shown sociopathic tendencies since she was a toddler. We both know that. It wasn't your fault that events conspired to tip her over the edge.' He held up his hand and ticked off his points one by one on stubby fingers: 'First she was furious because Vanessa took part of you away from her. Then she was jealous of Michael and your obvious liking for him. Then her exam results weren't up to the ridiculously high standards she'd set herself: that was the catalyst for what she did to that wretched cat. Then she fell in love with Toby Clifford and he paid her back by raping her. And finally Toby twisted the knife by pretending to flirt with Vanessa.'

There was a silence. It was not easy to allow others to share responsibility. I wanted to keep it all for myself.

'And then of course,' Peter said, 'there was Francis Youlgreave.'

I shrugged.

'You can't dismiss him.' He sipped his coffee, then added, 'Much as you'd like to. If nothing else, he gave Rosemary exactly the example she needed.'

'This is all very well, but it doesn't change anything. The point is, if I hadn't been with Joanna –'

'Exactly the same thing might have happened. In a sense, Joanna's got nothing to do with this. Has it occurred to you that you're hiding behind your guilt? It means you don't have to engage with the world again. With people. With God.'

'Rubbish.'

'Is it?' Shrouded in pipe smoke, he studied my face. 'Vanessa's dead. This is finished.'

I stared back. 'Rosemary's alive. So are Michael, and Audrey, and Toby. Not to mention Joanna.'

'There's a limit to what you can do for them. They won't let Toby out of jail until nineteen-eighty at the earliest. And you've been advised not to see Audrey. You know what happened last time.'

I had visited Audrey in the nursing home that James Vintner had found for her. Though heavily sedated, she had flung herself at me, covered my face with moist kisses, and begged me to take her home with me. She was suffering from the delusion that she was my wife.

'But Michael?' It was Michael's evidence which had clinched the case against Rosemary, and both of them had known it. 'The stress of it all, and then the way Rosemary threatened him . . .'

The memory of that summer evening was as vivid as the memory of Vanessa's lifeless face this morning. I had tried to talk to Rosemary while we waited in the Vicarage study for Inspector Jeevons. But you cannot talk to someone who is disintegrating in front of you. It was as if another person now inhabited the shell of my daughter and stared at me through her eyes and spoke to me through her mouth.

'How could you do this to me? I hate you, hate you, hate you. And God damn Michael, send him down to hell. I'll punish him if it takes me all my life. You wait and see . . . He's ruined everything, the little bastard. But he'll suffer for it, Father, I swear to God he will, and so will you . . .'

As the thick, barely recognizable voice was stumbling through its commination, I had looked up to see Michael in the doorway. His mouth was open but he said nothing. Through the open window came the distant sound of wings. I heard the wings at Roth, and I heard them now in the dining room of this hotel almost a year and a half later. Once again despair rolled towards me, grey and inexorable like a bore streaming down a tidal estuary.

'David? Stop that. Now.'

A hand gripped my arm. I opened my eyes and blinked across the table at Peter.

'Now listen to me. I know you're tired but you mustn't let your defences down.'

'But Michael heard –'

'Michael has his parents to care for him, as well as you. He's young. He'll manage perfectly well without you fussing over him.'

Peter released my arm, sat back and began to prod the contents of his pipe bowl with a spent match. Tension drained away from me. This time the wave had thrown me exhausted but alive on to the river bank.

'And as for Joanna,' he continued in a gentler voice, 'I had a letter from her last week. She's pregnant.'

Another silence stretched between us. I had not seen Joanna for nearly a year and a half. Peter had insisted on that. When he came back from Crete that summer, he had reinstated himself as my spiritual director and imposed several conditions on me. One of them was that I should not see Joanna again. It had been Peter who had arranged for her to go to the treatment centre, and he who made sure that she stayed. There she had met a medical student in his final year. After he had qualified, they had married and moved up to Northumberland, where he had been offered a partnership.

Peter had told me that Joanna was thinking of training as a nurse. I thought that the child would probably force her to postpone that. I found it hard to think of her married to another man, to think of her having another man's child.

'You need a change,' Peter went on remorselessly. 'Have you thought of doing some teaching again?'

'But my job –'

'You can't spend the rest of your life acting as someone else's curate in north-west London. You'd do far more good as a teacher.'

I shook my head.

'There comes a point when punishing yourself becomes a purely self-indulgent exercise. The real question is how you can put your talents to best use. Let's face it, they don't lie in the pastoral direction. You're a teacher, perhaps a scholar.

The last time I saw you baptizing a baby you held it as if it was going to explode.'

I looked at him and saw the glimmer of a smile on his face. 'In a manner of speaking, it did explode.'

'I heard of a teaching job in America the other day. It's an Episcopalian theological college in the Midwest. The chap who runs it trained at Pusey House. I used to know him quite well when I was up at Oxford. If you want I can put in a word. No need to decide now. But think about it.'

'I don't know. I really don't know.'

'You've done enough brooding. It would do you good to get out of this country.'

'There's Rosemary.'

'I'll keep an eye on her. I'll visit, and I'll see that other people do.'

'She was a victim too. For God's sake, Toby gave her a taste of heroin and *raped* her . . . She was so shocked and ashamed she couldn't even tell us what happened. And to make matters even worse he managed to wriggle out of that charge.'

'Rape's notoriously difficult to prove. I know Rosemary has suffered – and still does. But there's absolutely no point in your making her into another rod to beat yourself with.'

'I can't just run off and leave her.'

'You can – and in the circumstances I think you should.' Peter put his elbows on the table and leant towards me. 'You're using Rosemary as just one more excuse not to make a fresh start. Besides, if you take this job, you'd have a decent salary and plenty of opportunities to fly over and see her. If that's possible.'

'What do you mean by that?'

'You know very well that she doesn't want to see you. You have to accept that.'

I looked at him. Very good people can be as ruthless as very bad people.

'Come on, David,' he said softly. 'You can't go on drifting. You've got to leave all this behind you. You're carrying the past around like a dead weight.'

I sat back and stared out of the window. It had begun to snow again. The flakes were almost invisible against the pale grey of the sky. I thought of the little girl whom Toby had seen crying in the crystal ball. I did not think he had made it up. He had sounded so surprised – at what he saw? At his ability to see it?

When Joanna took me up to Francis Youlgreave's room in the tower, she had heard a child crying too. The same one? Had the child been merely the product of a drugged imagination? In that case, why had Toby seen it? Did that mean that the child was somewhere in the past or the future or another part of the present?

'There's so much I don't understand,' I said. 'The trouble is, I don't know whether a fresh start is possible. I don't know if all this is finished yet.'

'It is always possible to begin again. And even if it weren't, we should try.'

I stood up and smiled down at Peter, a round little man like Father Christmas without the beard. 'I wonder,' I said. 'I wonder.'

THE OFFICE
OF THE DEAD

For Vivien, with love and thanks

PART I

The Door in the Wall

1

'I'm nobody,' Rosie said.

It was the first thing she said to me. I'd just pushed open the door in the wall and there she was. She wore red sandals and a cotton dress, cream-coloured with tiny blue flowers embroidered on the bodice, and there were blue ribbons in her blonde hair. The ribbons and flowers matched her eyes. She was very tidy, like the garden, like everything that was Janet's.

I knew she was Rosie because of the snapshots Janet had sent. But I asked her name because that's what you do when you meet a child, to break the ice. Names matter. Names are hard to forget.

'Nobody? I'm sure that's not right.' I put down the suitcase on the path and crouched to bring my head down to her level. 'I bet you're really somebody. Somebody in disguise.'

'I'm nobody.' Her face wasn't impatient, just firm. 'That's my name.'

'Nobody's called nobody.'

She folded her arms across her chest, making a cross of flesh and bone. 'I am.'

'Why?'

'Because nobody's perfect.'

She turned and hopped up the path. I straightened up and watched her. Rosie was playing hopscotch but without a stone and with an invisible pattern of her own making. Hop, both legs, hop, both legs. Instead of turning to face me, though, she carried on to the half-glazed door set in the wall of the house. The soles of her sandals slapped on the flagstones like slow applause. Each time she landed, on one foot or two, the jolt ran through her body and sent ripples through her hair.

I felt the stab of envy, almost anger, sharp as John Treevor's knife. Nobody was beautiful. Oh yes, I thought, nobody's perfect. Nobody's the child I always wanted, the child Henry never gave me.

I'd been trying not to think about Henry for days, for weeks. For a moment his face was more vivid than Rosie and the house. I wished I could kill him. I wished I could roll up Henry and everything else that had ever happened to me into a small, dark, hard ball and throw it into the deepest, darkest corner of the Pacific Ocean.

Later, in one of those fragmentary but intense conversations we had when Janet was ill, I tried to explain this to David.

'Wendy, you can't hide away from the past,' he said. 'You can't pretend it isn't there, that it doesn't matter.'

'Why not?' I was a little drunk at the time and I spoke more loudly than I'd planned. 'If you ask me, there's something pathetic about people who live in the past. It's over and done with.'

'It's never that. Not until you are. It *is* you.'

'Don't lecture me, David.' I smiled sweetly at him and blew cigarette smoke into his face. 'I'm not one of your bloody students.'

But of course he was right. That was one thing that really irritated me about David, that so often he was right. He was such an arrogant bastard that you wanted him to be wrong. And in the end, when he was so terribly wrong, I couldn't even gloat. I just felt sorry for him. I suppose he wasn't very good at being right about himself.

Nobody's perfect.

2

When I was young, the people around me were proud of their pasts, and proud of the places where they lived.

My parents were born and bred in Bradford. Bradford was superior to all other towns in almost every possible way, from its town hall to its department stores, from its philanthropists to its rain. Similarly, my parents were quietly confident that Yorkshire, God's Own County, outshone all other counties. We lived in a tree-lined suburb at 93, Harewood Drive, in a semi-detached house with four bedrooms, a Tudor garage and a grandfather clock in the hall.

My father owned a jeweller's shop in York Street. The business had been established by his father, and he carried it on without enthusiasm. He had two interests in life and both of them were at home – his vegetable garden and my brothers.

Howard and Peter were twins, ten years older than me. They were always huge, semi-divine beings who took very little notice of me, and they always will be. I find it very hard to recall what they looked like.

'You must remember something about them,' Janet said in one of our heart-to-hearts at school.

'They played cricket. When I think about them, I always smell linseed oil.'

'Didn't they ever talk to you? Do things with you?'

'I remember Peter laughing at me because I thought Hitler was the name of the greengrocer's near the station. And one of them told me to shut up when I fell over on the path by the back door and started crying.'

Janet said wistfully, 'You make it sound as if you're better off without them.'

That's something I'll never know. When I was ten, they were both killed, Peter when his ship went down in the Atlantic, and Howard in North Africa. The news reached my parents in the same week. After that, in memory, the house was always dark as though the blinds were down, the curtains drawn. The big sitting room at the back of the house became a shrine to the dear departed. Everywhere you looked there were photographs of Peter and Howard. There were one or two of me as well but they were in the darkest corner of the room, standing on a bookcase containing books that nobody read and china that nobody used.

Even as a child, I noticed my father changed after their deaths. He shrank inside his skin. His stoop became more pronounced. He spent more and more time in the garden, digging furiously. I realized later that at this time he lost interest in the business. Before it had been his duty to nurse it along for Peter and Howard. Without them the shop's importance was reduced. He still went into town every day, still earned enough to pay the bills. But the shop no longer mattered to him. He no longer had any pride in it. I don't think he even had much pride in Bradford any more.

In my father's world girls weren't important. We were needed to bear sons and look after the house. We were also needed as other men's objects of desire so the men in question would buy us jewellery at the shop in York Street. We even had our uses as sales assistants and cleaners in the shop because my father could pay us less than he paid our male equivalents. But he hadn't any use for a daughter.

My mother was different. My birth was an accident, I think, perhaps the result of an uncharacteristically unguarded moment after a Christmas party. She was forty when I was born so she might have thought she was past it. But she wanted a daughter. The problem was, she didn't want the sort of daughter I was. She wanted a daughter like Janet.

My mother's daughter should have looked at knitting patterns with her and liked pretty clothes. Instead she had one who acquired rude words like cats acquire fleas and who wanted to build streams at the bottom of the garden.

It was a pity we had so little in common. She needed me, and

I needed her, but the needs weren't compatible. The older I got, the more obvious this became to us both. And that's how I came to meet Janet.

I suspect my father wanted me out of the house because I was an unwelcome distraction. My mother wanted me to learn how to be a lady so we could talk together about dressmaking and menus, so that I would attract and marry a nice young man, so that I would present her with a second family of perfect grandchildren.

My mother cried when she said goodbye to me at the station. I can still see the tears glittering like snail trails through the powder on her cheeks and clogging the dry ravines of her wrinkles. She loved me, you see, and I loved her. But we never found out how to be comfortable with one another.

So off I went to boarding school. It was wartime, remember, and I'd never been away from my parents before, except for three months at the beginning of the war when everyone thought the Germans would bomb our cities to smithereens.

This was different. The train hissed and clanked through a darkened world for what seemed like weeks. I was nominally in the charge of an older girl, one of the monitors at Hillgard House, whose grandmother lived a few miles north of Bradford. She spent the entire journey flirting with a succession of soldiers. The first time she accepted one of their cigarettes, she bent down to me and said, 'If you tell a soul about this, I'll make you wish you'd never been born.'

It was January, and the cold and the darkness made everything worse. We changed trains four times. Each train seemed smaller and more crowded than its predecessor. At last the monitor went to the lavatory, and when she came back she'd washed the make-up off her face. She was a pink, shiny-faced schoolgirl now. We left the train at the next stop, a country station shrouded in the blackout and full of harsh sounds I did not understand. It was as if I'd stepped out of the steamy, smoky carriage into the darkness of a world that hadn't been born.

Someone, a man, said, 'There's three more of you in the waiting room. Enough for a taxi now.'

The monitor seized her suitcase in one hand and me with the other and dragged me into the waiting room. That was where

I first saw Janet Treevor. Sandwiched between two larger girls, she was crying quietly into a lace-edged handkerchief. As we came in, she looked up and for an instant our eyes met. She was the most beautiful person I'd ever seen.

'Is that a new bug too?' the monitor demanded.

One of the other girls nodded. 'Hasn't turned off the waterworks since we left London,' she said. 'But apart from the blubbing, she seems quite harmless.'

The monitor pushed me towards the bench. 'Go on, Wendy,' she said. 'You might as well sit by her.' She watched me as I walked across the room, dragging my suitcase after me. 'At least this one's not a bloody blubber.'

I have always loathed my name. 'Wendy' sums up everything my mother wanted and everything I'm not. My mother loved *Peter Pan*. When I was eight, it was that year's Christmas pantomime. I sat hugely embarrassed through the performance while my mother wept happy tears beside me, the salty water falling into the box of chocolates open on her lap. They say that James Barrie invented the name for the daughter of a friend. First he called her 'Friendy'. Then with gruesome inevitability this became 'Friendy-Wendy'. Finally it mutated into 'Wendy', and the dreadful old man left it as part of his legacy to posterity in general and me in particular. The only character I liked in his beastly story was Captain Hook.

'Wendy,' Janet whispered as we huddled together in the back of the taxi on the way to school, squashed into a corner by a girl mountain smelling of sweat and peppermints. 'Such a pretty name.'

'What's yours?'

'Janet. Janet Treevor.'

'I like Janet,' I said, not wanting to be outdone in politeness.

'I hate it. It's so plain.'

'Shame we can't swap.'

I felt her breath on my cheek, felt her body shaking. I couldn't hear anything, because of the noise the other girls were making and the sound of the engine. But I knew what Janet was doing. She was giggling.

So that's how it started, Janet and me. It was January, the Lent Term, and we were the only new children in our year.

All the other new children had come in September and had already made friends. It was natural that Janet and I should have been thrown together. But I don't know why we became friends. Janet was no more like me than my mother was. But in her case – our case – the differences brought us together rather than drove us apart.

Hillgard House was a late-eighteenth-century house in the depths of the Herefordshire countryside. The nearest village was two miles away. The teaching was appalling, the food was often barely edible. When it rained heavily they put half a dozen buckets to catch the drips in the dormitories on the top floor where the servants' bedrooms had been, and you would go to sleep hearing the gentle *plop-plip-plop* as the water fell.

The headmistress was called Miss Esk, and she and her brother, the Captain, lived in the south wing of the house. There were carpets there, and fires, and sometimes when the windows were open you could hear the sound of music. The Esks had their own housekeeper who kept herself apart from and superior to the school's domestic staff. The Captain was rarely seen. We understood that he had suffered from a mysterious wound in the Great War and had never fully recovered. The senior girls used to speculate about the nature of this wound. When I was older, I gained considerable respect by suggesting he had been castrated.

We were always hungry at Hillgard House. It was wartime, as Miss Esk reminded us so often. This meant that we could not expect the luxuries of peace, though we could not help but notice that Miss Esk seemed to have most of them. I think now that the Esks made a fortune during the war. The school was considered to be in a relatively safe area, remote from the risks of both bombing raids and a possible invasion. Many of the girls' fathers were in the services. Few parents had the time and inclination to check the pastoral and educational standards of the school. They wanted their daughters to be safe, and so in a sense we were.

Janet and I never liked the place but we grew used to it. As far as I was concerned, it had three points in its favour. No one could have a more loyal friend than Janet. Because of the war, and because of the Esks' incompetence, we were left alone a great deal of the time. And finally there was the library.

It was a tall, thin room which overlooked a lank shrubbery at the northern end of the house. Shelves ran round all the walls. There was a marble fireplace, its grate concealed beneath a deep mound of soot. The shelves were only half full, but you never quite knew what you would find there. In that respect it was like the Cathedral Library in Rosington.

During the five years that we were there, Janet must have read, or at least looked at, every volume there. She read *Ivanhoe* and *The Origin of Species*. She picked her way through the collected works of Pope and bound copies of *Punch*. I had my education at second hand, through Janet.

In our final year, she found a copy of *Justine* by the Marquis de Sade – in French, bound in calf leather, the pages spotted with damp like an old man's hand – concealed in a large brown envelope behind the collected sermons of Bishop Berkeley. Janet read French easily – it was the sort of accomplishment you seemed to acquire almost by osmosis in her family – and we spent a week in the summer term picking our way through the book, which was boring but sometimes made us laugh.

In our first few terms, people used to laugh at us. Janet was small and delicate like one of those china figures in the glass-fronted cabinet in Miss Esk's sitting room. I was always clumsy. In those days I wore glasses, and my feet and hands seemed too large for me. Janet could wear the same blouse for days and it would seem white and crisp from beginning to end, from the moment she took it from her drawer to the moment she put it in the laundry basket. As for me, every time I picked up a cup of tea I seemed to spill half of it over me.

My mother thought Hillgard House would make me a lady. My father thought it would get me out of the way for most of the year. He was right and she was wrong. We didn't learn to be young ladies at Hillgard House – we learnt to be little savages in a jungle presided over by the Esks, remote predators.

3

I had never known a family like Janet's. Perhaps they didn't breed people like the Treevors in Bradford.

For a long time our friendship was something that belonged to school alone. Our lives at home were something separate. I know that I was ashamed of mine. I imagined Janet's family to be lordly, beautiful, refined. I knew they would be startlingly intelligent, just as Janet was. Her father was serving in the army, but before the war he had lectured about literature and written for newspapers. Janet's mother had a high-powered job in a government department. I never found out exactly what she did but it must have been something to do with translating – she was fluent in French, German and Russian and had a working knowledge of several other languages.

In the summer of 1944 the Treevors rented a cottage near Stratford for a fortnight. Janet asked if I would like to join them. My mother was very excited because I was mixing with 'nice' people.

I was almost ill with apprehension. In fact I needn't have worried. Mr and Mrs Treevor spent most of the holiday working in a bedroom which they appropriated as a study, or visiting friends in the area. John Treevor was a thin man with a large nose and a bulging forehead. At the time I assumed the bulge was needed to contain the extra brain cells. Occasionally he patted Janet on the head and once he asked me if I was enjoying myself but did not wait to hear my answer.

I remember Mrs Treevor better because she explained the facts of life to us. Janet and I had watched a litter of kittens being born at the farm next door. Janet asked her mother whether humans ever had four at a time. This led to a concise lecture on sex, pregnancy and childbirth. Mrs Treevor talked to us as if we were students and the subject were mathematics. I dared not look at her face while she was talking, and I felt myself blushing.

Later, in the darkness of our shared bedroom, Janet said, 'Can you imagine how they . . . ?'

'No. I can't imagine mine, either.'

'It's *horrible*.'

'Do you think they did it with the light on?'

'They'd need to see what they were doing, wouldn't they?'

'Yes, but just think what they'd have looked like.'

A moment afterwards Mrs Treevor banged on the partition wall to stop us laughing so loudly.

After Christmas that year, Janet came to stay with me at Harewood Drive for a whole week. She and my mother liked each other on sight. She thought my father was sad and kind. She even liked my dead brothers. She would stare at the photographs of Howard and Peter, one by one, lingering especially at the ones of them looking heroic in their uniforms.

'They're so handsome,' she said, 'so beautiful.'

'And so dead,' I pointed out.

In those days, the possibility of death was on everyone's minds. At school, fathers and brothers died. Their sisters and daughters were sent to see matron and given cups of cocoa and scrambled eggs on toast. The deaths of Howard and Peter, even though they had happened before my arrival at Hillgard House, gave me something of a cachet because they had been twins and had died so close together.

To tell the truth, I was jealous when Janet admired my doomed brothers, but I was never jealous of the friendship between Janet and my mother. It was not something that excluded me. In a sense it got me off the hook. When Janet was staying with us, I didn't have to feel guilty.

During that first visit, my mother made Janet a dress, using precious pre-war material she'd been hoarding since 1939. I remember the three of us in the little sewing room on the first floor. I was sitting on the floor reading a book. Every now and then I glanced up at them. I can still see my mother with pins in her mouth kneeling by Janet, and Janet stretching her arms above her head like a ballet dancer and revolving slowly. Their faces were rapt and solemn as though they were in church.

Janet and I shared dreams. In winter we sometimes slept together, huddled close to conserve every scrap of warmth. We pooled information about proscribed subjects, such as periods and male genitalia. We practised being in love. We took it in turns at being the man. We waltzed across the floor of the library, humming the Blue Danube. We exchanged lingering kisses with lips clamped shut, mimicking what we had observed in the cinema. We made up conversations.

'Has anyone ever told you what beautiful eyes you have?'

'You're very kind – but really you shouldn't say such things.'

'I've never felt like this with anyone else.'

'Nor have I. Isn't the moon lovely tonight?'

'Not as lovely as you.'

And so on. Nowadays people would suggest there was a lesbian component to our relationship. But there wasn't. We were playing at being grown up.

Somewhere in the background of our lives, the war dragged on and finally ended. I don't remember being frightened, only bored by it. I suppose peace came as a relief. In memory, though, everything at Hillgard House went on much as before. The school was its own dreary little world. Rationing continued, and if anything was worse than it had been during the war. One winter the snow and ice were so bad the school was cut off for days.

Our last term was the summer of 1948. We exchanged presents – a ring I had found in a dusty box on top of my mother's wardrobe, and a brooch Janet's godmother had given her as a christening present. We swore we would always be friends. A few days later, term ended. Everything changed.

Janet went to a crammer in London because the Treevors had finally woken up to the fact that Hillgard House was not an ideal academic preparation for university. I went home to Harewood Drive, helped my mother about the house and worked a few hours a week in my father's shop. There are times in my life when I have been more unhappy and more afraid than I was then, but I've never tasted such dreariness.

The only part I enjoyed was helping in the shop. At least I was doing something useful and met other people. Sometimes I dealt with customers but usually my father kept me in the back, working on the accounts or tidying the stock. I learned how to smoke in the yard behind the shop.

I got drunk for the first time at a tennis club dance. On the same evening a boy named Angus tried to seduce me in the groundsman's shed. It was the sort of seduction that's the next best thing to rape. I punched him and made his nose bleed. He dropped his hip flask, which had lured me into the shed with him. I ran back to the lights and the music. I saw him a little later. His upper lip was swollen and there was blood on his white shirtfront.

'Went out to the gents,' I heard him telling the club secretary. 'Managed to walk into the door.'

The club secretary laughed and glanced in my direction. I wondered if I was meant to hear, I wondered if the secretary knew, if all this had been planned.

It was a way of life that seemed to have no end. Janet wrote to me regularly and we saw each other once or twice a year. But the old intimacy was gone. She was at university now and had other friends and other interests.

'Why don't you go to university?' she asked as we were having tea at a café in the High on one of my visits to Oxford.

I shrugged and lit a cigarette. 'I don't want to. Anyway, my father wouldn't let me. He thinks it's unnatural for women to have an education.'

'Surely he'd let you do something?'

'Such as?'

'Well, what do you want to do?'

I watched myself blowing smoke out of my nostrils in the mirror behind Janet's head and hoped I looked sophisticated. I said, 'I don't know what I want.'

That was the real trouble. Boredom saps the will. It makes you feel you no longer have the power to choose. All I could see was the present stretching indefinitely into the future.

But two months later everything changed. My father died. And three weeks after that, on the 19th July 1952, I met Henry Appleyard.

4

Memory bathes the past in a glow of inevitability. It's tempting to assume that the past could only have happened in the way it did, that this event could only have been followed by that event and in the order they happened. If that were true, of course, nothing would be our fault.

But of course it isn't true. I didn't have to marry Henry. I didn't have to leave him. And I didn't have to go and stay with Janet at the Dark Hostelry.

During her last year at Oxford, Janet decided that after she had taken her degree she would go to London and try to find work as a translator. Her mother's contacts might be able to help her. She told me about it over another cup of tea, this time in her cell-like room at St Hilda's.

'Is it what you want to do?'

'It's all I can do.'

'Couldn't you stay here and do research?'

'I'll be lucky if I scrape a third. I'm not academic, Wendy. I feel I don't really belong here. As if I got in by false pretences.'

I shrugged, envious of what she had been offered and refused. 'I suppose there are lots of lovely young men in London as well as Oxford.'

'Yes. I suppose so.'

Men liked Janet because she was beautiful. She didn't say much to them either so they could talk to their hearts' content and show off to her. But she went out of her way to avoid them. Janet wanted Sir Galahad, not a spotty undergraduate from Christchurch with an MG. In the end, she compromised as we all do. She didn't get Sir Galahad and she didn't get the spotty undergraduate with the MG. Instead she got the Reverend David Byfield.

Early in 1952 he came over to Oxford for a couple of days to do some work in the Bodleian. He was writing a book reinterpreting the work of St Thomas Aquinas in terms of modern theology. That's where he and Janet saw each other, in the library. It was, Janet said, love at first sight. 'He looked at me and I simply *knew*.'

Even now, I find it very hard to think objectively about David. The thing you have to remember is that in those days he was very, very good-looking. He turned heads in the street, just as Janet did. Like Henry, he had charm, but unlike Henry he wasn't aware of it and rarely used it. He had a first-class degree in theology from Cambridge. Afterwards he went to a theological college called Mirfield.

'Lots of smells and bells,' Janet told me, 'and terrifyingly brainy men who don't like women.'

'But David's not like that,' I said.

'No,' she said, and changed the subject.

After Mirfield, David was the curate of a parish near Cambridge for a couple of years. But at the time he met Janet he was lecturing at Rosington Theological College. They didn't waste time – they were engaged within a month. A few weeks later, David landed the job of vice-principal at the Theological College. They were delighted, Janet wrote, and the prospects were good. The principal was old and would leave a good deal of responsibility to David. David had also been asked to be a minor canon of the Cathedral, which would help financially. The bishop, who was chairman of the Theological College's trustees, had taken quite a shine to him. Best of all, Janet said, was the house that came with the job. It was in the Cathedral Close, and it was called the Dark Hostelry. Parts of it were medieval. Such a romantic name, she said, like something out of *Ivanhoe*. It was rather large for them, but they planned to take a lodger.

The wedding was in the chapel of Jerusalem, David's old college. Janet and David made a lovely couple, something from a fairy tale. If I was in a fairy tale, I told myself, I'd be the Ugly Duckling. What made everything worse was my father's death

– not so much because I'd loved him but because there was now no longer any possibility of his loving me.

Then I saw Henry standing on the other side of the chapel. In those days he was thickset rather than plump. He was wearing a morning suit that was too small for him. We were singing a hymn and he glanced at me. He had wiry hair in need of a cut and straight, strongly marked eyebrows that went up at a sharp angle from the bridge of his nose. He grinned at me and I looked away.

I've still got a photograph of Janet's wedding. It was taken in the front court of Jerusalem. In the centre, with the Wren chapel behind them, are David and Janet looking as if they've strayed from the closing scene of a romantic film. David looks like a young Laurence Olivier – all chiselled features and flaring nostrils, a blend of sensitivity and arrogance. He has Janet on one arm and is smiling down at her. Old Granny Byfield hangs grimly on to his other arm.

Henry and I are away to the left, separated from the happy couple by a clump of dour relations, including Mr and Mrs Treevor. Henry is trying half-heartedly to conceal the cigarette in his hand. His belly strains against the buttons of his waistcoat. The hem of my dress is uneven and I am wearing a silly little hat with a half-veil. I remember paying a small fortune for it in the belief that it would make me look sophisticated. That was before I learned that sophistication wasn't for sale in Bradford.

John Treevor looks very odd. It must have been a trick of the light – perhaps he was standing in a shaft of sunshine. Anyway, in the photograph his face is bleached white, a tall narrow mask with two black holes for eyes and a black slit for the mouth. It's as if they had taken a dummy from a shop window and draped it in a morning coat and striped trousers.

A moment later, just after the last photograph had been taken, Henry spoke to me for the first time. 'I like the hat.'

'Thanks,' I said, once I'd glanced over my shoulder to make sure he was talking to me and not someone else.

'I'm Henry Appleyard, by the way.' He held out his hand. 'A friend of David's from Rosington.'

'How do you do. I'm Wendy Fleetwood. Janet and I were at school together.'

'I know. She asked me to keep an eye out for you.' He gave me a swift but unmistakable wink. 'But I'd have noticed you anywhere.'

I didn't know what to say to this, so I said nothing.

'Come on.' He took my elbow and guided me towards a doorway. 'There's no time to lose.'

'Why?'

The photographer was packing up his tripod. The wedding party was beginning to disintegrate.

'Because I happen to know there's only four bottles of champagne. First come first served.'

The reception was austere and dull. For most of the time I stood by the wall and pretended I didn't mind not having anyone to talk to. Instead, I nibbled a sandwich and looked at the paintings. After Janet and David left for their honeymoon, Henry appeared at my side again, rather to my relief.

'What you need,' he said, 'is a dry martini.'

'Do I?'

'Yes. Nothing like it.'

I later learned that Henry was something of an expert on dry martinis – how to make them, how to drink them, how to recover as soon as possible from the aftereffects the following morning.

'Are you sure no one will mind?'

'Why should they? Anyway, Janet asked me to look after you. Let's go down to the University Arms.'

As we were leaving the college I said, 'Are you at the Theological College too?'

He burst out laughing. 'God, no. I teach at the Choir School in the Close. David's my landlord.'

'So you're the lodger?'

He nodded. 'And resident jester. I stop David taking himself too seriously.'

For the next two hours, he made me feel protected, as I had made Janet feel protected all those years ago. I wanted to believe I was normal – and also unobtrusively intelligent, witty and beautiful. So Henry hinted that I was all these things. It was wonderful. It was also some compensation for a) Janet getting married, b) managing to do it before I did, and c) to

603

someone as dashing as David (even though he was a clergyman).

While Henry was being nice to me, he found out a great deal.
He learned about my family, my father's death, the shop, and
what I did. Meanwhile, I felt the alcohol pushing me up and up
as if in a lift. I liked the idea of myself drinking dry martinis in
the bar of a smart hotel. I liked catching sight of my reflection
in the big mirror on the wall. I looked slimmer than usual, more
mysterious, more chic. I liked the fact I wasn't feeling nervous
any more. Above all I liked being with Henry.

He took his time. After two martinis he bought me dinner at
the hotel. Then he insisted on taking me back in a taxi to my
hotel, a small place Janet had found for me on the Huntingdon
Road. On the way the closest he came to intimacy was when
we stopped outside the hotel. He touched my hand and asked
if he might possibly see me again.

I said yes. Then I tried to stop him paying for the taxi.

'No need.' He waved away the change and smiled at me.
'Janet gave me the money for everything.'

5

In those days, in the 1950s, people still wrote letters. Janet and I had settled into a rhythm of writing to each other perhaps once a month, and this continued after her marriage. That's how I learned she was pregnant, and that Henry had been sacked.

Janet and David went to a hotel in the Lake District for their honeymoon. He must have made her pregnant there, or soon after their return to Rosington. It was a tricky pregnancy, with a lot of bleeding in the early months. But she had a good doctor, a young man named Flaxman, who made her rest as much as possible. As soon as things had settled down, Janet wrote, I must come and visit them.

I envied her the pregnancy just as I envied her having David. I wanted a baby very badly. I told myself it was because I wanted to correct all the mistakes my parents had made with me. With hindsight I think I wanted someone to love. I needed someone to look after and most of all someone to give me a reason for living.

Henry was sacked in October. Not exactly sacked, Janet said in her letter. The official story was that he had resigned for family reasons. She was furious with him, and I knew her well enough to suspect that this was because she had become fond of him. Apparently one of Henry's responsibilities was administering the Choir School 'bank' – the money the boys were given as pocket money at the start of every term. He had to dole it out on Friday afternoon. It seemed he had borrowed five pounds from the cash box that housed the bank and put it on a horse. Unfortunately he was ill the following Friday. The headmaster had taken his place and had discovered that money was missing.

At this time I was very busy. My mother and her solicitor had decided to sell the business. I was helping to make an inventory of the stock, and also chasing up creditors. To my surprise I rather enjoyed the work and I looked forward to going to the shop because it got me away from the house.

When there was a phone call for me one morning I thought it was someone who owed us money.

'Wendy – it's Henry.'

'Who?'

'Henry Appleyard. You remember? At Cambridge.'

'Yes,' I said faintly. 'How are you?'

'Wonderful, thanks. Now, what about lunch?'

'What?'

'Lunch.'

'But where are you?'

'Here.'

'In *Bradford*?'

'Why not? Hundreds of thousands of people are in Bradford. Including you, which is why I'm here. You can manage today, can't you?'

'I suppose so.' Usually I went out for a sandwich.

'I thought the Metropole, perhaps? Is that OK?'

'Yes, but –'

Yes, but isn't it rather expensive? And what shall I wear?

'Good. How about twelve forty-five in the lounge?'

There was just time for me to go home, deal with my mother's curiosity ('A friend of Janet's, Mother, no one you know'), change into clothes more suitable for the Metropole and reach the hotel five minutes early. It was a large, shabby place, built to impress at the end of the century. I had never been inside it before. Only the prospect of Henry gave me the courage to do so now. I sat, marooned by my own embarrassment, among the potted palms and the leather armchairs, trying to avoid meeting the eyes of hotel staff. Time moved painfully onwards. After five minutes I was convinced that everyone was looking at me, and convinced that he would not come. Then suddenly Henry was leaning over me, his lips brushing my cheek and making me blush.

'I'm so sorry I'm late.' He wasn't – I'd been early. 'Let's have a drink before we order.'

Henry wasn't good-looking in a conventional way or in any way at all. At that time he was in his late twenties but he looked older. He was wearing a grey double-breasted suit. I didn't know much about men's tailoring but I persuaded myself that it was what my mother used to call a 'good' suit. His collar was faintly grubby, but in this city collars grew dirty very quickly.

Once the dry martinis had been ordered he didn't beat about the bush. 'I expect you've heard my news from Janet?'

'That you've – you've left the Choir School?'

'They gave me the push, Wendy. Without a reference. You heard why?'

I nodded and stared at my hands, not wanting to see the shame in his eyes.

'The irony was, the damn horse won.' He threw back his head and laughed. 'I knew it would. I could have repaid them five times over. Still, I shouldn't have done it. You live and learn, eh?'

'But what will you do now?'

'Well, teaching's out. No references, you see, the headmaster made that very clear. It's a shame, actually – I *like* teaching. The Choir School was a bit stuffy, of course. But I used to teach at a place in Hampshire that was great fun – a prep school called Veedon Hall. It's owned by a couple called Cuthbertson who actually *like* little boys.' For an instant the laughter vanished and wistfulness passed like a shadow over his face. Then he grinned across the table. 'Still, one must look at this as an opportunity. I think I might go into business.'

'What sort?'

'Investments, perhaps. Stockbroking. There's a lot of openings. But don't let's talk about that now. It's too boring. I want to talk about you.'

So that's what we did, on and off, for the next four months. Not just about me. Henry wooed my mother as well and persuaded her to talk to him. We both received the flowers and the boxes of chocolates. I don't know whether my mother had loved my father, but certainly she missed him when he was no longer there. She also missed what he had done around the house and garden. Here was an opportunity for Henry.

He had the knack of giving the impression he was helping

without in fact doing very much. 'Let me,' he'd say, but in fact you'd end up doing the job yourself or else it wouldn't get done at all. Not that you minded, because you somehow felt that Henry had taken the burden from your shoulders. I think he genuinely felt he was helping.

Even now it makes me feel slightly queasy to remember the details of our courtship. I wanted romance and Henry gave it to me. Meanwhile he must have discovered – while helping my mother with her papers – that my father's estate, including the house and the shop, was worth almost fifty thousand pounds. It was left in trust to my mother for her lifetime and would afterwards come to me.

All this makes me sound naive and stupid, and Henry calculating and mercenary. Both are true. But they are not the whole truth or anything like it. I don't think you can pin down a person with a handful of adjectives.

Why bother with the details? My father's executor distrusted Henry but he couldn't stop us marrying. All he could do was prevent Henry from getting his hands on the capital my father left until after my mother's death when it became mine absolutely.

We were married in a registry office on Wednesday the 4th of May, 1953. Janet and David sent us a coffee set of white bone china but were unable to come in person because Janet was heavily pregnant with Rosie.

At first we lived in Bradford, which was not a success. After my mother died we sold the house and went briefly to London and then to South Africa in pursuit of the good life. We found it for a while. Henry formed a sort of partnership with a persuasive businessman named Grady. But Grady went bankrupt and we returned to England poorer and perhaps wiser. Nevertheless, it would be easy to forget that Henry and I had good times. When he was enjoying life then so did you.

All things considered, the money lasted surprisingly well. Henry worked as a sort of stockbroker, sometimes by himself, sometimes with partners. If it hadn't been for Grady he might still be doing it. He once told me it was like going to the races with other people's money. He was in fact rather good at persuading people to give him their money to invest. Occasionally he even made them a decent profit.

'Swings and roundabouts, I'm afraid,' I heard him say dozens of times to disappointed clients. 'What goes up, must come down.'

So why did his clients trust him? Because he made them laugh, I think, and because he so evidently believed he was going to make their fortunes.

So why did I stay with him for so long?

It was partly because I came to like many of the things he did. Still do, actually. You soon get a taste for big hotels, fast cars and parties. I liked the touch of fur against my skin and the way diamonds sparkled by candlelight. I liked dancing and flirting and taking one or two risks. I occasionally helped Henry attract potential clients, and even that could be fun. 'Let's have some old widow,' he'd say when things were going well for us, and suddenly there would be another bottle of Veuve Clicquot and another toast to us, to the future.

When Henry met me I was a shy, gawky girl. He rescued me from Harewood Drive and gave me confidence in myself. I think I stayed with him partly because I was afraid that without him I would lose all I had gained.

Most of all, though, I stayed because I liked Henry. I suppose I loved him, though I'm not sure what that means. But when things were going well between us, it was the most wonderful thing in the world. Even better than dry martinis and the old widow.

Letters continued to travel between Janet and me. They were proper ones – long and chatty. I didn't say much about Henry and she didn't say much about David. A common theme was our plans to meet. Once or twice we managed to snatch a day in London together. But we never went to stay with each other. Somehow there were always reasons why visits had to be delayed.

We were always on the move. Henry never liked settling in one place for any length of time. When he was feeling wealthy we rented flats or stayed in hotels. When money was tight, we went into furnished rooms.

But I was going to spend a few days with Janet and David in Rosington after Easter 1957. Just me, of course – Henry had to go away on what he called a business trip, and in any case he didn't want to go back to Rosington. Too many people knew why he'd left.

I'd even done my packing. Then the day before I was due to go, a telegram arrived. Mrs Treevor had had a massive heart attack. Once again the visit was postponed. She died three days later. Then there was the funeral, and then the business of settling Mr Treevor into a flat in Cambridge. Janet wrote that her father was finding it hard to cope since her mother's death.

So we continued to write letters instead. Despite her mother's death, it seemed to me that Janet had found her fairy tale. She sent me photographs of Rosie, as a baby and then as a little girl. Rosie had her mother's colouring and her father's features. It was obvious that she too was perfect, just like David and the Dark Hostelry.

Life's so bloody unsubtle sometimes. It was all too easy to contrast Janet's existence with mine. But you carry on, don't you, even when your life is more like one long hangover than one long party. You think, what else is there to do?

But there was something else. There had to be, as I found out on a beach one sunny day early in October 1957. Henry and I were staying at a hotel in the West Country. We weren't on holiday – a potential client lived in the neighbourhood, a wealthy widow.

It was a fine afternoon, warm as summer, and I went out after lunch while Henry went off to a meeting. I wandered aimlessly along the beach, a Box Brownie swinging from my hand, trying to walk off an incipient hangover. I rounded the corner of a little rocky headland and there they were, Henry and the widow, lying on a rug.

She was an ugly woman with a moustache and fat legs. I had a very good view of the legs because her dress was up around her thighs and Henry was bouncing around on top of her. His bottom was bare and for a moment I watched the fatty pear-shaped cheeks trembling. The widow was still wearing her shoes, which were navy-blue and high-heeled, surprisingly dainty. I wouldn't have minded a pair of shoes like that. I remember wondering how she could have walked across the sand in such high heels, and whether she realized that sea water would ruin the leather.

I had never seen Henry from this point of view before. I knew he was vain, and hated the fact that he was growing older. (He secretly touched up his grey hairs with black dye.) The wobbling flesh was wrinkled and flabby. Henry was getting old, and so was I. It was the first moment in my life when I realized that time was running out for me personally as well as for other people and the planet.

Maybe it was the alcohol but I felt removed from the situation, capable of considering it as an abstract problem. I walked towards them, my bare feet soundless on the sand. I crouched a few yards away from the shuddering bodies. Suddenly they realized they were not alone. Simultaneously they turned their heads to look at me, the widow with her legs raised and those pretty shoes in the air.

Still in that state of alcoholic transcendence, I had the sense to raise the Box Brownie and press the shutter.

6

I don't keep many photographs. I am afraid of nostalgia. You can drown in dead emotions.

Among the photographs I have thrown away is the shot of Henry bouncing on his widow on the beach. I knew at once that it could be valuable, that it meant I could divorce Henry without any trouble. At the time, the remarkable thing was how little the end of the marriage seemed to matter. Perhaps, I thought as I took the film out of the camera, perhaps it was never really a marriage at all, just a mutually convenient arrangement which had now reached a mutually convenient end.

I still have a snap of us by the pool in somebody's back garden in Durban with Henry sucking in his tummy and me showing what at the time seemed a daring amount of naked flesh. There's just the two of us in the photograph, but it's obvious from the body language that Henry and I aren't a couple in any meaningful sense of the word. Obvious with twenty-twenty hindsight, anyway.

In my letters to Janet I had been honest about everything except Henry. I didn't conceal the fact that money was sometimes tight, or even that I was drinking too much. But I referred to Henry with wifely affection. 'Must close now – His Nibs has just come in, and he wants his tea. He sends his love, as do I.'

It was pride. Janet had her Mr Perfect and I wanted mine, or at least the illusion of him. But I think I'd known the marriage was in trouble before the episode with the widow. What I saw on the beach merely confirmed it.

'I want a divorce,' I said to Henry when he came back to our room in the hotel. By the smell of him he'd fortified himself in the bar downstairs.

'Wendy – *please*. Can't we –?'

'No, we can't.'

'Darling. Listen to me. I –'

'I mean it.'

'All right,' he said, his opposition crumbling with humiliating speed. 'As soon as you like.'

I felt sober now and I had a headache. I had found the bottle of black hair dye hidden as usual in one of the pockets of his suitcase. It was empty now. I'd poured the contents over his suits and shirts.

'No hard feelings,' I lied. 'I'll let you have some money.'

He looked across the room at me and smiled rather sadly. 'What money?'

'You know something?' I said. 'When I saw you on top of that cow, your bum was wobbling around all over the place. It was like an old man's. The skin looked as if it needed ironing.'

In the four months after I found Henry doing physical jerks on top of his widow, I wrote to Janet less often than usual. I sent her a lot of postcards. Henry and I were moving around, I said, which was true. Except, of course, we weren't moving around together. In a sense I spent those four months pretending to myself and everyone else that everything was normal. I didn't want to leave my rut even if Henry was no longer in there with me.

Eventually the money ran low and I made up my mind I had to do something. I came back to London. It was February now, and the city was grey and dank. I found a solicitor in the phone book. His name was Fielder, and the thing I remember most about him was the ill-fitting toupee whose colour did not quite match his natural hair. He had an office in Praed Street above a hardware shop near the junction with Edgware Road.

I went to see him, explained the situation and gave him the address of Henry's solicitor. I told him about the photograph but didn't show it to him, and I mentioned my mother's money too. He said he'd see what he could do and made an appointment for me the following week.

Time crawled while I waited. I had too much to think about and not enough to do. When the day came round, I went back to Fielder's office.

'Well, Mrs Appleyard, things are moving now.' He slid a sheet of paper across the desk towards me. 'The wheels are turning. Time for a fresh start, eh?'

I opened the sheet of paper. It was a bill.

'Just for interim expenses, Mrs Appleyard. No point in letting them mount up.'

'What does my husband's solicitor say?'

'I'm afraid there's a bit of a problem there.' Mr Fielder patted his face with a grubby handkerchief. He wore a brown double-breasted pinstripe suit which encased him like a suit of armour and looked thick enough for an Arctic winter. There were drops of moisture on his forehead, and his neck bulged over his tight, hard collar. 'Yes, a bit of a problem.'

'Do you mean there isn't any money?'

'I did have a reply from Mr Appleyard's solicitor.' Fielder scrabbled among the papers on his desk for a few seconds and then gave up the search. 'The long and the short of it is that Mr Appleyard told him your joint assets no longer seem to exist.'

'But there must be something left. Can't we take him to court?'

'We could, Mrs Appleyard, we could. But we'd have to find him first. Unfortunately Mr Appleyard seems to have left the country. In confidence I may tell you he hasn't even settled his own solicitor's bill.' He shook his head sadly. 'Not a desirable state of affairs at all. Not at all. Which reminds me . . . ?'

'Don't worry.' I opened my handbag and dropped the bill into it.

'Of course. And then we'll carry on in Mr Appleyard's absence. It should be quite straightforward.' He glanced at his watch. 'By the way, your husband left a letter for you care of his solicitor. I have it here.'

'I don't want to see it.'

'Then what would you like me to do with it?'

'I don't care. Put it in the wastepaper basket.' My voice sounded harsh, more Bradford than Hillgard House. 'I don't mean to seem rude, Mr Fielder, but I don't think he has anything to say that I want to hear.'

Walking back to my room along the crowded pavement I wanted to blame Fielder. He had been inefficient, he had been corrupt, but even then I knew neither of these things were true. I just wanted to blame somebody for the mess my life was in. Henry was my preferred candidate but he wasn't available. So I had to focus my anger on poor Fielder. Before I reached my room, I'd invented at least three cutting curtain lines I might have used, and also constructed a satisfying fantasy which ended with him in the dock at the Old Bailey with myself as the chief prosecution witness. Fantasies reveal the infant that lives within us all. Which is why they're dangerous because the usual social constraints don't operate on infants.

When I went into the house, Mrs Hyson, the landlady, opened the kitchen door a crack and peered at me, but said nothing. I ate dry bread and elderly cheese in my room for lunch to save money. I kept on my overcoat to postpone putting a shilling in the gas meter. Since leaving Henry I had lived on the contents of my current account at the bank and my Post Office Savings Account, a total of about two hundred pounds, and by selling a fur coat and one or two pieces of jewellery.

I wasn't even sure I could afford to divorce Henry. First I needed to find a job but I was not trained to do anything. I was twenty-six years old and completely unemployable. There were relations in Leeds – a couple of aunts I hadn't seen for years and cousins I'd never met. Even if I could track them down there was no reason why they should help me. That's when I opened my writing case and began the letter to Janet.

Looking back, I think I must have been very near a nervous breakdown when I wrote that letter. It's more than forty years ago now, but I can still remember how the panic welled up. The certainties were gone. In the past I'd always known what to do next. I often didn't want to do it but that was not the point. What had counted was the fact the future was mapped out. I'd also taken for granted there would be a roof over my head, clothes on my back and food on the table. But now I had nothing.

I looked for the letter after Janet's death and was glad I could not find it. I hope she destroyed it. I cannot remember exactly what I told her, though I would have kept nothing back except perhaps my envy of her. What I do remember is how I felt while I was writing that letter in the chilly little room in Paddington. I felt I was trying to swim in a black sea. The waves were so rough and my waterlogged clothes weighed me down. I was drowning.

Early in the evening I went out to post the letter. On the way back I passed a pub. A few yards down the pavement I stopped, turned back and went into the saloon bar. It was a high-ceilinged room with mirrors on the walls and chairs upholstered in faded purple velvet. Apart from two old ladies drinking port, it was almost empty, which gave me courage. I marched up to the counter and ordered a large gin and bitter lemon, not caring what they thought of me.

'Waiting for someone then?' the barmaid asked.

'No.' I watched the gin sliding into the glass and moistened my lips. 'You're not very busy tonight.'

I doubt if the place was ever busy. It smelled of failure. That suited me. I sat in the corner and drank first one drink, then another and then a third. A man tried to pick me up and I almost said yes, just for the hell of it.

There were women around here who made a living from men. You saw them hanging round the station and on street corners, huddled in doorways or bending down to a car window to talk to the man inside. Could I do that? Would you ever get used to having strange men pawing at you? How much would you charge them? And what happened when you grew old and they stopped wanting you?

To escape the questions I couldn't answer, I had another drink, and then another. In the end I lost count. I knew I was drinking tomorrow's lunch and tomorrow's supper, and then the day after's meals as well, and in a way that added to the despairing pleasure the process gave me. The barmaid and her mother persuaded me to leave when I ran out of money and started crying.

I dragged myself back to the bed and breakfast. On my way in I met Mrs Hyson. She knew what I'd been doing, I could see it in her face. She could hardly have avoided knowing. I must have smelt like a distillery and it was a miracle I got up those stairs without falling over. It was too much trouble to take off my clothes. The room was swaying so I lay down on top of the eiderdown. Slowly the walls began to revolve round the bed. The whole world had tugged itself free from its moorings. The last thing I remember thinking was that Mrs Hyson would probably want me out of her house by tomorrow.

7

I began the slow hard climb towards consciousness around dawn. For hours I lay there and tried to cling to sleep. My mouth was dry and my head felt as though there were a couple of skewers running through it. I was aware of movement in the house around me. The doorbell rang and the skewers twisted inside my skull. A few moments later there was a knock on the door.

Trying not to groan, I stood up slowly and padded across the floor in my stockinged feet. I opened the door a crack. Her nose wrinkling, Mrs Hyson stared up at me. I had slept in my clothes. I hadn't removed my make-up either.

'There's a gentleman to see you, Mrs Appleyard.'

'A gentleman?'

Mrs Hyson frowned and walked away. My stomach lurched at the thought it might be Henry. But I had nothing left for him to take. Maybe it was that solicitor, anxious about his cheque.

A few minutes later I went downstairs as if down to my execution and into Mrs Hyson's front room. I found David Byfield examining a menacing photograph of the dear departed Mr Hyson. He turned towards me, holding out his hand and offering me a small, cool smile. He didn't seem to have changed since his wedding day. Unlike me.

'I hope you don't mind my calling. I was up in town anyway, and Janet phoned me this morning with the news.'

'She's had my letter, then?'

He nodded. 'We're so sorry.'

How I hated that *we*. 'No need. It had been coming to an end for a long time.' I glared at him and winced at the stabs of pain behind my eyes. 'You should be glad, not sad.'

'It's always sad when a marriage breaks down.'

'Yes, well.' I realized I must sound ungracious, and added brightly, 'And how are you? How are Janet and Rosie?'

'Very well, thank you. Janet's hoping – we're hoping that you'll come and stay with us.'

'I can manage quite well by myself, thank you.'

'I'm sure you can.'

The Olivier nostrils flared a little further than usual. 'It would give us all a great deal of pleasure.'

'All right.'

'Good.'

He smiled at me now, showing me his approval. That's what really irritated me, the way I felt myself warming in the glow of his attention. Sex appeal can be such a depressingly impersonal thing.

David swiftly arranged the next stage of my life, barely bothering to consult me. His charity was as impersonal as his sex appeal. He was helping me because he felt he ought to or because Janet had asked him to. He was earning good marks in heaven or with Janet, possibly both.

A few hours later I was in a second-class smoking compartment and the train was pulling out of the echoing cavern of Liverpool Street Station. I still had the hangover but time, tea and aspirins had dulled the skewers of pain and made them irritating but bearable, like a certain sort of old friend. My suitcase was above my head and the two trunks would be following by road. I had bathed and changed. I'd even managed to eat and keep down a meal that wasn't quite breakfast and wasn't quite lunch. David wasn't with me – his conference ended at lunch time tomorrow.

The train lumbered north between soot-streaked houses beneath a smoky sky.

'Let's face it,' I told myself as the train began to gather speed and I fumbled for my cigarettes, 'he doesn't give a damn about me. And why the hell should he?'

It occurred to me that I wasn't quite sure which *he* I meant.

After Cambridge the countryside became flat. The train puffed on a straight line with black fields on either side. It was already getting dark. The horizon was a border zone, neither earth nor sky. I was alone in my compartment. I felt safe and warm and a little sleepy. If the journey went on for ever, that would have been quite all right by me.

The train began to slow. I looked out of the window and saw in the distance the spire of Rosington Cathedral. The closer we got to it, the more it looked like a stone animal preparing to spring. I went to the lavatory, washed a smut off my cheek and powdered my nose. David had telephoned Janet and asked her to meet me.

By the time I got back to the compartment, the platform was sliding along the window. I pulled down my suitcase and left the train. The first thing I noticed was the wind that cut at my throat like a razor blade. The wind in Rosington isn't like other winds, Janet had written in one of her letters, it comes all the way from Siberia and over the North Sea, it's not like an English wind at all.

Janet wasn't on the platform. She wasn't at the barrier. She wasn't outside, either.

I dragged my suitcase through the ticket hall and into the forecourt beyond. The station was at the bottom of the hill. At the top was the stone mountain. The wind brought tears to my eyes. A tall clergyman was climbing into a tall, old-fashioned car. He glanced at me with flat, incurious eyes.

Before I went to Rosington I didn't know any priests. They were there to be laughed at on stage and screen, avoided like the plague at parties, and endured at weddings and funerals of the more traditional sort. After Rosington, all that changed. Priests became people. I could believe in them.

I wasn't any nearer believing in God, mind you. A girl has her pride. Sometimes, though, I wish I could think that it was all for the best in the long run. That God had a plan we could follow or not follow, as we chose. That when bad things happened they were due to evil, and that even evil had a place in God's inscrutable but essentially benevolent plan.

It's nonsense. Why should we matter to anyone, least of all to an omnipotent god whose existence is entirely hypothetical? I still think that Henry got it right. It was one evening in Durban, and we were having a philosophical discussion over our second or third nightcaps.

'Let's face it, old girl,' he said, 'it's as if we're adrift on the ocean in a boat without oars. Not much we can do except drink the rum ration.'

At Rosington station, I watched the clergyman's car driving up the hill into the darkening February afternoon. I waited a few more minutes for Janet. I went back into the station and phoned the house. Nobody answered.

So there was nothing for it but one of the station taxis. I told the driver to take me to the Dark Hostelry in the Close. In one of her letters, Janet said someone told her that in the Middle Ages, when Rosington was a monastery, the Dark Hostelry was where visiting Benedictine monks would stay. The 'Dark' came from the black habits of the order.

The taxi took me up the hill and through the great gateway, the Porta, and into the Close. I saw small boys in caps and shorts and grey mackintoshes. Perhaps they were at the Choir School. None of the boys would remember Henry. Six years is a long time in the life of a school.

We followed the road round the east end of the Cathedral and stopped outside a small gate in a high wall. I didn't ask the driver to carry in my suitcase – it would have meant a larger tip. I pushed open the gate in the wall, and that's when I saw Rosie playing hopscotch.

'And what's your name?' I asked.

'I'm nobody.'

Rosie wasn't wearing a coat. There she was in February playing outside and wearing sandals and a dress, not even a cardigan. The light was beginning to go. Some children don't feel the cold.

'Nobody?' I said. 'I'm sure that's not right. I bet you're really somebody. Somebody in disguise.'

'I'm nobody. That's my name.'

'Nobody's called nobody.'

'I am.'

'Why?'

'Because nobody's perfect.'

And so she was. Perfect. I thought, *Henry, you bastard, we could have had this.*

621

I called after Rosie as she skipped down the path towards the house. 'Rosie! I'm Auntie Wendy.'

I felt a fool saying that. Auntie Wendy sounded like a character in a children's story, the sort my mother would have liked.

'Can you tell Mummy I'm here?'

Rosie opened the door and skipped into the house. I picked up my case and followed. I was relieved because Janet must have come back. She wouldn't have left a child that age alone.

The house was part of a terrace. I had a confused impression of buttresses, the irregular line of high-pitched roofs against a grey velvet skyline, and small deeply recessed windows. At the door I put down my case and looked for the bell. There were panes of glass set in the upper panels and I could see the hall stretching into the depths of the building. Rosie had vanished. Irregularities in the glass gave the interior a green tinge and made it ripple like Rosie's hair.

A brass bell pull was recessed into the jamb of the door. I tugged it and hoped that a bell was jangling at the far end of the invisible wire. There was no way of knowing. You just had to have faith, not a state of mind that came easily to me at any time. I tried again, wondering if I should have used another door. The skin prickled on the back of my neck at the possibility of embarrassment. I waited a little longer. Someone must be there with the child. I opened the door and a smell of damp rose to meet me. The level of the floor was a foot below the garden.

'Hello?' I called. 'Hello? Anyone home?'

My voice had an unfamiliar echo to it, as though I had spoken in a church. I stepped down into the hall. It felt colder inside than out. A clock ticked. I heard light footsteps running above my head. There was a click as a door opened, then another silence, somehow different in quality from the one before.

Then the screaming began.

There's something about a child's screams that makes the heart turn over. I dropped the suitcase. Some part of my mind registered the fact that the lock had burst open in the impact of the fall, that my hastily packed belongings, the debris of my life with Henry, were spilling over the floor of the hall. I ran up a flight of shallow stairs and found myself on a long landing.

The door at the end was open. I saw Rosie's back, framed in the doorway. She wasn't screaming any more. She was standing completely still. Her arms hung stiffly by her sides as though they were no longer jointed at the elbows.

'Rosie! Rosie!'

I walked quickly down the landing and seized her by the shoulders. I spun her round and hugged her face into my belly. Her body was hard and unyielding. She felt like a doll, not a child. There was another scream. This one was mine.

The room was furnished as a bedroom. It smelled of Brylcreem and peppermints. There were two mullioned windows. One of them must have been open a crack because I heard the sound of traffic passing and people talking in the street below. At times like that, the mind soaks up memories like a sponge. Often you don't know what's there until afterwards, when you give the sponge a squeeze and you see what trickles out.

At the time I was aware only of the man on the floor. He lay on his back between the bed and the doorway. He wore charcoal-grey flannel trousers, brown brogues and an olive-green, knitted waistcoat over a white shirt with a soft collar. A tweed jacket and a striped tie were draped over a chair beside the bed. His left hand was resting on his belly. His right hand was lying palm upwards on the floor, the fingers loosely curled round the dark bone handle of a carving knife. There was blood on the blade, blood on his neck and blood on his shirt and waistcoat. His horn-rimmed glasses had fallen off. Blue eyes stared up at the ceiling. His hair was greyer and scantier than when I'd seen it last, and his face was thinner, but I recognized him right away. It was Janet's father.

'Come away, Rosie,' I muttered, 'come away. Grandpa's sleeping. We'll go downstairs and wait for Mummy.'

As if my words were a signal, Mr Treevor blinked. His eyes focused on the two of us in the doorway.

'Fooled you,' he said, and then he began to laugh.

PART II

The Close

8

'I'm so sorry.' Janet was brushing Rosie's hair. The bristles caught in a tangle, and Janet began carefully to tease it out. 'He just *arrived*.'

'It doesn't matter,' I said.

'Oh, but it does.' Her eyes met mine, then returned to the shining hair. 'The doorbell rang at half past three and there he was. He'd come all the way from Cambridge in a taxi.'

Rosie was sitting on a stool on the hearthrug, her back straight, not leaning against her mother's knees. In her place I would have been fidgeting, or playing with a toy, or looking at a book. But Rosie seemed hypnotized by the gentle scratching of the brush.

'It didn't occur to him to telephone. He just came as he was. No luggage, no overcoat. He even forgot his wallet. I had to use the housekeeping.' Janet smiled but I knew her too well to be fooled. 'He was still in his slippers.'

We were in a narrow, panelled sitting room. The three of us were huddled round the hearthrug in front of the fire. Rosie was in her nightclothes. Janet had given me a gin and orange, with rather too much orange for my taste, and I was nursing it between my hands, trying to make it last.

'He'd forgotten his medicine too. Actually they're laxatives. He gets terribly concerned about them. That's why I had to pop out to the chemist's before it closed. And then the dean's wife swooped and I couldn't get away.' The brush faltered. Janet rested her hands on Rosie's shoulders. 'Poor Grandpa will forget his own name next, won't he, poppet? Now, say good night to Auntie Wendy and we'll put you into bed.'

When they went upstairs, I wandered over to the drinks tray and freshened my glass with a little gin. All three of us had tiptoed round what Mr Treevor had done upstairs. I wondered what Janet was saying to Rosie about it now. If anything. How *do* you explain to a child that Grandpa found a bottle of tomato ketchup in the kitchen, took it upstairs to his room and splashed it over him to make it look as if he'd stabbed himself to death? What on earth had he been thinking about? He had ruined his clothes and the bedroom rug. God knew what effect he had had on Rosie. The only consolation was that all the excitement had tired him out. He was resting on his bed before supper.

Glass in hand, I wandered round the room, picking up ornaments and looking at the books and pictures. I had grown sensitive to poverty in others as you do when your own money runs low. I thought I saw hints of it here, a cushion placed to cover a stain on a chair's upholstery, a fire too small for the grate, curtains that needed relining. David couldn't earn much.

There was a wedding photograph in a silver frame on the pier table between the windows, just the two of them in front of Jerusalem Chapel, David's clerical bands snapping in the breeze. I didn't have any photographs of my wedding, a hole-in-the-corner affair compared with theirs. My mother had thought we should have a white wedding with all the trimmings but Henry persuaded her to let us have the money instead for the honeymoon.

Janet came downstairs.

'Supper will have to be very simple, I'm afraid. Would cheese on toast be all right? There's some apple crumble in the larder.'

'That's fine.' I noticed her shiver. 'What's wrong?'

'I wanted it to be nice for you on your first evening especially. We haven't seen each other in such ages.'

'It's all right. It's lovely to be here. Will your father be coming down?'

'He's dozed off.' She went over to the fire and began to add coal. 'I didn't like to wake him.'

I sat on the sofa. 'Janet – does he often do things like that?'

'The tomato ketchup?'

I said nothing.

'He's always had a sense of humour,' she said, and threw a shovelful of coals on the fire.

'He kept it well concealed when I came to stay with you.'

Janet glanced at me. Tears made her eyes look larger than ever. 'Yes. Well. People change.'

'Come on.' I patted the seat of the sofa. 'Come and tell me about it.'

'But supper –'

'Damn supper.'

'I wish I could.' Suddenly she was almost shouting. 'You've no idea how much I hate cooking. In the morning the sight of a fried egg makes my stomach turn over.'

'Me too. Anyway, I'm going to help with supper. But come and sit down first.'

She dabbed her eyes with a dainty little handkerchief. She was one of the few people I've ever known who don't make a spectacle of themselves when they cry. Janet managed everything gracefully, even tears. I brought her another drink. She made a half-hearted attempt to push the glass away.

'I shouldn't drink this. I've already had one tonight.'

'It's medicinal.' I watched her take a sip. 'Tell me, how long's he been like this?'

'I don't know. I think it must have started before Mummy died. It's been very gradual.'

'Have you thought about putting him in a home?'

'I couldn't do that. He's not old. He's not even seventy yet. And it's not as if he's ill. Just a bit forgetful at times.'

'Has he seen the doctor?'

'He doesn't like doctors. That business with the tomato sauce . . .'

'Yes?'

'I think he was just trying to be friendly. Just trying to play a game with Rosie, to make her laugh. But he didn't realize the effect he would have.'

She hesitated and added carefully, 'He was never very good with children.'

'And what does David say?'

'I haven't liked to bother him too much. He's very busy at present. There's a possibility of a new job . . .'

'But surely he must have noticed?'

'He hasn't seen Daddy for a while. Anyway, for most of the time he's all right.'

I felt like an inquisitor. 'And what did Rosie say?'

'Nothing really.' Janet ran her finger round the rim of her glass. 'I told her that Grandpa was just having a joke, and it was one of those grown-up jokes that children don't always understand. And she nodded, and that was that.'

It turned into quite a nice evening in the end. Rosie fell asleep, and so did that dreadful old man upstairs. Janet and I ended up making piles of toast over the sitting room fire and getting strawberry jam all over the hearthrug. Janet gave me a chance to talk about Henry but I didn't want to, not then. So we ignored him altogether (which he would have hated so much) and I was happy. There was I acting the tower of strength while inside I felt like a jelly, just as I had all those years ago at school. Between them, Janet and Mr Treevor made me feel useful again. We choose our own families, especially if our biological ones aren't very satisfactory.

9

Even now, when I am as old as John Treevor, I dream about the day I came to Rosington. Not about what happened in the house. About talking to Rosie outside. The odd thing, the disturbing thing, is what Rosie says. Or doesn't say.

When I see her in the dream I know she's going to tell her joke, that she's called Nobody because nobody's perfect. But the punchline is scrambled. That's what makes me anxious – the fact I don't know how the words will come out. Perfect but nobody. Nobody but perfect. A perfect nobody. Perfect no body. No perfect body. Maybe my sleeping mind worries about that because it's less painful than worrying about what was going on in the house.

But the dream came much later. On my first night in Rosington I slept better than I had for years. I was in a room on the second floor away from the rest of the house. When I woke I knew it was late because of the light filtering through the crack in the curtains. The air in the bedroom was icy. I stayed in the warm nest of the bedclothes for at least twenty minutes more.

Eventually a bursting bladder drove me out of bed. The bathroom was warmer than my room because it had a hot-water tank in it. I took my clothes in there and got dressed. I went downstairs and found Janet's father sitting in a Windsor chair at the kitchen table reading *The Times*.

We eyed each other warily. He had not come downstairs again the previous evening; Janet had taken him some soup. He stood up and smiled uncertainly.

'Hello, Mr Treevor.'

He looked blank.

'I'm Wendy Appleyard, remember – Janet's friend from school.'

'Yes, yes. There's some tea in the pot, I believe. Shall I –?' He made a half-hearted attempt to investigate the teapot on my behalf.

'I think I might make some fresh.'

'My wife always says that coffee never tastes the same if you let it stand.' He looked puzzled. 'Good idea. Yes, yes.'

I was aware of him watching me as I filled the kettle, put it on the stove and lit the gas. He had put on weight since I had seen him last, a great belt of fat. The rest of him still looked relatively slim, including the face with its nose like a beak and the bulging forehead, now even more prominent because the hairline had receded further. His hair was longer than it used to be and unbrushed. He wore a heavy jersey that was too large for his shoulders and too small for his stomach. I wondered if it belonged to David. He did not refer to the incident yesterday and nor did I.

'I hope you slept well?' he said at last.

'Yes, thank you.'

'The noises didn't keep you awake?'

'The noises?'

'Yes, yes. You tend to get them in these old houses.'

'I didn't hear any. I slept very well.'

He gathered up his newspaper. 'I must be going. It's getting quite late.'

'Where's Janet?'

'Taking Rosie to school. Will you be all right? Can you fend for yourself?'

Once he'd established my ability to do this, at least to his own satisfaction, he pottered out of the kitchen. I heard him in the hall. A door opened, then closed and a bolt smacked home. He had taken refuge in the downstairs lavatory.

He was still in there after I'd drunk two cups of tea, eaten a slice of toast and started the washing-up. A bell jangled – one of a row of bells above the kitchen door. I guessed it must be the garden door, so I dried my hands and went to answer it. There was a small, sturdy clergyman on the doorstep. He touched his hat.

'Good morning. Is David in?'

'I'm afraid he's up in town at a conference. Janet's out but she should be back soon. May I take a message?'

'Do you happen to know when he's coming back?'

'This evening, I think.'

'I'll ring him tomorrow or perhaps drop in. Would you tell him Peter Hudson called? Thank you so much. Goodbye.'

He touched his hat again and walked briskly down the path where Rosie had played hopscotch to the gate in the wall. The lawn on either side of the path was still white with frost. At the gate, he turned, glanced back and waved.

That was my first meeting with Canon Hudson. A meek and mild little man, I thought at the time, with one of those forgettable faces and a classless voice that could have come from anywhere. If I had to have dealings with a clergyman, I thought, I'd much prefer he looked and sounded like Laurence Olivier.

10

In the evening David came home from London. The mood of the house changed. He arrived in the lull between Rosie being put to bed and supper. I hadn't been looking forward to seeing him. Janet and I were in the kitchen, Mr Treevor was dozing in the sitting room.

David kissed Janet and shook hands with me.

'Did you have a good time?' Janet asked him.

'Most of it was hot air but some useful people were there. Any messages?'

'On the desk in the study. Rosie might still be awake if you want to say good night to her.'

'Just a few phone calls I should make first.'

'Oh, and Peter Hudson called.'

Already at the kitchen door, David turned. His face was sharper than it had been. 'And?'

'It was this morning – Wendy saw him. He said he'd phone or drop in tomorrow.'

'He'll want to talk about the library. I'll see if I can get hold of him now.'

He left the room. I avoided looking at Janet.

'He's concerned about this library business,' Janet said hastily, as if in apology. 'There's a proposal to merge the Theological College Library with the Cathedral one. Hardly anyone uses the Cathedral Library, you see, and it would be much better for everyone if it was housed in the Theo. Coll. Peter Hudson's the new Cathedral librarian so his opinion's very important.'

'The marriage of two libraries? Gosh.'

She winced. 'It's more than that. You know David's boss is

getting on? It's an open secret he may retire at the end of the summer term.'

'And David wants the job?' I smiled at her and tried to make a joke of it. 'I thought the clergy weren't supposed to have worldly ambitions.'

'It's more that David feels he could do useful work there. Canon Osbaston likes him. He's the principal. So does the bishop. But the appointment needs the agreement of the Cathedral Chapter as well. It's a bit like a school, you see. The bishop and the others are like the college's board of governors.'

'So where's the problem?'

'Some of the canons aren't very enthusiastic about David getting the job. Including Peter Hudson.'

Janet began to lay the table. The Byfields usually ate in the kitchen because it was warmer and because the dining room was a day's march away up a flight of stairs and at the other end of the house.

'Hudson seemed quite a nice little man,' I said. 'Inoffensive.'

Janet snorted. 'That's a mistake a lot of people make.' She sat down suddenly and rubbed her eyes. 'God, I'm tired.'

I took the cutlery from her and continued laying the place settings. She fiddled with one of the napkin rings, rubbing at a dull spot on the silver.

'It's not really about this library,' she went on slowly. 'Or even about the job. It's about the college itself. They're talking about closing it down.'

'Why should they do that?'

'Because applications are down and money's tight. It's a problem all over the country. David says the Church of England needs between six and seven hundred ordinations a year at the minimum if it wants to keep its parishes going. But they haven't managed six hundred a year for nearly half a century. And meanwhile everything's more expensive. The Theo. Coll.'s a great barrack of a place. It simply eats up money.'

'Why does David want to be principal of it? Couldn't he do something else? Why can't he have a parish like normal priests?'

'He feels his vocation is to be a teacher and a scholar – perhaps even an administrator.' She straightened one of the knives. 'And – and I think it's the sort of job that gets you noticed. David wouldn't look at it like that, of course, but that's what it amounts to.'

'Sounds more like Imperial Tobacco than the Church of England.'

'The Church is an organization, Wendy. They all work the same way. The C of E isn't there to make money but it's still an organization.'

I was tempted to make a joke about God being the chairman for life but decided that Janet might think it in bad taste.

'The salary would be much better, too,' she said in a voice barely louder than a whisper.

It was at that point that a handful of suspicions coalesced into a certainty. 'Money's tight for you, isn't it?'

Janet said nothing. I remembered how David had paid my bill at Mrs Hyson's and bought my train ticket. I thought about the cost of Mr Treevor's taxi from Cambridge, and how having two extra mouths to feed – and in my case water – would affect a household budget.

I drew out a chair and sat down beside her. 'You've been very good to me,' I said. 'Both of you, real friends in need. But I shan't stay long.'

Janet lifted her face. 'I don't want you to go. I like having you here. Anyway, where would you go? What would you do?'

'I'll find something.'

She shook her head. 'Not yet. God knows what would happen to you.'

'Other people manage,' I said airily.

'You're not other people. You're Wendy. Anyway, what about Henry?'

My heart twisted. 'What about him?'

'You don't think –?'

'I told you in the letter. It's over. I'm going to divorce him. He can't contest it. He only married me for the bit of money I had.' I rubbed a patch of rough skin on my hand, trying to smooth away the hurt. 'I caught him making love to another woman and she was the ugliest bitch you've ever seen.'

'Oh, Wendy.'

She took my hand. I stared at them, her hand and mine lying on the scrubbed deal table.

Janet said, 'You must stay for a while.'

'Only if you let me pay something. And if you let me help you around the house.'

'You haven't got any money.'

'I've got one or two little bits of jewellery.'

'You're not to sell them.'

'Then I'll have to go.'

We glared at each other. She began to cry. So did I. While we finished laying the table we shared a brief companionable weep. By the time we'd dried our eyes, hugged each other and cleared the draining board we both knew that I would stay.

11

The first Saturday of my visit was cold but sunny. David took Janet and me up the west tower of the Cathedral. We climbed endless spiral staircases and edged along narrow galleries thick with stone dust. At last he pushed open a tiny door and we crawled out on to an unbearably bright platform of lead.

There was no wind. I swear it was colder and sunnier up there than it had been on the ground. I leaned against one of the walls, which were battlemented like a castle's. I was gasping for breath because of too many stairs and too many cigarettes.

I looked out. The tower went down like a lift in a horror film. The ground rushed away. I held on to the parapet, the roughness of the stone scouring my hands as I squeezed it more and more tightly.

Below me was the great encrusted hull of the Cathedral and the tiled and slated roofs of Rosington. Around them as far as the eye could see were the grey winter Fens. They stretched towards the invisible point where they became one with the grey winter sky.

For an instant I was more terrified than I had ever been in my life. I was adrift between the sky and the earth. All my significance had been stolen from me.

Then Janet put her hand on my arm and said, 'Look, there's Canon Osbaston coming out of the Theological College.' She lowered her voice. 'If tortoises waddled they'd look just like him.'

In those days Rosington was a small town – perhaps eight or nine thousand people. Technically it was a city because it had a cathedral, so its sense of importance was out of proportion to its size. It was also an island set in the black sea of the Fens, a place apart, a place of refuge. It was certainly a place of refuge for me. Even if he wanted to, Henry would hardly follow me to the town where he had made such a fool of himself.

David told me that in the Middle Ages the Isle of Rosington was largely surrounded by water. It was a liberty, almost a County Palatine, in which the abbots who preceded the bishops wielded much of the authority usually reserved for the king. Here the Saxons made one of their last stands against the invading armies of the Normans.

The city still felt a place under siege. And the Cathedral Close, a city within a city, was doubly under siege because the town around it nibbled away at its rights and privileges. The Close was an ecclesiastical domain, older than the secular one surrounding it, and conducted according to different laws. Its gates were locked at night by an assistant verger named Gotobed who lived beside the Porta with his mother and her cats.

Rosington wasn't like Bradford or Hillgard House or Durban or any of the other places I'd lived in. The past was more obvious here. If you glanced up at the ceiling while you were sitting in Janet's kitchen you saw the clumsy barrel of a Norman vault. The Cathedral clock rang the hours and the quarters. The Close and its inhabitants were governed by the rhythm of the daily services, just as they had been for more than a thousand years. I had never lived among religious people before and this was unsettling too. It was as though I were the one person capable of seeing colours, as if everyone else lived in a monochrome world. Or possibly it was the other way round. Either way I was in a minority of one.

When we were at school Janet and I used to laugh at those who were religious. Now I knew she went to church regularly, though it was not something we had talked about in our letters.

On my first Sunday morning in Rosington I stayed at home. Janet and Rosie were going to matins at ten thirty. The pair of them looked so sweet dressed up for God in their Sunday finery.

'If you don't mind I won't come to church,' I said to David at breakfast. I'd already made this clear to Janet but I wanted to say it to him as well. I didn't want there to be any misunder-standings.

He smiled. 'It's entirely up to you.'

'I'm sorry, but I'm not particularly godly. I'd rather do the vegetables.'

'That's very kind of you. But are you sure it isn't too much trouble?'

I don't know how, but he made me feel like the prodigal daughter a long way from home.

'I suppose you have to go to church,' I said to Janet as we were washing up after lunch. 'Part of your wifely duties.'

She nodded but added, 'I like it too. No one makes any demands on you in church. You can just be quiet for once.'

I was stupid enough to ignore what she was really saying. 'Yes, but do you believe in God?'

I didn't want Janet to believe in God. It was as if by doing so she would believe a little less in me.

'I don't know.' She bent over the sink and began to scour the roasting tin. 'Anyway, it doesn't really matter what I believe, does it?'

During my first fortnight in Rosington the five of us settled into a routine. Given how different we were, you would have expected more friction than there was. But David was out most of the time – either at the Theological College or in the Cathedral. Rosie was at school during the week – she was in her second term at St Tumwulf's Infant School on the edge of the town. Old Mr Treevor – I thought of him as old, though he was younger than I am now – spent much time in his bedroom, either huddled over a small electric fire or in bed. As far as I could see his chief interests were food, the contents of *The Times* and the evacuation of his bowels.

The house itself made co-existence easier. The Dark Hostelry was not so much large as complicated. Most of the rooms were small and there were a great many of them. David said the building had been in continuous occupation for seven or eight hundred years. Each generation seemed to have added its own eccentricity. It was a place of many staircases, some of which led nowhere in particular, small, crooked rooms with sloping floors and thick walls. The kitchen was in a semi-basement, and as you washed up you could watch the legs of the passers-by in the High Street, which followed the northern boundary of the Cathedral Close.

Although the Dark Hostelry was good for keeping people apart, it was not an easy house to run. A charwoman came in three mornings a week to 'do the rough'. Otherwise Janet had to do the work herself. And there was a lot of it – this was 1958, and the nearest thing Janet had to a labour-saving device was a twin-tub washing machine with a hand mangle attached. The last time the place had had a serious overhaul was at the turn of the century when the occupants could probably have afforded two or three servants.

In some ways I think Janet would have preferred to be a paid servant. She loathed the work but at least she would have been getting a wage for it. A simple commercial transaction has a beginning and end. It implies that both parties to it have freedom of choice.

Janet had the worst of both worlds. There was a dark irony in the fact that as well as running that ridiculous old house she also had to pretend to be its mistress, not its slave. Janet was expected to be a lady. When the Byfields came to Rosington she had visiting cards engraved. I've still got one of them – yellowing pasteboard, dog-eared at the corners, the typeface small and discreet.

Mrs David Byfield
The Dark Hostelry
The Close
Rosington

Telephone: Rosington 2114

When the Byfields arrived at the Dark Hostelry, the ladies of the Close and the ladies of the town called and left their cards. Janet called on them and left hers. It was a secular equivalent to what David was doing every day in that echoing stone mountain in the middle of the Close. A ritualistic procedure which might once have had a purpose.

I doubt if David knew what a burden he'd placed on her

641

shoulders. Not then, at any rate. It's not that he wasn't a sensitive man. But his sensitivity was like a torch beam. It had to be directed at you before it became effective. But it wasn't just a question of him being sensitive or not being sensitive. Everyone thought differently. This was more than forty years ago, remember, and in the Cathedral Close of Rosington.

Nowadays I think David and Janet were both in prison. But neither of them could see the bars.

12

It became increasingly obvious that something would have to be done about Mr Treevor.

He and I, a pair of emotional vampires, arrived on the same February afternoon and more than three weeks later we were still at the Dark Hostelry. I flattered myself there was a difference, that at least I did some of the housework and cooking. I sold my engagement ring, too. I'd never liked the beastly thing. It turned out to be worth much less than Henry had led me to expect, which shouldn't have surprised me.

Mr Treevor did less and less. He took it for granted that we were there to supply his needs – regular meals, clean clothes, bed-making, warm rooms and a daily copy of *The Times*, which for some reason he liked to have ironed before he would open it.

'He never used to be like that,' Janet said to me on Thursday morning as we were snatching a cup of coffee. 'He hardly ever read a paper, and as for this ironing business, I've no idea where that came from.'

'Isn't it the sort of thing they used to do in the homes of the aristocracy?'

'He can't have picked it up there.'

'Perhaps he saw it in a film.'

'It's a bit of a nuisance, actually.'

'A bit of a nuisance? It's a bloody imposition. I think you should go on strike.'

'I think his memory's improving. That's something, isn't it?'

I wondered whether it would ever improve to the point

where he would be able to remember who I was from one day to the next.

'He told me all about how he won a prize at school the other day,' Janet went on, sounding as proud as she did when describing one of Rosie's triumphs at St Tumwulf's. 'For Greek verses. He could even remember the name of the boy he beat.'

'He's getting old,' I said, responding to her anxiety, not what she'd said. 'That's all. It'll happen to us one day.'

Janet bit her lip. 'Yesterday he asked me when Mummy was coming. He seems to think she'd gone away for the weekend or something.'

'When's he going home?'

'On Saturday,' Janet said brightly. 'David's offered to drive him back.'

Early on Friday morning all of us realized that this would have to be postponed. Even on the top floor I heard the shouting. By the time I got downstairs everyone else was in the kitchen. Even Rosie was huddled in the corner between the wall and the dresser, crouching to make herself as small as possible.

Mr Treevor was standing beside the table. He was in his pyjamas, but without his teeth, his slippers and his dressing gown. He was sobbing. Janet was patting his right arm with a tea towel. David, also in pyjamas, was frowning at them both. There was a puddle of water on the table, and the front of Janet's nightdress was soaked. The room smelled of singed hair and burning cloth.

Afterwards we reconstructed what had happened. Mr Treevor had woken early and with a rare burst of initiative decided to make himself some tea. He went downstairs, lit the gas and put the kettle on the ring. It was unfortunate that he forgot you had to put water in the kettle as well. After a while, the kettle started to make uncharacteristically agitated noises so he lifted it off the ring. At this point he forgot two other things – to turn off the gas, and to cover the metal handle of the kettle with a cloth. The first scream must have been caused when the metal of the handle burnt into his fingers and the palm of his hand.

David stared at me. 'We must have a first-aid box somewhere, mustn't we?'

'Phone the doctor,' I said to him. 'Quickly.'

'But surely it's not a –'

'Quickly. Mr Treevor's had a bad shock.'

He blinked, nodded and left the room.

I pulled a chair towards the sink, and with Janet's help drew Mr Treevor down on to it. I turned on the tap and ran cold water over his hand and arm.

'Janet, why don't you take Rosie back to bed and fetch a blanket? Have you got any lint?'

'Yes, it's –'

'You'd better bring that as well. And then what about some tea?'

There's a side of me that derives huge pleasure from telling people what to do. No one seemed to mind. Gradually, Mr Treevor's sobs subsided to whimpers and then to silence. By the time the doctor arrived, all four adults were huddled round the kitchen boiler drinking very sweet tea.

The doctor was Flaxman. I recognized his name from Janet's letters – he had been helpful when she was pregnant. Later I came to know him quite well. He had a long, freckled face, flaking skin and red hair. He examined Mr Treevor, told us to put him to bed and said he would call later in the day.

In the afternoon, Flaxman returned. He spent twenty minutes alone with Mr Treevor and then came down and talked to us in the sitting room. David was still at the Theological College.

'How is he?' Janet asked.

'Well, the burns aren't a problem. He'll get over those. It could have been worse if you hadn't acted promptly.'

'We've Mrs Appleyard to thank for that.' Janet smiled at me.

Flaxman sat down. He didn't look at me. He began to write a prescription.

'Would you like a cup of tea? Or some sherry? It's not too early for sherry, is it?'

'No, thanks.' He tore off the prescription and handed it to Janet. 'These will help Mr Treevor sleep, Mrs Byfield. Give him one at bedtime. If he complains of pain, give him a couple of aspirin. Tell me, where does he live?'

'He has a flat in Cambridge.'

'Does he live alone?'

'There's a landlady downstairs. She cooks for him.'

'How long will he be staying with you?'

Janet wriggled slightly in her chair. 'I don't really know. My husband was going to take him back tomorrow but in the circumstances, I suppose –'

'I'd advise you to keep him here a little longer. I'd like to see him again over the next few days. I think his condition needs assessment. Perhaps you'd let me have the address of his GP.'

'He wasn't properly awake this morning,' Janet said, clutching at straws. 'He's not been sleeping well.'

'The sleeping tablets will help that. But the point is, he needs looking after. I don't mean he needs to be hospitalized, but he needs other people around to keep an eye on him.'

'Is – is this going to get worse?'

'It may well do. That's one reason why we need to keep an eye on him, Mrs Byfield – to see if he is getting worse.'

'And if he is?'

'There are several residential homes in the area. Some private, some National Health.'

'He'd hate that. He'd hate the loss of privacy.'

'Yes, but his physical safety has to be the main concern. Could he live with you or some other relative?'

'Permanently?'

'If you don't want him to go into a residential home, that would probably be the best solution, Mrs Byfield. At least until his condition deteriorates a good deal more.'

'But – but what exactly's wrong with him?'

'At this stage it's hard to be categorical.' He glanced quickly at us both. 'But I think he's in the early stages of a form of dementia.'

There was a long silence. I wanted to say to Janet, *You've got enough on your plate*, but for once I kept my mouth shut.

Then she sighed. 'I shall have to talk to my husband.'

13

Janet and I went to Mr Treevor's flat on Saturday. We drove over to Cambridge, another small victory for me hard on the heels of my display of Girl Guide first aid. In a sense I was beginning to shed my burdens just as Janet was shouldering more.

David had assumed that Janet would go by bus. It was after all cheaper than going by train.

'Why not the car?' I said on Friday evening, emboldened by my Girl Guide expertise and by a substantial slug from the gin bottle in my bedside cupboard.

'Janet doesn't drive.' David hardly bothered to glance at me. 'I'd take you myself, of course, but unfortunately I've got my classes in the morning and then there's a meeting first thing in the afternoon. The Finance Committee.'

'I'll take her,' I said.

This time David looked properly at me. 'I didn't realize you drove.'

'Well, I do. But what about insurance?'

'It's insured for any driver I give permission to.'

'There you are. Problem solved.'

'But have you driven recently, Wendy? It's not an easy car to drive, either. It's –'

'It's a second series Ford Anglia,' I interrupted. 'We had one for a time in Durban, except ours was more modern and had the 1200 cc engine.'

'I see.' Suddenly he smiled. 'You're a woman of hidden talents.'

I smiled back and asked Janet when she would like to go. I felt warm and a little breathless, which wasn't just the gin.

647

That's biology for you. David upset a lot of men in his time but I never knew a woman who didn't have a sneaking regard for him, who didn't enjoy his approval.

Janet and I had six hours of freedom. The charwoman agreed to come in for the day and keep an eye on Mr Treevor and Rosie. Rosie liked the charwoman, who gave her large quantities of cheap sweets which Janet disapproved of but dared not object to.

The road from Rosington to Cambridge is the sort of road made with a ruler. The Fens could never look pretty, but the day was unseasonably warm for early March and the sun was shining. It was possible to believe that spring was round the corner, that you'd no longer be cold all the time, and that problems might have solutions.

Mr Treevor's flat was the upper part of a little mid-Victorian terraced house in a cul-de-sac off Mill Road, near the station. I hadn't known what to expect but it wasn't this. The landlady, the widow of a college porter, kept the ground floor for herself. Mr Treevor and the widow and the widow's son shared the kitchen, which was at the back of the house, and the bathroom which was beyond the kitchen, tacked on as an afterthought.

The landlady was out. Janet let herself in with her father's key and we went upstairs. I must have shown what I was feeling on my face.

'It's a bit seedy, I'm afraid,' she said.

'It doesn't matter.'

'You didn't think he'd live somewhere like this, I suppose? He wanted to stay in Cambridge, you see, and it was all he could afford when Mummy died.'

Janet took me along the landing to the room at the front, which was furnished as a sitting room. It smelled of tobacco, stale food and unwashed bodies.

'She gives him his breakfast and an evening meal,' Janet said, meaning the landlady, 'and she's meant to clean for him as well and send his washing to the laundry.' She threw up one of the sash windows and cold, fresh air flooded into the room. 'I don't think she does very much. That's one reason why I didn't warn her we were coming.'

'I'm sorry. I – I suppose there was nowhere better available.'

'Beggars couldn't be choosers.' She turned round to face me. 'There was enough money when I was growing up. My mother was always working and she was good at her job. They were queueing up for her. And Daddy had a little money of his own. Not much, about a hundred a year, I think. They didn't have pensions or anything like that. I think they more or less lived up to their income.'

'It's all right,' I said awkwardly, because I was English and in those days the English hated talking about money, especially with friends. 'I quite understand.'

Janet was braver than me, always was. 'When Mummy was ill, the translation work dried up and they had to live on Daddy's capital. So what with one thing and another there wasn't much left when Mummy died.' She waved her arm. 'But he had this. He could be independent and he loves Cambridge.'

I said, suddenly understanding, 'You and David are helping to pay for this, aren't you?'

She nodded. 'Only a little.'

'That's something,' I said. 'You won't have to any more.'

But I knew as well as she did that they would have to pay for other things now, and in other ways.

John Treevor was still alive and less than twenty miles away in Rosington. Yet as we moved around his flat, sorting his possessions, it was as if he were already dead. His absence had an air of permanence about it.

His possessions dwindled in significance because of this. People lend importance to their possessions and when they're dead or even absent the importance evaporates. I remember there was a thin layer of grime on the windowsills, dust on the books, holes in most of the socks.

'It would be much simpler if we could just throw it all away,' Janet said as she closed the third of the three suitcases we'd brought with us. 'And what are we going to do about his post? He's not going to want to write letters.'

While I took the suitcases down to the car, Janet went through the drawers of the desk. When I came back there was a pile of papers on top and she was looking at a photograph, tilting it this way and that in front of the window.

'Look.'

I took it from her. The photograph was of her when she was not much older than Rosie, a little snapshot taken on the beach. She was in a bathing costume, hugging her knees and staring up at the camera. I handed it back to her.

'It was before the war. Somewhere like Bexhill or Hastings. We used to go down to Sussex to stay with my grandparents. I thought it was heaven. Daddy taught me to swim one summer, and he used to read me to sleep.' Her voice was trembling. 'There was a collection of fairy stories by Andrew Lang, *The Yellow Fairy Book*. I'd forgotten all about it.'

She foraged for her handkerchief in her handbag and blew her nose.

'Why did it have to happen to him?' she said angrily, as though it were my fault. 'Why couldn't he just have grown old normally, or even died? This is nothing. It's neither one thing nor the other.'

I said nothing because there was nothing to say.

Janet left a note for the landlady. I took her out to lunch and afterwards we walked in the pale sunshine through St John's College and on to the Backs. It wasn't much of an attempt at consolation but it was the only one I could think of.

Now the decision had been made, David felt there was no point in delay. Over the next few weeks we sold or gave away or threw away two-thirds of the contents of the flat.

Mr Gotobed, the assistant verger, helped David bring the rest of Mr Treevor's belongings back to the Dark Hostelry. Puffing and grunting, the two men carried some of the furniture – the desk, the chair, the glass-fronted bookcase – up to Mr Treevor's bedroom to make it seem homely. Janet arranged photographs on the desk, herself and her mother, both in newly cleaned silver frames. She brought her father's pipe rack and tobacco jar, not that he smoked any more, and put them where they used to stand on his desk.

I'm not sure this was a good idea. One morning, shortly after we'd finished the move, Mr Treevor emerged from the bathroom as I was coming down the stairs from my room. He laid his hand on my arm and looked around as if checking for eavesdroppers.

'There's funny things happening in this house,' he confided.

'They've got the builders in. They've been changing my room. It must be at night because I've never actually seen them at work. I've seen one of them in the hall, though. Furtive-looking chap.' He padded across the landing towards his room. At the door he glanced back at me.

'Better keep your eyes skinned, Rosie,' he hissed. 'Or there's no knowing what they'll get up to. Can't be too careful. Especially with a pretty girl like you.'

Rosie?

14

I have to admit the Cathedral came in handy when it was raining. You could walk almost the length of the High Street under cover. Or you could cut across from the north transept to the south door and avoid going right the way round the Cathedral outside. And sometimes if the choir was practising or the organ was playing I'd sit down for a while and listen.

That's where Peter Hudson found me.

It was raining heavily that morning, silver sheets of icy water sweeping across the Fens from the east. I had been to the Labour Exchange in Market Street. The woman I talked to disapproved of me. Was it my lipstick? The tightness of my skirt? The fact I'd forgotten to bring my gloves? I suspect she labelled me as louche, dangerously sophisticated and a potential husband-snatcher. Which tells you as much about the competition as it does about me.

At present the Labour Exchange had only two jobs for which I was suitably qualified. They needed someone behind the confectionery counter in Woolworth's. Or, if I preferred, I could earn rather more if I worked shifts at the canning factory on the outskirts of town. Neither of them had anything to be said for them except money, and there wasn't much of that on offer either.

I was beginning to think I'd have to go back to London. I didn't want to do that, partly because I thought Janet needed me but more because I knew I needed her. It wasn't just the breaking up with Henry. It was as if every mistake I had ever made in my life had come back to haunt me. It was rather like when you leave a hotel and they present you with a bill that's three times larger than you thought it was going to be.

I entered the Close by the Boneyard Gate from the High Street and ducked into the north door of the Cathedral to get out of the rain. Actually, it wouldn't have taken me much longer to stay in the open and reach the Dark Hostelry. But Janet was there and I wanted a moment or two by myself to catch my breath and decide what I was going to say to her.

Walking into the Cathedral was like walking into an aquarium, as if you were moving from one medium to another. Here the air was still, cool and grey. Gotobed, the assistant verger, gave me a quick, shy smile and scurried into the vestry. The building smelled faintly of smoke, a combination of incense and the fumes from the stoves that fired the central heating. I remember these stoves far better than anything else in the Cathedral. They were dotted about the aisles like cast-iron birdcages. The stoves were circular, domed, about the height of a man but much wider. Perched on top of each one was a cast-iron crown which would have fitted a very small child.

The choir was rehearsing behind the screen dividing the space beneath the Octagon from the east end. I couldn't see them but the sound of their voices welled into the crossing and poured into transepts and nave. Gotobed came out of the vestry, but this time he didn't look at me because he was on duty, carrying his silver-tipped wand of office and conducting Mr Forbury in a procession of one back to the Deanery.

I sat down on a chair, wiped the rain from my face and tried to think. Instead I listened to the sound of the voices spiralling up into the Octagon below the spire. The nearest I came to thinking was when I found myself wondering what Henry was doing at this moment, and where, and with whom. He must have found another woman by now, someone else willing to make a fool of herself because he flattered and amused her.

Then I noticed Canon Hudson coming out of the vestry. To my annoyance he came over towards me. That was one of the problems of Rosington. I had been used to the anonymity of cities.

'Hello, Mrs Appleyard. Enjoying the singing?'

'I don't know what it is but it's very restful.'

'We're rather proud of our music here. If you're here over Easter, you should –'

'I don't think I will be,' I said roughly, the decision suddenly made.

'You're leaving us?'

'I need to find a job. There's nothing down here. Or rather, nothing that appeals.'

He sat down beside me and folded his hands on his lap. 'And what exactly are you looking for, Mrs Appleyard?'

'I don't really know. But my husband's left me so I'm going to have to make my own living now.' I wished I could take the words back. My private life was none of his business. Janet had told other people that my husband was 'away'. I glanced at my watch and pantomimed surprise. 'Oh! Is that the time?'

'Difficult for you,' he said, ignoring my attempt to wind up the conversation. 'Am I right in thinking you'd prefer to stay in Rosington for the time being?'

'Well, it's a possibility.'

'You say you have no qualifications.'

'Apart from School Certificate.'

'And have you ever worked?'

'Only in my father's shop for a few years before I married. He was a jeweller.'

'What did that entail?'

I nearly told him to mind his own business, but he was such a gentle little man that being unkind to him seemed as wantonly cruel as treading on a worm. 'It varied. Sometimes I served in the shop, sometimes I helped with the accounts. I did most of the inventory when we sold the business.'

The music spiralled round and round above our heads. Just like me, it was trying to get out.

'How interesting,' Hudson said. 'Well, if you really are looking for something local, in fact I know of a temporary part-time job which might fit the bill. It's actually in the Close and to some extent you could choose the hours you work. But I don't know whether it would suit you. Or indeed whether you would suit it.' He smiled at me, taking the sting from the words. 'I want someone to catalogue the Cathedral Library.'

I stared blankly at him. Still smiling, he stared back.

'But I wouldn't know where to start,' I said. 'Surely you'd need a librarian or a scholar or someone like that? It's not the sort of thing I could do.'

'How do you know?'

'It's obvious.'

'Mrs Appleyard, what's obvious to me is that it could suit us both if you were able to help. So it's worth investigating, don't you think?'

I shrugged, ungracious to the last.

'Why don't you have a look at the library now? It won't take a moment.'

He was a persistent little man and in the end it was easier to do what he wanted than to refuse. He fetched a key from the vestry and then took me over to a door at the west end of the south choir aisle. He unlocked it and we stepped into a long vaulted room.

Suddenly it was much lighter. On the east wall, high above my head, were two great Norman windows filled with plain glass. A faded Turkish runner ran from the door along the length of the room's long axis towards a pair of tables at the far end. On either side of the runner were wooden bookcases, seven feet high, dividing the room into bays. The temperature wasn't much warmer than in the Cathedral itself, which meant it felt chilly even to someone inured to the draughts of the Dark Hostelry.

'Originally the room would have been two chapels opening out of the south transept,' Peter Hudson said. 'It was converted into a library for the Cathedral in the eighteen-seventies. No one knows for sure, but we think there must be at least nine or ten thousand books here, possibly more.'

We walked the length of the room. I looked at the rank after rank of spines, most vertical, a few horizontal, bound in leather, bound in cloth. The air smelled of dust and dead paper. I already knew I didn't have the training to do a job like this and probably not the aptitude either. But what I saw now was the sheer physical immensity of it.

One night at Hillgard House, Janet and I had sneaked out of our dormitory, slipped down the stairs and out of a side door. The sky was clear. We were in the middle of the country and in any case there was a blackout because it was wartime. We lay on our backs on the lawn, feeling the dew soaking through our nightdresses, and stared up at the summer sky.

'How many stars are there?' Janet murmured.

And I'd said, 'You could never count them.'

Terror had risen in me, a sort of awe. Facing all those books in the Cathedral Library I felt the same awe, only once removed from panic. Like the night sky, the library was too big. It contained too many things. I just wasn't on the right scale for it.

'I'm sorry, I don't think this will work.'

'Let's sit down and talk about it,' Hudson suggested.

At the end of the room were two large tables and an ill-assorted collection of what looked like retired dining chairs. Behind the tables was a cupboard built along the length of the wall. Hudson pulled out one of the chairs and dusted it with his handkerchief. I sat down.

'It's such a big job, and anyway I wouldn't know how to do it. I expect a lot of the books are valuable. I could damage them.'

He dusted another chair and sat down with a sigh of relief. Clasping his hands on the table, he smiled at me. 'Let me tell you what the job would entail before you make up your mind.'

'Aren't there medieval manuscripts? I wouldn't have the first idea how to read them.'

'The Cathedral does possess a few medieval manuscripts and early printed books. But they're not here. They're either under lock and key in the Treasury or they're on loan to Cambridge University Library or the British Museum. Nothing to worry about there.'

'If you say so.'

'You see, this library is a relatively recent affair. What happened was this – in the nineteenth century Dean Pellew left the Cathedral his books, about twelve hundred volumes. That's the nucleus of the collection. He also left us a sum of money as an endowment. So the chapter has a separate library fund which is there for buying new books and which can also be used for paying an assistant to manage the day-to-day work of the library. When the endowment was set up it was arranged that one of the canons should be the librarian and oversee the running of it. My immediate predecessor took over in 1931. He died in office last year so he had a long run for his money. But he didn't do much with the library.' Hudson smiled at me. 'And for the last ten years of his life, I doubt if he gave it a thought. Somehow it came to be understood that Cathedral librarian was one of those honorary posts. We've got enough of those on the Foundation, heaven knows. And then I took over.'

'Janet said there's a possibility the books might be given to the Theological College Library.'

He nodded. 'The dean and chapter have decided to close the Cathedral Library. It's not been formally announced yet but it's an open secret. The legal position's rather complicated – it's a question of diverting the endowment to something else relating to the Cathedral. And then there are the books, which is where you would come in. They're hardly ever used here, and frankly it's a waste of space having them here.'

'I wouldn't have thought space was a problem in this building.'

'You'd be surprised. It's our duty to make the best use of our resources we can. But to go back to the books. One possibility is that we give some or all of them to another library, and yes, perhaps the one at the Theological College might be appropriate.'

I noticed he did not mention the possibility that the Theological College might close.

'Or we may sell some or all of them. But we can't really decide what to do until we know what we've got. There's never been a complete catalogue, you see.' He stood up and lifted down a heavy foolscap volume from a shelf. He blew off the dust and placed it on the table. 'Dean Pellew's original collection is listed in here. Just authors and titles, nothing more, and I'd be surprised if we've still got them all. And then over the years there've been one or two half-hearted attempts to record acquisitions as they were made. Some of them are in here.' He tapped the book. 'Others are in the filing cabinet by the door.'

Hudson sat down again. He took out a pipe, peered into its bowl and then put it back in his pocket. I wondered what he would pay me and whether it would be enough to allow me to stay on in Rosington. He was going bald on top. Next I wondered whether he and his wife were fond of each other, and what they were like when they were alone together. Her name was June. She was one of the few ladies in the Close who not only recognized me but said hello when we met.

'Couldn't you get someone from a bookshop to look at the books?'

'We could. They would certainly do a valuation for us, I imagine. But we don't even know if we want to sell them yet. And if we wanted a catalogue, we'd have to pay them to do it.' He hesitated, and added, 'There's another reason why I'd like the books catalogued before we make up our minds what to do with them. There are a few oddities in the library. I'd like a chance to weed them out.'

'What do you mean exactly?'

'Apparently my predecessor found a copy of Mrs Beeton's *Household Management*. One or two novels have surfaced as well. Perhaps my predecessors muddled up some of their own books with the library's.'

'Look, it's very kind of you, but I still don't think I'd be suitable. I've never done anything like this before.'

He beamed across the table. 'Personally I've never found that a good reason not to do something.'

Hudson was persistent, even wily. He proposed I try my hand after lunch at half a dozen of the books under his supervision. If the results were satisfactory to me and to him then he suggested a trial period of a week, for which he would pay me three pounds, ten shillings. If we were both happy after this, the job would continue until the work was finished. All it needed, he said, was application and intelligence, and he was quite sure I had both of those.

The week passed, then another, then a third. It was easier to carry on with it than to try to explain to Hudson yet again why I wasn't suitable. The money was useful, too. I worked methodically round the room, from bookcase to bookcase. I did not move any of the books except when reuniting volumes belonging to a set. I used five-by-three index cards for the catalogue. On each card I recorded the author, the title, the publisher and the date. I added a number which corresponded to the shelf where the book was to be found and I added any other points which seemed to me to be of interest such as the name of the editor, if there was one, or the name of the series or whether the book contained one of Dean Pellew's bookplates, and had therefore been part of the original endowment.

It was surprisingly dirty work. On my first full day I got through several dusters and had to wash my hands at least half a dozen times. At Janet's suggestion, I bought some white cotton dusting gloves.

I reserved a separate table for the books which were in any way problematical. One of these was *Lady Chatterley's Lover*, which I found halfway through my second week sheltering in the shadow of Cruden's *Concordance*. I flicked through the pages, feeling guilty but failing to find anything obscene. So I borrowed it to read properly, telling my conscience that it wouldn't matter two hoots to Hudson if I found it today or next week.

I watched the cards expanding, inching across the old shoebox I kept them in until that shoebox was full and Canon Hudson found me another. My speed improved as I went on. The first time I managed to dust and catalogue fifty books in a single day, I went to the baker's and bought chocolate eclairs. Janet and Rosie and I ate them round the kitchen table to celebrate the achievement. As time went by, too, I needed to refer fewer and fewer queries to Canon Hudson.

At first he came in once a day to see how I was getting on. Then it became once every two or three days or even longer. There was pleasure in that too.

'You've got a naturally orderly mind, Wendy,' he told me one day towards the end of April. 'That's a rarity.'

Henry would have laughed at the thought of me in a Cathedral Library. But the job was a lifeline at a time when I could easily have drowned. I thought it came to me because of the kindness of Canon Hudson, and because I happened to be in the right place at the right time. Years later I found out there was a little more to it.

It was in the early 1970s. I met June Hudson at a wedding. I said how much the job in the Cathedral Library had helped me, despite everything, and how grateful I was to her husband for offering it to me.

'It's Peter who was grateful to you, my dear. At one point he thought he'd have to catalogue all those wretched books himself. Anyway, if anyone deserves thanking it ought to be Janet Byfield.'

'What do you mean?'

'It was her idea. She had a word with me and asked if I would suggest you to Peter. She said she hadn't mentioned it to you in case it didn't come off. But I assumed she'd have said something afterwards.'

'No,' I said. 'She never did.'

That increased my debt to Janet. I wish I knew how you pay your debts to the dead.

15

Then there was the business about the bishop's invitation. It was delivered by hand through the letter-flap from the High Street while Janet and I were having tea in the kitchen. She ripped open the envelope, which had the arms of the see on the back, read the note from Mrs Bish and pushed it across the table to me. She had asked the Byfields to dinner.

'That means *he's* asked us,' Janet explained. 'David will be pleased.'

'What's he like?'

'He was the Suffragan Bishop of Knightsbridge before he came here.' Janet blushed as she usually did when she was going to say something unkind. 'And some people say he was better at the Knightsbridge part than the bishop part.'

'You mean he's a snob?'

On that occasion she wouldn't say more. But after meeting the bishop once or twice I knew exactly what she meant. Like so many people in those days, he secretly felt that the Church should be a profession confined to gentlemen. His chaplain was a young man named Gervase Haselbury-Finch, who looked like Rupert Brooke and had a titled father, qualifications which as far as the bishop was concerned made up for his lack of organizational abilities. I don't mean to imply there was anything improper about the bishop's behaviour, not in the sense that makes tabloid headlines. He was married and had three grown-up children.

'The bishop likes to have little chats with David,' Janet went on. 'He says things like, "I'm expecting great things of you, my boy." He's very much in favour of keeping the Theo. Coll. going and he thinks that David would make a marvellous principal. So that's something in our favour. A very big something.'

'Is that how they choose someone?' I said. 'Because the bish likes their face?'

'Well, there's more to it than that. Obviously. But it helps.'

'It's not exactly fair.'

She made a sour face. 'The Church isn't. Not always.'

'It's like something out of the Middle Ages.'

'That's exactly what it is. You can't expect it to behave like a democracy.'

Later that evening we discussed the invitation over supper. David already knew about it because he had met the bishop at evensong. The only other people invited were the Master of Jerusalem and his wife. It turned out that the bishop had been at Jerusalem College too.

'I haven't anything to wear,' Janet said.

'Of course you have.' David smiled at her. 'Wear what you wore for the Hudsons. You'll look lovely.'

'I always wear that.'

'They'll notice your face not your dress.'

'Your mother had a very pretty dress at our engagement party,' Mr Treevor put in. 'I wonder if she's still got it. Why don't you ask her? Are there any more baked beans?'

Afterwards David took his coffee to the study and Mr Treevor went upstairs. Janet shook a small avalanche of powdered Dreft into the sink and turned on the tap so hard that water sprayed over the front of her pinafore and on to the tiled floor.

'What's up?' I said.

'It'll be ghastly. They'll make me feel like a poor little church mouse. I can never think of anything to say to the bishop. He pretends I must be frightfully intellectual because he's read some of Mummy's translations. So he tries to have conversations about the theme of redemption in Dostoevsky's novels and the irrationality of existentialism. It's dreadful. Meanwhile the women look at my shoes and wonder why they clash with my handbag.'

'Don't go,' I said.

'I've got to. David will be so upset if I don't. The bishop wants me to come, you see, and the bishop's word is law. And what about you?'

'Don't worry about me. I'd much rather stay at home.'

I hadn't been included in the invitation – I'm not sure the bish knew of my existence, not then. This suited me very well. Someone had to keep an eye on Rosie and Mr Treevor. Anyway, in my bedroom I had the bottle of gin and the unexpurgated *Lady Chatterley's Lover*. What more could a girl want?

'I suppose I could wear my blue dress. But there's that stain on the shoulder.'

'You can borrow my shawl if you like.'

In the end, though, Janet didn't go after all. On the day of the dinner party she developed a migraine. She had had them occasionally since we were children, usually when under strain. When I came back for lunch and found her flat out on the sofa, I made her go to bed and arranged to collect Rosie from school. David came in later, with just time to bathe and change before going out again. I told him what had happened, and said there was no chance that Janet would be well enough to go out to dinner.

'I'll go up and see her,' he said. 'Perhaps she's feeling better.'

'She's not. And if you try and persuade her she is feeling better, it'll only make her feel worse.'

'That's plain speaking.'

I sensed the anger in him. I even took a step backwards and felt the edge of the hall table pushing into the back of my thigh. 'That's what we do up in Yorkshire, David. Honestly, I don't mean to be rude, but I know what she's like when she has these migraines. And this one's a stinker.'

'I'll go and see her now.'

'But please let her stay in bed.'

He stared at me. There was so much anger in his face now that just for a moment I was frightened, physically frightened. He could strangle me now, I thought, and no one could stop him.

'I'll see how she is,' he said in a tight voice.

'While you're upstairs, perhaps you could say good night to Rosie. She was asking after you earlier.'

The jab went home. I saw it in his face. He went upstairs without another word. I felt guilty because I had been unkind

663

to him and angry for being scared. I tend to attack when I feel defensive. I told myself that it wasn't as if he didn't deserve what I'd said about Rosie. David knew, and I knew, that Janet thought he should try to spend a little more time with her. He doted on her as he doted on Janet. But he was a busy man, convinced of the importance of what he was doing and in his heart of hearts he was a complete reactionary. Looking after children was something that you left to women. That was what they were for, along with the other marital duties which he probably assumed had been ordained by God and man since time immemorial. I wonder now if David was a little scared of young children. Some adults are.

The upshot of that was that Janet didn't go to dinner with David and David didn't say good night to Rosie. I went up later after he had left the house and found Rosie still awake.

'Your light shouldn't be on,' I said.

She stared at me without saying anything. She was a child who knew the power of silence.

'What are you reading?'

Rosie angled the book towards me. It was a big illustrated volume called *Tales from the New Testament*, an impeccable choice for a clergyman's daughter. It was open at one of the colour plates. The picture showed the Angel Gabriel talking to the Virgin Mary. The caption read, 'Hail, thou that art highly favoured, the Lord is with thee: blessed art thou among women.'

She looked up at me with bright, excited eyes. 'He looks like Daddy. The angel looks like Daddy.'

'I suppose he does a bit, yes. Except the angel's got fair hair and it's rather long.' I tried to make a joke of it. 'And, of course, Daddy doesn't wear a white dress or have wings.'

'He sometimes wears a sort of white dress in church.'

'Yes, I'm sure he does.'

'Grandpa said he saw an angel.'

'What?'

'He told me. He looked out of his window and there the angel was, walking in the garden.'

'How interesting. Now, why don't I read you a story, just a quick one, and then you can settle down?'

I read her the story of the feeding of the five thousand, which

I chose on the grounds that it was short and contained no angels whatsoever. Some children like to sit with you, or on you, while you read to them. Rosie preferred me to sit in the chair by the window. She said it was so she could watch my face.

Later, when the story was over, I tucked her up and kissed the top of her head.

'Auntie Wendy?'

'What?'

'Was Lucifer an angel?'

'I don't know.'

'He'd be a sort of naughty angel. A wicked one who lives in hell.'

'You'll have to ask Daddy. He'll know.'

'Yes,' Rosie said. 'He knows all about God and things like that.'

Mr Treevor had settled into his new home surprisingly quickly. As long as there were no major deviations from the routine he had established he seemed quite content. Janet worried that he might try to repeat his mock-suicide attempt but there were no more incidents like that. (Janet asked him on several occasions why he'd done it. Twice he said it was a joke to amuse Rosie. Once he couldn't remember doing it at all. And the last time he said it was to see how much people loved him.)

If anything Rosie rather liked him. Perhaps it was because he was the nearest available man in the absence of a father. Sometimes he would go and say good night to her and an hour or so later Janet would find them both asleep, Rosie in bed and Mr Treevor in the armchair by the window. It was rather touching to see them together, asleep or awake. They didn't communicate much and they made few demands on each other, but they seemed to enjoy being in the same room.

The next day when the migraine had subsided, I told Janet what Rosie had said.

'An angel? Daddy must have been dreaming.'

'Most people settle for gnomes in the garden. I think an angel's rather classy.'

'Perhaps it was the milkman. He usually wears a white coat.'

665

'But he doesn't come to the garden door.'

'Daddy's getting a bit confused, that's all,' Janet said. 'Dr Flaxman said this might happen.'

Nowadays they would be able to narrow it down and perhaps delay the dementia's progress with drugs. Mr Treevor could have had a relatively early onset of senile dementia, either Alzheimer's or Multi-Infarct Dementia. Alzheimer's can be a pre-senile dementia as well. He wasn't a drinker so it can't have been alcoholic dementia. Other dementias can be caused by pressure in the brain, perhaps from a tumour, or by rare diseases like Huntington's or Pick's. But Pick's and Huntington's usually start when their victims are younger. If it was Huntington's it would have shown up when Rosie had the tests when she was an adult, even if she was not a carrier. The other main dementias, Creutzfeldt-Jakob disease and Aids dementia, developed later than 1958.

The worst thing, Janet said, was he knew what was happening. Not very often, but sometimes. He wasn't a fool by any means. And occasionally he was capable of acting completely rationally. That was why we took the story of the robbery seriously.

It happened while he was alone in the house. David and I were at work. Janet had gone to collect Rosie from school. When they got back they found Mr Treevor in a terrible state, trying to phone the police.

According to him, he had been dozing in his room when he heard somebody moving around downstairs. Thinking it was Janet, he had gone on to the landing and called downstairs, asking when tea would be ready. He heard footsteps, and the garden door slam. He looked out of the window and saw a man walking quickly down the garden and through the gate into the Close.

'He's been here before,' Mr Treevor said when he was retelling the tale for us at supper. 'I'm sure of it. He's stolen several of my things in the last few weeks. Those maroon socks, you remember, Janet, the ones Mummy knitted, and my propelling pencil.'

'The pencil had fallen down the side of your chair,' Janet reminded him.

He waved aside the objection. 'There's a ten-shilling note went from my wallet. That's what he took today.'

Janet glanced at me. I had been there yesterday morning when he'd produced a ten-shilling note and given it to Janet because he had a sudden urge for a box of chocolates.

'This man,' David said. 'What did he look like?'

'I only saw him from the back. Just a glimpse. A small dark man.' Mr Treevor stared thoughtfully at David and added, 'Like a shadow. That's it, David, tell the police that. He was like a shadow.'

16

Early in May the weather became much warmer. I no longer had to wear a coat and two cardigans when working in the library. The big room filled with light. The index cards marched steadily across the shoeboxes and everywhere I looked there was evidence of my industry. I felt better in other ways, too. On some days I hardly thought about Henry at all.

One Tuesday afternoon I was sitting at the table when I heard the door opening at the other end of the room. I assumed it was Canon Hudson or Janet or even Mr Gotobed, the assistant verger, who had a habit of popping up unexpectedly in the Cathedral or the Close. I turned in my chair and found myself looking up at David.

'I hope I'm not interrupting you. The dean's trying to track down a model of the Octagon, and there's a possibility it may be in here.'

I screwed the cap on my fountain pen. 'Not that I've seen, I'm afraid. But please have a look.'

He glanced round the library and smiled. 'It's looking much more organized than when I last saw it.'

'So it should be,' I said. 'Now what about this model?'

'The dean thought it might be in one of the cupboards.'

He nodded towards the long cupboard behind the table where I worked. It was about six feet high and built of dark-stained pine. Canon Hudson had told me that before the room was converted to the library, it had been used as the choir vestry and the cupboard had probably been built to house cassocks and surplices. It was full of rubbish now, he'd said, and when Gotobed had a spare afternoon he would investigate it properly.

I'd tried the doors but they were locked.

David produced a key and unlocked the nearest door. Then he opened the other two, pulling open the three sets of double doors so the whole cupboard filled with light. What I noticed first was the skeleton of a mouse lying at the foot of one of the doors. Dust was everywhere, soft and gritty. I saw a bucket, a small mountain of prayer books, an umbrella stand, a stack of newspapers, an object like a wooden crinoline with a torn surplice draped over it, a clump of candlesticks, some of which were taller than me, a lectern, empty bottles and a cast-iron boot-scraper. I bent down to pick up one of the newspapers. It was a copy of the *Rosington Observer* from 1937.

'There we are.' David lifted the ragged surplice from the ecclesiastical coat hanger. 'Extraordinary, isn't it? I wonder who made it.'

'Is *that* it?'

He shot me an amused glance. 'Were you expecting something more lifelike? This shows what you don't see – the skeleton supporting the whole thing.' He flapped the surplice at the model, dislodging some of the dust. 'It's very elegant. A mathematical figure in wood. If I get the dust off, do you think you could help me lift it out?'

I ended up doing the dusting myself. Then we lifted the model out of the cupboard. It stood like the skeleton of a prehistoric animal on the library carpet.

'It's as if it's got eight legs,' I said.

'Each of them rests on top of one of the pillars below. They're beams supporting almost all the weight. Amazing, really – nearly sixty feet long, and they taper from just over three feet at the base to twelve inches at the top where they meet the angles of the lantern.'

His long fingers danced over the wooden framework. I didn't understand what he was saying. I really didn't try. I was too taken up watching how his hands moved and the expression on his face.

'And then look how they twisted the lantern itself round so its sides are above the angles of the stone Octagon below. It splits the weight of each angle of the wooden Octagon between two pairs of these main beams that run down to the piers of the stone Octagon. Its legs, as you said.' Suddenly he broke off, frowning. 'But there should be a spire. Where do you think it's got to?'

I pointed into the cupboard at what I had assumed was an umbrella stand. Admittedly it was a peculiar shape for the purpose but it did have a broken umbrella jammed into it. With a cry of triumph David lifted it out. I applied the duster and then he raised it on top of the model of the Octagon. It slotted into place. We both stood back to admire it. The whole model now stood over six feet high. Nearly two feet of this was the slender framework of the spire, also octagonal.

'It's based on the Octagon at Ely,' David was saying. 'Ours is five or ten years later and rather smaller. In one sense it looks as if Ely was the apprentice work. Ours is much lighter – physically lighter, and also the windows in the lantern are larger. And we've got a spire which here is an integral part of the design.'

He was like a boy in his pleasure. It had never struck me before how attractive enthusiasm can be, the sort of enthusiasm that reaches out to other people.

'What are you going to do with this?' I asked him.

'We're planning an exhibition. The dean thinks we should do more to attract the tourists. Without the income we get from them it would be very difficult to run this place. Do you think I could leave it in that corner for now? He'll want to come and see it. But would it be in your way?'

We moved the Octagon where he suggested. David glanced at the table where I worked, which was underneath one of the windows.

'How are you getting on?'

'I'm nearly halfway, I think. I had to have a week off over Easter.'

'Any surprises?'

'*Lady Chatterley's Lover.*'

He stared at me, then threw back his head and laughed. 'What did you do with it?'

'I gave it to Canon Hudson.' I decided not to mention that I had read it first. 'Apparently it's the unexpurgated 1928 edition and it might be worth something.'

'But we'd have to sell it anonymously.' He gestured towards my card index. 'I'd like to have a look through there sometime, if I may.'

My excitement drained away. Indeed, up to that moment I hadn't been aware I was excited, only that I was enjoying myself. But now it was spoiled. Suddenly it seemed improbable he was interested in what was in the library for its own sake. Perhaps this was something to do with his campaign for the Theological College.

'I'm sure Canon Hudson wouldn't mind,' I said.

'I'd better leave you to your labours.'

At the door he paused. 'By the way, I should thank you.'

'It's nice to have an excuse for a break.'

'I don't just mean now. I mean at home. I don't know how Janet would have managed without you. Especially with her father around.'

I felt myself blush. I couldn't stand much more of this new David, considerate, enthusiastic and worst of all grateful.

'Of course, I'm not sure how long he'll be with us,' he said, and the old David emerged once again. 'In the nature of things it can't be for ever.' Then he smiled and the gears of his personality shifted again. 'Bless you,' he said, as priests do, and slipped out of the library.

I think coincidence is often a label we attach to events to confer a fake significance on them. But it makes me feel uncomfortable that on the same afternoon, a few minutes after David left, I had my first encounter with Francis Youlgreave.

I was cataloguing Keble's three-volume *Works of Richard Hooker*. On the flyleaf of the first volume, opposite the bookplate of the dean and chapter, was the name F. St. J. Youlgreave. Presumably Youlgreave had owned the book and later presented it to the library.

There was a strip of paper protruding from the second volume. I took it out. The top was brown and flaky where it had been exposed to the air but most of the strip had been trapped between the pages. It looked like a makeshift bookmark torn from a larger sheet. Both of the longer edges were ragged. One side was blank. On the other were several lines of writing in ink that had faded to a dark brown.

. . . a well-set-up boy perhaps twelve years old. He said he was going to visit his sister and their widowed mother who lodge in Swan Alley off Bridge Street. His name is Simon Martlesham and he works at the Palace where he cleans the boots and runs errands for the butler. It is curious how people of his class, even the younger ones, smell so unpleasantly of rancid fat. But when I gave him sixpence for helping me back to the house, he thanked me very prettily. He may be useful for . . .

Useful for what?

I made a note of where I had found the scrap of paper and put it to one side to show Canon Hudson. I didn't like the comment about the smell of rancid fat. I wondered what the boy had told his mother and sister when he finally reached home in Swan Alley. I made a note of Youlgreave's name on the index card for the *Works of Richard Hooker*.

I went back to the pile of books on my table and worked for another half an hour. I was on the verge of going out for a cigarette and a cup of tea when the door opened and Janet came in. She was rather pale and breathing hard.

'Help!' she said. 'You'll never guess what David's done. He's asked Canon Osbaston to dinner.'

17

Canon Osbaston, the principal of the Theological College, was the man whose job David wanted.

He had a taste for Burgundy and on Saturday morning David spent a good deal of money at Chase and Cromwell's, the wine merchants in the High Street. He also showed an uncharacteristic interest in the food Janet was intending to serve. David was trying to butter up the old man but I don't think he realized it. He could be astonishingly obtuse, especially where something he really cared about was concerned.

In honour of Canon Osbaston's visit we were going to use the dining room. I spent part of the morning polishing the table and cleaning the silver. What we needed, I thought, was a well-set-up boot boy to take care of these little jobs about the house.

Janet was unusually quiet at lunch. She wasn't irritable but her attention was elsewhere and there were vertical worry lines carved in her forehead. I assumed it was because of this evening. After lunch David went to play tennis at the Theological College. It was a fine day so I volunteered to take Rosie for a walk to give Janet a clear run in the kitchen. Rosie agreed to come on condition we went down to the river and fed the ducks. She was always a child who negotiated, who made conditions.

We walked down River Hill to Bishopsbridge. From there we went along the towpath until we found a cluster of mallards, two couples and their attendant families. We crumbled stale white bread and fed them.

'Would those ducklings taste nicer than ducks?' Rosie asked.

'I hadn't really thought about it.' The idea of eating one of those fluffy little objects, halfway to being cuddly toys, seemed absurd. 'Not as much meat on them as the older ones.'

'We like lamb instead of sheep, and veal instead of cow,' Rosie said. 'So I wondered.'

What she said made perfectly good sense. I was pretty sure that if a cannibal had a choice of me and Rosie on the menu he'd go for Rosie. I turned away from the ducks, looking for a change of subject. That's when I saw the Swan.

It was an L-shaped pub built of crumbling stone with an undulating tiled roof in urgent need of repair. A weather-beaten sign hung from one of the gable ends. I towed Rosie away from the river. There was a yard dotted with weeds in front of the pub, partly enclosed by the L. On one of the benches beside the front door an old man was sitting in the sunshine with his pipe and an enamel mug of tea.

'Hello,' I called out. 'It's a lovely afternoon.'

After a pause he nodded.

'I was wondering, is there somewhere called Swan Alley near here?'

'There is,' he said in a broad Fen accent, 'and then again there isn't.'

Oh God, I thought, not another old fool who thinks he has a sense of humour. 'Where is it?'

He took a sip of tea. 'Just behind you.'

I saw a piece of wasteland used as a car park, separated from the towpath by a mechanics workshop built largely of rusting corrugated iron.

I turned back. 'So it's not there now.'

'Just as well. Terrible place. Whole families in one room, and just a cold tap in the middle of a yard for all of them to share.' He shook his head, enjoying the horror of it. 'My old mother wouldn't let me go there because of the typhoid. They had rats as big as cats.' He studied me carefully to see how I took this last remark.

'How wonderful. That must have been a record, surely?'

'What was?'

'Having rats that size. I hope someone had the sense to catch a few and stuff them. Is there a museum where you can see them?'

'No.'

'What a pity.'

He started to light his pipe, a laborious procedure which told me the conversation was over. I felt a little guilty for spoiling his fun but not much. Rosie and I walked up the lane towards Bridge Street.

'Would baby rats be nicer to eat than full-grown ones?' Rosie asked, though unfortunately not loud enough for the old man to hear.

We crossed Bridge Street and went through the wrought-iron gates that led into the lower end of Canons' Meadow. The ground rose steadily upwards towards the Cathedral and, to the left of it, a mound of earth covered with trees, once the site of Rosington Castle. We walked up the gravel path to a gate into the south end of the Close. Canon Hudson was standing underneath the chestnuts on the other side talking to the bishop.

I tried to slip past them, but the bishop saw Rosie and beckoned us over. He was a tall, sleek man with a pink unlined face and fair hair turning grey. He was wearing a purple cassock that reminded me of a wonderful dress I'd once seen in a Bond Street window.

'Hello, Rosie-Posie. And how are you today?'

She beamed up at him. 'Very well, thank you, sir.'

Hudson introduced me to his lordship, who congratulated me briefly on my work in the library and then turned back to Rosie.

'And how old are you, my dear?'

'Four, sir. I'll soon be five. Not next week, the week after.'

'Five! Gosh! That's *very* grown up. What presents are you hoping to get?'

'Please, sir, I'd like an angel.'

'A what?'

'An angel.'

The bishop patted her shining head. 'My dear child.' His eyes swept from Hudson to me and he murmured, smiling, 'Trailing clouds of glory, eh?' Then he bent down to Rosie again. 'You must ask your daddy and mummy to bring you over to my house one day. You can play in the garden. It's lovely and big, and there's a swing and a pond with some very large goldfish. When you come I'll introduce you to them. And Auntie Wendy can come too. I'm sure she'd like to meet my fishies as well.'

And so on. The bishop seemed to have at his command an effortless flow of whimsicality. In an open contest he'd have knocked spots off J. M. Barrie. If anyone had told me at Rosie's age that I looked like the Queen of the Fairies I'd have curled up with embarrassment. But she accepted it as her due.

'I'm glad we bumped into each other,' Hudson said to me while the episcopal gush flowed on. 'I meant to drop in yesterday. Everything all right?'

'Fine, thanks.'

'I gather David found a model of the Octagon in the wall cupboard. Something for the dean's exhibition.'

'It was quite exciting, actually. It made a change from cataloguing books. Mind you, I'm not sure I'd have known what it was if he hadn't been there.' One memory jogged another. 'By the way, I came across a scrap of paper with some writing on. It was in a book that once belonged to someone called Youlgreave.'

'Ah yes. That would probably be Francis Youlgreave. He was the canon librarian about fifty years ago. What exactly did you find?'

'It looked like part of a letter or diary. Something about giving a boy sixpence for helping him.'

'He was a bit of an oddity, Canon Youlgreave. He had to retire after a nervous breakdown. If you come across anything else of his I'd like to see it. Would you make sure you do that?'

It wasn't what he said so much as the way that he said it. Hudson looked so mild and inoffensive that those rare times when I saw his other side always came as a shock. His voice was sharp, almost peremptory. He had just given me what amounted to an order.

'Of course,' I said. 'But now we mustn't keep you any longer. Come along, Rosie, we mustn't be late for tea.'

I dragged Rosie away from her mutual admiration society, said goodbye and walked towards the Cathedral and the Dark Hostelry. When we reached home, I opened the gate in the wall and Rosie ran ahead of me into the house. I found her and David waiting for me in the hall.

David was still in his tennis whites and his racket was on a polished chest near the door. I noticed that he'd knocked the vase of flowers on the chest, and a few drops of water glittered on the dark oak. Stupid man, I thought. If we didn't wipe off the water soon, it would leave a mark.

'Wendy, there you are.' His voice was casual to the point of absurdity, a tangle of elongated vowels and muted consonants. 'I thought I'd take Rosie downstairs and give her some tea.'

My face must have shown my surprise. But I managed a smile. 'OK. How nice.'

He moved towards the stairs to the kitchen, towing Rosie. 'Oh, by the way,' he said, interrupting Rosie who was telling him about the bishop and his fishies. 'Janet asked if you could pop up and see her if you had a moment. She's in our bedroom, I think.'

David give Rosie her tea? It was unheard of. Without taking off my hat, I went quickly upstairs and tapped on Janet's door. I heard her say something. I twisted the handle and went in. She was sitting on the window seat looking at the Cathedral.

'Are you all right?' I said, walking towards her.

She turned to look at me. The tears welled out of her eyes and ran down her cheeks.

'Wendy,' she said, 'I don't know what I'm going to do.'

I watched the tears running down her cheeks. 'What's wrong?'

She shook her head.

I went to her, put my hands on her arms and drew her towards me. She laid her head on my shoulder and began to sob. Between the sobs she muttered something.

'I can't hear you. What did you say?'

She lifted her tear-stained face. 'I can't bear it.' She hiccuped. 'Another one.'

'Another *what*?'

Janet pulled away from me and blew her nose. 'Another baby. I think I'm pregnant.'

18

Wine had a curious effect on Canon Osbaston, like water on a wilting plant. After two glasses of sherry and the first glass of Burgundy he moved on to a higher and more active plane of existence. As something of a connoisseur of the effects of alcohol, I watched with interest.

Osbaston had a big, unwieldy body, a long scraggy neck and a small bald head. My first impression was that he was like a tortoise, and this was not just because of his appearance. It was also because of the way he moved. You felt he should be encouraged to spend the winter in a cardboard box in the garage.

By the time we reached the veal cutlets, we were all rather merry. There were only the four of us round the table. John Treevor was capable of casting a blight on any social occasion, but fortunately he had been persuaded that he would be more comfortable having a tray upstairs. David was charming – he wasn't in competition with Osbaston, quite the reverse. I had fortified myself with a slug of gin beforehand so I was ready to relax and enjoy myself. So was Janet once the main course was on the table. With the second glass of Burgundy, Osbaston told an elderly joke involving chorus girls which was actually quite funny.

'Delightful to see such charming young ladies in the Close,' he boomed across the table to David. 'That's what the Theological College lacks, you know – a woman's touch. Mrs Elstree does her best, I'm sure, I don't want to imply she doesn't. But it's not the same. Mark you, there's bags of room for a family in the principal's quarters.' He nodded and if nods were words this one would have said, *A nod's as good as a wink*. The little head swivelled to face Janet. 'Which reminds me – how's young Rosie?'

'Asleep, I hope. She's very well.'

'A lovely name for a lovely child.' He swallowed more wine. 'It always reminds me of that story about dear old Winnington-Ingram when he was Bishop of London. Do you know it?'

'I'm not sure I do,' David said.

'I had it from his chaplain. The bishop was a great believer in cold baths, you see, and their moral value. One day he was talking in the East End and telling his audience how splendid it was to have a daily tub. Most of them didn't even have running water in their own homes, but I doubt if that occurred to the old boy. "And when I get out of my bath," he told them, "I feel rosy all over." At which a voice at the back of the hall pipes up, "'oo's Rosie, then?"'

We laughed enthusiastically. David turned the conversation to the previous occupant of the Principal's Lodging, a married man with a family.

'Yes, one of the daughters kept the library in order. What was her name? Sibyl, I think.' Osbaston inclined his head to me. 'Just as you are doing here in the Cathedral Library, Mrs Appleyard. Do you think librarianship is a job that women are particularly suited to? One could define it as a specialized form of housekeeping applied to books. It requires efficiency, a tidy mind. Splendid womanly virtues. Don't you agree?'

'Yes, indeed,' I said. 'In my experience, men tend to be both inefficient and untidy.'

His little brown eyes gleamed in the candlelight. 'Too true, Mrs Appleyard, too true.'

David got up to fetch the second bottle of Burgundy from the sideboard. Janet looked anxiously at me. I raised my glass to her and drained the rest of the wine.

Osbaston leant towards me. 'Once you've finished with the Cathedral Library, Mrs Appleyard, perhaps we should ask you to put our library in order for us.'

'So you've suffered from male librarians as well?'

'I think you'd find we're a little better organized than the Cathedral Library.' He turned back to David. 'The last time

I was in the Cathedral Library I happened to open Lowther Clarke's *Liturgy and Worship* to check a reference and I found half of it had been eaten.' There was a rumbling from deep in his interior. 'Mice, I suppose. I expect they found it pretty hard going. But undoubtedly edifying. No, Mrs Appleyard, you'd find our library much less daunting.'

'If the libraries are merged,' David said, 'Wendy's help could be particularly useful.'

'Doesn't that depend on Canon Hudson?' Janet said.

Osbaston nodded. 'And on others. We mustn't count our chickens, eh?'

'No news on that front, I suppose?' David asked, gesturing with the bottle towards Osbaston's glass.

'Not as far as I know. I gather Peter Hudson's rather taken up at present with the exhibition. Another of the dean's bright ideas.' While Osbaston's glass was being refilled he switched his attention to Janet and me. 'Trollope was perfectly right, I'm afraid. Cathedral closes are breeding grounds for eccentricity. Present company excepted. Let's hope the dean doesn't make an exhibition of *himself*. Ha, ha.'

Janet smiled politely.

I said, 'I gather some of the canon librarians have been a little eccentric. Francis Youlgreave, for example.'

'Oh, him.' Osbaston waved David and the bottle towards me. 'Mad as a March hare. Of course, he wrote poetry, which may explain it. Have you read any of his stuff?'

'I don't think I have.'

'There's quite a well-known one, "The Judgement of Strangers". Let's see, how does it go?' His voice dropped in pitch. '*Then darkness descended; and whispers defiled The judgement of stranger, and widow, and child.* Something along those lines.'

'What's it about?'

'No one's quite sure. My predecessor claimed it was based on a story Youlgreave found in the Cathedral archives. Something to do with a woman heretic being burnt at the stake. Can't say I've ever come across it.' Osbaston sipped his wine. 'Pity he didn't stick to poetry. He would have been all right then.'

'What do you mean?' Janet asked. 'What happened to him?'

'Went round the bend, my dear, had to resign. Unfortunately

it wasn't something that could be hushed up. But they must have seen it coming. If only they'd managed to persuade him to take leave of absence. The trouble was, they say the dean was a bit of a weakling, afraid of his own shadow. And I think there might have been a family connection between them. Anyway, Youlgreave was allowed to stay in residence far longer than he should have been. There were complaints, of course, but it's actually quite hard to get rid of a canon. We're protected by statute, you see. Finally the poor fellow lost all touch with reality and he simply had to go. Caused quite a scandal at the time, I believe.'

'But what did he do?' I asked.

'He preached a sermon in favour of ordaining women priests.' Another rumble of laughter erupted from deep in the interior. 'Can you believe it?'

After dinner David took Osbaston into the drawing room and gave him a glass of brandy while Janet and I cleared the table and made the coffee.

'It seems to be going quite well,' Janet said as she piled plates into the sink.

'If Osbaston has any more to drink we'll probably have to carry him home,' I said. 'Who'd have thought it?' I noticed Janet was leaning against the draining board. 'Are you OK?'

She glanced back at me. 'Just tired.'

I made her sit down at the kitchen table. All the standing up couldn't be good for her and she had been up since half past six. I suggested she went to bed but she wouldn't hear of it.

'It would be rude.'

'It would be common sense.'

She shook her head. 'I'm all right. I'll be fine after a little rest.'

I gave up. It had always been impossible to deflect Janet from something she considered to be her duty. Probably the woman they burnt at the stake suffered from a similar mentality.

I picked up the tray and we went into the drawing room. Osbaston and David broke off their conversation as we came in. They looked like conspirators. I wondered if they'd been scheming about the Theological College. Ever the little gent, David sprang up to take the tray from me.

'I was just telling David,' Osbaston said, rolling the brandy round his glass, 'my housekeeper can remember Canon Youlgreave.'

'Really?'

He eyed me in a speculative way I suddenly recognized. It was as if someone had thrown a glass of icy water in my face. The sort of life Henry and I had led contained a great many men who looked at me as Osbaston did. 'It's not that surprising,' he said, settling his glasses on his nose. 'I've never dared ask Mrs Elstree how old she is but she can't be much less than seventy. Youlgreave must have died about fifty years ago.'

'It's hard to think of someone alive actually knowing him. He's like a character out of history, somehow.'

Osbaston allowed one of his rumbles to emerge. 'You must come and meet her. Why don't you all have tea with me tomorrow? Mrs Elstree makes very good –'

There was a loud crash above our heads. Janet was into the hall first, with the rest of us close behind.

Mr Treevor was standing at the head of the stairs. His feet were bare and his greasy hair stood up around his head. His pyjama jacket was undone, revealing a tangle of grey hair, and his trousers sagged low on his hips.

'Daddy, what's wrong?' Janet cried. 'Are you all right?'

'There was a noise, footsteps, just like before,' Mr Treevor said in a thin whine. 'I went to see if Rosie was all right but I couldn't find my glasses. I must have – must have knocked something over. Janie, where *are* my glasses?'

As if on cue, Rosie began to cry.

19

In the end I talked to David about Janet. He didn't like it and nor did I. I was beginning to feel like an interloper in their marriage, in more ways than one.

It was after breakfast the next day, Sunday, which happened to be the fifth anniversary of my marriage to Henry. No one else remembered this and I did my best to forget it. David came back from celebrating the early communion service full of the joys of this world and the next. While he worked his way through two cups of coffee, two boiled eggs and several rounds of toast, Janet pecked at a slice of bread and butter. After I'd washed up I cornered him in his study where he was reading a book and making notes.

'Janet's not well,' I told him. 'She needs to rest.'

'What's wrong with her?'

'She tired herself out yesterday killing the fatted calf. And she was tired beforehand. And then there's her condition.'

His eyes were drifting back to the book on his desk.

'She's pregnant, David. And in the first three months women are particularly delicate. If she works too hard there's a danger she might lose the baby.'

That got his attention. 'I hadn't realized. In fact . . .' His voice tailed away and I laid a private bet with myself that he had been about to say, *In fact I'd forgotten she was pregnant*. He looked at me. 'What do you advise?'

'I think she should go back to bed. She's getting ready for church at present. Tell her you think she ought to rest. It's what she needs. I can do lunch. There are plenty of left-overs.'

'Do you think she'll be well enough to have tea with Canon Osbaston?'

'She's not *ill*, David. She's just tired and I really think she needs a day off. Rosie and I can come if you want.'

In one way it worked out very well. Janet spent most of the day in bed and the rest of us muddled along reasonably happily. In retrospect, I think Rosie may have been withdrawn. Usually she enjoyed being with her father but when we walked to the Theological College for tea with Canon Osbaston, it was my hand she decided to hold. None of this seemed significant then and even now I wonder if I'm reading too much into it. That's the trouble with trying to remember things – you end up twisting the past into unrecognizable shapes. I just don't know what happened the previous evening. If anything.

I do know the weather was wonderful that afternoon. I haven't imagined the feeling of sun on my arms as we walked through the Close and down to the Porta. Ink-black shadows danced along the pavement. We passed Gotobed planting pansies in his window box. He pretended not to see us. He was a large man who hunched his shoulders as if trying to make himself small. His face was delicate, with big ears and a tiny nose and chin. I thought he looked like a mouse and perhaps felt like one too. He would talk to me when I was by myself but I think he was scared of David. He was certainly terrified of the head verger, a swarthy man named Mepal who rarely spoke, but I think everyone was a little afraid of Mepal, including the dean.

Immediately outside the Porta was Minster Street, which ran along one side of a small green before plunging down Back Hill to the station and the river. On the other side of the green stood the Theological College, a large red brick building surrounded by lank shrubberies like coils of barbed wire.

David guided us up the drive and round to the lawn at the back. Four pink young men were playing lawn tennis. A little further on, four more were playing croquet. The Principal's Lodging, a self-contained wing of the main building, was beside the croquet lawn.

Canon Osbaston was dozing in a wing armchair in front of open French windows. The room behind him was long, high-ceilinged and densely populated with large brown pieces of furniture. He must have heard our footsteps on the gravel because his eyes flickered open and he struggled out of the chair.

'Must have nodded off. Meant to have the kettle on before you arrived. Is Janet with you?'

'She's a little unwell,' David said.

'Nothing serious, I trust. Such a pleasant evening.' He leered at me. 'I wonder if you would give me a hand making the tea, Mrs Appleyard? I'm afraid it slipped my mind yesterday evening, in the – ah – heat of the moment, that Mrs Elstree has Sunday afternoons off. She visits her widowed sister, I believe.'

'Perhaps Rosie can help as well,' I said. 'Many hands make light work.'

In the end, all four of us went into the kitchen. I felt as though I'd awakened a Sleeping Beauty. I wished I could find a way to send him to sleep again. We found that Mrs Elstree had left everything ready for us in the kitchen. Ten minutes later, we were sitting in deckchairs on the lawn.

We drank lapsang souchong and ate most of a Victoria sponge. It was warm in the sun and I felt pleasantly tired. Osbaston found Rosie some paper and a pencil and once she had finished her cake she sat on the lawn in the shade of a beech tree and drew.

The young men played croquet and tennis, and watching them gave me something to do with the forefront of my mind. Occasionally some of them would wander over to have a few words with Osbaston or David. More than one of them looked at me in a way that gave me pleasure. I might have no taste for elderly clergymen but after the dreariness surrounding the end of my marriage it was nice to be admired again, even by theological students.

David and Osbaston were talking about the syllabus for next year – something about the pros and cons of increasing New Testament Greek at the expense of Pastoral Theology. It was one of those lazy conversations full of half-sentences which happen when people know each other very well, so much so that each is usually aware what the other is about to say. I looked at David through half-closed eyes.

Before I knew what was happening, I found I had drifted into a daydream in which I was married to him and Rosie was our daughter. That was enough to make me sit up with a jerk. I hate the way the mind plays tricks when you're relaxing. I went into the house to powder my nose. By the time I came out the tennis and the croquet were finished and it was time to go. The men were turning their thoughts towards evensong.

'You must come and meet Mrs Elstree some other time, Mrs Appleyard,' Osbaston said. 'In the meantime I found something else which might interest you.' He pottered through the French window into his drawing room and came out a moment later with a hardback book bound in blue cloth. 'I thought I'd seen something about that fellow Youlgreave recently, and I was right. I looked it out after breakfast this morning. Do borrow it, if you'd like. I've put a marker in.'

I took the book and opened it automatically to the title page. *The Journal of the Transactions of the Rosington Antiquarian Society 1904.*

'I think it may be what gave him the idea for that judgement poem,' Osbaston said. 'You remember, the story about a heretic being burned? Take it with you, my dear, and study it at your leisure.' He edged a little closer to me. 'Perhaps we could discuss it when you come and meet Mrs Elstree.'

I smiled at him. 'Thanks.' I looked around for a diversion and found Rosie. 'What a nice drawing. May I see it?'

With obvious reluctance she gave it to me. David and Osbaston came closer and together we looked down at the sheet of paper in my hands. It was a child's drawing with no sense of perspective or proportion. After all, Rosie wasn't yet five, though in some ways she was very mature for her age. The pencilled figures were like stick insects with a few props attached. But you could see what Rosie had been getting at. A man wearing a white dress and a pair of wings was about to plunge a sword shaped like a cake slice into a small person with long hair cowering at his feet.

'Let me guess,' said Canon Osbaston, his head swaying towards Rosie. 'Could this be the sacrifice of Isaac?' He frowned and a heavy forefinger stabbed the man with the sword. 'But in that case this must be Abraham, despite the wings. After all, it can hardly be the Angel of the Lord.'

20

Osbaston had marked a letter, one of a number printed at the end of the *Journal*. I read it after supper when David was working in the study. Janet was trying to reconcile the butcher's bill with what we had actually received and said she would look at it later.

CORRESPONDENCE RECEIVED BY THE EDITOR

From the Revd Canon F. St J. Youlgreave:

Sir,

I write to apprise you and other members of the Society of an interesting discovery I have made in my capacity as Cathedral Librarian. I had occasion to examine the binding of a copy of the Sermons of Dr Giles Briscow, the Dean of Rosington in the reign of Queen Elizabeth, which was in a decayed condition, with a view to seeing whether it should be rebound. I discovered there were annotations on the end-paper at the back of the book. These are in a Secretary hand which I judge to be of the first half of the seventeenth century. The writing is in Latin and appears to have been copied from an older work, perhaps a Monkish Chronicle dealing with the history of the Abbey of Rosington.

Evidence on the flyleaf at the front of the book suggested to me that the volume had once been in the possession of Julius Farnworthy, who of course was Bishop from 1619 to 1628, and whose tomb is in the South Choir Aisle. It is possible, even probable, that Bishop Farnworthy, or one of his contemporaries at Rosington, was responsible for the memorandum inscribed on the end-paper.

For the time being I have entrusted the book to an acquaintance who has some skill at palaeography and who is also in a position where he may conveniently examine the Farnworthy Collection in the British Museum Library. First, however, I took the precaution of copying the memorandum in full. When the results of the palaeographical examination are known, and when I have had an opportunity to complete other researches, I hope to be in a position to present a paper on the subject to the Society. I intend to assess the authenticity and provenance of this curious discovery, and also to sketch in the background of the events which it describes insofar as this proves possible to do. In the meantime, I hope you will permit me to whet the appetite of my fellow members of the Society with my rendering of the memorandum into English.

'In the third year of King Henry's reign, plague swept this part of the country. Merchants and pilgrims alike dared not cross the Great Causeway for fear of infection. Houses were left empty, fields untended and animals starved for want of feeding.

'Men said openly that the devil was abroad in the land.

'In the village of Mudgley, the parish priest died in much agony. His housekeeper stood at the cross and told those that remained alive that the Devil had carried away his soul, but at the same time an Angel had protected hers. And she uttered this blasphemy: that the Angel had told her she was chosen among all women to be His first priest of her sex. And the Angel ordained her, saying unto her, "Am I not greater than any Bishop?"

'Whereupon the woman led the people into church and celebrated Mass. Hearing this, the Abbot, Robert of Walberswick, sent men to bring her to Rosington where she was tried before God and man for blasphemy. But the Devil would not leave her. She would not confess her sins nor repent of her evil so they burned her in the marketplace. Her name was Isabella of Roth.'

Robert of Walberswick was Abbot from 1392 to 1407. The

third year of King Henry's reign must refer to Henry IV and therefore date this episode to 1402. It is not clear whether the village mentioned is Mudgley Burnham or Abbots Mudgley. The Latin shows no signs of the influence of the Renaissance and it contains many characteristically Mediaeval contractions and turns of phrase. At present, at least, we can only speculate why the unknown writer of this memorandum should have wished to copy the passage. The whereabouts of the original is equally mysterious.

If I may be permitted to end on a personal note, you will notice that Roth is mentioned. I can only assume that this is the village of Roth in the County of Middlesex. Strange to say, this is a locality I know well, since my family has resided there for more than forty years.

I am, Sir, etc.

F. Youlgreave

I also found Youlgreave's poem, 'The Judgement of Strangers', in an anthology of Victorian verse in the dining-room bookcase. If I hadn't read the letter, I don't think the poem would have made any sense to me at all. But if you assumed it was Isabella's story, then everything fell into place. Well, perhaps not everything because some of it was almost wilfully hard to understand. But you could see that the poem might be an impressionistic account of a woman being martyred for her beliefs in a vaguely medieval setting.

I read both the poem and the letter again when I was in bed with rather a large nightcap. The gin gave a slight hangover later and probably caused the nightmare which woke me covered in sweat in the early hours. I dreamed I was in Rosington marketplace. Someone was burning rubbish near the cross and people were shouting at me. Just before I woke up, I glanced into a litterbin fixed to a lamppost and found a doll with no arms staring up at me.

'Theologically the idea's completely untenable, as Youlgreave would have known,' David said. 'The notion of women priests simply doesn't make sense.'

'Why?' I asked, not because I cared one way or the other. It was just that I wanted to keep David talking, and he was particularly appealing when he became passionate about something.

He glanced up at the Cathedral clock. 'I don't want to go into it now. There isn't time and it's a very complicated subject.'

'Come on. That's no answer.'

He stopped at the door to the cloisters. We had been walking round the east end of the Cathedral on our separate ways to work. It was another beautiful day. A wispy cloud hung behind the golden weathercock at the tip of the Octagon's spire. Every detail of the stonework was crisp and clean. A swallow appeared round one of the pinnacles at the base of the spire, banked sharply and swooped down the length of the nave towards the west end. Suddenly David smiled, and not for the first time I thought that there is something cruel about beautiful people. Their beauty sets them apart from the rest of us. From the beginning they are treated differently.

He said, 'I don't believe a woman can be a priest any more than she can be a father.'

'But being a priest's a job. If you can have a woman on the throne, why can't you have one in the pulpit?'

'Because God chose to become incarnate in a patriarchal society. He chose only male apostles. Just as he wanted a woman, the Virgin Mary, to have the highest possible human vocation.'

'We're not living in first-century Palestine any more.'

'I don't think God's choice of time and place was an accident. It would be absurd for a Christian to think that. There's nothing in Scripture to support the idea of women priests. So we can only conclude that a male priesthood is what God wanted. If it were just a matter of human tradition, of course it could be changed. But it's not. It's a divine institution.'

'I'll have to take your word for it. But can't the Church sometimes admit it's got it wrong? After all, it's changed its mind before. For instance, you don't go around burning people at the stake any more just because they don't agree with you.'

'The two things aren't analogous.'

You can't argue with fanatics, I thought. If David wanted to inhabit a fairy-tale universe conducted by fairy-tale laws, that was his business.

'I've got to do some work,' I said. 'I'd better go. Thanks for the theology lesson.'

For an instant I thought he looked disappointed, like a dog deprived of a bone. Perhaps he had seen me as a potential convert, the prodigal daughter on the verge of a change of heart. We said goodbye and he walked on towards the Porta and the Theological College.

I ducked into the cloisters and walked slowly towards the south door of the Cathedral. On my way I passed the entrance to the Chapter House, a large austere room with a Norman arcade running round the walls below the windows. Nowadays the chapter met in more comfortable surroundings and the room was used mainly for small concerts and large meetings. They were going to use the room for the exhibition. Hudson was in there talking to the dean, and he gave me a wave as I passed the doorway.

Before I started work I got out a couple of histories of Rosington and one of the county. There were references to Mudgley, both Abbots and Burnham, and to outbreaks of plague in the fourteenth and fifteenth centuries. But I found nothing about Isabella of Roth, women priests or angelic visitations.

After that I catalogued half a dozen books. But my attention kept wandering back to Francis Youlgreave and Isabella and to the boy called Simon, the one Youlgreave thought might be 'useful'. Finally I decided that I would take my coffee break early and skip the coffee part of it.

Instead I went to the public library which was housed in a converted Nissen hut in a street off the marketplace. Janet had taken me to join the library a few weeks before but I had never used it. The librarian in charge was a thickset man with a face like a bloodhound's and thick, ragged hair the colour of wire wool. I asked him if they had anything on Francis Youlgreave.

'About him or by him?'

'Either.'

'We've got a book of his poetry.'

'Good. Where can I find it?'

Wheezing softly, he stared at me. 'I'm afraid it's on loan.'

I felt like a child deprived of a treat. 'Can I reserve it?'

The book was called *The Tongues of Angels*. 'Is there a biography?' I asked as I handed the librarian the reservation card and my sixpence.

He glanced at my name on the card. 'Not that I know of, Mrs Appleyard. But he's in the *Dictionary of National Biography*, and there's also something about him in a book we have called *Rosington Worthies*. Chapter nine, I think. You'll find it in the reference section under Local History.'

I was impressed and said so.

'To be honest, I hadn't heard of him until last week. But someone happened to be asking about him.'

'Would that have been Canon Hudson, by any chance?'

'It wasn't him. No one I know.'

It was another little mystery, and one which irritated rather than intrigued me. I was surprised to find I didn't like the idea of someone else being interested in Francis Youlgreave. I felt he ought to be mine. A substitute for Henry, perhaps, safely dead and therefore able to resist the lures of widows with more money than morals.

I thanked the librarian, went into the little reference department and dug out the bones of Youlgreave's life. But, like the model of the Octagon we'd found in the library, the bones didn't give much idea of the finished article.

Francis Youlgreave was born in 1863, the younger son of a baronet. He published *Last Poems* in 1884 while he was an undergraduate at St John's College, Oxford. After coming down from the university he decided to go into the Church. These are facts, you can look them up for yourself in the *Dictionary of National Biography*. He was in fact one of the first ordinands at Rosington Theological College. Several curacies followed in parishes on the western fringe of London.

In 1891, still in London, Francis became the first vicar of a new church, St Michael's, Beauclerk Place, which is west of Tottenham Court Road. (That's how I came to think of him, by the way. As Francis, as if he was someone I knew.) In 1896 he published his second volume of poetry and then *The Four Last Things*. Four years later he became a canon of Rosington. Osbaston had been right about a family connection. The dean at the turn of the century was a cousin of Francis's mother.

His last book, *The Tongues of Angels*, was published in 1903. The following year ill health forced him to retire. He went to live in his brother's house, Roth Park in Middlesex, where he died on 30th July 1905. Nowadays he was best known for the one poem 'The Judgement of Strangers', said to have been admired by W. B. Yeats.

At lunch time there were usually only the three of us at the Dark Hostelry. Rosie was at school and David had lunch at the Theological College. Janet had found time to read Youlgreave's letter in *The Journal of the Transactions of the Rosington Antiquarian Society*. While we ate cold lamb and salad I told her about the failure of my attempt to find out more about Isabella. Meanwhile Mr Treevor chewed methodically through an immense quantity of meat.

'Why are you doing this?' Janet asked.

'It's such a strange story. And I can't help feeling sorry for the woman.'

'If she ever existed.'

'I think she did. Why would Francis have invented something like that?'

Janet looked across the table at me. 'I don't know. So you think the poem *was* inspired by Isabella?'

'Of course. Have you read it?'

'Not yet. I'll look at it after lunch.'

'The poem's in three parts.' I held up my hand and ticked off the fingers. 'First the soldiers come for her when she's in church. Then there's the trial scene. And finally there's the bit at the end where she's burnt at the stake.'

'When was it written?' Janet said.

'It was one of the poems in *The Four Last Things*, which was published in 1896. So –' I broke off as the implication hit me.

'And when did he write this letter to the Antiquarian Society?'

'In 1904. He'd become a canon of Rosington in 1901.'

Janet smiled at me. 'Then isn't it a little hard to see how a discovery he claimed to have made in the Cathedral Library could have inspired a poem published at least five years earlier?'

'Is there any more lamb?' asked Mr Treevor, looking at the remains of the joint.

For a moment I felt ridiculously depressed. Then I cheered up. 'I know – Francis was at the Theological College here. That must have been in the 1880s. So he could have come across the book then. Perhaps the students were allowed to use the Cathedral Library. And then he found it again when he came back to Rosington. That makes sense, doesn't it? He'd be bound to look for it.'

For a moment Janet concentrated on carving the meat. 'Why does it matter?'

'It's quite interesting. Especially in view of that sermon of his, the one about women priests that made them give him the sack. There must be a connection.'

'More?' Mr Treevor suggested.

Janet went back to the carving and Francis Youlgreave slid away from us, back into the void he had come from. Instead we talked about the Principal's Lodging at the Theological College, and whether it would make a better family home than the Dark Hostelry.

I was glad of the change of subject. I didn't want to think too much about why Francis was interesting me, or to allow Janet to delve too deeply into my motives. All right, I was bored. I needed stimulation. But another reason for my interest is painfully obvious now. But believe me, it wasn't then – in those days I fooled myself as well as everyone else.

I wanted to find a way of impressing David Byfield. I wanted to make him take notice of me. How better to do this than by making a scholarly discovery? It makes me squirm to think about it. I wouldn't say I was in love with David. Not exactly. What I felt about David had a lot to do with wanting to get back at Henry. But it wasn't entirely that. The thing you have to understand about David, the real mystery perhaps, is that despite his arrogance and his habit of patronizing the little women around him, he was actually very sexy.

Living in the same house I couldn't avoid him. Once I saw him naked. Despite its size there was only one bathroom at the Dark Hostelry. I came down one morning in my dressing gown, opened the door and there he was – standing in the bath, the water running off his white body, reaching for a towel draped over the washbasin. As the door opened, he stopped moving, apart from his head turning towards the door, and in that instant he was like a statue of an athlete, a young god frozen in time.

'So sorry,' I blurted out. I closed the door and bolted back to my room on the next floor. If it was anyone's fault it was his, because we always locked the door of the bathroom. But somehow I felt the blame was mine, that I had been prying like a Peeping Tom. Twenty minutes later we met at breakfast and both of us pretended it hadn't happened. I wonder if it stuck in David's memory over the years as it has in mine.

21

The dean's exhibition was taking shape in the Chapter House.
Janet told me that the idea had aroused considerable opposition
because it smacked of commercialism. I was never quite sure
whether the opposition was on religious or social grounds. In
the Close, it was often hard to tell where the one stopped and
the other began.

The dean had financial logic on his side. There was death-
watch beetle in the roof of the north transept. The windows of
the Lady Chapel needed re-leading and the pinnacles at the west
end were in danger of falling into Minster Street. The available
income barely covered the running costs, according to David,
and was incapable of coping with major repairs or emergencies.
Opening the Chapter House for an exhibition might be the first
step towards setting up a permanent museum. The real question
was whether the tourists would be prepared to pay the entry fee
for what was on offer.

'If this works, the dean's talking of having a Cathedral café,'
David told us one evening. 'It makes a sort of sense, I suppose.
Why should the tea shops in the town reap all the benefit from
the Cathedral's visitors?'

'But where would they put it?' Janet asked.

'If they close the library there would be plenty of room there.'

'But that's inside the Cathedral.'

He shrugged. 'They could move the exhibition into the library
and use the Chapter House or somewhere else in the Close for
the café.'

The collection included a good deal of medieval stonework
– fragments of columns, tombstones and effigies, some of the

grander vestments from the great cope chest, fragments of stained glass, and of course the model of the timber skeleton of the Octagon which David had found in the library cupboard. Canon Hudson asked me to keep an eye out for attractively bound or illustrated volumes in the Cathedral Library, particularly ones with a Rosington connection. I tried to make David laugh by suggesting they used the *Lady Chatterley* I had found, but he preserved a stone face and said he did not think it would be suitable.

The whole thing was done on the cheap. The dean had no intention of wasting money on new display cases or on extending the collection until there was evidence that the exhibition would make a profit. They had decided against hiring staff, too. One by one, the ladies of the Close were recruited for the exhibition rota. There was to be a grand opening in June with the bishop. The *Rosington Observer* had promised to send a photographer.

'I'm sorry you got landed with this as well,' Janet said to me on the evening of the day I was asked to join the rota. 'I don't think David should have asked you.'

'I don't mind. Anyway, it may never happen.'

'What do you mean?'

'I may not be here by then. This job isn't going to last for ever.'

Janet looked at me and I saw fear in her eyes. 'I hope you don't go. Not yet.'

'It won't be for a while,' I said, knowing that I would never be able to resist Janet if she asked for my help, if she asked me to stay. 'Anyway, the cataloguing may take longer than I think. You never know what's going to turn up.'

Or who. When I left the library the following afternoon I found Canon Osbaston loitering in the cloisters.

'Ah!' he said. 'Good Lord! I'd forgotten I might find you here, Mrs Appleyard. I was just examining the exhibition.'

Wheezing softly, he held open the door to the Close.

'You're going to the Dark Hostelry?'

'Yes.'

He fell into step beside me. 'Perhaps we might walk together. I'm on my way to the High Street to buy some tobacco.'

We walked for a little while without talking.

Suddenly he burst out, 'Youlgreave was mad, Mrs Appleyard. Absolutely no doubt about it. Don't you find it rather warm for the time of year?'

'It's lovely, isn't it?' I said.

'Let's hope the sunshine lasts. We have a jumble sale for the South American Missionary Society on Saturday.'

Our progress through the sun-drenched Close was slow, a matter of fits and starts. We stopped while Osbaston mopped his face with a large handkerchief. In honour of the weather he was wearing a baggy linen jacket and a Panama hat with a broken brim.

'When you say "mad",' I said after a moment, 'what do you mean exactly?'

'I understand Canon Youlgreave was considered eccentric when he first came to Rosington,' Osbaston said, edging closer to me. 'And then he grew steadily worse. But it was in ways that made it difficult for one to insist on his having the appropriate medical treatment. When I arrived here in 1933 there were many people living who had known him and all this was common knowledge.'

'So what did he *do*?'

'It was a particularly distressing form of mental instability, I'm afraid.' Osbaston glanced at my face as if it was a pornographic photograph. 'It seems that his private life may not have been above reproach. And then there was that final sermon. Caused rather a stir – there were reports in the newspapers. They had to bring in the bishop and I believe Lambeth Palace was consulted too. Fortunately the poor fellow's family were very helpful. No one wanted any scandal.' The little head nodded on the great body. 'So we have that much to be thankful for, Mrs Appleyard. And we mustn't judge him too harshly, must we? I believe he was always very sickly even as a boy.'

By now we were standing outside the door in the wall leading to the garden of the Dark Hostelry.

'I must say goodbye, Mr Osbaston.'

He moistened his lips just as he had on Saturday night when he was about to take a sip of Burgundy. 'I thought I might have a cup of tea at the Crossed Keys Hotel. I don't suppose you'd care to join me?'

'That's very kind, but I should go. Janet's expecting me.'

He raised his Panama. 'Some other time, Mrs Appleyard. Delightful to see you again.' He ambled away.

Janet was on her knees weeding a flowerbed near the door into the house. 'What have you got to smile about?' she said.

22

'How nice to see you again, Mrs Byfield,' Mrs Elstree said. 'Such a shame about the weather.'

'It's not a bad turnout all things considered,' Janet replied. 'By the way, this is my friend Mrs Appleyard. We were at school together. Wendy, this is Mrs Elstree.'

I shook hands with Canon Osbaston's housekeeper, a tall, drab woman who looked as though she had stepped out of a sepia-tinted photograph. She stared at the base of my neck. I wondered if my neck was dirty or if a button had come adrift and my bra was showing. But she smiled quite affably and then turned her attention back to Janet.

'Let's have some tea, shall we?' she suggested. 'I need to check they've remembered everything. I'm afraid some of our staff need watching like a hawk.'

The three of us made our way through the crowd to the urn controlled by the Theological College's cook. It was raining hard so the jumble sale was being held in the dining hall. Since the doors had only just opened, there wasn't a queue for tea. Most of the people here were middle-aged women in hats and raincoats, armed with umbrellas. They intended to let nothing get between them and a good bargain.

Janet insisted on buying the tea. Mrs Elstree examined the sugar bowl, felt the side of the urn and checked the level in the milk jug.

'Nothing to worry about, I'm glad to say,' she murmured in my ear. She had a Fen accent, its harsh edges softened by years of contact with clerical vowels. 'They know better than to try monkeying about with me.' She smiled at Janet's back and lowered her voice still further. 'Lovely lady, Mrs Byfield. Such a nice family to have in Rosington.' Then, at a more normal volume, 'I understand you work in the Cathedral Library, Mrs Appleyard.'

'For the time being,' I said. 'Which reminds me, Canon Osbaston told me you might be able to tell me something about Canon Youlgreave. I came across something he'd written in the library a week or so ago.'

'He was a strange man and no mistake.' She lifted her eyes to my face. The pupils were large and black. 'Not that I knew him well, of course.'

'Where did he live?'

'Bleeders Hall. Where the Hudsons are now. I was working next door in the Deanery. Of course they did things in a lot more style in those days. The dean had a butler and kept his own carriage.'

'Really? And what was it like at Canon Youlgreave's?'

'I couldn't say. I never had any call to go there. Of course, Mr Youlgreave was a bachelor and didn't need the sort of establishment the dean did. But he had the house redecorated – I remember that. He lived in the Dark Hostelry while it was being done.'

Janet brought the tea. 'Who lived in our house?'

'Francis Youlgreave,' I said. 'But Mrs Elstree says it was only for a short time. Apparently he had the house the Hudsons have got.'

'He wasn't liked, I'm afraid,' Mrs Elstree said. 'And of course he went mad in the end. Not that we were surprised. We could see it coming.'

'Did you hear the famous sermon about women priests?'

She shook her head and then, as if to make up for this failure, added, 'They say he was over-familiar with the servants. And some of his ideas were very strange. You know he did away with himself?'

'No, I didn't.' I watched her spooning sugar into her tea. 'I thought he'd not been well for some time and he just died.'

'That's not what we heard. And him a clergyman. But it didn't happen here. It was after they got rid of him.' She took a sip of tea and then turned to Janet. 'What I say, Mrs

Byfield, is that you're bound to get a few rotten apples in every barrel.'

'I don't suppose you knew a boy called Simon Martlesham in those days. He worked at the Bishop's Palace.'

'Simon Martlesham? Oh yes.' She hesitated and stirred her tea again, quite unnecessarily. 'I think he used to run errands for Canon Youlgreave sometimes. But he left Rosington years ago. He lives in Watford now. My brother bumped into him in the Swan.'

'I know. The pub by the river.'

She nodded. 'His family used to live down there. There was his mother and sister. By that time he was at the Palace, of course, the servants lived in . . . I don't remember a father. I expect he was in the area and thought he'd go and see his old home. Not that there's much to see.'

People swirled between us. Someone jogged my elbow and tea slopped in the saucer and on the sleeve of my mackintosh. Other conversations began. Later Janet bought a knitted golliwog in a blue boilersuit for Rosie's birthday and I found a Busy Lizzie for the kitchen windowsill.

Afterwards as we were walking home arm in arm under one umbrella, Janet said, 'So you're still interested in Francis Youlgreave?'

'Just something to pass the time.' I was afraid that Janet would sense my ingratitude, my boredom with Rosington, my shabby little thoughts about David. I rushed into speech. 'I imagine Mrs Elstree can be rather terrifying. But she was very pleasant to us.'

'Mrs Elstree tries as hard as she can to be nice to me,' Janet said. 'That's because if David gets Osbaston's job, she hopes we'll keep her on.'

'And will you?'

'Not if I can help it. I think she's too used to running the place, too set in her ways. Mr Osbaston leaves everything to her. But she's right about the work involved.' She looked sideways at me. 'Actually, I don't think it would be much fun being the principal's wife.'

We hurried through the rain in silence after that. David was at home working on his book in the study and in theory keeping

702

an eye on Mr Treevor and Rosie. In the Close a car passed us, splashing water over my shoes and stockings.

'Can you smell anything?' Janet asked when we were taking off our raincoats in the hall.

'Only damp.' I sniffed the air. 'And perhaps bacon from this morning.'

'No, it's something underneath that. Something not very nice. At least I think it is.'

It was the first time any of us mentioned the smell. Of course Janet must have imagined it or smelled something different from the later smell. There's no other explanation.

David came out of the study. 'Hello. How was it?'

'Much as you'd imagine,' Janet said. 'But wetter. Where's Rosie?'

'Somewhere upstairs with your father. I think they were going to play Snap.' Then his voice dropped a little in pitch. 'Ah – Wendy?'

Surprised, I looked away from my reflection in the mirror. I was wondering if my nose was unusually red. Was it becoming what my mother would have called a 'toper's nose'? I thought David was looking accusingly at me.

'I had a letter this morning,' he said. 'From Henry.'

I stared at him. I felt sick. What he'd said was as unexpected as a punch in the stomach. But David and Henry were friends, in the inexplicable way that men are friends. Which meant that it didn't necessarily matter that they hadn't seen each other for years, they rarely wrote to each other, and they had completely different outlooks on life. I wondered if they'd been plotting about me.

'He asked if you were here,' David went on.

I said nothing.

'I'll have to write back and say you are. Naturally.'

'All right.'

'He wants to see you. He says –'

'I don't want to see him,' I said loudly. 'Just tell him that. Now I'm going to get changed. I'm soaking wet.'

I ran upstairs, past the sound of giggling coming from Rosie's room and up the next flight of stairs to my own bedroom. When I got there I blew my nose and looked away from my reflection in the mirror on the dressing table. What I needed, I decided, was a very early nightcap.

Two days later, on Monday, I came across a copy of an Edwardian children's book in the library. It was by G. A. Henty and was called *His Country's Flag*. Though the spine had faded the colours of the picture on the jacket were still as vivid as the day it was new. The picture showed a young English boy in a red coat. He was harvesting a crop of frightened-looking Zulus with a sabre. I opened the book and there was that familiar handwriting on the flyleaf.

For Simon Martlesham on his thirteenth birthday with good wishes from F. Youlgreave. July 17th, 1904.

23

Rosie's fifth birthday was on Wednesday, 14th May. All of us except Mr Treevor got up a little earlier than usual so she could have her presents before going to school.

As I came downstairs I thought for an instant that I smelled something unpleasant, like meat that's beginning to go off. I remembered Janet mentioning a smell the previous Saturday when we returned from the jumble sale at the Theological College. But when I stopped in the hall and sniffed, there was nothing out of the ordinary. Only damp, old stone and yesterday's vegetables.

Rosie was very excited, darting round the kitchen like a swallow round the Octagon. On the table was a little heap of cards and presents.

'May I open them?' she demanded. 'May I, please?'

'Have some breakfast first,' Janet told her.

'I want them now. It's my birthday.'

'Yes, poppet, but you have to eat breakfast, even on your birthday. Afterwards.'

'Now. Please, Mummy.'

They stared at each other. Janet looked away first, about to concede.

I picked up the card and parcel I had put on the table. 'Well, you won't be needing this then.'

Rosie looked up at me, her gaze both curious and calculating.

'This is for a little girl who does what her mummy tells her to do.'

I smiled at her, wishing I hadn't interfered. Rosie was Janet's

705

business, not mine. A moment later Rosie sat down at her place and watched her mother pouring cornflakes into her bowl. If she had been a general, she would have called it a tactical withdrawal.

It took Rosie five minutes to eat her cereal and a slice of toast, and drink a glass of milk. Then she worked through the pile before her. First she opened the envelopes, glanced at the birthday cards and put them on one pile. The discarded envelopes went on another. But two postal orders and a Premium Bond went in a special pile of their own, weighted by a fork.

Next came the parcels. She allowed David to cut them open with scissors. The parcel which had come in the post contained a maroon cardigan.

'How nice of Granny Byfield,' Janet said without enthusiasm.

Rosie did not comment.

Now there were four parcels left, the ones from the adults in the house. First she opened Mr Treevor's. The old man had wanted to give Rosie an apple taken from the bowl on the dresser. Last night, he'd told Janet that an apple would be good for Rosie and would also be something she would enjoy eating. When he was a boy, he said, he had often wished for an apple but no one had ever given him one for his birthday. Janet said it was a lovely present and very thoughtful of him. But when she wrapped up the apple she added the blue golliwog she had bought at the jumble sale.

David's present was Lamb's *Tales from Shakespeare*, an illustrated edition with simplified language. Janet had bought her a new dress, very smart, in navy-blue needlecord covered with pale-pink horses and trimmed with pink lace. It had puffed sleeves and a Peter Pan collar. Rosie was enchanted. Before she went to school she took the dress up to her parents' room so she could put it on and look at herself in the big mirror.

But first she opened my present. I had asked Janet to find out what Rosie wanted. It turned out she wanted an angel. Janet and I decided that a doll might be an acceptable compromise. In the toy shop in the High Street I'd found a rather expensive one with long blonde hair and blue eyes which opened and closed according to whether the doll was vertical or horizontal. The legs and the arms were jointed where they met the torso and the head swivelled on the neck. If you pressed the chest it croaked 'Mama'.

The doll came complete with a pink dress, underwear, socks and shoes. This didn't seem quite the right outfit for a celestial being, so I'd made a long white gown out of a couple of old handkerchiefs and embroidered an A for Angel in blue cotton over the heart, or rather over the place where the heart would have been if the angel had possessed one. We dressed the doll in the gown and packed away the pink clothes in an empty cigar box.

'They can be her trousseau,' Janet had said.

'Or her disguise when she goes out among humans,' I replied.

When Rosie opened the box and saw her angel lying there, she didn't say anything for a moment. Then, very slowly and very gently, she picked up the angel and cradled it in her arms.

'Do you like it?' Janet asked. 'Go and say thank you to Auntie Wendy.'

Still carrying the doll, Rosie came to stand by my chair and waited for me to kiss her cheek.

'Happy birthday,' I said. 'I'm glad you like it.'

Janet explained about the trousseau and how I'd made the gown and about the doll's saying 'Mama'.

Rosie nodded. 'But where are the wings?'

'Not all angels have wings,' I said.

'They do,' Rosie said.

'Ask your father, dear,' Janet suggested. 'He knows about this sort of thing. And I'm sure he'd like to have a good look at your angel.'

In fact, David's attention was now divided between *The Times* and a slice of toast and marmalade. But he allowed himself to be diverted for long enough to agree that angels didn't always have wings, which allayed Rosie's doubts for the time being.

'Auntie Wendy,' she said to me when she and Janet were leaving for school. 'My angel is my favourite present.'

On Rosie's birthday I did not come home at my usual time. I wanted her to have her birthday tea, with the cake, with Janet and David. It was her birthday and she deserved to have her parents all to herself. So at lunch time I told Janet that I wanted to do some shopping and I would be a little later than usual.

Late in the afternoon I found another book that had once belonged to Francis Youlgreave, the *Religio Medici* by Sir Thomas Browne, in an edition published in 1889. I was keeping a separate list of everything that had been his, and I felt everything I found told me a little more about him. The book was bound in flaking leather that left crumbs of dead skin on my fingers, and the spine was cracked. I riffled through the pages, which rustled like leaves in autumn. I found a passage marked in the margin with a wavering line of brown ink.

> Nay, further, we are what we all abhor, Anthropophagi and Cannibals, devourers not onely of men, but of our selves; and that not in an allegory, but a positive truth: for all this mass of flesh which we behold, came in at our mouths; this frame we look upon, hath been upon our trenchers; in brief, we have devour'd our selves.

It took me a moment to work out what the writer was saying, and when I did I shivered. I thought of those pictures of snakes with their tails in their mouths.

'Not nice, Francis,' I said aloud. 'And why did you mark it?'

In the still air of the Cathedral Library, the words waited for an answer. Jesus, I thought with another shiver, I'm talking to myself, this is ridiculous.

I stood up and walked over to the old catalogue in the big foolscap volume. Here were listed the books in Dean Pellew's original bequest and a number of later additions. The last entry was dated 1899. No sign of the *Religio Medici*. I checked the cabinet by the door which contained the later records, equally patchy. The earliest of these was a commentary in German on the Pentateuch. The entry was dated November 1904 and was in a neat copybook hand, very unlike Francis's scrawl.

I now knew from the *Dictionary of National Biography* that Francis had come to Rosington in 1900 and had departed at some point in 1904. He might have left some books in the library, but I hadn't come across any trace of him in the various catalogues. It suddenly struck me that the catalogue entry for November 1904 might well mark the point when someone more conscientious had started to look after the collection. Which suggested Francis had probably been forced to resign in the late summer or early autumn of the year. Which in turn would make my job easier if I ever wanted to try to trace a public record of his last sermon.

Until then the idea of doing so hadn't occurred to me. But why not? Osbaston had said the sermon had been mentioned in the papers. It must surely have been reported in the *Rosington Observer*.

I glanced at my watch. I had planned to spend forty-five minutes dawdling round the shops before going back to the Dark Hostelry. But there was nothing I wanted to buy that couldn't wait.

The *Rosington Observer* had an office in Market Street. It was a weekly newspaper which told you all about markets and meetings, and announced auctions, births, deaths and marriages. Funerals were covered in obsessive detail. The main editorial policy was to mention the names of as many local people as possible and to include the word 'Rosington' at least once in the first sentence of every piece.

Two women sat behind a long, polished counter in the room overlooking the street. They were talking about someone called Edna while one of them typed with two fingers and the other knitted. I asked if they kept old copies of the newspaper, and the knitter took me into a room at the back whose walls were lined with deep steel shelving. There was a table under the window with a single chair beside it. The newspapers were stacked in chronological order.

'They're filthy,' the woman warned me. 'I'll leave you to it. We close at five.'

I had my cotton dusting gloves, so the dust and the ink didn't bother me. I worked my way round the shelves to the pile that included issues from 1904. That was when I began to get suspicious.

First, there was no dust on the top of the pile. But there was on the piles to the right and the left, and indeed on every other

709

pile in this part of the shelves. The pile covered 1903 to the first half of 1906, so you would have expected the issues for 1904 to be somewhere in the middle. But they weren't. They were on top.

I carried them over to the table and began to work back from November. I found a mention of Francis almost at once in a small item on the fifth page.

> The Revd J. Heckstall will give a series of four evening lectures on the Meaning of Advent, beginning Tuesday next at 7.30 p.m., at the Almonry. All are welcome to attend. These were previously advertised as being given by Canon Youlgreave. There will be a collection in aid of the Church Empire Society.

I worked backwards. In October the newspaper told its readers that Canon Youlgreave had resigned and left Rosington because of poor health, and that the dean and chapter thought it unlikely that his successor to the canonry would be appointed until the new year.

In September I expected to find details of the sermon that had led to the resignation and its consequences. Instead I found something that in a way was worse than nothing. Two issues had been mutilated. Someone had used a penknife to cut out a total of five items, two of them probably letters to the editor. They'd pressed so hard that the blade had sliced through two or three of the pages beneath.

I took the two newspapers into the front office. The knitter and the typist stopped talking and looked at me.

'They mustn't be taken out of the room,' the knitter said. 'It's the rules.'

I spread the papers out on the counter. 'Look. Someone's been cutting bits out.'

'People just don't care, do they?' the typist said. 'I mean, look at those Teddy boys.'

The knitter popped a peppermint in her mouth. 'Just couldn't be bothered to copy it out, I expect. Whatever it was.'

'Has anyone been in there lately?'

'Could have been done years ago.'

I doubted it because the cuts in the yellowing paper looked too clean. 'Perhaps. But has anyone been recently – in the last few weeks, say?'

'There was Mrs Vosper,' the typist said. 'Wanted to find out the date of her parents-in-law's wedding.'

The knitter gave a bark of laughter. 'A bit late for that.'

'And the solicitor's clerk came in on Friday, didn't he?' the typist went on.

'Which solicitor?' I asked.

'I don't know.'

'He *looked* like a solicitor's clerk,' the knitter explained. 'Quite a small man. Black jacket and pinstriped trousers.'

'And what did he want?'

'Didn't ask. We were too busy. A couple of people had come in to place advertisements, and someone else was moaning about something the editor had written, though why talk to us, I just don't know.'

'Anyway,' the typist said, regaining control of the conversation by raising her voice, 'why do you want to know?'

'It just seems an odd thing to do.'

'People do odd things every day,' the knitter said. 'You just wouldn't believe some of the stories we hear. You couldn't surprise us if you tried.'

'I don't suppose I could.'

The typist said, 'It's almost five o'clock. We have to close in a moment.'

So I went shopping after all. I bought cotton for Janet, a bar of chocolate for Rosie and a bottle of gin for me. At the wine merchant's, Mr Cromwell looked curiously at me, and for a moment I thought he was going to say something. Next time I needed gin I'd buy it in Cambridge.

And all the time I found it hard to concentrate because I was wondering who had been taking cuttings from the *Rosington Observer*, and why, and whether it was something to do with Francis Youlgreave.

It must have been almost six o'clock by the time I reached the Dark Hostelry. Janet rushed into the hall as I let myself into the house. When she saw it was me, disappointment flooded over her face.

'What's wrong?' A split second later, I asked, 'Where's Rosie? What's happened?'

'She's fine. She's in the kitchen. It's Daddy. You haven't seen him, have you?'

'No.'

'He was in the garden with Rosie while I was making the tea. When I called them in, only Rosie was there. She said he'd gone out. And that was nearly two hours ago. David's looking for him.'

Mr Treevor rarely left the house and garden, and when he did one of us always went with him. He hadn't been out by himself since he'd moved into the Dark Hostelry.

'He can't have got far. Have you told the police?'

'Not yet. David thought we should wait a little.'

We went down to the kitchen. Rosie was chatting to her new doll and did not look up as we came in. The remains of the birthday tea were still on the table. My bag clanked as I put it down on the dresser. I wondered if David had delayed calling the police because he was afraid of scandal.

'Rosie,' Janet said. 'Are you sure Grandpa didn't say where he was going?'

She glanced up, shaking her head. 'No, he didn't say where.'

There was a slight stress on the last word. That's what made me say, 'But did he say *why* he was going out?'

'He said he wanted to look for some wings.' Rosie stroked the doll's hair. 'For Angel. He said angels must have wings.'

At that moment we heard a key in the back door, the door that opened into the High Street and the marketplace. And then Mr Treevor was saying, 'I'm very hungry. Isn't it tea time yet?'

24

There was a devious side to David. The business about the phone call showed that.

Janet was on a committee, chaired by Mrs Forbury, the dean's wife, which met at teatime on Thursday afternoons at the Deanery. The Cathedral, Janet said, needed what Mrs Forbury called a Woman's Touch. So we used to refer to the committee members as the Touchies. They dealt with the flower rota, oversaw the cleaning and the maintenance of various fabrics, from altar cloths to choir boys' ruffs. There was even a sub-committee to deal with the complicated question of the manufacture, maintenance and disposition of kneelers. According to Janet, this was where an inner circle of Touchies decided all matters of importance.

That was why I left work early on Thursday afternoons. While Janet went to the Touchies, I gave Rosie and Mr Treevor their tea. Between four and five thirty, I was usually the only responsible adult at the Dark Hostelry.

David knew this.

The phone rang while I was washing up. Rosie was playing with Angel at the kitchen table and Mr Treevor was dozing in his room. His adventure yesterday had left him tired out. David had eventually found him in the High Street. Mr Treevor said he wanted to find some ducks so he could feed them. There weren't any ducks in the High Street, and in any case he had nothing to feed them with.

I went up to the study, where the phone was. It was David's room, dark, austere and full of books, and it always made me feel like a trespasser. I picked up the handset and recited the number.

'Wendy,' Henry said. 'It's me.'

I felt sweat breaking out on my forehead and on the palm of my hand holding the telephone.

'Wendy, don't hang up, please. Are you there?'

I stared at a crucifix on the wall over the fireplace. Christ's brass face was contorted. The poor man really looked in pain.

'Wendy?'

'I've got nothing to say.'

'I'm sorry,' Henry said. 'I was a fool. I miss you. I love you.'

'Oh, bugger off.'

I put the phone down. I stood beside the desk and glared at the telephone. I was trembling and the tears blurred my vision. After a while the phone rang again. I let it ring. It went on for thirty-six rings. I felt like a piece of elastic, and each ring stretched me a little further. David must have arranged this. David and Henry were friends, and no doubt David felt it no more than his pastoral duty to do his best to help repair a failing marriage. When at last the ringing stopped, it was as if someone had turned off a pneumatic drill. I turned to go. Rosie was in the doorway, with Angel in her arms. I scowled at her.

'What are you doing?'

'The phone kept ringing.'

'Yes,' I said.

'So why didn't you answer it?'

'I – I was busy.'

Rosie pressed the doll's chest. 'Mama,' it said.

The little black monster started to ring again.

'Are you going to answer it now?'

I turned round and picked up the handset.

'Wendy?' Henry said. 'Can't we talk? Please.'

What was there to talk about, I wanted to say – divorce? Henry's wobbling buttocks bouncing on top of the Hairy Widow? The way my money had disappeared? But I couldn't say any of this because Rosie was still in the doorway.

'I need to see you,' he went on. 'Whenever you want. Couldn't we meet for lunch? I've got some of your things. A bit of jewellery.'

'I'm surprised you haven't sold it,' I said. 'Or perhaps you haven't needed to.'

'If you're thinking about that woman,' he said, 'I haven't seen her since the day on the beach. I promise you.'

I turned away from the door because I didn't want Rosie to see me crying.

'We could meet in Cambridge,' he suggested. 'Would that be easier for you? Please, Wendy.'

'London,' I said.

'All right. Can you manage Monday? We could meet at the Café Royal. What time would suit you?'

'Twelve thirty,' I said. 'And if you aren't there when I arrive I won't wait. I've done enough waiting.'

I put the phone down. Rosie and I went back to the kitchen and I finished the washing up. Afterwards I went up to my bedroom and had an early nightcap. It seemed to me that I no longer had anything left to lose. It didn't matter if I made a fool of myself. I'd already done that in such a comprehensive way that any other follies barely registered.

So after I'd rinsed out the glass and done my teeth, I went back to the study and rang directory enquiries. It was very easy – they found the number almost immediately. I perched on the edge of the desk and listened to a phone ringing in a strange house in a strange town.

'Hello,' said a woman's voice, high and breathless. 'Who's speaking?'

'Hello,' I said. 'Could I talk to Mr Simon Martlesham?'

'Not here, you can't. We rent the house off him, you see.'

'Do you have a phone number or a forwarding address?'

'So you don't know him?'

'Not exactly. But we've a sort of mutual friend, and I've got something to return to him.'

'Hang on.' A moment's silence, then the rustle of paper. 'Are you ready?'

'As much as I'll ever be.'

She didn't laugh, but she gave me a phone number.

25

On Saturday morning there was a postcard from the library. The book I had reserved the previous Monday was now waiting for me. Immediately after lunch I went to fetch it.

It was another warm day and the same librarian was on duty. He was wheezing more than before and his wiry hair needed brushing. He was sitting at the table near the door, his hands fluttering over tray after tray of tickets. The library was almost empty because people were still at lunch. He looked up and the folds and wrinkles of his bloodhound face rearranged themselves into a smile.

'I've come to collect the book,' I said, and put down the postcard on his desk. 'That was quick.'

'We aim to please, Mrs Appleyard,' he said sadly. 'There's not much else one can do in this vale of tears, is there?'

'I can think of one or two other things,' I said.

He took a small green hardback from the shelf behind him and stamped it. I read the last due date, upside down, and worked out that the last borrower had taken out the book in the middle of last week.

'So who had it?' I asked. 'The man you mentioned before? The one who was asking about Francis Youlgreave?'

'What is it about Francis Youlgreave? Why's everyone so interested?'

'I can tell you why I am. I'm working in the Cathedral Library, and there are books that used to be his. So I'm just curious.'

'Just curious?' He had a way of speaking that made it sound as though he were testing everything, like a scientist with a laboratory full of instruments. 'I told you before, I didn't know who the borrower was.'

'But wasn't the name on the ticket?'

'Of course. But I didn't see the ticket. Someone else stamped the book. It was a busy time, and she couldn't remember the name. It was returned at a busy time, too. She thought it might have been Brown. Or Smith. Not a name that stood out.'

So he'd bothered to ask. He was getting curious too.

'So you don't know if it was the same person?'

'It seems likely. The man I talked to was middle-aged. Small, dark. I think he wore glasses and had a bald patch. Dressed quite formally. Looked very respectable.'

'A black jacket and pinstriped trousers? A bit like a solicitor's clerk?'

'Something like that, I suppose. Not that I know any solicitor's clerks.'

I thanked him and put the book in my bag.

'By the way,' he said, 'are you by any chance related to *Henry* Appleyard?'

It was as if the bloodhound had slapped me.

'Yes. How do you know him?'

The librarian waved orange-stained fingers. 'We used to bump into each other occasionally.'

In the betting shop? In the pub?

He was waiting for me to explain. He was curious about that as well.

'I haven't seen him for a while,' I said. 'Anyway, thanks for the book. 'Bye.'

I walked back through the sunshine, stopping to buy a pair of stockings, very sheer and very expensive, and also some new lipstick. On my way to the Close I went through the market. There were stalls around the cross and the cobbles were strewn with rotting vegetables and cardboard. A rubbish bin attached to a lamppost reminded me of my dream, but this one didn't contain a doll, only a woman's shoe without a heel and crumpled newspaper greasy from wrapping fish and chips. I wondered whether Isabella of Roth had really died here over five hundred years ago and, if she had, whether any trace of her agony remained apart from Francis's letter in the *Transactions of the Rosington Antiquarian Society*. Pain mattered, I thought, it should be noticed and remembered. Did Henry and his Hairy Widow add up to a pain that mattered?

From the market, it was only a few yards to the back door of the Dark Hostelry in the High Street. I let myself in. The house was cool and quiet. Nobody was around. I went upstairs to take off my hat and gloves. I saw David, Janet and Rosie from my window sitting in the dappled shade of the apple tree. They looked like an ideal family, self-contained in their beauty. You didn't often see them sitting together.

I lay on my bed and resisted the temptation to have a nip of gin as a reward for not minding the fact that I wasn't part of an ideal family. Instead I looked at *The Tongues of Angels*. The pages smelled of tobacco, strong and foreign, like French or Turkish cigarettes. When I tried to read a poem called 'The Children of Heracles' I couldn't concentrate. So I put the book in the cupboard by the bed and went down to join the others.

David was in a deckchair with a book on his lap, his shirt open at the neck and the sleeves rolled up. He looked like Laurence Olivier in a very good mood. Janet was sitting on a rug brushing Rosie's hair. Rosie was in her new dress because she was going to a party later in the afternoon and was brushing Angel's hair, the strokes of her brush exactly in time with Janet's. I felt like a trespasser, just as I had in David's study the other day.

'Oh good,' Janet said. 'Do you think these ribbons match?'

David sat up. 'Come and sit here. I'll go on the grass.'

'Don't move, please. And the ribbons look fine to me.' I knelt on the rug beside Janet and lit a cigarette.

'David's just had a phone call from Gervase Haselbury-Finch,' Janet said. 'Do sit still, poppet. You know, the bishop's chaplain.'

'In a sense it concerns you,' David said, 'and anyway there's no reason why you shouldn't know about it. It seems that the bishop's definitely in favour of diverting the Cathedral Library's endowment to the Theological College. He's written to the dean and chapter about it.'

'How nice.' I couldn't think of anything else to say.

'Do sit still, poppet,' Rosie said to Angel.

'Gervase went to the same school as David,' Janet said, and went back to the brushing.

718

I flicked ash on a fallen leaf. 'It's a small world.'

'He's got no direct influence over what the dean and chapter decide,' David went on, leaning towards me, 'but they are bound to take notice of what he thinks. The point is, the bishop wouldn't suggest diverting the endowment unless he intended the Theological College to stay open.'

'But I thought you already knew he was in favour of that.'

'Yes – he's said as much to me. But this shows he's actually prepared to do something about it. It's a step forward, believe me.'

The Cathedral's clock boomed the half-hour. Janet stood up suddenly and brushed her skirt with her hand.

'We must go. Time to do your teeth, poppet.'

'Time to do your teeth, poppet,' Rosie echoed to Angel.

'Mama!' Angel replied.

They went into the house. David told me how it would be perfectly possible not just to keep the Theological College open but to expand the number of students. It was a question of attracting the right type of ordinand and he had a number of ideas how they could do that. Accommodation wouldn't be a problem – they could convert the attics into study bedrooms.

'We'll be back at about five,' Janet called from the house. She grimaced at me. 'I've been roped in to help with the games.'

David told me about a programme of visiting lecturers he planned, about changes in the course structure to reflect new trends in theology, and about improvements to the social and sporting activities of the college. He gesticulated with long, graceful hands.

'After all, it's not a nunnery,' he said. 'There's no reason why they shouldn't have a bit of fun.'

'Oh, yes,' I said. 'We all need that.'

While David talked I nodded and occasionally commented or asked appropriate questions in the pauses. I was really engaged in admiring the line of his jaw, the colour of his eyes and his well-kept and beautifully shaped fingernails. I also wondered if he talked to Janet like this while they were alone. They didn't talk very much when I was there.

'By the way,' he said, leaning closer to offer me a cigarette, 'I know Henry was planning to ring.'

'Yes.' I sat up and shook my head to the cigarette. 'He phoned on Thursday.'

'Janet told me. Look, I hope you didn't mind my telling him when you might be in?'

'It's too late if I did,' I said. 'I'm going to see him on Monday.'

He nodded. 'I'm glad.'

'I don't know what I feel,' I said, suddenly reckless. 'It's all such a bloody mess.'

'Wendy,' he said, 'you know that –'

At this interesting moment the door to the house opened. We both turned, as if caught red-handed.

'He's out there,' Mr Treevor said in a thin, wavering voice.

'Who is?' David asked, standing up.

'The burglar. He was standing outside Chase and Cromwell's and looking up at my bedroom window.'

'The man you saw?' I said. 'The man like a shadow?'

'Yes. I told you. He's there. He's watching us. He's biding his time before he strikes again.'

'I don't think that's very likely, actually,' David said.

Mr Treevor pouted. 'He is. I saw him.'

'Why don't we go and see?' I suggested.

The old man's face crumpled. 'Don't leave me.'

'You can come as well.'

David sighed. 'This is absurd,' he murmured to me.

'Perhaps. But it won't do any harm, will it?'

'What are you whispering about?' Mr Treevor's voice rose to a squeal. 'Everyone's always whispering.'

'We're just talking about going out,' I said. 'Let's go this way.'

We went into the Close and walked down to the Sacristan's Gate and into the High Street. It was Saturday afternoon so the pavements were crowded with shoppers. But I couldn't see a little man in black outside Chase and Cromwell's, or indeed anywhere else. Mr Treevor's head made jerky little stabbing movements as if he was pecking the air with his nose.

'He's not there now, is he?' David said.

'He was,' Mr Treevor cried. 'I saw him. I did, I did.'

'All right.' I patted his arm which was hooked round mine. 'Let's go home.'

It was quieter in the Close and he calmed down almost immediately. We walked arm in arm, three abreast, with Mr Treevor in the middle, our prisoner. Canon Hudson was coming in the other direction. He waved to us and we stopped to talk near the gate to the Dark Hostelry.

'I was going to phone you this evening,' I said to him after we had agreed how unseasonably warm the weather was and how well Mr Treevor was looking. 'Do you mind if I take Monday off? I have to go to London.'

'Of course. Business or pleasure?'

'Business,' I said, avoiding David's eyes.

There was a clatter behind us. I turned to see Gotobed coming from the north door, carrying a bucket and a small shovel. Usually he walked in a stately fashion in the Close, as though leading an invisible procession. But now he was hurrying.

'Are you all right?' Hudson called to him.

Gotobed veered towards him. 'I'm all right, sir. But there's them that aren't.'

'What do you mean?'

'You'd better look at this.'

He motioned Hudson to one side, turned his back on the rest of us and held up the bucket.

Hudson wrinkled his nose. 'Not a nice sight, I agree. But we get plenty of pigeons in the Close, and sometimes they die.'

'He was under the bench in the north porch, sir.'

'Looks as if he'd been there for some time.'

'He was tucked under one of the legs. I wouldn't have seen him if I hadn't dropped my keys. He couldn't have got there by accident.'

'Perhaps a visitor pushed him under there to –'

'They did more than push him under the bench, sir,' Gotobed interrupted. His hands were trembling but there was no trace of his usual shyness. 'Have a proper look. Go on.'

Hudson peered into the bucket. 'Yes,' he said slowly. 'I see your point.'

'Let me see,' Mr Treevor said, pulling his arms free of David's and mine.

721

He skipped across the path to Hudson's side. David and I, taken by surprise, followed. I glanced into the bucket.

'Don't, Mrs Appleyard,' Gotobed said to me, his nose twitching. 'It's not nice.'

It was a very skinny, decaying pigeon with mangy feathers. One of its legs had been reduced to a stump. For an instant I thought it had died of natural causes.

Mr Treevor's head bobbed, and he turned away. 'Ugh!' he said. 'Isn't it time to go home? We mustn't be late for tea.'

The bucket swung in Gotobed's hand and the pigeon rolled slowly over. It was beginning to smell. Then I realized why it looked so skinny. There were wounds along its sides, ragged slits exposing flesh and bone and gristle. Someone had hacked the wings off the pigeon's body.

26

I felt like a fool on Monday morning. Part of me was also excited, as if I was going to a party.

When the train left Cambridge I went along the corridor to the lavatory. As I sat there I took off my wedding ring, which wasn't easy, and slipped it in my handbag. The skin where it had been was slightly paler than the rest of the finger. As far as the world was concerned, Mrs had turned into Miss, a magical transformation like frog into prince, or the other way round. Perhaps snakes felt this way when they sloughed off a dead skin, colder and suddenly more vulnerable, but also lighter than air.

I checked my make-up in the lavatory mirror for the third time since leaving the Dark Hostelry and then returned to the compartment. There were two men, one my age, one a little older, and they both glanced at me as I came in. The younger of the two was quite good-looking. He stared discreetly as I crossed my legs, and I was glad I was wearing the new stockings.

The Tongues of Angels was one of the two books in my shopping bag. I took it out and skimmed through the poems again. I thought I knew where Francis had found the title – I'd checked the phrase in David's dictionary of quotations. Almost certainly he'd taken it from the New Testament, from the opening sentence of the thirteenth chapter of I Corinthians. 'Though I speak with the tongues of men and of angels, and have not charity, I am become as sounding brass, or a tinkling cymbal.'

But the contents didn't have much to do with charity, not on the surface at least. The poems were divided into seven sections. Each of the sections had the name of an archangel. Uriel, Raphael, Raguel, Michael, Sariel, Gabriel and Remiel.

Oddly enough the poems themselves weren't about angels, arch or otherwise. They were mainly about children or animals, sometimes both. I'd read all of them at least three times but I still wasn't sure what most of them were really about.

But there was one thing I approved of. There was none of that J. M. Barrie nonsense for Francis. Quite the reverse. The children in 'The Children of Heracles' were cut up into little bits by their father, because a goddess had put him under a spell and made him think they were his enemies. Another poem was about the Spartan boy who ran with a fox gnawing his vitals and saved his country at the cost of his own life. At the end of it the fox ran off laughing. A third concerned a cat at the court of Egypt, a cat who was older and more mysterious than the Sphinx, a cat who watched with unblinking eyes as the children of the pharaoh died of the plague.

The longest poem was called 'Breakheart Hill'. It was about a hunt in a pseudo-medieval forest where people said 'prithee' and 'by our lady' at the drop of a hat, and varlets lurked on the greensward 'neath the spreading oaks. The quarry was a hart, the noblest in the country, and the king, his huntsmen and his hounds pursued it all day for miles and miles. At last the light began to fade and the king commanded the huntsmen to drive the stag up a steep hill near the royal hunting lodge, for it was time for it to die.

The king's son, who was on his first hunt, begged his father to spare the hart which had given them so much sport. But the king would not. The pack drove the stag up the hill, and there, on the summit, its great heart broke open and it died of exhaustion just before the hounds leapt at its throat. The young prince wept.

The king ordered his huntsmen to drive the dogs back. Then he took his son by the hand and led him to the stag. He drew his dagger, sliced open its breast and cut deep down to its broken heart. The king put his hand inside the broken heart and drew it out, dripping with blood. The prince watched. The king daubed blood on the boy's face and kissed his forehead.

> 'For hart's blood makes the young heart strong,' quoth he.
> 'God hath ordained it so. He dies that ye
> 'May hunt, my son, and through his strength be free.'

So what had angels to do with all this? Maybe Francis believed he'd cracked their code, and worked out what they talked about among themselves when not on official business. And their favourite topic of conversation turned out to be nasty anecdotes involving children and animals.

Or perhaps it was the other way round and the message was straightforwardly Christian. Heracles, the fox, the pharaoh's cat and the hunting king were all dominant types who either remained aloof from the crowd or got their own way. But was this of any use to them or anyone else, Francis was asking, without charity?

None of this made much sense. But with Francis I was used to that. I felt a kinship with him for that very reason. My life didn't make much sense either. At least I was going to London for the day. I crossed my legs again, glanced up at the younger man and caught him watching.

The train was slowing for Liverpool Street Station. I put the book in my bag and stared out of the window at bomb sites, the backs of grimy houses and new tower blocks. The last time I had seen this view I had been suffering from a king-sized hangover and more unhappy than I could ever remember being before. Life had improved. London was huge and full of possibilities. Excitement wriggled inside me as if the snake was escaping from another skin.

I took the tube to Chancery Lane. The noise, the crowds and the constant movement were partly scary and partly invigorating. So was the fact that no one knew who I was. I felt like someone who had emerged from months of seclusion – from a monastery, say, or hospital or prison. Rosington had been all three of those things to me.

When I left the station I had to ask directions to Fetter Passage. Not once but three times. It was that sort of place – people thought they knew where it was but turned out to be wrong. I found it at last, a lane curved like a boomerang, north of Holborn in the maze of streets between Hatton Garden and Gray's Inn Road. On one side were warehouses and offices, and on the other a small Victorian terrace, now incomplete because a bomb had ripped out one end of it. Most of the houses had shopfronts. The one nearest the bomb site was the Blue Dahlia

Café, the side wall shored up with balks of timber growing out of a sea of weeds. I lingered outside, looking through the window.

The café was about half full. The customers, men and women, seemed respectable. Office workers, I thought, perhaps having elevenses. Was one of the men Simon Martlesham? I went inside.

Layers of smoke moved sluggishly through the air. At the back was an archway masked by long multi-coloured strips of nylon which trembled in the draught. A radio played quietly. Few people were talking. A sad-faced woman was washing up at the sink behind the counter and a man was making sandwiches. They ignored me.

I waited at the counter. Eventually the woman dried her hands and shuffled over to me. She had sallow skin and black lank hair.

'My name's Appleyard. I've arranged to meet a Mr Martlesham here, but I'm a little early. Do you know him?'

She nodded.

'He's not here already?'

'You sit down and wait. You want something?'

I ordered coffee. She waved me to an empty table and said something in what sounded like Italian to the man making sandwiches. Then she slipped through the ribbons into the room beyond, her slippers slapping on the linoleum. A little man in a raincoat was reading a newspaper at the next table. He glanced up at me, squinting through his cigarette smoke, but turned away when I met his eyes.

While I waited, I dipped into *His Country's Flag*, the other book in my shopping bag. Soon I learned that young Harry Verderer had recently been orphaned, but his wealthy uncle intended to send him to Cape Town where there were openings at a bank with whom the uncle had connections. This was appropriate, because the man at the next table was going bald, and the patch of shiny skin on the top of his head was shaped rather like a map of Africa. Harry was frightfully cross because he wanted to join the army and become a hero like his father and grandfather before him. Instead he had to buckle down and do his duty at the bank for the sake of his kid sister Maud.

At that moment the woman brought my coffee. The man at the next table squirmed in his chair, brushing ash from his lap.

The ribbons fluttered again, and then I was no longer alone. A man limped towards my table, dragging his left leg across the floor. His left arm hung down at his side with a *Daily Telegraph* wedged near the armpit. He wore a worsted suit and carried a stick. His dark eyes were on the book, not me.

'Miss Appleyard?' He must have looked for a wedding ring.

'Mr Martlesham. And in fact it's "Mrs".'

We shook hands. I wondered why I'd been so keen to claim the 'Mrs' I could so easily have discarded with the ring.

Martlesham propped his stick against the table and sat down, lowering himself awkwardly into the chair. If his thirteenth birthday had been in July 1904, he must now be almost sixty-seven. He had neat, well-proportioned features and once must have been handsome. Still would have been if his face hadn't been lower on the left side than on the right. But the suit was brushed and pressed, his hair had been recently cut and his collar was spotless. He wore a gold tiepin, a horse's head inlaid with enamel. He smelled of shaving cream now, not rancid fat.

When he was settled, he glanced at the waitress and she went through the ribbons again.

'You've got them well trained,' I said.

'What?'

'The waitress. Is she fetching you something?'

'Coffee. Sorry. Is there anything else you would like?'

'No, thanks. Do you live near here now?'

'In a way.' He smoothed back his silver hair and nodded towards the book. 'Is that the one you mentioned?'

'Yes.'

Martlesham had sounded suspicious when I'd phoned him on Thursday, but had been too surprised to ask many questions. I hadn't been sure how he would take it – not everyone wants to be reminded of their childhood, me included. But he'd said he'd like the book, if it was all the same to me. I'd suggested the time for our meeting, and said I was coming up to Liverpool Street, and he'd suggested the Blue Dahlia Café. I assumed it was near where he lived or worked, but perhaps he had just thought it would be convenient for me.

'I don't mind telling you, that phone call of yours took me by surprise.' He had a strange accent, clipped as a suburban privet hedge, but the stroke had slurred his voice just as it had changed the shape of his face and crippled his left arm and leg. 'Still, it's very kind of you, I'm sure.'

'That's all right. I was coming up to town anyway.'

'Even so.'

'Actually, I was curious.'

'Why?'

'As I told you on the phone, I'm cataloguing the Cathedral Library.'

He nodded, impatiently. 'That's where you found the book.'

'Yes. By and large it's not exactly an exciting job. So anything out of the ordinary makes it more interesting. You see?'

'Can I have a look?'

'Of course.' I pushed the book across the table. 'After all, it's got your name in it.'

He opened the book and read what Francis had written on the flyleaf. I drew on my cigarette. I wasn't sure whom the book belonged to. I hadn't asked Canon Hudson if I could give it to Simon Martlesham. That would have involved showing him the inscription, and I was sure he would disapprove of my trying to find out anything to do with Francis.

The waitress brought Martlesham's coffee and a plate with two Rich Tea and two ginger biscuits on it. She stationed the plate between us and went away. Neither took any notice of the other. They might have been mutually invisible.

He looked up and stared across the table at me. I was shocked to see tears in his eyes. No reason for him to be sad. Perhaps the stroke had affected his tear ducts.

'What I don't understand is how you found me,' he said. 'I forgot to ask. I mean, you just rang up out of the blue.'

'Mrs Elstree told me you lived in Watford. So I asked directory enquiries, and a lady who was your tenant gave me your London number.'

'Who's Mrs Elstree?'

'I don't know what her maiden name was but she knew you

when you were a boy, when she worked at the Deanery. And she said her brother met you a year or two back, when you visited Rosington.'

'Oh yes. That'd be Alf Butler. The first and last time I've been back to Rosington. Just happened to be passing through and I thought I'd take a look at the old place. He was down by the Swan, and he recognized me right away.' He caressed the handle of the stick with his right hand. 'I looked different then.'

'You knew him when you were children?'

'Alf's parents used to have a little shop in Bridge Street. So Mrs What'sername must be Enid.' Martlesham gave me a crooked smile. 'I remember her. Always full of doom and gloom, that one.'

I smiled back. 'She's Canon Osbaston's housekeeper now. He's the principal of the Theological College.'

'Hang on a minute.' His forehead wrinkled. 'How come you were talking to her about me in the first place?'

'I wasn't,' I said. 'Not exactly. I was asking about Canon Youlgreave. Because he was the one who gave you the book.'

He moved sharply. The stick propped against the table began to slide. The coffee swayed in the cups. 'What's your interest in Canon Youlgreave, Mrs Appleyard?'

I caught the stick before it fell. A drop of coffee had fallen on the toecap of one of Martlesham's shoes. It looked like a grey star on a curved black mirror.

'He was the Cathedral librarian at one time,' I said. 'Some of the books I found used to belong to him. He seemed quite an interesting person.'

Martlesham stared out of the window. 'Compared to the rest of them, he certainly was that.' He turned back to me. 'Do you live in the Close, Mrs Appleyard?'

'I'm staying at the Dark Hostelry.'

'I remember. When I was a lad I think the precentor had it. Though Canon Youlgreave lived there for a few months, I remember. So is your husband a clergyman?'

'No.'

'Oh, really?'

I hurried on. 'I expect the Close has changed a good deal since you were there.'

'I doubt it. But I wouldn't know what it's like now. I haven't been there for years.' He glanced at me and went on, speaking more quickly than before, 'Never liked the atmosphere, to be honest. When I was growing up there wasn't much love lost between town and Close. Either you were one or t'other. Which made it awkward for the people like me. For the servants.'

'That's one thing that's changed.' I thought of Janet imprisoned in her own kitchen. 'I don't think there are many servants in the Close nowadays.'

'I was lucky,' he said.

'Because you worked at the Palace?'

He shook his head. 'Worst place of all. The bishop's butler could have given Stalin a few lessons. No, I meant I was lucky because I didn't have to work there very long. Not much more than a year. I've got Canon Youlgreave to thank for that. But I doubt if anyone remembers him now.' His voice roughened. 'Not as he really was. After all, it must be more than fifty years.'

'Some people do.'

'Not *him*. Not the man. If they remember anything, they'll remember what happened. But there was more to him than that. Those folk are meant to be Christians and yet they're as fond of scandal as anyone else.'

'More to him than what? You mean the poetry?'

'Yes, there's that. But I don't go in for that sort of thing myself. No, what I meant is that he did a lot of good in a quiet way. I know people thought he was strange. All right, he was a bit odd. But the long and the short of it is, if it hadn't been for him I wouldn't be here.'

'What happened?'

'I suppose you could say he took a fancy to me. First time we met was when he had a fall in the Close – he'd slipped on some ice and I helped him home. Later on he lent me some books. You know, encouraged me to think there was more to life than cleaning other people's boots.' He brought out a silver case and fumbled one-handedly for a cigarette. 'A lot of people were poor in those days. Really poor. Hard to imagine it now, isn't it? No one goes hungry any more. No one dies because they can't afford the doctor.'

730

'It's progress,' I said.

He nodded but his attention was elsewhere, on whatever he saw in his memory. 'Most people in the Close didn't give a damn about what was happening on their own doorstep. They'd only put their hands in their pockets if it was somewhere else. India, say, or even the East End. But they didn't want to see it themselves a few hundred yards from the Close.'

'In Swan Alley?'

'Maybe they thought poverty might be infectious, like the plague. Or maybe they'd have to realize it was their fault.' For a few words his accent changed – the vowels broadened and the Fen twang of his childhood emerged. 'But Mr Youlgreave wasn't like that.'

He put the cigarette in his mouth at last. I flicked the lighter under his nose.

After a moment I said, 'Did you hear that last sermon of his? The one that caused such a lot of fuss?'

'What sermon?'

'Apparently he said there was no reason why women couldn't be priests as well as men.'

Martlesham shook his head. 'I was in Canada by then. I'd lost touch with him. I heard him preach a sermon about Swan Alley, though. Said it was a blot on God's earth. They didn't like that, either. He was a good man.'

A good man? So unlike the other epitaphs for Francis Youlgreave.

'What did you mean about scandal? You said that's what people would remember.'

'Scandal? That's the whole point. What scandal? If you ask me, it was all smoke, no fire. He didn't fit in, you see. And they made him suffer for it.'

Why didn't he fit in? Wasn't his father a baronet and his mother the cousin of the dean? Fifty years later I didn't fit in either. But at least I knew why. My lipstick was too bright and I'd mislaid my husband. And something else was niggling at me, something to do with now, with the Blue Dahlia Café.

'Mr Youlgreave paid for me to emigrate,' Martlesham went on. 'He had a friend on the committee of this organization, the Church Empire Society. If they liked you, if you had good references, they'd put up half the money if someone else would put up the rest.' He laid his right hand on the book, the cigarette still smouldering between his fingers. 'That's why I'm glad to get this. A bit late, but in a way that makes it all the better.'

'So you never had it at the time?'

He shook his head. 'Do you know where I was on my thirteenth birthday? In the middle of the Atlantic on the *Hesperides*. He probably bought it and forgot to give it to me before we sailed. But how did it get in the library?'

'There were several of his books there. He was ill when he left Rosington, so perhaps they just got left behind. It's nothing out of the ordinary. No one's sorted out that library for years and I've found all sorts of odd things.'

Like *Lady Chatterley's Lover*, for example, unexpurgated but disappointingly dull. Meanwhile my sense of unease was growing. I glanced round the room. What was so familiar about the Blue Dahlia Café? There were fewer customers now. Perhaps this was the lull before lunch. The waitress met my eyes for an instant and then looked away. The man with the bald patch like Africa turned another page of his *Daily Express*. I glanced at my watch. I was going to be late for Henry if I wasn't careful. Not that it mattered. He could wait or stay as he pleased.

'He wanted me to have a chance to make something of myself,' Martlesham was saying. 'In the colonies everyone was as good as everyone else. No one cared who your parents were. The Church Empire Society made sure you learned a trade.' He looked at his hands. 'I was a carpenter. Did quite well, too. I had my own little business in Toronto. Then came the war, the Great War, I mean, and that was the end of that.'

'You joined up?'

'Hard not to. So there I was, back in England. But at least I had a trade. Probably saved my life, that did. Most of the chaps I joined up with died in the trenches. Me, I spent most of the time on Salisbury Plain teaching heroes like them how to saw props for dug-outs.'

'It must have been nice to see your family again.'

'What family?'

'I thought – Mrs Elstree mentioned your mother, and a sister.'

He stubbed out his cigarette. 'Mother died before I went to

Canada. As for Nancy, she was in Toronto. Mr Youlgreave saw to that as well.'

'She went with you?'

'Yes. The society had an orphanage. She was adopted almost as soon as we got there. Best thing that could have happened to her.'

'It must have been a wrench for you, though. Your last link with home.'

He shrugged. 'It's a long time ago. I can't remember. I didn't go back to Rosington. No point. Nothing to go back to. But I stayed here.'

'Why?'

'Met a girl at a dance in Winchester.' He was looking not at me but through me. 'It was Armistice Day. Vera.' He swallowed, and his eyes focused on me again. 'Died last year.'

'I'm sorry.'

'Anyway. So I let the house in Watford and moved back to town. I've got the flat over the café. That's the story of my life, for what it's worth.' He smiled, revealing a sudden glimpse of the charm he must have had as a younger man. 'I don't know why a pretty young woman like you should bother to listen, but thanks. And I'm glad to have the book.'

'It was no trouble.' I looked at my watch again, this time more obviously. 'I really should be going. I've an appointment.'

'Hope I haven't made you late.' He pushed back his chair. 'Don't worry about paying for your coffee, Mrs Appleyard. Least I can do.'

'Thank you. That's very kind. Don't get up, there's no need.'

We shook hands, and I almost ran out of the café. It was half past twelve and I was going to be very late. Not that it mattered. Anyway, it wasn't that. It was because I'd suddenly realized why the Blue Dahlia Café was making me uneasy.

Turkish tobacco, or something very similar to it. Someone in the café had been smoking it. Perhaps even Martlesham himself. After all, there had been a touch of the dandy about him, from the tiepin to the glistening shoes, from the spotless collar to the silver cigarette case. It was perfectly possible that Francis Youlgreave himself had smoked cigarettes like that at the turn

733

of the century, oval Sullivan Powells, perhaps, or Kyprinos from Cyprus.

The sort of cigarette that made the café smell like *The Tongues of Angels* in my handbag.

27

A gypsy was selling lavender at Piccadilly Circus.

'Have a sprig, sir,' she said to the man in front of me. 'Bring you luck.'

He side-stepped, trying to get round her, but she wouldn't let him. 'Just a little bit,' she whined, 'and bless you, so much luck.'

He brushed her arm from his sleeve and hurried towards the steps to the tube.

'God rot you in hell,' she shouted after him. Then she saw me and the anger left her face and the whine returned to her voice. 'A little bit of lavender, missy? Bring you luck. Young ladies need luck as well as a pretty face.'

I didn't want her to curse me. I felt I had enough bad luck to cope with already. Meeting Martlesham had settled nothing. It had just made matters worse. And now I had to deal with Henry.

I found my purse and gave the gypsy sixpence. A hand like a monkey's paw snatched the money and dropped the lavender in the palm of my hand. The hand was damp and left a smear of dirt on my pale leather glove.

I hurried up Regent Street. It was nearly ten to one. Still clutching the lavender, I hurried through the revolving door of the Café Royal.

If Henry had waited for me, I expected to find him in the bar. But he was standing just in front of me in the lobby and looking almost as dapper as Simon Martlesham in a dark-blue suit with a faint pinstripe. He had a white carnation in the buttonhole and a silk handkerchief poking out of the breast pocket. For an instant

I saw him with Rosington eyes. Mrs Forbury and her Touchies would have thought him a bit of a cad.

'Wendy.' He lunged towards me. 'You're looking beautiful.'

I couldn't stop him embracing me but I turned my head and all he succeeded in kissing was my ear. He smelt familiar, but as smells from the past do. The sort of smells that belonged to you at another time, when you were another person.

'We must celebrate,' he was saying. 'Let's have a drink. Why are you carrying that bit of lavender?'

I looked at the sprig. I had been holding it so tightly that the stain had spread further. The glove was probably ruined.

'I bought it from a gypsy just now.'

'Not like you to be superstitious.' Henry was always quick. 'Is that the effect of Rosington?'

I shook my head and said what about that drink.

We went into the bar. I wrapped the lavender in a handkerchief and dropped it in my handbag. When the waiter came Henry ordered dry martinis.

'Just like when we first met,' he murmured.

'Don't be sentimental. It doesn't suit you.'

But I was glad he'd chosen dry martinis. I needed a slug of alcohol.

'We can have lunch here if you like,' he was saying. 'Or if you'd rather we could go somewhere else. I wondered about the Savoy, perhaps.'

'Where does all this money come from?' I asked. 'Your Hairy Widow?'

'I told you on the phone. I haven't seen her since – since the day I last saw you.'

Luckily the drinks arrived at this moment.

'Cheers,' Henry said, and we drank.

For the next few minutes, neither of us found much to say. We smoked cigarettes, finished our drinks and ordered another round. Henry asked how the Byfields were, and I said they were very well, and that Janet and David sent their love.

'How's Rosie?'

'Very well.'

'Isn't her birthday around now?'

'Last Wednesday.'

736

'She must be – ah –?'

'Five.'

'Perhaps I should send her a present.'

Once again the conversation languished.

'We should talk about the divorce,' I said at last.

'I meant what I said on the phone. I love you.' He sat up, squaring his shoulders. 'I was a bloody fool. Can't we start again?'

'There's no point. There'd be someone else. Some other poor fat widow with a big bank balance.'

'There won't. Because –'

'And where did you go to, anyway? Your solicitor told mine that you'd just vanished.'

'It was a business trip, and I was a little short of cash.' Henry stared at his hands. 'I left a letter with him for you. Did you get it?'

'I told my solicitor to put it in the wastepaper basket.'

It had been about the only useful thing poor Fielder had ever done for me. His unpaid bill was still in my bedroom at the Dark Hostelry. The amount seemed rather large for what he'd achieved.

I said, 'I'm saving up to divorce you.'

'Is there someone else?'

I stared at Henry. He had a little dimple in his chin which made him look like an overgrown baby. I had always found it rather attractive. I wondered what he'd say if I said, *Yes, there is someone else. David.*

'It's none of your business any more.'

'I owe you some money.'

'You owe a lot of people some money.'

'Do you remember Grady-Goldman Associates?'

'I'll hardly forget.'

He nodded. 'When Grady went bust I ended up with about thirty per cent of the stock in Grady-Goldman.'

Aloysius Grady lived like a rich man and talked like one too. He had wanted Henry to set up a European property portfolio for him and then to manage it on his behalf. Henry had put in a lot of work. He had even lent Grady a lot of money for him to give to his daughter, who was studying in the UK, and taken

737

company stock as collateral on the loan. When the crash came, our money vanished and the stock plummeted.

'Just after you – you left,' Henry went on, 'I had a cable from Louis Goldman. A subsidiary of Unilever wanted to buy the company and the shares had gone through the roof. He was the other major shareholder, and he thought we could get them higher if we worked together.'

'Come on, Henry.'

'What?'

'This sounds like another one of your fairy tales.'

'It's not, I promise. That's why I had to leave the country. Louis bought me a ticket. It was all in that letter.'

I tried to remember the Grady-Goldman place. A big compound with a wire fence and lots of huts roofed in corrugated iron. A black watchman making tea. Grady's Rover driving into the compound in a cloud of dust. Cigar smoke catching the back of my throat in a small, hot office. And Grady himself, a big, balding man with wispy red hair who tried to pinch my bottom.

'What did they do? Why did Unilever want to buy them?'

'Machine tools,' Henry said. 'That's why Grady-Goldman seemed a good bet to me in the first place. There're not many people who make them south of the Sahara. Louis had got the company up and running again. They weren't into profit because of the debts Grady had left. But they had the trained workers, they had the plant, and they had the customers.'

'If you're trying to tell me your financial acumen has made you rich, I just won't believe you.'

'It wasn't my financial acumen. It was Louis's. But it was my luck.' He hesitated. 'To be precise, just over forty-seven thousand pounds' worth of luck.'

'Good God.' I thought about the sprig of lavender in my bag. It seemed to have worked retrospectively, and for the wrong person. 'What are you going to do with it?'

'I'm going to give you some.'

I said nothing.

'I've been thinking about all sorts of things lately,' Henry went on, sounding pleased with himself.

'Good for you. It's a big responsibility, isn't it, having all this money to waste?'

'That's just it. Change of plan. I've come to the conclusion that gambling as a career doesn't suit me. I'm thinking of becoming a schoolmaster again.'

I laughed.

'It's not such a silly idea. I was a schoolmaster when you first met me. I rather enjoyed it.'

'Henry,' I said. 'Have you forgotten what happened at the Choir School? They more or less chucked you out. No one's going to give you a job without a reference.'

He looked smug. 'I've thought of that. Though to be honest, I didn't have to do much thinking. Someone else did my thinking for me.'

'Like Louis Goldman? I wish you'd stop being mysterious.'

'You remember I taught at another school before Rosington? Veedon Hall. The Cuthbertsons want to sell up. A friend of mine who's still on the staff wrote to me out of the blue and asked if I knew anyone who might be interested in going into partnership with him. It's a going concern, waiting list as long as your arm, and old Cuthbertson always had a soft spot for me. The price is a snip, too. All it would take is thirty thousand.'

'Then there's nothing to stop you going ahead.'

'I don't want to do it by myself. I want us to do it.'

I shook my head.

'It wouldn't be like burying yourself in the sticks.' He stretched out a hand towards me which I pretended not to see. 'It's not far from Basingstoke. You could be up in town in no time.'

'It's too late.'

'I shouldn't have blurted it out like this. I'm sorry. Look, why don't you think about it for a few days? A few weeks, if you like. Talk to Janet. Let's go and have some lunch.'

After that, my mood changed. I don't know whether it was the alcohol or what Henry had said, but I felt much happier. Perhaps the lavender was doing its job. We took a taxi to the Savoy and had lunch in the Grill Room. Henry wanted champagne.

'Not Veuve Clicquot,' I said. 'I've had enough of widows.'

So he ordered a bottle of Roederer instead. 'Talking of widows,' he said. 'That reminds me.'

He launched into a long, involved story about Grady's widow

739

and her attempts to entrap a Unilever executive for herself or, failing that, for her daughter. He ended up making me laugh. Later I told him about the Dark Hostelry and my job. We compared notes about the inhabitants of the Close.

'There's no need for you to stay in that job if you don't want to,' Henry said over coffee.

'I need to earn my living now,' I said as lightly as I could.

He took an envelope from his jacket pocket and laid it on the table between us. 'That's up to you.'

'What is it?'

'A cheque for ten thousand.'

'You're paying me off? Is that what it is?'

'Don't be silly, Wendy. It's yours. I want you to have it.'

'A divorce settlement?' My voice was rising. 'Is that it?'

His lips tightened. 'At least you won't have to work in a dead-end job if you don't want to, and you won't have to live in Rosington.'

'I'm going to finish the job.'

'You don't *have* to. You can just walk away from it.'

'It wouldn't be fair to Hudson.'

'Wendy, you don't owe him anything. You've done some work for him, he's paid you for it, but there's no reason why you should work any longer than you want to.'

'I know, but I'd like to finish it.'

I watched Henry putting two cigarettes in his mouth, lighting them both and giving one to me. It seemed such a natural thing to do. He hadn't asked, either, just taken it for granted that as he was having a cigarette I would have one as well.

I said, 'Actually, there's another reason.'

'I thought there might be. There *is* someone else, isn't there?'

'It's none of your business. Not now.' Then I laughed at his face, which was pink with champagne and anger. 'OK, there is someone. His name's Francis Youlgreave.'

He ran a hand through his hair, leaving a tuft of it standing up, the way he always did when he was puzzled. 'Youlgreave? Who?'

'You might have come across him at Rosington.'

'The bastard,' Henry muttered.

'He's been dead for fifty-two years. He was one of the canons in the early nineteen-hundreds, and a minor poet as well. He caused a bit of a scandal and they made him leave.'

Henry's face brightened. 'Then Francis and I have got something in common. Besides you, I mean.'

'There's a lot of unexplained things about him. For example, no one seems to know whether he died naturally or committed suicide.'

'At Rosington?'

'No – he died a little later, after they'd made him resign. The story was that he was forced out because he preached a sermon in favour of having women priests.'

Henry raised his eyebrows. 'If you did that in Rosington even today you'd probably get tarred and feathered.'

'There was more to it than that. I keep finding traces of him *now*. But the strangest thing, the thing that worries me, is that something's going on, something I don't understand.'

'What do you mean?'

'Someone else is interested in Francis Youlgreave, someone else is trying to find out about him.'

'Well, why not?'

'No reason. But I think they're doing it secretly.'

'You don't sound very sure.'

I sighed. I wasn't sure. No one seemed to know the little man who looked like a solicitor's clerk, but that didn't mean he was trying to hide his identity. There could be a perfectly innocent explanation for his interest in Francis. And apart from him, what else had I got to worry me? The fact that Mr Treevor kept seeing little men hanging around the Dark Hostelry? Senile dementia does not make for reliable witnesses. Or the pigeon with its wings cut off? Someone's idea of a joke, perhaps, or just a schoolboy with an absorbing interest in biology. Nothing necessarily suspicious, nothing to do with Francis. The smell of what might have been Turkish tobacco clinging to *The Tongues of Angels*? Coincidence.

'It's nothing,' I said. 'Anyway, thank you for lunch. I really ought to be going now.'

'Don't go yet. There's no hurry.'

'I want to go shopping before I catch the train back.'

'Where?'

'I thought I'd start in Piccadilly and walk up Bond Street and then down Oxford Street. And then I can catch a tube or a bus back to Liverpool Street.'

'Sounds arduous. Can't I come too? Carry the parcels? Fight off the footpads?'

'No, Henry. In any case, you'd be bored.'

'I'd like to buy you a present.'

'I don't want a present, thanks. I doubt if I'll buy anything. You wouldn't understand – I just want to look. Shopping in Rosington is like shopping in 1953.'

'I tell you what. I'll buy you some gloves.' He picked up the pair on the table. 'Look at those. Filthy. You *need* some more.'

'All right.' I smiled at him. If money was no object I might as well make the most of it. 'In that case you can buy me a pair from the Regent Glove Company. But they won't be cheap.'

'I should hope not.'

Henry paid the bill and we walked up to the Strand. He wanted to hail a taxi but I had a fit of remorse and wouldn't let him.

'Listen, Henry, you're taking taxis everywhere, you've just given me lunch at the Savoy, you're about to buy me the most expensive pair of gloves I've ever had – the way you're going, that money will be gone in a few months. And why do we need a taxi? There's nothing wrong with a bus.'

'I think Rosington must have given you ideas below your station.' But he took my arm and we walked towards the bus stop. 'After you've done your shopping, let's have a drink before your train. Perhaps even dinner. Or what about a show?'

'Stop it, Henry. Anyway, I won't have time.'

'We could just have a quick drink at Liverpool Street if you want.'

'I don't think that would be a good idea.'

'Why not?'

I stopped so sharply that a man behind us bumped into Henry and swore.

'Henry, nothing's changed. It's over between us. I promised I'd see you for lunch but that's all.' I thought of the Hairy Widow and hardened my heart. 'I'm not going to meet you for a drink.'

He stared at me, looking hurt and angry at the same time. 'But Wendy –'

'I'm sorry, there's nothing you can say that will change my mind.'

I pulled my arm away from his and we walked the rest of the way to the bus stop in silence.

It was about a minute later I changed my mind. The bus came almost at once. It was a double-decker, and I led the way upstairs. I wanted to look out of the window at the streets of London, pretend to be a tourist and not have to talk to my husband.

Henry followed me up the stairs. He was closer than I liked. His nearness oppressed me. It made me nervous and also gave me a pleasure I didn't want. I turned round, meaning to glare at him. As I turned, something caught my eye.

Passengers were still filing on to the platform of the bus. I was just in time to see a small, dark man in a raincoat moving towards a seat on the lower deck. He wasn't wearing a hat. He was bald.

From my vantage point on the stairs, I saw quite clearly that the bald patch was roughly the shape of a map of Africa.

28

The western side of the Cathedral's spire was coated with evening sunlight as heavy as honey. I walked up from the station, occasionally glancing down at my new gloves, which were fine black suede, lined with silk. It was almost a crime to wear them.

In one way it had been a mistake to see Henry, I knew, like scratching a scab until the blood welled up again. On the train I'd kept thinking of him bouncing on top of his Hairy Widow. Henry with his bare, wobbling bottom like a plump baby's, and the widow waving her legs in the air and wearing those oh-so-desirable, dark-blue, high-heeled shoes. It was there in the photograph, captured for all eternity in black and white, in my bedside table at the Dark Hostelry.

I trudged slowly up the hill towards the Porta. I wasn't drunk and I didn't have a hangover, though this was a matter of luck rather than good judgement. But I wasn't exactly sober either. It was more than alcohol. Emotions can intoxicate you as well, even sadness.

Part of the sadness, tied up with Henry in some inexplicable way, was the knowledge I was here in Rosington again. That was one reason why I was walking slowly. I felt as though I were thirteen years old and trying to postpone the moment when I had to go back to Hillgard House at the beginning of term.

The first person I saw when I went into the Close was Mr Gotobed. He was sitting on a bench beside the door of his house, reading the sports page of the *Rosington Observer* and stroking a large ginger cat. He was still in his cassock, which he wore when he was being a verger and conducting the clergy about the Cathedral. When he heard my footsteps, he glanced over the top of the paper.

'Mrs Appleyard.' He stood up quickly, dislodging the cat. 'Lovely evening.'

'Isn't it?' The cat rubbed itself against my leg so I bent down and stroked it. 'This is a fine animal. Is he yours?'

'My mother's. He's not bothering you, is he?'

'Not at all.' The cat purred like a distant aeroplane. 'What's his name?'

'Percy.' Gotobed was blushing. 'My mother says it ought to be spelt with a U and an S.'

I stared blankly at him for a moment. His blush deepened. Then I realized that Gotobed had made a joke. 'Oh, I see! Pursy. Because of his purring. Very good.'

'She's ninety-three, my mother,' confided Gotobed. 'But she's still got her sense of humour and she's as bright as a button. Which reminds me. I told her about that pigeon. You remember?'

'It's not something you're likely to forget in a hurry.'

'Sorry – maybe I shouldn't have mentioned it.'

'No, I'm interested. What did your mother say?'

'She said perhaps there's a loony on the loose in the Close. Like there was last time.'

'Last time?'

'Fifty or sixty years ago. Someone started doing things to animals and things. Not at all nice.'

'What exactly happened?'

He clasped his hands in front of him and his nose twitched. He looked so unhappy I would have liked to stroke him rather than Pursy.

'It's all right,' I said. 'You don't have to worry about shocking me. It just can't be done.'

He gave me a tentative smile. 'If you're sure you want . . . Well, they found a rat without any legs outside Bleeders Hall one morning. And there was a headless cat in the north porch. Mother wasn't sure, but she thought there might have been a bird without any wings as well.'

'And did they ever find out who was doing it?'

'Turned out to be one of the canons. He'd gone queer in the

head, poor chap.' Gotobed was staring at me now, his eyes clear and intelligent. 'You wouldn't have thought many people would remember it now. It's a long time ago. But if someone did, they might be trying to play games with us, don't you think? Like pretending to be a ghost.'

'Do you believe in ghosts, Mr Gotobed?'

'Not me, Mrs Appleyard.' He slapped his hand against his thigh, and there was a *crack* that bounced off the wall of the Porta. 'I only believe in what I can see and touch.'

I made a rapid calculation. If Mrs Gotobed was now ninety-three, she must have been about forty when Francis had left Rosington. 'Was your mother living in the Close then?'

'I don't rightly know. It must have been around then she married Dad. But the way she talked about it, everyone knew what was going on.'

'She must remember a lot about the old days.'

'She remembers more about what happened when she was a girl than what happened yesterday. You know what these old folks are like.' Gotobed beamed like a proud parent. 'Of course, she gets a bit muddled. Thinks I'm Dad sometimes.'

'Do you think she might let me talk to her?' I added hastily, 'I'm interested in the old days because of the Cathedral Library and the dean's exhibition.'

'I could ask her. Mind you, she doesn't see many people now.'

I told him it didn't matter and said good night.

The Cathedral clock struck half past eight. The swallows and martins were doing their evening acrobatics around the Octagon. I walked slowly, aware of my tiredness. In London, I'd found it hard to concentrate on the shops. I suppose the alcohol hadn't helped. And meeting Henry had made me weary too, and so in another way had that business with Simon Martlesham and the little man on the bus.

No doubt tiredness was the reason why I felt someone was watching me. The feeling increased as I neared the door to the cloisters. It was almost as if Francis were pursuing me rather than the other way round. Which was absurd. Ghosts were no more plausible than gods and the idea that either of them, should they exist, should be interested in the living was equally silly. I remembered the lavender in my bag and wondered why I'd been fool enough to buy it.

Better to concentrate on the questions belonging to the here and now. What was Simon Martlesham up to? Was the little bald man the one who had borrowed the library book and stolen cuttings from the 1904 backfile of the *Rosington Observer*? And was he also the man Mr Treevor had seen in and outside the Dark Hostelry, the little dark man who looked like a ghost?

Now the Cathedral was between me and the sun. The path round the east end was in shadow. I walked more quickly. I was within fifty yards of the door to the garden of the Dark Hostelry when I heard the wings.

At first I thought one of the swallows had swooped down to hawk for insects near the ground, and that it had passed close to my ear. But the wing beats were slower and deeper than a swallow's could ever be and I swear I felt the air move. On the other hand, I was in a suggestible mood and everyone knew that the acoustics of the Close were almost as strange as the acoustics of the Cathedral itself. The Close was a network of stone canyons with a battery of idiosyncratic sound effects. David said there was a spot outside the north door where a whisper could be heard clear as a bell at the Sacristan's Gate.

All this galloped through my mind in not much more than a second. I looked up, half expecting to see a bird darting away. There was nothing. A trick of the mind, I told myself; I was tired.

I pushed open the gate of the Dark Hostelry. The sun was on the upper windows of the house and they gleamed like slabs of polished brass. The garden was in shadow. I noticed, as I had on that first day three months ago, how impossibly neat and tidy it was. The Byfields couldn't afford a gardener, and it was all Janet's work. How did she manage, especially now she was pregnant? And why did she bother? She had always been neat, in her possessions as well as in her person. At Hillgard House, her locker in the fourth-form common room had been displayed to all of us as a model of what a locker should be.

I made a resolution that in future I should at least mow the lawn. I walked up the path. I had missed supper but I didn't mind that. It was a long time since lunch at the Savoy but I wasn't hungry.

As usual the door was unlocked. I stepped into the hall. The house was silent. There was definitely an unpleasant smell now. Perhaps it was the drains or a rat had died under a floorboard. But there were no floorboards in the hall, only stone flags. David would have to talk to the chapter clerk.

For a moment I was seized with a dread that history was about to repeat itself, that soon there would be a child's scream from upstairs. The doors to the sitting room, the dining room and the study were all open. I left my hat on the hall table and went down to the kitchen to show Janet my new suede gloves.

She was sitting at the table with the tradesmen's account books in front of her. The books were closed and she was smoking a cigarette. She looked very pale.

'Hello. How did it go?'

'Glad it's over.'

She started to get up. 'I'll put the kettle on.'

'Don't bother.' I sat down beside her. 'Are you all right?'

'Tired. I thought I'd take the weight off my feet.'

'You ought to be in bed.'

'I'll perk up in a moment.'

'Where's David?'

'There's a meeting at the Theo. Coll.' She pushed the cigarettes and matches towards me. 'But tell me, how was Henry?'

'He bought me some very nice gloves.'

Janet stroked them. 'They're beautiful. I won't ask how much they cost.'

'And he also gave me this.'

I took the envelope from my handbag and passed it to Janet. I watched her opening it, watched her eyes widening.

'Wendy, is this a joke?'

'I don't think so.' I explained about Louis Goldman and about Henry going to South Africa. 'Anyway, if I pay it in I'll soon find out.'

'If?'

I concentrated on lighting a cigarette. Then I said, 'He wants to buy a share in a prep school, Veedon Hall, the one he used to teach in before he came here. He asked if I'd come back, if we could start again.'

'And will you?'

'I don't know.' I blew out smoke. 'Half of me thinks, what's the point? You can't take away the past. I'm not even sure I want to.'

Janet said nothing.

'You think I should go back to him, don't you?'

'I don't know.' Suddenly her face began to crumple like a sheet of paper. 'I don't know what I think about anything.'

'It'll be all right. Don't worry.'

She sniffed and a tear fell on the table, just missing Henry's cheque. 'It's probably because I'm pregnant. It's as if all your emotions suddenly belong to someone else.'

I leant across the table and put my arm round her. Her shoulders were shaking.

'Sorry,' she said, 'sorry. I'm not really like this, but I think I must have been bottling it up until you came back. I don't want to bother David with it at present, he's so busy.'

'It's not your fault. Blame the baby. My mother had a craving to eat grass when she was pregnant with me.'

She clung to me for a moment and then relaxed. How could David leave her in this state?

'You've been doing too much,' I said harshly.

'Don't be cross.'

'I'm not cross with you. I'm cross with me.'

'Don't be silly.' She pulled away and looked at me. 'What is it? Something's wrong, isn't it? Was it seeing Henry?'

'I thought it was over. I thought I was past the worst.' I stubbed out my cigarette, wishing the ashtray was the Hairy Widow's face. 'But on the train coming back I kept thinking about – about that woman. At least David doesn't . . .'

'David's got God instead.' She smiled at me to show the words were meant as a joke.

'I'd like to kill the wretched woman,' I said. 'And torture Henry for a very long time.'

'Of course you would.'.

'I must be going round the bend. When I was walking through the Close this evening I had the strangest feeling. I heard wings.

749

It was as if a bird swooped down behind me. Not a swallow or anything like that. Something much larger.'

'It's the acoustics. And you're tired.'

'That's what I told myself.' I looked at her. 'And to be honest I had too much to drink in London. I don't suppose that helped.'

'Don't worry. It's a difficult time.'

'But it's always difficult.'

'You need an early bed. We all do.'

Neither of us spoke for a moment. It was the first time I'd mentioned the drinking, though she must have known about it. But Janet never tried to change me. She always took me as I was. She let me believe I was the strong one.

After a moment she looked at her watch. 'I must go and check on Rosie. I promised I'd go up in ten minutes after I settled her down, and that was ages ago.'

'I'll go.' I stood up, eager to show that I wasn't a complete failure. 'I bought a couple of postcards for her, and if she's awake she can have them now. I need to take my things up anyway.'

I went slowly upstairs, back to that faint but definitely increasing smell in the hall. The sun was completely behind the Cathedral now and the whole house was in shadow. On the next flight, I heard Rosie giggling, an unusual sound – she was not a child that laughed much, partly because she had too much sense of her own dignity. I walked along the landing to the open door of her room. The curtains were still open and through the window I saw the Octagon and the spire, dark against a darkening sky. Rosie giggled again.

'Hello, Rosie, I've –' I broke off.

The room was full of soft, grey light. It was perfectly obvious that there were two heads on the pillow.

'Mr Treevor,' I said.

He sat up in the bed. Rosie was still laughing, snuffling with excitement. Mr Treevor wore his maroon striped pyjamas. His hair looked like a wire brush and he was not wearing his teeth. His eyes were huge in his shrunken face.

'What are you doing here?'

'I was cold,' he said, pushing out his lower lip. 'Rosie's keeping me warm.'

'I'm tickling Grandpa,' Rosie announced, 'and Grandpa's tickling me.'

'Nice and warm now,' Mr Treevor said.

'Then perhaps you'd better go to bed,' I suggested. 'I think it's time for Rosie to go to sleep.'

He extricated himself with some difficulty from the bed-clothes. In the end I had to help him. He tottered out of the room and across the landing. He and Rosie did not say good night to one another. His door closed with a gentle click. I decided the postcards could wait until the morning.

'Are you all right?' I asked Rosie as I tucked her in again.

She nodded, settling her head into the pillow. Her face rolled towards me. The excitement had faded away.

'Where's Mummy?'

'Downstairs. She'll be up to see you soon.'

'But why isn't she here *now*?'

'She will be. She –'

'But I want her.'

'Why? For a particular reason?'

'She always came to see me before.'

'Before what, dear?'

'Before you came.'

'And she does now. But I happened to be passing, and I heard you and Grandpa, and –'

'You take Mummy away from me,' she interrupted. 'You stop her seeing me. You *make* her stay downstairs.'

'Don't be silly, Rosie. You know that's not true.'

She put a thumb in her mouth as though corking it would stop further words falling out. In the fading light her face had become the colour of lard, like one of the marble monuments in the Cathedral and just as hard. I stroked her hair. She turned her head away, dislodging my hand.

'Mummy,' she muttered, so quietly I could pretend not to hear her. 'I want Mummy.'

Didn't Rosie understand I was trying to *help* Janet? Did she really believe I had taken her mother away from her? The trouble with children, I thought, is that they see things differently from grown-ups, and it's so easy for them to get hold of the wrong end of the stick.

751

She muttered something else, in an even lower voice, and this time I really couldn't hear what she said. Not for sure. But it might have been, 'I hate you.'

'Mummy will be up very soon. Don't worry about anything, and sleep tight.'

I squeezed Rosie's shoulder and left the room. Least said, soonest mended. I'd let Janet know that Rosie had wanted her, I thought, as I climbed the stairs up to the second floor and my own bedroom. But perhaps it would be better not to mention Mr Treevor and the tickling. Janet would worry that Rosie might have been scared. She would be concerned about her father, at this further sign that he was growing worse.

This was 1958. We were more innocent then. And adults can get hold of the wrong end of the stick, too.

29

In the morning I went back to work. My visit to London seemed to have given me extra energy. I catalogued more books than ever before. This was despite the fact that I had three visitors.

The first was Canon Hudson, who wanted me to check a draft of the pamphlet for the exhibition in case there were any errors.

My next visitor was Mr Gotobed who stood in the doorway fiddling with the badge of the Cathedral which he wore on a chain round his neck as part of his verger uniform.

'I mentioned to Mother what you said, Mrs Appleyard.' He gabbled the words out as though they were hot. 'She says she'd be pleased to see you if you'd like to drop in for a cup of tea tomorrow afternoon. But she says she hopes you won't mind her not being up and dressed. Of course, if you can't spare the time –'

'It's very kind of her. Please tell her I'd love to come.'

Mr Gotobed coloured. 'Mother's a bit deaf, I'm afraid, so you may have to speak quite loudly.'

'That's all right. Tell her I'm looking forward to it.'

Finally, just as I was thinking of packing up at the end of the day, Canon Osbaston arrived. Under his arm was a large flat package wrapped in brown paper and tied up with string.

'Good afternoon, Mrs Appleyard. I hope I haven't interrupted your labours at a crucial point.'

'Not at all.' I watched him moving down the library, deliberate as a tank.

'Mrs Elstree knew I would be passing nearby and she entrusted me with an errand.'

He ran out of breath and began to puff. I drew out a chair for him and he sat down heavily and laid his package on the table. It was a big chair but his body overflowed around it. He took out a handkerchief and dabbed the bald patch on his little head.

'Dear me, Mrs Appleyard, it is still unseasonably hot.'

'One of the advantages of working here is that the temperature never gets that far above freezing.'

He chortled like a schoolboy in a Billy Bunter story. 'Very droll, Mrs Appleyard. And how are your researches into Canon Youlgreave progressing?'

'Slowly,' I said, playing safe.

He edged his chair a little closer to mine and leant towards me. 'It's really very odd, but someone else has been asking questions about him.'

'Asking you?'

He shook his head. 'Mrs Elstree. Apparently a man came up to her as she was leaving the Theological College one day. It was in the morning, she was going shopping. He said he was writing a book about him. According to Mrs Elstree, he looked quite respectable but he certainly wasn't her idea of a writer.'

'How strange. Did she say anything else about him?'

'Not really. She sent him off with a flea in his ear.' Canon Osbaston settled his glasses more firmly on his nose so he could see me better. 'I wondered if he might be some sort of journalist. But why would a journalist be interested in Canon Youlgreave?'

'I've no idea,' I said with perfect truth.

'Of course, in your case it's very different. In a sense you're treading in his footsteps. Which brings me to my reason for being here.' He smiled, and if tortoises have teeth they must be just like Canon Osbaston's. 'Mrs Elstree was up in the attics the other day. There's a possibility that we may convert some of them into study bedrooms. Be that as it may, she chanced upon something she thought might interest you. As she knew I was practically passing the library door, she asked me to deliver it.'

He moved the parcel a little closer to me. Clearly I was expected to examine it there and then. This took some time because Canon Osbaston felt that dealing with knots was a man's responsibility. This meant he had to find his penknife, cut the string, close the knife, roll the string into an untidy ball and unwrap the brown paper, a process that is far less tedious to describe than it was to watch. The result of his labours was a framed photograph measuring perhaps fifteen inches by twelve. The frame was heavy and dark, its varnish dulled, and the photograph itself was spotted with damp. It showed about twenty people on the lawn in front of a building, which I recognized almost immediately as the Theological College. They were on the croquet lawn in front of the French windows of the Principal's Lodging. On the far left of the photograph were branches from what must have been the beech tree under which Rosie had sat drawing a picture of an angel with a sword.

Several of the people in the photograph were wearing costumes of some sort. Of those who weren't, three of the men were dressed as clergymen.

Canon Osbaston leant closer still. His breath was sour, smelling of ginger. He tapped a long knobbly forefinger against one of the clergymen.

'According to Mrs Elstree, that's Canon Youlgreave.'

So at last I saw Francis, though not as clearly as I would have liked. He was the smallest of the men and he stooped towards the camera as if he'd seen something rather interesting at the base of the tripod. He was wearing a hat, but what I could see of his hair was dark. His nose was long and his eyes were dark, blank hollows.

Canon Osbaston leant a little closer and peered at the photograph. As he did so he rested his right hand as if for support on my left knee.

'Have you noticed the curious clothing, Mrs Appleyard? I wonder if they were engaged in a dramatic production of some sort.'

'Excuse me,' I said, 'your hand.'

He glanced down at his hand and my knee as though seeing them for the first time. 'Good heavens! I'm so sorry.' He removed the hand, although without obvious haste, and gave me another of his tortoise smiles. 'I think the clergyman in the centre must be Canon Murtagh-Smith, one of my predecessors.'

I stood up, moved round the corner of the table and stretched. 'Pins and needles,' I explained.

'How tiresome. I believe regular exercise is the only answer. As for the third clergyman, both Mrs Elstree and I are baffled. In those days we had our own chaplain, so it may be him, or perhaps one of our lecturers.' Seizing the back of his chair with one hand and resting the other on the table, he pushed himself to his feet. 'But I mustn't keep you any longer from your work, Mrs Appleyard.'

'Do thank Mrs Elstree for me. And tell her I know Mrs Byfield will be interested to see the photograph as well.'

'Yes, indeed,' said Canon Osbaston, his eyes bright with understanding. He knew as well as I did that Mrs Elstree had produced the photograph for Janet, not for me. It was Janet who might be the wife of the next principal.

He shuffled down the library, gave me a wave and left. I turned back to the photograph. There were several children in it, including two little girls in white dresses. One of them was standing next to Francis, part of her shielded from the camera lens by his right arm. I stared at her, wishing there were more detail in the print. Then I remembered the magnifying glass in the tray where I kept my pens and pencils. I could see everyone a little more clearly under the glass. If only I could climb into the photograph, I thought, I would understand everything. As it was, all I really discovered was that the two little girls seemed to have white protuberances attached to their shoulders. A moment later, I realized what they were. Wings.

The little girls were dressed up as angels.

30

'You're a big girl,' Mrs Gotobed observed. 'That's nice.'

'Mother!' Mr Gotobed set down the tea tray on a brass table between my chair and his. 'She doesn't always realize what she's saying,' he murmured to me.

'Like me,' Mrs Gotobed continued. 'Wilfred's father used to say I was built like a queen.'

'How lovely.' Nobody had ever told me I was built like a queen but I wished they had.

Mrs Gotobed nodded. She was sitting in a wing armchair with her feet up almost on top of the little coal fire that smouldered in the grate. Her legs were covered with a crocheted blanket. She was wearing what looked like a tweed coat. Her face was long and bony, with pale, dusty skin like tissue paper.

'Milk, Mrs Appleyard? Sugar?'

Watched by Pursy, who was lying in a patch of sunlight on the window ledge, Mr Gotobed blundered around the over-furnished little room. He was wearing an apron over a dark suit made of stiff, shiny material that looked as if it would stand up by itself if its owner suddenly evaporated. The tea service was bone china speckled with little pink roses. We had lovingly laundered napkins, so old that their ironed creases were now permanent, apostle teaspoons, two sorts of sandwiches and two sorts of cake.

'You've gone to an awful lot of trouble,' I said as I accepted a fishpaste sandwich.

'It's no trouble,' Mrs Gotobed replied. 'Wilfred enjoys it. I always say he'll make someone a lovely wife.'

'Mother!'

For the moment we devoted ourselves to eating and drinking. The Gotobeds' house was next to the Porta. Through Pursy's window I saw the Theological College across the green. Rain fell steadily from a sky the colour of the slates of the college's roof. As I watched, two familiar figures emerged from the driveway, the one sheltering under an umbrella held over him by the other.

'There's the bishop,' I said.

Mrs Gotobed looked up. 'And Mr Haselbury-Finch. The dean and Canon Hudson went in a little earlier.'

'Mother knows everything that's going on,' said Mr Gotobed proudly. 'Inside or outside the Close.'

Directly opposite Pursy's window was another which over-looked the chestnuts, the entrance to Canons' Meadow and the road up to the cloisters and the south door.

'So you live in the Dark Hostelry with Mr and Mrs Byfield?'

'That's right.'

'They're a handsome couple. And that little girl of theirs is a beauty. I saw you and her the other day talking to His Lordship and Canon Hudson.'

'Mrs Appleyard is working in the Cathedral Library for Canon Hudson,' Mr Gotobed said in a loud voice, speaking in the vocal equivalent of capital letters.

'I know that, dear. I'm not stupid.'

'No, Mother. Try a slice of this fruit cake, Mrs Appleyard. It was made by one of the Mothers' Union ladies.'

'Just a small slice,' I said. 'I mustn't spoil my supper.'

Mr Gotobed cut three substantial slices and handed them round. Once again silence descended. It was clear that in this household eating and talking were not combined.

'Not bad,' Mrs Gotobed said, wiping her fingers on her napkin, 'though not as good as the ones I used to make. They don't put in enough fruit nowadays.'

'Mrs Appleyard,' announced Mr Gotobed, 'is very interested in the *old* days.'

'There's no need to shout, Wilfred.'

'Because of working in the library and helping with the exhibition. You remember the exhibition, Mother? The one the dean's having in the Chapter House.'

She sniffed. 'Next thing we know they'll be selling cups of tea in the Lady Chapel. I don't know what your father would have said.'

'The dean and chapter have to make ends meet, same as everyone else.'

'It's not right,' Mrs Gotobed said. 'It's the thin end of the wedge, you mark my words.' She cast her eyes up to the ceiling as if searching for consolation there. 'You'd think they'd remember Jesus throwing the moneylenders out of the Temple, being educated men and all.'

'That's not the same thing at all, Mother.'

'Why not?'

I said, 'You must have seen a lot of changes over the years, Mrs Gotobed.'

'Changes?' She snorted, then began to choke. But a second later I realized she wasn't choking, she was laughing. After a moment, she brushed the tears from her eyes with a grubby forefinger. 'This is the sort of place where everything changes and everything stays the same.'

'Now, Mother, that doesn't quite make sense. Do you mean –'

'Mrs Appleyard knows what I mean.'

'Were you thinking about the pigeon your son found?' I asked.

'Oh, that. I suppose so. That and other things.'

'Mr Gotobed said you'd told him it'd happened before, about fifty years ago.'

'Not pigeons, I think.' She took a sip of tea and stared into the glowing coals of the fire. 'I remember a cat. That had lost its head. They found it in the north porch. And there was a rat, too – they found that in Canons' Meadow. And I think there was a magpie that had lost its feet. No pigeons, though.'

'And they found who was responsible?' I prompted. 'One of the canons who wasn't quite right in the head?'

'Oh, no.' Mrs Gotobed held out her cup to her son. 'More.'

He took the cup. 'But, Mother, I'm sure you said –'

'You're getting muddled again, Wilfred.'

She turned to me. 'He sometimes says it's me that's muddled, Mrs Appleyard, but half the time it's him.'

'I'm sure you said it was one of the canons.'

759

'I said they *thought* it might be one of the canons, Wilfred. That's a very different thing. There was a lot of gossip, I remember, a lot of wagging of nasty tongues.'

'Was the canon Mr Youlgreave?'

'Yes, that's the name. How do you know?'

'Just a guess. He used to be the Cathedral librarian so I've come across a few references to him.'

'They didn't like him, that was the long and the short of it. He tried to rock the boat, Mrs Appleyard, and nobody likes people like that.'

'How did he rock the boat?'

'There used to be some dreadful places in Rosington then. Down by the river. He made a fuss about them, tried to get something done.'

'Like Swan Alley.'

'How do you know about Swan Alley?' she snapped.

'Someone mentioned there was slum housing down there.'

'All the land down there was owned by the dean and chapter. They'd let it out, of course, but it was still their land. So they didn't like him pointing the finger. Well, they wouldn't, would they? It's human nature, isn't it? Mind you, Canon Youlgreave did have some funny ideas. They got rid of him in the end. Ganged up on him, I shouldn't wonder. He wasn't a well man.' She shook her head sadly. 'But such a lovely gentleman.'

Mr Gotobed was looking bewildered. 'So it wasn't him after all.'

'What?'

'Cutting up birds and things.'

'How can it be? He's been dead for fifty years.'

'Not now, Mother. Then.'

'There's a copycat about if you ask me.' She stared dreamily into her teacup and then looked at me. 'Like I said, Mrs Appleyard, things don't change, not around here. I said as much to Dr Flaxman only the other day.'

'But who would want to copy something like this?' I asked. 'And who would know about it in the first place?'

'Plenty of people,' she shot back. 'You'd be surprised. Fifty years isn't really a long time.'

'Not when you're your age, Mother,' said Mr Gotobed, beaming nervously and brushing the crumbs from his apron. 'Next thing we know we'll be seeing your telegram from the Queen and your photo in the *Observer*. That *will* be a treat.'

She shook off his interruption like a fly. 'Fifty years isn't long in Rosington.' She waved a hand at the window overlooking the Close. 'Especially out *there*.'

'Just some lad, I expect,' Mr Gotobed said. 'Fiddling around with his penknife. I dare say he didn't mean any harm.'

Mrs Gotobed wrinkled her nose, sipped her tea and wrinkled her nose again. 'This is stewed, Wilfred. That's not very nice for our visitor, is it? Couldn't you make some fresh?'

In an instant Mr Gotobed was on his feet, apologizing, gathering teacups, dropping teaspoons on the carpet, and denying that making a fresh pot would be in the slightest bit troublesome. He picked up the tray and then realized he would have difficulty opening the door. I stood up to do it for him. He edged out of the room, keeping as far away from me as possible.

'Close the door,' Mrs Gotobed told me. 'There's a draught.'

On my way back to the chair, I paused by the mantelpiece. There was a photograph of a boy in a chorister's cassock and ruff.

'Is this Wilfred, Mrs Gotobed?'

She nodded. 'He cried when his voice broke. Always was a silly boy. But kind-hearted, I'll say that.'

I sat down. Now we were alone, she looked younger, as if age was part of a disguise she wore when her son was in the room.

'Have you lived in this house a long time?' I asked.

'That's one good thing about a place like this, about it not changing. They'd had a Gotobed in the Close for the past hundred years, so they didn't want a change when his dad died. Just as well. I don't know what he'd have done otherwise. I don't know where we'd have lived.'

A short, uncomfortable silence followed. Pursy woke and looked first at Mrs Gotobed and then at me. Coals settled in the grate, and the window looking out on the Close rattled in its frame as a squall of rain spattered against the glass.

'If it wasn't Canon Youlgreave cutting up animals,' I said, 'then who was it? Did you ever find out?'

She glanced at me, her face at once sly and unsurprised. 'Not for certain.'

'But you had an idea?'

'There was a boy.'

'Can you remember his name?'

'Simon. Was it Simon?' Her head nodded on to her chest and her eyelids closed. 'Don't mind me if I nod off,' she mumbled. 'And don't go. Wilfred will bring the tea, that will wake me up.'

'Simon who?'

'Simon,' she repeated. 'Good-looking boy. He went away.'

Then the door opened and Mr Gotobed walked backwards into the room carrying the tray. For the rest of my visit the three of us took part in short, intense bursts of conversation, punctuated with pauses when Mrs Gotobed nodded off for a moment.

She was curious about Mr Treevor. She had heard that he was living in the Dark Hostelry.

'I thought I saw someone who might be him the other day,' she said. 'Old gentleman, with a big head, not too steady on his pins. Went into Canons' Meadow. He was by himself.'

'Mr Treevor doesn't go out much,' I said. 'Not by himself.'

But he had gone out on his own on Rosie's birthday. He said he'd gone to feed some ducks.

'That's Mother all over,' Mr Gotobed whispered as he showed me out of the house. 'Likes to know everything about everyone.'

It was only as I was walking back through the Close that I realized Mrs Gotobed had asked me very few questions about myself, and none about how I came to be living in the Dark Hostelry, or the whereabouts of my husband. She must have known that Henry had been sacked from the Choir School. She must have noted my surname. If she asked no questions, then presumably she knew the answers already.

At the Dark Hostelry I found Janet, Rosie and Mr Treevor in the kitchen. Rosie and Mr Treevor were eating cheese on toast. Rosie's doll was on the chair beside her.

'How did it go?' Janet asked.

Rosie pressed the doll's chest. 'Mama!' it said.

'Angel wants more,' Rosie interpreted.

'Coming, darling,' Janet said mechanically.

'It was interesting.' I sat down at the table. 'And she was very protective of Wilfred.'

'Wilfred?'

'Mr Gotobed to you. Mrs G. was a hen with one chick. I think I was being sized up.'

Janet giggled. 'As a future Mrs Gotobed?'

It was the first time I had heard her laugh for days. 'I don't think the current Mrs Gotobed would approve of a woman in my situation.'

I tried to speak lightly but Janet wasn't fooled. All the laughter drained from her face.

'Did you learn anything about Francis Youlgreave?' she asked.

'Not really. Except Mrs Gotobed's a supporter. A real gentleman, she said. She thinks he wasn't liked in the Close because he ruffled too many feathers about the slums by the river. Apparently the dean and chapter owned the freehold.'

I didn't mention Simon. David had told Janet about the pigeon Mr Gotobed had found, but I hadn't yet passed on Mr Gotobed's information that someone else, fifty years earlier, had a penchant for cutting up small animals in the Close. The Byfields had other things on their minds at present, and also I didn't think Janet would thank me, or that David would approve. When I was in Rosington that year, I often had the feeling he was looking for reasons to disapprove of me.

'So Canon Youlgreave remains a man of mystery,' Janet said, cutting the slice of bread into two, half for Rosie, half for Angel.

'What about mine?' Mr Treevor demanded.

'Just coming, Daddy.'

There was something in her voice that alerted me. 'How have you been?'

Janet pushed her hair from her forehead. 'Fine, really. A bit tired.'

Our eyes met. She was tired, so she should rest. But how could she rest with these people in this house?

I said, 'When the weather's cleared up, I'll mow the lawn.'

Janet began to speak, but was interrupted by the slamming of the door in the hall above. She straightened up. Suddenly the tiredness was smoothed away.

'David's home early,' she said. 'That's nice, isn't it, poppet?'

Rosie nodded.

'You've got crumbs on your chin,' Janet went on. 'Wipe them off with your napkin and sit up.'

Rosie obeyed.

Usually David would come down to the kitchen to say hello when he got back from the Theological College, if only for a moment.

Janet took some toast from the grill, added a layer of grated cheese and slid it back. 'I'll just pop up and see if he needs a cup of tea.'

'I'll keep an eye on the toast,' I said.

I listened to Janet's slow footsteps on the stairs to the hall. A moment later I gave Mr Treevor his second slice of cheese on toast.

'Thank you, Mummy,' he said, and seized it with both hands.

He had almost finished by the time Janet came back down-stairs. I knew by her face something was wrong.

'Janet –'

'There was a meeting of the trustees this afternoon,' she said dully. She leant on the table, taking the weight from her feet. 'They've decided to close the Theological College after all.'

31

I was still angry on Thursday morning when the parcel came. I was in the drawing room doing the dusting. The postman knocked at the back door and David answered. He brought the parcel up to me, which I suppose was meant as an olive branch. I recognized the handwriting at once and so I expect did he.

He gave me the parcel and said, 'Wendy, I must apologize.'

'What for?'

'Last night. I know I was upset but I shouldn't have taken it out on you.'

'And on Janet and Rosie,' I reminded him, rubbing salt into the wound. I was in no mood for an apology, and I thought if David was going to put himself on a pedestal as a clergyman, he should have had all the more reason to act like a civilized and Christian human being.

'Yes,' he said mildly. 'You're right.' But the Olivier nostrils flared momentarily and I realized that I was trespassing yet again on the wrong side of an invisible line. Not that I cared. 'In any case,' he went on, 'it was unforgivable of me.'

Suddenly there was no longer any satisfaction in attacking him. 'It's all right. Anyway, it's not me you have to worry about, is it? It's Janet.'

He nodded curtly and left the room. I knew it was pointless to goad him, but if he was angry with me then I was angry with him. There hadn't been much point in his shouting at Janet over supper last night, or in his storming out of the kitchen in the middle of the meal and slamming the door behind him.

If David hadn't been a priest, if he hadn't been a man who habitually kept his emotions so tightly under control, it would have been less shocking. After he'd left, Janet had wept into a tea towel, Rosie had played with Angel in the corner by the dresser, and Mr Treevor had quietly finished off all the untouched food on everyone else's plates.

I sat down on the sofa, turning Henry's parcel over and over in my hands. On Monday Henry had said he wanted to buy a birthday present for Rosie and in the end there hadn't been time that afternoon. He had the cheek to ask me to do it for him, but I'd refused.

It was odd seeing my name in Henry's handwriting, as subtly unsettling as receiving a self-addressed envelope. I undid the string and unwrapped the brown paper. Inside were three books and a letter. *Noddy Goes to Toyland* and *Hurrah for Little Noddy* were by Enid Blyton. He had written Rosie's name inside but in a way they were meant for me. The third book was a slim green volume almost identical to the library book in my bedside cupboard upstairs. It was a copy of Francis Youlgreave's *The Tongues of Angels*.

I opened the letter, which was written on notepaper from Brown's Hotel. He was obviously still doing his best to run through the £47,000 as soon as possible.

My dear Wendy

I hope Rosie likes the Noddy books. Noddy looks like an odious little twerp to me, but perhaps I'm not the best judge.

Anyway, over to Youlgreave. I've done a little checking. There is a Farnworthy collection listed in the catalogue of the British Museum Library – mainly theology. It doesn't include the sermons of Dr Giles Briscow, though the library does have a late-seventeenth-century copy of that. So presumably it's not the one that Youlgreave had, if Youlgreave's ever existed.

Now for the big news. On Tuesday I went to the Blue Dahlia only to find your little bald man just leaving. I followed him back to Holborn. He's got an office over a tobacconist's. Harold Munro, Ex-Detective Sergeant Metropolitan Police, Private Investigations & Confidential Enquiries Undertaken. That's what it said on his card in the tobacconist's window. And I know it's him, because he came

into the shop for some cigarettes while I was there and the
tobacconist called him Mr Munro.

Munro asked the tobacconist to take any messages the next
day, that was Tuesday, because he had to be out of the office.
The tobacconist said where was he going, and hoped it was
somewhere nice. And Munro said it was a place called Roth,
up the Thames near Shepperton.

There were footsteps in the hall and I looked up. Mr Treevor
had come up from the kitchen and was moving towards the
downstairs lavatory.

'Mr Treevor?' I called.

He paused, his hand on the lavatory door. 'Yes?'

'You know the man you saw watching the house from the
High Street?'

'I've seen him before,' Mr Treevor said. 'I'm pretty sure he's
a ghost.'

'Was he bald?'

'Might have been.' Mr Treevor twisted the handle of the
lavatory door. 'Yes, I think he was.'

'And can you remember the shape of his bald patch? You must
have seen it from above when he was in the High Street.'

'It wasn't a nice shape. He wasn't a nice man.'

'Was it triangular? A bit like a map of Africa?'

'I expect so,' said Mr Treevor obligingly, vanishing into the
lavatory and locking the door behind him.

I went back to Henry's letter.

So next morning I went down to Waterloo and caught a train
for Shepperton – Roth is too small to have a station. In fact,
Roth hasn't got much of anything besides a church, a bus
shelter and a pub. It's one of those villages that got swallowed
by the suburbs and apart from a whacking great reservoir and
one or two fields that the builders forgot, all you can see are
houses.

But there's a sort of green where the bus shelter is and
the pub. This seems to be the centre of the place and
I reckoned if Munro came to Roth he'd probably come
there sooner or later. I spent about an hour having a

cup of coffee in a ghastly little café, all chintz and horse brasses. No luck there. When it was opening time, I pottered along to the pub. Luckily our Harold had had the same idea. He was talking to an old codger in the snug, so I nipped into the lounge bar, got myself a drink and settled down for a spot of eavesdropping.

I wonder if he's ex-Metropolitan Police because they kicked him out for inefficiency. I sat at the bar pretending to read the paper. I could hear some of what they were saying. Munro seemed to be asking about the Youlgreaves. They mentioned someone called Lady Youlgreave who lives in the Old Manor House (just down the road). Unfortunately some people came in and I couldn't hear very well, because people were talking loudly on the other side of me.

But I heard the name Francis Youlgreave several times. The old codger was rabbiting on about a place called Carter's Meadow. I think Youlgreave may have upset a neighbour by doing something beastly to a cat there.

Munro left soon afterwards. The last I saw of him, he was walking fast down the road to the station.

I didn't want to follow, because I thought it might make my interest in him a little too obvious. So I had a look at the church, which is small and old. Francis Youlgreave is buried here – there is a memorial tablet in the chancel to him. All very discreet – just the family crest, his name and the dates of his birth and death.

The only other thing was the poems. There was a box of second-hand books near the door, threepence each, all profits to the Church Restoration Fund. One of them was some poems by Francis Youlgreave, which I thought you might like. I had a look at it on the train back to town, and I couldn't make head or tail of it. Nutty as a fruit cake, as your mother used to say.

On Thursday, I'll try and find out something about Martlesham and I'll give you a ring in the evening. With luck you'll get this before I phone.

I meant everything I said on Monday. I know I've been a bloody fool but don't let's throw it all away. If you haven't cashed that cheque, please do.

All my love,

Henry

I don't know why, but that letter made me want to cry. I suppose it underlined how far Henry and I had travelled since we married, and especially since I found him with his Hairy Widow on the beach.

I went up to my room with the parcel. I'd have to find some paper to wrap up the present for Rosie. The house was very quiet. Janet had taken Rosie to school, David was in his study and Mr Treevor was in his room. I mounted the second flight of stairs up to my landing. When I put the books in my bedside table, I noticed the sprig of lavender resting on Henry's cheque beside the gin bottle. I didn't feel lucky. Just miserable.

I lit a cigarette. I was in no hurry to go to work. I stared at the photograph Canon Osbaston had lent me. It was propped up on an old washstand in the corner of the room behind the door. The trouble was, nothing made sense, then or now. What the hell were Martlesham and Munro up to? If they wanted to find out about Francis, why couldn't they do it openly? Perhaps there was some obvious explanation staring me in the face which I couldn't grasp because I was too busy making a mess of my life and watching Janet and David making a mess of theirs. Where did the mutilated pigeon come in? And what about the little man Mr Treevor saw, the little man like a shadow who might or might not be the same as, or at least overlap with, Harold Munro, the private investigator with a bald patch the shape of Africa?

I picked up the photograph and took it to the window so I could see it better. There, according to Mrs Elstree, was Francis Youlgreave. Hero or villain? Madman or saint? If I could climb into the blurred monochrome world of the photograph and talk to him for five minutes, I would at least find the answers to those questions. And perhaps I would also find the answers to others in the present.

I stubbed out my cigarette and got ready to go to the library.

When I went downstairs I found David in the hall. He was wearing his hat and raincoat and bending over the oak chest. He poked his umbrella between it and the wall.

'What's up?' I asked. 'Lost something?'

'It's this smell.' He jabbed the umbrella viciously downwards. 'I wondered if there's something got trapped down here. I can *feel* something.'

'Why don't we move the chest out?'

'It may not be terribly pleasant. If it's a dead rat, for example. And wouldn't the chest be rather heavy for you?'

'No, it wouldn't,' I said. 'But are you sure you can manage?'

Those nostrils flared, but he bit back the temper and nodded. There were handles at either end of the chest. We lifted it a few inches away from the wall, easy enough with two of us, though hard for one person to do without scraping the chest on the flagstones.

Wedged in the angle between the wall and the floor was a mass of feathers and bone. The smell was suddenly much stronger.

David said, 'What the hell –?'

I touched his arm. 'We must get it out of the way before Janet sees it.'

Not it – them.

As if on cue, the kitchen door slammed, and we heard Janet's footsteps coming up the stairs to the hall.

32

'He'll have to go,' David said. 'You must see that, Janet.'

She chewed her lower lip. 'We don't know it was him.'

'Who else could it have been?' He sighed, rather theatrically. 'Rosie?'

'Of course not.'

'It's a symptom of severe mental illness. He needs to be under proper medical supervision.'

'But he'd *hate* it if we put him in a home.'

There was a sudden rushing of water and the bolt on the door shot back. Mr Treevor slipped out, walking backwards as if from a royal presence, peered into the empty lavatory and carefully closed the door. Only then did he turn round and see the three of us.

The chest was still pulled away from the wall. David and Janet were facing each other across it. I was on my hands and knees, eavesdropping while sweeping up the mess with the coal shovel and brush from the drawing-room fireplace. The smell was worse, so I was breathing through my mouth. I tried not to look too closely at the wings because I thought there might be maggots.

Mr Treevor was carrying *The Times*. He tapped it importantly and said, 'Good morning. I can't stop and chat, I'm afraid. I must check my investments.'

'Daddy –' Janet began.

He paused, his foot already on the first stair. 'Yes, dear?'

'Nothing.'

He smiled at all three of us. 'Oh well, I must be on my way.'

We listened to his footsteps mounting the stairs and waited

for the slam of his bedroom door. I shovelled the wings on to a sheet of newspaper, part of yesterday's *Times*, and wrapped it into a parcel. I could cover it with brown paper and string, put a stamp on it, and send it through the post. To Henry? To his Hairy Widow? I shook my head to shake the madness out of it. Perhaps madness was infectious, and this house was riddled with its germs.

David glanced at his watch. 'We'll talk about it this evening,' he said to Janet. 'But I'm afraid he can't stay here.'

'It could have been anyone,' Janet burst out. 'We don't lock the door in the day. They could have just walked in.'

'Why should they bother?' David picked up his briefcase. 'I have to go. Canon Osbaston's expecting me.'

He and David were meeting to discuss ways of reversing the decision to close the Theological College. The trustees' change of heart was due to the diocesan architect's unexpectedly gloomy report on the fabric of the Theological College. Apparently it needed thousands spent on it, quite apart from the cost of the proposed modernization programme. But there were a number of other considerations which had not been taken into account. David had lectured Janet and me about them last night. There was the question of whether the trustees were legally entitled to close down the college and divert its endowment to the wider needs of the diocese. In any case, shouldn't they seek a second opinion from another, and more objective, surveyor? There was also the point that one of the trustees had been absent. It might be possible to raise extra funds from sources outside the diocese. And then there was the bishop. David was seriously disappointed in him. Instead of throwing his weight behind the Theological College, as he'd led everyone to expect he would do, he had abstained when it came to the vote. But if there were a new vote, he might be persuaded to change his mind.

'It's the dean and Hudson who are the real problem,' David had told us, not once but several times. 'Not that report – they're just using it as an excuse. But they don't realize what they're destroying. Once the college is closed, they'll never be able to get it started again.'

I watched him through the glazed door as he strode down the garden path to the gate into the Close, the rain pattering on his umbrella. What he hadn't mentioned last night, but what Janet and I knew, was that if his career was a boat, it had just hit a rock. The principal's job would have been perfect for him, and according to Janet it would have almost certainly led to higher things.

But with that no longer a possibility, what was David going to do? He couldn't stay here as a minor canon for ever. Unless a friendly bishop could be persuaded to pull a tasty rabbit out of a hat, at best he'd have to become a chaplain to a school or college and at worst he'd end up as a parish priest in the back of beyond.

I put the parcel in the dustbin. Before going to the Cathedral Library I had a cup of coffee with Janet because that was the only way I could persuade her to sit down for ten minutes.

'I'm sorry about David being so rude,' she said. 'He's so upset he doesn't know what he's doing.'

'It's not surprising.'

'But it's not fair of him to take it out on everyone.'

'I'm not sure I'd behave much better if I was in his shoes. Losing a job you've –'

'It's not just the job. It's Peter Hudson.'

'I don't understand.'

Janet wrinkled her forehead. 'He's the only person in the Close David really admires. He says he's got a first-class brain.'

'Lucky him.'

'David respects him. He'd like Peter to *like* him.'

'So it must have made it worse that he was the one who wanted to close the Theo. Coll.?'

She nodded. 'I think he hoped that Peter would change his mind at the last moment. Not that there was ever much chance of that.'

'Men can be such babies.' I took our cups and saucers to the sink.

'The funny thing is, I think Peter *does* like David. June said something once . . . Wendy, leave the washing-up. You must go to work.'

Janet became almost cross when I tried to help, so I left her in the kitchen, with the suds up to her elbows. At the library, I began with the proofs for the Chapter House exhibition, which didn't take long. Despite his poetry, Francis hadn't earned a place in the dean's roll of honour. When I'd finished, I took the marked-up proofs to the Chapter House. Canon Hudson was there with Mr Gotobed, directing two of the Cathedral workmen as they moved display cases around the big room. Mr Gotobed beamed shyly at me as I came in.

'Thank you for tea yesterday,' I said. 'It was nice meeting your mother too.'

Hudson looked sharply at me. I was about to give him the proofs when I saw that there was another person in the Chapter House. Mr Treevor perched like a little black bird in one of the niches which ran round the walls below the great windows. He was very close to the model of the Octagon and was staring at it with huge, fascinated eyes.

'Thanks for doing that.' Hudson skimmed through the proofs. 'Not too many problems, then?'

'No. Is Mr Treevor all right?'

'He's no bother.' Hudson looked up. 'He wandered in a few minutes ago.'

'It's just that he doesn't normally go out by himself now.'

'Then if Mrs Byfield is at the Dark Hostelry, perhaps you could take him home? I wouldn't like her to be worried.'

I went over to Mr Treevor, laid a hand on his arm, smiled at him and told him it was time to go. He nodded and put his arm through mine. In the archway leading to the cloisters he stopped to wave at the men in the Chapter House. They waved back.

Outside it was still raining. I put up my umbrella. The pair of us walked slowly through the Close.

'I saw him going into the Chapter House,' Mr Treevor confided.

'Who?'

'The dark little man. I saw him in the garden, you see, so I followed him. He went into the Chapter House but he must have gone when I wasn't looking. He wasn't there when we left.'

'Do you see him a good deal?'

Mr Treevor considered the question. There was a drop of moisture on the end of his nose and I didn't think it was rain. I watched it trembling and wished it would fall.

'Yes, he's often around. You don't think he could be my brother?'

'I didn't know you had one.'

'Nor did I, but I think I might. It's possible they didn't tell me. And it would make sense, wouldn't it?'

In the Dark Hostelry, we found Janet in the kitchen scrubbing the floor. She hadn't noticed her father's departure.

'You shouldn't be doing that,' I said. 'Leave it for the char-woman.'

'I was going to,' Janet said, 'but Daddy spilled porridge on the floor this morning and then Rosie stepped in it.'

'Then you should have asked me.'

'I can't ask you to do everything. It's not fair.'

'Why not? After all, you won't be pregnant for ever. Anyway, I must run. I'll see you at lunch time.'

'You know I've got the Touchies this afternoon?'

Mr Treevor wandered into the kitchen. He drew back the sleeve of his jacket and ostentatiously consulted his wristwatch. 'I see it's lunch time. I've washed my hands.'

Janet glanced at her own watch. 'Did you forget to wind your watch last night? It's only quarter past ten.'

'But I'm hungry.'

'That's all right, Daddy. Don't worry. You can have some bread and dripping to be going on with.'

Mr Treevor looked at his watch again. 'But I was sure it was one o'clock.'

'What's on your wrist?' Janet said, taking a step nearer to him. 'Have you cut yourself?'

He held out his arm, and stood, head bowed, waiting for her to examine it. Janet pushed back the watch. The strap had partly concealed a gently curving scratch about two inches long. Part of it had been deep enough to draw blood, now dried. The blood was on the inside of Mr Treevor's shirt cuff. The second hand was still sweeping round the dial of the watch. The hour and minute hands stood at seventeen minutes past ten.

'How did you do that?' asked Janet.

'I must have caught it on a nail when I went out for my walk.'

Janet and I exchanged glances. Mr Treevor sat down at the

kitchen table and asked how many slices of bread and dripping he could have. I went back to work. For the next two hours I catalogued library books. There were no surprises either, not unless you count a bound volume of *Punch* for 1923. I was bored, but the boredom was a kind of relief. It was better to be bored than to worry about Janet and about Mr Treevor and his ghostly brother and about what Simon Martlesham might be up to.

At a quarter to one I locked the library and went back to the Dark Hostelry for lunch. We had bread and soup, followed by cheese and fruit. Mr Treevor ate in silence as though his life depended on it. Janet and I made sporadic attempts to start a conversation, but our minds were on different things and in the end we gave up.

After lunch I washed up while Janet went to lie down for half an hour. I took her a cup of tea, but she was so deeply asleep I tiptoed away without waking her.

I had my own tea in solitary state in the drawing room. I fetched *The Tongues of Angels* to read, the copy Henry had sent me. It was just possible, I thought, I might be able to trace the former owner of the book, who might have known him. Or there might be marginal notes. Or the book might turn out to be Francis's own copy.

But Francis hadn't read this book. No one had – the pages were still uncut. I fetched the paperknife from Janet's bureau and worked my way through, reading scraps of verse as I turned each page. There were my old friends Uriel, Raphael, Raguel and Co. There were the children of Heracles, sliced into bits by their dreaming spellbound father. There was the cat watching the pharaoh's children die, and the slaughter of the stag on Breakheart Hill.

I turned back to the beginning of the book and noticed something I'd missed when I'd looked at it before. There was an epigraph, and I knew at once where it had come from, knew the very book Francis had taken it from.

Nay, further, we are what we all abhor, Anthropophagi and Cannibals, devourers not onely of men, but of our selves; and that not in an allegory, but a positive truth: for all this

mass of flesh which we behold, came in at our mouths; this
frame we look upon, hath been upon our trenchers; in brief,
we have devour'd our selves.

I'd found this very passage marked in the *Religio Medici* which
had once belonged to Francis. It was an oddly intimate discovery, as though I had sliced open his mind with Janet's
paperknife, and now I was seeing something that perhaps only
he himself had seen before.

I turned the page and glanced at the table of contents. For
one vertiginous moment I thought I was falling. Or rather that
everything else was falling away from me. It was exactly the
sensation I had felt on the afternoon near the beginning of my
stay in Rosington when David had taken Janet and me up the
west tower of the Cathedral. This time there was no Janet to put
her hand on my sleeve and murmur that if tortoises waddled,
they would waddle like Canon Osbaston. I shut my eyes and
opened them again.

Nothing was altered. I hadn't imagined it. The table of contents wasn't as it should have been. As before, it listed all
the poems in the collection under their appropriate angelic
sub-heading. But there weren't seven archangelic sub-headings
now, as there were in the copy of the book I had borrowed from
Rosington Library. There were now eight. The new sub-heading
came at the end – 'The Son of the Morning', which sounded like
a suitable pseudonym for an angel – and it contained only one
poem, 'The Office of the Dead'.

I think now that the oddest thing of all was the violence of
my reaction. The poem shocked me before I'd read it, before I
knew why it was shocking. It didn't make sense, any more than
the fact I had smelled something unpleasant in the hall before
Mr Treevor could have put the pigeon's wings there. There are
some things I still don't understand.

I turned back to the title page. At last I saw what should have
stared me in the face as soon as I opened Henry's parcel. I had
expected this book to be called *The Tongues of Angels*. After all,
it looked like *The Tongues of Angels* and Henry had said it was
The Tongues of Angels. And most of its contents were identical in
every way to those of *The Tongues of Angels*.

This book was called *The Voice of Angels*.

I turned back to the title page. Instead of being published by Gasset & Lode, *Voice* had been 'privately printed for the author'. Everything else was the same as far as I could tell – the date, the typeface, even the paper.

I turned the pages to the end of the book. The new section had its own epigraph, taken apparently from the fourth section of the *Celestial Hierarchies* of Dionysius the Areopagite, whoever he was.

> They, above all, are pre-eminently worthy of the name Angel because they first receive the Divine Light, and through them are transmitted to us the revelations which are above us.

The poem was long and very obscure, even by Francis's standards, and written in the painfully archaic language he had liked so much. I skimmed through it. As far as I could tell, it was in the form of a conversation between the poet and a passing angel. The angel told Francis why he'd left his principality and come down among the sons and daughters of men. The angels had the gift of eternal life, it seemed, and they wanted to share it with a handful of suitably qualified humans. In fact, according to the angel, he and his friends had just about everything in their gift.

I didn't like the poem – it made me feel uncomfortable, and I certainly didn't begin to understand it. On the whole, I thought it was just another version of the old Christian claptrap about death being just a gateway to eternal life. What was so wonderful about life that you should want it to go on for ever?

I closed the book with a snap and tossed it on to the table by the sofa. It slid across the polished wood and almost fell off. Why had Francis bothered to print a separate edition of *The Tongues of Angels*? Was there something about 'The Office of the Dead' that he didn't want the rest of the world to see? If so, what? Or was it simply that Gasset & Lode had refused to print it in the commercially published edition because it was such a bad poem?

The rain had stopped at last and a pale sun was trying to force its way through the clouds. I decided to have a walk before I went back to work. I needed to clear my head. I put on my hat and raincoat and went into the Close. There was a farm on the other side of the Theological College. If the ground wasn't too muddy I'd get out of the city for half an hour and walk among fields, dykes and hedgerows that sloped down to the Fens.

But I never even left the Close. Just as I reached the Porta, I heard the tinkle of a handbell, uncannily similar to the one we used in the Dark Hostelry to let people know a meal was ready. Then came a jangling crash. I looked towards the Gotobeds' cottage. One of the first-floor windows was open. A hand fluttered in the room behind the window.

I walked over to the cottage and looked up. 'Hello, Mrs Gotobed. How are you?'

The hand appeared again, beckoning me. I couldn't see her face, but the sound of her voice floated down to me.

'The door's unlocked. Come upstairs.'

I picked up the bell from the flagstone path, went inside and up the stairs to the little sitting room. There were several changes since I had seen it last. For a start, Mrs Gotobed was sitting at the window overlooking the Close with Pursy on the ledge between her chair and the glass. Secondly, the room had not been smartened up for a visitor. The remains of her lunch were on a tray beside her, the commode was uncovered, and she looked as if she hadn't bothered to brush her hair since yesterday.

'Is there something I can do?' I asked.

'Have you seen him?' she hissed at me.

'Mr Gotobed? Not recently, not since this –'

'Not him. That man who was trying to get in.'

'What man?'

'There was a fellow in a black overcoat trying to get in.' Her voice was shaking, and she looked older than she had yesterday. 'I've never seen him before. Though I didn't get a good look at him, me being above and him wearing a hat.'

'What happened?'

'He knocked on the door. I was asleep, nodded off after my dinner, didn't hear him at first. Then I looked out to see who it was and there he was. He tried the door handle. He was about to come in, murder me in my sleep, I shouldn't wonder. I called down, "What do you think you're doing?" and he glanced up at me and scarpered. Out through the Porta, and the Lord knows where he went then. If I'd been a couple of years younger, I could have got to the other window to see where he went.'

'It's all right,' I said, drawing up a chair and sitting beside her. I took one of her hands in mine. Her skin was as cold as a dead person's. 'Would you like me to fetch Mr Gotobed, or the police?'

She shook her head violently. 'Don't go.'

'I won't. Can you remember anything else about this man?'

Her fingers gripped mine. 'Black hat, black coat. I think he was a little fellow, though I can't be sure as I was above him, you see.' She breathed deeply. 'Bold as brass,' she muttered. 'In broad daylight, too, and in the middle of the Close. Wouldn't have happened when I was a girl, I'll tell you that. It's been one of those days, Mrs Appleyard, I don't mind telling you. I was all shook up to start with, but I didn't expect something like this.'

'Shall I make you a cup of tea?'

'Later.'

'I'm sure he won't come back. Not now you've frightened him off.'

'How can I be sure of that?'

There wasn't any way you could be sure. Once you're frightened, you're frightened and common sense doesn't come into it.

'Could the man have been a tramp?'

'He could have been a parson for all I know. All I saw was the black hat and black coat, I told you.' Suddenly she paused and stared at me. 'Tell you one thing, though, his shoes were clean. If he was a tramp, he was a very particular one.'

Another possibility was that Mrs Gotobed had misinterpreted the situation altogether. Perhaps it had been a door-to-door salesman paying a perfectly innocent call. He might have been as frightened of her as she was of him.

'What a day, eh?' said Mrs Gotobed. 'First poor Pursy, and now this.'

We both looked at the cat who was still sprawled at his ease on the window ledge. He had taken no notice of either of us since I had come in.

'He came in this morning like a bat out of hell,' Mrs Gotobed said. 'Through the kitchen window, we keep it open a crack for him, and Wilfred said he broke a vase he was in such a hurry. Came streaking up here and jumped on my lap. He doesn't do that very often unless he wants something. Cats aren't stupid.'

She rested her hand on Pursy's fur. He turned his head and stared out of the window, ignoring her. It was only then that I saw that his left ear was caked with blood.

'What happened to him?'

'Must have got into a fight. The other fellow nearly had his ear off.'

I scratched the cat gently under its chin with one hand and with the other smoothed aside the matted fur round the base of the ear. It looked as if a single claw had sliced through the skin near where the ear joined the scalp. A claw or a knife? At least the blood had dried and if the wound wasn't infected it should heal easily. Pursy pulled his head away from me and examined me with amber eyes.

'Poor little fellow,' Mrs Gotobed mumbled. 'When he was a kitten, he was such a scrap of a thing. Just like a little baby.' Her hands turned and twisted in her lap. 'You've not had children then, you and Mr Appleyard?'

'No.'

'Not yet,' she amended. 'Don't leave it too long. I didn't have Wilfred till I was forty, and then it was too late to have more.' Her jaw moved up and down, up and down as if she were chewing her tongue. 'I never had much time for children. But it's not the same when it's your own. You feel differently somehow. And it never goes away, neither. Sometimes I look at Wilfred and I feel like he's a baby all over again.'

'I'm sure he's a good son.'

'Yes. But that's not to say he isn't a silly boy sometimes. I don't know what he'll do without me to look after him, and that's the truth. Lets his heart rule his head, that's his problem. If he could find himself a nice wife, I'd die happy.'

I wondered if she suspected I was dallying with her son's affections and was therefore warning me off. For a moment we sat in silence. I stroked Pursy, who rewarded me with a purr.

'This cut,' I said. 'I think this might have been done with a knife.'

Mrs Gotobed wrinkled her nose. 'Shouldn't be surprised. They're everywhere, you know.'

'Who are?'

'Mad people. Ought to be locked up.'

'Does this remind you of what happened before?'

'That pigeon Wilfred found?'

I nodded.

'What I'd like to know is where the wings went.'

'And it's not just the pigeon, is it? What about fifty years ago and all the things that happened then?'

Her shoulders twitched. 'Same thing, another person.'

'You said in those days a boy was doing it. A boy called Simon.'

'Did I?'

'It couldn't be him, could it?'

She shook her head. 'He went away. Years ago.'

'But he might have come back.'

'Why would he do that? Nothing to come back *for*.'

'I don't know. Was his surname Martlesham, by the way?'

'Might have been. I can't remember. Why?'

'I found something in the Cathedral Library which mentioned him meeting Canon Youlgreave. Was there a boy called Martlesham?'

'Oh, yes.'

'Who was he?'

'He used to clean the boots and things at the Palace.'

'Where were you living then?'

'Down by the river.'

'In Swan Alley?'

She sighed, a long broken sound like rustling newspaper. 'No – Bridge Street. Over a shop.'

'Not far away. Did you know the Martlesham family?'

'Everyone knew the Martleshams.' She licked her lips. 'The mother was no better than she should be. Called herself missus but she was no more married than I was in those days.'

'Let's see if I've got this right. Simon was the eldest, and he worked at the Palace. And then there was a sister?'

'Simon was always going to make something of himself. Ideas above his station. Nancy must have been five or six years younger. Funny little thing, black, straight hair, always watching people, never said very much. Never heard her laughing, either, not that there was anything to laugh about in Swan Alley.'

'What happened to them?'

'The mother died in childbirth. Don't know who the father was. It was around that time Simon went a bit queer in the head. But Canon Youlgreave helped him.'

I waited. Pursy's paw dabbed at a fly on the windowpane. The sun had broken through the clouds. There was a big puddle near the chestnuts and two schoolboys in short trousers were trying to splash each other.

'He heard their mother had died, and he helped Simon emigrate. Paid for him to learn a trade, as well. And he found someone to adopt Nancy.'

'So Nancy emigrated as well?'

'Might have.' Blue-veined lids drooped over the eyes. 'I can't remember.'

The front door opened. I turned in my chair, half fearing and half hoping that the little man in black had come back. But Mrs Gotobed didn't stir. There were footsteps on the stairs, heavy and confident. Then Mr Gotobed came into the room. He saw me, and the air rushed out of his mouth in a squeak of surprise.

'It's all right,' I said. 'Your mother's had a bit of a shock, but she's all right now.'

'It's all wrong,' Mrs Gotobed said, 'frightening people like that.'

33

As the evening went on, I felt increasingly annoyed with Henry. It was true that we hadn't arranged a time for him to ring, but I naturally assumed he'd phone while Janet was out with the Touchies, as he had last week. He didn't.

I made beans on toast for Rosie and Mr Treevor. I banged the plates down on the table, not that they noticed, and had a minor tantrum when I couldn't find the vegetable knife. They didn't notice that either. It was stupid, but I wanted to talk to him. He might be able to make more sense out of *The Voice of Angels* and what Mrs Gotobed had said than I could.

After I'd washed up and done the vegetables for the grown-ups' supper, I fetched the book and went through 'The Office of the Dead' again. There were some grisly bits which reminded me of 'The Children of Heracles' and 'Breakheart Hill'. Blades sliced through flesh, bones cracked asunder. There was a particularly disgusting passage about a bleeding heart. I was trying to work out what the angel wanted the poet to do with this when Mr Treevor tottered into the kitchen.

'Am I Francis Youlgreave?' he asked.

'No,' I said. 'You're John Treevor.'

'Are you sure?'

'Absolutely sure.'

'It's only that I thought someone said I was Francis Youlgreave. But if you're sure I'm not I must be John after all.'

'Who said you were Francis Youlgreave?' I asked.

'Someone I saw this morning. When I was out.'

'In the Chapter House, do you mean?'

'Yes. He was the little man near the winkle thing.'

'The what?'

'You know, that thing that's a bit like a willie when it's big.' He stared at me, his face suddenly aghast. 'Oh dear. Shouldn't I have said that?'

'It's all right. Don't worry. The thing to remember is, you're John Treevor.'

'Yes,' said Mr Treevor. 'I know.'

He went upstairs again, leaving me to remember the scene in the Chapter House with the model of the Octagon, which was like no willie I'd ever seen. Besides Mr Treevor, the other men in there had been Mr Gotobed, Canon Hudson and two of the Cathedral workmen. Mr Gotobed and the workmen were all big and burly. Canon Hudson was small but not particularly dark. I gave up the puzzle just as the garden door opened and Janet called downstairs that she was back.

'That was extraordinary,' she said when she came down to the kitchen. 'You'll never guess who the Touchies talked about.'

'Henry?'

'Francis Youlgreave.' She filled the kettle at the sink, raising her voice to be heard over the rushing water. 'According to Mrs Forbury, they used to call him the Red Canon.'

'How does she know?'

'Because she grew up in Rosington. Her father was the vicar of St Mary's.'

'She can't have known him personally, can she? She doesn't look much more than fifty.'

Janet shook her head. 'She remembers people talking about him when she was growing up. Did you know he used to smoke opium?'

'She's pulling your leg.'

'She wasn't. *She* believes it, and so do all the other Touchies.'

'The Red Canon – so he was a Socialist?'

Janet shrugged. 'Or he had one or two vaguely Socialist ideas. I doubt if they'd seem very radical now. There was that business about the slums near the river. Youlgreave made himself unpopular by going on about it ad nauseam at chapter meetings. And what was worse, much worse, he was far too free and easy with the servants. Mrs Forbury said he invited working-class children into his house and gave them unsuitable ideas.'

'What does that mean exactly?'

'She was far too coy to say. But she mentioned his experiments with animals. Someone claimed he'd cut up a cat, so people started talking about witchcraft. There were complaints to the dean, who was in a very awkward position because Youlgreave was some sort of cousin. But he had to do something about it because the police were involved. Not officially, I think, but someone had a word in the ear of the chief constable.'

'They certainly laid it on with a trowel,' I said. 'So he's a drug addict and a revolutionary, and practises black magic on the side.'

'He was also a heretic as well, or the next best thing. When he preached that sermon about women priests, he played into everyone's hands. Mrs Forbury said it was so obviously loopy, it made his position untenable.'

'That's Rosington logic,' I said. 'They could cope with drug-taking and witchcraft, but they couldn't let him get away with heresy.'

'One of those people who live in the wrong time.'

'And the wrong place. Don't forget the place.'

All at once I felt depressed. It seemed to me that whatever Francis had been guilty of, he wasn't alone with his guilt. I thought of the Touchies smacking their lips around a tea table in the Deanery. How did you calibrate guilt? How did you measure one guilt against another?

'I don't suppose they mentioned the names of any children, did they? A boy called Simon Martlesham?'

'I don't think so. And *was* there a boy? I thought Mrs Forbury said something about a little girl.'

Then Rosie came downstairs and we started talking about other things. One of them was Mr Treevor. I didn't tell Janet about his willie-winkle remark because that would have only added to her worries. But she was concerned that he'd gone out by himself again this morning. I suggested we start locking the doors, even when one of us was at home, so he couldn't slip out without our knowing.

Underneath this was the other conversation that we weren't having. Finding the wings this morning had brought matters to a head. Though I wasn't going to say so to anyone, least of all

Janet, for once I agreed with David. Mr Treevor ought to go into a home, for his sake and everyone else's.

I knew he would be miserable, but if he stayed here he wouldn't be particularly happy either, and he'd make at least two other people miserable as well. And, as the dementia took hold, there was always the risk that he'd do something far worse than he'd already done. At the back of my mind was the possibility that he might already have done worse things than kill a pigeon and cut off its wings.

'And it's going to be difficult when the baby comes,' Janet was saying. 'I'll have to go into hospital for a few days, I can't see any way round that.'

'I'll come and hold the fort if you want.'

I saw alarm flicker in Janet's face. She was looking over my shoulder. I turned. Rosie was in the room, sitting on the floor with Angel on her lap in her corner by the dresser. She met my eyes and I knew she had heard us talking about the baby, and understood what it meant as well. Whatever else Rosie was, she was never stupid. Janet and David had decided not to tell her about it until the pregnancy was past the first twelve weeks.

'Oh,' Janet said. 'I didn't see you down there, darling. I wish you wouldn't sit on the floor. You'll get your school dress dirty.'

'All right.'

She got up and wandered round the table, a thumb in her mouth.

'Where are you going?' Janet said.

'Up to my room.'

Rosie broke into a run as she reached the doorway. Her feet pattered up the stairs.

'Oh, Lord,' Janet said. 'This would happen now.'

The evening continued to roll downhill. David came home but communicated mainly in grunts before going to ground in the study. Rosie had a tantrum, which ended in her lying rigid and bright red on the floor, screaming as loudly as possible. Mr Treevor climbed into his bed and pulled the covers over his head. David came out of the study and shouted upstairs, 'Can't you control her, Janet? I'm trying to work.' Meanwhile, I made an egg-and-bacon flan with too few eggs and not enough bacon.

I went upstairs for a bracing nip of gin. I hadn't touched my bottle since the trip to London on Monday but these were special circumstances. On the first-floor landing I heard voices in Rosie's room and paused to eavesdrop.

'Are we really having a baby?' Rosie was saying in a singsong, babyish voice.

'Yes, darling,' Janet said. 'Isn't that nice?'

'Will it be a boy or a girl?'

'We don't know yet. We have to wait till it comes. We can't be absolutely sure it's coming yet – that's why Daddy and I haven't told you before. Would you like a little brother or a little sister?'

'Rosie doesn't want a baby,' she said in the same silly voice. 'Angel doesn't want one, either. Never, never, never.'

Things improved slightly at supper time, partly because of the gin. Mr Treevor was lured out of bed at the thought of food. Rosie was so exhausted that she fell asleep. Even David cheered up a little, after drinking two glasses of sherry before we ate. Meanwhile, Janet carried on as usual. She was, of course, the one person in the house who wasn't allowed to be depressed or have tantrums, or act strangely or brace themselves with fortifying nips of gin. Someone at the Dark Hostelry had to be reliable, and we had chosen her.

After supper, she went up to check on Rosie and settle Mr Treevor. I washed up, made coffee and took it up to the drawing room. David was reading *The Voice of Angels*. I poured the coffee. He looked up as I handed him the cup.

'Thanks. Is this yours?'

'Yes. Henry sent it. He found it in a box of second-hand books.'

'It's absolute tosh, isn't it?' He smiled up at me as he spoke, making it obvious that the sting in the words was not directed at me. 'I knew Youlgreave was eccentric, but I hadn't realized he was quite such a bad poet.'

'I think he was very unhappy,' I said.

'Quite possibly. But is that an excuse?'

Part of me was annoyed with David for criticizing Francis, and another part of me had treacherously abdicated its responsibilities and turned into a mass of goo because he'd smiled at me.

I sat down and lit a cigarette. David shut the book and put it gently on the side table by his chair. He always treated books as though they were infinitely fragile.

'Why are you spending so much time on Youlgreave?'

'I'm interested in him,' I said, blowing smoke out of my nostrils like an outraged dragon. 'He was an interesting person.'

David smiled at me again. He opened his mouth to speak but then Janet came back into the room. I finished my coffee and said there was something I needed to do upstairs. I wasn't sure whether the result of leaving David and Janet alone would be a quarrel or a reconciliation, but I knew I had to let them try and find out.

On the first floor, Rosie's room was dark and silent. Mr Treevor's door was closed. I went upstairs to my room. The first thing I did was open the bedside cupboard and take out the gin bottle. The cupboard smelled of lavender. The light gleamed on the green glass like the smile on the face of a welcome friend. I poured myself a comfortable inch and sat on the bed, sipping slowly and feeling liquid fire run down my throat and into my belly. Who needed babies when you had London Dry Gin?

Bloody Henry.

So I took out the photograph of Henry and his Hairy Widow and looked at it again, something I'd sworn not to do. I looked at her legs waving in the air and his quaking bottom between them and thought I would probably need another glass of gin in a moment. To delay this, I put the photograph away and looked around for a distraction.

My eyes fell on the other photograph, the one of the clergymen and the children in front of the Theological College. I lifted it down from the washstand and held it under the bedside light. Francis, the little man with the long nose and the black shadows where his eyes should be, was face to face with me.

I rubbed the glass with my finger, trying to see him better. Once again, I wished I could pass through it into that world and find out what they were doing in the photograph and who they all were. I took another sip of gin and at that very moment, as though the liquid brought inspiration with it, I realized that there was a way.

I turned the photograph over. The frame was wooden, and the photograph was backed by a thin sheet of plywood held in place by tacks. I levered some of them up with a nail-file and then pulled out the plywood. I pushed the glass up from underneath and pulled out the cardboard, the mount and the photograph in one go. I peeled the photograph and mount away from the cardboard. There was writing on the back of the photograph. I had gone through the glass.

In that other time it was high summer. 'Tableaux Vivants at the Principal's Garden Party: first prize Oberon, Titania, and attendant fairies. August 6th, 1904.'

Not angels after all.

Underneath, written in the same faded brown ink, were the names. 'The Revd Canon Murtagh-Smith, Principal – the Revd J. R. Heckstall, Vice-Principal, Canon Youlgreave . . .' But it was the name next to his that leapt up at me.

'N. Martlesham'.

In my haste I knocked the glass as I turned the photograph over. Drops of gin slopped on to the frame. So that was Nancy, the little girl standing literally in Francis's shadow. She was the real mystery, not Simon, not Francis. What was a little girl from Swan Alley doing with wings sprouting from her shoulders at a Theological College garden party?

There was something else, too, something whose unsettling significance gradually crept over me. I reached for my glass. At that moment the phone began to ring downstairs.

I went on to the landing and hung over the banisters. David went to answer it in the study. The ringing stopped, and a moment later David came out and called softly up to me. By the time I reached the hall, the drawing-room door was tactfully closed and he and Janet were on the other side.

'Wendy, darling!' said Henry's disembodied voice.

'A character in *Peter Pan*.'

It was an old joke, dating back to the days of our engagement. It wasn't funny any more. Instead it had become a sort of emotional nursery food, something one of us would produce when the other was feeling low, a way of saying everything was all right and some things never change. I don't know what made me produce it then, and if I could have withdrawn the words I would have done. They were implying quite the wrong thing to Henry.

'How are you, dearest?' he burbled. 'Have you had the parcel?'

'It came this morning,' I said. 'Listen, I need to see you. Can I come up to town tomorrow?'

'Wonderful! Come tonight. I'll hire a car and come and fetch you.'

'I don't mean like that. Listen, there're several things I want to do.'

'Concerning your friend Francis?'

'Yes. That book you sent me was very interesting. It's not like the one I got from the library after all. The title's different, and there's a poem in it which isn't anywhere else. I'll come up on the same train – can you meet me at Liverpool Street?'

'Of course I can. But what's –?'

'The most important thing to do is talk to Simon Martlesham. So we need to go to the Blue Dahlia. But first I'd like to –'

'Hang on. Why do you want to see Martlesham again?'

'Because he told me he had his thirteenth birthday on the *Hesperides* in the middle of the Atlantic.'

'What's wrong with that?'

'He said his sister Nancy was with him on that voyage, and we know that his birthday was in July 1904 from that children's novel Francis was going to give him.'

'So?'

'I've just found a photograph that shows Nancy on the lawn of the Theological College. It's dated the sixth of August. So why was Simon lying? And what happened to Nancy?'

34

I wish I hadn't gone to London, not on Friday.

The shouting started a little after six o'clock. I was in that uncomfortable state between sleep and waking and at first I thought it came from my dream. I was with Simon Martlesham on the *Hesperides* and there were icebergs ahead and he and everyone else said we were going to sink. And I kept saying but it's July so there can't be any icebergs.

I snapped into consciousness. I'd slept badly all night. Too excited, I supposed, and too curious. There was also the question of Henry. I was half looking forward to seeing him and half reluctant.

After a second or two, I realized the shouting wasn't in the dream. I scrambled out of bed and struggled into my dressing gown. At this stage I couldn't make out the words, or even who was shouting. I opened my door and went on to the landing.

'You disgusting old man.' David's voice. 'Get into your room and stay there.'

A keening sound like the wind in the chimney. Mr Treevor?

Running feet, bare soles thudding on the linoleum, then Janet saying, 'What is it, what is it?'

I paused at the head of the stairs. She wouldn't want me down there, not now.

'What's he *done*?' she said.

'God knows,' David snarled. 'He was in bed with Rosie. Cuddling her.'

'He was probably just lonely or cold. You know how fond of –'

'There's nothing to discuss. He has to go.'

The keening rose in volume.

'David, I –'

'It's a question of what's best for him as well as for everyone else in this house. In the long run it's kinder to everybody if he goes into a home.'

'What's *happening*?' moaned Mr Treevor.

'Shut up and get in your room,' roared David.

The door slammed.

'You can't do this,' Janet said.

'Can't I?' David said. 'Why not?'

I slipped back into my room and shut the door very quietly. I climbed into bed, lit a cigarette and told myself that Janet loved David. If I was really Janet's friend, I couldn't come between her and him, however well-meaning I felt my intervention was. Two's company in a marriage. The Hairy Widow had taught me that.

I don't know what David actually saw. I never dared ask him then or later. The possibility that there might have been some sort of sexual contact between Mr Treevor and Rosie didn't even occur to me, not until years later. I thought he'd just been monkeying about in some way and that his actions showed that he'd sunk still further into his second childhood. But if this had happened now, over forty years later, I would automatically have placed a sexual interpretation on it. Whether I would have been right to do so is another matter. I just don't know what was going on in Rosie's bedroom.

All I know is that I heard David shouting and that hindsight can play tricks on you just as any other kind of vision can.

So I pretended I'd heard nothing. It was the action of a coward, a well-mannered guest and even a loyal friend. I was all three of those, though not usually at the same time. I stayed in bed until my alarm went off. When I went downstairs, only Janet and Rosie were in the kitchen.

'Sleep well?' Janet asked.

'Like a log, thanks. And you?'

'Not bad.' Janet patted her tummy. 'Felt a bit queasy but it didn't come to anything. Unlike yesterday. I don't know if that's progress or not.'

'David not down?'

'He was up early. He went to do some work at the college. He's going to see the diocesan architect today.'

'It's a very worrying time,' I said.

'I expect something will come up. David's already put out a few feelers.'

Breakfast went on as usual. Janet took a tray up to Mr Treevor. She asked if I needed sandwiches for London and sent her love to Henry. She carefully avoided saying anything I could have interpreted as a hope that he and I would get back together again. And I carefully avoided mentioning the shouting. Our friendship was about what we didn't say as well as what we did.

'There's no real urgency about going to London,' I said as I was washing up. 'Perhaps I should go next week. It's not a bad day and I could give you a hand in the garden.'

'The garden can wait. You go to London and enjoy yourself. Have you told Canon Hudson, by the way?'

'No, not yet. I'll phone after breakfast. But I do wonder if I should mow the lawn instead.'

Janet looked up through the basement window of the kitchen. If you leaned forward far enough you could see a rectangle of sky above the roofs of the houses on the other side of the High Street. 'Anyway, I think it might rain. There's really no point in your staying.'

'Let me take Rosie to school before I go. There's plenty of time.'

She agreed to that, saying that she was a little tired. Now I wonder if she knew me better than I knew myself, and she allowed me to walk Rosie to school to soothe my conscience.

When I got back I phoned Simon Martlesham and arranged to meet him in the Blue Dahlia at two thirty. His clipped voice showed no sign of surprise. He bit back emotions as well as words. When he asked why I wanted to see him, I said I'd found something to do with his sister, something which would interest him. And then I put the phone down. I know it was melodramatic of me, but I felt that Simon Martlesham had been making a fool out of me, and now it was my turn.

I borrowed a music case from Janet to carry the photograph and the two books, *The Tongues of Angels* and *The Voice of Angels*.

On the train to London I read the poems again, but the more I read them the less I understood them. At one point I persuaded myself that 'The Office of the Dead' was a punning title, meaning both a funeral service for the dead and the job the dead did for the living. But if Francis was not only mentally unbalanced but also taking opium, it was quite possible that the poem was never anything more than nonsense.

The train journey passed quickly. Travelling to London already seemed like a habit, and an enjoyable one at that. Whatever I decided to do about Henry, I had established that a life outside Rosington was a possibility.

Henry was waiting at the barrier, which surprised me a little because punctuality was not one of his virtues. He took my arm and insisted on carrying the music case.

'What do you want to do?' he asked. 'A cup of coffee?'

'I'd like to go to the Church Empire Society, please.'

'I beg your pardon?' We stopped to allow a porter wheeling a barrow to go by. 'What on earth's that?'

'The organization that sent Simon Martlesham to Toronto, with a little help from Francis Youlgreave. And according to him, his sister went into one of the society's orphanages.'

'Can't we phone them up?'

I had looked up the Church Empire Society in David's copy of *Crockford's Clerical Directory*. There was an address in Westminster, but no telephone number.

'I think a personal visit would be better.' I smiled at him. 'I thought you'd enjoy being a relative trying to trace your long-lost uncle and aunt.'

He smiled back. 'And who will you be?'

'I'll be your little wifey, of course. Reluctantly indulging my husband's whims.'

'I'd like that.'

Once again our eyes met. This time neither of us smiled.

We took a taxi from the station. On the way I told Henry what I knew about Simon and Nancy Martlesham's emigration.

As we were coming down to Blackfriars, Henry said, 'I went to Senate House yesterday afternoon.'

'What senate?'

'It's the University of London Library in Bloomsbury. I thought

I'd see if I could track down anything about Isabella of Roth. No luck.'

'I'm not surprised. She was probably one of Francis's inventions.'

'But I did find something that might be relevant in *English Precursors of Protestantism in the Later Middle Ages*.' He looked smugly down his nose at me. 'Murtagh-Smith and Babcock, London 1898. Perhaps I should give up teaching and become a scholar instead.'

'What was the name of the first author?'

His smile faded. 'Murtagh-Smith. Ring a bell?'

'He was the principal of the Theological College in Youlgreave's time. Anyway, what did he have to say?'

'Not a lot that helped, I'm afraid. But apparently at the end of the fourteenth century, the Lollard Movement was trying to reform the Church. They had lots of revolutionary ideas – they thought people should read the Bible in their own language and that warfare was unchristian. Oh, and they didn't like the Pope, either. They thought every Christian had the right to work out what they really believed by reading the Bible and meditating on it. According to Murtagh-Smith and his friend, the Peasants' Revolt was partly to do with the Lollards. The government didn't like them, naturally, and in 1401 they passed the first English law to allow the burning of heretics.'

'Well, it fits so far. But were the Lollards in favour of women priests?'

'I doubt it. But they didn't approve of clerical celibacy.' He grinned at me. 'They claimed it led to unnatural lusts. But this is the point. Murtagh-Smith says that several people were burned at the stake for preaching Lollard heresies in Rosington.'

'When?'

'In 1402.'

'Same date. But nothing about women priests?'

He shook his head. 'Perhaps that was another of Francis's little ideas. Just a little modification of history. After all, that's what poetic licence is all about, isn't it?' Suddenly he changed the subject. 'Do you think it's a good idea to go to this society? What are you trying to prove?'

'That Simon Martlesham was lying.'

'He might have made a mistake. Anyway, what's the point in turning over stones? It's not going to help anyone now, is it?'

I didn't answer. I stared out of the window. We were on the Victoria Embankment now, with Big Ben rearing up ahead. How could I explain to Henry that when everything was wrong in my life Francis had thrown me a line, a thread of curiosity. More than that – I felt about Francis as I'd felt about Janet, all those years ago at Hillgard House. He was weak, and I wanted to protect him.

'Sorry,' said the new, reformed Henry. 'I don't want to be nosy. It's none of my business.'

The Church Empire Society occupied a shabby little house in a street off Horseferry Road. There were two dustbins and a bicycle in what had once been a front garden. I rang the bell and a moment later it was answered by a tall tweedy lady, very thin, with a sharp nose and chin set between cheeks that bulged, as though crammed with illicit sweets.

Henry raised his hat. 'Good morning. So sorry to bother you. But I wonder if you could help us.'

Suddenly, and quite unexpectedly, Henry and I were a team again, just as we had been with his clients. I didn't have to do much because Henry did most of the talking – I was cast in the role of the grumpy wife, who thought it stupid that her husband should waste so much time chasing after a family black sheep. So he had a double claim on the tweedy lady's sympathy.

She was the sole permanent employee of the society and her name was Miss Hermione Findhorn. Her office occupied the front room on the ground floor. It must have been about twelve feet square and there was barely room for two people, let alone three. This was because the office, and as far as I could see the whole house, was filled with outsized paintings and pieces of furniture.

'I'm frightfully sorry, Mr Appleyard,' Miss Findhorn said in a voice which seemed to emerge from her nose. 'The problem is, we were bombed. We used to have a rather larger house in Horseferry Road. We managed to save quite a lot, as you can see.' She waved a chapped hand with bitten fingernails around the room, around the house. 'But alas, our records were stored in the attics and we recovered none of them.'

797

Henry persevered. Miss Findhorn said it was perfectly possible that the society had arranged for the passage of two orphan children to Toronto in 1904. In those days, they trained young people for useful trades. They had in fact maintained an orphanage in Toronto. Unfortunately that had been closed in the 1920s. But they'd managed to save the scrapbooks which in those days the society maintained to record its achievements. Miss Findhorn produced a tall, leather-bound volume covering 1904. She and Henry turned the pages. I knew from the way Henry was standing that he had found nothing, that this was a waste of time. Then he stiffened, and pointed to a clipping. I craned my head to see what he was looking at. A name leapt up at me.

Sir Charles Youlgreave Bt.

'There was someone of that name in Rosington,' Henry said casually. 'Canon Youlgreave, I think it was. I wonder if there's a connection.'

'Quite possibly,' said Miss Findhorn, angling her glasses so she could read the newsprint. 'Sir Charles was on our Committee of Management. Usually members sit for three years, and I think in those days they often took a personal interest in the young people they helped. Perhaps Canon Youlgreave suggested your uncle and aunt as suitable candidates.'

'Very likely,' Henry said.

We said goodbye and found another taxi in Horseferry Road. Henry suggested lunch at the Ritz, but I wouldn't let him. In the end we went to a chop house off the Strand, a dark, low-ceilinged place divided up into wooden booths so you could be private if you wanted to be. We got there before one, so we found a quiet table without difficulty.

'Are you still wasting money at Brown's Hotel?' I asked.

'I'm leaving today.' Henry offered me a cigarette. 'I'm going to find a nice little private hotel with a landlady who'll mother me.' He leaned forward with his lighter. 'You're wearing your wedding ring today.'

It was part of my social camouflage in Rosington. I said, 'I needed it for Miss Findhorn. After all, we were supposed to be man and wife.'

'We still are. Have you paid in that cheque yet?'

'No.'

'Why not?'

'I don't know if I want to.'

'But it's ten thousand pounds. Where is it?'

'In my bedside cupboard.' *With a sprig of lavender on top to make it smell better.*

'Listen, Wendy, it'll be safer if you have it. Then I can't spend it. And it's only fair.'

'I thought you were going to buy a share of that school.'

'I am. It's all going ahead. I promise. But if I've got this extra money, I'll just waste it.'

I smiled at him. 'I'll see.'

'You've changed.'

'And why do you think that is?'

Suddenly we were on the verge of a quarrel neither of us wanted. He must have sensed it as well because he threw a question about Janet and David at me. Soon I was telling him about the Dark Hostelry, about the collapse of David's hopes for the Theological College and about the odd behaviour of Mr Treevor.

Later I showed him the two books, *Tongues* and *Voice*, and also the photograph. Henry read 'The Office of the Dead' while demolishing a helping of steak-and-kidney pudding.

'In a way, it's like Christianity gone mad.' He sat back and wiped his mouth with his napkin. 'You eat the body and blood, and in return you get eternal life.' He glanced down at the open book. 'Or the secret of youth or something. Hard to know exactly what he *does* mean.' He turned over a page. 'And what's all this stuff about the angel sitting at his shoulder telling him what to write? It makes it sound as if he's got his own personal Angel of the Lord. He must have been completely round the bend.'

'I don't know. He was obviously a bit eccentric –'

'That's one way of putting it.'

'But you can't deny he did a lot of good. Some of his ideas were just a little ahead of his time.'

'And ours,' Henry said. 'I can imagine how David feels about women priests.'

'What worries me is the girl.' I pointed to the little figure beside

Francis. 'What happened to her? Why should Martlesham lie about it?'

'There's probably a perfectly innocent explanation. Anyway, he might have made a mistake.'

'About something like that, his own sister coming with him to Canada?'

'It happened over fifty years ago, Wendy. And he's had a stroke since then, remember.'

Henry ordered more beer and by common consent we talked about other things, mainly about his plans for Veedon Hall. We both skated round my role in these, if any. At ten past two we went back to the Strand and took a taxi to the Blue Dahlia Café.

As we drew up outside, Henry touched my arm. 'Look!'

I followed the direction of his pointing finger. There were several people walking down Fetter Passage but I recognized none of them.

'Right at the end,' Henry said. 'Just turning the corner.'

'Who?'

'I'm sure it was Munro.'

'What do you think?' Henry said as we stood on the pavement after paying off the taxi. 'Martlesham's got Munro to follow us after we leave him?'

I shook my head. 'More likely he's been following us already.'

'But how?'

'If Martlesham told him I was coming to see him this afternoon, all Munro needed to do was go to Liverpool Street and keep an eye on trains from Rosington.'

Fetter Passage was very quiet after the bustle of Holborn. But was someone watching us, Munro or a colleague? I glanced up at the windows above the café, wondering which belonged to Martlesham's flat.

Henry said, 'In that case he'll know about the Church Empire Society.'

'And what about if he was in the chop house? If he was in the booth next to ours, he might have heard something.'

'Nothing we can do about it now.' He looked up and down the terrace. 'Bit of a dump.'

'But not as bad as Swan Alley.'

I opened the door of the café. The ribbons swayed like seaweed across the archway at the rear of the room. We had arrived in the dead time between lunch and tea and there were few customers. The sad-faced woman was cutting bread at the counter. She didn't look up as we came in.

'I've come to see Mr Martlesham,' I said to her.

'I tell the boss you're here.'

Without meeting my eyes, she put down the knife and shuffled through the archway. A moment later, she parted the ribbons again and beckoned us.

Beyond the archway was a small room used for serving food. Immediately opposite us was an open door leading to a kitchen. She gestured to another door on our left.

'Knock,' she commanded.

I tapped on the door and I heard Martlesham telling us to come in.

The room was equipped as an office with what looked like cast-off War Department furniture. Martlesham was sitting behind the desk and facing us. Behind him was an open window looking into a sunny yard full of bicycles and dustbins. He didn't get up, but stared past me at Henry.

'Who's this?'

'My husband, Henry Appleyard. Henry, this is Mr Martlesham.'

Henry smiled and extended his hand across the desk. Martlesham shook it for the shortest possible time.

'You'll excuse me if I don't get up. Please sit down.'

I chose a hard chair in front of the desk. I felt as though he was interviewing me. I said, 'Do you own the café?'

'I own the whole terrace.' He sounded bored with his possession.

I heard Henry suck in his breath beside me.

'It must mean a lot of work for you,' I said, not because it was an intelligent thing to say but because it was the first thing that came into my mind.

'Not really. I have someone to take care of the details. It's a long-term investment, really.'

'You're planning to develop the site?' Henry said.

'Yes. Everyone's on short tenancies except for a couple of leaseholders at the far end of the terrace. I'm waiting for them to die or move.' He gave us a twisted smile. 'And they're probably waiting for me to do the same.'

A fleck of ash marred the brilliantly white surface of his left-hand shirt cuff. He put down his cigarette and carefully brushed it off. There was a freshly ironed handkerchief in the breast pocket of his jacket and his hands had been manicured. I wondered who looked after his appearance now Vera was dead. Perhaps he had planned Fetter Passage to be a nest egg for their shared old age. For the first time it struck me that Vera's death might have had something to do with his hiring Munro. Perhaps he'd wanted to find out if he still had a family. It isn't easy to be lonely. I knew all about that.

'What did you want to see me about?'

'About Nancy,' I said. 'I wondered if she might have any memories of Canon Youlgreave.'

He shrugged. 'Quite possibly. But you'd have to find her.'

'So you don't have an address?'

He shook his head. 'I told you, she was adopted almost as soon as we got to Toronto. The couple who took her were moving down to the States, and the lady at the orphanage said it would be better for her if she didn't have any contact with her old life.'

'That must have been terrible for both of you.'

His heavy lids drooped over dark eyes. 'Better than Swan Alley, Mrs Appleyard, I tell you that. She was going to a good home, with good people. I had a job, somewhere to live, prospects. They didn't give us much time to think about it, anyway. After the *Hesperides* docked, I saw her maybe twice in the next six weeks. Then that was that.'

'That's a pity,' I said.

'Why?'

'Because if you had an address for her, she might have been able to explain this.' I lifted Janet's music case on to the desk and took out the photograph. I put it in front of him, on his unblemished green blotter. 'But perhaps you can explain it instead.'

Slowly he put on a pair of glasses. For what seemed like several minutes he stared down at the photograph. His expression didn't change. Henry fumbled in his pocket and a moment later lit a cigarette. As if the flare of the match was a signal,

Martlesham raised his head and transferred his stare to me.

'Well?'

'I wondered if you recognized it.'

'The place? No, I don't.'

'It's Rosington Theological College. The lawn at the back.'

'Very possibly. I never went there. Wasn't it that red brick place near the Porta?'

'Do you recognize anybody?'

'There's Canon Youlgreave, of course. And that man there, the old clergyman, wasn't he another canon? Some of the ladies look familiar but I wouldn't be able to put a name to them, not now.'

'What about the children?'

For the first time there was a hint of anger in those dark eyes. 'Why are you asking me all this?'

'Look at the girl next to Canon Youlgreave,' I said.

He glanced down, then back to me. He said nothing.

'Is that your sister?'

'Could be.' He spoke as though I were grinding the words out of him one by one. 'Hard to tell.'

'She's dressed up, Mr Martlesham. Looks like a pair of wings. Does that ring any bells?'

'Maybe they were doing some kind of play. Canon Youlgreave was always involved in anything artistic, you see, being a poet. Maybe not a play. Might have been dancing, or something, and they needed a little girl.'

'According to the writing on the back, it *is* your sister.'

He looked at me as if I'd stung him. Then, clumsily with his one good hand, he turned the photograph over. He read the row of names on the back.

'So you knew it was Nancy all along, Mrs Appleyard.' He glared at me and I was suddenly glad that Henry was in the room. 'Why come and pester me about it?'

'Because of the date at the top.' I watched him looking at it. Then I went on, 'Your birthday was on the seventeenth of July. According to you, you and your sister were in the middle of the Atlantic on the *Hesperides* on that day. So what's she doing with a pair of wings on the lawn of the Theological College over two weeks later?'

Martlesham took off his glasses, folded them and put them away in their case. Only then did he look at me. 'I must have made a mistake about the date.'

'We can easily check that,' said Henry suddenly. 'The date of the sailing would have been in the newspapers.'

Martlesham ignored him. 'Or whoever wrote the names on the back made a mistake. Simple as that. Or they put the wrong date.'

'I don't think that's very likely, Mr Martlesham. You thought that was Nancy and there are plenty of people in Rosington we can ask, people who will remember her as she was then. There's Mrs Elstree, for one. And I expect we can check when the principal's garden party was. If we need to.'

Martlesham sighed and reached for his cigarette case. He said in a low voice, almost as if talking to himself, 'I could ask you to leave.'

'And then your private investigator could follow us and see what we did next.'

'What are you talking about?'

'Harold Munro, ex-detective sergeant, Metropolitan Police.'

'Never heard of him.'

'Who else would bother to hire him?'

'How should I know?' He tapped a cigarette on the case and put it in his mouth. 'Anyway, what's he been doing?'

'He's paid several visits to Rosington in the last few weeks. He's stolen cuttings about Francis Youlgreave from the backfile of the *Rosington Observer*. He borrowed a copy of one of Youlgreave's books from the public library. He tried to question a number of people, including Mrs Elstree, and nearly frightened one old lady to death. He's been seen watching the Dark Hostelry, it's even possible he's been inside the house. He followed me after I met you here on Monday and he's got an office in Holborn. My husband saw him ten minutes ago at the other end of Fetter Passage.'

'Very mysterious, Mrs Appleyard. Sounds like a job for the police, especially if you think this man's broken into the Dark Hostelry.'

I picked up the photograph and returned it to the music case. His hand twitched as I picked it up, and for a moment I wondered if he would try to stop me taking it.

'What would you think, Mr Martlesham?' Henry said. 'If you were in our position.'

'I'd think it was time to stop poking my nose in other people's business.'

'You haven't any children, have you?'

Martlesham shook his head.

'And your wife has just died, Wendy tells me,' Henry went on. 'It would be very natural if you wanted to trace members of your family.'

'Well, I don't,' Martlesham said. 'What would be the point?'

'I would have thought the answer to that was obvious,' Henry said gently. 'It's not much fun being by yourself.'

Martlesham fiddled with his lighter. Then he looked at me and sighed. 'You've got it all wrong. I suppose there's no reason why you shouldn't know. I don't want to trace Nancy now for the same reason that I didn't want to trace her when I came to England in 1917. I don't want to *embarrass* her. That's the long and the short of it.'

'Embarrass?' I said. 'I don't understand.'

His mouth twisted. 'The last thing she said to me was, "You sold me. I hate you."'

'At the orphanage?' I said.

'There never was any orphanage, Mrs Appleyard. And she didn't come to Canada, either. She stayed here. That's why she's in that photo.'

He lit the cigarette at last and puffed furiously. Smoke billowed across the desk, pushed by the draught from the window. I sniffed.

Virginia tobacco, not Turkish.

35

'Did you believe him?' asked Henry.

'I don't know.' I stroked the cool, silky glass in front of me. 'I'm sure some of it was true. The question is how much.'

Henry was good at finding nice little pubs. He'd found one near Liverpool Street Station, a place of engraved mirrors, burnished brass, dark, gleaming woodwork and stained-glass lights in all the windows. The downstairs bar was full of office workers snatching a quick drink before going home. Henry and I were in the little upstairs bar, which was much quieter. We had a table in the window and could talk without the risk of being overheard. Not that there was any sign of Harold Munro.

'I think he's a gambler by nature,' Henry said. 'You don't start life in Swan Alley and end up fifty years later with a slice of Holborn unless you're prepared to take chances.'

'So what are you saying?'

Henry shrugged. 'Just that he may have been taking another gamble with us. Admitting part of the story as a way of keeping the rest of it concealed. I mean, he couldn't really get away from the date on that photograph. You set a trap for him and he walked right into it. When you come down to it, there's very little he told us that can be proved. Anyone who could have supported the story is dead.'

'Except perhaps the sister.'

Henry cocked an eyebrow, a trick I'd seen him practise in the mirror. 'You think she's still alive? After what Martlesham told us?'

The story had emerged by fits and starts. It was as if Martlesham was in the witness box, reluctantly disgorging information, volunteering nothing, and leaving the cross-examining counsel to do as much of the work as possible. The Martlesham children's mother had died in childbirth. At the time there wasn't a man living with them. 'Pregnancy scared them off, I reckon,' Simon told us. 'And she was getting very sickly.' He never actually said, but it was clear that Mr Martlesham had not been seen for many years. Simon hinted that his parents might not have been married and there was even some question as to whether his father was also Nancy's.

Simon had met Francis during the winter before his mother's death. The relationship sounded innocent, even praiseworthy. Francis lent Simon books and encouraged him to go to evening classes in English literature and arithmetic. He invited both Simon and Nancy to tea at the Dark Hostelry, where he was living at the time. Francis was looked after by two elderly servants, a cook-housekeeper and a maid who disapproved of the Martlesham children.

'For me and Nancy,' Martlesham said, 'it was like a glimpse of paradise. Sitting on a comfortable chair in a clean house. Afternoon tea with sandwiches and as much cake as you wanted to eat. Youlgreave gave me a penknife and let me carve my initials on a walnut tree in the garden, to show how well I could make the letters. He used to put Nancy on his knee and read us stories. Is the walnut tree still there?'

'No,' I said. 'There's only an apple tree now.'

When the mother died – 'I heard her screaming,' Martlesham remarked in a matter-of-fact voice – the only other relative in Rosington had been an aunt, the mother's elder sister who worked in a haberdasher's in the High Street. 'She'd come a long way from Swan Alley, Aunt Em had,' Martlesham said. 'Us kids were just a burden to her. And she was walking out with someone she wanted to marry, a very respectable man with a house and everything. She didn't want us queering her pitch. Hard woman. But I can't say I blame her.'

That was when Francis had stepped in. He helped to pay for the mother's funeral. One evening he called on Aunt Em with a proposal. He was willing to arrange for Simon to go to Canada, where he could learn a trade and make a fresh start in life. And he had an even more alluring offer for Nancy.

A lady and gentleman who lived near his brother's house in Middlesex were unable to have children. They wanted to adopt a little girl and bring her up as a lady. Nancy would be perfect for them. She was quick, intelligent and pretty. Her eyes were the same colour as the lady's. She would live in a house with a big garden and have a pony and a room of her own.

'Aunt Em was pleased, of course, then she said I was old enough to make up my own mind. Nancy said she wanted to stay with me, but there was nothing I could do for her. Or not for years, until I got myself established. No, it was the right choice, no doubt about that.'

'You said she accused you of selling her,' I said. 'What did you mean by that?'

His face darkened. I guessed he hadn't meant to tell us that, that the words had slipped out. He wasn't angry, I realized a moment later, he was embarrassed.

'Just before I left Rosington, Mr Youlgreave gave me fifteen pounds.' He hesitated, selecting the right words. 'To help me settle in Canada. But Nancy was only a kid, she misunderstood what was going on.'

Now, in the upstairs room of the pub, Henry said, 'We've only Martlesham's word that Nancy was adopted. As we've only got his word about so much else. There's another reason why he might not have tried to get in touch with his sister when he got back to England. Perhaps he knew there was no point.'

'How do you mean?'

'What if he *knew* she was dead?'

'That's horrible.'

'It's where all this is going, if you ask me.' Henry lit two cigarettes and passed one to me. 'There was a very strange side to Francis Youlgreave – that's obvious from the poems. And Martlesham got very worked up when you asked him about the animals.'

He had come the nearest I'd seen him to losing his temper. He said that was typical of all he hated about Rosington. People had said that Canon Youlgreave was mad, going around cutting up animals for sadistic reasons of his own. But he, Simon Martlesham, knew better, and so did many other people, including Canon Youlgreave's servants. Mr Youlgreave had an

808

interest in animal physiology. Once or twice Simon Martlesham had helped him to dissect small animals. There was one occasion when Simon had found a drowned kitten floating in the river and had fished it out for Youlgreave, who had rewarded the boy with half a sovereign for his pains. But the twisted minds of others had soon interpreted this absolutely innocent scientific enquiry into something sinister.

'Call themselves Christians?' Martlesham had said, just as he had done on the first occasion I met him and echoing Janet a few hours earlier. 'They were no more Christian than this desk is. And from what you say, it sounds like things haven't changed.'

'Suppose he's feeling guilty?' I said to Henry, wondering if there was time for another drink. 'He's had a stroke, he's lost his wife, he's got no children. Suppose this is the first time in his life he's had time to think about what he did to his sister. I think he needs to find out if she's still alive.'

'Because he wants to see her again?'

'Not necessarily. He might just want to reassure himself that Francis was telling the truth, that she was adopted, that she did grow up to be a lady. He feels guilty. He simply doesn't *know* what happened to her.'

Henry picked a shred of tobacco from his lip. 'I suppose it would explain a lot. The private investigator going to Roth, going to Rosington, taking an interest in us. This isn't just about Youlgreave.'

'If she – she died in 1904, do you think *The Voice of Angels* tells us anything about how?'

'For God's sake, Wendy.' Henry stared at me. 'You're not suggesting that Youlgreave took that tripe *literally*?'

I shrugged and pushed aside my empty glass. 'It's time I went.'

There was a scrap of pleasure to be derived from the knowledge that I'd shocked Henry. It was usually the other way round. He walked with me to the station. I wouldn't let him see me on to the train. At the barrier, I paused to say goodbye. Suddenly he leaned forward and put his arms around me. He was clumsy about it, which was unlike him. He tried to kiss my lips. I turned aside so he kissed the lobe of my right ear instead. I pulled his arms away from me and stepped back.

809

'Wendy, listen, when can I see you again?'

'I don't know. I expect I'll be coming up to London sooner or later.'

'Can't we fix a time? If it would help, I could come to Rosington.'

If Henry was seen in Rosington, the Touchies would really have something to gossip about and he'd run the risk of being snubbed as he came round every corner.

'I don't think that would be a good idea.'

'I thought perhaps the wedding ring meant –'

'You thought wrong.'

'Wendy, please –'

Suddenly furious, I turned on my heel and left him. I had my ticket punched at the barrier and walked up the length of the train. I knew Henry was still watching me but I didn't turn round and wave.

How dared he think he could snap his fingers and I'd come running back? Damn Henry, I thought, as I squeezed myself into a compartment already crowded with commuters, damn Francis and damn everything.

Between Cambridge and Rosington I indulged in an unpleasant fantasy conversation with Henry. I told him that I fancied his friend David much more than him, that David was much better looking and had a much nicer body. David's bottom didn't wobble, I told Henry, and his skin wasn't so flabby it looked as if it needed ironing. I knew I'd never say any of these things, and I felt rather sick for even thinking them.

At Rosington, I walked quickly up the hill and went into the Close by the Porta. There was no sign of Mr Gotobed, or indeed of anyone I knew, and for that I was glad. I didn't want to make conversation.

I opened the gate to the Dark Hostelry garden. Rosie's tricycle was standing on the lawn. Janet made a fuss about things being left out in the garden overnight, so I picked it up and put it in the little shed in the corner by the honeysuckle.

The garden door was unlocked. I went into the hall.

'Nurse!' called a man's voice from the landing on the floor above. 'Is that you?'

Dr Flaxman's head appeared over the banisters. He frowned when he saw me.

'Come up here,' he barked. 'Come and make yourself useful.'

36

It wasn't just the baby that died.

Janet's miscarriage was the turning point of the whole business. Until then, I'd never thought much about miscarriages. They were something that happened to queens in the history books whose husbands were desperate for an heir. Or to characters in novels. Or to quiet little women I didn't know very well because they didn't go out much. A miscarriage was hard luck for all concerned, I assumed in so far as I thought about it at all, but not the end of the world.

It was a day or two before I learned the full story. On Friday morning, after I had left for London, Janet had finished the housework before going into the garden to mow the lawn. The pains started coming at tea time. They grew steadily worse in the early evening. David was late home, and both Rosie and Mr Treevor were demanding food and attention and I wasn't there to share the load. Janet meant to sit down and rest for a moment, but every time she was about to do so there would be another demand.

'Anyway, I thought I was just having a few twinges,' she wailed to me when I went to see her on Saturday morning in hospital. 'It's like the curse – you carry on and sooner or later they go away. But this time they didn't. They got worse.'

Janet had gone to the lavatory and that was when she realized that things were very wrong. Even then, she wouldn't phone David. She phoned the doctors' surgery instead, and was lucky enough to catch Flaxman as he was about to go home. That was the only piece of luck she had that day.

'It's all my fault,' she said in the hospital. 'I killed him.'

'Look,' I said awkwardly, 'that's nonsense. It wasn't your fault. And in a way it wasn't a proper baby yet. You don't even know it was a boy.'

'Of course it was a proper baby,' she snarled at me. 'And I know it was a boy, I always did. His name was going to be Michael. *Michael*.'

For a moment she held my eyes with hers. She looked as if she wanted to strangle me. Then she started crying again and held out her arms, asking for comfort.

Later she told me what Dr Flaxman had said when he had visited her earlier in the morning. 'He told me I had to put it behind me and get pregnant again. What does he know? He made it sound as if I'd had a tooth out and another would grow in its place.'

No matter how often I told her not to be silly, no matter how often I told her the miscarriage was nobody's fault, no matter how often she said that she quite agreed, she still felt she was to blame on some level I couldn't reach. In the end, no one reached her there.

In the meantime I rather enjoyed myself. I had the agreeable sense that other people thought I was rising to the crisis. I tried to comfort Janet. I looked after Rosie and Mr Treevor, whose needs were almost identical. I ran the Dark Hostelry after a fashion. And I listened to David when he needed to talk.

'I had a note from the bishop this afternoon,' he told me on Saturday evening. 'Asking after Janet, and so on. But he said that there's a combined living becoming vacant at the end of the summer. Asked if I might be interested.'

'Where is it?'

'Tattisham with Ditchford. It's about thirty miles away. Near Wisbech.'

'So it's in the depths of the Fens?'

He nodded. 'You can't get much more remote. It would be a struggle financially too – the stipend's nothing special and one would have to run a car. I don't know how Janet would manage. There would be no one for her to talk to.'

Nor for David, I thought, who was one of those people who wherever they live never quite leave university.

'Still, perhaps she would like the change,' he went on. 'A

chance for a new start. How's Rosie, do you think? This must be very unsettling for her.'

'She's OK, I think,' I said with the assurance of the child-less. 'Of course, she's very young, and children that age are self-absorbed.'

'Does she know about the baby?'

'I told her Mummy had to go into hospital, and that she wouldn't be having a baby after all.'

'How did she take it?'

'In her stride.'

This was entirely true. When I told Rosie the news, she smiled up at me and said, 'Good.' I thought David might find this upsetting. Now I'm old and times have changed, I see things rather differently. It strikes me as faintly ridiculous that Janet and I, two grown women, should have spent so much time and effort worrying about David's feelings. We treated him as if his heart was made of eggshells.

Janet came home on Sunday morning with orders to rest as much as possible for a few days. She was very weak and still depressed. Flaxman told us that the best thing to do was to try to jolly her out of it, and David and even I colluded with this. I think this was probably the worst thing we could have done. Every time David or Flaxman said, 'Never mind, Janet, you'll soon get over it, and then you can get pregnant again and have another baby', he was telling her that she wasn't allowed to mourn for the one she'd just lost. No one else was mourning, not really. We were being relentlessly bloody jolly. So Janet had to grieve inside herself, and confined griefs grow bitter.

On Sunday afternoon Janet said to me, 'I'm worried about David.'

'Because of Tattisham with Ditchford?'

She shook her head. 'Because I'm ill, I won't be able to – well, he'll have to do without it for a while.'

'I'm sure he'll manage.' It would have grated if either of us had used the word sex.

'It's different for men, I suppose.'

'Each to his own,' I said, wondering whether Henry was doing without it at present and why he hadn't phoned me. I'd tried to phone him at Brown's on Saturday but he had already paid

814

his bill and left the hotel. He had not left a forwarding address. Perhaps he'd had enough of me.

Sunday went from bad to worse. Mr Treevor went to bed early, Janet had her supper in bed, and David and I ate in the kitchen. Afterwards David went upstairs to collect Janet's tray. A moment later I followed him up because he had forgotten to take Janet's coffee. I found David ushering a whimpering Mr Treevor across the landing. The old man wasn't wearing his teeth and his face had collapsed in on itself.

'What's up?'

'He was in Rosie's room again.' David glared at me as if it was my fault. 'I'm not having this.'

Suddenly Mr Treevor flung himself on his knees and embraced David's legs. 'Don't send me away,' he wailed. 'Please don't put me in a home.'

I tried to help him to his feet but he clung to David.

'Come on, Mr Treevor,' I urged him. 'Why don't you get into bed and I'll bring you a nice warm hot-water bottle and a cup of cocoa?'

'Don't send me away!'

I noticed that Rosie was watching from the doorway of her room. It could only be a matter of seconds before Janet appeared.

White-faced, David bent down, gripped Mr Treevor's wrists and broke his hold. He pulled the old man to his feet. David's eyes were so bright that it seemed to me that it wasn't him looking through them but someone else.

'Get back in your room,' he said softly, and his fingers squeezed the frail old wrists until Mr Treevor squealed. 'You've caused enough trouble.'

He pushed Mr Treevor away from him. The old man would have fallen if I had not put out an arm to steady him. He stared at David as if he was seeing his son-in-law for the first time, which in a sense of course he was.

'I wish I was dead,' Mr Treevor said. 'Please kill me. I don't want to live.'

'Of course you do,' I said briskly, taking him by his arm and drawing him towards his room. 'We all love you very much, Mr Treevor, but we're all a bit upset now because

Janet's not well. But things will seem much better in the morning.'

Suddenly the fight went out of him. I led him into his room. He allowed me to put him into bed. I tucked him in.

'Night, night,' I said. 'Don't get out of bed again, and I'll come and see you soon.'

He held up his face to me. 'Kiss,' he ordered.

I bent down and kissed his forehead. It was like kissing an old newspaper. Then I went back to the landing, which by now was empty. I peeped into Rosie's room. She was in bed, pretending to be asleep with Angel on the pillow beside her. Rosie had never held up her face and asked me to kiss her. Janet and David's door was closed and I heard voices on the other side.

I felt very sorry for myself. So I went down to the drawing room, mixed myself a large gin and Angostura, stretched out on the sofa and lit a cigarette. Things would get better, I told myself without conviction. I thought that David had behaved appallingly. And I also thought that, given the right circumstances, or rather the wrong ones, I might have behaved in exactly the same way.

After a while, he came downstairs. I didn't bother to take my feet off the sofa or try to hide the glass. He sat down beside the empty fireplace.

'I'm sorry about that,' he said. 'I lost my temper. I shouldn't have done that with anyone, but with poor John it's even more inexcusable.'

I lit another cigarette and let him stew.

'You won't know, but I've caught him in with Rosie before. It's – ah – not normal behaviour – a symptom of course of the dementia.'

'But it was all harmless, really, wasn't it? He wasn't hurting her.'

'I don't think we need discuss this further. It's a medical matter. In point of fact, Janet and I had already decided he would have to go into a nursing home. There's no question about it now. I'll ring Flaxman in the morning.'

There was a silence. I searched desperately for something worth saying.

'Are you sure it's the best thing to do?'

'Are you implying it isn't?' His voice hardened, and the stranger looked out of his eyes. 'John can only get worse. He needs trained help. And Janet and I have to think of Rosie as well.'

I nodded. 'I know. And you're right. But he's going to be so upset.'

'It's a question of what's best for all concerned.' David's voice was gentler now. 'Naturally we'll visit him regularly. But the probability is that he soon won't recognize any of us, so it really doesn't matter where he is.'

This time the silence was longer.

'I never asked,' David said abruptly. 'How was Henry when you saw him the other day?'

'Much the same. He sent his regards.'

'And is he helping with your researches?'

It was odd that David couldn't mention my search for Francis without sounding patronizing about it, even when he was trying to be nice to me.

'Very well, thank you,' I said primly. 'But now there's another puzzle. Someone else is interested.'

'In Youlgreave?'

'Yes. They've hired a private investigator called Harold Munro to dig around.'

David frowned. 'But that's absurd. You don't hire a detective to find out about a dead poet.'

'No. Henry said much the same thing on Friday evening.'

'So he knows about this?'

What David meant was that if Henry knew about Harold Munro, then the private investigator couldn't be dismissed as a fantasy created by a credulous woman.

'It was Henry who followed Munro and found out who he was,' I said.

'In London?'

'Yes. But Munro's also been to Rosington. It may have been him watching the Dark Hostelry the other day – you remember when Mr Treevor saw a man staring up at the house?'

'Do you think he might be interested in you rather than Youlgreave?'

'He borrowed one of Youlgreave's books from the public

library. He took cuttings about him from the *Rosington Observer*. He's even been pestering Mrs Gotobed and Mrs Elstree.'

'How very odd. Perhaps we should have a word with the police.'

'And tell them what?' I asked. 'Has anyone committed a crime?'

Once again David shrugged. I knew his mind had wandered off to something else, probably the Theological College or his brilliant career rather than Mr Treevor, Janet or the dead baby. So I sat there nursing my glass and wondered if there had in fact been a crime, not in 1958 but over fifty years earlier.

David would have said I was imagining things. But I hadn't imagined Nancy Martlesham, who to all intents and purposes had vanished in a puff of smoke from the lawn of the Theological College on August 6th, 1904.

37

I had talked to Canon Hudson over the weekend and he told me to take as much time off work as I needed. On Monday morning I walked Rosie to school. David had already gone to the Theological College, so it meant leaving Janet alone at the Dark Hostelry with Mr Treevor.

'Are you sure you can manage?' I asked her.

'I'll be fine. Anyway, I'd like to stay with Daddy.'

Mr Treevor had refused to get out of bed. David had already phoned Dr Flaxman about a nursing home.

It was a fine morning. Rosie answered my attempts at conversation with monosyllables. When we reached the gates of St Tumwulf's, she didn't want me to come in. But she gave me Angel, and watched carefully as I stowed the doll in the shopping bag I had brought for the purpose. She allowed me to drop a kiss on the top of her shining head. I watched her walking through the playground, which was full of children standing or playing in groups. She didn't talk to any of them, just threaded her way among them to the door of the school.

It was nearly a mile back to the Close. I spent most of the time thinking about the shopping and the menus for the next few days, and also thinking about how strange it would be to sit down to meals in the kitchen without John Treevor in the Windsor chair at the end of the table.

After crossing the main road, I passed St Mary's and went into Palace Square. Directly in front of me was Minster Street with the west front of the Cathedral rearing up on the far side of it. I was just in time to intercept Mrs Elstree.

'Hello,' I said. 'How are you?'

'Very well, thank you.' She made to move on, without even asking how Janet was. I hadn't seen her for a few days, and in the interval she seemed to have become more sepia-tinted than ever, as if she was gradually losing all her colours except brown.

'There was something I wanted to ask you,' I said.

'I'm afraid I'm in a bit of a hurry.'

'It was about the Martlesham children, Simon and Nancy. Apparently they had an aunt who worked at a haberdasher's.'

'Really?'

By now she was past me and moving away towards the High Street. I turned and walked beside her.

'I wondered if you could remember anything about her.'

'It's a very long time ago, Mrs Appleyard. I'm afraid I can't help you. Now you must excuse me.'

She hurried on. Short of seizing her arm, there wasn't much I could do to stop her. I thought I knew what had happened. Now the decision had been taken to close the Theological College, there was no longer any need for Mrs Elstree to waste unnecessary time and effort on the Byfields, let alone on me as Janet's friend. Unless there was more to it than that – had Mrs Elstree decided that she had had enough of talking about Francis Youlgreave?

But there was someone else who might remember the Martleshams' aunt. I walked along Minster Street and into the Close by the Porta. But Dr Flaxman's Riley was parked outside the Gotobeds' house. I moved towards the chestnuts, meaning to cut through the cloisters. I heard a door slamming behind me.

I looked back. Dr Flaxman walked round his car and came towards me, moving as usual at one-and-a-half times the speed of a normal person.

'I think I've found a room for Mr Treevor,' he said, touching his hat with a forefinger. 'Would you tell Mrs Byfield? It's in the Cedars, so it should be quite convenient.'

'Where's that?'

'On the outskirts of town. A couple of hundred yards beyond the infants' school. But the room won't be ready until the beginning of next week. The Byfields will need to phone the matron. I wonder whether in the meantime we should take him into hospital. I'd like to have a proper look at him, and it would be one less thing for Mrs Byfield to worry about.'

'Do you want me to mention that to her now as well?'

'Please. She may want a word with her husband. Tell her to ring the surgery as soon as possible and let me know if it suits.'

He nodded and turned back to his car.

'Is Mrs Gotobed all right?' I said quickly. 'I was wondering about calling on her this morning.'

'I wouldn't do that if I were you.' He jingled his car keys in his hand. 'I've just been to see her – she had one of her turns in the night.'

I went back to the Dark Hostelry. Mr Treevor was still in his room but Janet had dragged herself down to the kitchen, where she was sitting at the table and staring at the washing up from breakfast which I hadn't yet had time to do.

'You should be back in bed,' I said, 'or at least resting.'

'There's so much to do.'

'Yes, and I'm doing it. It's all arranged.' I put the kettle on. 'Go on – put your feet up in the drawing room and I'll make us some coffee.'

She did as I asked. I washed up while the water was coming to the boil. I took the coffee upstairs and gave her Dr Flaxman's message.

'I still think we should keep him for a little bit longer,' she said. 'I'd feel so guilty if he went now. Perhaps if I had a week or two to talk to him about it.'

'It wouldn't do any good.' I lit a cigarette and perched on the window seat with my coffee. 'He's already too much for us to cope with.'

Janet lay back on the sofa twisting a damp handkerchief between her fingers. I felt I was failing her, and she felt she was either failing her father or failing David and Rosie. That was silly. The only person who was failing was Mr Treevor himself, and that through no fault of his own.

'Janet, trust me. This is the right decision. And in a week or two you'll agree. It's just that you feel ghastly at present, because of the baby.'

The tears overflowed. I knelt by the sofa and put my arms around her. This is what Flaxman and David never understood. Janet needed to cry. Someone she loved had died. The fact that the person was less than three months old and she had never seen him was beside the point.

After a while Janet drew away from me and blew her nose. 'I *despise* people who dissolve into tears at every possible opportunity.'

'You cry all you want,' I said.

I turned away so she wouldn't see the tears in my own eyes and took a sip of cold coffee. My cigarette had burned itself out in the ashtray on the window seat. I picked up the packet and shook out another. As I did so I heard the clack of the latch on the gate. I looked out of the window. The dean's wife came in from the Close and strode down the path towards the house.

'Oh, damn and blast,' I said viciously, channelling all my anger towards the woman in the garden. 'It's Mrs bloody Forbury. Shall I head her off? I'll tell her you're resting.'

Janet shook her head. 'I'd better see her. It's very kind of her to come.'

'More like nosy.'

'I'll have to see her sooner or later so I might as well get it over with.'

I wiped the scowl off my face and went to answer the door. Mrs Forbury swept past me into the hall.

'Good morning. It's Mrs Appleyard, isn't it?'

'Yes, indeed.' I added, not to be outdone, 'And you must be Mrs Forbury. I believe Janet's mentioned you.'

She was already stripping off her gloves. I took her into the drawing room. Janet asked if I would make some fresh coffee. When I came back, Mrs Forbury was describing how her mother treated miscarriages with wonderful sang-froid, insisting that they were tiresome but hardly serious, like the common cold. Janet took it well, though there was a brief chill between the two women when she said she didn't think she would be up to coming to the Touchies at the Deanery on Thursday afternoon, and that she might not be able to do the flowers in the Lady Chapel next week.

In a perverse way, dealing with Mrs Forbury seemed to do

Janet good. She treated her in much the same way as she had treated Miss Esk, our headmistress at Hillgard House, with an appearance of deference masking a calm determination to get her own way as far as was possible. Nor did the dean's wife bear her any ill will for this. Quite the reverse. It made me realize that Janet fitted in here. Mrs Forbury liked her. Janet could be trusted to play by the rules of the Close. Janet suited Rosington in a way that I never could.

Mrs Forbury mellowed. She even accepted one of my cigarettes.

'I don't usually smoke before lunch but I'm feeling a little naughty today.' She sat back, smoke dribbling from both nostrils, and bestowed a smile on me. 'Janet tells me you've found traces of the Red Canon in the Cathedral Library.'

'A few books. I gather he was still talked about when you were a child.'

She chuckled. 'Hardly surprising, Mrs Appleyard. He caused a few ripples in his time, I'm afraid. It wasn't just his Socialist ideas, though those were bad enough. In religious terms he became very eccentric indeed. My poor dear father used to say that he should never have been allowed to stay for as long as he did. Especially after the business with the animals.'

'The ones that were cut up?'

Mrs Forbury raised her eyebrows. 'You *have* been doing your homework. If I remember rightly, there was some question as to whether he did it himself or whether he encouraged a boy from the town to do it for him. Anyway, it was all rather unpleasant. He was far too friendly with those children.'

'Children?'

'There was a little girl as well.' Her eyes met mine for an instant and slid away. 'The boy's sister. Canon Youlgreave made rather a pet of her, rather like Lewis Carroll and that Oxford girl. You know, the one they say was Alice. But that was rather different, of course – after all, Alice was the daughter of a don.'

'What happened to the children?'

'Heaven knows.' Mrs Forbury stubbed out her cigarette. 'Went back to where they came from, I suppose.' She snorted with laughter but her face wasn't amused. 'My old nanny used to say that if I was naughty the Red Canon would come and take me away. There was a lot of talk, I'm afraid.' She helped herself to one of the Rich Tea biscuits which I had brought out in her honour. 'But eventually they persuaded Mr Youlgreave to resign his canonry and leave Rosington, and then everything calmed down.'

So perhaps the sermon in favour of women priests had only been their excuse for easing him out of Rosington, a convenient ecclesiastical scandal used as a smokescreen for something worse. But had he left Rosington with or without Nancy?

Mrs Forbury glanced up at the mantelpiece at a little silver clock Janet had salvaged from her father's possessions. 'I must fly. I haven't even begun to think about lunch.'

I saw her out of the house. On the doorstep she beckoned me to follow her outside.

'I'm glad you're here, Mrs Appleyard,' she murmured, though there was no risk of Janet overhearing us. 'If ever Janet needed a friend, it's now.'

I blinked. 'I'll do my best.'

'I'm sure you will. This can't be an easy time for her, what with her father and the Theological College closing.' Her face suddenly puckered, and wrinkles appeared so she looked like a pink walnut. 'I've had three miscarriages myself so I know what it's like. One tries to be cheerful about these things but it's not easy. Keep an eye on her, won't you?'

She patted me on the arm and marched down the path to the gate. Momentarily flabbergasted, I stared after her. I'd long since written off Mrs Forbury as a snobbish, domineering, insensitive cow. She might be all of these things but now I'd learned she was something else as well. It was unsettling. I wished people didn't have to be so messy and confusing.

I went back into the house to find that Mr Treevor had crept downstairs to the drawing room. He had made an attempt to dress himself. His flies were undone and the bottom button of his cardigan had been pushed through the buttonhole at the top. He was sitting in the chair where the dean's wife had sat, and his trousers had ridden up to reveal the fact that he was wearing only one sock. As I came in, he turned eagerly towards me.

'Is it lunch time, Mummy?'

'No, dear,' I said. 'Not yet.'

Janet exchanged glances with me. Then she said, 'Daddy, there's something –'

'Daddy?' he said wonderingly, looking around the room. 'Where?'

Janet looked at me again and gave a tiny shake of her head.

'I thought you meant *me* for a moment.' Mr Treevor frowned and nibbled his lower lip, just as Janet sometimes did. 'But I'm not Daddy, am I? I'm Francis.'

38

Several hours later, just before David came home, Janet finally managed to tell Mr Treevor that he was going into hospital. He took it badly, both at the time and afterwards. I'm not even sure he understood what she was saying to him but he must have sensed her distress.

'I feel like a murderer,' Janet said to me afterwards. 'How can we do this to him?'

When David came home he did his best to reassure both Janet and Mr Treevor, but his best wasn't good enough in either case. Rosie sensed the strain and started to play up, spilling her milk on the kitchen table and talking in a babyish lisp very unlike her normal precise voice. I took her upstairs, bathed her and read her one of the Noddy books which Henry had sent.

Hurrah for Little Noddy was about a little puppet who lived in Toyland. The plot involved the theft of a garageful of cars by a gang of sinister goblins. Noddy was wrongfully accused of the crime and flung into jail. Fortunately his best friend, a gnome named Big Ears, was able to clear his name. After the arrest of the goblins, Noddy was rewarded with a car of his own. If only life were that simple, I thought.

While I read, Rosie cuddled Angel and stared at me with large eyes. As I was nearing the end, I heard Janet coming upstairs with Mr Treevor. He was sobbing quietly. 'I wish I was dead,' he said. 'I wish I was dead.'

I raised my voice and hurried on with the story.

'It doesn't make sense,' Rosie said when I had finished.

'What doesn't?'

'This book. How could they think he'd stolen all the cars?

There're at least six in the picture. He couldn't drive them all at once.'

'Perhaps they thought he drove them away one by one. Or he had some friends who came and helped.'

'It's silly.' Rosie shut the book with a snap. 'Doesn't make sense. I don't like that.'

'Nor does anyone.' I got up and closed the curtains. 'Time to settle down now. I'll ask Mummy and Daddy to come and say good night, shall I?'

'Why does Grandpa want to die?'

I hesitated in the doorway. 'I don't think he does really.'

'But he keeps saying he wants to. Is it nice being dead?'

Rosie wasn't my child so I didn't say what I thought. 'When you're dead you go to heaven. That's what Mummy and Daddy believe.'

'I know that. But is it *nice*?'

'Very nice, I expect.'

If it existed, it couldn't be much worse than the life that some people left behind them. Like poor Isabella of Roth, if *she* had existed, burning to a cinder in Rosington marketplace for believing the wrong thing at the wrong time about something that didn't exist in the first place.

'Do they have nice food in heaven?' Rosie asked, settling herself down in bed.

'I'm sure they do. Nothing but the best.'

'Angels eat food too, don't they? It's not just for the dead people?'

'You'll have to ask Daddy. He's the expert. Now, sleep well and see you in the morning.'

I bent to kiss her. Rosie's nightdress and the doll's angelic uniform blended with the pillowcase and sheet. For an instant in the half-light it looked as if there were two fair disembodied heads resting like head-hunters' trophies on the pillow. A memory stirred. Someone's father at a party in Durban, talking about head-hunters and why they did it.

The phone began to ring. I heard Janet talking in Mr Treevor's room and David's footsteps crossing the hall. I went down to the drawing room. A moment later, David poked his head around the door.

'It's Henry.'

I went into the study, wishing I'd had time to have a drink or a cigarette, or even to touch the sprig of lavender for luck. It wasn't easy seeing him again. I had grown used to his absence.

'Wendy!' Henry's enthusiasm bubbled down the line. 'How are you, darling?'

'All right, thanks.' I was so glad to hear him that I decided to postpone reminding him that I wasn't his darling any more. 'What have you been up to?'

'I'll tell you in a minute. What's up with David?'

'I'm sorry,' I said. 'I tried to let you know.'

'Let me know what? What's happened? Are you OK?'

'It's not me. When I got back on Friday, I found that Janet had lost the baby.'

Henry whistled. 'It never rains but it pours, eh?'

'There's more. Mr Treevor's going into hospital tomorrow morning, and then to a nursing home next week. Permanently.'

'Sounds quite sensible – I'd have thought that would be a relief.'

'It is sensible and it will be a relief, but it doesn't stop Janet feeling awful about it. And Mr Treevor hasn't taken it well, either.'

'Why didn't David say something to me? I'm meant to be his friend.'

'You know him. His idea of a heart-to-heart chat is to ask you if it's stopped raining yet.'

Neither of us spoke for a moment. It was a trunk-call. I wondered how much the silence was costing.

'Wendy?'

'What?'

'I'm sorry about the other day. At Liverpool Street. I shouldn't have said all that.'

'It's all right.' I felt a surge of pleasure I didn't want to think about too much. 'I got a bit carried away too.'

There was another pause. I heard the scrape of a match as Henry lit a cigarette.

'I bet the atmosphere's pretty grim. You must need a holiday.'

'Sounds wonderful. When Janet's better I think I'll probably have one.'

'Have you paid in that cheque yet?'

'No.'

'Damn it. Why not?'

'I haven't had time.'

'Would you like me to do it for you?'

I laughed. 'It's not like you to be careful with money.'

'I'm a reformed character nowadays. Economizing like mad. I've left Brown's.'

'I know. I tried to phone you on Saturday.'

Another expensive silence went by.

'I thought about phoning,' Henry said at last. 'But I wasn't sure you'd want to hear from me.'

'Where are you staying?'

'That's why I was phoning you, actually. To let you know. I've got a room at the Queen's Head.'

'Where's that?'

'It's the pub at Roth.'

'What on earth are you doing there?'

'Sleuthing. That's the technical term, isn't it? I had to go somewhere, so I thought why not here? The Queen's Head is very cheap, compared to Brown's at any rate. The food's not bad, and it turns out they've got quite a good cellar. I went to church yesterday – the vicar's about ninety-nine and quite inaudible – and I've had tea at the café on the green, which is run by some terrifyingly refined ladies.'

'How long are you staying?'

'I haven't made my mind up. Why?'

'I just wondered –'

'You see, dearest,' Henry said quickly, 'without your organizational powers I go to pieces. I need you to make the decisions. I wish you were here.'

'So do I.' I'd spoken without thinking but immediately realized I might have given him the wrong impression. I rushed on before he had time to comment. 'Have you got anywhere? With the sleuthing, I mean.'

'I tried to call at the Old Manor House this morning. I had it all worked out. I was going to be an architectural historian writing an article about interesting houses in the area. But I didn't have a chance to say anything. A woman in a pinny answered the door and said Lady Youlgreave wasn't at home. And there were a couple of dogs, too.' His voice became plaintive. 'Savage brutes. One was an Alsatian. It kept trying to bite me.'

I don't think anyone except myself knew that Henry was afraid of dogs. When he was a kid he had been bitten in a sensitive place by a long-haired collie.

'I tried the library, though, and that wasn't a complete washout. There was a pile of old newspapers on a table at the back. The local rag, the *Courier*.'

'Don't tell me. For 1904 or 1905?'

'Both. The librarian just said that another reader had left them out.'

'So Munro's been back to Roth?'

'Presumably. Though nothing had been cut out. No chance, I suppose. I had a look through. There was a certain amount about the Youlgreaves and Roth Park, charitable stuff mainly, but nothing about Francis leaving Rosington.'

'The Youlgreaves probably owned a chunk of the newspaper.'

'And hushed up the Rosington business as far as they could?' Henry said. 'Maybe. He was mentioned in December 1904, though, as one of a list of local worthies who gave money to the village school. Then there's nothing till the report of his death the following summer.'

'That's something. What exactly happened?'

'There was an inquest but the official line was that it was a pure accident. Youlgreave's room was quite high up in the house and apparently he fell out of his window one night. A maid found the body the following morning. Accidental death. That was the story. The coroner said he must have leant out a bit too far trying to get a breath of air. It was a very warm night.'

'When are you going back to London?'

'Tomorrow morning, probably. Any chance of your coming up to town in the next few days?'

'Not really. There's too much I need to do here.'

'How would it be if I came to see you?'

'In Rosington?' I couldn't keep the disbelief out of my voice.

'They've got long memories here, you know. If Oliver Cromwell turned up, they'd probably present him with a bill for damaging the carvings in sixteen forty-something.'

'I don't mind that. Why don't I come up tomorrow? I've got a date with the Cuthbertsons but I can easily put them off. We could have lunch at the Crossed Keys.'

'The Cuthbertsons?'

'I told you – they own Veedon Hall. I'd arranged to run down and spend the day with them looking over the school and so on. But they won't mind if –'

'You mustn't cancel that.'

'All right, then I'll come and take you to lunch on Wednesday. So that's settled. I've looked up the trains. There's one that gets to Rosington at about twelve thirty-five.'

'But Janet –'

'She can come too, if you like. And David, I suppose. Though I'd much rather it was just you.'

I gave in, mainly, I told myself, because it would mean I wouldn't have to cook lunch.

'That's wonderful,' he said. 'And afterwards we can go to the bank and pay in your cheque.'

I couldn't help myself. I laughed. Henry was like a terrier with a sense of humour. He made me laugh and he never let go.

He cleared his throat. 'Anyway, I'd better leave you to make cocoa or whatever you do for fun at this time. I love you. I'm going to put the phone down now so you don't have to reply to that.'

There was a click and the line went dead. I stared at the handset for a moment and then replaced it on its base. I felt happier than I had done for months, which was stupid of me. I heard Janet's footsteps on the stairs and went to tell her that Henry had invited us to lunch the day after tomorrow. She must have had a bath while I was on the phone because she was already in her nightclothes – a dressing gown over a cotton winceyette nightdress, cream-coloured and with a pattern of small pink bows. It was a thick winter dressing gown, which made me think that even a bath had failed to warm her up. But her face lit up when I told her Henry was coming.

'How lovely,' she said. 'I'm so glad.'

'It doesn't mean anything's changed,' I warned her. 'But there's no reason why we shouldn't behave like civilized human beings, is there?'

'No, of course not.'

'It's Tuesday tomorrow,' I said hastily, knowing I was beginning to blush, and seizing on an exit line. 'I'd better put the rubbish out.'

I was still feeling happy when I went to bed that night. Before going to sleep, I reread 'The Office of the Dead' whilst smoking a final cigarette.

> *Enough! I cried. Consume the better part,*
> *No more. For therein lies the deepest art . . .*

The words triggered the memory that had begun to surface when I was talking with Rosie. Or rather parts of a memory, about the conversation with someone's father in Durban. The man who knew about head-hunting.

It had been at one of Grady's parties. This one had been just before the company crashed, and with it Henry's investment. My memory of it was partial because even by Grady's standards, the party had been particularly drunken.

The ex-colonial administrator had stuck out because he didn't resemble any of the other guests. He was somebody's father on a visit from England. He was a little, hunched man with a creased yellow face. I remember him early on in the evening standing in a corner with a glass of orange juice in his hand watching us making fools of ourselves. I felt sorry for him because I thought he was obviously lonely, and anyway I was trying to escape from Grady, so I went to talk to him. I asked him if he was bored.

'No,' he said. 'It's fascinating.'

'What is?'

He smiled up at me and gestured with his glass towards the crowd of people swirling through the room and spilling on to the terrace and down into the garden and around the pool. 'All this. Ritual behaviour is one of my interests.'

I laughed. 'You're teasing me.'

He shook his head and explained that his work had encouraged him to develop an interest in anthropology.

'Yes, but that's about savages – primitive people, I mean.'

'All human societies have their rituals, Mrs Appleyard, how-ever sophisticated they may appear to be on the surface. Think of the ritual mourning we indulged in when the King died. And look at this – intoxication, formalized sexual display and childish games, many of them of an aggressive nature. I could give you plenty of parallels from tribal cultures in West Africa.'

'But that can't be the same,' I said. 'Their reasons for doing it must be completely different from ours.'

'Why?'

'Because we're Europeans and they're Africans.'

'It makes no difference. That is one of the interesting things that anthropology shows. On a ritual level, human societies are strikingly similar in many respects. Take cannibalism, for instance.'

I made a face at him. 'Rather you than me.'

'I don't mean cannibalism from necessity or inclination, of course, where eating other human beings is a matter of survival, or an addition to the diet. No, I mean ritual cannibalism, which has nothing to do with nourishment. It's often allied to head-hunting. I came across a certain amount of it in West Africa and also in the East Indies. There were various reasons for it, but the most common, found in most cultures at some point or another, is that by eating something of a person you acquire his soul, or perhaps a part of him you particularly value. His courage, for example, or his prowess in battle.'

'Not in Europe, surely? Or at least not since we all lived in caves and went around knocking each other over the head with rocks.'

'There's evidence to show that the practice persisted in England and Scotland until the Middle Ages. And there were cases in other parts of Europe much later than that. There was one in the Balkans, in Montenegro, in 1912. And a diluted version of this lasted much longer. Think of hair, for example. Other people's hair.' He smiled grimly at me. 'You wouldn't necessarily eat it, of course, not nowadays. But I can remember my aunts wearing mourning brooches and rings containing locks snipped from the loved one's head. What they were really doing, of course, was carrying around a little bit of the soul of a person they'd lost. Rather like the head-hunters do in parts of Borneo. More genteel than eating his brain as they might have done at another time or in another place, but the principle's exactly the same.'

The rest of what he'd said had been drowned in dry martinis or lost in the blue haze of cigarette smoke. It didn't matter. The question was what had Francis wanted that a child might possess? Youth, health and life? Had Francis believed that the purpose of dead children was to feed the living with life? How did that compare with buying a sprig of lavender from a nasty old woman in the hope it would bring you luck?

I turned over the pages of *The Voice of Angels* until I came to 'Breakheart Hill'.

> *'For hart's blood makes the young heart strong,' quoth he.*
> *'God hath ordained it so. He dies that ye*
> *'May hunt, my son, and through his strength be free.'*

Time sanitizes all but the most dreadful horrors. There I was, entertaining the bizarre idea that a clergyman of the Church of England might have considered eating bits of children in the crazy belief that this would somehow extend his life. But it was only a speculation, and the fact that Francis had died more than fifty years ago removed it one stage further from here and now. So I felt pleased with myself. I was even looking forward to telling Henry about the idea tomorrow.

I put out the cigarette and settled down. I thought of Henry briefly, that he had his good points as well as his bad, then I slid into a deep sleep. There must have been dreams, though I don't remember any of them, and they must have been happy ones because I was still feeling happy when I woke up.

It was one of those times when there's very little transition between sleep and being awake. It's like swimming up from the bottom of a pool, the sense of urgency and speed, the sense of breaking out of one element into another.

The room was full of light. I knew it was still early because the light had that soft, almost colourless quality you get in the hour or two after dawn. I opened my eyes and saw Janet in the doorway. She was wearing a long pale-blue nylon nightdress and her hair was loose and unbrushed.

'Wendy,' she said. 'Wendy.'

I sat up. 'What is it?'

She seemed not to have heard me. She looked so cold, an ice woman. You could see the shape of her body through the nylon of the nightdress. With a twist of envy I wondered if she'd bought it to make herself look pretty for David.

'Janet, what's happened?'

'Wendy.' She took a step into the room, then stopped and blinked. 'Daddy's *dead*.'

39

Blood is the colour of a scream.

Neither of us said anything as we stood in the doorway looking down at the body of John Treevor. But that's what I thought. *Blood is the colour of a scream.* There was nothing logical, nothing rational, about it. I couldn't scream for fear of waking Rosie.

Who would have thought he had so much blood in him?

Really we should get the sheets and the pillowcase in a bath full of cold water as soon as possible. Soak blood in cold water, said my mother, who was a sort of walking housewife's manual. But the bedding was so saturated I doubted if it would ever be clean again. And there was nothing we could do about the mattress. It wasn't just the cover. The blood would have soaked right into the horsehair.

I knew Janet was right, that he was dead. He was so very still, you see, and the blood had stopped flowing.

There were red splashes on the bedside rug. The rug would have to go, too. Mr Treevor's false teeth, clamped for ever shut, were in the glass on the bedside table. His knees had drawn up under the eiderdown. He was lying on his back and it looked as if he had two open mouths, one redder than the other. All the redness cast a sombre glow through the room, neutralizing the pale dawn light.

On the rug was a knife, the vegetable knife we'd lost. Oh well, I thought, that's something. None of the other knives in the kitchen drawer were nearly as good for peeling potatoes. Mr Treevor's eyes were open and he stared up at the ceiling towards David's heaven. Except that David was far too sophisticated to believe in a common-or-garden traditional heaven located above the sky.

Janet stirred. 'At least he's at peace now.'

Peace? Is that what you call it? 'I'm going to be sick.'

I pushed past her, went into the bathroom and locked the door. When I came out, Janet was waiting for me on the landing. She had a key in her hand and the door to Mr Treevor's room was closed. Without exchanging a word we went down to the kitchen.

I filled the kettle and put it on the stove. While Janet laid the tea tray, I leant against the sink and watched her. I remember how she fetched the cups and saucers and aligned them on the tray, how the teaspoons were polished on the tea towel, how the milk jug was filled and then covered with a little lacy cloth designed to keep out the flies. I remember how deft her movements were, how she made a little island of order amid all the chaos, and how beautiful she was, though she was still pale and her face was rigid with shock.

She must have sensed me watching her, because she glanced up and smiled. For an instant it was as if she'd struck a match behind her face, and the flame flared, warmed the chilly air for a moment, and died.

I made the tea. Janet poured it and added three teaspoonfuls of sugar to each cup.

'It's my fault,' she said after the first sip.

'Of course it isn't.'

She shook her head. 'He couldn't face going away. We were putting him out like a piece of rubbish for the dustmen. My *father.*'

'He was going into hospital for his sake as much as for yours.' I reached across the table and touched her hand. 'You know how he's been lately. He could have done this at any time, for any reason. Or for no reason at all. He wasn't himself.'

Janet gasped, a single, ragged sob. 'Then who was he?'

'At one point he thought he was Francis Youlgreave,' I said. 'Listen, all I'm saying is that part of him had already died. The important part, the part that was your father.'

Janet took a deep breath. 'I must phone someone. Dr Flaxman, I suppose.'

I touched the key lying between us on the table. 'You've locked the bedroom door?'

She nodded. 'In case Rosie –'

'What about David?'

Janet blinked, wrinkled her forehead and looked up at the clock on the dresser. 'He'll be getting up in a moment to say the morning office.'

'Janet, why did you go into your father's room?'

'I woke up and I couldn't get back to sleep. I – I thought I'd just peep in and see if he was all right. He was so upset. When do you think –?'

'I don't know.' I remembered how still everything had been in Mr Treevor's bedroom, how the blood had soaked into the bedding, how dark the blood had been. 'Probably hours ago.'

'What a way to end.'

'If he'd had the choice, he'd probably have preferred it. I'd much rather go like that than get more and more senile.'

Water rustled in one of the pipes running down the wall. Janet pushed back her chair.

'That's David,' she said.

I wondered why she'd come to me not him after she found her father.

Death wasn't something I'd had to deal with very often. I hadn't had the practice. I didn't know the procedures. I thought that Mr Treevor had somehow cheated death by killing himself. Part of me, the little selfish child that lives within us all, was glad he was dead. In the long run, it would save everyone a lot of trouble.

I just wished he hadn't made such a mess of his exit. Literally. Why hadn't he done it sensibly and discreetly somewhere in the wings of our lives? A nice quiet overdose, perhaps, almost indistinguishable from a natural death, or at least something Janet could have told herself was an accident, like stepping in front of a bus. At times like this I was glad of the privacy of the mind. If my thoughts had been public property, the world would have labelled me a psychopath.

Janet slipped away to talk to David. I went upstairs to dress. Afterwards I took another cup of tea into the drawing room and smoked a cigarette. David was now in the study talking on

838

the phone. The doors were open and I could hear what he was saying.

'No, there's no doubt at all, I'm afraid . . . can't you come sooner than that?'

I stared through a window at a garden varnished with dew. The spire gleamed in the early morning sun. Francis must have stood in this room, looked out of this window, seen this view.

'I appreciate that,' David was saying. 'Very well . . . Yes, all right, I'll ring them straightaway . . . Goodbye.'

He put down the phone and came to join me in the drawing room.

'Flaxman can't manage it before half past eight.'

'I'll take Rosie to school.'

'Thanks.' I doubt if he heard what I'd said. 'Poor Janet,' he went on. 'All this on top of the miscarriage.'

'I think she needs to be in bed.'

'Would you tell her about Flaxman? I'd better phone the police, and the dean.'

I persuaded Janet to go back to bed. Then I got Rosie up, made breakfast and walked her to school. It felt unnatural to be doing normal things. Everything should have become abnormal in deference to Mr Treevor's death. But Rosington ignored his absence. The city was the same today as it had been yesterday, which was *wrong*.

I looked at Rosie as we drifted down the hill towards St Tumwulf's. She had Angel clamped under her arm and she was sucking her thumb. The doll was wearing its pink outfit because it was moving in disguise among mortals, and so she matched Rosie in her pink gingham school dress. I thought Rosie was paler than usual. She'd been as fond of Mr Treevor as anybody.

During breakfast, David had told her that Grandpa had gone to heaven in the night.

'Will he be coming back?' she had said.

'No,' David replied. Rosie nodded and went back to her cornflakes.

At the school gates, I asked Rosie if she was feeling all right.

'*I'm* all right. But Angel's got a tummy ache.'

'A bad one?'

'A little bit bad.' Rosie's face brightened. 'I'm going to finish sewing Angel's shawl today and it'll go nicely with her dress. That'll cheer her up.'

'She'll look very pretty.'

'We're sisters now,' Rosie told me. 'Both in pink.'

'Makes the boys wink, doesn't it?'

She gave me the doll and went into the playground. It seemed to me the other children parted before her like the Red Sea. I found the headmistress in her office, told her what had happened and asked her to keep an eye on Rosie.

'A death in the family, in the home,' the headmistress said. 'It's a terrible thing for a child.'

When I got back to the Dark Hostelry, I found Dr Flaxman in the drawing room talking to David and Janet.

'I'd better have the key,' he was saying. 'If you wouldn't mind.'

David frowned at him. Janet moved along the sofa and patted the seat beside her. I sat down.

'I don't understand,' David said.

'It's common practice in cases like this, Mr Byfield.'

'What do you mean?'

'Cases where the coroner will have to be notified.'

'I can understand that of course, but –'

'And particularly where there's an element of doubt about the death.'

'I should have thought that was plain enough.'

Flaxman's eyes flickered towards me and then returned to David. 'Perhaps I could have a word in private.'

Janet said, 'That's not necessary. Whatever you can say to my husband you can say to Mrs Appleyard and me.'

David nodded. 'Of course.'

'Very well.' Flaxman continued to speak to David, ignoring Janet and me. 'It's possible that Mr Treevor killed himself. But any death like this needs careful investigation.'

'Surely you're not suggesting –?'

'I'm not suggesting anything,' Flaxman said. 'I'm just doing my job. May I use your phone?'

People came and went, doing their jobs, while we sat by and watched. Dr Flaxman waited until two uniformed police officers appeared on the doorstep. David took the police to see Mr Treevor. They didn't stay long in the room and they said very little. But when they came out, one of them went away and the other lingered like a ghost on the landing in front of Mr Treevor's door.

I took him up a cup of coffee and a biscuit. He looked at me as if I were a Martian and blushed. But he said thank you and then broke wind, which embarrassed him more than it did me.

Our next visitors were also police officers. But these were detectives in plain clothes. Inspector Humphries was a tall, hunched man with short, fair hair which looked as if it would be as soft as a baby's. He had a broken-nosed sergeant called Pate, all bone and muscle. I later discovered Pate played fly-half for the town's rugby football fifteen. David introduced me and explained that his wife was in bed.

Humphries grunted. 'Perhaps you'd like to take us upstairs, sir,' he said. 'Who was it who actually found the body?'

'My wife. Then she woke Mrs Appleyard and me.'

'I see.' The inspector had a Midlands accent and a way of mumbling his words that made it sound as if he was speaking through a mouthful of thick soup. 'And when was Mr Treevor last seen alive?'

'About half past ten the previous evening. My wife looked in to say good night.'

Humphries grunted again. We had reached the landing. At a nod from the inspector, the constable on guard unlocked Mr Treevor's door. I heard Pate sucking in his breath. Then the two detectives went into the room and closed the door behind them. Then the doorbell rang and David and I went downstairs and answered it together.

The doorbell kept ringing all morning. First there was another doctor, the police surgeon. Then came Peter Hudson, who asked if there was anything he could do and said that he would take over David's responsibilities at the Cathedral for the time being. Later on in the day we found in our letterbox a stiff little note from the dean, addressed to Janet, expressing polite regret at the death of her father.

Canon Osbaston turned up in person, suddenly frail, his little head wagging like a wilting flower on the long stalk of his neck.

David put him in the drawing room and I brought him a glass of brandy.

'Poor Janet,' he said, 'it's so very hard. Sometimes it seems so meaningless.'

'Yes,' said David.

'So pointless,' Osbaston murmured. 'It really makes one wonder.' Then he glanced at his watch, finished his brandy and struggled to his feet. 'Give my love to Janet and let me know if there's anything I can do. But I'll call again tomorrow, if I may. Perhaps I'll see you at evensong, David.'

In that moment I liked him better than I had ever done.

June Hudson appeared just as Osbaston was leaving. She was holding a large earthenware dish.

'Just a little casserole,' she said, handing it to me. 'I thought you might not have time to cook a proper meal tonight.' She shifted from one foot to the other. 'And how's Janet?'

'Very shaken, naturally,' David said. 'She's resting now.'

'Let me know when you think she might like a visitor.'

'You're very kind.' David made it sound like an accusation.

June Hudson smiled at us both and almost fled down the garden towards the gate to the Close.

Shortly after this, they took the body away. They brought an ambulance into the Close and backed it up to the gate into our garden. People lingered to watch, swelling to a small crowd when the police raised screens. Sergeant Pate suggested that it might be better if we kept out of the way. So the three of us sat in Janet and David's room and tried to resist the temptation to peer out of the window.

We heard the tramp of feet on the stairs. They took away the mattress and the bedding as well as the body. They also removed some of Mr Treevor's possessions. They gave David a receipt. Janet wanted to say goodbye to her father, but David wouldn't let her. He said there would be other opportunities. He meant when the mortuary had cleaned him up.

'I'm trying to remember him now as he used to be,' Janet said carefully, like a child repeating a lesson. 'Before Mummy died.'

Then it was time for me to collect Rosie. David offered me the use of the car but I refused, because it was garaged at the

Theological College and fetching it would have meant one of us having to walk through the Close. Besides, I thought it would be better for Rosie if everything that could be normal was normal.

I met no one I knew on my way to school with Angel. None of the mothers and grandmothers at the school gate talked to me, though one or two of them gave me curious looks. They did that anyway. When Rosie came out I gave her the doll.

'I've done the shawl,' Rosie said. 'It's pink. I've got it in my satchel. Where's Mummy?'

'She's having a rest at home.'

'But it's daytime.'

'You know she hasn't been very well recently. And of course she's very sad at present because of Grandpa.'

'Grandpa's in heaven,' Rosie announced, with a hint of a question mark trailing at the end of the sentence.

'Yes, that's what Daddy said.'

She took my hand because it was less effort for her if I towed her up the hill to the town. 'Angel says, perhaps he went to hell.'

'Why would he go there?'

'If you do bad things, you go to hell.'

'Did Grandpa do bad things?'

Rosie conferred silently with her doll. 'Angel doesn't know. What's for tea?'

'That's something *I* don't know. I expect we'll find something.'

We didn't talk for the rest of the way. There was a men's outfitters with a large plate-glass window in the High Street, and as usual Rosie lingered as we passed to admire her reflection. The proprietor was fetching a rack of ties from the window display for a customer standing a yard or two behind him. It was the dean. For an instant his eyes met mine and then he turned away to examine a glass-fronted cabinet containing cufflinks and tiepins.

We went into the Close by the Sacristan's Gate. Mr Gotobed was shooing a group of schoolboys off the sacred grass around the east end of the Cathedral, the skirts of his cassock fluttering in the breeze. He turned as he heard our footsteps on the

843

gravel, abandoned the children and walked quickly and clumsily towards us.

'Mrs Appleyard.'

I smiled at him.

'Mother and me were sorry to hear about Mr Treevor. She asked me to send her condolences.'

'Thank you. I'll tell the Byfields.'

His eyes were full of yearning. I told him Rosie needed her tea and that I had to rush.

When we got home, Rosie went up to see her mother. There was a knock on the garden door. A small man with no chin and a very large Adam's apple was standing on the doorstep. He waved at me. When I opened the door he edged forward, smiling, and I automatically stepped back into the hall.

'*Rosington Observer*, miss. I'm Jim Filey. I called about the sad fatality.'

'I see.'

'I gather there'll have to be an inquest. Very distressing for the family, I'm sure.' He pulled out a notebook. 'And you are?'

It was the way he stared at me that made up my mind. He was younger than me and acting like a hard-bitten newshound. I didn't like anything about him, from his over-greased hair to the fussy little patterns on his gleaming black brogues.

'My name's none of your business.' I began to close the door. 'I'll say goodbye.'

'Here, miss, wait. Is it true Mr Treevor cut his throat?'

'I'd like you to go, Mr Filey.'

But he was no longer looking at me. He was looking over my shoulder, into the hall.

'Get out,' David said very quietly.

I stepped aside from the doorway. David moved towards Filey. For an instant I thought that he was going to hit the reporter. Filey took a couple of steps backwards. David shut the door and locked it. Filey scowled at us through the glass and then walked rapidly down the garden to the gate.

'Thanks,' I said. 'He was beginning to be a pest.'

'You shouldn't have to put up with that sort of thing.'

He had calmed down now. The whole episode had lasted less than a minute. What really shook me was not that nasty little reporter but what I'd glimpsed in David. There was so much rage in him. Perhaps that was why he needed to believe in God, to find something greater than himself that would contain and repress whatever was swirling around inside him and trying to find a way out.

I said, 'This may be a sign of things to come.'

His eyebrows shot up. 'Surely not?'

I'd lowered my voice to a whisper, as had he. 'This is going to get in the newspapers.'

'You may be right. I'd better phone my mother.'

He returned to the study to phone Granny Byfield. I went downstairs to the kitchen. I wanted to talk to someone who didn't belong in Rosington, who wasn't part of the little world of the Close. That wasn't the whole truth – I wanted to talk to *Henry*.

In the kitchen I opened the larder door and wondered what to do for Rosie's tea. At least we had the Hudsons' casserole for supper. All at once the idea of living in Henry's prep school seemed wonderfully attractive. At least there would be staff to take care of the cooking and cleaning, the washing and ironing.

I turned round to put a loaf of bread on the table. For a moment I thought Mr Treevor was sitting in the Windsor chair at the end of the table. Suddenly the knowledge that he would never be there again, demanding a second helping before some of us had even started our first, made my eyes fill with tears.

40

On Wednesday morning our first visitor was Mrs Forbury. She came through the gate to the Close, glancing over her shoulder like a thief as she slipped into the garden.

'It's the Queen Touchy,' I told Janet, who was lying on the sofa in the drawing room. 'I'll send her away.'

'No, don't,' Janet said. 'It's kind of her to come.'

You can never predict how people are going to react. When Mrs Forbury saw Janet lying there in her dressing gown, she bustled over to her, put her arms around her and gave her a hug. Janet hugged her back and started to cry.

'There, there,' said the Queen Touchy. 'There, there.'

'Would you like some coffee?' I said.

Mrs Forbury looked over Janet's head at me. 'I'd better not, thank you. I mustn't stay long. I just popped in on impulse, you see, and Dennis wouldn't know where to find me if – if he happened to want me.'

In other words, she hadn't told her husband she was coming here. She didn't stay long. She slipped out of the house as furtively as she'd come in. When she said goodbye, Janet clung to her hand. At the time I couldn't understand it, but now I think that Janet and Mrs Forbury were joined together by dead babies.

'It *was* kind of her,' Janet said when I came back.

I nodded offhandedly, miffed that I had been temporarily dislodged from my position as Comforter-in-Chief.

'I must do a bit of shopping this morning,' I said. 'You remember that Henry's coming?'

'David will stay with me. You go out to lunch with him by yourself. It'll do you good.'

'But what about you?'

'I'll find something. I'm not very hungry.'

'But Janet –'

'I'm not ill. I wish you wouldn't mother me.'

The doorbell rang again.

I went into the hall. Inspector Humphries and Sergeant Pate were standing with their backs to the house, apparently admiring the sun-filled garden. When I opened the door they turned together to face me in a movement so synchronized it might have been choreographed.

'Good morning, Mrs Appleyard,' Humphries mumbled, his lips scarcely moving. 'Is Mr Byfield in?'

'I'm afraid you've missed him. He's at the Theological College.'

'May we come in?'

I stood back to let the two men into the house.

'Who is it?' Janet called from the drawing room.

'The police.'

Humphries moved so that he could see Janet on the sofa through the doorway of the drawing room. 'Mind if I have a word, Mrs Byfield?'

The policemen sat down one on either side of the fireplace. I perched on the arm of the sofa. Pate took out a notebook and fiddled with the piece of elastic which held it together.

Humphries cleared his throat. 'I'm afraid I shall have to have a look in Mr Treevor's room again, Mrs Byfield. And perhaps elsewhere in the house.'

'All right.'

I said, 'Is there something in particular you're looking for?'

'One or two things we'd like to clear up,' he said, still looking at Janet.

'Such as?' Janet asked.

'If you don't mind, I'd rather talk to your husband about this,' Humphries said.

'Why?'

'Well, there are some things that aren't suitable for ladies, really.' He stirred in his chair. 'No need to make things worse than they are, is there?'

'Mr Treevor was my father,' Janet said. 'I want you to talk to *me*.'

I saw Pate wince, as though expecting an explosion. Humphries ran his fingers through his baby-soft hair. But he didn't clam up. Quite the contrary.

'Very well, Mrs Byfield, I'll tell you what I would have told your husband. There's some doubts about the circumstances of your father's death. You know what a pathologist is?'

'Of course I do.'

'He had a look at the body last night. Now, when someone cuts their throat, you normally get a clean cut and they arch their heads back, which means the carotid arteries slip back. And that means that the knife misses them, so there's less blood than you'd expect. Follow me so far?'

For a moment the scene in Mr Treevor's room flashed in vivid technicolour behind my eyes.

'There was quite a lot of cuts on your father's throat, and a lot of blood. The bedclothes were in a mess, too, which suggests he struggled. Tell me, Mrs Byfield, was your father right-handed or left-handed?'

'Right-handed,' she muttered, and Sergeant Pate had to ask her to repeat her answer.

'If a right-handed person is cutting his throat, Mrs Byfield, he usually does it from left to right. Understand? But the cuts on your father's throat were from right to left. So. Perhaps you can see now why I wanted to talk to your husband, and why we'd like to have a look around a little more, and ask a few questions.'

I stood up. 'This is absurd,' I said. 'You know Mr Treevor wasn't a well man. As Dr Flaxman will tell you, he was going senile. He wasn't acting normally. Nothing he's done in the last few months could be called *normal*. So it hardly seems strange that the way he killed himself was rather unusual.'

Inspector Humphries had stood up as well. With his head hunched forward on his shoulders, he looked like a bird of prey in an ill-fitting suit. 'Unusual, Mrs Appleyard? Oh yes, *very* unusual. For example, this is the first suicide I've seen where the perpetrator killed himself, then got up and washed the knife, left it on the floor at least a yard away from the bed, climbed back into bed and carried on with being dead.' He sucked air between his teeth. 'Very unusual indeed, I'd say. Wouldn't you agree, Sergeant?'

Janet shifted her body on the sofa. 'What would you say if I asked you to leave?'

'I'd say that was your right, Mrs Byfield, but if you do it won't take me long to come back with a search warrant. And if this goes any further, your refusal will look very bad. Whatever happens there will have to be an inquest, you know. It will probably be adjourned so we can make further enquiries.'

Janet sighed. 'You can look round, if you want.'

'Good.'

'Do you want me to go with them?' I said to her.

Janet shook her head. 'It doesn't matter.'

Neither of us spoke for a moment when Humphries and Pate left the room. We heard their heavy footsteps on the stairs and the key turning in the lock of Mr Treevor's room.

'Why was he so unpleasant to you?' I asked.

She looked at me for a long moment. 'Why should he be nice?' she said at last. 'They'll look everywhere.'

'Everywhere?'

'Of course they will. It's their job.'

I wanted to laugh. What would they make of the bottle of gin in my bedside cupboard, not to mention the sprig of lavender resting on a cheque for ten thousand pounds?

'Janet, you don't think –'

'I don't know what to think.' She swung her legs off the sofa. 'I'd better ring David.'

There was another ring at the doorbell.

It was a boy with a telegram addressed to David and Janet. Janet tore open the envelope, read the message and passed it to me.

ARRIVING 12.38 TRAIN. MOTHER.

'Damn it,' Janet said, running her fingers through her hair. 'I thought this might happen.'

'It must be the train Henry's on. Ask David to bring round the car, and I'll meet them both if you want.'

'We'll have to make up a bed for her, and then there's supper.'

At least David's mother had given us something to do, something to distract us from the heavy feet moving about upstairs, and what the presence of the police officers might mean to all of us. While Janet phoned David, I explained what had happened to Inspector Humphries and made up the bed for old Mrs Byfield in the little room next to Rosie's. Mrs Byfield was a demanding visitor, and Janet asked me to make sure there was a hot-water bottle to air the bed, and on the bedside table a carafe of water, a glass and a tin of biscuits in case she should feel peckish in the night. She might be chilly at night, so extra blankets had to be found and a fire had to be laid.

While I was doing this, David came home, and I heard his raised voice first in the hall and later in Mr Treevor's room. I was glad to see him, because we soon had other distractions in the shape of two more journalists, whom David turned away, and the bishop's chaplain. I stood on the landing and eavesdropped on his conversation with David in the hall below.

'I say,' said Gervase Haselbury-Finch, 'this is awful. The bishop sent me round to say how sorry he is. He says you and Mrs Byfield are much in his mind at present. And in his prayers, naturally.'

'How very kind of him,' said David in a voice that suggested the opposite. 'Do thank him.'

'Um – I should say – the chief constable telephoned him this morning.'

'Really?'

'I gather there are one or two things that the police will have to clear up about Mr Treevor's death. He – the bishop, that is – would very much appreciate it if you could keep him informed.'

'I'm sure he would,' said David.

'There are wider issues to be considered.' Haselbury-Finch was almost gabbling by now. 'The bishop feels that the matter could be a sensitive one for the diocese, even for the church as a whole.'

'Thank him for his advice, Gervase. In the meantime, I have got rather a lot to do.'

'Eh? Oh yes, I see. You must be awfully busy. I'll say goodbye then.'

The garden door opened and closed. I went downstairs and found David lighting a cigarette.

'I heard that,' I said.

'I could have strangled him,' David said, and to my surprise smiled at me. 'Not poor Gervase. The bishop.'

'I'd better go down to the station.' I studied my reflection in the hall mirror. I would have to go as I was. There was no time to repair make-up or brush hair.

'I'll see if I can get rid of the policemen before my mother comes. I'm sorry you're being dragged into this. Just drop my mother off here and then go and have lunch with Henry. Try and forget all about it.'

'Not so easy.'

'No.'

We seemed to have blundered into a world where the ordinary rules were temporarily suspended. So I said, 'What do you think really happened to Mr Treevor?'

David rubbed his forehead. 'God knows. It simply doesn't make sense.'

Our eyes met. I felt sick. It was as if we were all in a lift going down a shaft, and the cables had snapped and we were falling, and all we could do was pretend we were calm and wait for the crash at the bottom.

David let me out of the back door into the High Street. The car was parked in the marketplace. I drove down River Hill and cut through Bridge Street to the station. I was a few minutes late and when I got there I found Mrs Byfield asking a porter to be more careful with her suitcases while Henry was pretending to be absorbed in a poster advertising the Norfolk Broads.

Henry pecked my cheek. 'I'm so sorry. How are David and Janet?'

'I'll tell you later.'

'There were journalists on the train.'

I smiled at Granny Byfield. To look at her was to get an impression of what David would look like when he was old. I introduced myself, and then Henry. She had met us at David and Janet's wedding but we had not lingered in her memory. I drove them back to the Dark Hostelry. Henry tried to make

851

conversation – he'd have tried to talk to a Trappist monk – but Mrs Byfield kept him in his place with monosyllabic replies and the occasional glare.

We parked in the marketplace. Mrs Byfield gazed out of the window while she waited for Henry to fetch the suitcases from the boot and me to open the door for her. Her hip was painful and I had to help her out.

'I'm sure I've seen that woman before,' she said, leaning heavily on my arm. 'Do you know her?'

I was just in time to see a small woman wearing a dark-blue headscarf going into the Sacristan's Gate.

'No, I don't think so.'

'I never forget a face,' announced Mrs Byfield. 'I probably met her when I've stayed here before.'

'Damn,' I murmured.

'I *beg* your pardon.'

Jim Filey was leaning on the back doorbell of the Dark Hostelry. There was another man with him, a camera and flash slung round his neck.

Henry followed my gaze. 'Trouble?'

'What is it?' demanded Mrs Byfield.

'There's a journalist and a photographer outside the house.'

At that moment the door opened and I glimpsed David's face. The flash went off.

'Intolerable,' Mrs Byfield said. 'It shouldn't be allowed.' She limped down the pavement towards the Dark Hostelry, with Henry and me trailing behind her. She tapped Filey on the arm with her stick. 'Excuse me, young man. You're blocking our way.'

Filey swung round. So did the photographer, raising his camera. There was another flash.

'Come in, Mother,' David said. 'These gentlemen are just leaving.'

'Mrs Byfield?' Filey said, his Adam's apple bobbing in excitement. 'I wonder if you'd care to comment on the tragic death of your daughter-in-law's father. Was he someone you knew well?'

'I don't want to talk to you, young man. I shall complain to your editor.'

Filey jotted something down in his notebook. 'Have you come down to stay with your son and his family, Mrs Byfield?'

She compressed her lips as if to stop the words falling out. David took her arm and drew her gently into the house. I followed, with Henry dragging the cases behind me. David shut the door and put the bolts across.

'Well!' Mrs Byfield said. 'This is a fine welcome, I must say.'

'It's getting worse.' David kissed his mother's cheek.

'Worse?'

'They were peering through the kitchen window just before you came.'

'But when all's said and done, it's none of their business.'

'That's not how they see it, Mother.' He hesitated and then went on, 'It seems that there's a possibility that Janet's father didn't commit suicide after all.'

She frowned. 'Some kind of accident?'

'The police think not.'

'But that's ridiculous.' She was nobody's fool and saw where this was leading. 'Then someone broke in. A thief.'

'Perhaps. Janet's father did say he'd seen a strange man in the house, but we rather dismissed that. As you know, he hadn't been himself in the last few months.'

'I'd like to sit down now.' She looked tired and old.

'Come up to the drawing room. Let me take your coat.'

'Where's Janet?'

'Resting in bed.'

Granny Byfield grunted as she moved towards the door to the stairs, either because of the pain from her hip or because she disapproved of Janet's resting in bed.

David looked at Henry and me. 'I'm sorry about this. Why don't you two go to lunch?'

'Isn't there something I should do here?' I said. 'Your mother will need some lunch as well.'

'Just go,' David said wearily. 'Please. I'll need to talk to her, and it'll be easier if there's no one else around.' He glanced at his mother, who had begun the long haul up the stairs, and turned back to us. 'I'm sorry to sound so unwelcoming.'

I don't know why, but I put my hand on his shoulder and kissed his cheek.

41

A few minutes later Henry and I slipped into the High Street and walked down to the Crossed Keys. I thought the lobby of the hotel smelled faintly of Turkish tobacco, but no one I recognized was there or in the bar.

The big, panelled dining room was almost empty. We ate tinned tomato soup, a steak-and-kidney pie with far too much kidney, and a partially cooked bread-and-butter pudding. Not that it mattered. Neither of us had much appetite. We had a couple of gins beforehand and shared a bottle of claret with the meal.

While we ate, or rather for most of the time failed to eat, I told Henry what had happened. It wasn't until the pie arrived that I realized something that should have struck me at the station. I laid down my fork.

'You *knew*,' I said. 'You knew about Mr Treevor.'

'There was something in the *Telegraph* this morning. Not much – police are investigating the death of a sixty-nine-year-old man in the Cathedral Close at Rosington. That sort of thing. They didn't mention him by name but they made it clear he was a resident. So I was half expecting it. And then I asked the ticket collector at the station, and he confirmed it.'

'Filey.'

'Who?'

'He's a reporter on the local paper. He was the one asking the questions when we arrived at the Dark Hostelry. I bet he sold the story to the *Telegraph*.'

'How's Janet taking it?'

'Not very well. It's come on top of David losing his job, and the miscarriage. It would be bad enough if he had just died. But to have it happen like this . . . David's been good. I think they've learned who their friends are.' I thought of the dean's wife. 'And sometimes they're not who you'd expect.'

We sat in silence for a moment. There had been a party of rowdy men, perhaps journalists, in the bar, but the only other person in the dining room was a well-dressed woman sitting twenty feet away with her back to us and staring out of the window into the street. I thought she might be the woman that Mrs Byfield had recognized in the High Street, but I wasn't sure.

Henry broke the silence. 'No sign of Munro?'

'It seems rather unimportant now, whatever he and Martlesham are up to.'

Henry glanced across the table at me. 'After what happened to Janet's father?'

I nodded.

'I suppose they are unconnected.'

'They must be.' I pushed aside the small mountain of bread-and-butter pudding. 'Martlesham hadn't got anything to do with Mr Treevor. They probably didn't even know of each other's existence.'

Henry shook his head. 'Not necessarily. When Munro came to Rosington, he might have been finding out about the Dark Hostelry as well as about Youlgreave. So Martlesham could have known about Mr Treevor. I bet it was an open secret in the Close that he was going senile. And Munro would have told Martlesham.'

I thought about the stroke-blighted man we had met. 'Martlesham was hardly in a position to nip down to Rosington and cut somebody's throat, even if he had a motive for doing it.'

'No. I agree.' Henry threw down his napkin and reached for his cigarettes. 'Nothing quite fits. I wish you'd come away with me. *Now*. Not go back to that bloody house. I don't like thinking of you there.'

'I've got to stay. They need me.' I gave him a weak smile. 'Besides, Granny Byfield will fight off any intruders.'

'But this could go on for ever.'

'Nonsense.' I glanced at my watch. 'Listen, we can't stay too long. I've got to collect Rosie from school.'

'I'll come with you.'

'There's really no need. I'll take the car.'

'I'd like to come. And I'm going to book myself into a room here.' He flapped a hand at the smoke between us. 'Have you paid that cheque in yet?'

I shook my head.

'Then that's something else I can do, isn't it? You see – I can make myself useful.'

'Henry –'

'Wendy.'

We looked at each other across the table.

'Yes?'

'I wish,' he said, and stopped.

'I do too.' For an instant I laid my hand on top of his and watched the expression of shock leap into his eyes. I moved the hand away. 'I don't think I want any coffee.'

'What about a small brandy?'

'Not for me.'

When we got back to the Dark Hostelry, we found Janet crying on the sofa, David looking harassed in the hall, and Granny Byfield standing in the doorway between them, explaining what she was going to do. She glanced at us as we came up the stairs from the kitchen.

'I'm sure Mr and Mrs Appleyard will agree with me.'

'Agree with what?'

'That the Dark Hostelry is no place for a child at present.'

'I take your point, Mother,' David said. 'But the question is whether Rosie would find it more upsetting to go back with you than to stay here.'

'I'm surprised at you,' she fired back.

'Take her,' Janet said.

David slipped past his mother into the drawing room. 'Darling, are you sure?'

Janet blew her nose. 'Your mother's right. Especially *now*.'

Now that the police were treating Mr Treevor's death as suspicious.

Granny Byfield wheeled on Henry and me. 'The sooner the better, don't you agree? I wonder if one of you would be kind enough to drive us to the station. I'll get ready to leave while you pick Rosie up from school. There's a train back to town at ten to four.'

'I'm coming as well,' Janet said.

'Where?' Granny Byfield asked.

'To the station, of course.'

The old woman nodded. 'But you won't come up to town with us?'

'No,' Janet said.

Janet and I went upstairs to pack a suitcase for Rosie.

'Are you sure this is sensible?' I murmured.

'She's right. I don't like to have to admit it but she is.'

'They needn't go by train. If you want I could drive them, and you could come too.'

Janet thought about it for a moment and then shook her head. 'It would only prolong the agony.'

'Where exactly does she live?'

'She's got a flat in Chertsey. It's quite large, and very nice.'

I knew her well enough to understand what she wasn't saying. 'But no place for a child?'

'As Granny Byfield has said herself. More than once. But at least she'll be away from all this. No, don't pack Angel. Rosie will need her on the train.'

I carried the suitcase down to the kitchen. Janet launched into a desperate conversation with Granny Byfield about Rosie's likes and dislikes. Semolina would make her sick, and she wasn't very fond of porridge. Could she have the landing light on when she went to sleep? She usually had a glass of orange squash in the middle of the morning and the middle of the afternoon.

'We'll see,' Granny Byfield said. 'I don't approve of cosseting children.'

Henry and I slipped out to fetch the car.

'Poor Rosie,' Henry said as we walked up the High Street. 'I'd pay quite a lot of money to avoid a few days alone with Granny B.'

'She's a tough little kid.'

'She'll need to be.' He touched my arm. 'Funny how they vary – kids, I mean. I wonder what a child of ours would be like.'

'I wonder.' I stopped by the car and unlocked the driver's

door. 'By the way, aren't you going to have to buy a toothbrush and so on if you're staying the night?'

Henry accepted the diversion and we moved on to safer subjects. We drove down to St Tumwulf's and collected Rosie. She was shy at first with Henry but willing to flirt with him – she always preferred men to women. Then I told her that Granny Byfield had come to take her on a little holiday. Her face froze for a moment as though briefly paralysed.

'Can Angel come?' she said at last.

'Oh, yes.'

I drove round to the High Street door of the Dark Hostelry. There were no journalists, which was just as well. Granny Byfield was not in a mood for compromise, she would probably have attacked them with her umbrella. Janet and I loaded her into the car while David put the suitcases in the boot.

David said, 'Wendy, if you don't mind, I'll take them down to the station.'

'Is this wise?' his mother said through the open window of the car. 'Having both Mummy and Daddy there might give Rosie a bit of a swollen head.'

'I don't think so,' David said.

He started the engine. His mother was beside him in the front. Rosie sat in the back holding Angel, both in pink to make the boys wink.

We're sisters now.

As the car drew away from the pavement, Janet glanced up at me, her face unsmiling. No wave, no words, just an expression that said, *Now I have lost two children.*

Henry and I went back to the Dark Hostelry. As I was unlocking the back door, Henry brushed my arm.

'Look. There he is. I'm sure it's him.'

I swung round. A large black car had just passed us, moving slowly up the High Street towards the marketplace. I glimpsed the profile of a man sitting in the front passenger seat. The driver was very small and his head was turned away from us, towards the passenger. It was impossible to see clearly because of the reflections in the glass.

'Munro?' I said.

'I think so.'

'Who's driving?'

'It looked like that woman. The one who was having lunch in the Crossed Keys.'

'Perhaps she works for Martlesham too.'

The car turned left and vanished round the corner.

'Hell of a car,' Henry went on. 'A Bentley. He must be simply rolling. Do you think Martlesham could have been in the back?'

'I don't think anyone was.'

He looked at his watch. 'I need to draw some cash. We've just got time before the bank closes.'

'Do you still have an arrangement here?'

He shook his head. 'But I can give you a cheque made out to you and you can draw the money out of your account.'

'All right.' I patted my handbag. 'I've got a cheque book.'

We walked down the High Street to Barclays Bank. It was a dark, gloomy building both inside and out. Henry and I sat facing each other at one of the tables in the banking hall and wrote our cheques. I reached for a paying-in slip.

'Wouldn't this be a wonderful opportunity to pay in that cheque for ten thousand?' he suggested.

'I've not made up my mind about that yet.'

'Then pay it into your account and make up your mind afterwards.'

'Don't try and bully me.'

'After all, your handbag might be stolen.' He slid the new cheque across the blotter to me. 'And there's the other one.'

I don't know what I would have done if we hadn't had the interruption. I'd been dimly aware of a tall man in a dark suit standing at the counter with his back to us. At that moment, he turned around, sliding a wallet into the inside pocket of his jacket. It was the dean. Mr Forbury saw me at the same time that I saw him.

'Good afternoon, Mrs Appleyard.' He nodded in a stately way.

Henry pushed back his chair and stood up, his hand out-stretched. 'Good afternoon, Mr Forbury.'

As chairman of the Choir School governors, the dean had had a good deal to do with Henry's resignation. But Henry wasn't the sort of person to bear a grudge. He wouldn't have wanted this meeting, but now it had happened he was going to make the best of it.

'Good afternoon.' If the dean's face had been a pool of water, you'd have said it had frozen over. 'Goodbye, Mrs Appleyard.'

He ignored Henry's hand and stalked out of the bank. I noticed that the tips of Mr Forbury's ears were pink.

'Horrible man,' I said.

Henry shrugged. 'It had to happen sooner or later.'

He spoke lightly but I wasn't fooled. Henry liked people to like him. It was his little weakness. The episode with the Hairy Widow hadn't just been about money.

'The bank's going to close in a moment,' I said. 'We'd better get a move on.'

He was always quick to seize an advantage. 'You'll pay in both cheques, won't you?'

I scribbled the long row of noughts on the paying-in slip. Just because of the dean.

'Good girl,' Henry said.

I stood up. 'Don't push your luck.'

We were the last customers to leave the bank. I stood in the doorway searching for my keys in my handbag and listening to the heavy doors closing behind us and the soft metallic sounds of turning locks.

'Excluded from paradise,' Henry said. 'Again.'

'We'll have to go back through the Close. I haven't got my back-door key.'

The Boneyard Gate was only a few yards from the bank. As we went through the archway, the full length of the Cathedral was in front of us, stretching east and west like a great grey curtain.

Henry said, 'It will get worse, you know. Much worse.'

'That business with Mr Treevor?'

He nodded. 'You don't have to stay here.'

'I do.'

We walked a few yards in silence. Our squat shadows slithered along the path in front of us. The sun was in the south-west and another shadow lay beside the nave of the Cathedral like a canal of black water.

Henry glanced at me and smiled. 'By the way, now David's mother's gone, there must be a spare room at the Dark Hostelry. Do you think Janet might let me ask myself to stay?'

I smiled back. 'Nothing to do with me.'

At that moment Mr Gotobed shepherded a group of tourists out of the north door. They broke away from him and scuttled down the path round the east end, towards the cloisters and the Porta. I raised a hand in greeting.

'Do you mind if I have a word with him?'

'With Gotobed? Why?'

'His mother's ill. I'd like to know how she is.'

'It's hard to believe you've actually met the mother.'

'Why?'

'It's rather like someone claiming they've met a leprechaun. No one ever sees her, you see, not close up. The boys used to claim she died years ago, and that Gotobed –'

'She certainly wasn't dead when I had tea with her.' I opened my bag. 'Look – here are the keys. Why not make yourself useful and put the kettle on?'

I veered across the close-cropped grass towards Mr Gotobed, who was still standing at the north door. Henry had irritated me. I liked the Gotobeds. They weren't there to be laughed at.

As I drew near, Mr Gotobed bobbed his head as though I were the dean and he had come to conduct me from the vestry to my stall.

'How's your mother?'

'As well as can be expected, thank you. She's had these turns before but this one's worse.'

'She's still at home?'

'Won't go to hospital. Put her foot down. Doctor says it's best to let her be. But people come in to help.'

Mr Gotobed was very pale, his skin dry and flaking. There were more lines than ever before. He blinked often, the sandy eyelashes fluttering like agitated fingers.

'Is there anything I can do?'

'You've got enough on your plate.'

'I'd like to help.'

He looked at me. 'Thank you. It might cheer her up to see you. But perhaps you wouldn't want to –'

'I'll come. When's the best time?'

'Could you manage this evening? About six o'clock?'

I nodded.

'The nurse comes to settle her down about six-thirty. But by six I will have given her tea, and as a rule she's quite perky after that. It's a good time.'

'I'll be there.'

'Don't be surprised at the change. Her mind wanders more. You know?'

'I know,' I said.

We said goodbye. Mr Gotobed went back into the Cathedral and I walked on to the Dark Hostelry. On the way it occurred to me that Mr Gotobed hadn't called me 'Mrs Appleyard' once. He hadn't been nervous, either, or embarrassed. Between them, Mr Treevor and Mrs Gotobed had succeeded in dissolving the formality between us.

I don't know what made me stop at the gate of the Dark Hostelry. Some people claim we have a sixth sense that tells us when we're being stared at, which strikes me as an old wives' tale. Nevertheless, something made me look over my shoulder.

At first sight I thought the green between the Cathedral and the Boneyard Gate was empty. Then a movement near one of the buttresses caught my eye. Someone was standing in the great pool of shadow that ran the length of the Cathedral.

Not standing – walking. The sun was in my eyes. It was as if a drop from the pool of shadow had broken away and taken independent life. The smaller shadow became a man in dark clothes. Around him glowed the brilliant green of the lawn. He was coming towards me, but he must have seen me watching because he swung away towards the Boneyard Gate as if trying to avoid me.

Francis?

Then I blinked. It was Harold Munro, dressed as usual in his drab, old-fashioned clothes. He might be flesh and blood but he had no right to haunt us.

'Hey! You!'

At my shout he stopped. He stared across the lawn. I began to walk, almost run.

'Mr Munro! I'd like a word with you.'

He said nothing, just waited, cigarette in hand. A moment later I was within a yard of him. Because of my heels I was an inch or two taller than him. In my stockinged feet we would have been about the same size. There were flecks of dandruff on his black jacket and his pinstripe trousers needed pressing. He wore a grubby hard collar and a greasy, tightly knotted tie. A silver chain stretched across the front of his black waistcoat. The bald patch the shape of Africa glistened with sweat. The only cool thing about him were his eyes, which were grey and slanting.

'Why are you spying on us?'

'Me, miss?'

Anger bubbled out of me, surprising me as much as it surprised Munro. 'You can go back to Simon Martlesham and tell him we're sick and tired of having you turn up like a bad penny round every corner. And what's more, you can tell him I'll be notifying the police about a suspicious character hanging round the Close and harassing old ladies.'

I paused, partly because I had run out of things to say and partly because I wanted to hear his reaction. But he said nothing. He sucked on his cigarette and stared up at me with his little grey eyes while the sweat ran like tears down his cheeks.

'So you'll tell Martlesham?' I put my hands behind my back because they had clenched into fists. 'I've had enough. We've had enough. Can't you see?'

Munro nodded.

'He's looking for his sister, isn't he? That's what this is all about.'

He bobbed his head again and smiled – not at me but at something he saw in his mind. He flicked the cigarette end into the air. We watched it falling to the ground. Then he slipped away, a black shadow gliding silently across the grass towards the Boneyard Gate.

I sniffed the air like a rabbit scenting danger. I smelled Turkish tobacco.

42

The little sitting room was even more crowded than before because they'd moved a bed into it. A bank of coal glowed in the grate. The windows were closed. The smells of old age were stronger. The body was decaying in advance of death.

Mrs Gotobed's tissue-paper skin covered the bones of her face like a sagging tent. 'Wilfred, go and have your tea,' she said.

'I'm all right.' Mr Gotobed smiled uneasily at me. 'Mother likes to make sure I'm eating properly.'

'That's why you must have your tea. Mrs Appleyard will sit with me.'

'Of course I will.'

Mr Gotobed left the room.

'I don't know what he'll do when I'm gone,' Mrs Gotobed said as soon as the door had closed. 'No more sense than a new-born baby.'

'How are you?'

'Tired. Very tired. Sit by the window where I can see you.'

I sat on a hard chair near the window overlooking the Close. Pursy stared incuriously at me from the window seat. A golden slab of sunshine poured through the opposite window. Dust swam in the air and lay thickly on the horizontal surfaces. I wished I could turn back time for Mrs Gotobed, and for myself, until we reached a golden age when pain had not existed. The lids fluttered over Mrs Gotobed's eyes.

'Still looking for Canon Youlgreave?' she said.

I nodded. 'In a way.'

'He was a good man, a good man.' The eyes were open now to their fullest extent. 'Do you hear what I say? A *good* man.'

What I say three times is true. But why was it so important to her even now, when the life was almost visibly seeping out of her.

'What about the Martlesham children's aunt? What happened to her?'

The old woman's shoulders twitched.

'*You* must have known her.' Urgency made me raise my voice. 'What was she like? What did *she* feel about the children?'

Mrs Gotobed shook her head slowly from side to side. She blew out through loosely closed lips, making a noise like a dying balloon.

'I'm a fool, aren't I?' I said. 'It was you all along. You were the aunt.'

She continued to blow out air. Then she stopped and smiled at me. 'I wondered if you'd ever guess.'

'You didn't want the children. You had a good job, and then you were getting married. Would they have been in the way?'

'I was his queen,' Mrs Gotobed mumbled. 'Last chance for me. But I knew Sammy didn't want the children. Can't say I blamed him. *Her* children, especially.'

'Your sister's?'

'Everyone knew what she'd been like. Better off dead, that one. Bad blood.'

'Canon Youlgreave helped.'

'He was very kind. And there's no denying the money came in handy.'

'Simon went first?'

'Couldn't wait. He left just after his ma died, before me and Sammy got engaged. Nancy lived with me for a bit after that.' She screwed up her face. 'I told you, I had lodgings in Bridge Street. Landlady kept complaining about the children. Couldn't abide the trouble and the mess they made, and the noise, and she wouldn't look after them when I was at work. *I'll thank you to remember I'm not a nursemaid*, that's what she said. Silly woman, with a front tooth missing . . . I can see her now. Wilfred never made much noise. He always was a quiet boy, right from the start.'

'Nancy,' I reminded her, trying to keep her to the point. 'What was *Nancy* like?'

There was a pause. Then Mrs Gotobed said slowly, as though

865

the words were being pulled out like teeth, 'Out for what she could get. Nice as pie with Mr Youlgreave, oh yes, but when she was at home with me it was another matter. Nasty piece of work when all's said and done.'

'When did she leave?'

'Sammy and me were wed in the autumn. October the fourteenth. It was before that.'

'And before Canon Youlgreave left Rosington?'

'I think so. But it can't have been long before. He said he'd give Sammy and me a wedding present, and he did – he sent us some money. But he'd gone by then.'

'Where did he take Nancy?'

'To a lady and a gentleman who were friends of his. No children of their own, he said. They were going to bring her up a lady. Always had the luck of the devil, that one. Trust her to fall on her feet.' The eyelids drooped again. 'Little bitch.' The lids flickered. 'Sorry. It slipped out. Really, I'm sorry.'

'It doesn't matter.'

'No one else knew, apart from Sammy. Not about the money. Not about the children. Sammy thought it was for the best. We said I'd had them adopted by relations in Birmingham. It was for their own good.'

'You never heard from them again?'

'I did from Simon. He sent me a letter from Canada. And I'm sure Mr Youlgreave wouldn't have hurt the kiddies, he was a clergyman. Anyhow, why would he do them any harm?'

There were footsteps on the stairs. Suddenly her face became cunning.

'You won't tell Wilfred? You promise? A Bible promise?'

'Of course I won't tell him,' I said. And the fact that she needed me to say that made it obvious that she must have at least suspected that Nancy was not going to live in a gentleman's house and grow into a fine lady.

The door opened and Wilfred Gotobed edged into the room. 'Are you all right, Mother?'

She was still looking at me. 'When will this end? I've had enough.'

I stood up. 'I hope I haven't tired you.'

The old woman shook her head.

'Does Mother the power of good to see a new face,' Mr Gotobed said. 'Doesn't it, Mother? When you're feeling better, we could get a wheelchair and –'

'Goodbye, dear,' Mrs Gotobed said to me, and turned her head away.

'Goodbye.'

'It was a long way from Swan Alley,' she said as I reached the door. 'You'll remember that, won't you?'

I nodded. Mr Gotobed stumbled towards me but I said I would see myself out.

A moment later I was breathing the sweet, fresh air of the Close. They said there was one law for the rich and one for the poor. Perhaps rich and poor had different moralities as well.

Now I knew or could guess what had happened in 1904. Perhaps Francis had buried what was left of the body in one of the gardens of the Close. Or put it in a weighted sack and dropped it in the river like a litter of unwanted kittens. No one had wanted to know what he had done, not to Nancy Martlesham, because she wasn't the sort of little girl who belonged in the Close or anywhere else.

I felt no sense of achievement. It wasn't just that I liked old Mrs Gotobed and I did not like what I'd heard of Nancy Martlesham. There was another problem. Something niggled. Something didn't make sense. And I didn't think I would ever see Mrs Gotobed again, and so I would never find out what it was.

43

It was as if they sensed blood. During that long evening, the reporters seemed to be everywhere. Two of them tried to talk to me on my way back to the Dark Hostelry. As I unlocked the garden gate, the photographer raised his camera. While Henry and I were making supper, they rang the back-door bell seven times. Until I drew the kitchen curtains, they crouched down on the pavement of the High Street and peered through the window.

We ate on trays upstairs in the drawing room. None of us said very much, Janet least of all. Her pale, perfect face gave nothing away. At one point David and Henry tried to have a conversation about cricket. I wanted to kick both of them.

Halfway through the meal the phone rang. Henry went to answer it. He'd started answering the phone after David swore at one of the reporters. Janet wouldn't let us take the phone off the hook because Granny Byfield or Rosie might try to get in touch.

This time it wasn't one of the journalists, it was the dean. David went to talk to him and came back looking even angrier than before.

'He suggests we ask the police if we can move out for a while. He feels we'd be happier. And that this sort of attention is bad for the atmosphere of the Close.'

'It mightn't be a bad idea.' I looked from Janet to David. 'You won't get any peace here, not for a day or two. You could take the car.'

'Wouldn't it cost a lot of money?' Janet said vaguely, as if she was thinking of something completely different.

'Blow the money,' Henry said.

David put down his tray on the carpet and picked up his cigarettes. 'Perhaps we *should* go away. It's like living in a goldfish bowl.'

'You must let me know if I can help,' Henry said to David, in the awkward voice he used when he wanted to do someone a good turn.

'We'll manage, thanks.'

Janet stood up suddenly, knocking over an empty glass. 'You all seem to have made up your minds about what we're doing. I'd better go and think about what needs to be packed.'

She closed the door behind her and we listened to her feet on the stairs.

David cleared his throat. 'Yes, no time like the present.'

He and Henry continued to talk about cricket. When it comes to burying heads in the sand, a man can out-perform an ostrich any day. I found Janet in Rosie's room. She was sitting on the bed, her hands clasped together on her lap, staring out of the window. I sat beside her and the bed creaked. When I put my arm around her she felt as cold and stiff as a waxwork.

'Listen,' I said. 'You know what they say – the darkest hour's before dawn.'

'I thought I'd better see if there was anything of Rosie's we should send on.'

'I thought you were packing for you and David.'

'Rosie's more important.'

'I'm sure she's all right.' I gave Janet's shoulder a little shake. 'Ten to one, you'll find that Granny Byfield's met her match.'

'You're too kind to me. You've always been too kind for me. I'm not worth it.'

'Don't be silly.'

A door closed downstairs. The men's footsteps crossed the hall. They were talking about the last test match in the West Indies.

'Silly to worry, isn't it?' Janet said. 'It doesn't change anything.'

'Would you like a hand with the packing?'

'I don't even know if we're going anywhere yet.'

'I really think you should.'

She turned her head and smiled at me. 'You're right. No point in staying here. But if you don't mind, I think I'll do it tomorrow. I'm feeling rather tired.'

I remembered belatedly that she was still coping with the miscarriage. I persuaded her to have a bath and go to bed. I went downstairs and bullied the men into making themselves useful. Half an hour later I took Janet some cocoa. She was already asleep. On impulse, I bent down and kissed her head. Her hair wasn't as soft as usual. It needed washing.

I went to bed early myself. After a long bath, I got into bed to read. I flicked over the pages of *The Voice of Angels*. The poems were nasty pretentious rubbish, I thought, sadistic and unnecessarily difficult. But as well as all those things, they were also sad. As I picked my way through the verses, I hardly noticed the rest, only the sadness.

I heard footsteps on the stairs, my stairs, the ones to the second floor. There was a tap on the door and I said, 'Come in.'

Henry smiled uncertainly at me from the threshold. He had a bottle of brandy under one arm and was carrying a couple of glasses.

'David's gone to bed. I saw your light was on. I wondered if you'd fancy a nightcap.'

I nodded and moved my legs so he could sit on the end of the bed. He poured the drinks and passed me a glass.

'Cheers.'

I said, 'Not that there's much to be cheery about,' and drank.

'David's in an awful state.'

'Is he? I thought he was concentrating on cricket this evening.'

Henry shrugged. 'It's what he doesn't say. I suggested they go to London. They could see Rosie.'

'That's assuming Inspector Humphries lets them.'

'Do you think . . . ?'

I took another sip. 'I don't know what to think. But if Humphries is right, Janet's father didn't kill himself.'

'It doesn't bear thinking about.'

'Do you know, before he died, Mr Treevor was beginning to think he might be Francis Youlgreave?'

'He was going senile. Wendy?'

I looked at Henry. 'What?'

'I'm sorry. Sorry for everything.'

He patted my leg under the bedclothes. We sat there for a moment, as awkward as teenagers. I thought about my schoolgirl passion for David and decided that even though it hadn't actually come to anything, I didn't have much to be proud about either. And I also thought about the Byfields and Mr Treevor and Francis Youlgreave. There was too much suffering in the world already. I held out my hand.

Henry took it and kissed it. Then our lips were kissing and we both spilt our glasses of brandy.

'Phew,' Henry said, as the bottle rolled off the bed and fell to the rug without breaking. 'And thank God I put the cork in it.'

In the morning, we were still together, naked in that narrow bed, and the brandy bottle was still where it had fallen. It was like that other morning when Janet came into my room to tell me that Mr Treevor was dead. The light had the same pale, colourless quality.

But it was David, not Janet, in the doorway. He was in his pyjamas, unshaven, his hair tousled.

Henry grunted and turned towards the wall. I looked at David and he looked at me.

'It's Janet,' he said. 'This time it's Janet.'

PART III

The Blue Dahlia

44

Time doesn't heal, it just gives you other things to think about.

'How are you feeling?' Henry said, speaking gently so as not to startle me.

'I'm fine, thank you.'

'Are you sure?'

'Darling, I wish you'd stop treating me like a restive horse.'

He had been like this since we had discovered I was pregnant. I'd never seen him so excited, so happy. I was less certain about my own feelings. Over the years I had grown used to not being pregnant. So the possibility that I might be had been unsettling, like a threatened invasion. And the knowledge that I actually was left me breathless with excitement and fear.

'Would it be better if I drove?' Henry asked.

'If you drive I'll be holding on to the seat for the whole journey.' I changed down for a corner and threw a smile at him. 'I feel much more secure if I've got the steering wheel.'

We drove for a moment in silence through the gentle Hampshire countryside. It was September, and the afternoon still had the warmth of summer. I kept the speed down, dawdling along the A31 in our new Ford Consul, because we'd been invited to tea and I didn't want to be early. Granny Byfield liked punctuality in others.

'I wish the old hag wasn't going to be there,' Henry said. 'It'll be bad enough as it is.'

'Not for you, surely. At least you've talked to David on the phone.'

'It's not the same. The sooner he gets another job, the better.'

'And for Rosie.'

I didn't want to see David, and I wanted to see Rosie even less. They would remind me of Janet.

'If it's a girl,' I said, 'I'd like to call her Janet.'

Henry touched my hand on the steering wheel. 'Of course.' He squeezed my fingers for an instant. 'Darling, at least we're making a fresh start now. Everything else is in the past.'

'Yes, Henry,' I said, and added silently to myself, *They're all in the past, Francis, Mr Treevor and Janet, and even your Hairy Widow with those wonderfully frivolous navy-blue shoes*. You can never really go back to what you once were, not unless you grow senile like Mr Treevor. You can never forget what you and others have done.

Granny Byfield's flat in Chertsey was in a small block near the centre of the town. David answered the door. I was shocked at the change in him. He had never been fat, but he had lost a lot of weight in the last few months. Suffering had made him less handsome than he had been, but in a strange way more attractive. He brushed my cheek with cold lips.

'You look fit,' Henry said.

They shook hands awkwardly.

'I managed to do quite a lot of walking up in Yorkshire.' David had spent nearly two months immured in an Anglo-Catholic monastery, a sort of gymnasium for the soul which Canon Hudson had found for him. 'Mother and Rosie are in the sitting room. By the way, she doesn't like one to smoke.'

Granny Byfield and Rosie were sitting at a tea table in the bay window. The room was large for a modern flat, but seemed smaller because it was filled with furniture and ornaments, and because the walls were covered with dark, striped paper like the bars of a cage.

Rosie had Angel in her arms. The doll was in her pink outfit, now rather grubby. Rosie seemed unchanged from that time six or seven months ago when I had first seen her in the garden of the Dark Hostelry. She was wearing a different dress, of course. This one was green with white flecks – I remembered Janet making it for her. But she must have grown a little since then, because the dress was getting small for her.

We shook hands with Granny Byfield, who looked us up

876

and down but did not smile. I bent and kissed the top of Rosie's head.

'Hello, how are you?'

Rosie looked up at me. She said nothing. I hugged her, and it was like hugging a doll, not a person.

'You must answer when you're spoken to, Rosemary,' Granny Byfield said. 'Has the cat got your tongue?'

'Hello, Auntie Wendy,' Rosie said.

'How's Angel?'

'Very well, thank you.'

'Mama!' said Angel, as if in confirmation.

'Now sit down and make yourself comfortable,' Granny Byfield ordered. 'I'll make the tea, and David can bring it in.'

The little tea party went on as it had begun. It would have been a difficult meeting at the best of times. But with Granny Byfield there we had no chance of success whatsoever. She could have blighted a field of potatoes just by looking at it.

I tried to talk to Rosie, but on that occasion I didn't get very far. She answered in monosyllables except when I asked if she was looking forward to going to school.

'No,' she said. 'I want to go home.'

'I expect you and Daddy will soon have a new home, and then you –'

'I want the home we had before.' She stared at the top of the doll's head. 'I want *everything* to be like before.'

We stayed less than an hour. David came downstairs with us, pulling out a packet of cigarettes as we reached the communal front door of the flats. We left Rosie helping her grandmother clear the tea table, a small, blonde slave poised on the verge of mutiny.

Henry accepted a cigarette and produced his lighter. 'Any news about a job?'

David shook his head.

'Is it because of Janet?' I asked.

His face didn't change at the name but I felt as if I'd kicked him. 'I don't think it helps. But really it's simply that the right sort of job hasn't come along yet.'

'A university chaplaincy, perhaps?' Henry suggested. 'You'll want to carry on with your book and so on, I expect.'

'I thought I might go into parish work. I'm helping out here.'

I was surprised but didn't say anything.

'I did a lot of thinking in Yorkshire,' David went on, answering our unspoken questions. 'And praying. I came to the conclusion it was time for a change of direction.'

Henry said, 'Wendy and I thought – well, if you ever want a job in a prep school, you've only got to ask.'

'I don't think I'd be very good at teaching small boys. Or small girls, come to that.'

'But you'll come and stay, won't you?' I said. 'Come now, if you like. And Rosie. There's bags of room.'

'Thank you. I'll bear that in mind.'

He turned away from me as he spoke because gratitude never came easily to David. I glanced up at the window of the flat and saw Rosie looking down at us.

'It would be nice for Rosie, of course,' Henry said. 'And I expect she'd be a civilizing influence on our little barbarians.'

'Is she all right?' I asked. 'She seemed rather quiet.'

'She wants her mother.' David stared at the tip of his cigarette. 'I think she'd like to be four years old again and stay that way for ever. Of course, there's not much for her to do here, and that doesn't help.' He moistened his lips. 'It's not been easy for her. Or for my mother, come to that.'

'Your mother must seem quite – quite formidable to a small child,' I said.

'Mother has very firm ideas about children and how they should behave.' He glanced at me, and I thought I saw desperation in his face. 'She thinks Rosie's very babyish, for example. So she tries to encourage her to be more grown up. Once she took that doll away from her, and there was a terrific fuss.'

'Rosie told me she wanted to go back home.'

'She still finds it hard to accept what's happened.'

'To accept that it can't be changed?' I thought of the Hairy Widow. 'To know that it's something she'll never escape from, for the rest of her life?'

Henry cleared his throat. 'Poor little kid, eh? Still, time's a great healer.'

David was still looking at me. 'Mother's right, in a way. Rosie *is* being babyish at present. But that's only because on some level she thinks it might somehow cancel out what's happened. You see?'

'Like a sort of magic?'

'Yes. But she can't go on doing that for the rest of her life.'

'What about clothes?' I said.

'What?'

'I couldn't help noticing that dress was rather small for her. Getting some new clothes might help her start making a break with the past.'

'When in doubt, go shopping,' Henry said. 'It's every woman's motto, young and old.'

David rubbed his forehead. 'I don't think Rosie's had anything new since we left Rosington.'

'Then why don't I take her up to town? I'm sure she'd enjoy that – it would take her out of herself, give her something new to think about. We could make a day of it.'

'I couldn't possibly –'

'Why not? I'd enjoy it too. It would be nice if we could do it this week. We'll be pretty busy after that.'

'I must admit it would be very useful. Mother's not as mobile as she was. She doesn't really like shopping. And perhaps you're right – perhaps it would help Rosie come to terms with things.'

'That's settled then.' I took out my diary. 'What about Thursday?'

'Fine, I think. I'll ring to confirm, shall I?' He turned to Henry. 'Are you sure this won't cause problems? When does term start?'

'Next week. I'm as nervous as hell, actually.'

'Teaching's like riding a bicycle,' David said. 'Once learned, never forgotten. Mother's the same with people. Never forgets a face.'

It wasn't the teaching that worried Henry. It was the responsibility.

David looked at me. 'Which reminds me – my mother remembered whom she saw in Rosington.'

I looked at him blankly for a moment, and then nodded as the memories flooded back. I'd just driven Granny Byfield up from the station and she'd seen a woman whose face was familiar going into the Close by the Sacristan's Gate. Henry and I had seen her lunching at the Crossed Keys a few hours earlier. Also, according to Henry, later that afternoon she'd driven up Rosington High Street in a big black car with Harold Munro beside her.

All this on the last day of Janet's life. And at this moment I didn't give a damn who the woman was. The only thing that mattered at present was David, who was trying to mention the day of Janet's death as if it had been any other day. I wished I could hug him as I'd hugged Rosie.

'My mother met her last month at a charity lunch in Richmond. It's Lady Youlgreave.'

'What on earth was she doing in Rosington?' Henry said. 'Did your mother find out?'

'Oh yes. They had quite a chat once they discovered they had something in common. She'd been on a motoring holiday in East Anglia and she stopped for lunch in Rosington. Apparently Francis Youlgreave was her husband's uncle.'

I dared not look at Henry. An idea slipped into my mind, as unwelcome as a thief in the night. If Harold Munro had been in Lady Youlgreave's car, then didn't that suggest that Simon Martlesham wasn't Munro's employer? Didn't it make it much more likely that Martlesham was Munro's quarry?

45

The Old Manor House at Roth smelt to high heaven of old money. Quite a lot of it. I pulled over to the side of the road and we sat and admired the view.

It was a long, low house a few hundred yards away from the Queen's Head, where Henry had stayed. The windows were large and the walls had recently been painted a soft bluey-green that shimmered like water. Between the house and the road was a circular lawn with a raked gravel drive running round it and meeting at the front door. An offshoot of the drive ran down the side of the house to the back. The leaves of the copper beech were changing colour in the garden behind. Outside the front door was a large car, its paintwork like a black mirror.

'Is that the same car?' I asked. 'It looks as if it might be.'

Henry grunted. He was grumpy because he hadn't wanted to come. 'It's a black R Type Bentley Continental, and so was the one we saw in the High Street. You don't see many of them around.'

I took the keys from the Ford's ignition and felt for the door handle. 'OK. Let's go and see if the owner's at home.'

'Wendy – can't we leave it?'

I turned to face him. 'I'd like to know what she was up to. And why.'

'She was curious about her uncle. What's so strange about that?'

'If she's only a Youlgreave by marriage, then he wasn't her uncle.'

'That's hair-splitting. You know what I mean. You don't think perhaps that because you're pregnant, you're –'

'Making too much of things? All right, tell me why she was being so mysterious about it? She could have come to Rosington and asked all those things herself. Instead she hired that nasty little man. If it's nothing more than simple family curiosity, it just doesn't make sense.'

Henry shrugged. I knew what he was thinking – that I was behaving no less oddly than Lady Youlgreave. I knew I could never begin to tell him the muddled reasons why Francis was so important to me, and why he would never quite be able to understand me even if I tried. The answers were tied up with him, as well, and with the Hairy Widow and David Byfield and above all with Janet. I'd failed with Janet. I didn't want to fail with this.

'Wendy –'

I didn't wait to hear what he had to say. I pushed open the door and swung my legs out of the car. A moment later I was walking down the drive towards the front door. Behind me I heard the slam of Henry's door and his footsteps hurrying after me. I rang the doorbell. The front of the house was in shadow and the air on my bare forearms was suddenly cool. Henry came up beside me. When I glanced at him he grinned.

'Just be polite, darling,' he murmured. 'That's all I ask.'

I rang the doorbell again. 'If she's in.'

'Remember – she might have grandsons who could come to Veedon Hall.'

There was a pattering on the gravel behind us, and suddenly Henry was dancing up and down while something brown and hostile snapped at his ankles.

'Beast!' said a voice behind us.

Henry swore in a way unlikely to impress the average grand-mother. I kicked the dog in the ribs.

'Beast! Come here!'

The dog, a dachshund, reluctantly abandoned Henry and sidled back to its mistress by a roundabout route. For the first time I got a good look at Lady Youlgreave. She was a small, stooping woman with dark dyed hair. Her face was lined like a monkey's and in no way beautiful, but expertly and expensively made up. She was wearing well-cut slacks and a silk blouse. Once upon a time, men had probably found her attractive. I thought she could have been any age between fifty-five and seventy-five.

A large Alsatian strained at the leash held in her right hand. Pulled by the dog, Lady Youlgreave moved towards us in a series of darting movements like a bird's. The dachshund kept between us and his mistress, ready to intervene again if things grew nasty.

'And what can I do for you?'

The voice had the calm assurance of someone who has always had money, who has always told other people what to do. There was no warmth in it, no friendliness.

'I'm Wendy Appleyard,' I said. 'This is my husband, Henry.'

I watched the name register on her face. It was like watching someone respond to a mild electric shock. The Alsatian sniffed the toe of my shoe, the one that had kicked the dachshund.

'Is this Beauty?' I asked.

Lady Youlgreave nodded and waved the dog away from me with a hand whose fingernails were thickly encrusted with purple varnish.

'Are we right in thinking you're Lady Youlgreave?'

She nodded, looking faintly surprised I'd had to ask. Then she waited, leaving me to say why we were here.

'You know Mrs Byfield, I understand?'

'Slightly, yes.'

'We've just been having tea with her and her son and grand-daughter.'

She stared up at me with large, dark-brown eyes like muddy ponds. 'It was a sad business at Rosington,' she announced.

'Yes, it was.'

'I think Mrs Byfield mentioned you were living in the house at the time?'

'I think you already knew that. Harold Munro would have told you.'

For an instant the monkey face was blank. Then the wrinkles rearranged themselves into an expression that could have been a grimace or a grin. 'I want to take the weight off my feet. Let's sit in the garden, shall we?'

She led us down the side of the house to a formal rose garden. We passed under an archway of greenery and on to a large square lawn bisected by a stone-flagged path. Round the enclosure ran an old brick wall lined with trees and shrubs. Beyond the wall were the roofs of a sea of box-like houses. The garden was a green island, embattled and existing on sufferance, like Rosington surrounded by the Fens, and the Close surrounded by Rosington.

Lady Youlgreave made a beeline for a cluster of garden furniture – four wicker armchairs with cushioned seats and a table with splayed bamboo legs. She perched in the largest chair, which had a tall back like a throne, and waved at us to sit down as well.

'I can only spare a few minutes.'

'Then I'll keep this brief,' I said. 'Munro was working for you.'

Her shoulders lifted. 'Was he?'

'Would you mind telling us what you wanted him to do?'

'I don't think it's any business of yours, Mrs Appleyard.'

'I don't agree. You see, he was watching me some of the time. That makes it my business. He tried to talk to all sorts of people in Rosington. Did you know he almost frightened one old lady to death?'

The dogs had settled down on the grass by Lady Youlgreave's feet. But something in my tone made them both raise their heads. She scratched the Alsatian between its ears and then examined her hands, which wore more rings than I'd ever owned in my life.

'I hired Mr Munro to make some enquiries on my behalf about one of my husband's relations.' She looked up at me. 'That's the long and the short of it. By the way, what was the name of the old lady you mentioned?'

'Mrs Gotobed.'

There was no mistaking the pleasure in Lady Youlgreave's face. 'But she recovered?'

'For a short time. She died a few weeks later.'

Henry drew in his breath sharply. 'Of course, my wife isn't actually implying that Mr Munro caused Mrs Gotobed's death. Just that –'

'He certainly gave her a bad fright,' I said. 'I saw her just after it had happened. She thought Munro was trying to break in.'

Lady Youlgreave nodded, not committing herself.

'He traced Simon Martlesham,' I went on. 'Why would you want him to do that?'

'To trace Martlesham? Because as a boy he'd known Francis Youlgreave.'

'I think what really interested you was why Francis Youlgreave left Rosington. There was a scandal, wasn't there?'

'That's common knowledge.' She raised plucked eyebrows, black as ink. 'Women priests – I wonder where he got that one from. I don't think he even liked women very much. Frightened of them, probably. A lot of men of that generation were. But there's no great secret about that, Mrs Appleyard. Mr Munro even found me a report in *The Times*.'

'He also ripped out everything about it from the backfile of the *Rosington Observer*. Straightforward theft, was it, or was he trying to muddy the trail for anyone who came after him?'

'Mr Munro did have a tendency to cut corners, I give you that.'

'Did?'

'I'm no longer employing him. He finished the job I wanted him to do.'

'But your uncle was involved in another scandal, Lady Youlgreave, and this one wasn't ecclesiastical. I think they just used that sermon about women priests as an excuse to get rid of him.'

'How very melodramatic.'

'It was to do with Simon Martlesham and his family.'

She leant forward, and her fingers stopped scratching the Alsatian's scalp. 'Go on.'

'Mrs Gotobed was Simon Martlesham's aunt. The Martleshams were very poor. They came from a part of Rosington called Swan Alley, a slum by the river – it no longer exists. Simon cleaned the boots in the Bishop's Palace. And he had a little sister called Nancy. But you know all this, don't you?'

'I know a lot of things, Mrs Appleyard.'

'Then the mother died, and the children became the responsibility of their aunt. She was working in a haberdasher's shop then – she hadn't married Mr Gotobed. The children were a burden to the aunt, partly because she wanted to get married.

Mr Gotobed was the head verger, and he had a house in the Close. He didn't like the idea of children who came from Swan Alley. Perhaps he wanted his own children. Is this making sense to you?'

Lady Youlgreave nodded in a way that suggested she didn't much care whether it made sense or not. Henry stirred in the chair beside me and the wicker creaked.

'Luckily a solution was at hand,' I went on. 'Canon Youlgreave knew the Martlesham children. Simon had helped him when he fell over in the Close. And Canon Youlgreave had taken an interest in the boy, given him books to read and so on. And he'd done the same for Nancy, the sister, as well. I expect all that increased his reputation for eccentricity.'

'I don't want to hurry you, Mrs Appleyard, but I do have another engagement.'

I nodded. 'This won't take long. Mrs Gotobed said that people in the Close thought he was being over-friendly with children from Swan Alley. Anyway, he came to the rescue as far as the Martleshams were concerned. He paid for Simon to emigrate to Canada, and learn a trade there. But this is where it gets confusing. When I first talked to Simon, he said that Francis Youlgreave had also paid for Nancy to emigrate with him. But then we found a photograph that proved that Nancy had stayed in Rosington. So Simon changed the story. He said Canon Youlgreave had arranged for Nancy to be adopted by wealthy friends. But as far as I can see, there's no evidence that he actually did that. After the summer of 1904, Nancy Martlesham simply vanished.'

Henry wriggled and cleared his throat. 'Nothing necessarily sinister in that, of course.'

'Do go on,' drawled Lady Youlgreave. 'It's so interesting to have another perspective on Uncle Francis.'

'I've talked to people who knew him,' I said. 'I've read his poetry. Did Mr Munro tell you that he was in the habit of cutting up animals? Or did you know that already from something you'd found here?'

I paused. But she said nothing. She stared at me with those opaque brown eyes.

'I think he believed that eating a child might make him stay young.'

Lady Youlgreave hooted briefly with laughter, a surprisingly loud sound in that quiet garden. 'Uncle Francis was eccentric, I grant you that. It's common knowledge. Unbalanced, even. Did you know he was addicted to opium? But I doubt if he had the strength to kill a fly. Just think about it, Mrs Appleyard. Think about the practicalities of killing something, even a cat.'

'How did you know there was a cat?' I asked sharply.

She dismissed the question with a wave of her hand. 'Munro turned up something.'

'So he *was* strong enough.'

'More likely the animal was already dead.'

'He was strong enough to kill himself, by all accounts.'

She glanced pointedly at her watch. 'Aren't we getting rather hypothetical, Mrs Appleyard?'

'You're interested in the Martleshams as much as Francis Youlgreave. I think you were trying to trace them. And in particular you were looking for Nancy. Because something you'd found or heard made you think that Francis had killed her.'

This time Lady Youlgreave laughed properly. It was one of those well-bred laughs that don't express mirth. When she'd had enough, she sat up in her chair and smiled at me. It unsettled me, that smile, because it didn't belong on this face at this time. I could have sworn it was a smile of relief.

'How imaginative you are, Mrs Appleyard. But I'm afraid I have to disappoint you. I've never for a moment thought that Uncle Francis killed her. And for a very good reason. I'm Nancy Martlesham.'

46

Veedon Hall was a place with aspirations, a tall, ugly house built by a nineteenth-century manufacturer of corsets. It had a large garden which the school prospectus referred to as the Park, a pond known as the Lake and a ditch called the Ha-Ha. One of the bedrooms was said to be haunted by the ghost of an aristocratic girl abandoned by her lover.

The reality was kinder than the aspirations and almost cosily suburban, despite the fact we were in the depths of rural Hampshire. The rooms were large, airy and well-lit. Generations of small boys had humanized the place. I liked Veedon Hall very much, which was just as well because I now owned twenty per cent of it.

The previous owners, the Cuthbertsons, had invited us to stay the week after Janet's death. When Henry told me, I assumed there had been an element of calculation in the invitation, that they wanted to safeguard the sale they had agreed with Henry. It's always easier to believe the worst about human nature than the best. But when I met them, I soon realized they simply wanted to help.

Henry and I had spent much of the summer term at Veedon Hall, gradually growing used to the place and to each other. I was surprised to discover that as far as the school was concerned I was one of Henry's advantages. His new partner was what we used to call a confirmed bachelor and, as Mrs Cuthbertson told me, the mothers liked to think there was a woman about the place. As for Henry, he slotted into the rhythms of the school as though he'd never been away.

'The boys actually work for him,' Mr Cuthbertson said. 'Lord knows why, but there's not many of us you can say *that* about.'

I was fond of Veedon Hall for what it was and what it could be. Best of all, it wasn't the Close at Rosington. It was another miniature world, but this one was dominated by a hundred and seventeen fairly healthy little savages. The boys had to learn about the subjunctive of *Amo* and simultaneous equations, which fortunately was not my province, but they also had to be fed and watered, looked after when they were ill and comforted when they were sad. One of the junior matrons left suddenly when her mother fell ill and I took on some of her duties.

It made me feel as if I was someone else now, knowing that I was not only pregnant but owned part of the school. Henry had put both our names in the contract. So far I'd enjoyed the school more than the pregnancy. Henry and his partner might be wonderful teachers but neither of them had the slightest idea how to organize the place or control the money. Gradually I began to take over the administration. I had come a long way from 93, Harewood Drive, Bradford, but part of me was still the daughter of a Yorkshire shopkeeper.

So I was busy. During the summer term and afterwards, I didn't have much time to brood or to grieve about Janet. I didn't have much time to think about what had happened. That suited me very well. But I could run away from Rosington for the rest of my life. I could never run away from Janet.

Janet. However busy I was, she was always there in the back of my memory, waiting patiently. I'd kept cuttings about the case in a large manila envelope because I knew sooner or later I would have to read them again.

One of the newspapers carried the headline THE WOMAN WHO DIED FOR LOVE. The *News of the World* said Janet was an Angel of Mercy who had killed to save suffering. She had done the wrong thing for the right reason, and had made herself pay the price. The general verdict was that she was kind-hearted but fatally weak. It was taken for granted that suicide was a coward's way out. I didn't understand that, and still don't. Killing yourself must take more courage than I ever had.

None of the accounts mentioned David's lost job or indeed

David's failings as a husband. He and Rosie were confined to the margins of the drama. Janet would have been glad of that. She wasn't vindictive, and she cherished her privacy. At some point before swallowing the rest of her father's sleeping tablets, she wrote three letters and put them under her pillow.

The coroner's letter was read out at the inquest. Janet said she was sorry to be such a trouble to everyone. She'd decided to take an overdose and kill herself because she'd killed her father. She had not been able to bear him going senile, and she knew how desperately unhappy he was, and how much more unhappy he would be when he went to the nursing home. He had begged her to kill him, she wrote. She added that she couldn't stand living with the knowledge of what she had done, and that in any case she was very depressed after losing a baby. The coroner saw the letters to David and me but did not think it necessary to read them out in open court.

I never knew what was in Janet's letter to David. Mine was short and to the point, and more than forty years later I can recite it word for word.

There's nothing anyone can do, even you. The police know I killed Daddy and I think it's only a matter of hours before they arrest me. You've always been a sort of guardian angel to me, but please don't think this is your fault.

This way it's better for everyone, especially David and Rosie. I want so much for them to be free to make a fresh start and they can't do that if I'm here. I know you'll help them if you can. Thank you for everything.

Do you know how much Henry needs you? Give him my love and to you, as always, my special love.

Janet

The coroner was scrupulously fair and even sympathetic. The evidence presented by the police left no doubt that Mr Treevor had been killed. A number of witnesses, including David and myself, had testified that Mr Treevor was very unhappy and had on several occasions asked to be killed. Dr Flaxman had told the court that Mrs Byfield was seriously depressed after losing her baby and that he was worried about her mental health.

Then came the clinching piece of evidence. The police had visited the council dump. A few hours after Mr Treevor's death, early on Tuesday morning, the dustmen had done their round. So detectives painstakingly picked their way through a mound of rubbish until they had found items from the Dark Hostelry.

Inspector Humphries testified that these included envelopes addressed to the Byfields and to me, and an empty Worcestershire sauce bottle with Janet's fingerprints on it. A few inches away they found a damp bundle of newspaper, the *Church Times*, as it happened, containing potato peelings and a quantity of wet rags. Under examination, the rags had proved to be part of a cotton winceyette nightdress, Inspector Humphries said, originally cream-coloured and with a pattern of small pink bows.

Much of the fabric was stained with what forensic tests established was blood identical to Mr Treevor's blood type. The police believed that Janet had tried to wash the nightdress and herself after killing her father, and had then decided to cut up the nightdress with scissors and put it out with the rubbish. On the hem of the nightdress was a laundry label which had been traced back to the Dark Hostelry. David himself confirmed that his wife had owned such a nightdress. Neither he nor the police had been able to find it in the house. He was almost sure that his wife had been wearing it on the evening before her father's death.

So she hadn't put on the pale-blue nylon nightdress to make herself look pretty for David after all. I wished I believed in God so I could at least pray for Janet's soul. I'd failed her, you see, because I was so tied up with my own affairs, with Henry and Francis Youlgreave. I hadn't noticed that my best friend was driving herself into a corner.

The coroner said it was a tragedy, which I suppose it was, and that Janet had loved not wisely but too well. I wondered if there had been hatred mixed up with the love. Nowadays the psychologists would say that Mr Treevor had behaved 'inappropriately' with Rosie on several occasions, perhaps many. Had he also behaved 'inappropriately' with Janet when she was a child? I couldn't imagine her hating anyone enough to kill them. Except of course herself, the person she always hated most of all.

But what about David? I'd seen the way he had looked at Mr Treevor when he had found him in Rosie's bed, heard the tone of his voice. Hatred turned David into someone else. If hatred alone could kill, then Mr Treevor would have died long before he bled to death.

Janet loved David. In a sense she'd lived for him. When I stopped feeling numb, and when I stopped trying to distract myself with the doings of a hundred and seventeen small boys, I started to think again. It was then that it occurred to me that Janet might have done more than live for David. She might have died for him as well.

47

On that Sunday we didn't talk much as we drove back from Roth to Veedon Hall. When we turned into our drive relief dropped over me like an eiderdown. I must have sighed.

'What is it?' Henry said.

'Do you know, this is the first proper home we've ever had?'

'Better late than never.'

After supper we went for a gentle walk in what we had taken to calling the Parklet. Mist was already creeping up the lawn towards the terrace. When I glanced back at Veedon Hall, for once it looked beautiful, a house from a fairy tale.

I slipped my arm into Henry's. 'It's so quiet.'

'Wait till the little hooligans get back. Then we'll know what noise means.'

Because of my pregnancy Henry insisted on strolling at a pace suitable for a funeral procession. He was also smoking his pipe, a messy habit which at least kept away the midges. The pipe was a recent innovation designed to make him look solid and dependable in front of parents. Henry hadn't quite mastered the art so he was practising in private with me.

'After all,' he said, 'you'll soon be a parent.'

There was a stone bench beside what we naturally called the Lakelet, and we sat here for a while, despite the fact the midges were worse near the water. Henry was convinced I needed a rest. It was still light but now the sun had gone the air was rapidly cooling. Ducks sent ripples swirling across the silver water. I thought of the mallards I'd fed with Rosie near the place where Swan Alley had once been, and wondered if Nancy Martlesham had fed their ancestors when she was a child growing up by the river.

'She hasn't any,' Henry was saying. 'That's one consolation.'

I'd missed something. 'Who hasn't? And hasn't any what?'

'Grandsons. Lady Youlgreave's got no children at all. So we don't have to be nice to her on that account.'

'You *asked* her?'

'No, it was when you went to the lavatory. I happened to mention you were pregnant, you see. And she said she was glad she'd never had children because looking after herself was a full-time job as it was.'

'Do you think she's happy?'

Henry shrugged and sent a wavering plume of smoke across the water. I suspect he was trying to blow smoke rings.

I said, '*I* don't think she lets herself think whether she's happy or not.'

Henry sucked on the pipe, which made a gurgling sound. 'I don't see what she's got to complain about. She's obviously not short of a bob or three.'

Lady Youlgreave told us that Uncle Francis had never lived in the Old Manor House. In his day the family's home was Roth Park, a red brick mansion whose chimneys were visible over the roofs of the newer houses. He died at Roth Park, too, jumping from the sill of his bedroom window to the gravel beneath. In his way he had been very kind to her, Lady Youlgreave said, and she used to call him Uncle Francis.

It wasn't Francis she'd hated. It was the people who had sold her to him. Her mother's sister Aunt Em and her brother Simon Martlesham. She didn't use the word hate, but that's what I thought I saw in her sallow little face as she sat on her white wicker throne in the garden of the Old Manor House.

'Uncle Francis thought he was acting for the best. But it's never nice for a child to be torn away from her family.' Lady Youlgreave smothered a little yawn, as though either we or the subject bored her, possibly both. 'Especially if your mother has just died. At first he sent me to live with a dreadful woman in Hampstead. She'd been a governess to the Youlgreave children when he was a boy. She taught me how to mind my p's and q's.

She bought me clothes.' Her lips curled. 'She gave me elocution lessons.'

'How long were you there?'

'A couple of months. It seemed like centuries. But Uncle Francis was being cruel to be kind. He didn't want me to come as too much of a shock to the couple who'd agreed to adopt me. And I didn't. I settled in very well. Father' – she gave the last word a faint ironical inflection – 'was a solicitor in Henley. We had a house by the river. I had my own governess. My father's aunt had married a man named Carter who owned land in Roth. That's how Francis knew him. I rather think Francis had been in some sort of legal trouble and Father helped him out.'

'Why?' I'd said. 'Why this business with Harold Munro?'

'After all these years – is that what you mean? You'll understand when you're my age, Mrs Appleyard. When you're young you've no time to look back. But when you're old there's little else to do. Besides, I wanted to know what had happened to my brother.'

'And your aunt.'

She laughed. 'That was a bonus. I'd assumed she was dead. She must have been over ninety.'

'But all the secrecy –'

'Why should I have made a song and dance about it? Tell me, Mrs Appleyard, if you'd been brought up in Swan Alley, if you'd been bought and sold as a child, would you like the world to know? Of course you wouldn't. That's why I chose a private investigator. A journalist would probably have ferreted out the information more efficiently, but I couldn't have relied on him to be confidential. The only obvious alternative would have been a lawyer. But that would have been much more expensive.' She stared haughtily at us down her nose, which was small and pitted. 'I'm not made of money, you know.'

All the while she was talking, I had the feeling she was laughing at us.

'When I first talked to your brother, he said you'd gone to Canada with him.'

'That's Simon all over. Wouldn't want to put himself in a bad light, the one who'd abandoned his little sister. He always was a dreadfully *smarmy* boy. You should have seen him with Uncle Francis. He'd have said black was white if Uncle Francis wanted him to. At least Aunt Em was quite open about it. She didn't want children wrecking her last chance of marriage, especially not children from Swan Alley with a mother like ours and no father worth mentioning. To hear her talk about Sammy Gotobed, you'd have thought he was the Archbishop of Canterbury.' She twisted her features into a pop-eyed, hollow-cheeked mask and intoned in a deep voice, 'The acme of respectability.'

'You've read the poems, of course?'

Her head dipped. 'Of course. Munro sent me a copy of *The Tongues of Angels* he found in Rosington Library. But there was no point. I already have it.'

'Do you have *The Voice of Angels*?'

'It's the same thing. A privately printed edition of *Tongues*. For some reason he changed the title slightly.'

'He also added another poem.'

She stared without expression across the white table. 'So? Perhaps his publishers wouldn't let him include it in the edition they produced.'

'It's rather an odd poem.'

'You could say that of almost all of them.'

I was the first to drop my eyes. What she said was reasonable by its own lights. It was probably the truth.

Henry murmured that perhaps we had taken up too much of Lady Youlgreave's time. He had been very patient with me. I found that was one of the few advantages of being pregnant. People tended to humour you when you had whims. You were almost expected to behave irrationally.

It was then that I asked to use the lavatory. Lady Youlgreave took me into the house by a side door. Shaky bladder control was one of the many things I didn't like about being pregnant. But I admit I was nosy too. The part of the house I saw was full of battered furniture and paintings in tarnished frames. Nevertheless it smelled of money, just like the car, the sort of money that has been part of your life for so long that you no longer notice it.

As she walked down the hall with me, Lady Youlgreave said, 'I hope you won't mind treating this as confidential, Mrs Appleyard.'

'I suppose so,' I said.

'I'm sure you understand that it's not very pleasant to have one's family secrets displayed in public. As poor Mr Byfield has found out.' She waved towards a door. 'It's in there.'

'Don't think I'm prying – well, I am, I suppose – but how did you come to marry into the family?'

'It's not so very strange. My parents' – once again that ironic inflection – 'used to visit my great-aunt's house here. The Carters. Most of their land is under the Jubilee Reservoir now, and the house too. They had a dance for their daughter's twenty-first and that's where I met my future husband.' She looked at the door of the lavatory, barely trying to conceal her impatience. 'So you see – it's all quite simple.'

The lavatory had rich mahogany woodwork, brass taps and blue-and-white tiles. The pan was raised on a dais and I felt like a queen as I sat there hoping to squeeze out more than the usual two teaspoons'-worth so I wouldn't need a lavatory again before we got home.

But I found it hard to concentrate. I felt uneasy, a sensation that was almost physical, like a mild form of morning sickness. Perhaps I was wrong, and certainly I had only first impressions to go on, but Lady Youlgreave seemed an arrogant, self-sufficient woman with so much money and so few ties that she had no reason to worry about the opinions of others. She had no reason to talk so frankly to a strange woman who turned up with her husband out of the blue on Sunday afternoon.

So why had she answered my questions so frankly?

Another perk of pregnancy was early-morning tea. You need perks when your body has been invaded by a demanding little stranger, your hormones are behaving like disruptive toddlers, and your digestive system is in the throes of a revolution.

Henry was so convinced of my infinite fragility that he would get up early to make the tea. In the back of both of our minds was the memory of what had happened to Janet and the baby she had thought was a boy.

On Monday morning he put the tray by the bed and kissed me. Being together had become a routine, though not I think one we would ever take for granted. He poured the tea and wandered over to the window, twirling the cord of his dressing gown.

'Lovely morning.' He sat down in the chair by the window and fumbled in his pocket for cigarettes. 'There's a letter for you on the tray.' He paused just long enough to alert me. 'A Rosington postmark.'

I sipped my tea and then picked up the envelope. The handwriting was familiar but I couldn't put a name to it. I slit the envelope with the handle of a spoon, pulled out the letter and glanced at the signature. It was from Peter Hudson.

My dear Wendy

I imagine you're both very busy, on the verge of the new term. I am writing partly so June and I can wish you and Henry the best of luck with your new venture.

The cataloguing of the Cathedral Library has at last been finished! James Heber (a friend of Mrs Forbury's nephew) spent the summer finishing what you so ably began. He has just completed the History Tripos at Cambridge and is going on to do his MA at Durham. He found no more surprises, thank heaven! No decision has yet been made about what we shall do with the books, nor with those in the Theological College Library.

The dean's exhibition in the Chapter House has been a success, you will be glad to hear – so much so that there are plans to expand it and make it permanent. So the dean asked young Heber to have a look at the Rosington Archive in Cambridge University Library to see if there was anything worth including. It's a collection of records and other material, some monastic but most Post-Reformation, relating to the Cathedral and the diocese. It was lodged in the University Library by Canon Youlgreave. Someone catalogued it in a rather perfunctory way in the 1920s, but only in part.

Heber turned up several possible exhibits. He also came across a reference in the Sacrist's Accounts for 1402 to the cost of fuel and other expenses relating to the burning of heretics. There was some debate about who should be ultimately responsible for meeting these expenses – the Abbey felt it was the King's responsibility, not theirs. The interesting point is that those burned were named – two of them came from the village of Mudgley, and one of those was called Isabella. So perhaps that poem of Youlgreave's had some foundation in fact after all. Unfortunately there was no mention of the precise charges.

There's one other thing. I had a letter last week, addressed to me as Cathedral Librarian, from a man named Simon Martlesham. He said he had been trying to get in touch with you at the Dark Hostelry, had found out you had moved, and wondered if I had a forwarding address. He said you knew how to contact him so I've dropped him a line saying that I've passed his request on to you.

We hope to see David and Rosie in October if all goes well. I know you have been in touch too. Remember us to them when you see them.

June sends her affectionate good wishes to you both,

as do I,

Peter

I passed the letter to Henry and watched him read it as I finished my tea. I saw the frown shooting up between his eyebrows as he neared the end.

'I think we should call it a day,' he said after he'd finished.

'Call what a day?'

'All this Youlgreave-Martlesham stuff. You're not going to get in touch with Martlesham, are you?'

'I don't know.'

'It's all in the past. You have to put it behind you.'

Some things I would never put behind me, among them Janet and the Hairy Widow. 'I'll see,' I said.

'Let it be,' Henry advised. 'Please.'

'Is there anything more to know?' I peered into my cup, looking for my fortune among the leaves. 'And is there any more tea in the pot?'

48

Three days later, on Thursday, I met David, Rosie and Angel under the clock at Waterloo Station. Henry had offered to come with me, but I persuaded him to stay at school. I didn't want a fractious husband in tow. Henry didn't enjoy buying clothes, even for himself.

'You won't overdo it,' he had said when he drove me to the station. 'Promise.'

'I promise.'

David looked relieved to see me. He had a briefcase under his arm and dark smudges under bloodshot eyes. I wondered whether his God was being much help to him now. Rosie was wearing another dress I recognized, navy-blue needlecord dotted with pale-pink horses, with puffed sleeves and a Peter Pan collar. It was the one Janet had given her for her fifth birthday. Someone had plaited her hair rather badly. In one hand she carried Angel. In the other she clutched a miniature handbag made of plastic and intended to look like patent leather.

'Are you sure this won't be too much trouble?' David asked.

'Not at all. I shall enjoy it.'

'You must let me pay for your lunch as well.' He took out a worn wallet. 'And you'll need something for taxis. How much do you think one should budget for the clothes? About ten pounds?'

'There's no need,' I said. 'This is my treat.'

'I can't allow that.'

Rosie stared up at us, her eyes moving from David's face to mine. Her expression was intent, as though the fate of the world rested upon the result of the conversation. The fingers holding the handbag strap whitened. For a moment I said nothing because there was no need for me to say the words aloud.

Let me do this for Janet's sake.

'Where and when would you like to meet?' David asked.

He had capitulated and we both knew it. As soon as we had arranged a rendezvous, he couldn't wait to get away. He was going to have a day of unbridled fun working on his book on Thomas Aquinas in a library. I think he was so relieved to escape from Granny Byfield that he would have enjoyed anything, even shopping for clothes with Rosie and me.

Later, when David had left and Rosie and I were queueing for a taxi, she slipped her hand into mine, which wasn't something she often did voluntarily. She tugged my arm as though pulling a bellrope for service in an old-fashioned hotel.

She turned her perfect face up to mine. 'Auntie Wendy? Do you think I could have a dress with a *belt*?'

'I should think so.'

We went to Oxford Street and spent most of the morning shopping. I spent a small fortune – I was reasonably confident that neither David nor his mother would have an accurate idea of the cost of children's clothes in the West End. Angel was never far from Rosie, and before we bought anything Rosie went through the ritual of asking the doll's opinion.

After Selfridge's, we were both exhausted so we found a restaurant and had lunch.

'It looks as if Angel could do with a few new clothes as well,' I said as we were waiting for our pudding. 'What do you think?'

'Yes, please. Angel would *love* that, wouldn't you?'

'Mama!' squawked the doll, because Rosie had pushed her chest.

I studied Angel. The fabric of her dress had shrunk and in places the pink had run.

'Granny washed her clothes,' Rosie said. 'It didn't do much good.'

'We'll see what we can do.'

She nodded and bestowed a small, prim smile on me. She was a well-brought-up child, and had done this whenever I had offered to buy her something. I would have preferred it if she'd thrown her arms around me and kissed me. Or better still, said she loved me, though in my heart of hearts I knew even then it could only be cupboard love. But Rosie was such a pretty little girl, and my best friend's daughter. I wanted to hear her say she loved me. I wanted to believe it, too, and I still hoped that one day she might mean it.

I realize now that Rosie disliked me. No, it was worse than that, much worse, though it hurts me to admit it. She *hated* me. They'd been a happy little family at the Dark Hostelry until I turned up, or Rosie thought they had. Then I'd taken her mother away from her for ever and ever, and there was nothing anyone could do to bring her back. So here I was, trying to make up for an absence, trying to compete with a ghost.

'We can go to Hamley's after we've finished here,' I said, still playing the game I was doomed to lose. 'Have you been there before?'

She shook her head.

'It's a very big toy shop. I'm sure they'll have something.'

'I want some more angel clothes for her. The dress you made got messed up.'

'That's a pity. But never mind. Perhaps we'll find something better.'

Limpid eyes stared across the table. 'Mummy soaked it in cold water but it was no use.'

Then the waitress arrived with our ice-creams coated with chocolate sauce and decorated with two wafers in the shape of fans. Rosie picked up her spoon and dug it into the ice-cream. I sat there staring across the table at her. I searched my memory, trying to remember what Angel had been wearing, and when. Especially when.

'Rosie, what was on the angel dress? What made it messy?'

She had just put a spoonful of ice-cream in her mouth. She ate it very slowly, looking at me all the while through her lashes. She was not the sort of child who talked with her mouth full. Finally she dabbed the corners of her mouth with her napkin.

'Mummy said it was a secret.'

A stain you soak in cold water?

'Mummy's not here now,' I said, suddenly ruthless. 'Only you and me.'

Rosie considered this for a moment. 'But Mummy *said*.'

'How would it be if I just made a suggestion? You could nod your head. Or shake it. So you wouldn't be actually *saying* anything.' Another spoonful of ice-cream. Then she swallowed and nodded her head.

I ignored the faint clamour of my conscience, pushed the bowl away and reached for my cigarettes. 'Was it something like – like tomato ketchup?'

Another nod.

'I wonder if it was Grandpa's?'

A third nod.

I shook a cigarette out of the packet. My hand trembled as I put it in my mouth and at first I couldn't make the lighter work. I was conscious of Rosie watching me, of her continuing to eat ice-cream. I felt simultaneously hot and cold and in dire need of a dry martini. I inhaled fiercely, and the smoke scorched my lungs.

'How did it get on the dress?'

She swallowed. 'Angel fell into it. But Mummy said I mustn't tell. Never ever.'

'It's all right.'

'She cut up the dress and put it down the lav.'

'And Grandpa?'

'Grandpa? It's what he *wanted*.'

Her spoon scraped round the bowl, greedy for the last crumb of wafer, the last smear of cream and sauce. What was *implied* was important, not what was said. I remembered Mr Treevor wishing he was dead, the last words I heard him say, and Rosie had heard him too. And afterwards she'd asked me about dying. I'd confirmed that dead people go to heaven, and that heaven was very nice.

'You knew where he kept the knife?'

Rosie nodded. 'It was one of our secrets.' She wriggled in her chair, a flirt's twitch. 'We hid it at the back of the fireplace in his room. He was going to get me some more wings for Angel. Can I have your ice-cream if you don't want it?'

I pushed the bowl across the table to her. 'Mummy found you? Afterwards?'

'She came in just after I'd done it. He moved when I put it in and he knocked Angel out of my hand. Angel was all messy.'

'What did Mummy do?'

'She tried to wake Grandpa but he was asleep. Then she said we'd have to tidy ourselves up.' Suddenly the face crumpled – the beauty vanished and all I could see was a frightened child. 'I wish Mummy was here.'

'So do I, darling.'

At last it made sense. First Janet hoped that the death of her father would be taken as suicide. When that had failed, she valued herself so little that taking the blame on herself seemed the best thing to do from everyone's point of view. Perhaps she'd welcomed the chance. I don't think she wanted to live any more. She must have thought that by killing herself, and by taking the blame for her father's death, she was sparing David something even worse. She was preventing Rosie being labelled as a murderer for the rest of her life.

Later on I found in a bookshop one of those formidable blue Pelican paperbacks that used to march across the shelves in David's study at the Dark Hostelry. This one was about criminal law. As I turned to the chapter about juveniles, my fingers left damp smudges on the pages. The author quoted the precise wording of Section 50 of the Children and Young Persons Act of 1933.

It shall be conclusively presumed that no child under the age of eight years can be guilty of any offence.

'The presumption,' Mr Giles commented, 'is irrebuttable.'

In other words Rosie could never have been tried because by law she could not commit a crime. So she could not have been labelled as a murderer. Had Janet known that? Even if she had known, would it have mattered? Janet must have wanted to do what was best, or rather least bad, for Rosie and David. If she had told the truth to David and me, to Dr Flaxman and Inspector Humphries, the law would have said Rosie could not commit a crime – but people weren't so scrupulous.

You can never hide from malicious curiosity. Even if the

Byfields had changed their names and gone to live in Australia, someone would have found out.

I don't know. Perhaps I'm making it too complicated. Sometimes things are heart-breakingly simple and not at all rational. Perhaps Janet didn't want to live very much. Perhaps she was looking for death and her daughter showed her how to find it.

I said to Rosie, 'Have you told anyone else?'

She shook her head and spooned the last of my ice-cream from the bowl.

'If I were you, Rosie, I wouldn't. Will you promise?'

She touched her mouth with the napkin. 'All right.'

I did it for Janet, I swear. It spared David even more pain, and Granny Byfield and Rosie herself. Would it have helped anyone if I'd told David the truth, if I'd rung up Inspector Humphries and informed him that my best friend had pulled the wool over his eyes and mine? Above all I wonder, would it have saved other lives later?

If I shut my eyes I see Rosie with the knife in one hand and Angel in the other. I see Janet bending over her father and the blood pulsing slowly out of his neck. But you can never know what would have happened if you'd made another choice. I hold on to that.

The waitress was hovering and I asked for the bill.

'Will we ride in a taxi to Hamley's?' Rosie asked.

'It's not very far.' I saw her face fall. 'Would you like to?'

'Yes, *please*.'

The taxi question was a welcome diversion. We had enough parcels to justify the extravagance to myself, and Henry would be pleased because I would be taking his advice and not overdoing it. A short journey meant a small fare. I wanted to give Rosie a treat. It sounds odd that I was thinking of things like that when my world had been shaken so violently to its foundations. But I did. We are odd, all of us. We distract ourselves with details. It's a way of coping.

At Hamley's we struck lucky, or rather Rosie did. We found an assistant who was willing to take the question of dolls' clothing very seriously indeed. After much discussion we bought two outfits for Angel. The first was a short multi-coloured cocktail dress in synthetic taffeta with a wide off-the-shoulder wrapover neckline and a fitted bodice. The skirt was bell-shaped and had a special petticoat to go under it. The outfit included a pair of high-heeled shoes.

'She'll look so lovely at parties,' the assistant said. 'Won't she?'

Rosie pressed Angel's chest. 'Mama,' the doll said.

Fifteen minutes later, we decided on the second outfit. Angel could now dress casually in a sleeveless cream blouse with a low square neckline, and a pair of fitted navy-blue linen shorts. The assistant persuaded us that Angel would be underdressed on holidays without a pair of blue leather mules and a straw hat with a ribbon round the brim.

'After all,' she said, 'you wouldn't want her to wear high-heeled shoes when she's yachting or on the beach. She'd look silly.'

Finally, we managed to find a plain white nightdress which fitted. It was trimmed with lace at the neck and cuffs and perhaps rather low-cut for an angel, but Rosie did not mind.

While the assistant was wrapping our purchases, Rosie wandered round the department examining other dolls, their clothes, their houses and their furniture. She sidled over to me as I was writing the cheque.

'Auntie Wendy?'

'Yes?' I tore out the cheque and looked down at Rosie. Despite everything, I found myself envying her. She was so beautiful, you see, then and later, and so self-contained, which armoured her against suffering.

She towed me over to a display of baby dolls and the equipment which went with them. 'Do angels have babies?'

'No, dear. I don't think they do. They don't bother with that sort of thing.'

'Are you sure?'

'Pretty sure. You can ask Daddy, though.'

'Angels don't have babies,' Rosie said, 'because angels don't *need* babies.'

Her tone of voice made it clear she was advancing this as a possibility rather than stating it as fact.

'I'm sure you're right.' I didn't want to have to buy a baby doll as well, and of course a baby doll would need a pram and a cot and a complete wardrobe. 'But Daddy will know.'

She nodded. 'I don't want to have babies.'

'Why?'

'They're too much trouble. They make too much mess. I expect that's why angels don't have them.'

She slipped away from me and went to smile at the assistant, who was all too ready to be smiled at. I sat down heavily on a chair in front of a counter.

Babies are too much trouble. They make too much mess . . .

Rosie's words went round and round in my mind, speeding up like a merry-go-round, and the faster they went the worse I felt. I remembered something that Simon Martlesham had said and linked it for the first time to one of Mrs Gotobed's remarks, or rather to its implication.

All the dolls on the displays were staring at me, their painted faces masks of horror, their perfect eyebrows arched in shocked surprise like Lady Youlgreave's. I needed someone to say it wasn't true, I'd made a mistake.

'Madam? Madam?'

I looked up at the assistant stooping over me.

'Are you all right, madam?'

'I'm fine, thanks. Just a little faint.'

'It's rather hot in here. They find it so hard to get the temperature right.'

'Let's get a taxi,' Rosie suggested. 'Then you won't have to walk anywhere.'

I breathed deeply. The baby inside me needed air. *Concentrate on the baby. My baby.*

'A taxi?' I said. 'Good idea. But I'd like to make a phone call first.'

'Where are we going?' Rosie asked.

'What would you say to another ice-cream?'

49

I damned the expense and told the taxi driver to wait. Rosie and I went inside the Blue Dahlia Café. The sad-faced woman was behind the counter polishing an already gleaming urn. When she saw Rosie, she brightened as if inside her a candle had burst into flame.

'I've come to see Mr Martlesham,' I said. 'He's expecting me.'

'Just a moment, miss. I see if he's ready.'

'I wonder if you could look after Rosie while I'm talking to him.'

'Oh, yes.' The woman smiled down at Rosie, who smiled back, scenting an easy conquest. 'That's a pretty dolly. What's her name?'

'Angel.'

'What a pretty name. Does Angel like ice-cream?'

Rosie nodded and stared at her feet.

'When Mummy talks to Mr Martlesham, I make you an ice-cream and her an ice-cream. You can help me.'

Rosie said nothing and nor did I, but Angel squawked, 'Mama.' The woman went through the archway and for a moment the multi-coloured strips of nylon ribbon fluttered like a broken rainbow.

Rosie squeezed my hand as if ringing a bell for service. When I looked down, she said, 'Will the lady let me eat Angel's ice-cream?'

'I expect so.'

A moment later the woman came back. 'He see you now.'

'You be good, Rosie. I shan't be long.'

'We make ice-creams,' the woman said. 'Lovely ice-creams for little angels.'

She swept Rosie round the counter, ignoring a customer at the table in the window who was trying to attract her attention.

I went through the archway and tapped on the door to the left. Martlesham told me to come in.

At first sight he was unchanged, as dapper as ever. He sat behind the big desk, the chair angled so I saw only the right side of his face, the side undamaged by the stroke. Today he was wearing a blazer and a loosely knotted cravat. Gold gleamed in the folds of the cravat, the tiepin with the horse's head inlaid with enamel. He extended his hand over the desk to me.

'Forgive me if I don't get up.' He wrenched the words out of himself. 'Not too fit at present.'

'I'm sorry.'

We shook hands. His skin was dry and cold, like a snake's.

'Someone in Rosington passed on my message?'

'Yes.'

'Good of you to come in person, Mrs Appleyard. I thought you might write or phone. Have you come far?'

'Hampshire. My husband and I are living there now.'

Everything about Simon Martlesham was as immaculate as ever. What had changed was something inside. He wasn't fighting any more.

'I was ill during the summer.' He wasn't asking for sympathy, merely stating a fact. 'I would have written to you sooner. I was sorry to hear about your friends. What was their name?'

'Byfield.'

'I saw it in the papers.'

'Their daughter's in the café now. She's having a lovely time and lots of ice-cream.'

'Claudia likes children. Now Franco's grown up, what she needs is grandchildren. Do you want anything, Mrs Appleyard? Tea or coffee?'

'No, thank you.'

'I don't like loose ends,' he said. 'It wasn't me who hired that private detective. I think I've seen him once or twice, watching the café. Claudia noticed him too . . . They're very good to me, in their way, her and Franco. But I didn't hire the man, I promise you that.'

'I know.'

'But I want to know who did. It's a worry, you see.'

'I got it the wrong way round, Mr Martlesham. It wasn't you trying to find your sister. It was your sister trying to find you.'

In his shock he turned to face me. The left-hand side of his face was worse than it had been before. I guessed he'd had another stroke over the summer. He licked his lips and leant across the desk, cupping his ear with his hand.

'Who?'

'Your sister Nancy.'

He sat back in his chair. Breathing heavily, he pulled a handkerchief from his trouser pocket, dabbed his forehead and blew his nose. 'Tell me, please. What happened?'

So I explained that Francis Youlgreave had kept his promise and that Nancy was indeed a lady, and in more senses than one. I said I'd talked to her, and tried to describe the Old Manor House. He listened, nodding his head slowly.

'Do you want her address?' I said.

'No.'

For a moment neither of us spoke. The old man's mouth worked, as though he was chewing words. I thought of him as old, though he was only sixty-seven.

'He was a good man,' Martlesham said at last. 'Canon Youlgreave. I always said he was.'

'I know you did.'

Now I had the opportunity. Now I had a chance to ask the question. Perhaps the last chance. And I didn't want to do it. Because Martlesham was dying and none of us can face too much undiluted truth, whether about other people or ourselves. I looked around the room with its battered ex-War Department furniture. I wanted to go home, back to Veedon Hall and Henry.

'Do you think he was a good man?' Martlesham barked, making me jump. 'Do you, do you?'

The colour had risen in his face. His right hand, the one unaffected by the stroke, was trembling on the blotter. I thought he might be on the verge of another stroke.

'I think he did some good things,' I said. 'And he did some bad things too. Like most of us. But perhaps he went to extremes, and in both directions.'

'What do you mean?'

'Your sister, Lady Youlgreave – she hired Munro to trace you and to find out what people knew about Francis Youlgreave. Why do you think she did that?'

He shrugged one shoulder. 'How do I know?'

'I think perhaps you could guess. Why don't you want to see her now?'

'I told you why.'

'You said that in the past, when you came back to England, you would have been an embarrassment to her, and that she thought you'd sold her. Maybe both those things were true, but there was something else, wasn't there?'

His right hand raised itself on its fingers and scuttled slowly across the blotter. He stared at his hand, not me.

'Did you know your aunt was alive until very recently, until June?'

He raised his eyes. Slowly he nodded.

'And did you know you've got a cousin, too – Wilfred Gotobed?'

'You talked to them?'

'Yes.'

'*Aunt Em* talked to you?'

'She was careful what she said, of course, she had to be. For the same reason you had to be, and Lady Youlgreave. Lady Youlgreave most of all.'

His nails scraped the blotter, as though trying to scratch out something. 'I'm tired. I must ask you to leave.'

'I will.' I stood up, smoothed down my skirt and picked up my handbag. 'But before I go, Mr Martlesham, I'll tell you what I think happened. Mrs Gotobed said that when she wanted to get married, the children were a problem, her sister's children, because Sammy Gotobed didn't want them. At the time I thought she meant you and Nancy. But that didn't make sense, because you were more or less off her hands. You were working at the Bishop's Palace before your mother died, and living there too. Then Canon Youlgreave sent you off to

Canada. Either way, you wouldn't have been much of a burden on your aunt.'

'She was an old woman. She got confused about how old I was.'

'And then you told me, the last time I saw you, that your mother had died in childbirth. Mrs Gotobed said that before she married her verger, she lived in lodgings and your mother's children came to live with her. The landlady complained about the trouble and the mess they made. "I'm not a nursemaid," that's what she said.'

The hands were completely still now.

'Even if you *had* been living with them, a thirteen-year-old boy with a job of his own wouldn't have needed a nursemaid.'

Martlesham had old man's eyes surrounded by crumpled skin and swimming with moisture. I watched a tear gathering on the lower lid of the right eye.

'*Children*,' I said. 'More than one.'

He said nothing. He blinked, and the tear vanished.

'What happened to the baby?'

He didn't answer, would never answer. Nor would any of them. Francis Youlgreave had given the three of them a future, Simon, Nancy and Aunt Em, and in return he took the baby. It had been simple. All that remained were a few fragments of the crime.

'I could find out,' I said. 'I could go to Somerset House and look for the birth certificate.'

Martlesham's head twitched and something like a smile crept across the ruined face.

I knew then it was no use. The birth hadn't been registered. This was a slum baby, an orphan, unwanted by the living and expected to die. So even the victim had been legally non-existent, just as Rosie legally could not be a murderer.

A new-born baby is so small. Not very different in size from a cat or a chicken, and much less able to defend itself. Simon and Mrs Gotobed might not have known what would happen, though perhaps they had guessed. But Nancy?

Simon Martlesham wouldn't meet my eyes. I left the room, closing the door quietly behind me. I wiped my eyes and blew my nose. On the far side of the ribbons, Rosie was sitting in state at one of the tables surrounded by an audience of admiring women and finishing a bowl of ice-cream daubed with chocolate sauce. It took me a while to drag her away. The sad-faced woman would not let me pay the bill.

The taxi driver looked up from his *Post* as we came out of the café. I shook my head and pointed at the telephone box on the corner of Fetter Passage. I took Rosie's hot, sticky hand and tugged her towards it. I opened the door of the box and a warm waft of urine and vinegar swept out.

'It's smelly,' Rosie said. 'Who are you ringing?'

'Just someone I know. You can wait outside.'

She stood by the box and talked to Angel while I phoned directory enquiries. I was lucky – I had been afraid the Old Manor House number might be ex-directory, and I knew that if I didn't try now, I never would. *Consume the better part, No more. For therein lies the deepest art . . .* Pregnant women have odd fancies and sudden, overwhelming fears. That's what Henry would think when I told him about this.

If I told him.

The voice of a woman I didn't recognize crackled in my ear. I pressed the button, gave my name and asked for Lady Youlgreave.

'Tell her it's about Uncle Francis,' I said.

I waited, my left hand resting on my stomach, my baby.

A moment later, Lady Youlgreave came on the line. 'Mrs Appleyard. What can I do for you?'

'I've just seen Simon.'

'Who?'

'Your brother.'

'I hope you didn't give him my address.'

'He doesn't want to see you.'

'Why have you been pestering him now?'

I was bobbing on a great tide of emotion, anger and fear, revulsion and pity, rising higher and higher. 'I know what happened. I know about the baby.'

'Do you indeed. Which baby might that be?'

'Your little brother or sister. The one that Francis Youlgreave bought. What sex was it? Did you even give it a name?'

'I beg your pardon?'

'Did you help him kill it?'

'What a vivid imagination you have,' Lady Youlgreave said, and put down the phone.

'Why are you crying?' Rosie said as we walked down Fetter Passage towards our taxi.

I couldn't be bothered to pretend. 'Because people are such a terrible mixture of good and bad.'

Rosie tossed her head as though I'd said something so childish it was beneath contempt.

'Nobody's perfect,' she said. 'Except Angel.'